The Lily Bard Omnibus

Shakespeare's Landlord
Shakespeare's Champion
Shakespeare's Christmas
Shakespeare's Trollop
Shakespeare's Counselor

Charlaine Harris

GOLLANCZ
LONDON

First published in Great Britain in 2010 by
Gollancz
An imprint of the Orion Publishing Group
Orion House, 5 Upper St Martin's Lane,
London WC2H 9EA
An Hachette UK Company

A CIP catalogue record for this book
is available from the British Library

ISBN 978 0 575 09643 1 (Cased)
ISBN 978 0 575 09644 8 (Export Trade Paperback)

1 3 5 7 9 10 8 6 4 2

Typeset at The Spartan Press Ltd,
Lymington, Hants

Printed in Great Britain by Clays Ltd,
St Ives plc

The Orion Publishing Group's policy is to use papers
that are natural, renewable and recyclable products and
made from wood grown in sustainable forests. The logging
and manufacturing processes are expected to conform to
the environmental regulations of the country of origin.

www.charlaineharris.com
www.orionbooks.co.uk

'Lily Bard is one of the best-drawn and most compelling characters in contemporary mystery fiction – complex, smart, streetwise, tough'   *Booklist*

Shakespeare's Landlord

'Riveting . . . Lily's triumphant progress from scarred loner to fierce fighter is very rewarding. Bravo, Ms Harris!'
                                                    Pen & Dagger

Shakespeare's Champion

'Full of surprises, this second fast-paced and gripping Lily Bard adventure showcases the amateur sleuth's strength, determination and martial arts prowess . . . An engaging puzzler that's propelled along by Lily's easy, no-frill narration'   *Publishers Weekly*

Shakespeare's Christmas

'Harris has reached a new high. Don't miss it'   *Booklist*

Shakespeare's Trollop

'An ending that will take everyone by surprise . . . An extremely compelling read'   *Romantic Times*

Shakespeare's Counselor

'Lily Bard . . . is the equal of Kay Scarpetta, Kinsey Millhone, and V.I. Warshawski'   *Library Journal*

Shakespeare's Landlord

For all my fellow inmates
in Doctor Than's House of Pain:
especially Martha, John, and Wayne

Chapter One

I gathered myself, my bare feet gripping the wooden floor, my thigh muscles braced for the attack. I stepped forward on the ball of my left foot, pivoting as I moved, and my right leg swung up, bent at the knee. My foot lashed out, returned instantly. The black Everlast punching bag rocked on its chain.

My right foot touched down, and I pivoted lightly on the ball of that foot, my body oriented this time facing the bag. My left leg came forward to deliver a longer, harder, thrusting mae geri. I continued the kicking, the pivoting, alternating the side kicks with the front kicks, practicing my weaker back kicks, my breathing growing deeper but never losing its rhythm – exploding out with the kick, coming in deep with the retraction.

The bag danced on the end of its chain, swinging back and forth, requiring more and more concentration on my part to plant the next kick accurately. I was tiring.

Finally, I lashed out with my stronger right leg, using all my power, dodged the backswing, and struck seiken, my hand in a smooth line with my arm, my knuckles driving into the bag.

I had finished my exercise. Automatically, I bowed, as I would have if I'd had a live sparring partner, and shook my head in disgust at my own foolishness. I reached for the towel hanging on its appointed hook by the doorknob. As I patted my face, I wondered whether my workout had been enough; if I took a shower now and got in bed, would I sleep? It was worth a try.

I washed my hair, soaped and rinsed, and was out within five minutes. After I dried myself, I put mousse on my hair and stood before the mirror to fluff it out with my fingers and a pick; I had tucked the towel around me so I couldn't see my chest in the mirror.

My hair is short and light blond now. One of my few extravagances is getting it colored, permed, and cut at Terra Ann's, the fanciest hairdressing salon in Shakespeare. Some of my employers get their hair done there; they never know quite what to say when they see me.

Most bodybuilders consider a deep tan part of their regimen, but I'm pale. The scarring doesn't stand out so much that way. But I do get rid of excess hair; I pluck every stray eyebrow, and my legs and armpits are shaved smooth as a baby's bottom.

Once upon a time, years ago, I thought I was pretty. My sister, Varena, and I had the usual rivalry going, and I remember deciding my eyes were bigger and a lighter blue than hers, my nose was straighter and thinner, and my lips were fuller. Her chin was better – neat and determined. Mine is round. I haven't seen Varena in three years now. Probably she is the pretty one. Though my face hasn't changed, my mind has. The workings of the mind look out through the face and alter it.

Sometimes, some mornings – the ones after the really bad nights – I look in the mirror and do not recognize the woman I see there.

This was going to be one of those really bad nights (though I had no idea how bad it was going to get). But I could tell there was no point in going to bed. My feet itched to be moving.

I dressed again, throwing my sweaty workout clothes into the hamper and pulling on blue jeans and a T-shirt, tucking in the T-shirt and pulling a belt through the belt loops. My hair was only a little damp; the blow-dryer finished the job. I pulled on a dark windbreaker.

Front door, back door, kitchen door? Some nights it takes me a while to decide.

The back. Though I keep my doors greased so they swing back and forth almost noiselessly, the back door is the quietest.

The back door is directly opposite the front door, making my house a shotgun house; from my back door, I can look down the hall and through the living room, which occupies the width of the front of the house, to check to make sure the dead bolt is shot.

It was, of course; I am not one to neglect security. I locked the back door as I left, using another key to turn the dead bolt from the outside. I pushed the key down to the very bottom of my front pocket, where it couldn't possibly fall out. I stood on the tiny back porch for a minute, inhaling the faint scent of the new leaves on the climbing rose vines. The vines were halfway up the trellis I'd built to make the little porch prettier.

Of course, it also obstructed my view of anyone approaching, but when the first roses open in about a month, I won't regret it. I have loved roses since I was a child; we lived on a large lot in a small town, and roses filled the backyard.

That yard of my childhood was easily five times as big as this backyard, which extends less than twenty feet, ending abruptly in a steep slope up to the railroad tracks. The slope is covered with weeds, but from time to time a work crew wanders through to keep the weeds under control. To my left as I faced the tracks was the high wooden privacy fence that surrounded the Shakespeare Garden Apartments. It's slightly uphill from my house. To my right, and downhill, was the equally tiny backyard of the only other house on the street. It's nearly an exact copy of my house, and it's owned by an accountant named Carlton Cockroft. Carlton's lights were off, not too surprising at this hour of the night. The only light I could see in the apartment building was in Deedra Dean's place. As I glanced up, her window fell dark.

One o'clock in the morning.

I silently stepped off my little back porch, my walking shoes making almost no noise in the grass, and began to move invisibly through the streets of Shakespeare. The night was still and dark – no wind, the moon only a crescent in cold space. I could not even see myself. I liked that.

An hour and a half later, I felt tired enough to sleep. I was on my way home, and I was not trying to conceal myself anymore; in fact, I was being sloppy. I was using the sidewalk that borders the arboretum (a fancy name for an overgrown park with some labels on trees and bushes). Estes Arboretum takes up a block of

definitely unprime Shakespeare real estate. Each of the four streets
edging the park has a different name, and my street, Track, on the
park's east side, is only a block long. So there's little traffic, and
every morning I get to look out my front window and see trees
across the street instead of someone else's carport.

I rounded the corner from the south side of the arboretum,
Latham Street, to Track; I was opposite the little piece of scrub-
land that no one claimed, just south of Carlton Cockroft's house. I
was not careless enough to linger under the weak streetlight at the
corner. There is one at each corner of the arboretum, as Shakespeare's budget can't run to putting streetlights in the middle of
the block, especially in this obscure part of town.

I hadn't seen a soul all night, but suddenly I was aware I was
not alone. Someone was stirring in the darkness on the other side
of the street.

Instinctively, I concealed myself, sliding behind a live oak on
the edge of the park. Its branches overhung the sidewalk; perhaps
their shadow had hidden me from the presence across the street.
My heart was pounding unpleasantly fast. Some tough woman
you are, I jeered at myself. What would Marshall think if he saw
you now? But when I'd had a second to calm down, I decided that
Marshall might think I was showing some sense.

I peered around the oak's trunk cautiously. In the middle of the
block, where the person was, the darkness was almost total; I
couldn't even tell if I was watching a man or a woman. I had a
flash of an unpleasant recollection: my great-grandmother, in the
act of saying, 'Blacker than a nigger in a coal mine with his mouth
shut', and embarrassing everyone in the whole family quite
unconsciously. Or maybe not; maybe that little nod of satisfaction
had not been over a well-turned phrase but over the pained looks
she'd intercepted passing between my parents.

My great-grandmother would have stomped out to the middle
of the street and inquired what the person's business was, quite
assured of her own safety in doing so, too.

But I know better.

The person was pushing something, something on wheels.

Peering intently into the darkness, I tried to remember if I'd ever seen anyone out on my street before when I was up and wandering. I'd seen a few cars go by, residents or visitors of people in the apartment building, but I couldn't recall ever meeting up with anyone on foot in the past four years – at least in this part of town.

On the bad nights, when I ghost all the way downtown, it is sometimes a different story.

But here and now, I had something to worry about. There was something furtive about this odd incident; this person, this other inhabitor of the night, was pushing what I could now tell was a cart, one with two wheels. It had a handle in the middle of the longer side, and legs on it, so that when you let go of the handle and set it upright, it would be steady and straight. And it was just the right size for two thirty-gallon garbage cans.

My hands curled into fists. Even in the dark, I could identify the familiar shape of the cart. It was my own. I'd bought it at a yard sale from some people who were moving; the man of the house had made it himself.

It was loaded down with something wrapped in dark plastic, like the sheets you buy to put in flower beds to keep weeds down; I could see the faint shine off the smooth plastic surface.

I felt a rage I hadn't experienced in a long time. Something illicit was happening, and the cart thief was trying to involve me in it. The peace that I'd worked so hard to achieve was going to be ripped away, through no fault of my own. I could not confront this thief directly; that wouldn't make sense – the thief might be armed, and was obviously in the middle of doing something he or she wanted to conceal.

So I clenched my teeth, and watched and waited.

Across the rough surface of neglected Track Street, the thief trundled the garbage-can cart with its heavy burden; I could tell it was heavy because of the strain in the cart thief's posture.

This was absolutely eerie; I found myself shivering. I pulled the sides of my dark windbreaker together and, with a tiny sound, zipped it shut. With deliberate movements, I pulled a thin dark scarf from my pocket and tied it over my light hair. All the while, I was tracking the cart thief's laborious progress. The thief was heading for the park; I felt my lips twitch up in a smile as I observed the thief trying to get the cart from the pavement up onto the sidewalk. Wheelchair accessibility had not been a priority when those sidewalks were paved many years ago.

Finally, the cart bumped up onto the sidewalk and across it. The thief's feet had to hurry to catch up. Into the darkness of the arboretum, following one of the narrow paved paths, the thief rolled the loaded cart. I began to count seconds. In three minutes, the thief returned, still pushing my cart.

Now it was empty.

My anger was taking second place to curiosity, though that would only be temporary.

I watched the thief roll the cart up my driveway, barely making it through the narrow walk space between my car and the carport wall. The thief reappeared from the back of my house, walking quickly, and had to go down my driveway to the curb and then walk around the end of the fence to walk up the apartment building's south driveway. The thief circled around back; he or she would enter the building through the quieter back door; the front door squeaked. I always remember things like that.

I am in and out of that apartment building quite a lot.

Sure enough, the thief didn't reappear at the other side of the apartment building. It was someone living there, or the overnight guest of someone living there. With one single woman and four single men living there, overnight guests are not infrequent.

For a few more seconds, I hugged close to the trunk of the tree, waiting to see if a light would come on. From where I was, I could see the side windows on the south side of the apartment building and the front windows, too; no lights came on in any of them. Someone was being extra careful.

Well, I, too, would be careful. I waited five minutes, according to my digital watch, before I made a move. Then I went deeper into the arboretum, following no trail, moving as quietly as possible in the darkness. I'd estimated where I'd intersect the path; I was as familiar with the layout of the arboretum as I was with the floor plan of my house. I'd spent hours wandering Shakespeare by night.

It was so black in the thick of the trees that I wondered if I would even be able to find what the thief had dumped. If my jeans hadn't brushed the plastic, which emitted that typical dry rustle, I might have groped around the path for another hour.

But the second I heard that rustle, I dropped to my hands and knees. Patting around in the darkness, I discovered the wrapping was not plastic sheeting but two large garbage bags, one pulled from the top and another from the bottom to overlap in the middle covering – something soft and big. I poked the bag; there was something hard under the softness. Something bumpy. Something an awful lot like ribs.

I bit my lower lip to keep from making noise.

I struggled silently with an almost-overwhelming urge to jump up and run. After several deep breaths, I won. I steeled myself to do what I had to do, but I couldn't face doing it in the dark.

I reached into my windbreaker pocket and pulled out a narrow, lightweight, powerful little flashlight that had caught my fancy at Wal-Mart. I shifted in my squatting position so that my body was between the apartment building and what was on the ground. I switched on the flashlight.

I was angry at myself when I saw my hand was shaking as I separated the bags. I fumbled them apart some four inches and stopped. I was looking at a torn, rather faded shirt, a man's plaid shirt in green and orange. The chest pocket had caught on something; it was partially ripped from its stitching and a fragment was missing.

I recognized the shirt, though it hadn't been torn when I'd seen it last.

I worked the bag up a little at the side and found a hand; I put my fingers on the wrist, where a pulse should be.

In the chilly Shakespeare night, I squatted in the middle of the trees, holding hands with a dead man.

And now I'd left my fingerprints all over the plastic bags.

*

About forty minutes later, I was sitting in my bedroom. I was finally tired to the bone.

I'd taken the bags off the corpse.

I'd confirmed the corpse's identity, and its corpsedom. No breath, no heartbeat.

I'd worked my way out of the arboretum, knowing I was leaving traces but helpless to avoid it. My incoming traces were unerasable; I'd figured I might as well make a trail out, too. I'd emerged from the bushes on Latham and crossed the street there, well out of sight of the apartments. I'd gone from cover to cover until I circled Carlton Cockroft's house, silently crossing his yard to arrive in my own.

I'd found that the cart thief had replaced my cart and reinserted the garbage cans, but not as I'd had them. The blue garbage can was always on the right and the brown on the left, and the thief had reversed them. I'd unlocked my back door and entered without turning on a light, then opened the correct kitchen drawer, extracted two twisties, and lifted out and sealed the garbage bags already lining the cans. I'd relined the cans with the garbage bags that had been used to cover the body, then put the bagged garbage in them, sealing the second set of bags over the first set. I'd figured I couldn't examine the cart in the middle of the night, and wheeling it inside would have created too much noise. It would have to wait until morning.

I'd done all I could do to erase my own involuntary complicity.

I should have been ready for bed, but I found myself biting my lower lip. My bedrock middle-class upbringing was raising its strong and stern head, as it did at unexpected and inconvenient times. The mortal remains of someone I knew were lying out there in dark solitude. That was wrong.

I couldn't call the police department; possibly incoming calls were taped or traced in some way, even in little Shakespeare. Maybe I could just forget about it? Someone would find him in the morning. But it might be the little kids who lived on Latham . . . And then it came to me – whom I could call. I hesitated, my fingers twisting and untwisting. The back of my neck told me this was not a smart move. Get it over with, I told myself.

I pulled out my little flashlight and was able to read my tiny Shakespeare phone book by its dimming glow. I punched in the right numbers, listened to three rings; then a groggy male voice said, 'Claude Friedrich here.'

'Listen,' I said, surprised at how harsh and ragged my voice came out. I waited a beat.

'Okay.' He was alert now.

'There's a dead man in the park across the street from you,' I said, and hung up the phone. I crept across the hall to the room with the punching bag, my workout room. Through its window, I could see the light come on in Claude Friedrich's apartment, which was on the second floor, by Deedra Dean's.

Now I'd done all I could.

With a pleasant feeling of having discharged a responsibility, I climbed out of my clothes and into a nightgown. I heard a car in the street outside, and I padded into my dark living room to look out the window. Friedrich had taken my phone call seriously; he was out there in hastily thrown-on clothes, talking to one of the night patrolmen, Tom David Meiklejohn. As I watched, they started down the same path into the park that the cart thief had taken, each carrying a powerful 'skull-buster' flashlight.

Incident closed, I thought, going back to my bedroom and crawling into my double bed. I pulled the fresh sheets up, settled my head on my pillow, and instantly, finally, fell asleep.

Chapter Two

The next day was a Tuesday. On Tuesday mornings, I take care of Mrs Hofstettler. Marie Hofstettler's son Chuck lives in Memphis. He worries about his mother, but he doesn't worry enough to make the drive over to Shakespeare to see her. So he pays me handsomely to spend time with his mother twice a week.

I always do a little cleaning, channel Mrs Hofstettler's clothes through the washer and dryer, and occasionally take her to a friend's house or Kmart or Kroger's, if Mrs Hofstettler is having what she calls a 'limber' day.

I walked over from my house to the apartment building, letting myself in the squeaking front door and rapping lightly on the first door to my left to let Mrs Hofstettler know I was coming in. I had a key. Mrs Hofstettler was already up, a good sign; on her bad, stiff days, she is still in bed when I get there.

'I didn't sleep at all last night!' she said by way of greeting. Marie Hofstettler, now eighty-five, is as wrinkled as a dried apricot. Her hair is white and silky and thin, and she wears it pulled back in an untidy bun. (I know what pain it costs the old lady to raise her arms to form the bun. In a stupid moment, I had suggested Mrs Hofstettler have her hair cut short, and I had been treated to a huffy hour-long silence.) This morning, Mrs Hofstettler's teeth were already in and she had managed to pull on a red-and-blue-striped housedress, so the excitement had done her good.

'I saw there was crime-scene tape across the path going into the park', I commented in as neutral a voice as I could manage. No true Shakespearean would call Estes Arboretum anything but 'the park'. I'm finally getting the hang of being a true Shakespearean after four years.

'Didn't you hear all the commotion, girl?'

'I didn't hear a thing,' I answered truthfully. 'I slept real heavy last night.' I went down the hall to Mrs Hofstettler's bedroom to fetch the wash from the hamper.

'Then you are an amazing sleeper,' Mrs Hofstettler called after me. 'Honey, there were police cars up and down the street, and people coming and going, and an ambulance, too.'

'And I don't know anything about it to tell you,' I said, trying to sound regretful. I'm not normally chatty with clients, but I admire Marie Hofstettler; she doesn't whine and she isn't clingy.

'Let's turn on the radio,' Mrs Hofstettler said eagerly. 'Maybe we can find out what happened. If that don't work, I'm calling Deedra at the courthouse. She always knows what's going on.'

I started the washing machine. All eight apartments, of course, have the same layout, with the east apartments mirroring the west. There are four units upstairs and four downstairs. The building's front door and back door are locked at eleven, and residents aren't supposed to give anyone a key. Marie's apartment is a ground-floor front apartment on the north side. She's had it since the building was erected ten years ago; Marie and Pardon Albee are the only original tenants. In Marie's apartment, as in all of them, the common hallway door opens directly into a living room, with an area to the rear used for dining. Across from this dining area is the kitchen, of course, which is well lined with cabinets and counters for an apartment kitchen. The hall starts where the kitchen and dining area end, and to your right (in Marie's apartment) is the closet containing the washer and dryer and shelves used for linens and cleaners and odds and ends. Almost opposite this closet is the door to the master bedroom, which is a nice size and has a very large closet. On the same wall as the wash closet is the door to the much smaller guest bedroom, and at the end of the hall is the bathroom, with a large frosted-glass window, which is supposed to be the second line of escape in case of fire.

I've always appreciated the fact that the front doors are not centered, so that when a tenant answers his or her front door, the caller can't see down the hall directly into the bathroom.

The builder and resident landlord, Pardon Albee, had had the gall to call these the Shakespeare Garden Apartments because the front ones overlook the arboretum. The back ones at the ground floor overlook only the paved area that lies between the apartment and the garage, divided into eight stalls not quite wide enough for two cars each. The second floor apartments at the back have a scenic view of the train tracks, and beyond them the back lot of a hardware and lumber-supply store.

After I'd turned on the radio for Mrs Hofstettler, I began dusting the larger bedroom. Mrs Hofstettler turned up the radio loud so I could listen along, after a conscientious discussion about whom it might bother; no one, the old woman decided, since T. L. and Alvah York next door should be out for their morning walk, and Norvel Whitbread, whose apartment was above, was already at work, or drunk, or both.

The area station, which covered most of Hartsfield and Creek counties, plays so-called classic rock. It is a preprogrammed station. The song that came on first was one I'd liked long ago, before the time when my life's agenda had gotten so . . . simplified. I smiled as I lifted the old china figurines on the dressing table and dusted them very carefully. The song ended, I glanced at my watch, and right on cue the local announcer began to speak, her southern Arkansas accent so broad that even after four years in Shakespeare, I had to listen quite carefully.

'In local news' ('In lawcol nyus'), twanged the conscientiously serious voice, 'in Hartsfield County, Shakespeare real estate developer Pardon Albee was found dead in Estes Arboretum at approximately two-thirty A.M. by Police Chief Claude Friedrich, who was acting on an anonymous phone tip. The cause of death is not known at this time, but police suspect foul play. Albee was a lifelong resident of Shakespeare and a member of the Shakespeare Combined Church. In other news, a Creek County judge sentenced Harley Don Murrell to twenty years for the abduction and rape of a local—'

'Oh no!' Mrs Hofstettler exclaimed in real distress.

I carefully put down the shepherdess I'd been dusting and hurried into the living room. 'Lily, this is horrible! Oh, Lily, do you suppose he was killed and robbed right here? And who will we pay rent to now that Pardon Albee's dead? Who'll own the building?'

I automatically handed Mrs Hofstettler a Kleenex, thinking it was very like her to come right to the point. Who indeed owned the building now? When I'd recognized Pardon Albee's ugly green-and-orange plaid shirt last night, that hadn't been what I'd thought of.

The answer would not affect me directly, for I'd bought my house from Pardon, as had my neighbor. And Pardon had sold the lots at the north end of Track and around the corner on Jamaica Street to the Shakespeare Combined Church, a coalition of splinter churches that had thrived most unexpectedly. As far as I knew, the only property that Pardon still owned outright was Shakespeare Garden Apartments, and he'd enjoyed owning it to the hilt. In fact, he'd seen himself as the pivotal character in some kind of television drama – the kindly landlord who helps all his tenants solve their problems and knows all their most intimate secrets.

He'd worked hard on making the last part come true, anyway.

'I've got to call – Lily, I'm so glad you're here today!'

Mrs Hofstettler was more upset than I'd ever seen her, and I'd heard her fume for two weeks over the altar boy at St Stephen's Episcopal Church lighting the wrong candle during Advent.

'Who did you want to call?' I asked, putting down the dust cloth.

'The police. Pardon was here yesterday. It was the first of the month, you know. I get a check from Chuck toward the end of the month, and I deposit it, and every first, here comes Mr Albee, regular as clockwork. I always have my check made out and sitting on the table for him, and he always . . . Oh, I think I should tell the police he was here!'

'I'll call, then.' I hoped Mrs Hofstettler could ease her agitation with a phone call. To my surprise and dismay, the dispatcher at the Shakespeare Police Department said someone would be right by to listen to Mrs Hofstettler's story.

'You'd better make some coffee, Lily, please,' the old lady said. 'Maybe the policeman will want some. Oh, what could have happened to Pardon? I can't believe it. Just yesterday, he was standing right *there*. And now he's dead, and him a good twenty-five years younger than me! And Lily, could you pick up that tissue there, and straighten that pillow on the sofa? Oh, durn these stiff old legs! You just don't know, Lily, how frustrating being old can be.'

There was no safe response to that, so I straightened the room very quickly. The coffee was perking, everything in the apartment was dusted, and I'd given the bathroom a quick once-over by the time the doorbell rang. I was pulling the clothes from the dryer, but I'd become infected by Marie's house-pride, so I hastily carried the clean wash back to deposit in the guest bedroom and shut the louver doors that concealed the washer and dryer on my way back to answer the bell.

I had expected some underling. With a pang of dismay, I recognized the chief of police, the man I'd called in the middle of the night, Claude Friedrich.

I stood aside and waved him in, cursing my conscience-stricken call, afraid anything I said would cause him to recognize my voice.

It was the first time I'd seen Claude Friedrich close up, though of course I had glimpsed him driving in and out of the apartment house driveway, and occasionally passed him in the hall when I was in the building on a cleaning job.

Claude Friedrich was in his late forties, a very tall man with a deep tan, light brown hair and mustache streaked with gray, and light gray eyes that shone in the weathered face. He had few wrinkles, but the ones he had were so deep, they might have been put in with a chisel. He had a broad face and a square jaw, broad shoulders and hands, a flat stomach. His gun looked very natural on his hip. The dark blue uniform made my mouth feel dry, made something inside me twitch with anxiety, and I reacted with anger.

Macho man, I thought. As if he could hear me, Friedrich suddenly turned to catch me with my brows raised, one side of my mouth pulled up sardonically. We locked stares for a tense moment.

'Mrs Hofstettler,' he said politely, transferring his gaze to my employer, who was twisting a handkerchief in her hands.

'Thank you for coming – maybe you didn't even need to,' Mrs Hofstettler said in one breath. 'I would hate to bother you. Please have a seat.' She gestured toward the flowered sofa at right angles to the television and to her own favorite recliner.

'Thank you, ma'am, and coming here is no trouble at all,' Friedrich said comfortingly. He knew how to be soothing, no doubt about it. He sat down gratefully, as if he'd been standing for a long time. I moved into the kitchen, which has a hatch cut in the wall behind the counter, and opened it to stick out the coffeepot behind our guest's back. Mrs Hofstettler, thus reminded, went into her hostess mode, helping her regain her calm.

'I'm not being polite,' Mrs Hofstettler accused herself, turning her mild, faded blue eyes on her guest. 'Please, have some coffee. Do you take cream and sugar?'

'Thanks,' Friedrich said. 'I'd love some coffee. Black, please.'

'Lily, would you mind bringing Chief Friedrich some black coffee? I don't believe I want any. But you get yourself a cup and come join us. I believe, young man, that I knew your father . . .' And Mrs Hofstettler was off on the inevitable establishing of connections that made southern introductions so cozy and drawn-out.

Knowing it would please Mrs Hofstettler, I fixed a tray with napkins, a plate of cookies (a secret indulgence of Marie's – she likes Keebler Elves, chocolate with chocolate filling), and two generous cups of coffee. While I was assembling the tray, I was listening to Friedrich telling Marie about his years as a police officer in Little Rock; his decision to return to Shakespeare when, in quick succession, his father died, he himself divorced his wife, and the position of chief of police became vacant; and his pleasure at rediscovering the slower pace of life in little Shakespeare.

This guy was good.

As I aligned the napkins in overlapping triangles on the brightly painted tole tray, I admitted to myself that I was worried. After all, how long could I go without speaking before it looked just plain peculiar? On the other hand, he'd been asleep when I'd made the call. And I'd said so little, maybe he wouldn't recognize my voice?

I lifted the tray easily and carried it out to the living room. I handed Friedrich his cup. Now that I was close to him again, I was even more aware of how big he was.

'I'm sorry, I don't believe I've actually met you . . .' Friedrich said delicately as I perched on the hard armchair opposite him.

'Oh, you'll have to excuse me!' Mrs Hofstettler said ruefully, shaking her head. 'This awful news has just taken away all my manners. Chief Friedrich, this is *Miss* Lily Bard. She lives in the house next to our apartment building, and Lily has become the mainstay of Shakespeare since she moved here.'

Trust Mrs Hofstettler not to ignore a matchmaking opportunity; I should have anticipated this.

'I've seen you around, of course,' the big man said, with the courtly implication that no man could ignore me.

'I clean Deedra Dean's apartment,' I said briefly.

'Did you work in this building yesterday?'

'Yes.'

He waited for me to continue. I didn't.

'Then we need to talk later, when you're not working,' he said gently, as if he was talking to a shaky centenarian, or a mental deficient.

I nodded curtly. 'I have a break between four and five-thirty.'

'I'll come to your house then,' he said, and without giving me any time to agree or disagree, he focused his light gray eyes on his hostess.

'Now, Miss Marie, you tell me about seeing Mr Albee yesterday.'

'Well,' Mrs Hofstettler said slowly, gathering herself together with a kind of morbid pleasure, 'Pardon always comes about nine in the morning on the first day of the month . . . to collect the rent. I know he likes the other tenants to stop by his apartment, but he comes to me because I have limber days and I have stiff days, and I never know till I open my eyes in the morning which it's going to be.' She shook her head at the vagaries of illness and old age, and Friedrich responded with a sympathetic rumble.

'So he rang the doorbell, and I let him in,' Mrs Hofstettler said, concentrating hard on her narrative. 'He was wearing an orange-and-green plaid shirt and dark green polyester pants . . . kind of bad colors for anyone, but for a fair man, really not . . . well, that's neither here nor there. But especially if you're kind of heavyset . . . well . . . So he commented on the weather, and I answered – you know, the usual kind of thing people say to old ladies they don't know very well!'

Claude Friedrich smiled at this particular sharp old lady, took a sip of his coffee, then raised his cup to me in silent appreciation.

'Did he say anything about his plans for the day?' the police chief rumbled. His voice was like the sound of far-off thunder; it made you feel quite safe right where you were.

I was *really* going to have to be careful. I stared down into my coffee cup. I was so angry that I'd embroiled myself in the death of Pardon Albee, I pictured myself hurling the coffee cup against Mrs Hofstettler's dead-white wall. Of course, I wouldn't; Marie was not to blame for my predicament. I sighed silently, then looked up to meet Claude Friedrich's intent gaze. Damn.

'He just said he had to go back to his place to wait for everyone to come by with the rent. Since you've been living here, Mr Friedrich, you know how Pardon was about getting the rent right on the dot. He did say something about interesting things on the news . . .'

'Local news? National news?' Friedrich queried gently. He wasn't breaking into Mrs Hofstettler's stream of thought, I observed. He was more directing it with a gentle insinuation every now and then. It was skillful. And I noticed that somehow he'd managed to make two cookies vanish, without my ever seeing him chew.

'He didn't say.' Marie Hofstettler shook her head regretfully. 'He was kind of cheerful about it, though. You know, Pardon was – I don't know how to say it, now that he's gone – he liked to know things,' she finished delicately, with a tiny contraction of her brows and a little bob of her head.

He had called it 'taking a neighborly interest'.

That wasn't what I had called it.

'Now, yesterday, did you see any of your neighbors here?' Friedrich asked Mrs Hofstettler.

She thought, her lips pursed.

'I thought once I heard Alvah and T. L. next door, but they weren't due to come in until late last night, so I must have been mistaken. And I heard people knocking on Mr Albee's door – to pay their rent, you know – several times during the morning and afternoon. But I'm almost always watching the TV or playing the radio, and I don't hear quite as well as I used to.'

'When you thought you heard the Yorks, do you mean you heard their voices, enough to identify them, or do you mean that you just heard someone next door?'

Again, Mrs Hofstettler thought carefully. 'I believe I just heard movement next door.'

'It might have been me,' I said. 'I bought some groceries for them and put them in the kitchen and was supposed to water the plant.'

'Well, I heard this sound about three in the afternoon. I'd just gotten up from my nap.'

'That was probably me.'

Friedrich made a note in a little hot-pink spiral-bound notebook that suddenly appeared in his hands.

I glanced at my watch. I had to leave in thirty minutes to get to my next cleaning job, and I had yet to put away Marie's clean laundry.

'Excuse me,' I murmured, and took the tray back to the kitchen, feeling Friedrich's bright gaze on my back. I quickly washed and dried the dishes, then dodged out of the kitchen and into the guest bedroom. Nothing I'd washed needed ironing, so I was able to get everything put away in a few minutes. I went down a mental checklist; I'd done everything for Marie I usually do on Tuesday mornings, and I'd be coming back again on Saturday. Marie was almost out of Glass Plus. In the kitchen, I left a note affixed to the refrigerator with an 'I Heart Grandma' magnet. Marie gets money from Chuck to pay me, too; she'd write me a check on Saturday.

The police chief was gone when I emerged from the kitchen. I'd been waiting to hear the front door close behind him.

'Good-bye, Mrs Hofstettler,' I said. Marie was staring into space, her hands quiet in her lap. She seemed startled that I was still there.

'Good-bye, Lily,' the old woman said wearily. 'I'm so glad you came in today. This would have been hard to cope with on my own.'

'Maybe you should give your son a call today.'

'I hate to bother Chuck,' Marie protested.

'This is a very awful thing that's happened.' I remembered just how awful it had been in the narrow glow of my flashlight, in the dark, in the trees, in the middle of the night. But with a mental exercise as familiar as my bicep curls, I blocked it out. It would surface at another time and place, but by then I would be alone.

Tuesdays are always busy for me. Today was rougher than usual because I hadn't had enough sleep the night before and had endured great stress.

I ran in my house to grab some fruit to eat in the car on the way to my next job.

The garbage hadn't been picked up yet; Tuesday is also garbage day for my part of town. My cart was out in front, the garbage cans sitting in it correctly. No one could know or suspect that the garbage within those cans was double-bagged, that one set contained the traces of human remains. I had lifted the cans quickly that morning to see if any vestige of Pardon Albee's last ride was visible on the cart. To the naked eye, the metal looked quite clean.

As I went out the kitchen door to my carport, I could hear the rumble of the garbage truck coming. I couldn't resist standing there, one foot in the car and one arm propped on the open door, watching the truck approach. A middle-aged black man wearing a blue jumpsuit with 'City of Shakespeare' stitched on the back hoisted out the garbage cans, one after another, dumped the bags into the back of the truck, and returned the garbage cans to the cart.

I closed my eyes in relief as the garbage truck moved up the street to the apartments. The clumsy vehicle turned cautiously to navigate the staple-shaped driveway. But it didn't idle long enough behind that building; I heard it moving again much sooner than it should have. I found myself wishing I could see through the privacy fence.

I was willing to bet that on the other side of it, policemen wearing rubber gloves were going through the apartment garbage cans.

It struck me as a sophisticated concept for the Shakespeare police force.

Though I had no way of finding out for sure, my guess was that the idea had originated with Chief Claude Friedrich.

I stood in the doorway of Bobo Winthrop's room and eyed it grimly. Bobo is a husky seventeen-year-old, full of hormones in overdrive, as I'd discovered last summer. He was at school today, but his room was evidence that Bobo had been home at least to sleep and change clothes often during the past week. There was furniture in the room, somewhere, under all the mess, and I remembered it was good furniture, just as Bobo, I had a gut feeling, was a good kid – under all the mess.

In other words, he didn't leave his room like this to spite me after I'd thumped him in the guts for putting his hand on my bottom. It's just that Bobo has been accustomed all his life to having someone clean up after him.

Days like this, I feel like I'm following an elephant in a parade, armed only with a puppy's pooper-scooper.

But since I am well paid by Beanie Winthrop to clean her house, I shouldn't grumble, I reminded myself sternly. Faced with Bobo's room, it was hard to remember why I'd chosen housecleaning as my means of support.

I was a National Merit Scholar, I reminded myself, dragging the plastic wash basket behind me as I worked my way across the room, tossing in soiled clothes as I went. I was top of my high school class. I finished college. My grade point average was 3.9.

On Tuesdays, that is my mantra.

Bobo had also ordered pizza one evening while his parents were out, I discovered. Probably – I evaluated by the layers of clothing over the cardboard box – about three days ago.

'Yoohoo!' came a light sweet voice from the kitchen, accompanied by the slam of the door leading into the garage. 'Lily! I'm just stopping by on my way to my tennis lesson!'

'Good afternoon,' I called back, knowing my voice was (at best) grim. I much preferred seeing none of the Winthrops – not Beanie; her husband, Howell Junior; her oldest son, Bobo; or his younger siblings, Amber-Jean and Howell Three.

Beanie's maiden name had been, incredibly, Bobo: Beatrice ('Beanie') Bobo. The Bobos were sixth-generation Arkansas aristocrats, and I suspected Beanie had a slave-owning gene still in her DNA.

'Here I am, Lily!' Beanie cried with exaggerated joy, as though I had been on tenterhooks waiting for her appearance. And Beanie always makes appearances; she never just walks into a room. She popped into the doorway now like she was appearing in an English comedy: Attractive Lady Beatrice, on her way to play tennis, stops to speak to the parlor maid.

Beanie is undeniably attractive. She's in her middle forties, but her body doesn't know it. Though her face is not actually pretty, Beanie is a past mistress at maximizing what she has. Her long, thick hair is colored a discreet chestnut brown, her contacts make her brown eyes darker, and her tan is always touched up in the winter with a sun-bed session or two a week.

'Listen, Lily, wasn't that awful about Pardon?' Beanie was in her chatty mode. 'I went to high school with his little sister! Of course, even then Pardon wasn't the easiest person to get along with, but still . . . to be killed like that! Isn't it awful?'

'Yes.'

'Ah . . . well, Lily, if you find Bobo's checkbook, please leave it on my desk. He hasn't balanced it in six months, and I promised him I'd do it. Though when he thinks I'll find the time, I don't know!'

'All right.'

'Oh, and Lily – Bobo tells me you take karate. Can that be true?'

'Yes.' I knew I was being uncooperative. I was in a bloody mood today. And I hated the idea of the Winthrops discussing me. Most days, I find Beanie amusing but tolerable, but today she was irritating beyond measure. And Beanie felt the same way about me.

'Well, now, we always wanted Bobo to take tae kwan do, but there never was anyone here to teach it, except that man who went broke after six months. Who do you take from?'

'Marshall Sedaka.'

'Where does he teach it? At his gym?'

'He teaches goju karate to adults only on Monday, Wednesday, and Friday nights in the aerobics room at Body Time, seven-thirty to eight-thirty.' Those three nights were the highlights of my week.

Beanie decided I was experiencing some kind of warming trend, and she beamed at me.

'So you don't think he'd teach Bobo? After all, Bobo's seventeen, and as much as I hate to admit it, he's practically an adult – physically, at least,' Beanie added rather grimly.

'You can ask him,' I replied. There wasn't a hope in hell of Marshall taking on a spoiled kid like Bobo, but it wasn't my business to tell Beanie that.

'I just may do that,' Beanie said, making a little note in the tiny spiral-bound notebook she keeps in her purse all the time. (That's something Beanie and Claude Friedrich have in common, I reflected.) And Beanie would call, too; one of the few things I find to admire about the woman is her devotion to her children. 'Well,' Beanie said dismissively, looking up and turning slightly as if she was already half out the door, 'I'm just going to freshen up for a minute and then I'm off to the club. Don't forget about the checkbook, please!'

'I won't.' I bent over to retrieve a sweatshirt Bobo had apparently used to clean his car's windshield.

'You know,' Beanie said reflectively, 'I think Pardon was that Marshall Sedaka's partner.'

'What?' The sweatshirt slipped from my fingers; I groped around for it, hoping I hadn't heard correctly.

'Yes,' said Beanie firmly. 'That's right. Howell Junior told me, and I thought it was funny at the time, because Pardon was the most unfit man I've ever seen. He wouldn't walk down the street if he could ride. That gym's been a great success. It must have made Pardon a lot of money. Wonder who he left it all to?'

I just kept tossing clothes into the plastic wash basket. When I finally looked up, Beanie had gone, and a moment later I heard splashing noises from Beanie's big bathroom off the master bedroom.

After I heard the slam of the door to the garage, I said out loud, 'I best start being nice to the mistress, else she sell me down the river.' I really shouldn't be rude to her, I told myself seriously. Since they pay for me twice a week.

I go to Mrs Hofstettler twice a week, too, but I charge her less – a lot less – because it takes me far less time and effort to straighten a two-bedroom apartment than it does the large Winthrop home, and also because the Winthrop children don't do the slightest thing to help themselves, at least as far as I can tell. If only they would put their own dirty clothes in the hamper and pick up their own rooms, they could save their parents quite a bit of my salary.

Normally, I am able to maintain my indifference to the

Winthrops' personal habits, but this morning I was thrown off balance by what Beanie had said. Had Marshall and Pardon Albee really been in business together? Marshall had never mentioned a partner in the business he'd built up from scratch. Though Marshall and I knew each other's bodies with an odd, impersonal intimacy from working out at the same time and taking karate together, I realized we really knew little about each other's daily lives.

I wondered uneasily why I would worry about Marshall Sedaka, anyway. What difference would a partnership between Pardon and Marshall make? No matter how dim the light, I knew I'd have recognized Marshall if he'd been the person wheeling Pardon Albee's body into the park.

That realization made me feel even more uneasy.

Bending my mind ferociously to the job at hand, I found Bobo's errant checkbook and propped it on his mother's dressing table, where she'd be sure to spot it. Thinking was slowing me down; I still had to do Howell Three's room, and though he isn't the pig Bobo is, he isn't neat, either.

On my Tuesday at the Winthrops', I pick up, do the wash and put it away, and clean the bathrooms. On my Friday visit, I dust, vacuum, and mop. The Winthrops also have a cook, who takes care of the kitchen, or they'd have to hire me for a third time slot. Of course, on Fridays, too, I have to do a certain amount of picking up just to reach the surfaces of things I need to dust, and I get aggravated all over again at the people who are lazy enough to pay me to clean up their mess.

I soothed myself with a few deep breaths. Finally, I realized I was upset not because of the unthrifty Winthrops – their habits are to my benefit – or even because of Marshall Sedaka's possible involvement with Pardon Albee, but because right after I'd finished here, I had to meet with Claude Friedrich.

Chapter Three

He was exactly on time.

As I stepped back to let him in, I was again impressed by his size and presence.

The big thing about fear, I reminded myself, is not to show it. Having braced myself with that piece of personal junk philosophy, I found myself unable to show the policeman much of anything, besides a still face that could be construed as simply sullen.

I watched him scanning my sparse furniture, pieces that were on sale at the most expensive local stores, pieces I'd carefully selected and placed exactly where I wanted. It is a small living room, and I'd chosen with its size in mind: a reclining love seat with a footrest, rather than a sofa; a wing chair; small occasional tables; small pictures. I have a television set, but it, too, is not large. There are no photographs. There are library books, a large stack, on the bottom level of the table by my chair.

The prevailing colors in both upholstery and pictures are dark blue and tan.

'How long have you lived in this house?' Friedrich asked when he'd finished looking.

'I bought it four years ago.'

'From Pardon Albee.'

'Yes.'

'And you bought it when you came to Shakespeare?'

'I rented it at first, with an option to buy.'

'What exactly do you do for your living, Miss – is it Miss? – Bard?'

Titles are not important to me, nor is political correctness. I didn't tell him to call me Ms. But I saw that he had expected me to correct him.

'I clean houses.'

'But a few things more than that?'

He'd done his research. Or maybe he'd always known about me, every detail of my life here in Shakespeare. After all, how much could the chief of police in this town have to occupy his mind?

'A few things.' He required elaboration, his lifted eyebrows implying I was being churlish with my short answers. I suppose I was. I sighed. 'I run errands for a few older people. I help families when they go out of town, if a neighbor can't. I get groceries in before the family comes home, feed the dog, mow the yard, and water the plants.'

'How well did you know Pardon Albee?'

'I bought this house from him. I clean some apartments in the building he owned, but that is by arrangement with the individual tenants. I worked for him a couple of times. I saw him in passing.'

'Did you have a social relationship with him, maybe?'

I flared up to speak before I realized I was being goaded. I shut my mouth again. I breathed deeply. 'I did not have a social relationship with Mr Albee.' As a matter of fact, I'd always had a physical aversion to Pardon; he was white and soft and lumpy-looking, without any splendors of character to counterbalance this lack of fitness.

Friedrich studied his hands; he'd folded them together, fingers interlaced. He was leaning forward, his elbows resting on his thighs.

'About last night,' he rumbled, shooting a sudden look over at me. I'd seated him on the love seat, while I was in the wing chair. I didn't nod; I didn't speak. I just waited.

'Did you see anything unusual?' He leaned back suddenly, looking straight at me.

'Unusual.' I tried to look thoughtful, but felt I was probably just succeeding in looking stubborn.

'I went to bed about eleven,' I said hastily. I had – the first time, when I'd found I couldn't sleep. 'Marie – Mrs Hofstettler – told me this morning there was a lot of activity outside, but I'm afraid I didn't hear it.'

'Someone called me about two-thirty in the morning,' Friedrich said gently. 'A woman. This woman said there was a body in the park, across the street from me.'

'Oh?'

'Oh yes, Miss Bard. Now I think this woman saw something, something about how that body got into that park, and I think that woman got scared, or knew who did it and was scared of that person, or maybe had a hand in Pardon Albee's turning up out there and just didn't want the poor man to lie in the park all night and get covered in dew this morning. So I think whoever it was, for whatever reason, had some concern about what happened to Pardon's remains. I sure would like to talk to that woman.'

He waited.

I did my best to look blank.

He sighed, heavily and wearily.

'Okay, Miss Bard. You didn't see anything and you don't know anything. But if you think of something,' he said with heavy irony in his voice, 'call me day or night.'

There was something so solid about Police Chief Claude Friedrich that I was actually tempted to confide in him. But I thought of my past, and of its emerging, ruining the sane and steady existence I'd created in this little town.

And at this moment, I knew the man was dangerous. I came out of my reverie, to find he was waiting for me to speak, that he knew I was contemplating telling him something.

'Good-bye,' I said, and rose to show him to the door.

Friedrich looked disappointed as he left. But he said nothing, and those gray eyes, resting on me, did not look hostile.

After I'd locked the door behind him, I realized, apropos of nothing, that he was maybe the fifth person who'd entered my house in four years.

On Tuesday evenings at five-thirty, I clean a dentist's office. When I first moved to Shakespeare and was living off my savings (what was left after I'd finished paying what the insurance didn't cover on my medical bills), while I built up my clientele, Dr Sizemore had stayed until I got there, watched me clean, and locked the door behind me when I left. Now I have a key. I bring my own cleaning supplies to Dr Sizemore's; he prefers it that way, so I charge him a little more. It is a matter of indifference to me whether I use my own supplies or the client's; I have my favorites, but they have theirs, too. I want to be Lily Bard who cleans; I don't want to be Busy Hands or Maids to Go or anything business-sounding.

Strictly privately, I call myself Shakespeare's Sanitary Service.

I'd thought of housecleaning as the ultimate in detachment when I'd decided how I would try to support myself, but cleaning has turned out to be an intimate occupation. Not only have I found out physical details about the people who employ me (for example, Dr Sizemore is losing his hair and has problems with constipation) but I've learned more about their lives, involuntarily, than I feel comfortable with.

Sometimes I amuse myself by writing a fictional column for the biweekly *Shakespeare Journal* while I work. 'Dr John Sizemore recently received a bill from a skin magazine – and I don't mean the kind for dermatologists – so he's hiding the copies somewhere . . . His receptionist, Mary Helen Hargreaves [when the locals said it, it sounded like Mare Heln] does her nails at work and reads English mystery novels on her lunch hour . . . His nurse, Linda Gentry, finished a package of birth control pills today, so next cleaning night, there'll be Tampax in the bathroom.'

But who would be interested in a column like that? The things I've learned are not things of real interest to anyone, though I was among the first to know that Jerri Sizemore wanted a divorce (the summons from the lawyer had been open on John Sizemore's desk), and I learned last week that Bobo Winthrop was practicing safe sex with someone while his parents were at the country club dance.

There are lots of things I know, and I've never told anyone or even thought of it. But this thing I know, about the death of Pardon Albee . . . this, I thought, I might have to tell.

It would lead to exposure, I felt in my bones.

My life might not be much, but it's all I have and it's livable. I've tried other lives; this one suits me best.

I was through at Dr Sizemore's at seven-thirty, and I locked the door carefully, then went home to eat a chicken breast, a roll, and some broccoli sprinkled with Parmesan cheese. After I'd cleaned up the kitchen, I fidgeted around the house, tried a library book, slammed it shut, and at last resorted to turning on the television.

I'd forgotten to check the time. I'd turned the TV on during the news. The pictures were among the worst: women holding screaming children, bombs exploding, bodies in the street in the limp grip of death. I saw the face of one desperate woman whose family was buried in rubble, and before my finger could punch the channel changer, tears were running down my face.

I haven't been able to watch the news in years.

Chapter Four

Wednesday mornings are flexible. It's the time I set aside for emergencies (special cleanings for ladies who are going to host the bridge club or give a baby shower) or rare cleanings, like helping a woman turn out her attic. This Wednesday, I had long been scheduled to help Alvah York with her spring cleaning. Alvah observes this rite even though she and her husband, T. L., live in one of Pardon Albee's apartments now that T. L. has retired from the post office.

Two years before, I'd helped Alvah spring-clean a three-bed-room house, and Alvah had started work before I arrived and kept on going at noon when I left. But Alvah has gone downhill sharply since the move, and she might actually need help for the two-bedroom apartment this year.

The Yorks' apartment is on the ground floor of the Garden Apartments, next to Marie Hofstettler's, and its front door is opposite the door of the apartment Pardon Albee kept for himself. I couldn't help glancing at it as I knocked. There was crime-scene tape across the door. I'd never seen any in real life; it was exactly like it was on television. Who was supposed to want to get into Pardon's apartment? Who would have had a key but Pardon? I supposed he had relatives in town that I didn't know of; everyone in Shakespeare is related in some way to at least a handful of the other inhabitants, with very few exceptions.

For that matter, how had he died? There'd been blood on his head, but I hadn't investigated further. The examination had been too disgusting and frightening alone in the park.

I glanced at my man-sized wristwatch. Eight on the dot; one of the primary virtues Alvah admires is punctuality.

Alvah looked dreadful when she answered the door.

'Are you all right?' I asked involuntarily.

Alvah's gray hair was matted, obviously uncombed and un-curled, and her slacks and shirt were a haphazard match.

'Yes, I'm all right,' she said heavily. 'Come on in. T. L. and I were just finishing breakfast.'

Normally, the Yorks are up at five-thirty and have finished breakfast, dressed, and are taking a walk by eight-thirty.

'When did you get home?' I asked. I wasn't in the habit of asking questions, but I wanted to get some response from Alvah. Usually, after one of their trips out of town, Alvah can't wait to brag about her grandchildren and her daughter, and even from time to time that unimportant person, the father of those grand-children and husband of that daughter, but today Alvah was just dragging into the living room ahead of me, in silence.

T. L., seated at their little dinette set, was more like his usual bluff self. T. L. is one of those people whose conversation is of 75 percent platitudes.

'Good morning, Lily! Pretty as ever, I see. It's going to be a beautiful day today.'

But something was wrong with T. L., too. His usual patter was thudding, and there wasn't any spring in his movement as he rose from the little table. He was using his cane this morning, the fancy silver-headed one his daughter had given him for Christmas, and he was really leaning on it.

'Just let me go shave, ladies,' he rumbled valiantly, 'and then I'll leave the field to you.'

Folding the paper beside his place at the table, he went down the hall. T. L. is a big, shrewd gray-haired man, running to fat now, but still strong from a lifetime of hard physical work. I watched T. L. duck into the bedroom doorway. Something else was different about him. After a moment, it came to me: This morning, he walked in silence. T. L. always whistles, usually country-and-western songs or hymns.

'Alvah, would you like me to come back some other time?'

Alvah seemed surprised I'd asked. 'No, Lily, though it's right sweet of you to be concerned. I may as well get on with spring cleaning.'

It looked to me as if it would be better for Alvah to go back to bed. But I began carrying the breakfast things into the kitchen, something I'd never had to do at the Yorks' before. Alvah had always done things like that herself.

Alvah didn't comment at all while I did the dishes, dried them, and put them away. She sat with her hands wrapped around a cup of coffee, staring into the dark fluid as if it would tell her the future. T. L. emerged from the bedroom, shaven and outwardly cheerful, but still not whistling. 'I'm going to get a haircut, honey,' he told his wife. 'You and Lily don't work too hard.' He gave her a kiss and was out the door.

I was wrong again in thinking Alvah would be galvanized by her husband's departure. All she did was drink the coffee. I felt the skin on the back of my neck prickle with anxiety. I'd worked with Alvah side by side on many mornings, but the woman at the table seemed altogether different.

Alvah suffers from a pinched nerve in her back and is having increasing problems getting around, but she is normally a practical, good-natured woman with decided ideas about how she wants things done and a plain way of expressing them. She could offend by this straightforwardness, and I've seen it happen, but I've never minded her ways myself. There are few unexpressed thoughts hanging around in Alvah York's head, and very little tact, but Alvah is a good person, honest and generous.

Then I saw the supplies I'd brought in for the Yorks on Monday afternoon were exactly where I'd left them. The butter was in the refrigerator in the same place I'd laid it down, and the lettuce beside it hadn't been washed. At least the paper towels had been unwrapped, put on the dispenser, and used, and the bread had been put into the bread box.

I couldn't say anything more than I'd already said. Alvah wouldn't tell me what to do. So I mopped the kitchen.

Alvah has her own way of spring cleaning, and I thought I remembered she began by getting all the curtains down; in fact,

the pair that hung in the living room on the window facing the
street had already been removed, leaving the blinds looking curiously naked. So until very recently, Alvah had been operating
normally. I cleaned the exposed blinds. They were dusty; Alvah
had stopped just at that point, after she'd taken down the first pair
of curtains.

'Is something wrong?' I asked reluctantly.

Alvah maintained her silence for so long that I began to hope
she wouldn't tell me whatever it was. But finally, she began
speaking. 'We didn't tell anyone around here,' she said with a
great weariness. 'But that man over in Creek County – that
Harley Don Murrell, the one who was sentenced for rape – well,
that man . . . the girl he raped was our granddaughter Sarah.'

I could feel the blood drain from my face.

'What happened?' I sat across from Alvah.

'Thank God they don't publish the victim's name in the paper
or put it on the news,' Alvah said. 'She's not in the hospital anymore, but T. L. thinks maybe she should be – the mental hospital.
She's just seventeen. And her husband ain't no help – he just acts
mad that this happened to her. Said if she hadn't been wearing
that leotard and tights, that man would have left her alone.'

Alvah heaved a sigh, staring down at her coffee cup. She would
have seen a different woman if she'd looked up, but I was hoping
she wouldn't look up. I was keeping my eyes open very wide so
they wouldn't overflow.

'But he wouldn't have,' I said. 'Left her alone.'

Wrapped in her own misery, Alvah replied, 'I know that, her
mother knows that, and you know that. But men always wonder,
and some women, too. You should have seen that woman
Murrell's married to, her sitting up there in court when she should
have been at home hiding her head in shame, acting like she didn't
have any idea in the world what her husband was up to, telling
the newspaper people that Sarah was . . . a bad girl, that everyone
in Creek County knew it, that Sarah must have led him on . . .'.

Then Alvah cried.

'But he got convicted,' I said.

'Yes,' Alvah said. 'He cried and screamed and said he'd got the Lord. It didn't do him a bit of good; he got convicted. But he'll get out, less someone kills him in prison, which is what I pray for, though the Lord may damn me for it. They say that other prisoners don't like rapists or child molesters. Maybe someone will kill him some night.'

I recognized the tone, the words. I had to fight panic hard for a second. I was grateful for Alvah's absorption in her own troubles. My hand went up to my chest, touched the light yellow of my T-shirt, felt the ridges of the scars underneath it.

'Alvah, all I can do is clean,' I said.

'Well, let's do that,' Alvah said shakily. 'We might as well.'

For three hours, we worked in the small apartment, cleaning things that had never been dirty and straightening things that had never been messy. Alvah likes her life streamlined – she would live well on a boat, I've always thought. Everything superfluous was thrown away ruthlessly; everything else was arranged logically and compactly. I admire this, having tendencies that way myself, though I'm not as extreme as Alvah. For one thing, I reflected as I wiped the cabinets in the bathroom, Alvah has such limited interests that cleaning is one of her few outlets for self-expression. Alvah does a little embroidery of an uninspired kind, but she doesn't read or sew and is not particularly interested in cooking or television. So she cleans.

Alvah is a warning to me.

'What about the camper?' I asked when I thought we were almost through with the apartment.

'What?' Alvah said.

'We usually do the camper, too,' I reminded her. The Yorks have a camper they pull behind their pickup truck, and when they visit their daughter, they park in her driveway and live in the camper. They can make their own coffee in the morning, go to bed when they feel like it, they've often told me. I'd been remembering while I worked how many times the Yorks had mentioned their granddaughter Sarah; youngest of their daughter's children, Sarah had been spoiled and had just last year made a bad marriage to a boy as young as she. But the Yorks have always doted on Sarah.

'You remember all the arguments Pardon gave us about that camper?' Alvah asked unexpectedly.

I did indeed. At each end of the residents' parking garage is a space about car width between the wall of the garage and the surrounding fence. The Yorks had asked permission to park their camper in the north space, and initially Pardon had agreed. But later, he'd reneged, insisting it stuck out and inconvenienced the other residents.

It had never been my business, so I'd paid little attention to the whole brouhaha. But I'd heard the Yorks carry on about it, and I'd seen Pardon standing out in the parking area, shaking his head at the camper as if it were a difficult child, puttering around it with a yardstick. Pardon Albee had been a fusser, a man apparently unable to let anything be.

He would never let a sleeping dog lie.

Now Alvah was weeping again. 'You'd better go, Lily,' she said. 'This whole thing has just got me where I don't know if I'm going or coming. These past few days, when we were there for the trial, they have just been like hell. I'll do better next week.'

'Sure, Alvah,' I said. 'Call me when you want to get your curtains back up, or if you want to clean the camper.'

'I'll call you,' Alvah promised. I didn't remind her that I hadn't been paid; that was an indicator, too, since Alvah is always scrupulous about paying me on the dot.

I can always drop back by tomorrow, I thought. By then, perhaps some of the shock of Murrell's trial would have worn off.

Of course, Sarah's suffering would continue, for weeks and months and years . . .

I realized it for sure wasn't my day as I was leaving the building. Deedra Dean came in the front door before I could get out of it.

I can't stand Deedra, especially since our conversation last week. We'd been standing right inside Deedra's upstairs apartment door. Deedra had come home for lunch and was ready to return to Shakespeare City Hall, where she almost earns a living as an office clerk.

'Hi, housekeeper!' Deedra had said chirpily. 'Listen, I been meaning to tell you . . . last week I think you forgot to lock the door behind you when you left.'

'No,' I had said very firmly. Reliability is very important in my work, maybe even more important than doing an impeccable cleaning job. 'I never forget. Maybe you did, but I didn't.'

'But last Friday, when I came home, my door was unlocked,' Deedra had insisted.

'I locked it as I left,' I'd insisted right back. 'Though,' I'd added, struck by a sudden recollection, 'Pardon was on his way up the stairs as I was coming down, and of course he has a master key.'

'Why would he go into my apartment?' Deedra had asked, but not as if the idea was so ridiculous. As it sunk in even further, Deedra'd looked . . . well, a strange combination of angry and uneasy. I'd been intrigued by the sight of thought processes echoing through Deedra's empty head.

Deedra Dean, Deedra of the shiny blond hair, voluptuous figure, and a face completely undermined by its lack of chin. Deedra is always brightly made up and maniacally animated to distract the eye from that damning absence. Deedra moved into the apartment building three years ago and had screwed every male who had ever lived in the building except (maybe) Pardon Albee and (almost certainly) T. L. York. Deedra's fond mother, a sweet, well-to-do widow who recently remarried, subsidizes Deedra heavily. Lacey Dean Knopp is apparently under the impression that Deedra is dating around until she finds Mr Right. To Deedra, every man is apparently Mr Right, for a night or two, anyway.

I've told myself often that it isn't any of my business, and I've wondered why Deedra's habits infuriate me. Gradually, I've come to the conclusion that Deedra's total lack of self-respect dismays me, Deedra's risk taking frightens me, and the ease with which Deedra has sex makes me envious.

But as long as I get paid on time by Deedra's mama, I keep

reminding myself every ten minutes that Deedra is an adult, nominally at least, who can arrange her life as she chooses.

'Well, just don't let it happen again,' Deedra had lectured me last week, with a lame attempt at sternness, after she'd accused me of leaving the door unlocked. Even Deedra's feeble brain had finally registered my anger. 'Oh, gotta run! I had to come back to get my insurance card. I've got to get my car inspected on my lunch hour and get that tag renewal notice in the mail.'

I'd wanted to say something to Deedra about her lifestyle, something that would make a difference, but I knew nothing I could say would make an impression. And it was truly none of my business; Deedra was supposed to be grown up. I'd watched out the window as Deedra hurried from the front door to her red sports car, left idling at the curb. Deedra's mother had made the down payment on that unreliable but flashy car; Deedra'd told me that quite casually.

'Did you ever find out if Pardon had been in your apartment?' I asked today. There was no one else in the ground-floor hall, and I kept my voice low. I had been following my own train of thought so intently, I'd forgotten that Deedra might be thinking of something quite different, and she looked at me now as if I was a very peculiar person.

'No,' she said fiercely. I raised my eyebrows and waited. 'And you better not tell the police you talked to me about that, either!'

'Oh?'

'You won't get any work in Shakespeare ever again,' Deedra threatened. 'I don't want to be involved in that old bastard getting killed.'

'Do you seriously think,' I said, one side of my mouth curling up in a very dry smile, 'that anyone in this town would give up an excellent and reliable maid like me to protect your hide?'

Deedra's blue eyes widened in shock. A door opened on the second floor, and down the stairs came the Garden Apartments' only black tenant, Marcus Jefferson. Marcus, a handsome man in his late twenties, gave us a startled look, muttered a greeting, and pushed past us to the front door, which gave its heavy groan as it inched shut behind him.

This building was full of people behaving peculiarly today. When I looked back at Deedra, her face was brick red and she was watching the front door close on Marcus Jefferson.

Uh-oh. I had a flash of what might have finally prodded Pardon Albee into 'doing something' about Deedra.

'Did you want me to come back on my regular day?' I asked. Perhaps Deedra didn't want my services anymore. I clean Deedra's apartment on Friday mornings. That is prime time, since everyone wants a house clean for the weekend, and I half-hoped Deedra would fire me.

'Oh . . . oh, yes. Listen, really, let's just forget all about that conversation we had last week, about the door. I left it unlocked, okay? I just remembered it later. I'm sorry I even thought you might have done it. You're just the most reliable . . .' Deedra's voice trailed off, a phony smile pasted to her face, where it looked quite at home.

As I walked down the sidewalk to my own house, I wondered if Pardon had indeed been in Deedra's apartment the week before. What would he go in there for? What would he have found if he did?

If he was looking for trash on how Deedra lived her private life, he'd have found plenty. In her top dresser drawer, Deedra keeps some pornographic pictures some lover had taken of her in exotic lingerie and some of her naked. I certainly hadn't wanted to know this little fact, but Deedra expects me to do her wash and put it away during the afternoon I spend cleaning the apartment, and that drawer is her lingerie drawer. Deedra also keeps some erotica and some ghastly magazines actually stuck under the bed (where I am obliged to vacuum), and of course the sheets are always a mess. There are probably other 'incriminating' things there, too, things Deedra's mother might be interested to know about.

Would Pardon Albee actually have dared to call Deedra's mother, the very proper Lacey Dean Knopp?

By God, that would be just like him.

Five minutes after I had entered my own house, the doorbell rang. I checked my peephole and opened the door.

My visitor was surprising but nonthreatening – my seldom-seen neighbor, Carlton Cockroft. I've spoken to Carlton only three or four times a year since I bought the house.

There is something very 'edible' about Carlton. He always reminds me of hot chocolate and caramels in the winter, or the coconut smell of tanning lotion and the tang of barbecue in the summer. Carlton is in his early thirties, like me. He has black hair and dark brown eyes, a cleft chin, and thick arched brows. He smells good. He is maybe four inches taller than I am, about five ten. My neighbor is polite, busy, and heterosexual – and that is the sum total of my knowledge.

'Hello, Lily,' he said, his voice pleasant but not cheerful.

'Carlton.' I nodded in greeting, then opened my door so he could step inside.

He looked very surprised, and I realized I'd never asked him in before. He looked at the room very quickly and didn't seem to know what to do with himself, quite unlike my assured visitor of the day before.

'Have a seat,' I said, taking the wing chair.

'Lily, I'll come straight to the point,' Carlton began after he'd settled himself on the love seat. He leaned forward, putting his elbows on his knees. He was wearing an unremarkable plaid shirt in navy blue and white, pleated blue jeans, and Reeboks; he looked informally prosperous and comfortable.

I waited for him to come straight to the point. Most people seem to think you should respond when they tell you they're about to do something, but I've always thought it more interesting to wait and see if they actually do it.

He kept his eyes on me for a moment, as if expecting something from me, sure enough.

I made an open-hands gesture – okay, the point?

'I saw you out walking the night of the murder.' He waited for me to shriek in alarm. 'I got up to get a sinus pill.'

I shrugged. 'So?'

'Lily, that puts you in a bad position. I didn't tell Friedrich, but he asked me an awful lot of questions about you. If anyone else saw you, I'm afraid he may even suspect you of having something to do with Pardon's death.'

I thought for a moment, my hands folded on my lap.

'So, why are you here?' I asked.

'I just wanted to warn you,' Carlton said, straightening from his intent-but-relaxed pose. 'I've always worried about you some.'

My eyebrows flew up.

'Yes, yes, I know,' he said with a little smile. 'None of my business. But you're a woman alone, a pretty woman, and since I live next to you I feel a little responsible . . . I sure don't want anything bad to happen to you.'

I felt a terrible impulse to pull up my shirt and let him have a good look. The bad thing, the worst thing, had already happened to me. But I knew he was trying to shelter me, shield me from harm. I knew that Carlton perceived that as the right stance for a man to take. And I thought, as I so often do when dealing with them, that men are frequently more trouble than they're worth.

'Carlton, I live next to you, and since you're a good-looking guy living alone, I feel responsible for you,' I said.

Carlton turned red. He started to get up, restrained himself. 'I guess I deserved that. I should have turned it around in my own head to hear how it sounded, before it came out. But dammit, Lily, I'm trying to be your friend.'

'I see that, Carlton, but why do you feel responsible for my possible trouble with the police? How do you know I'm not guilty of killing Pardon?'

My handsome neighbor looked at me as if I'd grown a snake's head and hissed. He was hurt, his gallant impulse rebuffed.

'Well . . .' he began stiffly, 'well . . . I've just wasted my time. And yours.'

I looked down at my right hand; my ring-finger nail had an aggravating notch in it. I'd have to get out my emery board before it got worse.

He said unbelievingly, 'I'm trying to be nice to you.'

I looked up at him steadily, debated whether or not to speak. 'Carlton, you've dated too many women who thought you were just what they were looking for,' I said. I had observed the parade to and from his little house for four years. A good-looking guy with no visible vices and a steady income in a town this size? USDA prime.

'But thanks for not telling the police you saw me. As it happens, I don't know who killed Pardon, and I'd rather not spend a lot of time convincing the police of that.'

I thought I'd been fairly agreeable. But Carlton said, 'Good-bye, Lily,' and stalked out in a huffy way. He remembered just in time not to slam the door behind him.

As I went to get my emery board, I shook my head. There was a good guy in there somewhere under a few layers of crusted manure. I wondered how Carlton had imagined his visit would go.

'Lily, I'm the handsome male next to you and I'm showing you by my silence that I'm gallant and dependable. You should develop a crush on me.'

'Thank you, hunk who has never noticed me before. I was out late at night on a mysterious but innocent errand. I am truly not the peculiar person I sometimes seem, and I am so grateful you have shielded me from interrogation by the rough police. I am absolutely innocent of everything but a strong urge to go to bed with you and/or hire you to prepare my next tax statement.'

I had a little laugh to myself, which was something I needed before I went to my next job.

The Shakespeare Combined Church secretary had called a few days before to ask me to serve and clean up after a board meeting for the SCC preschool, so I left home on foot at 4:55. After passing the apartment building, I began walking by the large parking lot,

which is at the end of Track Street. The preschool building, which
on Sundays houses the Sunday school, is set at the back of the
parking lot and is one long two-storey wing. An L-shaped covered
walkway runs across the front of the preschool and up the side of
the church proper, which faces Jamaica Street. The white-spired
church is traditional red brick, but I know little about that part of
the establishment. The offices of the minister and his secretary are
on the second floor of the Sunday school wing.

If I ever resume going to church, my choice won't be Shakespeare Combined, or SCC, as the locals invariably call it. SCC was
formed when lots of conservative splinter groups amazingly
coalesced to combine incomes and hire a minister and build a
facility that would serve them all.

They'd found the Reverend Joel McCorkindale and they'd fund-
raised and collected until they'd had enough to build the church,
then the Sunday school building. The Reverend McCorkindale is a
super fund-raiser. I've seen him in action. He remembers *everyone's* name. He knows everyone's family connections, asks after
ailments, condoles about losses, congratulates on successes. If
he is ever at a loss, he humbly confesses it. He has a spanking-
clean wife and two toothy, clean boys, and though I believe Joel
McCorkindale truly loves his work, he makes the skin on my neck
crawl.

I've learned not to ignore the skin on my neck.

As far as I know, Joel McCorkindale has never broken the law.
Probably he never would. But I feel his potential to do something
truly dreadful simmering right beneath the surface. I have lived
one step away from losing my mind for years. I am quick and
accurate in spotting unstable streaks in others.

So far, that strange streak has only shown itself in his hiring
of the church janitor. Norvel Whitbread had shown up on
the church doorstep one morning drunk as a skunk. Joel
McCorkindale had taken Norvel in, given him a good dose of the
Spirit (rather than spirits), and taken him on as church maintenance man. Like his boss, Norvel looks good on the outside; he
is supposedly now sober, he has a genuine knack for fixing things,

and he keeps a smile on his face for church members. He is voluble in his gratitude to the minister and the congregation, which makes everyone feel good.

Though Joel McCorkindale may have a dark monster inside, it may never surface; he's done a great job so far, keeping it contained and submerged. Norvel, however, is simply rotten inside, through and through. All his cheer is a sham, and I am sure his sobriety is, too. He is the most touched-up of whited sepulchres.

SCC pays Norvel's rent at the Shakespeare Garden Apartments, and a salary besides, and members of the church are always inviting him home to meals. In return, Norvel keeps the church bathrooms and the church floors clean, washes the windows twice a year, empties the garbage cans daily, picks up trash in the parking lot, and attempts minor repairs. He also does a little work for Pardon Albee at the apartments. But he won't do anything remotely domestic, like loading the huge church dishwasher or making and serving coffee. So I get the overrun of church duties, if none of the sisters of the church are available to serve for free.

This quarterly board meeting, comprising those elected to sit for staggered terms on the preschool governing board, is always a lively event, and I'm almost always hired to set up the coffee and cookie trays, because any sisters of the church overhearing this group would be liable to (depending on their individual temperaments) die laughing, or stomp out in exasperation.

Norvel Whitbread was lounging in the church kitchen, which is at the end of the preschool building farthest from the church, when I came in. A large broom and dustpan were leaning against the counter, establishing his bona fides.

'How're you [har yew] today, Sister Lily?' he drawled, sipping from a soft-drink can.

'I'm not your fucking sister, Norvel.'

'You want this job, you better watch your mouth, woman.'

'You want this job, you better stop spiking your Cokes.' I could smell the bourbon from four feet away. Norvel's thin, nose-dominated, undernourished face showed plain shock. I could tell it had been a while since someone had spoken to the church's pet convert in plain terms. Norvel was dressed in clothes passed on by a member of the congregation: the baggy brown pants and loose striped shirt had never been Norvel's choices.

While I got out the twenty-cup coffeepot, Norvel rallied.

'I'm a member of this church, and you ain't,' he said, his voice low and mean. 'They'll take my word.'

'I'll tell you what, Norvel. You go on and tell them what you like. Either they'll believe you and fire me – in which case, the next woman they hire will be more than glad to tell them about your drinking habits – or they'll fire you, at the very least keep a closer eye on you. As I see it, Norvel, either way, you lose.' My policy has always been to avoid or ignore Norvel, but today I was set on confronting him. Maybe my restraint with Carlton had worn out my quota of 'nice' for the day; maybe this was just one face-to-face encounter too many. I often go for a week without talking to as many people as I'd talked to today.

Norvel struggled with his thought processes while I got the coffee apparatus assembled and perking and found a tray for the white-boxed assortment of bakery cookies that had been left on the counter.

'I'll get even with you for this, bitch,' Norvel said, his sunken cheeks looking even more concave under the merciless fluorescent lighting.

'No, you won't,' I said with absolute certainty.

Inspired by the liquor or the devil or both, Norvel made his move. He grabbed his broom with both hands and tried to jab me with it. I grabbed the stretch of handle between his hands, ducked under his arm, twisted the broom, and bent. Norvel's arm was strained over the handle. It was excruciatingly painful, as I'd learned when Marshall taught me this particular manoeuvre, and Norvel made a high squeak like a bat's.

Of course, the Reverend Joel McCorkindale came in the kitchen right then. Before I saw him, I could tell who it was by the scent of his aftershave, for he was fond of smelling sweet. I slid my right foot behind Norvel's leg, raised it slightly, and kicked him in the back of the knee. He folded into a gasping mess on the clean kitchen floor.

I folded my arms across my chest and turned to face the minister.

Joel McCorkindale never looks like himself on the rare occasions when I see him with his mouth shut. Now his lips were compressed with distaste as he looked down at Norvel and back up at me. I figured that when he was an adolescent, McCorkindale had looked in the mirror and seen a totally forgettable male and then had vowed to become expert in using strength of personality and a remarkable voice to overcome his lack of physical distinction. He is of average height, weight, and unremarkable coloring. His build is average, neither very muscular nor very flabby. But he is an overwhelming man, able to fill a room with his pleasure, or calm, or conviction.

Now he filled it with irritation.

'What's going on here?' he asked, in the same marvelous voice God could have used from the burning bush – though I hoped God was above sounding peevish.

Norvel whimpered and clutched his arm. I knew he wouldn't try anything on me with his meal ticket standing there. I turned to the sink to wash my hands so I could return to arranging the cookies.

'Miss Bard!' boomed the voice.

I sighed and turned. Always, always, there was a payback time after I enjoyed myself.

People said so much they didn't need to say.

'What has happened here?' the Reverend McCorkindale asked sternly.

'Norvel got red-blooded, so I cooled him down.'

This would require the least explanation, I figured.

And the minister instantly believed me, which I had figured, too. I'd seen him give me a thorough look once or twice. I'd had a strong hint he wouldn't find a man making a pass at me unbelievable.

'Norvel, is this true?'

Norvel saw the writing on the wall (so to speak) and nodded. I'd wondered if his shrewdness would overcome his anger.

'Brother Norvel, we'll have a talk later in my study, after the meeting.'

Again, Norvel nodded.

'Now, let me help you up and out of here so Sister Lily can complete her work,' said McCorkindale in that rich voice with its hypnotic cadence.

In a minute, I had the large kitchen to myself.

As I searched for napkins, I decided that Norvel's drinking couldn't have escaped the overly observant Pardon Albee, since he saw Norvel at the apartments, too, as well as at church here. I wondered if Pardon had threatened Norvel with exposure, as I had done. Norvel would be a natural as Pardon's murderer. As a janitor, he might even be more likely to notice my cart as it sat by the curb on Tuesdays, and thus more likely to remember it when he needed to transport something bulky.

I grew fonder and fonder of that idea, without really believing it. Norvel is disgusting, and it would please me if he was gone from the apartments next door to my house. But I didn't really think Norvel had the planning ability to dispose of Pardon's body the way it had been done. Maybe desperation had sharpened his wits.

I put a bowl of artificial sweetener and a bowl of real sugar on the coffee tray. I got out two thermal coffee carafes and poured the perked coffee into them. By the time the board members had all assembled in the small meeting room right next to the fellowship hall, the cups, saucers, small plates, napkins, coffee carafes, and cookie trays had all been arranged on the serving table in the boardroom. I had only to wait until the meeting was over, usually in an hour and a half, to clean up the food things. Then I could go to my martial arts class.

For maybe a quarter of an hour, I straightened the kitchen. It was a good advertisement to do a little extra work and it kept me from being bored. Then I went out into the fellowship hall. The fellowship hall is about forty by twenty, and has tables set up all the way around the sides, with folding chairs pushed under them. The preschool uses the tables all week, and they get dirty, the chairs not evenly aligned, though the teachers carefully train the children to pick up after themselves. I neatened things to my satisfaction, and if I ended up close to the door where the meeting was taking place, well, I was bored. I told myself that like the things I happen to see in people's homes when I clean, the things I might happen to hear would never be told to another person.

The door to the meeting room had been left ajar to help the air circulation. This time of year, in a window-less room, the air tends to be close. Since I hadn't brought a book, this would help to amuse me till it was time to clean up.

One of the preschool teachers had mentioned evolution in her class during the course of Dinosaur Week, I gathered after a moment. I tried hard to imagine that as being important, but I just couldn't. However, the members of the board certainly thought it was just dreadful. I began wondering what enterprising child had turned in the teacher, what message it would send that child if the adult was fired. Brother McCorkindale, as they all addressed him, was for having the teacher in for a dialogue (his term) and proceeding from there; he felt strongly that the woman, whom he described as 'God-fearing and dedicated to the children,' should be given a chance to explain and repent.

Board member Lacey Dean Knopp, Deedra Dean's widowed and remarried mother, felt likewise, though she said sadly that just mentioning evolution had been a bad mistake on the teacher's part. The six other board members present were all for firing the woman summarily.

'If this is typical of the people we're hiring, we need to screen our employees more carefully,' said a nasal female voice.

I recognized that voice: It belonged to Jenny O'Hagen, half of a husband-and-wife Yuppie team who managed the local outlet of a nationally franchised restaurant called Bippy's. Jenny and Tom O'Hagen manage to pack their lives so full of work, appointments, church functions, and phone calling connected to the various civic organizations they join (and they join any that will have them) that they've found a perfect way to avoid free time and conversation with each other.

Jenny and Tom live in the ground-floor front apartment at the Shakespeare Garden Apartments, the one right by Pardon Albee's. Naturally, they don't have a minute to clean their own apartment, so they are clients of mine. I'm always glad when neither one is home when I'm working. But most often, whichever one has been on the night shift is just getting up when I arrive.

I hadn't known the O'Hagens belonged to SCC, much less held a position on the board, but I might have figured. It was typical of the O'Hagen philosophy that childless Jenny had managed to finagle her way onto the preschool board, since the preschool is the most important one in Shakespeare and the waiting list for it is long. Jenny had probably made an appointment with Tom to conceive a child on October fifteenth, and was putting in her time on the board to ensure that infant a place in the preschool.

Since my clients were involved, I began listening with heightened attention to the heated words flying around the boardroom. Everyone got so excited, I wondered if I should have made decaf instead of regular coffee.

Finally, the board agreed to censure, not fire, the hapless young woman. I lost interest as the agenda moved to more mundane things like the church school's budget, the medical forms the children had to fill out . . . yawn. But then I was glad I hadn't drifted away to clean some more, because another name came up that I knew.

'Now I have to bring up an equally serious matter. And I want to preface it by asking you tonight, in your prayers, to remember our sister Thea Sedaka, who's under a lot of strain at home right now.'

There was dead silence in the boardroom as the members (and I) waited in breathless anticipation to find out what was happening in the Sedaka household. I felt a curious pang that something important had happened to Marshall and I was having to find out this way.

Brother McCorkindale certainly knew how to use his pauses to good effect. 'Thea's husband is no longer – they have separated. Now, I'm telling you this very personal thing because I want you to take it into account when I tell you that Thea was accused by one of the mothers of one of the little girls in the preschool of slapping that child.'

I sorted through the sentence to arrive at its gist. My eyebrows arched. Slapping children was a great taboo at this preschool – at any preschool, I hoped.

There was a communal gasp of dismay that I could hear clearly.

'That's much, much worse than mentioning evolution,' Lacey Dean Knopp said sadly. 'We just can't let that go, Joel.'

'Of course not. The welfare of the children in our care has to be our prime concern,' the Reverend McCorkindale said. Though he spoke as though he'd memorized a passage from the school manual, I thought he meant it. 'But I have to tell you, fellow brothers and sisters in Christ, that Thea is deeply repentant of having even given the child cause to think she was slapping her.'

'She denies it?' Jenny O'Hagen had thought that through before anyone else.

'What Thea says is that the child spoke back to her, not for the first time, but for the seventh or eighth time in one morning. Now, Thea knows part of her job is to endure and correct behavior like that, but since she is under such a particular strain, she lost some of her self-control and tapped the child on the cheek to get her to pay attention. Like this, is how she showed me.'

Of course, I couldn't see or hear the Reverend McCorkindale's demonstration.

'Were there any witnesses?' Jenny asked.

I decided Jenny had potential as an interrogator.

'No, unfortunately, Jenny. Thea and the child were alone in the room at the time. Thea had kept the child in from recess to discuss improving her behavior.'

There was a silence while presumably the board members mulled this over.

'I think we have to call her on the carpet, Joel,' rumbled the voice of one of the older men on the board. 'Corporal punishment is a choice for the parents, not for the teachers at this school.'

I nodded.

'So you want her to keep her job?' Joel McCorkindale inquired pointedly. 'We have to reach a decision; she's waiting to hear. I must remind you that Thea is a steady churchgoer and she is in a very stressful situation. The parents of the little girl have said they would abide by our decision.'

They practically begged McCorkindale to drive directly over to Thea's house and tell her all was forgiven – provided she didn't repeat the offense.

The minister didn't have any more bombshells to drop, and the meeting was clearly winding down. I took care to be out of sight in the kitchen when the board members emerged. It crossed my mind that Joel McCorkindale would come in the kitchen to ask more about my confrontation with Norvel, but after the board members had gone, I heard his steps ascend to his office on the second floor.

As I washed the dishes and sealed the plastic bags containing the leftover cookies, I found myself wishing that I'd stayed in the kitchen during the whole meeting. I would see Marshall Sedaka in minutes, and knowing something about his private life that he himself had not chosen to tell me made me uncomfortable. I glanced down at my big waterproof watch, then hurriedly wrung out the washcloth and folded it neatly over the sink divider. It was already 6:40.

Since I had only minutes to change into my gi, I was less than pleased to see Claude Friedrich leaning against his official car, apparently waiting for me. He'd pulled the car right up to the curb in front of my house. Was that supposed to fluster me?

'Hello, Miss Bard,' he rumbled. His arms were crossed over his chest in a relaxed way. He was out of uniform, dressed casually in a green-and-brown-striped shirt and khakis.

'I'm in a real hurry now,' I said, trying not to sound snappy, since that would imply he had succeeded in upsetting me.

'Isn't one of the advantages of a small town supposed to be the slower pace?' he asked lazily.

I stopped in my tracks. Something bad was coming.

'Shakespeare is quieter than, say, Memphis,' he said.

I felt a sharp pain in my head. Though I knew it was emotional, it hurt as much as a migraine. Then I felt a wave of rage so strong that it kept me up straight.

'Don't you talk about that,' I said, meaning it so much, my voice sounded strange. '*Don't bring it up.*'

I went into my house without looking at him again, and I thought if he knocked on the door, he would have to arrest me, since I would do my best to hurt him badly. I leaned against the door, my heart pounding in my chest. I heard his car pull away. My hands were sweating. I had to wash them over and over before I pulled off my cleaning clothes and put on my spotless white gi pants. The top and belt were already rolled up in a little bag; I would just wear a white sleeveless T-shirt to Body Time and then put on the rest of my gi. I put my hand in the bag and touched the belt, the green belt that meant more to me than anything. Then I looked at the clock and went out the kitchen door to the carport.

I pulled into the Body Time parking lot just at seven-thirty, the latest I'd ever been. I pushed through the glass doors and hurried through the main room, the weights room. At this hour of the evening, only a few diehards were still working with the free weights or machines. I knew them enough to nod to.

I went quickly through the door at the back of the weights room, passing through a corridor along which doors lead to the office, the bathrooms, the massage room, the tanning-bed room, and a storage closet. At the end of the corridor are closed double doors, and I felt a pang of dismay. If the doors were closed, class had begun.

I turned the knob carefully, trying to be quiet. On the threshold, I bowed, my bag tucked under my arm. When I straightened, I saw the class was already in shiko dachi – legs spraddled, faces calm, arms crossed over their chests. A few eyes rolled in my direction. I went to one of the chairs by the wall, pulled off my shoes and socks, and faced the wall to finish putting on my gi, as was proper. I wound the obi around my waist and managed the knot in record time, then ran silently to my place in line, second. Raphael Roundtree and Janet Shook had unobtrusively shifted sideways to make room when they saw me enter, and I was grateful.

I bowed briefly to Marshall without meeting his eyes, then sank into position. After a few seconds of regulating my breathing, I peeked up at Marshall. He raised his dark eyebrows slightly. Marshall always makes the most of his quarter-Oriental heritage by working hard on inscrutability; his triangular face, its complexion somewhere between the pink of Caucasian and the ivory of Asian, remained calm. But the bird-wing eyebrows said volumes – surprise, disappointment, disapproval.

Shiko dachi is a position very like sitting on air, and it is painful and demanding even after long practice. The best way to get through it is to concentrate on something else, at least for me. But I was too upset to go into meditation. Instead, I scanned the line of fellow sufferers reflected in the mirror lining the opposite wall.

Newcomers are always at the end of the line. The newest man's head was bowed, his legs trembling – so probably the class had been in position for a minute and a half or two minutes. I hadn't missed much.

After a few seconds, I began to relax. The pain required my attention and the anxiety of my encounter with the policeman began to fade. I started my meditation on the kata we would practice later. Ignoring the ache in my quadriceps, I visualized the various moves that made up geiki sei ni bon, I reminded myself of mistakes I habitually made, and I anticipated further refining the grace and power of the kata, a series of martial arts strikes, blocks, and kicks woven together in what becomes almost a dance.

'Three minutes,' said the first-in-line student, a huge black man named Raphael Roundtree. His watch was strapped to his obi.

'Another minute,' said Marshall, and I could feel the dismay, though no one made a sound. 'Be sure your thighs are parallel with the floor.'

There was a general ripple of movement down the line as students corrected their stance. I stayed rock-still; my shiko dachi was as perfect as I could make it. My feet were the correct distance apart, pointing outward at the correct angle; my back was straight.

I emerged from my reverie for a moment to glance down the line in the mirror. The last-in-line man was in serious trouble. Though he was wearing shorts and a T-shirt, sweat was streaming down his face. His legs were trembling violently. With some amazement, I recognized my next-door neighbor, Carlton Cockroft, who had so generously let me know he'd seen me out walking in the night.

I shut my eyes and tried to refocus on the kata, but I was too full of surprise and conjecture.

When Raphael called, 'Four minutes,' it was as much relief to me as it was to the rest of the class.

We all stood, shifting from leg to leg to shake off the pain.

'Lily! Stretches!' Marshall said, his gaze just grazing me as it swept down the line. He retreated to a corner, where he watched us all for the slightest sign of slacking.

I bowed and ran to face the rest of the class. There were only eight that night. Janet and I were the only women, and we were much of an age, though I thought Janet might be thirty to my thirty-one. The men ranged from twenty to perhaps fifty-five.

'Kiotske!' I said sharply to bring them to attention. 'Rai,' I instructed, bowing to them. They bowed to me in return, Carlton only a beat behind. He was keeping a sharp eye on the man in line next to him, picking up on his cues. I wondered again why he was here. But the class was waiting for my directions, and I extended my right leg, balancing carefully on my left. 'Big toe up . . . and down . . .' I said. A few minutes later, I was concluding with lunges to alternating sides, my hands extended to the front for balance.

I bowed to Marshall and ran back to my place.

'Teacher's pet,' hissed Raphael out of the side of his mouth.

'Late, too.' Raphael and I pretty much alternate leading the stretches. Raphael is a high school math teacher, so I figure karate gives him a chance to blow off steam.

'First time,' I whispered defensively, and saw his teeth flash in a grin.

Marshall told us to take a short break, and after a gulp of water from the fountain in the weights room, I strolled over to Carlton. He looked overdone, rather than edible. His face was red and his hair was wet with sweat. I'd never seen him approach tousled, much less disheveled.

Raphael drifted up behind me before I could say anything to my neighbor, and I introduced them. I consider Raphael a friend, although I never see him outside of class. Now I might get to know Carlton in the same way, after living next door to him for four years. He had apparently rethought something after our prickly conversation.

'So what made you decide to come to class, Carlton?' Raphael was asking with open curiosity. It was obvious Carlton was no workout buff.

'I keep Marshall's books,' Carlton explained, which was news to me. 'And I've seen Lily heading out for class for four years now, since I bought the house next door to her. She always looks like she is happy to be going. I called Marshall today and he said to give it a shot. What comes next? I barely survived that shigga – whatever.'

'Next,' said Raphael, with an openly sadistic grin, 'comes calisthenics.'

'More?' Carlton was horrified.

I looked up at Raphael. We began laughing simultaneously.

I was still lacing up my shoes when the last class member left. I'd deliberately dawdled so I could talk to Marshall without asking him to preselect a time, which would have upset the balance of whatever relationship we have.

'Late tonight,' Marshall commented, folding his gi top carefully and putting it in his gym bag. In his white T-shirt, his arms bare, the warm ivory tinge to his skin was more apparent. Marshall's grandmother had been Chinese and his grandfather American, he'd told Raphael in my hearing one night. Aside from his skin tone and his straight black hair and dark eyes, it would be hard to tell. He is a little older than I am – about thirty-five, I figure – and only three inches taller. But he is stronger and more dangerous than anyone I've met.

'Police,' I said, by way of explanation.

'What – about Pardon?' Marshall gave me his attention.

I shrugged.

'Something was bothering you tonight,' he said.

Marshall had never said anything more personal than 'Good kick,' or 'Keep your hand and wrist in line with your arm,' or 'You've really worked on those biceps.' Because of our long camaraderie, I felt obliged to answer.

'A couple of things,' I said slowly. We were sitting on the floor about four feet apart. Marshall had one shoe on and was loosening the laces on the other, and he slipped it on and tied it while I was pulling on my second sock.

Marshall crossed his legs, wrapping them together in a yoga position, and pushed against the floor with his hands. He was suspended off the floor, his arms and hands taking all his weight. He 'walked' over to me like that, and I tried to smile, but I was too uncomfortable with our new situation. We'd never had a personal conversation.

'So talk,' he said.

I took as long as I could lacing up my shoe, trying to decide what to say. I looked over at him while he was distracted by the faint sound of the telephone ringing in his office. It cut off after the second ring; one of the employees had answered it.

Marshall's face is markedly triangular, with narrow lips and a nose that has been flattened a few times. He has a distinctly catlike look, but he doesn't have a cat's sleekness. He is built much more like a bulldog.

Well, I should either talk or tell him I'm not going to, I thought. He was waiting patiently, but he was waiting.

'Was Pardon Albee your partner?' I said finally.

'Yes.'

'So what happens now?'

'We had a contract. If one of us died, the other got the whole business. Pardon didn't have anyone else to consider. I had Thea, but Pardon didn't want to deal with her. So he carried a heavy insurance policy on me, and Thea would get that money if anything happened to me, instead of getting a share of the business.'

'So . . . you own Body Time now.'

He nodded. His eyes were fixed on me. I was used to being on the dispensing, rather than the receiving, end of fixed stares, and it was an effort not to fidget. Also, Marshall was a good bit closer to me than people were in the habit of getting.

'That's good,' I said, with an effort.

He nodded again.

'Have the police talked to you yet about Pardon?' I asked him.

'I'm going to go talk to Dolph Stafford tomorrow at the police station. I didn't want them to come here.'

'Sure.' I thought I could hardly bring up Thea; Thea's slapping the little girl was something I wasn't supposed to know, though if I knew the Shakespeare grapevine, everyone in town was hearing some version of the incident by now. And I couldn't just blurt out a question as to why Marshall and Thea had separated.

The air was getting pretty thick with something, and I was feeling increasingly nervous.

'So . . . the other thing?' he asked quietly.

I glanced over at him quickly, then back down at my hands, fidgeting with the damn shoelaces. 'Nothing else I can talk about,' I said dismissively.

'I've left Thea.'

'Oh.'

We stared at each other a little more, and I felt a bubble of hysterical laughter rising in my throat.

'Don't you want to know why?'

'What? Why what?' I knew I sounded stupid, but I just couldn't seem to concentrate. It was taking an effort to keep still. A private conversation, physical closeness, personal talk – these are unnerving things.

Marshall shook his head. 'Nothing, Lily. Can I ask you something in return?'

I nodded rather warily. I wondered if we looked like two of those wooden birds on the stand, bobbing at each other.

'Where'd you get the scars?' he asked gently.

Chapter Five

The room was suddenly airless.

'You don't really want to know,' I said.

'Of course I do,' Marshall said. 'We're never moving beyond where we are now unless I know that.'

I looked at the mirror beyond Marshall's shoulder. I saw someone I didn't recognize.

'People never feel the same about me once they know,' I said. My mouth was suddenly so dry, it was hard to speak.

'I will,' he said.

He wouldn't. It would ruin the unspoken bond between us – a bond with which, evidently, he was no longer content.

'Why do you want me to talk about it?' My hands were clenched and I could see them shake.

'I can never get to know you better until I know that,' he said with patient certainty. 'And I want to get to know you better.'

With one quick movement, I jerked off my T-shirt. Under it, I was wearing a plain white sports bra. Marshall's breath hissed as he got a good look at the scars. Not meeting his eyes, I turned a little so he could see the ones that crossed my shoulders like extra bra straps; I rotated back to show him the ones that striped my upper chest; I sat up straight so he could see more thin white scars in an arc pattern descending into the waistband of my pants.

And then I looked him in the eyes.

He did not blink. His jaw was fixed in a hard line. He was making a heroic struggle to keep his face still.

'I felt them when I gripped your shoulder in class last week, but I didn't know they were so . . .'

'Extensive?' I asked savagely. I would not let him look away.

'Are your breasts cut, too?' he asked, with a creditable attempt at keeping his voice neutral.

'No. But all around. In *circles*. In a *pattern*.'

'Who did this?'

What had happened to me had cut my life in two, more deeply and surely than the knives that had traced bloody festoons on my skin. Unable to stop, I remembered once again, descending into a familiar hell. It had been hot that June . . .

It had already been hot for a month. I had graduated from college and had been living in Memphis for three years. I had a nice apartment in east Memphis and a desk job at the city's largest maid and janitorial service, Queen of Clean. In spite of the stupid name, it was a good place to work. I was a scheduler. I also did spot checks on site and made courtesy calls to customers to see if they were satisfied. I earned a decent salary, and I bought a lot of clothes.

When I left work that Tuesday in June, I was wearing a short-sleeved navy blue dress with big white buttons down the front and white leather pumps. My hair was long and light brown then, and I prided myself on my long, polished fingernails. I was dating one of the co-owners of a bottled-water supply company.

My worst problem was the transmission of my car, which had already required extensive repairs. When I left work, I began to worry that it was going to eat up more of my money.

The car made it down the freeway to the Goodwill Road exit before I had to stop. There was a service station in sight on Goodwill, and lots of traffic, people everywhere. I walked down the exit ramp, nervous about how narrow it seemed when it had to accommodate a woman on foot and cars. Unexpectedly, a van coming slowly down the ramp stopped beside me. I thought, They're going to offer me a ride to the service station.

The passenger door was thrown open by someone sitting in the back, who immediately retracted into his crouch behind the passenger's seat. The man in the driver's seat was holding a gun.

When I accepted it for what it was, rather than trying to

imagine it was something else, my heart began racing, its thud so loud, I could hardly make out what he was saying.

'Get in or I'll shoot you where you stand.'

I could jump off the exit ramp and get hit by a car speeding on the road below, or I could tell him to shoot, or I could get in the van.

I made the wrong decision. I got in.

The man who had picked me up, I found out later, was an accomplished kidnapper named Louis Ferrier, called 'Nap' by his customers in acknowledgment of his expertise in stealing women and children, most of whom vanished forever. The abducted victims who did resurface were without exception dead, either mentally or physically. Nap had done jail time, but not for his specialty.

I was handcuffed the minute I got in the van by the man crouched behind the passenger's seat, an occasional accomplice of Nap's named Harry Wheeler. Harry reached around the seat, grabbed my hands, cuffed them, and held the chain that led from the cuffs. Then he blindfolded me. The windows of the van were heavily tinted. No one noticed.

During that dreadful ride out of Memphis, they just talked as if I wasn't there. I was in such a state of terror, I hardly knew what they said. I could feel death sitting in my lap.

At the end of the ride, which had led north from Memphis, Nap and Harry exited the highway and met with a representative of a biker gang at a prearranged rendezvous. Nap had rented me to the gang for one night, though I didn't know that.

Four men and one woman took me to an abandoned shack in the middle of some fields. One of the men had grown up around there and was familiar with the place. They attached the chain through my handcuffs to the metal head rail of an old cot. I was still blindfolded. The men drank, ate, and raped me. When that got old, they used the knife on my chest. They cut a circle around the base of each breast. They cut zigzags in the flesh covering my chest. They cut a target on my stomach, with my navel as the bull's-eye. They laughed as they did this, and I, chained to a dilapidated bed, screamed and screamed, until they slapped me and told me to stop or the knife would go deeper. And they raped me again.

The woman said very little during all this. I refused to believe, at first, that a woman could be present and not help me. When I realized the softer voice did indeed belong to a woman, I pleaded with her and begged her for help. I got no reply, but during a time when the men all seemed to be sleeping or outside urinating, the woman's voice came close to my ear and said, 'I lived through it. You can, too. They're not cutting you bad. You haven't lost anything but a little blood.'

I had not known that Nap was supposed to return for me, that I had been rented, not sold. I expected to die when the men tired of me and were ready to leave; I had had eighteen hours to anti-cipate my death.

I'd attached the name Rooster to the largest man. Rooster had a wonderful idea as they packed up their gear the next day. He had a cheap little revolver he'd picked up on the street, and he left it with me. He also left me one bullet.

'Now, you can use this on yourself,' he said genially. 'Or you can save it for Nap, when he comes back to get you, and use it on him. I figure it'll take you from now till he gets here to learn how to use it.'

'Be better if we killed her ourselves,' said a voice I hadn't attached to a name or weight.

'But look at it this way,' urged Rooster. 'If she kills Nap, we can always say she wanted to have sex with us, if worse comes to worst and somehow she finds us, though that ain't likely. But if we kill her, Nap'll come after us when we least expect it. Ain't you kind of sick of him? I know I am.'

This made good sense to the rest. Leaving me with a gun appealed to their sense of humor, too. As they left, they were laughing over Nap's surprise, and placing bets over whether or not I would choose to kill him or myself.

For some minutes after I heard the motorcycles buzz down the dirt road to rejoin the blacktop, I lay in a stupor. I could not believe I was still alive. I didn't know if I was glad or not. I wondered how long I would survive, with the wounds I had. My vaginal area was at best badly bruised; at worst, I had internal rips. I was oozing blood from the cutting, and the pain was dreadful, though I knew the cuts were not deep.

Very gradually, I realized I really was still alive, still alone, and the sense of what Rooster had said began to filter in. I raised my cuffed hands and worked off the blindfold.

The man who had kidnapped me was coming to retrieve me, to rent me out again for more of the same.

I had a gun and one bullet. It was so tempting, the thought of being out of all this. But what stopped me was the thought of my parents. They would know by now I was gone; people would be looking for me. I might not be found for years out here in this shack, and in all that time they would worry about me, pray for me, refuse to believe I was dead.

It suited me better to kill the man they called Nap. After a moment, I began to look forward to it.

Every moment cost me pain, but I figured out how to load the revolver, though the handcuffs made it difficult; at least there was enough slack in the chain to move my arms. I loaded, emptied out the bullet, and reloaded several times, until I had mastered it and knew the bullet was in the chamber that would fire. Then I tucked the gun down by my side and waited in the stinking, hot shack for Nap to come for me. I could see the sky through a hole in the roof; when the sun was almost overhead, I heard a van coming down the dirt road. I remembered the second man, and prayed he hadn't come this time.

I shut my eyes when the footsteps came close.

'How you feeling this morning, honey?' Nap asked jovially. 'Where did Rooster leave that key? Shit, they messed you up. It's gonna take you a while to get over this . . .' I could tell he was angry that I was too damaged to be useful for a while. I opened my eyes and looked at him, straight at him, and what he saw made him stop in the act of picking up my discarded blindfold.

I raised the gun and pointed it as carefully as I could, then fired.

It caught Nap in the eye.

He died far too quickly to suit me.

Of course, I had no idea where the key to the handcuffs was. Nap had said he'd left it with Rooster. I slid off the cot, then hitched myself across the floor, dragging the cot behind me. With incredible difficulty, I searched Nap just to make sure it wasn't on him. It wasn't.

It seemed to me there must be a way I could get out of the shack, but trying to get myself and the cot through the door was too hard for me. By that time, I was weak.

So I got to lie on the bed in the shack with the dead man for another day. Bugs came, and my cuts got infected, and the body began to smell.

By the time a farmer working in the adjacent field came to investigate Nap's van, maybe twenty-four hours later, I was running a high temperature, but not high enough to make me delirious. I longed for unconsciousness the way people in hell want ice water. The farmer saw the body of Nap lying on the floor inside the open door and ran to call for help. The flood of people who arrived after that had no idea a live person was inside the shack. The horror on the faces of the men who came to investigate the body told me that I had gone beyond some boundary.

I had passed; I had become the thing that had happened to me.

No one who saw me chained to that bed would ever be able to imagine that I'd had a dog named Bolo when I was little, that I'd enjoyed playing with dolls, that I'd gotten three raises in the past two years, that I came from a home as clean and orderly as any of theirs.

In the slow weeks of recovery, after repeated questioning by law-enforcement officials on several levels, after enduring a media drench that sensationalized what was already sensational, I realized that returning to my former life was no longer possible. It had been stolen from me. My boyfriend was still posing for the newspapers as my boyfriend, but he wasn't any longer. My parents simply could not cope with the horror of my ordeal or my execution of the man responsible.

I began to suspect that, in their secret hearts, they thought I had made the wrong choice in my use of the bullet.

My younger sister, Varena, was a rock at first, but gradually my slow physical and mental recovery wore Varena's lighthearted nature down and then defeated it. Varena was ready for me to rise from my bed and walk. Varena was ready to refer to my crisis in the past tense, to have conversations that did not refer to it even in terms of my recovery. After a few increasingly acrimonious exchanges that included such statements as 'Pull up your socks and get on with your life' and 'You can't go on living in the past,' Varena drifted back to her normal routine of nurse's duties at the little hospital in our family's town, teaching Sunday school, and dating a local pharmacist.

For a month longer, I stayed with my parents, with my belongings stored in their attic and toolshed. There was a healing quality in the house with the big front porch and the rose garden, the known neighbors. But most of those neighbors found it impossible to be natural around me; the best managed it, but the sheer horror of my victimization defeated the rest.

I tried hard not to be a tragic figure, tried desperately to reclaim my past, but I finally acknowledged defeat. I had to leave Bartley, to forget Memphis, to go somewhere new.

'And why did you pick Shakespeare?' Marshall asked me.

'The name,' I said, almost surprised that someone else was with me. I pulled my T-shirt back over my head. 'My name is Bard, as in the Bard of Avon. This is Shakespeare.'

'You picked it off the map like that?'

I nodded, stood. 'I'd tried a couple of places earlier that didn't work out, so random selection seemed as good a method as any.' I stood still for a moment. It was such an effort to move.

'I'll see you later,' I said. 'I don't want to talk any more now.' I lifted the bag with my gi and obi inside and strode out, not forgetting to turn and bow as I reached the door.

I drove home automatically, trying to keep my mind blank. It had been years since I had told my story, years since I had relived it in full. They had been good years, having people look at me quite normally, as if I was a full woman, not a thing, not a victim.

Now Chief Friedrich had indicated he knew who I was, so he knew I'd killed someone. Maybe he'd think I had had some kind of flashback and killed Pardon Albee, too. The pointed question about a personal relationship might mean that he suspected I'd killed Pardon because he'd paid me unwelcome attention. Knowing Pardon, that was a strange idea.

I sat on the side of my bed when I got home. I tried to picture myself as a vigilante, as some kind of – who was the girl who'd been raped in *Titus Andronicus?* Lavinia . . . yes, Lavinia, whose hands and tongue had been cut out by her attackers so that she could not reveal their identity. But Lavinia, I remembered, managed to tell her brothers somehow, and served the attackers to their mother as lunch, since the mother had permitted the rape to happen.

I wasn't set on gaining some kind of vengeance on all men for what had happened to me. But I certainly wasn't a trusting person anymore, and I definitely never expected much of people, and I would never be surprised to hear of any perfidy again.

I did not believe in the underlying goodwill of men or the unspoken sisterhood of women.

I did not believe that people everywhere are really the same, or that if you treat people kindly you will get kindness in return,

I did not believe in the sanctity of life.

If all the men were lined up in front of me, the four rapists and the man who cuffed me, and I had a loaded gun . . . I would kill them all, I thought. But I'm not scouring biker bars across America and I'm not standing in the post offices looking at wanted posters to see if they've done anything else. I haven't hired a private investigator to look for them.

Did that speak to my sanity, or did that say I would commit murder only if it was convenient? I felt a tingling all over, like a hand that had been asleep prickling as it woke up. I'd felt that before after the times when I couldn't dodge remembering. It was the rest of my personality seeping back into the shell I became when I immersed in the memory.

I turned down my covers, checked that my alarm clock was set, and gratefully crawled into bed. I reached over to switch out the lamp.

I'd kill the woman, too, I thought, feeling a wave of weariness sweep through my body. The woman I'd never seen. The bikers I'd never actually seen, only heard, felt.

But Pardon Albee – could Friedrich really believe I'd kill someone like that, someone I knew in the ordinary course of my life?

Of course he could.

I wondered what weapon had been used to kill the landlord. I hadn't seen much blood, though I hadn't examined Pardon very carefully. Since I'd been taking Goju from Marshall for two years or more, I thought maybe I could kill someone with my hands if I needed to – that had originally been my reason for studying a martial art.

That, too, would enter Friedrich's picture of me: a very fit woman . . . in conjunction with a middle-aged, nosy, presumably heterosexual man who lived very close to me . . . Put like that, it seemed pretty obvious to me that I must have killed Pardon in my sleep.

Starting tomorrow, I decided as I rolled onto my left side, I have to find out who killed the landlord. In the stage before sleep, it seemed that simple.

Chapter Six

I was on my way into the house to shower after my morning workout at Body Time – Marshall's assistant had opened the gym this morning, to my relief – when I saw Marcus Jefferson and a little boy. My hair was wet with sweat and big dark patches spotted my gray T-shirt and shorts. I was about to unlock my front door when I heard someone call my name.

'Good morning, Lily,' Marcus said from the sidewalk. It was the first time I had ever seen him smile, and I understood the attraction he has for Deedra. Marcus is well-muscled and tall, the color of coffee with one tablespoon of milk. His brown eyes have a golden cast. The little boy looked even more attractive, smiling and immaculately dressed, with long, curly eyelashes and huge dark eyes.

Though I longed to go right inside and get in the shower, out of courtesy I strolled down my driveway to the sidewalk and squatted down in front of the child.

'What's your name?'

'Kenya,' the boy said with a beaming grin.

'Kenya, that's a nice name,' I said. 'How old are you?' I supposed I was asking the right questions, since Marcus and the child both seemed pleased.

The boy held up three fingers. I had to repress a shudder at seeing how tiny those fingers were. The terrible vulnerability of children frightens me so much, I am leery of liking one. How could I ever be vigilant enough to protect something so frail and precious? Yet other people don't seem to share this terror, are foolish or defiant enough to have children and expect those children will live to adulthood without being harmed.

My face had gone wrong, I could tell. The child's uncertain eyes and faltering smile recalled me to my senses.

I yanked my lips into a grin and very gently patted the boy's shoulder. 'You'll grow up to be a big man, Kenya,' I said, and rose to my feet. 'Is this your son, Marcus?'

'Yes, this is my only one,' he said proudly. 'My wife and I have been separated for a few months, but she and I agree that I should spend as much time with Kenya as I can.'

'You must have worked four to midnight,' I said, pretty much at a loss for conversation topics.

Marcus nodded. 'I came home and got some sleep; then I got Kenya from his mom before she left for work – she works at the welfare office.'

'So, what are you two going to do today?' I asked politely, trying not to look at my watch. Thursday mornings, I have to be at the Drinkwaters' at eight-thirty.

'Well, we're going to McDonald's for breakfast,' said Marcus, 'and then I think we'll go to my place and play Candy Land, and maybe we'll watch Barney. That suit you, sport?'

'McDonald's, McDonald's,' Kenya began to chant, pulling on his father's hand.

'I better take this boy to get some food in him,' Marcus said, shaking his head at the boy's impatience. But he was grinning at the same time.

'I guess,' I said, 'you couldn't have him here, with Pardon being the way he was about the apartments being adults only.'

'I had Kenya over one time, and Mr Albee let me have it,' Marcus said, watching the child trot down the sidewalk. 'I'm wondering what the next owner will do. Would you know who that's going to be?'

'No,' I said slowly. This was the second time the subject had come up. 'No, I have no idea. But I'm going to try to find out.'

'Let me know,' Marcus said, and raised a hand in goodbye.

'Cute kid,' I said, and watched the young man trot to catch up with the little boy before I turned to go into my own house.

Mel and Helen Drinkwater have me in once a week for an

all-morning cleaning job. They are both in their fifties and work, he as county supervisor, she at a bank, and they are not messy people. But they have a large old house and their grandchildren, who live down the street, come in and out several times a week.

Helen Drinkwater is a woman who likes things done exactly to her taste, and she has a room-by-room checklist of things I should accomplish in the three and a half hours I am there. At first, Mrs Drinkwater actually tried to get me to check things off the list and leave a checked list in each room, but I wouldn't. In fact, as I was learning the Drinkwater house, the list was helpful, but it would have felt like a paint-by-numbers kit if I'd checked the little boxes.

Mrs Drinkwater (I have sworn never to call her Helen) hadn't said a thing. I'd left the list in the exact middle of the room each time I'd cleaned the house the first few visits.

Then Mrs Drinkwater had left a pile of dirty clothes by the washer with a note asking me to 'pop these in the washer and dryer for me.' The first time it happened, I had fumed and done it; the second time, I left a note myself, which said, 'Not on any of my lists,' and after that, Helen Drinkwater had not added to my duties.

The two-storey turn-of-the-century family home looked especially pretty in the clear, warm morning light. The house is pale yellow, with white trim and dark green shutters, and it is set far back from the street. Of course, a house like this is in the oldest surviving section of Shakespeare, and it has at least half an acre of woods behind it, which the Drinkwaters have left untouched.

This morning, I had a lot to think about. Marshall had said he was separated from Thea, and he'd said it as if that was significant to me. As I scrubbed the second-floor bathroom, I wondered if Marshall still had that spark of feeling for me after last night. The few times in the past I'd felt more than calm acceptance of a man, all I'd had to do to make him run was to tell him what had happened to me. Except one man, who'd gotten so excited that he'd tried to force himself on me. I'd hurt him, but it had taken time and a struggle. After that, I'd been ready to try martial arts, which has turned out to be the most pleasurable element in my life.

These thoughts tapped at my consciousness like raindrops hitting the sidewalk, thoughts that were significant but not wholly engrossing. I was also thinking about the Drinkwaters' bathtub ring, and what to do with the comic book I'd found behind the toilet. So it wasn't until the floorboards downstairs creaked a second time that I came to attention.

I became absolutely still, the sponge in my hand held motionless an inch from the surface of the sink. I was looking into the mirror over the sink, but I was not seeing myself. I was trying to make sense of the floorboards.

The Drinkwaters always leave the kitchen door unlocked when they depart at eight-fifteen, knowing I will be here at eight-thirty. I lock it behind myself when I get here, though daytime burglaries are unknown in this section of Shakespeare.

Someone had gotten in the house in that fifteen minutes.

I shut my eyes to listen harder. I tried to pull off my rubber gloves without making a sound. I set them in the sink. He'd not yet started up the stairs; I could improve my position.

There wasn't time to take off my shoes. I stepped silently out of the bathroom, trying to remember where the creaking boards upstairs were. If I could flatten myself against the wall at the beginning of the hall, which leads off at right angles from the stairs, I would be ready to strike when the intruder reached the top.

I crept closer to the stairs, flexing my hands to loosen the muscles. My heart had begun pounding heavily, and I felt a little light-headed, but I was ready – I would not be afraid; I would fight.

I should relax; I felt the tightness of my muscles; it would slow me down . . . so many things to think of.

He was on the stairs.

My hands clenched into fists and my leg muscles were hard and tense. My blood pounded harder through my heart.

A little noise, like material brushing against the wall. Very close.

Then there was a tiny sound I couldn't interpret. I felt a frown pull my brows together.

Had it been something metal?

And another creak of the stairs.

Surely – the creak had been from a lower step?

I shook my head, puzzled.

The next sound was from even farther, off the steps entirely, all the way into the kitchen . . .

Getting *away*, the son of a bitch was getting away!

I flew down the stairs, ignoring something white as I pelted down, rage lifting me out of myself so that I barely felt my feet touch the floor. But I heard the slam of the back door as I came through the kitchen doorway, and though I was only seconds behind him, it was enough for the intruder to conceal himself in the woods in back of the Drinkwaters' house.

I stood in the door for a minute or more, panting. For the first time, I understood the phrase 'spoiling for a fight'. Then common sense prevailed and I retreated, locking the kitchen door behind me.

I suffered an immediate reaction to the adrenaline my body had pumped into my blood to prepare me for action; at every step, I felt my flesh sag on my bones. With a terrible reluctance, I went to see what had been left on the stairs. A spotless white handkerchief was tented over something about halfway up. I reached out slowly and pulled off the handkerchief.

Shining in the sun pouring through the stained-glass window at the landing was a set of cheap metal toy handcuffs. By them was a plastic gun.

I sank onto the stairs and buried my head in my hands.

Three days ago, my past life had been a secret, or so I'd thought.

Now Claude Friedrich knew about my misfortunes. I'd told Marshall. Who else knew?

The life I had so carefully constructed was falling apart. I tried to find something to hold on to.

And I recognized, once again, the bleak truth: There was nothing but myself.

I searched the house. I talked to myself the whole time, telling myself that after it was searched and safe, I would finish cleaning it, and I did. It was a tremendous relief to leave the house and return to my own. I called Helen Drinkwater at work and told her that on my drive to work, I'd seen a suspicious man at the edge of the yard.

'I think you shouldn't leave it unlocked even for the fifteen minutes before I come,' I said. 'So either I have to get there while you're there, or you need to give me a key.' I could feel the woman's suspicions coming over the phone line, along with a tapping sound. Helen Drinkwater was tapping her teeth with a pencil. Mrs Drinkwater doesn't actually like to see me; she just likes to enjoy the results of my having been there. Before this morning, that had suited me just fine.

'I guess,' she said finally, 'you better come earlier, Lily. You can just wait in the kitchen until we leave.'

'I'll do that,' I said, and hung up.

The vicious game played with me today would not be repeated. I lay down on my bed and thought about the incident. It could be that the intruder had not known I could hear the little sound of the boards creaking; perhaps he'd just anticipated that I'd start down the stairs at some later time and find the cuffs and gun. Of course the intruder hadn't planned on any kind of confrontation; that was plain from the way he'd rabbited out the back door. But somehow, it made a difference whether or not the intruder had intended me to be aware of his presence before he left the house.

I would have to think about it. Maybe ask Marshall.

And that brought me upright on the bed instantly. I slapped myself on the cheek.

Marshall was on the edges of my life; he had probably left it completely after our conversation the night before. I won't start to think of him as part of my life, I promised myself. He'll go back to Thea. Or he's completely gone off me, since I told him about the scars. Or his common sense will tell him he doesn't need someone like me.

After that, I swore off thought for the day. I ate a hasty sandwich, then left the house.

I have two clients on Thursday afternoons, and I felt it had been a very long day when I left the last one, a travel agent's office, at six-thirty. The last thing in the world I wanted to see was Claude Friedrich at my doorstep.

You'd think he has the hots for me, I thought sardonically.

I parked the car in the carport and walked around to the front door instead of entering by the kitchen door, as I usually did.

'What do you want?' I asked curtly.

He raised his eyebrows. 'Not very polite today, are we?'

'I've had a long day. I don't want to talk about the past. I want my supper.'

'Then ask me in while you fix it.' He said this quite gently.

I couldn't think of what to do, I was so surprised. I wanted to be alone, but I would sound peevish if I told him to go away – and what if he didn't?

Without answering, I unlocked the door and walked in. After a minute, he walked in behind me.

'Are you hungry or thirsty?' I said, fury just underneath the words.

'I've had my supper, but I'd appreciate a glass of tea if you have some,' Friedrich rumbled.

Alone in the kitchen for a moment, I put my arms on the counter and rested my head on them. I heard the big man's footsteps sauntering through my spotless house, pausing in the doorway of my exercise room. I straightened and saw that Friedrich was in the kitchen, watching me. There was both sympathy and wariness in his face. I got a glass out of the cabinet and poured him some tea, plonking in some ice, too. I handed it to him wordlessly.

'I'm not here to talk about your past. I've had to check up on everyone connected to Pardon, as you can understand. Your name rang a bell . . . I remembered it, from the newspapers. But what

I'm here to talk about today . . . a client of yours was in to see me,' Friedrich said. 'He says you can verify his story.'

I raised my eyebrows.

'Tom O'Hagen says he came in from playing golf on his day off, Monday, at about three o'clock.'

He waited for my reaction, but I had none to give.

'He says that he then went over to Albee's apartment to pay his rent, found the apartment door ajar, looked inside, and saw that the area rug was rumpled up, the couch pushed crooked, and no one answered his call. He left his rent check on the desk right inside the door and left.'

'So you're thinking Pardon may already have been dead at three o'clock.'

'If Tom's telling the truth. You're his corroborating witness.'

'How so?'

'He says he saw you going into the Yorks' apartment as he came down the stairs.'

I thought back, trying hard to remember a perfectly ordinary day. I hadn't known until I was coming home from my night walk that it would be a day I needed to remember in detail.

I closed my eyes, attempting to replay that little stretch of time on Monday afternoon. I'd had the bag in my hand with the supplies the Yorks had wanted me to put in their apartment, anticipating their return. No, two bags. I'd had to put them down to fish out the right key – poor planning on my part. I remembered being peeved at my lack of foresight.

'I didn't hear anyone walking across the hall, but I did hear someone coming down the stairs, and it may have been Tom,' I said slowly. 'I was having trouble getting the right key separated from the bunch on my key chain. I went in the Yorks' place, put down the bags . . . put some things in the refrigerator. I left the other things out on the kitchen counter. I didn't need to water the asparagus plant because it was still very wet, and the shades in the bedroom were already open – I usually open them for the Yorks – so I left.' I replayed locking the door, turning to leave . . .

'I did see him! He was walking away from Pardon's apartment

to go to his own and he was hurrying!' I exclaimed, pleased with myself, Tom O'Hagen isn't my favorite person, but I was glad I was able to verify his story, at least to some extent. If it had been Tom I'd heard coming down the stairs, and then I'd seen him again leaving Pardon's in the two or three minutes I'd spent in the Yorks' apartment, surely he wouldn't have had time to kill Pardon. But why would Tom have been upstairs? He has a ground-floor apartment. Deedra? Nope. She'd been at work.

'I hear you know Marshall Sedaka,' Friedrich said abruptly.

The comment was so unexpected that I actually looked at him directly.

'Yes.'

'He was down to the station this morning, talking to Dolph Stafford. Dolph tells me he inherits that business now that Pardon Albee's dead. Pardon had a lot of irons in a lot of fires.'

I raised both hands, palms up. What of it?

'No one here knows much about Marshall,' Friedrich commented. 'He just blew into town and married Thea Armstrong. No one could figure out why some man hadn't snatched Thea up years ago, her being so pretty and smart. Marshall got lucky, I figure. Now I hear he's moved out of the house, got himself a little rental place on Farraday.'

I hadn't known where Marshall was living. Farraday was about three blocks away. I reached in the refrigerator, got out a container of soup I'd made over the weekend, and put it in the microwave.

It was a long two minutes until the timer beeped. I propped myself against the counter and waited for the police chief to go on.

'Pardon Albee was killed by one hard blow to the neck,' Friedrich observed. 'He was struck first on the mouth, and then got a crushing blow to the throat.'

I thought of how strong Marshall is.

'So you're thinking,' I said as I ladled soup into a bowl, 'that Marshall dumped Thea for me and killed Pardon Albee so he'd own his business, now that he doesn't have Thea's twelve-thousand-dollar-a-year salary from SCC?'

Friedrich flushed. 'I didn't say that.'

'That's the only point I can grasp from all this. Could you tell me any other implication I might have missed?' I stared at him for a long moment, my eyebrows raised in query. 'Right. Now, here's something real. Investigate *this*.' I held out the handkerchief, plain white, with a design of white stripes of different widths running around the border. Inside the handkerchief were the bumpy shapes of the gun and the handcuffs.

'You want to tell me about this?' Friedrich said.

Briefly and, I hope, unemotionally, I described what had happened at the Drinkwaters' that morning.

'You didn't call us? Someone was in the house with you and you didn't call us? Even if you were all right, what if they took something of Mel and Helen's?'

'I'm sure nothing was taken. I know everything in that house, and nothing was out of order. Nothing was rummaged through, or moved out of place, no drawers left open.'

'You're assuming that these items were left by someone who knows about what happened to you in Memphis.'

'Isn't that a logical assumption? I know you've found out. Have you told anyone?'

'No. It wasn't my business to do that. I did call the Memphis Police Department a couple of days ago. Like I said, I remembered where I'd heard your name – after I thought about it awhile. I've got to say, I'm kind of surprised you didn't change it.'

'It's my name. Why would I change it?'

'Just to avoid anyone recognizing it, wanting to talk about what happened.'

'For a while, I thought about it,' I admitted. 'But they'd already taken enough away from me. I wanted to keep at least my name. And then . . . it would have been like saying I had done something wrong.' And I glared at Friedrich in a way that told him clearly he was not to comment. He sipped his tea thoughtfully.

I wondered if Pardon had known the truth about my past. He'd never even hinted as much to me, but he had been a man who liked to know things, liked to own a little piece of the people around him. If Pardon had known, surely he would have hinted around to me. He wouldn't have been able to resist it.

'So, did the Memphis police send you a report of some kind, something on paper?' I asked.

'Yes,' he admitted. 'They faxed me your file.' He put his hand to his pocket, asked me if he could smoke his pipe.

'No,' I said. 'Where'd you leave the fax?'

'You think someone at my office has spread this around? You yourself haven't told anyone in this town about what happened to you?'

I lied. 'I haven't told anyone. And whoever left these on the steps at the Drinkwaters' house knows I got raped, and knows the circumstances. So the knowledge had to come from your office, as far as I can tell.'

Claude Friedrich's face darkened. He looked bigger, tougher, mean. 'Lily, maybe someone has known since you moved here. Maybe they've just had the good taste not to mention it to you.'

'Then they lost their good taste with a bang,' I said. 'You need to go. I have to work out.'

He took the handkerchief, handcuffs, and gun with him when he left. I was glad not to have them in my house anymore.

Normally, I don't work out on Thursday nights, especially when I've already gone to Body Time in the morning. But the day had been one long accumulation of fear and anger, interrupted by the boredom of everyday work. I needed to do something to relax my shoulders, and the punching bag didn't appeal to me. I wanted weights.

I pulled on a pink spandex shorts and bra set, covered it with a flowered T-shirt, grabbed my workout bag, and drove to Body Time. Marshall doesn't work on Thursday nights, so I wouldn't have the emotional strain of seeing him while he was still trying to digest what I'd told him.

Derrick, the black college student who picks up the slack for

Marshall in the evenings, waved a casual hand as I came in. The desk is to the left of the front door, and I stopped there to sign in before going over to the weight benches, unzipping my gym bag as I walked. There were only a couple of other people there, both serious bodybuilders, and they were doing leg work on the quad and calf machines and the leg press. I knew them only by sight, and after returning my nod, they ignored me.

The rest of the building was dark – no light in Marshall's office, the doors closed on the aerobics/karate room.

I stretched and did some light weights to warm up, then pulled on my weight-lifting gloves, padded across the palm and with the fingers cut off at the knuckle. I pulled the Velcro straps tight.

'Need me to spot?' Derrick called after I'd done three sets. I nodded. I'd done twenties, thirties, and forties, so I got the fifty-pound dumbbells from the rack and sat on one of the benches, lying down carefully with a dumbbell in each hand. When I felt Derrick's presence at my head, I checked my position. The dumb-bells were parallel with the floor and I was holding them down at shoulder level. Then I lifted them up and in until they met over me.

'All *right*, Lily!' Derrick said. I brought the dumbbells down, then back up, fighting to maintain my control. Sweat popped out on my face. I was happy.

By the sixth repetition, the lift had begun to be a struggle. Derrick gripped my wrists, helping me just enough to enable me to complete the move. 'Come on, Lily, you can do it,' he murmured. 'Push, now.' And my arms rose yet another time.

I put the fifties on the rack and got the fifty-fives. With a great deal of effort, I lay down on the bench and struggled to lift them; the conventional wisdom at the gym is that the first time is the hardest, but in my experience, if the first time is really difficult, it's likely all the succeeding lifts will be tough, too. Derrick held my wrists as my arms ascended, loosened his grip as my arms came down. I lifted the fifty-fives six times, my lips pulled back from my teeth in a snarl of concentrated effort.

'One more,' I gasped, feeling that treacherous exhaustion

creeping through my arms. I was so focused on making my lift that until the dumbbells were triumphantly in the air, I didn't realize that the fingers helping me were ivory, not black.

I held the lift until my arms collapsed abruptly. 'Going down!' I said urgently. Marshall moved back from the bench, and down came the weights, though I managed to stop short of dropping them from a height. I made a controlled drop, letting my bent arms hang down either side of the bench and releasing the dumbbells so they hit the rubber mat without rolling.

I sat up and swung around astride the bench, so pleased with my set that I overcame the anxiety of seeing Marshall for the first time after my true confessions session. Marshall was wearing what I thought of as his working clothes, a tank top and exotically patterned muscle pants from the line of exercise clothes clients could order through the gym.

'What happened to Derrick?' I asked, reaching for my gym bag to extract my pink sweat towel.

'I've been cruising all over town looking for you.'

'What's wrong?'

'Have you been here all evening?'

'No. I got here . . . oh, thirty or forty minutes ago.'

'Where were you before that?'

'At my house,' I said, an edge coming into my voice. If anyone had been asking but Marshall, I would have refused to answer. The big room was very quiet. For the first time, I noticed that we were alone.

'Where's Derrick?' I asked again.

'I sent him home after your fifty set. Was anyone at your house?'

I stared at him while I patted my chest and face dry.

'What's your point?' I asked.

'Lily, about an hour and a half ago, someone came in Thea's back door while she was in the living room and left a dead rat on the kitchen table.'

'Yuk,' I said in disgust. 'Who on earth would do something like that?' Suddenly, the dime dropped. 'You think—' I was so outraged, I was sputtering for words, and my hands tightened into fists.

Marshall sat astride the other end of the bench; he reached over to put a finger to my lips. 'No,' he said urgently. 'Never, I never thought so.'

'Then why the questions?'

'Thea . . . she has this . . .'

I'd never heard Marshall flounder before. He was acutely embarrassed.

'Thea thinks I did it?'

Marshall looked at the blinds drawn over the big front window, closed for the night. 'She thinks it might be you,' he admitted.

'Why?' I was bewildered. 'Why on earth would I do something like that?'

A flush spread across Marshall's cheeks.

'Thea has this idea that we're separated because of you.'

'But Marshall . . . that's just crazy.'

'Sometimes Thea is – crazy, I mean.'

'Why would she think that?'

Marshall didn't answer.

'You can go back and tell Thea – or I will be more than glad to do it myself – that I had an unwelcome visit from the chief of police, at my home, until right before I left to come here. So I have what you might call a golden alibi.'

Marshall drew a breath of sheer relief. 'Thank God. Now maybe she'll leave me alone.'

'So explain. Why would she think you two separated because of me?'

'Maybe I mentioned your name once too often when I was talking about karate class, or people who work out here.'

Marshall's eyes met mine. I swallowed. I was suddenly, acutely, aware that we were alone. I could never remember being alone with Marshall before, truly alone in an empty building. He reached out and flicked the light switch, leaving us only in the light that came through the blinds from the street. It fell in stripes across his face and body.

We were still sitting astride the bench, facing each other. Slowly, giving me plenty of time to get used to the idea, he leaned forward until his mouth touched mine. I tensed, expecting the flood of panic that had marked my attempts to have a close relationship with a man during the past few years.

The panic didn't come.

My mouth moved against Marshall's, welcoming. He slid closer, his legs going under mine until I lifted mine to wrap around him, my feet resting on the bench behind him. My arms went around his back and his hands were behind my back, pressing me to him.

Maybe it was the unexpectedness of it, maybe it was the unthreatening setting, or maybe it was because I had known Marshall as a friend first, but suddenly what had been so difficult became easy and urgent.

Marshall's hand lifted my T-shirt over my head. He had already seen the scars: I didn't have that moment to fear. I pulled off his tank top, my hands shaking. His tongue moved in my mouth. My hands ran over his torso for the first time. He pulled up my athletic bra and my breasts popped out; his tongue found a new target. I made an anguished little sound as a part of me I'd thought was atrophied came surging back to life. My hands conveyed my urgency, and after a moment, I stood, still straddling the bench, to work down my spandex shorts. He kissed my stomach as I stood before him, and then his mouth slid lower. In seconds, I rested one knee on the bench and turned to take my shorts off, and I heard cloth rustling in the darkness. Then bars of light fell across Marshall's heavily muscled bare body. In a few moments, Marshall was kneeling at the end of the bench while I lay back on it, filled with him, and the words he was whispering made me very happy, and everything worked beautifully.

Chapter Seven

I woke up cheerful, a condition so rare, I didn't even recognize it for a few minutes. I stretched in the bed, feeling a little sore in a most unusual way for me. Since I had had such a good workout the day before (and I smirked to myself when I thought that), I decided to do some pushups at home rather than trek in to Body Time. I turned on the coffeepot and went into the room with the punching bag, then hit the floor and did fifty quick ones. I showered quickly and pulled on some loose-cut jeans and a T-shirt, my ordinary working clothes.

I have never figured out how other women think they are going to fight – *or* clean house – in skintight jeans.

After retrieving my paper, I sat down for some cereal and coffee. I was conscious all the time of being extraordinarily relaxed and pleased, a mood so unusual, I hardly knew how to handle it.

I caught myself beaming out the kitchen window at the lovely morning. It's truly amazing what a good screw can do for your outlook, I thought. And it wasn't just the wonderful physical sensation; it was the successful completion of the sex act without a panic attack or a wave of revulsion for my partner.

I found myself wondering if Marshall would call me that day. What would happen at class tonight? I crushed those thoughts ruthlessly. It had been what it was, good sex, nothing more. But boy, it sure was nice to remember.

I glanced at my watch, then reluctantly gathered up my portable caddy of cleaning materials and rags to set out for the first job of the day, Deedra Dean's apartment.

Deedra is supposed to be at work by eight, but today she was still getting ready when I knocked on the door before using her key. This wasn't the first time Deedra'd been late.

She had hot curlers in her hair and a black lace slip on her body. Marcus Jefferson was coming out of his door as Deedra opened hers, and Deedra made sure he got a good look at the slip. I stepped in and turned to shut the door, catching a good look at Marcus's face as I did so. He looked a little . . . disgusted – but excited.

I shook my head. Deedra stuck her tongue out at me as she flounced back to her bathroom to finish her face. I had to make a great effort not to slap her cheek in the hope of knocking some sense into her head; there must be some intelligence rattling around in there, since Deedra is able to hold down a job where she actually has to perform work.

'Lily!' she called from the bathroom as I stared grimly around the chaos of the apartment. 'Are you a racist?'

'No, Deedra, I don't believe I am,' I called back, thinking pleasurably of Marshall's ivory body. 'But you're just playing – you're not serious about Marcus. And sleeping with a black man is still such a delicate thing that you really have to be serious about him to take the crap you're going to be handed.'

'He's not serious, either,' Deedra said, peeking out for a minute, one cheek pink and the other its natural white.

'Well, let's do something totally meaningless,' I muttered, and began to pile up all the magazines and letters and bills scattered over the coffee table. I paused in midact. Was I the pot calling the kettle black? No, I decided with some relief, what Marshall and I did had some meaning. I'm not sure what yet. But it meant something.

I went about my business as though Deedra wasn't there, and I certainly wished she wasn't. Deedra hummed, sang, and chattered her way through the rest of her toilette, getting on my nerves to an incredible degree.

'What do you think will happen to us now that Pardon's dead?' Deedra asked as she buttoned up her red-and-black-striped dress. She slid her feet into matching pumps simultaneously.

'You're the third person to ask me what the fate of the apartment building will be,' I said testily. 'How should I know?'

'Why, Lily, we just figure you know it all,' Deedra said matter-of-factly. 'And you never tell; that's the nice thing about you.'

I sighed.

'Now, that Pardon, what a son of a bitch,' Deedra said in the same tone. 'He sure was a pain to me. Always hovering, always asking me how my mama was, as if I needed reminding she's paying my rent for me. Always saying how nice it was I was dating so-and-so, if it was anybody white and professional, lawyer or doctor or bank president. Trying to scare me into living right.'

I would have tried that, too, if I'd thought it would work, I admitted to myself. Deedra was able to be flippant about Pardon Albee now that he was dead, but she'd been deathly afraid at the very idea of his searching her apartment the last time I'd talked to her.

The final button secured, Deedra went back to the bathroom mirror to add the finishing touches to her elaborately tousled blond hair.

She began in her nasal voice: 'When I went to pay my rent Monday afternoon' – I jerked to attention – 'I was going to have to plead with that old fart to keep his mouth shut about Marcus. He was asleep on the couch, though.'

'What time was that?' I called, trying to sound casual.

'Ahm . . . four-thirtyish,' Deedra said abstractedly. 'I left work for a few minutes. I forgot to take him a check at lunchtime, and you know how he was about being paid by five.' I walked down the hall so I could see her reflection in the mirror. Deedra was redefining an eyebrow.

'Did the apartment look okay?'

'Why, did you clean his, too?' Deedra said curiously, throwing down the eyebrow pencil. She began moving quickly to gather things up now that her face and hair were perfected. 'Actually, the couch with its back to the door was pushed out of place. You know, it was on rollers. One end of it was touching the coffee table, and the throw rug in front of it was all rumpled up.'

'You stepped in and had a good look, huh?'

Deedra stopped dead in the act of reaching for her purse on the

table by the door. 'Hey, wait a minute,' she said. 'Hey, Lily, I just
went inside the room when he didn't answer my knock. I thought
maybe he was in the back of his apartment, since the door was
unlocked. You know he was always home on rent day, and I
thought it would be a good day to talk to him. I should have
known better. It had already been a shitty day – my car wouldn't
start, my boss shouted at me, and then on my way back to work I
almost hit the camper. But anyway, I thought I heard a sound in
the apartment, so I opened the door, and there he was, out like
a light. So I left my check on the desk, since I saw some there
already, and I tried to talk loud to wake him up a couple more
times, but then I left.'

'He wasn't asleep,' I said. 'He was dead.'

Deedra's mouth fell open, obscuring her minimal chin entirely.

'Oh no,' she whispered. 'I never thought . . . I just assumed he
was asleep. Are you sure?'

'Pretty sure.' Though how to reconcile that with Tom
O'Hagen's story – the rumpled rug, the couch sitting askew, but
no body, an hour or more earlier – I couldn't fathom.

'You have to tell the police this,' I said as Deedra continued to
stand there in a stupor.

'Oh, I already did,' Deedra said absently. 'But they didn't tell
me – Are you sure?'

'Pretty sure.'

'So that's why he didn't hear me. And I was talking real loud.'

'And did you tell them why you wanted to talk to Pardon?'

A glance at her tiny gold watch lit a fire under Deedra.

'Hell no! I just said I went down there to pay the rent.' Deedra
grabbed her keys, then glanced at herself once more in the big
mirror over the couch. 'And don't you tell, either, Lily Bard! They
don't need to know anything about my personal life.'

I had a lot to ponder after Deedra was out the door.

Pardon Albee's body had been on the couch of his apartment at
four-thirty, give or take fifteen minutes. It hadn't been there at
three. But at three, when Tom saw it, the room was disarranged,
the door left ajar, as though a struggle had taken place.

Where had the body been in the hours before I had watched it being trundled across the street into the arboretum?

I gathered up my cleaning things when Deedra's apartment looked habitable again, then locked the door behind me carefully. I didn't want to hear any more accusations like Deedra's last week. I went down the stairs slowly to the O'Hagens'. Cleaning their apartment would use up the rest of my Friday morning.

Jenny answered my knock, so I knew she'd had the two o'clock to ten o'clock shift at Bippy's the night before. After closing, the O'Hagen on night duty usually got home by eleven or twelve and slept in the next morning, while the other one had to get up at five o'clock to make the six o'clock opening. Shakespeare is a town that rises early and beds early.

Jenny has red hair and freckles, a flat chest, and wide hips, and she dresses well to camouflage those features. But today in her flowered bathrobe, she was not aiming to impress me. Jenny likes to regard me as part of the furniture, anyway. After saying hi indifferently, Jenny plopped back in her recliner and lit a cigarette, her eyes returning to a talk show I had never thought of watching.

Jenny was the only person I'd seen in the past five days who was acting completely normal.

The O'Hagens do their own laundry, but Jenny and Tom hate cleaning their kitchen, not too surprising when you consider they manage a restaurant. So I almost always have plenty to load in the dishwasher, sometimes what I estimate to be a whole week's worth, and the garbage is always full of microwave meal trays and heat-and-eat cans. It also isn't too surprising, I figure, that they don't want to cook when they are home.

Jenny ignored me utterly as I moved around the apartment, to the point of not reacting at all when I took everything off the TV tray table set up next to the recliner and dusted the tray, putting its contents back in pleasing order afterward. I hate Jenny's cigarette smoke; she is the only client I have who smokes, I realized with a little surprise.

The phone rang after I'd been working an hour. I heard Jenny pick it up and turn down the volume on the television set.

Without trying, I heard Jenny murmur into the receiver for a few minutes, then thunk it back in its cradle.

I had worked my way back to the master bedroom, where I changed the sheets in a flash and snapped the bedspread back into order. I dumped the ashtray on Jenny's side of the bed (red hair on that pillow) and was walking around the bed to empty Tom's ashtray when Jenny appeared in the doorway.

'Thanks for backing up Tom,' she said abruptly.

I glanced up, trying to read the round freckled face. All I could see was reluctance. Jenny didn't like feeling beholden.

'Just told the truth,' I said, dumping the butts into the garbage bag and wiping out the ashtray. I replaced it with a little clunk on the bedside table. I spied a pencil on the floor, stooped to pick it up, and dropped it in the drawer of the bedside table.

'I know Tom's story sounded a little funny,' Jenny said tentatively, as though she was waiting for my reaction.

'Not to me,' I said crisply. I scanned the bedroom, couldn't spot anything I'd missed, and started out the door to the second bedroom, which the O'Hagens had fitted up as an office. Jenny stepped back to let me pass.

I'd tucked the corner of the dust cloth into my belt as I finished the bedroom. Now I whipped it out and began dusting the office. To my surprise, Jenny followed me. I glanced at my watch and kept on working. I was due at the Winthrops' by one, and I wanted to have something for lunch before I got there.

The glance wasn't lost on Jenny. 'Keep right on working,' she said invitingly, as though I wasn't already. 'I just wanted you to know we appreciate your remembering correctly. Tom was relieved he didn't have to answer any more questions.'

One had occurred to me during the morning. In the normal course of things, it wouldn't have crossed my mind to ask Jenny, but I was fed up with Jenny alternately ignoring me and following me around.

'So, did the police ask him what he was doing coming down the stairs from the other apartments, when he lives on the ground level?' I asked. I had my back to Jenny, but I heard a sharp intake of breath that signaled shock.

'Yes, Claude did, just now,' Jenny said. 'He wanted to ask Tom about that, since Tom hadn't mentioned that earlier.'

I could see why Claude Friedrich would think of asking, since his own apartment was on the second floor, opposite Norvel Whitbread's.

'And what did Tom say?'

'None of your business,' flashed Jenny.

Now, this was the familiar Jenny O'Hagen.

'Guess not,' I said. I ran the dust cloth over the metal parts of the rolling chair behind the desk.

'Well . . .' Jenny trailed off, then turned and marched into her bedroom, closing the door behind her firmly.

She emerged just as I finished cleaning – which I did not exactly consider a coincidence – clad in a bright green camp shirt and gray slacks.

'It looks great, Lily,' Jenny said without looking around. So she'd reverted to the new Jenny. I preferred the familiar rude Jenny; at least then I knew where I stood.

'Um-hm. You want to write me a check now, or mail it to me?'

'Here's the money in cash.'

'Okay.' I wrote a receipt, tucked the money in my pocket, and turned to leave.

I could feel Jenny moving up behind me, and I spun quickly, to discover she was much closer.

'It's okay!' Jenny said hastily, backing up. 'I just wanted to tell you that Tom wasn't doing anything wrong on the second floor, okay? He was up there, but it was okay.' To my amazement, Jenny looked red around the eyes and nose, as though she was about to cry.

I hoped that Jenny wouldn't actually weep; I would not pat Jenny O'Hagen on the back.

Evidently, Jenny felt the same way. 'See you next week,' she said in a clogged voice.

I shrugged, picked up my caddy of cleaning materials, and left. 'Good-bye,' I said over my shoulder, to prove I was not uncivil.

I'd closed the door briskly behind me as if I intended to leave the building at my usual clip. But I stopped and looked up and down the hall. There was no one in sight; I could hear no movement in the building. It was about noon on a Friday, and aside from the Yorks and Mrs Hofstettler, everyone should be at work.

It had occurred to me that the closet under the stairs (where Pardon kept odds and ends like extra lightbulbs and the heavy-duty vacuum for the halls) would have been an excellent temporary resting place for Pardon's wandering corpse.

And it just so happened I had a key.

Pardon himself had given it to me three years before, when he'd taken the only vacation I could remember. He'd gone to Cancún with a bus tour made up mostly of other Shakespeareans. While he'd been gone, I'd had the job of cleaning the halls and the glass panels in the back door, making sure the parking lot was clear of garbage, and channeling all the residents' complaints to the proper repairman. Pardon had given me the key then, and he had never asked for its return, perhaps anticipating more package tours in his future.

But all his fussing about his health had proved to have some basis, finally, when a specialist in Little Rock had told Pardon his heart actually had some small problem. Pardon had sworn off tours forever, for fear he'd have some kind of crisis in a foreign place, and he never tired of showing people his Cancún photos and telling them of his near brush with death.

I'd marked all the keys entrusted to me with my own code. If they were stolen, I didn't want the thief to be able to get into my clients' homes and offices. The code I used was not sophisticated: I just went down to the next letter of the alphabet, so the key to the closet of Shakespeare Garden Apartments had a little strip of masking tape on it with the initials THB in heavy black ink.

I tossed my key ring up and caught it with my right hand while I debated whether to look or not.

Yes, I decided.

The disappearance and reappearance of Pardon's body, and its ultimate disposal in the park via my cart, had opened a vein of curiosity and anger in me. For one thing, it revealed unexpected depths in one of the people I saw often – for I didn't think it possible that the killer could be someone other than an apartment resident.

I didn't know I'd reached that conclusion until I had the key in the lock and was turning it.

I looked inside the large closet. It opens facing the hallway, and since it conforms to the rise of the staircase, it is much higher at the left end than the right. I reached up for the long string that hangs down from the bare bulb overhead. Just as my hand touched it, a voice spoke behind me.

'What you looking for, Miss Lily?'

I gasped involuntarily, but in a second, I recognized the voice. I turned around to face Claude Friedrich.

'Anything I can help you with?' he continued as I looked up, trying to read the broad face.

'God Almighty, where *were* you?' I asked ferociously, angry at myself that I hadn't heard him, angry at him for the fear he'd made me feel.

'In Pardon's apartment.'

'Just skulking?'

I was not going to be able to provoke him into anger so he'd forget to ask me again, I saw.

'Examining the scene of the crime,' he said genially. 'And wondering, as I suspect you are, how come one person sees a body on the couch at four-thirty after someone else saw an empty couch at three o'clock, though at three o'clock the apartment looked like someone'd had a fight.'

'Pardon could've survived for a while,' I said, surprising myself by simply telling the policeman what was on my mind.

He looked equally surprised, and rather pleased.

'Yes, indeed, if it'd been another kind of wound.' Friedrich nodded his head of thick graying hair slowly. 'But with that blow to the neck, he would have suffocated pretty quick.'

And he looked down at my hands, empty now, since I'd put down the cleaning caddy when I opened the door. My hands looked thin and bony and strong.

'I could have killed him,' I said, 'but I didn't. I had no reason to.'

'What if Pardon had said he was going to spread the story of your bad time all over town?'

'He didn't know.' I'd come to that conclusion early this morning. 'You know what Pardon was like. He loved knowing all about everyone, and he'd bust a gut to tell whoever it was that he'd found out something about them. He'd have loved to *sympathize* with me about what happened. No one knew until you called Memphis and left that report lying around.' That was something else I'd have to do on my own – find out who in the police department had been talking, and to whom. I thought it quite likely that whoever had planted the cuffs and gun on the Drinkwaters' stairs had learned the significance of those items from a loose-mouthed police department employee.

'Probably you're right on that,' Friedrich admitted, giving me a pleasant surprise in return for the one I'd given him, 'and I'm looking into it. So you're checking out the closet to see if that's where he was stowed?'

I blinked at the change of subject. Friedrich was touchy about my reference to the poor security at the police department, as well he might be.

'Yes.' I explained how I came to have the key.

'Well, let's look,' Friedrich suggested, with a geniality I distrusted.

'You've already looked,' I said.

'Actually, no. Pardon's key ring hasn't turned up. We didn't want to break down the door. A locksmith was coming this morning to open it up, but now you've saved the city of Shakespeare a little money. I never thought of asking you if you had a key.'

It didn't seem a good time to tell him that I had keys to the front and back doors of the building, too.

'Why didn't you ask Norvel Whitbread?' I asked. 'He was supposed to be working for Pardon one morning a week.'

'He said he didn't have a key. And it seemed likely to me that Pardon wouldn't trust him enough to give him one, that Pardon would unlock the closet for him if Norvel needed to get in.'

I tucked the puzzle of Pardon's missing key ring in with all the other elements involved in the strange death of the landlord.

Friedrich stepped past me, reached up to pull the string, and scanned the closet when the light flooded into every corner. Pardon, whatever his faults, had not been stingy with wattage.

'Does it look like it always does, as far as you can tell?' Friedrich asked after we'd both taken a good look.

'Yes,' I said, a little disappointed. The shelves to the rear and left side of the closet were neatly lined with necessities – garbage bags, lightbulbs, cleaning materials – and odds and ends that Pardon had thought might be useful someday – mousetraps, vases, a door-knob, the big doorstop Pardon used to hold the front door when he got the hall carpet cleaned, and it was still damp. The big vacuum cleaner took up the right side of the closet. It was ancient, huge, and parked neatly, with its cord wrapped in a precise coil. That proved Norvel hadn't vacuumed last; Norvel would never wind a cord that pretty, I thought admiringly.

But Norvel was supposed to be doing the janitorial work.

Friedrich was looking over the shelves carefully and thought-fully, apparently doing an item-by-item inventory.

I reached over to touch his sleeve, then thought the better of it. 'Excuse me,' I said.

'Yes 'm?' Friedrich said abstractedly.

'Look at the cord on the vacuum.' I waited till he'd taken a good look. 'Someone other than Norvel Whitbread put that vacuum in here, and Norvel was supposed to do it.' I explained why I thought so.

Friedrich looked mildly amused. 'You got any idea who might

have put the vacuum in here, based on the way the cord is coiled?' he asked, and I realized he was gently pulling my leg.

Ho-ho. 'Yes, I have. I've seen the way Pardon put things away. That's the way Pardon did it. Every Monday morning, before he went to church, Norvel was supposed to vacuum and clean the glass in the doors, sweep the front walkway, and pick up trash in the parking area in the back. It doesn't seem he did that on Monday.'

'That's a lot to infer from a vacuum cleaner.'

It was an effort to shrug indifferently.

I took the key to the closet off my ring and handed it to Friedrich. Before he could say anything, I hoisted my caddy and strode out the front door, evicting Friedrich from my thoughts. I cast around in my mind for any reason I needed to go in my house; all of a sudden, I wasn't hungry anymore. Maybe I should jump right in the car to go to the Winthrops' house.

But there was yet another bump in my path – a car parked, blocking mine, in my driveway, and someone standing in my carport, leaning against my Skylark. My heart lurched when I recognized Marshall. I stood there awkwardly, not knowing what to do or say, feeling my cheeks get hot.

He took the caddy from me and put it on the ground. He drew me farther up under the carport and put his arms around me. After a moment, my arms went around his neck.

'I couldn't call you,' he said in my ear. 'I didn't know what to say over the telephone. I don't know what to say now.'

If he didn't, I sure wasn't going to venture anything. I was managing to enjoy being held, but I didn't like being in the carport; I didn't want to be seen. But the intoxication of Marshall's nearness, his remembered smell and touch, began to chip away at my anxiety. I felt a little dizzy. His tongue touched my lips.

'Marshall, I have to work,' I managed to say.

He held me a little away, looked at me sharply.

'Lily, are you putting me off because you don't want to be with me? Are you sorry about last night?'

'No.' I shook my head to reinforce it. 'No.'

'Are you having trouble, remembering what happened to you?'

'No . . .' I hesitated. 'But you know, having had sex once successfully doesn't mean I'm never going to live in the shadow of the rape again. The rest of my life, I'll have to deal with it.'

I am not a trouble-free woman. I am not always user-friendly. He had to have that brought to his attention, if he was trying to ignore it.

'But really, and I regret this, I'm late to my next cleaning job,' I finished prosaically.

'Lily,' he said again, as if he enjoyed saying it. I'd been looking down at the spot where our chests were touching. Now I met his eyes. His mouth came toward mine, and I could feel he was ready.

'We can't now,' I whispered apologetically.

'Tonight, after class?'

'Okay.'

'Don't eat first; we'll fix something at my place.'

I never ate before calisthenics, anyway. I nodded, and smiled at him. A red car going by in the street alerted me to the passage of time. I looked at my watch over his shoulder, wishing I could afford to call the Winthrops and tell them I was sick. But Marshall was an anomaly, and my work was the norm.

I was beginning to hope that with Marshall I could be exactly who I felt like being. The Memphis Lily, the Lily with long brown hair, who puffed and panted after twenty minutes on the tread-mill, would never have done what blond strong Lily did to Marshall next. My caress made him shiver all over.

'You don't know what it's been like,' he said when he could speak. I realized that Marshall had a story to tell, too.

'If you're sure you don't have ten extra minutes now,' he went on breathlessly, 'I guess I'll have to wait until tonight. We better not spar together in class!'

I found myself smiling at the thought of Marshall seething with desire while blocking my kicks, and seeing me smile made him laugh out loud.

'See you then,' I said, with a sudden resurgence of shyness. I gently extricated myself from his arms and went to my car. As he passed me to go to his Toyota, I had a back view of broad shoulders and tight butt to admire.

It had been so long since my plans had extended beyond my latest batch of library books or a movie I'd rented that I hardly knew what to think of as I drove the familiar route to my next job. I would be sweaty after class. Could I shower at his house? Would he expect me to stay the night, or would I come home to sleep? Where would I park my car? It was nobody's business that I would be visiting Marshall's rental house. I liked my life private.

As I slid out of my car at the Winthrops' back door, I decided I was excited, and scared. But most of all, I felt unsettled, a feeling I was having trouble enjoying. I'm not used to having so many variables to contend with, I realized.

But I had to put all that away in the back of my mind and get to work. I let myself in, locked the door behind me, and looked around the kitchen. The cook, Earline Poffard, had been at work; the counter was spotless and there was a full garbage can under the sink. Earline comes in twice a week, and she cooks enough suppers for the Winthrops to eat until she comes again. I had never met Earline face-to-face, but I knew her from her work; Earline labels everything she prepares, all her garbage lands in the bag, and she scours all the dishes herself, drys them, and puts them away. I have only to clean the outside of the microwave and the door of the dishwasher from time to time, and mop, and the kitchen cleaning is done.

For the first time, it occurred to me that I would like to meet Earline. Perhaps Earline was equally curious about me.

The habits of years reasserted themselves, and I set to work. I didn't want to be late to class this night; I looked forward to seeing Marshall my lover, and I didn't want Marshall my sensei to be shooting me the disapproving look he'd given me last time.

I'd gotten the dusting done and was getting the mop out of the closet when I heard a key in the lock.

'Hey, Lily,' called a casual male voice.

'Hi, Bobo,' I replied, making a mental note to tell Beanie she needed a new mop.

'Hey, what about that old guy getting killed over by your place?' Bobo said, his voice getting closer.

I glanced over my shoulder. The boy – the six-foot-two boy – was leaning against the kitchen sink, looking spectacular in cutoffs and an Umbro shirt. His grin betrayed his age, but his body had grown up ahead of him. I answer the phone while I'm working at the Winthrops', and most of the calls in the summer are inevitably for Bobo. He has his own phone, of course, but he gives only particular friends that number, much to his mother's irritation.

'He died,' I said.

'That's no answer, Lily! C'mon, you must know all about it.'

'I'm sure you know as much about it as I do.'

'Is it true someone called old Claude Friedrich while he was sacked out and told him where the body was?'

'Yes.'

'See, now that's the kind of thing I want you to tell me.'

'You already knew that, Bobo.' My patience had almost evaporated.

'Well . . . give me the inside scoop. You gotta know something that wasn't in the paper, Lily.'

'I doubt it.' Bobo loved to talk, and I knew he'd follow me around the house if I gave him the slightest encouragement.

'How old are you, Bobo?' I asked.

'Oh, I'm a senior. I'm seventeen,' he said. 'That's why I'm outta class early today. You gonna miss me next year when I go off to college, Lily?'

'You know it, Bobo.' I got the Mop & Glow from the cupboard, then turned the sink water to hot. 'For one thing, I ought to charge your parents less money because I won't have your mess to clean up.'

'Oh, by the way, Lily . . .'

When he didn't finish his sentence, I glanced over, to see Bobo was blushing a bright red.

As I raised my eyebrows to show I was waiting for him to finish his sentence, I squirted some cleaner on the floor. The water was running hot; I squeezed out the excess water and began to mop.

'When you were cleaning my room the other day, did you happen to find . . . something . . . ah, personal?'

'Like the condom?'

'Um. Right. Yeah.' Bobo stared at something fascinating by his right foot.

'Um-hmm.'

'What'd you do with it?'

'What do you mean? I threw it away. You think I was going to sleep with it under my pillow?'

'I mean . . . did you tell my mom? Or my dad?'

'Not my business,' I said, noting that Howell Winthrop, Jr, came a decided second on the list of people Bobo feared.

'Thanks, Lily!' Bobo said enthusiastically. He met my eyes briefly, his shoulders relaxed: He was a man looking at blue skies.

'Just keep using them.'

'What? Oh. Oh, yeah.'

And Bobo, if possible, grew redder than before. He left with a great show of nonchalance, jingling his keys and whistling, obviously feeling he'd had an adult conversation about sex with an older woman. I was willing to bet he'd be more careful disposing of personal items in the future, as well he ought.

I found myself singing as I worked, something I hadn't done in years. I sing hymns when I'm by myself; I know so many, from the countless Sundays I'd spent sitting with my parents and Varena in church – always in the same pew, fifth from the front on the left. I found myself remembering the mints my mother always had in her purse, my father's pen and the notepad he produced for me to draw on when I got too restless.

But thinking of my childhood seldom brings me anything but pain. Back then, my parents hadn't cast their eyes down when they spoke to me. They'd been able to hold conversations without tiptoeing verbally around anything they thought might distress their ravaged daughter. I'd been able to hug them without bracing myself for the contact.

From long practice, I was able to block out this unproductive and well-traveled train of thought. I concentrated on the pleasure of singing. It's always an amazement to me that I have a pretty voice. I'd had lessons for a few years; I used to sing solo in church, and perform at weddings from time to time. Now I sang 'Amazing Grace'. I reached up to brush the hair out of my face when I was finished, and it was a shock to find it was short.

Chapter Eight

I'd almost forgotten my sedentary neighbor's participation in the Wednesday-night class. It sure hadn't looked like he was having a good time, so I was surprised to see Carlton warming up when I bowed in the doorway. He was trying to touch his toes. I could tell from the way his mouth twisted that movement was painful.

'The full soreness has set in, huh?' I said as I sat on the floor to pull off my shoes.

'Even my hair hurts,' he said through clenched teeth as he strained downward. His fingers just managed to touch the tops of his feet.

'This is your worst day,' I told him.

'Is that supposed to make me feel better?'

'I thought maybe it would help to know that tomorrow won't be so bad.' I rolled my socks in a neat ball and stuck them in my right shoe. I stood, rotated my neck gently, then bent from my waist and put my hands flat on the floor. I gave a sigh of pleasure as my back stretched and the tension of the day flowed out.

'Show-off,' Carlton said bitterly.

I straightened and looked him over. Carlton was wearing shorts and a T-shirt. To the untrained eye, he would have looked pretty good, but I could see the lack of definition and development in his arms and thighs. Overweight, he wasn't; in shape, he wasn't.

Marshall came in and gave me a private smile before one of the other students approached him with a question. I followed him with my eyes for a moment and then considered Carlton, who was on the floor, his legs spraddled to either side, trying to touch his chest to the right leg, then the left. Carlton's thick black hair, normally gelled and swept behind his ears, was getting wild as he straightened and bent, straightened and bent. I pulled the top of my gi out of my gym bag and slid into it, then tended to the tying of the belt.

'So, Carlton. Remember the subduing hold we practiced last time?' I asked. Carlton scrambled to his feet.

'Ah . . . no. I had so much to learn that one night.'

Marshall was laughing with a knot of the younger men in the class.

'Okay. Reach out to grab my gi with your right hand . . . That's right. Now, grip hard.' Apparently scared he'd pull me off balance, Carlton barely took hold of the loose material. 'No, Carlton. You really have to hold on, or you'll think I was able to do this because you weren't exerting full strength.'

Carlton, while increasing the force of his grip, looked distinctly anxious. 'Oh, I wouldn't think that!' he protested.

'Now, remember? I reach up with my right hand, like so . . . I sink my thumb into the pit between your thumb and forefinger, to hit the pressure point – I got it, I see – and then I twist your hand so that the outside of it, the side of your little finger, is pointed toward the ceiling . . . Of course that rotates your whole arm, right?'

I could tell Carlton was remembering.

'Now I press your knuckles to my chest, being careful to keep your arm rotated. My fingers are wrapped around your hand, to keep the tension on . . . My thumb's still applying pressure . . . and now I—'

'Nooooo,' moaned Carlton, dropping to his knees as I applied counterpressure with my left hand on his upper arm and then bent over from the waist.

'Remember the distress signal Marshall showed you last time?' I asked.

Carlton shook his head, deeply involved with his pain.

'Slap your thigh with your free hand.'

He lost no time slapping, and I let go instantly. He looked up at me, his brown eyes wide in a pleading spaniel look that I suppose had been very effective on other women.

'That really hurt,' he said after a significant pause.

'We don't apologize, Carlton,' I said gently. 'I taught you something. We all get hurt.'

Carlton stood up, shook himself. He was having a little struggle with pride; his sensible side won.

'Well, here I am, learning,' he said ruefully. 'So I assume, to show you I learned it correctly, I get to do it to you?'

I reached out and grabbed his T-shirt.

I had to talk Carlton through the steps of hurting me enough for it to count. 'Sorry, I don't have to go down . . . Twist my hand a little more . . . Now go slow. You really don't want to break my arm. Wait for a real fight for that . . . Raphael, what is Carlton doing wrong?'

'He's not keeping you close enough,' diagnosed Raphael.

'Okay, Carlton, you're backing off, which means I can get free, or I can at least kick you and make you let go . . .' To demonstrate, I lashed out with my foot suddenly, but I pulled back in time just to tap Carlton's groin.

With a gasp, Carlton let go.

'We'll practice later,' I said. 'You might feel better doing this with Raphael or one of the other guys, because most men get so anxious about hurting a woman partner that they don't give it their best shot.'

'That bother you?' he asked.

'It used to. Now I think that in the real world, it would work to my advantage, and since women don't have men's upper-body strength, I need all the edge I can get.' I eyed Carlton with my own curiosity. 'Why'd you really start coming?'

'I wanted to see what you were so gung ho about. Three nights a week, for years . . . never missing, always on time. I thought it must be something that was a lot of fun.'

'It is,' I said, surprised that it could be seen differently.

'The fun is not apparent yet,' Carlton said. I hadn't known his voice could be so dry.

'Oh, it will be. You just have to learn a little, and it won't be so confusing.' Marshall was about to begin class, so I went to my place in line. I wasn't convinced that Carlton found me of such overwhelming interest that he felt like following my schedule, especially after our little exchange at my house earlier in the week.

'Kiotske!' Marshall called, and the class came to attention.

At water-break time, after calisthenics, Marshall drifted over to me. I could tell he was aiming for me, I was aware every minute of what he was doing as he said a word to this student or that. I was excited by his nearness, but I had not the slightest idea what to say to him.

'Did you hear anything else about what happened to Thea?' I asked after we'd given each other a little nod of greeting.

'No. The police said fingerprinting the doors didn't bring up anything unusual, and none of her neighbors saw anything. That little house has a grown-up backyard, so that's not too surprising. At least the rat was probably just caught in a trap, not tortured or anything.'

'Was she very shook-up?'

Marshall's expression was peculiar. 'Thea's pretty emotional,' he said.

I wondered if Thea had pleaded with him to come home for her protection, a thought I found distasteful. I didn't want to set foot in the situation between Marshall and Thea. But of course if you have sex with a man, I told myself wryly, you're part of the situation between him and his wife automatically.

As I practiced buntai with Janet Shook, the only other woman who consistently came to class, it occurred to me that the hideous practical joke played on me at the Drinkwaters' might be related to the equally hideous prank played on Thea. Was someone else so enamored of Marshall that she was doing horrible things to women she perceived as being involved with him?

As much as the thought made my skin crawl, it at least made some kind of sense out of an otherwise-bewildering incident.

'Lily!' Marshall called. Janet and I stopped our striking-and-blocking practice, and I bowed to Janet briefly before running over to Marshall. He was standing with Carlton, and he looked a little exasperated. 'You're a good teacher, Lily. Carlton and I are not – we're not meshing gears on star drill, and I need to help Davis on his kata. Could you . . .'

'Sure,' I said. Marshall patted my shoulder and moved on to Davis, a weedy twentyish man who sold insurance.

'Sorry you're stuck with me,' Carlton said, though he didn't look particularly sorry.

'What part of this exercise are you having trouble with?'

'The whole thing.'

I sighed, not too quietly.

'Okay, specifically, I'm having trouble remembering the sequence.'

'All right. Get in shiko dachi . . . No, turn your feet out . . . Now squat some more.'

Carlton moaned.

I dropped into position facing him. 'Now, *you* face that way,' I told him, pointing to my right, 'and *I'll* face this way . . . No, keep your hips in position; just turn the upper torso . . .'

'Explain to me again why we're whacking our arm bones together,' Carlton said pathetically.

'To make them tougher. So we don't feel as much pain when we fight.'

'We go through it now so we don't feel it later?'

'Ah . . . right. Now, forearms down, up . . . switch sides! Forearms down, up, switch!'

'So,' he puffed after a few more seconds, 'what would you do right now if I leaned over and kissed you on the neck?'

'Well, you're standing in a position that leaves your genitals wide open. So I'd probably strike you seiken – that is, with a powerful jab, in the groin, and then when you doubled over, I'd get you with an elbow to the back of the neck, and when you were all the way on the floor, I'd kick you repeatedly.'

'Better not do that, then.'

'Better not.'

'Just wanted to find out.'

'There is something else I want from you.'

'Name it.'

'I want to know who's inheriting the apartments and all Pardon's other land holdings, if he has any.'

Carlton grunted as I accidentally elbowed him. 'A niece of Pardon's, the daughter of Pardon's dead sister. She called Pardon's lawyer yesterday, who called me, since she's going to be coming to town day after tomorrow to arrange for Pardon's burial. Ow, Lily! Not so hard! And go over his books with me. This gal lives in Austin, Texas. I'm sure you're gonna love her. She's a tae kwon do instructor. Pardon had mentioned her to me one time.'

'Could that be why you're suddenly interested in coming here, rather than curiosity about my schedule?'

'Fifty-fifty, I'd say.'

'I'd better warn you, goju is really different from tae kwan do. Philosophy, fighting technique, stances.'

I shut up and accelerated the star drill until Carlton suddenly gave out. I'd been picking up the signals (shaking legs, increased sweating, a desperately determined set to his mouth) but had ignored them ruthlessly.

'Give me a break!' Carlton said, and I felt a little shame at driving him so hard.

'Don't scare him away, Lily,' Marshall said behind me.

'No, sir.' I tried to look repentant.

'Back in line,' Marshall called to the paired students, and we scampered (or hobbled) back into place.

'Kiotske!' We came to attention. 'Rai!' We bowed. 'Class dismissed!'

'My favorite words,' Carlton murmured to Janet, who laughed – too much for such a feeble joke, I thought.

Marshall came up to me and said very quietly, 'I'll pick you up at your house,' which answered all my questions.

I sat on the floor to pull on my shoes. After I tied them, it was an effort to get up smoothly, but it was also a point of pride. Carlton was sitting in one of the folding chairs that lined the room, his head cocked. He was looking at me as if he was examining a suspect hundred-dollar bill.

'Good night,' I said briefly.

'Good night,' he answered, and bent to tie his sneakers, a scowl on his handsome face.

I shrugged and went through the double doors, passing Marshall's office and waving to him. He was looking at employee time sheets. The main room was empty except for Stephanie Miller, one of Marshall's hired hands who teaches some of the aerobic classes. Stephanie was running the big industrial vacuum cleaner over the worn green carpet. I gave her a casual nod and passed through the front door and over to my Skylark, one of four cars left in the parking lot. There was something on the hood of my car.

I wouldn't let myself stop, but I slowed down to get a better look. It was a . . . doll?

Then I was standing a foot away and I dropped my gym bag. It was a doll, a Ken doll.

The eye had been defaced with red nail polish. It was fresh. I could smell it from where I stood. It had been used to create artistic drops of blood down the doll's face. Someone had made the doll look as if it had been shot in the left eye, the eye I had hit when I shot Nap.

I remembered exactly how it had looked, the sound the man had made, the way he'd hit the floor. He hadn't looked anything like a Ken doll . . .

'What's wrong?' Carlton asked. 'Car trouble?'

I was glad to be dragged back from the edge of the nightmare. I stood back so Carlton could see.

'Was this on your car?'

'Yes. I left the car locked, so someone put it on the hood.'

I shivered at the malignancy of the 'gift'.

'What's up?' Marshall asked. He'd just locked the front doors of the gym. Across the parking lot, Stephanie got in her car and pulled out to go home.

I pointed to the doll. I couldn't bring myself to touch it.

'Oh, Lily, I'm sorry,' he said after a moment.

'I get the feeling there's something about this I don't know?' Carlton asked.

I puffed out my cheeks with a gust of air. I was so tired. 'I guess I ought to take this by the police station,' I said.

'Lily, let it wait until tomorrow,' Marshall said. 'Go on home now. I'll see you in a little while.'

'No. I want to get rid of it. I'll call you when I get home.'

'Lily, do you want me to go to the police station with you?' Carlton asked.

I had almost forgotten Carlton was still there. I found myself feeling the unaccustomed emotions of warmth and gratitude toward my neighbor.

'That's very kind of you,' I said stiffly, wishing I could sound more gracious. 'But I think I better go by myself. Thank you for offering.'

'Okay. If you need me, call me.' Carlton hobbled over to his Audi and went home, doubtless anticipating a hot bath and a welcoming bed.

I watched him go because I didn't want to turn to meet Marshall's eyes.

'I'm wondering,' I said, still looking into the night, 'whether you have a secret admirer – someone who could find out my history and leave these little gifts for me, someone who could kill a rat and leave it on Thea's table.'

'So, it's scaring you off, and we should forget about us?' Marshall leaped to the thought. He was upset and angry.

Well, I'm not exactly happy, either, I fumed to myself.

'No, that's not what I'm saying.'

'Are you saying you don't want to see me tonight?'

'I don't know. No, that's not what I'm saying. I've been looking forward to it as much as you have.' I raised my hands, palms upward, in a gesture of frustration. 'But this is bad, isn't it? To think someone's watching me? Sneaking around with things like this?' I waved my hand toward the doll. 'Thinking about what to do to me next?'

'So you'll let that person make your life even more miserable?'

I swung around to face Marshall so suddenly that his shoulders tensed. I had so many thoughts, it was a struggle as to which one would be voiced first. 'I think I gave that up a good many years ago,' I said. I was stiff with fury, felt like hurting him. 'And while I looked forward to screwing you tonight, missing it would not make me miserable.'

'I wanted to sleep with you, too,' Marshall said, equally angry now. 'But I also wanted just to be with you. Just talk to you. Have a normal conversation with you – if that's possible.'

I struck, aiming for his diaphragm. Like a senseless person who didn't want teeth anymore, I told myself later. Quicker than I could block with my left arm, Marshall's hand shot out and gripped the wrist of my striking right arm when my knuckles were within an inch of his abdomen. His other hand had formed the knife, and was starting for my neck. For a long moment, we stared at each other, eyes wide and angry, before coming to our senses. His hand relaxed and he placed his fingers gently against my throat, feeling my pulse racing. My fist uncurled and fell to my side.

'Almost got you,' I said, embarrassed to find my voice was shaking.

'Almost,' he admitted. 'But you would've been down first.'

'Not so,' I argued. 'The diaphragm blow would've doubled you over and you would've missed my neck.'

'But the blow would've landed somewhere,' he argued back, 'and the force would have knocked you backward. Admittedly, after you had already hit me . . .' His voice trailed off and we looked at each other sheepishly.

'Maybe,' I said, 'I'm not the only person who has trouble carrying on a "normal" conversation?'

'You're right. This is probably pretty weird.'

Very carefully, as though we were covered with thorns, we eased into each other's arms.

'Relax,' whispered Marshall. 'Your neck muscles are like wires.'

I tentatively laid my head on his shoulder. I turned my mouth into his neck. 'What I'm going to do,' I said gently, 'is take the doll to the police department, tell them where I found it, and go home. When I get there, I'll call you. You'll come get me. We'll eat at your place, and then we'll do good things together.'

His hand massaged my neck. 'I can't get you to reverse the order?'

'I'll see you soon,' I promised, then slid from his arms and got in the car, stowing the grotesque doll on the seat beside me. I drove to the police department, which is housed in a former drugstore a couple of blocks from the center of town. There was only one police car in the parking lot, a dark blue city of Shakespeare car with a big number 3 on the side.

Tom David Meiklejohn was sitting inside, his feet propped up on a desk. He had an RC Cola in one hand and a cigarette in the other. Tom David, whom I know by sight, is good-looking in what I think of as a honky-tonk way. He has short, curly hair, bright, mean eyes flanking a sharp nose, and thin lips, and he dresses western on his days off. He'd been sleeping with Deedra around last Christmas, and during that month or two I'd seen him go in and out of the Garden Apartments regularly.

Tom David had been married at the time to a woman as hard-edged as he was, or so one travel agent had told another as I was cleaning their office. A few months later, I had seen the Meiklejohns' divorce notice in the local paper.

Now, Tom David, whom I'd observed patrolling many times during my night prowls, was slowly looking me up and down, making a show of trying to figure out my all-white outfit.

'Going to a pajama party?' he asked.

So much for courtesy to the public he serves, I reflected, though I'd anticipated as much. Not every policeman was a Claude Friedrich. Friedrich might make mistakes, but he didn't mind admitting them.

'This was left on my car outside of Body Time,' I said briefly, and deposited the doll on the desk in front of his feet. I'd wrapped it in a paper towel from a roll in my housekeeping kit. Now I spread the towel open.

Tom David gradually uprighted himself and put the RC Cola down. He stubbed out his cigarette, staring at the Ken doll.

'That's ugly,' he said. 'That's real ugly. Did you see anyone around your car?'

'No. I was in Body Time for over an hour. Anyone could have pulled into the parking lot, put the doll on my car, and pulled out without anyone seeing them. Not many people there tonight – most people don't work out on Friday evenings.'

'You were at that martial arts class that Marshall Sedaka runs?'

There was something about the way he said Marshall's name . . . not just distaste but also personal dislike. I went on full alert.

'Right.'

'He thinks he's tough,' Tom David remarked. There was a cold light in his mean, bright eyes. 'Orientals think they can order women around like they was sheep or something.'

I raised my eyebrows. If anyone thought of women as interchangeable parts, it was Tom David Meiklejohn.

'Sedaka see this?'

'Yes,' I said.

'He have a chance to put it on your car? You two have any personal relationship?'

'He didn't have a chance to put it on my car. He was inside Body Time when I got there, and he left after I did.'

'Listen, I'm the only one here right now, and when Lottie comes back with her McNuggets, I gotta go on patrol. You want to come back in tomorrow and make a statement?'

'Okay.'

'I'll try fingerprinting this, and we'll see what happens.'

I nodded and turned to go. As my hand touched the door, Tom David said abruptly, 'I guess you *would* be interested in self-defense.'

I could feel the color draining from my face.

I looked out through the glass door into the darkness.

'Any woman should be interested in self-defense,' I said, and walked out into the night.

I drove home tense with rage and fear, thinking of the bloody-eyed Ken doll, thinking of Tom David Meiklejohn mulling over what had happened to me with his buddies over a few beers. I had found the source of the leak in the police department, I was pretty sure.

I parked the car where it belonged, unlocked the back door, and threw everything but my keys and my driver's license into the house. Those I stuck in my T-shirt pocket, where they made a strange bulge over my breast. I had to walk. It was the only thing that would help.

The street was deserted at the moment. It was about 9:00 P.M. The night was much warmer than it had been the last time I walked, the humidity high, a precursor of the dreadful hot evenings of summer. It was fully dark, and I drifted into the shadows of the street, padding silently along to pass through the arboretum. Marshall's house on Farraday was not far. I didn't know the number, but I would see his car.

It relaxed me, moving through the night invisibly. I felt more like the Lily who had had a stable existence before the murder of Pardon Albee. Then, my only problem had been the sleepless nights, which came maybe twice a week; other than that, I'd had things under control.

Standing concealed in the undergrowth of the arboretum, I waited for a car to pass on Jamaica Street, so I could steal across.

I hadn't considered my route at all, but now sheer curiosity led me to drift toward the house Marshall had up until recently called home. There is very little cover on Celia Street, which is one of modest but spruce white houses with meticulously kept yards. I planned my approach. It was earlier than I usually walked, and there were more people on the move, which in Shakespeare isn't saying a hell of a lot – a car would pass occasionally, or I would see someone come out of his house, retrieve something from a pickup or jeep, and hurry back inside.

In the summer, children would be playing outside till late, but on this spring night, they all seemed to be inside.

I worked my way down the street, trying to be unobtrusive but not suspicious, since there were people still up and active. It was not a workable compromise. I'd rather be seen than reported, so I moved at a steady pace rather than drifting from one cover to another. After all, I was wearing white, hardly a camouflage color. Still, no one seemed to notice me, and curtains up and down the little street were uniformly drawn against the dark.

I only saw the police car when I was directly opposite Marshall's former home. It was parked up against Thea's next-door neighbor's hedge, which divides their yards from the street to the back of the lot. The cruiser was pulled right up behind a car that I assumed must be Thea's, which looked dark red or brown in the dim light of the streetlamp. So it didn't exactly seem the driver was paying an official visit; in fact, I concluded, Tom David Meiklejohn, whose car number 3 was parked in the driveway, was inside chitchatting with the rat-plagued Mrs Sedaka, while he was supposed to be patrolling the streets of Shakespeare to keep them safe for widows and orphans.

Instead, it seemed Tom David Meiklejohn was personal body-guard to one about-to-be-divorcée.

I had a fleeting desire to make yet one more anonymous phone call to Claude Friedrich, before I reflected that not only would that be sneaky and dishonorable but also that a possible relationship between Thea and Tom David was none of my business.

I began moving again, ghosting silently down the dark, quiet street, thinking hard as I passed from shadow to shadow.

In five minutes, I was on Farraday. Marshall's car was parked in the gravel driveway of the house on the corner, a little house smack in the middle of a small lot needing a great deal of yard work. The rental was definitely a step down from Celia Street.

I wondered if it had been hard for Marshall to leave the Sedaka house in Thea's possession.

The porch light was glowing yellow, but I continued on through the yard and around to the back door, my eyes adapting quickly to the darkness. I rapped three times, hard, and heard Marshall's quick footsteps.

'Who's there?' he asked. He's not a man who likes surprises, either.

'Lily.' He opened the door quickly. I went up the step and into the house. And despite what he had said about having an evening of conversation, the minute the door shut, his arms went around me and his mouth found mine. My hands snaked underneath his T-shirt, eager to touch his body again.

I did not have time to marvel at my ability to have sex without fear; I did not have time to wonder if what I was doing was wise, since I carried burdens enough for two, and Marshall was not exactly an unencumbered man. But we did take a moment for protection this time, and I hoped we wouldn't pay for our previous stupidity.

Afterward, it was hard to feel the limitations of my own skin, to feel myself shrinking back into the mold in which I'd cast myself before I'd come to Shakespeare. For the first time in years, it felt confining rather than comfortable.

And yet, as I looked around Marshall's Spartan bedroom – the queen-sized mattress and box spring on a frame, no headboard or footboard; a dresser clearly retrieved from someone's attic; a thrift store night table – I felt uneasy at being out of my own home. In many months, I hadn't been in anyone's house except to clean it.

We'd been lying together quietly since making love, my back to his front, his arm around me. Every now and then, Marshall would kiss my neck or stroke my side. The intimacy of the moment both excited and threatened me.

'You know Thea is seeing someone else,' I said quietly.

If he wanted to get divorced, he needed to know that. If he wanted to reconcile with Thea, he needed to know that.

'I thought so,' he said after a long moment. 'Do you know who it is?'

'What will you do if I tell you a name?' I turned over to face him, automatically reaching down for the sheet to cover my scars. Before he answered, he took the sheet, pulled it back down, and kissed my chest.

'Don't hide from me, Lily,' he whispered.

My hands twitched with the effort I was making not to grab the sheet. Marshall moved even closer to me so that his body covered the scars, and I gradually relaxed against him.

'Are you thinking I might track him down and beat him up for Thea's honor?' he asked after letting enough time pass to let me know he didn't consider Thea's affair a personal thing.

'I don't know you well enough to know what you would do.'

'Thea is a hometown sweetheart, because she's pretty and she was born and bred here. She knows when to act charming and sunny. She's good with children. But the people you won't find talking about Thea with this exaggerated awe are the men she's dated for a while – the men she's dated long enough to go to bed with.'

I pulled back a little to look at Marshall's face. He looked as if he had a bad taste in his mouth.

'Lily, by the time I came to town, Thea had run through the few locals she felt were worthy of her. She could tell, I think, that people were starting to wonder why pretty, sweet Thea couldn't seem to form a lasting relationship with anyone, so she dated me and married me quickly. I didn't go to bed with Thea before I married her. She said she wanted to wait and I respected that, but I found out after maybe a month, that was just because she didn't want me to back out like other men had.'

'She doesn't like sex?' I asked hesitantly. I should be the last one to criticize a woman who had problems dealing with men.

Marshall laughed in an unamused way. 'Oh, no. She likes it. But she doesn't like it like we do it,' and his hand ran down my back, caressed my hips. 'She likes to do . . . sick things, things that hurt. Because I loved her, I tried to oblige, but it ended up making me feel bad. Sad.'

Degraded, I thought.

'Then she decided she wanted a baby, and I wondered if that might save our marriage, so I tried to oblige. But I'd lost my interest by then, and . . . I couldn't.' This cost Marshall a great deal to say. 'So she called me names and taunted me, only in private, only when no one else could hear. Not because she cared about me, but because she didn't want anyone else to know she was capable of saying those things. Going home was like going to hell. I couldn't stand it anymore. I haven't had sex in six months, Lily, but that wasn't the worst of it, not by a long shot. So here I am, in this dump, wondering how to file for divorce without Thea taking my business away from me.'

I had no response to his money worries. I have very little available cash myself because I am saving strenuously against the day when I have to have a new car, or a new roof, or any of the sudden catastrophic expenses that can wipe out a one-income household. But at least all my finances, good or bad, are dependent on me and me only. I can't imagine how I'd feel if I had to give half of my business away to someone who had found pleasure in degrading and humiliating me.

'Tom David Meiklejohn.'

His eyes had been focused far away, staring past my shoulder at a bleak vista. Now he looked at me.

'The cop.' His dark eyes stared into mine. I gave a tiny nod. 'I'll bet she loves the handcuffs,' he said.

I tried not to shrink at the thought of a woman handcuffed, but my breath came out in a little whine that drew Marshall's attention to me instantly. 'Don't think of it, Lily,' he said quietly. 'Don't think of it; think of this.' And his hand slid gently between my legs, his mouth found my breast, and I did indeed think of other things.

'Marshall,' I said afterward, 'if you hadn't noticed, I wanted to tell you I have absolutely no complaints about your virility.' He laughed a little, breathlessly, and for a while we dozed together.

But I woke soon, anxious and ill at ease. Moving as quietly as I could, I got up and began pulling on my clothes. Marshall's breathing was still heavy and even and he shifted position, taking up more of the bed now that I wasn't in it. For a moment, I bent over the bed, my hand an inch from his shoulder. Then I drew back. I hated to wake him: I felt compelled to leave.

I eased out of the back door, punching in the button on the knob so it would lock behind me.

I'd begun thinking, as Marshall talked about Thea, of the dead rat someone had left on Thea's kitchen table in that neat white house on Celia. When I'd woken, the rat had worried me more and more.

The Ken doll, the toy handcuffs, the dead rat. Obviously, the tokens left for me referred to my past. The dead rat seemed cut from an entirely different pattern. A thought trailed through my mind like a slug: Had Thea perhaps tortured animals in her childhood? Was the rat also from Thea's past? I grimaced as I moved through the darkness. I could not bear cruelty to a helpless thing.

At this time of night, the streets were deserted, the town deep in sleep. I wasn't being as careful as I usually was. The only people likely to see me at this hour were the two patrolling policemen, and I knew where one of the two was; I'd checked on my way home, and Tom David was still at Thea's. Surely he'd gone off duty; wouldn't the dispatcher be trying to raise him otherwise?

I was yawning widely as I walked up my driveway. I'd pulled my keys from my pocket and was about to step off the drive to go to my front door when the attack came. Tired and inattentive as I'd been, I had trained for this moment for three years.

When I heard the rush of feet, I whirled to face the attacker, the keys clenched in my fist to reinforce my blow. But the man in the ski mask had a staff, maybe a mop or broom handle, and he swung it under my guard and whacked my ribs. I kept myself upright by a supreme effort, and when my assailant tried to swing the staff again, I let the keys fall, grabbed the staff with both hands, swung up my leg, and kicked him hard in the chest – not a very effective kick, but it was the best I could do under the circumstances. He did have to let go of the staff, which was good, but I staggered when he released it and dropped it myself, which was bad.

My kick had made him fall back, too, though, and that gave me time to recover my footing before he launched himself at me with a savage growl, like a dog out of control.

I was close to that point myself. When I saw the face coming toward me, shrouded in a ski mask but otherwise unguarded, I inhaled deeply, then struck as hard as I could with my fist, exhaling and locking into position automatically. The man screamed and began falling, his hands going up to clutch his nose, and on his way down, my knee came up, striking him sharply under the chin.

And that was the end of it.

Though I stood in a fighting stance in the dim light, the man was rolling and gurgling in a whipped way on my grass. Lights were coming on in the apartments – the man's scream had been piercing, if not long – and Claude Friedrich, the man used to dealing with emergencies, dashed around the dividing fence with a speed rather amazing for a man of his age. His gun was drawn. I took him in at a glance, then resumed guarding the man on the grass.

Friedrich stopped short.

'What the *hell* are you doing, Lily Bard?' he asked rather breathlessly. I glanced at him again, long enough to notice that he was clad only in khaki slacks. He looked pretty good.

'This son of a bitch attacked me,' I said, very pleased to hear my voice come out even.

'I would think it was the other way around, Miss Lily, if he didn't have a mask on and you weren't in your own yard.'

I saw no point in responding. I kept my attention focused on the writhing, whimpering figure.

'I think he's pretty much whipped,' Friedrich said, and I thought I detected a note of sarcasm. 'What I really wish you would do, Lily, is go inside your little house there and call the police station and tell them I need some backup here.'

What I longed to do was jump on my attacker and hit him a few more times, because the adrenaline was still pumping through my system, and by God, he had startled me. But Friedrich was making sense; there was no point in my getting into trouble. I stood straight, dropping my hands, and took a cleansing breath to relax. I took a step toward my house and felt a stab of pain, sharp enough to cause me to stop dead.

'You all right?' Friedrich said sharply, anxiously.

I found I was aching from more than the wish to punish my attacker. His first blow had been a good one, and he'd managed to rake my face with his fingers, though I couldn't remember how or when. As the rage ebbed away, the pain seeped in to take its place.

'I'll make it,' I told him grimly, and reached out to pull my keys from the grass. To my dismay, the little chain had snapped and the keys had scattered under our feet. I could find only one, but at least that one was my house key. I hobbled into the house, making my way to my bedroom. I called the police station first. After I hung up, my hand stayed wrapped around the receiver. I had no idea what I'd said to the dispatcher, the unseen Lottie. It was now one-thirty in the morning.

Marshall had made me promise to call him if I had trouble.

I checked the little piece of paper he'd scrawled his new phone number on, and I punched it in.

'Yes?' Marshall asked, a little groggy but conscious.

'I'm at home, Marshall,' I said.

'I knew you'd left,' he said curtly.

'I had a fight.'

'Are you all right?'

'Not entirely. But not as bad off as he is.'

'I'm out the door.'

And suddenly, I was talking to a dial tone.

I wanted more than anything else to lie down on the bed. But I knew I could not. I forced myself to get to my feet again, to move slowly back out to where Claude Friedrich was still holding a gun on 'the whiner', who had covered his now-blood-soaked ski mask with both hands.

I still didn't know the identity of my attacker.

'I guess you get to pull off his mask, Lily,' Friedrich said. 'He can't seem to manage.'

I bent painfully over, said, 'Put your damn hands down,' and was instantly obeyed. I grasped the edge of the ski mask with my right hand and pulled it up. It couldn't come off entirely because the back of his head pinned it down, but enough of the knit front slid up for me to recognize its wearer.

Blood slid from Norvel Whitbread's nostrils. 'You done broke my nose, you bitch,' he said hoarsely, and my hand snapped back to strike. Norvel cringed.

'Cut it out!' barked the chief of police, no trace of comforting rumble in his official voice, and with an effort of will, I relaxed and stepped away.

'I can smell the bourbon from here,' Friedrich said disgustedly. 'What were you doing when he came at you, Lily?'

'I was walking up to my own house in my own yard, minding my own business,' I said pointedly.

'Oh. Like that, huh?'

'Like that,' I agreed.

'Norvel, you are the stupidest son of a bitch who ever drew breath,' the chief of police said conversationally.

Norvel did some moaning and groaning and then he vomited.

'Good God Almighty, man!' exclaimed Friedrich. He looked over at me. 'Why you think he did this, Lily?'

'He gave me some trouble at the church the other day when I was working there, so I thumped him,' I said flatly. 'This is his idea of revenge, I guess.' Norvel seemed to stick to tools of his trade when he planned an assault. I was willing to bet the staff was the same broom he'd tried to hit me with at the church, with the straw sawed off.

A city police car came around the corner, lights rotating but siren silent, which was something to be thankful for.

A thought struck me and I squatted a few feet away from Norvel, who now smelled of many unpleasant things. 'Listen, Norvel, did you leave that doll on my car tonight?' I asked.

Norvel Whitbread responded with a stream of abuse and obscenity, the burden of which was that he didn't know what I meant.

'What's that about?' asked Friedrich.

'Okay, let's try again, Norvel,' I said, struck by a sudden inspiration. I held up a wait-a-minute hand to Friedrich. 'Why did Tom O'Hagen go upstairs to see you the day Pardon was killed?'

'Because he couldn't keep his dick in his pants,' snarled Norvel, in no mood to keep anyone else's potentially lucrative secret any longer. 'He gave me sixty lousy bucks not to tell his wife he's been screwing Deedra.'

Claude Friedrich was standing closer now. He'd moved in imperceptibly when he heard my question. Now he exploded in a cold kind of anger. 'Little something you forgot to mention to me, Norvel?' he asked furiously. 'When we get you into a cell after a side trip to the hospital, we're going to have a serious conversation.' He nodded to the deputy who'd trotted over from the patrol car, a young man I mentally classified as a boy.

While the deputy handcuffed Norvel and inserted him into the patrol car, Claude Friedrich stood by my side and stared down at me. I was still squatting, just because I knew getting up was going to hurt pretty bad. Tucking his gun in his waistband, Friedrich extended a hand. After a moment's hesitation, I reached up to grasp it, and he pulled hard. I rose with a gasp.

'No point asking you where you've been – well, maybe I don't need to,' he said, eyeing Marshall's car as it pulled in behind the patrol car. He let go of my hand, which he'd retained.

Marshall launched himself out of his car with gratifying speed. He did not grab me or hug me; he looked me over carefully, as if he was scrutinizing a piece of sale furniture for scratches and dents.

'We need to go inside,' he muttered. 'I can't see well enough out here.'

Claude Friedrich stirred. 'Mr Sedaka, good evenin',' he said.

Marshall looked at him for the first time. 'Chief,' he acknowledged, with a brief nod, before going back to his scrutiny of my facial scratches. 'Her face is bleeding,' he informed Friedrich, 'and I need to take her in and clean the cuts up so I can see their depth.'

I felt a sudden urge to giggle. I hadn't been examined this carefully since my mother had gotten a letter from the school about head lice.

'Norvel Whitbread attacked Lily,' observed the older man, who was beginning to feel the cool air against his bare chest, judging from the goose pimples I could see popping up. Friedrich seemed determined to push Marshall into acting like a proper boyfriend, perhaps consoling me on my ordeal and threatening death to Norvel.

'I'm assuming you whipped his butt,' Marshall told me.

'Yes, sensei,' I said, and suddenly the giggle burst out.

Both men stared at me in such complete amazement that I giggled all the harder, and then shook with laughter.

'Maybe she should go to the hospital along with Norvel?'

'Oh, he has to go to the hospital?' Marshall was as proud as if his much-coached Little Leaguer had hit a home run.

'Broke his nose,' I confirmed between the sporadic giggles that marked the wind-down of my fit.

'He armed?'

'Broomstick, I think,' I said. 'It's over there.' The staff had landed in the low shrubs around my front porch.

Friedrich went over to retrieve it. Evidence, I assumed.

'Lily,' he rumbled, carrying the wood gingerly by one end, 'you're gonna have to come in tomorrow and make a statement. I won't make you come in tonight. It's late and you need some attention. I'm prepared to take you to the hospital if you want.'

'No thank you,' I said soberly, completely over my mirth. 'I really want to go into my house.' More than anything, I was realizing, I wanted a shower. I'd had my usual workday, then karate class, two longish walks, sex, and a fight. I felt, and surely was, pretty gamy.

'Then I'll leave you to it,' Friedrich said quietly. 'I'm glad you came out on the good side. And I'm assuming when I go into the station I'll find out what this is about a doll left on your car?'

I could not forbear raising my eyebrows significantly in Marshall's direction. It was lucky my good sense had propelled me to the police station earlier in the evening. Marshall glared at me. I smiled back. 'Yes, sir,' I said, trying not to sound smug. 'I reported it earlier, to Tom David Meiklejohn. He wanted me to come in tomorrow and make a statement, too.'

'You got jobs on Saturday morning?'

'Yes, I do, but I'll be in at noon, anyway.'

'I'll see you then. Good night to you both.' And the policeman strode off, carrying the broom handle.

With his departure, my exhaustion hit me in the face.

'Let's go in,' I said. I scanned the grass, dimly lit by the streetlights at the corners of the arboretum. My key ring had broken. Luckily, the broken key ring was my personal one, with only my house, car, and lockbox key on it. I spotted a gleam of metal in the grass – my car key. Without thinking, I bent to retrieve it and felt a ripple of pain in the side that had taken the brunt of the first blow. I gave a little hiss of shock, and Marshall, who'd been staring after the departing lawman, helped me straighten.

I spotted my lockbox key on the way to the porch, and Marshall retrieved it for me. He helped me up the steps and into the house. Until I saw him look around, I had forgotten he'd never been in it.

He said, 'We need the bathroom,' and waved me into preceding him. Marshall undressed me quite . . . clinically. First, he cleaned the scratches on my face, put antibiotic ointment on them, and then he turned his attention to my ribs. He ran his fingers over each rib, gently but firmly, asking me questions as his fingers evaluated my injury.

'Take two aspirin and call me in the morning,' he said finally. 'I don't think anything's broken. But you'll have a bad bruise and you'll be sore. I'll tape you. It's lucky he's a sedentary alcoholic, or you'd be in the hospital now. How much warning did you have?'

'Not as much as I should have,' I admitted. 'He was waiting for me in the carport, with the mask and dark clothes on. But still . . .' and my voice trailed off, as I found I could not put one coherent thought together. He got my first-aid kit from the little linen closet and worked on me for a while.

'I have to shower,' I said. 'Out.'

'Keep the tape dry. Turn that side away from the water.'

'Yes, sensei.'

'I'm sleeping on your couch tonight.'

'It's a love seat. You'll get cramped.'

'Sleeping bag?'

'Nope. Don't like camping.'

'Floor.'

'You can sleep with me. It's queen-sized.'

I could tell he wanted to ask me why I'd left his bed earlier in the night. I was glad he was too decent to badger me when I was so exhausted. He helped me off with the rest of my clothes and then just left, without saying a word. I felt immense gratitude and relief. I turned on the shower and as soon as the water ran warm enough, I stepped in, pulled the curtain closed, and just let the water run over me. After a few seconds, I got the soap and shampoo and made as thorough a job of it as I could with Marshall's strictures. I even shaved under my arms, though bending over for my legs was too difficult.

When I stepped out into the steamy room and brushed my teeth, I felt much more like myself. My nightgown was hanging on the hook on the back of the door, and I pulled it over my head after my automatic deodorant, skin cream, and cuticle remover routine. I'd almost forgotten Marshall was there until I went in my bedroom. It was a shock to see the black hair on the pillow next to mine. He'd civilly taken the inside of the bed and left me the outside by the night table, and he'd left the bedside lamp switched on. He was sound asleep, on his left side, turned away from me.

Moving as silently as I could, I checked the front and back doors and all the windows – my nightly routine – and turned off the lamp. I slid into bed cautiously, turned on my right side, my unbandaged side, so my back was to his, and despite the strangeness of having someone in my house and bed, I was sucked down into sleep like water circling around the drain in my sink.

My eyes flew open at eight o'clock. The digital clock on the bedside table was right in front of me. I tried to think what was so different . . . Then I remembered the night before. My back felt very warm; it was pressed against Marshall's. Then I felt him move behind me, and his arm wrapped around my chest. My nightgown was thin and I could feel him pressing against me.

'How are you?' he asked quietly.

'Haven't moved yet,' I murmured back.

'Want to move some?'

'You have something specific in mind?' I asked as I felt his body respond to contact with me.

'Only if it won't hurt you . . .'

I arched harder against him and felt him press against me fiercely in response.

'We'll just have to try it out, see if it hurts,' I whispered.

'You sure?'

I turned over to face him. 'Sure,' I said.

His strength enabled him to hold his weight off me, and his eyes showed nothing but pleasure. In view of my scratched face and the black bruises on my side, I found this touching and amazing. I realized I'd already gotten used to his acceptance of the scars. So it was doubly dismaying to me, after we had finished lovemaking and were lying side by side holding hands, when he said, 'Lily, I've got to talk to you about something.' His voice was serious, too serious.

I felt my heart shrivel.

'What?' I asked, trying to sound casual. I pulled the sheet up.

'It's your quads, Lily.'

'My . . . *quadriceps?*' I said incredulously.

'You really need to work on them,' Marshall told me.

I turned to stare at him. 'I have scars all over my abdomen, I have scratches across my face, I have a huge bruise on my ribs, and your only remark about my body is that I need to work on my quads?'

'You're perfect except for your quads.'

'You . . . jerk!' Torn between amusement and disbelief, I pulled the pillow from under my head and hit him with it, which immediately activated the pain. I couldn't hold back my exclamation of dismay, and clapped my hand to my side.

'Lean back,' Marshall urged me, sitting up to help. 'Lean back, slowly . . . there. Raise your head a little.' He slid my pillow back under my head.

'Lily,' he said when he could tell the worst had passed. 'Lily, I was teasing.'

'Oh.' I felt abruptly and totally like a fool.

'Well, I guess I'm hardly social anymore,' I said after a moment.

'Lily. Why'd you leave last night?'

'I just felt restless. I'm not used to sharing time, or space, with anyone. I'm not used to visiting people's homes as a guest. You're still married. You're used to having someone else around. Probably you and Thea were invited places, right? But I'm not. I don't date. I'm just . . .' I hesitated, not sure how to characterize my life of the past few years.

'Coasting?'

I considered. 'Existing,' I said. 'Going from day to day safely. Doing my work, paying my way, not attracting any attention. Left alone.'

'Not lonely?'

'Not often,' I admitted. 'There are not that many people I like or have respect for, so I hardly want their company.'

Marshall was propped up on one elbow, his muscular chest a treat for my eyes. And I thought of it that way, as a treat: a seldom-achieved, rare thing that might not happen again. 'Who do you like?' he asked me.

I thought about it. 'I like Mrs Hofstettler. I like Claude Friedrich, I think, in spite of everything. I like you. I like most of the people in the karate class, though I'm not partial to Janet Shook. I like the new doctor, the woman. But I don't know any of those people that well.'

'Do you have any friends you don't know through work or karate class, anyone your own age that you . . . go shopping with, go to eat in Little Rock with?'

'No,' I said, my voice flat and verging on anger.

'Okay, okay.' He raised a placating hand. 'I'm just asking. I want to know how uphill this is going to be.'

'Pretty uphill, I'm afraid.' I relaxed with an effort. I glanced at the clock again. 'Marshall, I don't want to leave, but I have to work.'

'Are you just having a flash of antisocializing, or do you really have to work this morning?'

'I really have to work. I have to clean the doctor's office this morning, visit Mrs Hofstettler, go to the police station, and do my own shopping this afternoon.' I keep grocery expenses down by making a careful list and following it to the letter on my one visit to the grocery store a week.

'How are you going to manage with your ribs?'

'I'll just do what I have to do,' I said with some surprise. 'It's my job. If I don't work, I don't get paid. If I don't get paid, I go down the drain.'

'I have to open up the gym, too,' he said reluctantly. 'At least it opens late on Saturday, but I don't have anyone to work until one today, so I do have to get there.'

'We have to start moving,' I suggested, but I was suddenly reluctant to crawl out of the warm bed with its odor of him and sex.

'Can I take you out to supper tonight?'

I had that pressed feeling again. I almost balked, said no. But I told myself sternly that I'd be cutting my own throat. Marshall was throwing out a lifeline and I was refusing to grasp it.

'Sure,' I said, aware that I sounded stiff and anxious.

Marshall studied me.

'You pick the place,' he suggested. 'What do you like?'

I had not eaten in a restaurant in longer than I cared to add up. On nights I decide I don't want to cook, which isn't that often, since I enjoy cooking and it is cheaper than eating out, I pick up food and bring it home.

'Um,' I said, drawing on an old memory, 'I like Mexican food.'

'Great, so do I. We'll go to El Paso Grande in Montrose.'

Montrose was the nearest large town to Shakespeare, and the one where Shakespeare residents did most of their shopping when they didn't want to drive the hour and a half to Little Rock.

'All right.' I carefully sat up and swung my legs over the side of the bed. I bit my lip and I stayed there, trying to feel like getting up and brushing my teeth. I wanted Marshall to ignore my struggle, and miraculously he did, letting me take my time and rise on my own, then walk stiffly to the bathroom for a quick sponge bath and a meticulous brushing of my teeth and hair. I applied makeup quickly and thoroughly, hoping the scratches would be less conspicuous. I turned my face from side to side, checking it in the mirror, and decided I looked much better.

But I still looked just like a woman who'd been in a fight.

I walked out, still holding myself stiffly upright, to let Marshall have his turn.

By the time he emerged, having showered and used a tooth-brush in a plastic wrapper I'd put out for him on my sink (the dentist gives me a new one every time he cleans my teeth, but it is a brand I don't like), I'd managed to dress myself in the cheap clothes I wore to work: loose-leg blue jeans and an old dark red college sweatshirt with lopped-off arms. I hadn't been able to cope with pulling on socks, so I'd slid my feet into loafers instead of my usual cross-trainers.

Marshall started to speak, stopped, thought the better of it, and finally settled with saying, 'Pick you up at six?'

I approved of his skipping all the 'Are you sure you can do it? Why don't you call in sick today? Let me help you' stuff I'd been afraid he was going to put us through.

'Sure,' I said, showing him gratitude with my smile.

'See you then,' he said briefly, and went out to his car, which was still parked rather crookedly in front of the house.

Moving slowly but keeping going, I gathered together what I needed for the day and drove over to the doctor's office. As usual, I parked in the paved area behind the building, intended for the doctor and staff. I noticed without much interest that Dr Thrush's car was there, too. Dr Thrush is new in town and I had just started cleaning for her three weeks ago.

I used my key and stepped uncomfortably over the high thresh-old. Carrie Thrush was sticking her head out of her office, her brows drawn together with anxiety.

'Oh, thank goodness it's you, Lily!' the doctor exclaimed. 'I forgot it was time for you to come.' Then, as I moved down the hall, the relieved smile gave way to concern. 'Good God, woman, what happened to you?'

'I had a fight last night,' I said.

'In a bar?' The young doctor looked amazed, her dark brown eyebrows raised above eyes just as dark and brown.

'No, a guy jumped me in my yard,' I said briefly, explaining only because she'd asked with so much concern.

I didn't have much energy to spare today, so I had to focus on the job at hand. I opened the door of the patients' bathroom in the hall. That was the worst place, so that was where I always started. I had a strong feeling that between my own scheduled cleaning times, Dr Thrush came in every morning and gave it a light going-over herself. That bathroom would be even dirtier otherwise. I pulled on my gloves and started in.

I cleaned the little double-doored space where patients put their urine samples, then wiped off the knob of the little door into the lab. I laid a fresh paper towel down for the next patient's sample. I remembered I hadn't tested this pair of rubber gloves for leaks, and reminded myself to do that when I got home. The last thing I needed was to catch a bug here.

I became aware that Dr Thrush was standing in the bathroom doorway staring at me.

'You surely can't work in that condition!' Carrie Thrush said.

She has a firm voice that I believe she assumes to keep people mindful she is indeed a doctor. Carrie Thrush is shorter than I am and pigeon-plump. She has a round face with a determined jaw, unplucked eyebrows, and acne scars. She wears her chin-length black hair parted and brushed back behind her ears. Her dark brown eyes are round and clear, all that saves the doctor from plainness. I set her age at about my own, early thirties.

'Well, yes I can,' I said, since she was waiting for a response. I was not in the mood for arguing. I sprinkled powdered cleanser in the sink and wet the sponge to scour it. I compressed my lips in what I hoped was a determined line.

'Could I just look at your ribs? That's your problem, right? Listen, you're in a doctor's office.'

I kept on scrubbing, but my good sense conquered my pride. I laid down the sponge, pulled off my gloves, and pulled up my shirt.'

'Oh, someone taped you, I see. Well, let me just take this off . . .' I had to endure all the probing again, to hear a bona fide doctor tell me just as Marshall had that none of my ribs were broken but that the bruise and pain would last for a while. Of course Carrie Thrush saw the scars, and her lips pursed, but she didn't ask any questions.

'You shouldn't be working,' the doctor said. 'But I can tell that nothing I could say would stop you, so work away.'

I blinked. That was refreshing. I began to like Carrie Thrush more and more.

Cleaning the Shakespeare Clinic was an exasperating task because of paper. Paper was the curse of the doctor's office. Forms in triplicate, billing forms, patient health histories, reports from labs, insurance forms, Medicare, Medicaid – they were stacked everywhere. I had to respect each stack as an entity, lift it to dust and put it down in the same spot; so the office shared by the receptionist and the clerk was in and of itself a land mine. Compared with the office, the waiting room and examining rooms were cakewalks.

For the first time, it struck me that someone must also be cleaning those more often than once a week. As I vacuumed, I mulled this thought over. Nita Tyree, the receptionist? I couldn't picture Nita agreeing to that as part of her job. I barely know Nita, but I do know she has four children, two of whom are young enough to be in day care at SCC. So Nita leaves when the last patient walks out the front door, no matter what is sitting on her desk.

Gennette Jinks, the nurse, was out of the picture. I'd been behind the fiftyish Gennette in line at the Superette Food Mart only the week before and had heard (as had everyone else in a five-foot radius) about how hard it was to work for a woman, how young Dr Thrush wasn't accepting the wisdom she (Gennette) had attained with years of experience, at which point I had tuned out and read the headlines on the tabloids instead, since they had more entertainment value.

So the surreptitious weekday cleaner had to be the good doctor herself. I had stacked up the bills. Without wanting to, I knew how much Carrie Thrush still owed for her education, and I had a feeling that some weeks it was hard for Carrie to pay even me, much less Gennette and Nita.

I chewed this over as I mopped, having dusted and vacuumed around the doctor as she sat at her desk, a stack of the omnipresent paper on every available inch of surface.

When I had everything gleaming and smelling at least clean, if not sweet, I stuck my head in the office door and said, 'Good-bye.'

'Oh, let me write you a check,' said Dr Thrush.

'No.'

'What?' Carrie Thrush paused, her pen touching her checkbook.

'No. You examined me. Call it bartering.'

I was sure that was against some doctors' rules, but I was also sure the offer would appeal to my employer. And I was right. Carrie Thrush smiled broadly, then said, 'Thank God! No paper to fill out.'

'Thank God, no insurance to file,' I answered, and left, feeling that Carrie Thrush and I, cleaning woman and doctor, had, if not a relationship, at least the beginning of good feelings between us.

Chapter Nine

My bruised side ached more and more as Saturday dragged by. I moved through Mrs Hofstettler's apartment like a snail, but she was having one of her bad days and didn't seem to notice. I wondered what it would be like to feel this way many days and to know for a certainty it would last the rest of my life.

I made my statement at the police station, sitting bold upright and taking shallow breaths. The man who took it down was a detective, I had to assume, since he wasn't wearing a uniform. He told me he was Dolph Stafford and that he was mighty glad to meet me. He glanced at me out the corners of his eyes, and I saw pity in his elaborate courtesy. I knew he, too, had heard my old story, which I dragged around with me wherever I went, like the albatross around the Ancient Mariner's neck.

As I drearily went through the details of the Ken doll and Norvel's attack, I pondered an old problem. Now that my past was out, should I move? Before, the answer had always been yes. But I'd been in Shakespeare for four years now, longer than I'd been anywhere since I was raped. For the first time, I wondered if I might not just weather it out. The thought crossed my mind, and in crossing, it stuck there: When Dolph Stafford dismissed me, I went home to lie down, finally giving in to the pain. I'd just have to go grocery shopping Sunday or Monday.

My reluctance to go to the store wasn't wholly due to the pain. I knew by now the story about Norvel's attack would be all over town, and I just didn't want to encounter sympathetic looks or horrified questions.

Carrie Thrush had slipped me a few sample pain pills when I'd left her office. Normally, I'd think twice before taking Tylenol, but I was positively longing for whatever relief the pills might bring.

Swallowing two of the capsules with some water, I was just about to leave the kitchen to ease myself onto the bed when I heard someone knocking at the door.

I nearly decided to ignore it. But it was the brisk kind of rap-rap-rap that tells you that the caller is both impatient and persistent. I was already peeved when I got to the door and looked through the peephole, so discovering the caller was my sometime employer the Reverend Joel McCorkindale did not make me any happier. I shot back the bolt reluctantly.

The minister's 'happy to see you, sister' smile faltered as he took in the scratches on my face and the awkward way I was standing.

'May I come in?' He was wisely settling for dignified sympathy.

'Briefly.'

Taking that in his stride, McCorkindale stepped across the threshold and surveyed my tiny domain.

'Very nice,' he said with great sincerity. I reminded myself I must be careful. Sincerity was the Reverend McCorkindale's middle name.

I didn't offer him a chair.

This, too, he absorbed without comment.

'Miss Bard,' he began when he'd taken measure of my attitude, 'I know that you and Norvel Whitbread have had a personality conflict' – here I snorted – 'ever since you've had to work together at the church. I want you to know I'm extremely disturbed that he was so stupid last night, and I want you to know Norvel himself is very, very sorry he frightened you so badly.'

I had been looking down, wondering when he'd get through blathering, because my bed seemed to have acquired a voice and it was calling me louder and louder. But now I looked up at Joel McCorkindale.

'I was never frightened,' I said. 'Mad, yes. But not frightened.'

'Well, that's . . . good. Then, he's apologetic for having hurt you.'

'I beat the shit out of him.'

The minister flushed. 'He is definitely a sad sight today.'

I smiled.

'So, cut to the chase,' I prompted.

'I have come to ask you, most humbly, if you would consider dropping the charges against Norvel. He is repentant. He knows he should not have been drinking. He knows it is wrong, very wrong, to hold grudges. He knows it is against God's commandments to harm another person, much less a woman.'

I closed my eyes, wondering if he'd ever listened to himself.

The bad thing was, I reflected as McCorkindale expanded on Norvel's mental anguish, that if I hadn't had my little life-altering experience, I might be tempted to listen to this crap.

I held up a hand, indicating for him to stop.

'I am going to prosecute him to the full extent of the law,' I said flatly. 'I don't care if you ever hire me again. You've known he was drinking again for weeks; you had to have known. You know whatever convictions he expresses are going to vanish when he sees another bottle. That's his religion. I have never been able to understand why you kept him on when that became apparent to anyone who cared to look. Maybe he has something on you. I don't know and I don't care. But I will not drop charges.'

He took this well, like the shrewd man he is. He looked off to one side thoughtfully, turning something over in his mind.

'Lily, I have to tell you some members of our little church have felt the same way about you. They've wondered why I haven't let you go. You know, Lily, you're not everybody's cup of tea.'

I felt an intense desire to laugh. The medication was undoubtedly kicking in.

'You're a mysterious and violent woman,' McCorkindale prodded further. 'Some people have wondered out loud to me if you should still be working in Shakespeare, or at least at our little church.'

'I don't care if I work at your little church or not,' I said. 'But I'll tell you, if I catch you pressuring my employers to fire me because I'm "mysterious and violent", I'll sue you. Anyone who cares to can look up my past. And as for violent, present me with a list of fights I've started, or times I've been in jail, and I'll be real interested to read it.'

Ashamed of myself for offering even that much defense of charges that were indefensible, I waved the minister out of the door and locked it firmly behind him.

My bed was screaming now, and I never could ignore a scream. I floated down the hall and didn't even register the painful process of lying down.

When I woke up, there was a note on my bedside table.

I'd have to admit, were the Reverend McCorkindale to chance by, that this *did* scare me.

It was from Marshall.

'I came by at six to take you to supper in Montrose,' the note began, in Marshall's tiny, angular handwriting. 'I knocked for five minutes, and then you came to the door. You let me in, walked back to your bed, got in, and went back to sleep. I was worried till I found the little envelope with "For Pain" written on it. Call me when you wake up. Marshall.'

I read it over twice while I recovered from my flash of fear.

I looked at the clock. It read 5:00. Hmm. I rolled over somewhat gingerly to exit the other side of the bed. I peered between the blind slats. Black outside. It was five in the morning.

'God Almighty,' I said, impressed with Dr Thrush's medicine. I took a few steps around the room, and I was pleased to discover that I felt much better after my long rest. The worst of the soreness seemed to be gone. It worried me that I'd let Marshall in. Had I known it was Marshall? Would I have let just anybody in? If so, it was lucky that no one else had knocked. Or had they?

Suddenly anxious, I went through the whole house. Everything was exactly as it had been the day before; the only addition was Marshall's note and the pill envelope, still containing two capsules.

After I stowed the remaining pills away with great respect, I made some coffee and wondered what to do with the day. Sunday is my day off, not because it is a church day, but because it is the least desirable day of the week to clean, from my clients' standpoint. And I feel I deserve one whole day off every week. Usually I clean my own house or mow my lawn in the morning. When Body Time opens at one, I walk in the doors. I often stay for two hours, then come home to cook for the week. I rent movies from Rainbow Video ('Cinema across the Spectrum'), and every once in a while I call my parents.

Since I'd risen so early, and since all week had been unusual, somehow none of this sounded appealing at all.

After I had skimmed through my big Sunday Little Rock paper, treading my difficult reading path around stories of battered wives, neglected children, and starving, abandoned elders to arrive at those I could actually read (which pretty much boiled down to escaped dangerous pets – this week a boa constrictor – politics, and sports), I dressed in a gingerly way, hoping the bending wouldn't wake up my side. To my pleasure, the terrible ache did not return; there was a certain amount of tenderness, and leaning in some directions was painful, but nothing nearly as bad as it had been the day before.

All right, then. I'd just quell those rebellious feelings I had, this discontent.

My house needed cleaning.

I put on my rubber gloves with what was very nearly pleasure. It crossed my mind to call Marshall, or to drift through the dawn to his house and share his bed again. But I put those thoughts aside; I was in danger of counting on him, of thinking of my life as substantially changed. I found myself wistfully staring at my gloves and thinking of the pleasures of sex with Marshall, of the wonders of his body, of the excitement of being desirable.

But I began serious cleaning.

It is a small house, which never gets very dirty anyway, and I know it very well. In an hour and a half, by the time the rest of the world was waking up, my house shone and I was looking forward to a shower.

The quiet tap on the back door came as I was about to step in. With a curse, I wrapped my white terry robe back around myself and padded quietly to the door. I looked through the peephole.

Marshall looked back. I sighed, not knowing if I was glad to see him or sorry that he kept raising my expectations. I unlocked the door.

'If you don't stop this,' I said flatly, 'I'll think you really like me.'

'Hi to you, too,' he said, his eyebrows arching in surprise. 'Are you conscious this time?'

'Why don't you get in the shower with me,' I said over my shoulder as I went back to my hot running water, 'and find out?'

As it turned out, I was fully conscious.

As he kissed me while the water ran over us, I had a terrifying feeling that I wanted to save this moment, that it was precious. I knew the fallacy inherent in planning on anything lasting, I knew the degradation I'd undergone had altered me permanently, and I was afraid.

Afterward, I loaned him my terry robe and I put on my bright, thin one, and we watched an old movie on cable together. I put a bowl of grapes between us on the love seat, we put up the footrest, and we had a pleasant time appreciating the actors and laughing at the plot. When the movie ended close to noon, I got up to return the grapes to the refrigerator. Through the open blinds of the living room window, I observed a vaguely familiar red car driving by very slowly.

'Who's that, Marshall?' I asked sharply, the outside world coming back with a rush.

He was on his feet quickly and stared out the window.

'That's Thea,' he said. His voice was tight with controlled fury.

'She's driven by other times.' It was the car that had passed the day Marshall was kissing me in the carport. I'd seen it several times over the past few days.

'Shit, Lily,' he said, 'I'm sorry. I wish the divorce had already gone through. No judge would believe, with her sitting there looking so Southern belle, what she's capable of.'

I was still staring out of the window, lost in thought, when the Yorks walked by. Alvah and T. L. were holding hands, moving rather slowly, and wearing everyday clothes. They were missing church, an unheard-of occurrence.

But I was not as amazed as I might have been days ago. This past week had been full of atypical behavior on the part of almost everyone I knew, including myself.

Pardon had somehow talked himself into getting killed.

The upright, churchgoing Yorks had been derailed by the rape of their granddaughter.

Norvel Whitbread had shown his true colors after two years of being smarmy.

Tom O'Hagen had cheated on Jenny O'Hagen.

Deedra Dean had seen a dead body.

Claude Friedrich had been careless with a report.

Carlton Cockroft had exercised and revealed a wholly unexpected interest in his neighbor.

Marcus Jefferson had gotten to entertain his son in his own apartment.

Marie Hofstettler had had an interview with the police.

The Reverend Joel McCorkindale had visited me in my home.

Marshall Sedaka had taken a personal interest in one of his students.

One of his students had taken a personal interest right back.

Someone had rolled a body into the arboretum.

Someone else had deposited handcuffs where I would find them; killed a rat; left a painted Ken doll on my car hood.

'Overall,' I said, turning to Marshall, 'it would be hard to top last week.'

'We can give it a shot,' he suggested, and was surprised when I laughed.

'Let me tell you what happened last Monday night,' I said, and for the first time I told Marshall what I'd seen when I was out walking.

'You saw the murderer?'

'I saw the person dumping the body.'

Marshall thought my story over. 'I can understand why you didn't want to tell the police,' he said finally. 'With your cart being used. And since they didn't arrest anyone yet, you might be putting yourself in danger.'

'How so?'

'The killer might think you had seen more than you actually saw,' Marshall said. 'At least, killers always do in the movies. They're always coming after the person they think knows something, whether or not it's true.'

'Yeah, but that's the movies. This is Shakespeare.'

I suddenly realized what I'd said and I laughed. Marshall looked at me warily; I had to explain.

'Lily, I think the sooner the police arrest someone for this, the better it'll be for you.'

'No argument there.'

'Then we can concentrate on finding out who's playing these tricks on you and Thea.'

There was something in his voice that alerted me. 'Has something else happened to her?' I asked.

'She called me about six this morning. Someone came to the back door and spray-painted "Bitch" across it.'

'Is that so.' Marshall looked a little surprised at my lack of horror.

'So, Marshall, did you come over here to enjoy my company or see if I was gonna walk back up in my yard with a spray can in my hand?'

Marshall closed his eyes and took a deep breath. 'Lily, I think if you were mad at Thea, you would challenge her to fight, or ignore her for the rest of your life. I can't imagine you sneaking around in the dark spray-painting a woman's back door.'

But I wasn't so sure he believed that down to his bones. Hadn't there been a moment, a flicker, of something else – of relief – when I challenged him?

I sank down in the armchair and looked at him intently. 'I don't know if I'm at fault, if I'm being overly prickly, or if Thea has undermined your confidence in your own judgment so much that you can't trust your own instincts.'

Marshall was not quick to respond, and I was glad. I wanted him to think about this.

'Maybe both,' he said finally. 'Come on, it's almost time to work out.'

As I pulled on my ancient gray sweatpants and a dark blue T-shirt, I pondered the fact that he was quite willing to have sex with me even though he hadn't exactly given me a rousing vote of confidence. Did that mean he was so delighted with his returned virility that he just didn't care whether I was tormenting his wife?

Dealings between men and women are all too often like picking through a minefield, I thought with some disgust. Marshall was out in the living room waiting for me. He'd walked over in workout clothes, blue sweatpants and a maroon Body Time T-shirt.

It was strange that I could stand in the hall and watch Marshall stretch that wonderful body and feel a wave of lust, that I could love the way he didn't flinch at the horrible story I'd told him. But still, I drew back from him from time to time.

This was one of the times.

We didn't talk much on the way to Body Time in my car, but the prospect of doing something I enjoyed with Marshall, who also enjoyed it, made me feel more relaxed.

Janet Shook was on the treadmill when we entered. Her eyes widened. She clearly was adding two and two in her head. I waved casually. Marshall exchanged a few words with Derrick, who'd opened for him, and then we mapped out our workout. It was legs days – not my favorite – but doing legs was not so bad with company.

It was very convenient and pleasant having Marshall there to take the weights on and off and spot for me; it was equally pleasant being able to return the favor.

People who before had only nodded to me came up to speak, since I was with Marshall. Of course, everyone knew him. And I found that they knew who I was, too: They all called me Lily. Though my scratched face got some sideways glances, no one mentioned Norvel Whitbread.

This, too, was pleasant, but I found that after greetings had been exchanged, I had nothing to say. I just listened as they chatted with Marshall. Marshall is a kind of community clearing-house. Everyone who approached him had some piece of gossip or news to relate and seemed to feel free to speak in front of me. I wondered why.

I found, as the second gossiper in a row referred to it, that I had a reputation for being closemouthed. It surprised me to think that people thought of me at all, but I should have remembered: In small towns, there is no such thing as an invisible life.

Despite twinges in my side, I had finished leg-pressing three hundred pounds when Brian Gruber, an executive at the mattress-manufacturing plant that was one of Shakespeare's larger employ-ers, drifted by in the course of his workout to murmur quietly in Marshall's ear. Marshall listened grimly, doing a lot of curt nod-ding. This was so definitely a man-to-man talk that I did an extra set so they could finish. After all, Marshall had said my quads needed work.

When I was through, I just lay there and panted. Brian wandered away to do bicep curls while Marshall added a twenty-five to each side of the leg press for his set, looking thoughtful and grim. He didn't meet my eyes as I made way for him. I reached for my sweat towel and began dabbing at my forehead.

Damned if I was going to ask.

Marshall slid into position. He put his feet up on the push board, aligned them carefully. He pushed a little, taking the pressure off the relief bars, which he flipped to the side simultane-ously. Then he bared his teeth in a snarl of effort and began his set. Maybe he was trying to make me feel equal; three hundred was my top weight, and I knew Marshall could do double that. I waited stonily till his set was over and he'd flipped the bars back into place. He beckoned to me to crouch down where he lay.

So, here came the bad news.

'Brian just heard that Thea's been telling everyone at her church that she's going to put me through the wringer as far as property goes. But he also told me the same thing you did – that she'd been having overnight company, which'll count against her in court.'

'You've been having company, too.' I watched his face go blank.

I stood up and covered my face with the towel as though I was bathed in sweat, when in fact I'd cooled down. I had to get my indifferent face back on. I felt a strong inclination to pick up my workout bag and leave without a word, but that would be cowardly.

I shifted so my back was to the leg press, and I stared at a pretty teenager who was having the time of her life showing Bobo Winthrop how hard it was for her to bench-press two ten-pound dumbbells. Bobo looked over at me, his eyes widening as he took in my marred face. His mouth formed the words *You okay?* I nodded. Then the girl on the bench said something to claim his attention. I looked in another direction so Bobo wouldn't meet my eyes again and feel obliged to come over to talk to me.

I felt hands on my shoulders, and I twitched like a horse trying to dislodge a fly.

'So, I'll just have to find some other toehold,' Marshall said calmly. He began to take off the twenty-fives he'd added.

'Leave them on,' I said. I slid into position, braced my feet, flipped the braces to the side, and began to push.

I managed five reps before I could tell that serious pain was just around the corner.

To finish up, we did three sets, thirty each, of lunges and leg lifts in the aerobics room. When we sat up after a short rest, I said what I thought he was waiting for me to say. 'I don't think we should see each other until you're really divorced. Thea is unstable; she's in trouble at work and at home. There's no point making things worse for her, which will only make it worse for you in the long run – your property settlement and all.'

'I don't want a sick woman like that dictating what my life will be like,' Marshall said. He meant it, but he was also relieved. I could hardly blame him; I'd worked hard for what I had, too.

'Then there's the trick-playing thing,' I went on after a calculated pause. 'I can't go on being scared every time I step out of my house that someone's going to put something on my doorstep or leave something on my car. Maybe if we don't see each other for a while, that'll let up. If it's the same person who's playing tricks on Thea, it's someone who has serious feelings about you; maybe he, or she, will let you know about those feelings if I'm not around. You can deal with it, and I'll be clear of it.'

'I don't know what to say, Lily,' Marshall said. 'I don't want to lose you now that we finally . . .'

'I'm not going anywhere,' I said, and got to my feet, ignoring the reawakened pain in my side. 'We'll see each other in karate class, and here sometimes.' I left before Marshall had to think of something else to say.

As I drove home, I became aware that I was feeling something I hadn't felt in years: disappointment.

No sooner had I turned the corner to Track Street than I saw the police car at the curb outside my house. Leaning against it was Claude Friedrich, as solid and immovable as if he had all the time in the world.

I made a sudden decision to go grocery shopping, and after checking the traffic behind me, I backed up before Friedrich could see me and reversed my direction in a convenient driveway. I didn't want to talk to anyone right now, least of all the all-too-perceptive Friedrich.

I hadn't been to the store without a list in years. Sunday is the day I usually cook ahead, and my little freezer was almost empty.

The last time I'd been in Kroger's, I'd been shopping for myself and for the return of the Yorks . . . Hey, they'd never reimbursed me for the groceries, or for the work I'd done last Wednesday. I hated the thought of bothering them, knowing how devastated they were by the trial of their granddaughter's assailant, but if they felt better to the extent of being able to take a walk, they could pay me.

I was trying to remember all the ingredients of my favorite tortilla casserole when a cart slammed into mine. I looked up sharply and realized the anger rolling around inside me had found an excellent focus, here to my left, wearing a modest shirtwaist dress and loafers.

The woman pushing the other cart was Thea Sedaka. Thea had bumped my cart on purpose; the stare she fixed on me aimed at contrite but never made it past loathing.

It had been a long time since I'd seen Thea this close. She was as pretty as ever. Tiny and small-boned, the future ex-Mrs Sedaka has a sweet oval face outlined with shoulder-length dark hair cut to frame it perfectly. Thea had always made me feel like a hulking milkmaid to her dainty princess. I'd never known if the effect was intentional or a result of my own touchiness.

Now that I had the inside scoop on Thea's character, I could see how she achieved my displacement. She looked up, far more than she actually needed to, to make me feel even taller, and she pushed her cart with a little frown, as if it was almost too heavy to manage.

Thea's dark green dress was covered with teeny-weeny flowers in a sweet pink; nothing splashy or florid for Thea. She curled her lip at my workout clothes.

She guided her cart until she was at my side, right in the middle of the canned vegetables. I watched her lips curve in a venomous grin, and I knew she was about to say something she hoped would be painful.

So I beat her to the punch.

I leaned down to Thea and said with the widest smile I could stretch my lips into, 'Drive past my house one more time and I'll have Claude Friedrich arrest you.'

Thea's expression was priceless. But she snapped back together quickly.

'Marshall is mine,' she hissed, reminding me vividly of my seventh-grade school play. 'You're trying to break up a happy marriage, you home-wrecker.'

'Not good enough,' I said. 'You'd better warn Tom David to find another parking place.'

Once again, Thea was disconcerted. But being Thea, belle of Shakespeare, she rallied.

'If you're the one leaving those awful things at my house' – and here she actually managed tiny tears – 'please stop.' She said this just loudly enough for an older lady who was comparing soup cans to absorb her meaning and then eye me in horror.

'What things?' I asked blankly. 'You poor little gal, has someone been leaving things on your doorstep? What did the police say?'

Thea turned red. Of course she hadn't called the police; the police, in the person of Tom David Meiklejohn, had already been on hand.

'You know,' I said, with as much concern as I could muster, 'I'm sure Claude would station someone outside your house all night if you think there's a prowler.' The older woman gave me an approving nod and ventured down the aisle to compare the prices of tomato sauce.

I hadn't said anything insincere in so long that it actually felt refreshing and creative.

Thea had to content herself with a low-voiced 'I'll get you' and a flounce as she laboriously pushed her cart toward the meat counter. A very weak finale.

I left the grocery store with several bags, and I managed to feel almost like myself when I got home.

Damned if the chief of police wasn't still there. He'd just moved his car, probably to its parking space behind the apartments, but he'd returned his body to my carport. I pulled into my driveway and unlocked my trunk. I would not be kept out of my own home. Friedrich uncrossed his arms and sauntered over.

'What is it with you?' I asked. 'Why do you keep turning up here? I didn't do anything.'

'I might think I wasn't welcome if I didn't know better,' Friedrich rumbled. 'Your face is looking a lot better. How's the side?'

I unlocked my kitchen door and pitched in my purse and workout bag. I went back to the car for the first two bags of groceries. Friedrich wordlessly gathered the next two and followed me into the kitchen.

In silence, I put the cans away in the pantry, stowed the meat in the refrigerator, and slid the juice containers into the freezer of my side-by-side. When all that was done, when the bags were folded and put under the sink in their designated place, I sat down at my plain wooden table opposite Friedrich, who'd seated himself, and said, 'What?'

'Tell me what you saw the night Pardon was killed.'

I looked down at my hands. I thought it over carefully. My goal in keeping quiet had been to keep the police from asking questions about my past. Well, Friedrich had done that anyway, and been too trusting of his subordinates; my past was out, and the results hadn't been as dreadful as I'd always thought they would be. Or maybe I had changed.

If only Claude Friedrich was here to listen to me tell it, and I didn't have to go down to the police station again, why not tell him the little I knew?

And maybe Marshall had spooked me a little, with his 'woman who knows too much' scenario.

Friedrich was waiting patiently. I would feel much more comfortable in this big man's presence if I had nothing to conceal; he would then drench me with his warm approval. My mouth went up at one corner in a sardonic grin. This ambience was undoubtedly what made Claude Friedrich such a good policeman.

'I'll tell you what I saw, but it won't make any difference,' I told him, making my decision abruptly. I looked him in the eyes and spread my hands flat on the table. 'That's why I didn't see the need to tell you before.'

'It was you that called me that night, wasn't it?'

'Yes. It was me. Partly because I didn't want him to lie out there all night, but mostly because I was scared some kids might find him.'

'Why didn't you tell me all this to begin with?'

'Because I didn't want to come to your attention. What I saw wasn't important enough for me to risk you calling Memphis, getting the story about what happened to me. I didn't want people here to know. And yet it's happened, anyway.' And I looked him directly in the eyes.

'That's a mistake I can't make up to you,' he said. 'I regret letting that report sit around on my desk, more than I can tell you. I'm taking steps to minimize the damage.'

That was as much apology as I'd ever receive; and really, what more could he say?

I shrugged. My anger against him deflated gently. I had known all along that someday it was inevitable that my past would block my path again.

'What I saw was someone wearing a raincoat with a hood, wheeling Pardon over to the arboretum,' I said flatly. 'I don't know who it was, but I'm sure it was someone from the apartments. I figured you already knew that, since Pardon's body appeared and disappeared so many times. Gone when Tom O'Hagen paid his rent, back when Deedra paid hers. It had to have been hidden in a different apartment, though I can't imagine why anyone would move Pardon's corpse around.'

'How was the body moved over to the arboretum?'

'It was in some garbage bags, one pulled on from the feet and another pulled on from the head. Then it was loaded in my garbage-can cart and rolled over there.' I felt mad all over again when I thought of the use of my cart.

'Where are the garbage bags?'

'Gone to the incinerator.'

'Why'd you do that?'

'My fingerprints were on them. I checked to see if Pardon was dead.'

Friedrich gave me the strangest look.

'What?' I asked.

He shook his head. 'Start at the beginning,' he rumbled.

I began with my walk. Friedrich's eyebrows went up when he realized I walked by myself in the dead of night quite frequently, but he said nothing until I had given him the whole account.

'Do me a favor, Lily,' he said finally.

I raised my eyebrows and waited.

'Next time, just call me to start with.'

It took me a moment to realize he was joking. I smiled. He smiled back, no great big grin, but companionable. He was letting that warmth wash over me, and I was enjoying it just as much as any other suspect who'd just come clean. Why not? I thought, forgoing scolding myself for being a chump. I was prepared for Friedrich to take his leave, but there he stayed, seemingly content at my clean, bare kitchen table.

'So,' the policeman said. 'Happening in the same time frame, we have the murder of Pardon Albee and the strange persecution of Lily Bard and Thea Sedaka. Thea never called us in, officially. But Tom David said a few things to Dolph, who figured he better tell me. I like to know what's going on in my town. Don't you think it's strange, Lily, that so many unusual things are happening at the same time in Shakespeare?'

I nodded, though I had my own ideas about the 'strange persecution'. Moving quietly, I gathered my cutting board, a knife, and a package of chicken breasts. I began to skin and debone the chicken.

'The Yorks were gone on Monday. They returned that night late,' Claude said. I worked and listened. 'Mrs Hofstettler was there all the time, but she's partially deaf and sometimes almost immobile. Jenny O'Hagen was at work, and Tom O'Hagen was sleeping. When he got up, he played a round of golf at the country club. He came home and went upstairs to pay blackmail to Norvel Whitbread, who was home from work "sick". Then Tom went down to pay his rent. You were unlocking the Yorks' apartment. When Tom found Pardon's door open, the body wasn't there, but the furniture was not in its usual order. An hour and a half later, Deedra came home from work, went upstairs to get her mother's check, then went down to pay the rent. And Pardon's traveling body was back on the couch, but arranged naturally enough that Deedra thought he was asleep.'

'When did all the others pay their rent?' I asked over my shoulder as I scrubbed my hands at the sink. I thought this show-and-tell time was very strange, but I was enjoying it.

'I'd slipped my check under his door on my way to the station that morning,' Friedrich said. 'Norvel's rent was paid by the church. The secretary mailed Pardon a check, the Reverend

McCorkindale told me. Marcus Jefferson says he'd also slid his rent check under Pardon's door on his way out to work that morning, and Pardon must already have made a trip to the bank right when it opened, because Marcus's check, mine, and Mrs Hofstettler's were credited to Pardon's account when I called the bank.'

'What about the one the church mailed?'

'Didn't get to Pardon's mailbox until the day after he died.'

It would have been typical Pardon behavior to go by the church or up to Norvel's to ask about the rent, I thought, and raised my eyes to Friedrich's.

'But Norvel says Pardon didn't come to his apartment,' the big man said, and I bent back to my work before I realized how strange the little exchange was.

'He's lying, though,' I said.

'How do you figure?'

'Because Pardon did the vacuuming Monday himself. Remember the way the cord was wrapped? So he must have gone up to find out why Norvel hadn't done it. He's supposed to go in late to the church on Monday, after he's cleaned the apartment building's halls. The church gets a discount on his rent.'

For the first time since I'd known him, Claude Friedrich looked surprised.

'How do you know all this, Lily?'

'If it's about cleaning, I know it. I think Pardon told me all that when he explained why Norvel was going to be cleaning the building instead of me.' Pardon had just wanted to talk, as usual. It was fine with me not to have the poor-paying and tedious job of working under a constantly supervising Pardon.

Claude (as I now thought of him) looked at me a moment longer before resuming his running narrative of the day of the landlord's death. 'So that morning Pardon stopped by Mrs Hofstettler's to get her check, then went to the bank with three of the rent checks.'

I put together a marinade and popped the strips of chicken breast in the bowl. I had a hankering for stir-fry tonight. I began to brown stew meat in a skillet while I chopped potatoes, carrots, and onions to go in the stew pot. I stirred the sauce for the tortilla casserole. I had some leftover taco meat to dump into the sauce, and a tomato, and after that I shredded three flour tortillas. I handed Claude the grater and the cheese. Obediently, he began to grate.

'How much?' he asked.

'Cup,' I said, putting one on the table by him. 'You were saying?'

'And he talked on the telephone several times,' Claude continued. 'He called the plant where Marcus works; we don't know who he talked to, there. Of course, that might be completely unrelated to Marcus. At least two hundred other people work there. About eleven, he called someone in rural Creek County, a pal he went to school with at UA, but the guy is on a business trip to Oklahoma City and we haven't been able to track him down yet.'

I dumped all the stew ingredients into the slow cooker and got out my wok. While it was heating, I layered the tortilla casserole, including the grated cheese, and popped it in the freezer. Claude's voice provided a pleasant background sound, like listening to a familiar book on tape.

The stir-fry would provide two meals, I figured, the stew at least three; one night, I would have a baked potato and vegetables; the remaining meal could be the tortilla casserole and a salad.

After I put the rice in the microwave, I began stir-frying the chicken and vegetables. I was hardly aware that Claude had stopped talking. I stirred quickly, conscious only of the quiet content that came when I was doing something I could do well. The rice and the meat and vegetables were done at almost the same time, and I faced a little dilemma.

After a moment's hesitation, since sharing this meal represented yet another disruption, in my formerly pristine schedule, I got two plates out of the cabinet and heaped them with food, then put a fork, a napkin, and a glass of tea in front of the policeman. I set a plate in front of him, then put my own glass and fork on the table and retrieved my plate. I put the soy sauce within reach, added the salt and pepper, and sat down. I gave Claude a curt nod to indicate everything was ready, and he picked up his fork and began to eat.

I kept my eyes on my plate. When I looked up, Claude had finished his food and was patting his mouth with his napkin, carefully making sure his mustache was clean.

'Real good,' he said.

I shrugged, then realized that was not a gracious response to a compliment. I forced my eyes to meet his. 'Thank you,' I said stiffly. Never had I felt my long abstinence from society more keenly. 'Would you like some more?' I made myself add.

'No thank you, that was a gracious plenty,' he responded correctly. 'You finished?'

I nodded, puzzled. I found out why he'd asked in the next minute, when he reached across, took my plate and fork, and went to the sink. He turned on the faucets, located my dish-washing liquid, and began to wash all the dishes stacked on the counter.

I sat at the table with my mouth hanging open for a few seconds, then snapped out of my daze to get up and put away the leftovers in appropriate containers. Hesitantly, I set the now-empty wok by the sink for Friedrich to wash. I wiped the table and counters with a clean rag while he finished, and I swept the floor. Then, not knowing what else to do, I dried the dishes he'd put in the drainer and stowed them away.

The instant we were done with the homely procedure, before I could tense up again wondering what was to follow, Claude stuck out his huge hand, shook mine, and said, 'I appreciate the good cooking. I get mightily tired of my own,' and went to my front door.

I followed him as I ought to, but I wrapped my arms across my chest protectively. 'Good-bye,' I said, feeling I should say something more, but I couldn't think what. He gave me a totally unexpected smile, and I realized I'd never seen him like that, his wrinkles deepening as his lips curved up, his gray eyes suddenly slanting as the smile reached them.

'Good night, Lily,' he rumbled, and then went down my driveway to the sidewalk. He turned toward the apartments, He didn't look back.

I shut the door, locked it mechanically, and went back to make sure the kitchen was spotless before going to bed. I was smiling, I saw in the bathroom mirror. I caught myself actually wondering what Claude Friedrich would be like in bed, and I shook my head at my reflection in the mirror. 'You are going to the dogs, Lily,' I said to the mirror. My face in the mirror looked rather pleased at the prospect.

Chapter Ten

The telephone rang while I was putting on my makeup. I blew out a breath of exasperation. I'd hoped with the new workweek beginning, my life would get back to normal.

'Yes?' I said curtly.

'Lily Bard?' asked a faintly familiar voice.

'Yes.'

'This is Alvah York. T. L. and I just happened to remember yesterday that we owed you money.'

'I can stop by this morning at ten-thirty.' I'd be through with my first client by then.

'We'll be here.'

As I checked my supplies and loaded my car, I wondered if I should ask the Yorks how their granddaughter was doing, or just ignore the subject. I'd feel more comfortable myself just ignoring it, I decided. It was time to get back to my old familiar distance.

As I was giving the Althaus home its weekly two hours (it could have used five, but the two was all the Althaus budget would stand), I thought long and hard about the people in the apartment building. One of those tenants had killed Pardon Albee, whose somewhat irritating presence was already growing faint in my memory. For all his petty faults – his enjoyment in knowing about the lives of other people, his determined gossip gathering – Pardon hadn't deserved what had happened to him.

While I scraped determinedly at a wad of chewing gum one of the many Althaus children had dropped on the kitchen linoleum, I pondered Pardon's violent death and the disrespect shown his body.

Once again, I wondered where that body had been hidden in its curious journeys.

Well, it could have been in the back of Pardon's own apartment. But surely Claude, who'd been so amazingly forthcoming the night before, would have told me if traces supporting that idea had been found. So the body had been close, but not in Pardon's own apartment. Not in the closet under the stairs; Pardon and I had apparently had the only keys, and the killer had not used Pardon's keys, as the clean and orderly closet bore witness.

So, somewhere in the apartment house, or maybe in the garage? It seemed to me as if there was a thought in the back of my head, if I could just summon it up, something one of the tenants had told me, something that had made me wonder at the time . . . but God Almighty, I'd been talking to so many people lately. No wonder I couldn't remember. It would pop to the top of my mind if I just ignored it. I began thinking about hiding places for Pardon's body again.

I felt sure I could eliminate Mrs Hofstettler's and Claude's apartments. Marie Hofstettler was very much on the ball despite her aches and pains – she'd have to be totally senile to miss a dead body – and Claude . . . just hadn't killed Pardon. I didn't know why I was so sure, but I was. The Yorks had been out of town until late. That left the O'Hagens – which meant Tom, since Jenny had been at work – Deedra Dean, Norvel Whitbread, and Marcus Jefferson.

As I plugged in the ancient Althaus vacuum cleaner, I thought about Tom O'Hagen. What if Tom had lied about Pardon's living room being empty? What if Pardon's body had been lying on the couch, as Deedra said it had an hour or so later?

I worked over that idea determinedly but got nowhere. I simply could not think of a good reason for Tom O'Hagen to lie about that. He could have said he thought Pardon was asleep, as Deedra had. He could have said everything looked as normal, so he assumed Pardon had stepped out or retreated to the bathroom for a moment. Instead, Tom had insisted the furniture had been moved, the throw rug rumpled, as if something had taken place in the room.

Finally, I abandoned Tom O'Hagen in disgust. It was Marcus

Jefferson's turn in the lineup of suspects. Marcus was certainly strong enough to move Pardon's body. Marcus also had a grudge against Pardon; he obviously adored the little boy Pardon's policies prevented him from bringing home. But that was hardly sufficient motivation to strike Pardon hard enough to kill him, at least to my mind. I could only picture that happening if Pardon had provoked Marcus in some way – had threatened to tell Marcus's ex-wife that Marcus was having a fling with a white woman, say. Could Marcus's former wife have kept the child away from Marcus if she'd received that information? Would it make such a difference to her, in this day and age? And Pardon had called Marcus's workplace the day he died. But then, two hundred-odd people worked in the factory besides Marcus – among them, I recalled, was Deedra Dean's stepfather, Jerrell Knopp, whom I knew as an upright, polite, softspoken bigot, who would undoubtedly have violent feelings about any relationship his stepdaughter might have with a black man.

But Jerrell, if he killed anyone, wouldn't kill Pardon. He'd kill Marcus. Surely Marcus was supposed to work from eight to five? And Pardon had almost certainly died sometime before five. Marcus could have killed Pardon on his lunch hour, maybe. After all, if anyone had seen or heard from Pardon after the phone call he'd placed to his friend at eleven and Tom's knocking on Pardon's door at three, I hadn't heard about it.

Well, then, Deedra. Deedra had been at work until about four-thirty. She'd left her job early to give Pardon her rent check. Every Shakespeare Garden Apartments tenant knew Pardon was a stickler for getting paid on the dot. Why would the living room be in disarray at three if Deedra killed Pardon later? I tried to picture Deedra enraged, Deedra lifting something heavy and striking her landlord the crushing blow that had killed him. What would Deedra lift? There was nothing at hand there by the door to the apartment, and I didn't think Pardon had been fool enough to stand talking to a young woman with a poker in her hand. Besides, if I knew Deedra, Deedra was more likely to vamp her way out of a bad situation than to resort to violence. I sighed. Scratch Deedra.

Then there was the hopeless, hapless Norvel, at this moment languishing – desolately, I hoped – in the Shakespeare jail, which was so outdated and decrepit that the town was wondering when, instead of if, it would be ordered to build a new one. Norvel was certainly dumb enough to commit murder at a time when other people were in and out of the apartment building. He was panicky enough to try to hide the body. He was prone to get angry enough to attack, as I knew from firsthand experience.

But though I tried to picture it while I gathered the waste-baskets from each room, I could not imagine anything Pardon could have on Norvel that would provoke Norvel to that much rage. Norvel was not especially strong after years of drinking, eating improperly, and avoiding hard work. The blow that had killed Pardon had been delivered by someone strong and someone furious. It could have been Norvel, by some extraordinary circumstance, but I was inclined to doubt it.

As I carried bags of garbage out to the Rubbermaid trash receptacles, dropped them in, and clamped the lids shut against loose dogs or raccoons, I felt glad I'd chosen housecleaning as my livelihood and not private detecting. This murder, I thought, pausing to stretch my back muscles, had been a murder of impulse, though whose impulse, I hadn't the foggiest notion.

Pardon had finally spoken the sentence, the one sentence in his lifetime of watching, prying, and telling, the hearer could not bear to hear.

And that person had struck two blows, the second one closing Pardon's mouth forever.

I locked the door to the Althaus home behind me, feeling satisfied at having, however temporarily, restored neatness to the Althauses' chaotic environment. I could not figure out the identity of the murderer of Pardon Albee, but I could bring order to chaos.

I actually work harder for Carol Althaus than for any client I have, because frankly, Carol arouses my pity, which is not an easy thing to do. Carol is a nice, plain woman coping with a blended family of two children of her own and two of her husband's, and Carol has limited brainpower to handle the load. She works hard at a low-paying job, comes home to try to feed and chauffeur four children under ten, and every now and then fields a phone call from her husband, whose job involves a lot of traveling. I often picture Jay Althaus in his quiet motel room, all alone, bed with clean sheets, TV with remote control that he alone wields, and contrast Jay Althaus's evenings with Carol's.

I had a break from ten-thirty to noon; at noon, I'd clean a lawyer's office during his lunch hour. During this time every week, I usually run errands and pay bills. The first thing on my list for today was collecting the money owed me by the Yorks. As I drove back into town, for the very first time it occurred to me that Jay Althaus might be longing desperately for his wife and children every night he spends on the road.

Nah.

Rather than park on the street, which was too narrow for my comfort, I drove behind the apartment building. At this time of day on a weekday, there would be plenty of spaces empty.

Since I'd been considering the garage as a possible storage place for Pardon's body, I took the time to look it over. I pulled into Norvel's parking space – the apartment number is above each space, the effect remarkably like horse stalls at a big racetrack – and stood back to scan the white-painted wooden structure.

The garage, never a thing of beauty, didn't look its best empty. Since Shakespeare Garden Apartments doesn't have a basement, always a chancy thing in Arkansas, everyone in the building uses his or her stall for storage.

Starting from the left, the gap between the first stall and the fence surrounding the apartments was filled by the controversial York camper. The first stall is Norvel's. He doesn't own a car, but he'd leaned a broken framed mirror and a set of fireplace instruments in his allotted space: scroungings, I figured, that he hoped to sell. Marcus had put a wooden crate in the corner of his stall, and from it protruded a fat red plastic baseball bat and a tiny basketball goal. Claude Friedrich had put in a set of metal shelves that held car repair odds and ends and some tools. Deedra's space held a folded tent and a pair of muddy rubber boots. I have always thought it an odd sidelight to Deedra that she enjoys camping; of course, she doesn't enjoy camping alone. But it has always interested me that Deedra is willing to get away from her hot curlers for a weekend every now and then.

The first-floor tenants had scantier pickings. Marie has a car that I drive her around in, but other than that, her stall was empty. The Yorks, like Claude, have a set of shelves, but they were almost empty, and I thought they'd even been dusted; that was typical of Alvah. The O'Hagens had two expensive bicycles, covered with a tarp, at the back of their stall, and Pardon's car and a lawn mower were parked in his stall. I felt a little bleak as I looked at them. There is something melancholy about a dead person's possessions, no matter how impersonal they are, and there's nothing personal about a lawn mower.

This careful examination had told me absolutely nothing. The stalls are so open to view, it was hard to see how Pardon's body could have been hidden in any one of them. Maybe at the back of the stall between Mrs Hofstettler's car and the wall? Or the same place in Pardon's stall? Those were the only two cars the killer could have counted on remaining in place. Self-consciously, I checked the two stalls. Not a stain or a thread from the green-and-orange shirt.

The camper would be a great hiding spot, but the Yorks had been driving it home at the time Pardon died.

Well, I had to get my money from those upright people. I turned to go into the building and got an unpleasant shock. Norvel Whitbread was standing in the doorway.

'How'd you get out?' I asked.

'Church put up my bail.' He grinned at me, an unnerving sight, since Norvel is missing some teeth. Perhaps I'd knocked one of those out myself? I hoped so. His nose was many-colored and swollen.

'Get out of my way,' I said.

'Don't have to. I live here and you don't.' Norvel hadn't wasted any time consoling himself for his ordeal, I saw, and smelled.

'This time, the police won't come and I won't stop,' I said.

I could tell from his eyes that Norvel had made up his mind to move, but before he could shift his feet, a shove from behind sent him flying out the door, staggering to keep his feet under him.

T. L. stood in the doorway, his arm still extended, his mouth in a tight line of anger.

'You piece of trash,' he told Norvel, who had spun around to face this unexpected attack, 'if the next landlord don't evict you, it won't be for lack of my trying. You leave this woman alone. I don't care where you go, but you get out of my sight.'

T. L. was absolutely sincere, and that evidently impressed Norvel, no matter what Norvel's condition was. He looked sullen, but he acted swiftly, heel-and-toeing it out of the parking area.

Now I had to thank T. L., and I didn't much want to.

'Lily, you probably wanted to get in a few more licks,' T. L. said, with a smile that looked like his old self. 'But I just can't sit still when I hear something like that. And I am the acting landlord. At least the lawyer asked me to lock the doors at night like Pardon did.'

I had to smile. 'I appreciate it, T. L.,' I said.

'You come to see us? Alvah said you were going to drop by.'

'Yep.'

'Come on in.'

The door to the York apartment was still open. I couldn't help glancing over at Pardon's. The crimescene tape was still across the door. I followed T. L. into his living room, where Alvah was cross-stitching something blue and pink.

If T. L. was close to recovery, Alvah was not. I was sorry to see her face looked old, far older than it had the week before. She moved slowly and stiffly as she rose to get my money.

'Will you be needing me to help finish up?' I asked. I was babbling, but there was something awful and self-conscious about Alvah's sudden decline that made me want to fill the silence.

'I pretty much done it,' Alvah said listlessly. But the curtains were still off the windows, and the ceiling fan above their little dining table hadn't been dusted, a quick look told me.

T. L. had sat himself down in his favorite chair, a leather easy chair with a pouch hanging over one arm that held a *TV Guide*, the remote control, and a *Sports Illustrated*. He opened the *Sports Illustrated*, but I had a feeling he wasn't really reading the page in front of him.

'Harley Don Murrell killed himself,' Alvah said, handing me the money.

'Oh,' I said slowly. 'Well, that's . . .' My voice trailed off. I had no idea what that was. Good – a bad man dead? Bad – he hadn't had time to get the full horror of being in prison? A relief – their granddaughter no longer had to fear the day he got out on parole?

'How'd he do it?' I asked briskly, as if it mattered.

'He was on the third tier. He jumped over the rail and landed on his head.' Alvah's eyes were fixed on my face, but I didn't think she was seeing me any more than T. L. was reading *Sports Illustrated*.

'Quick then,' I said, almost at random. 'Well, see you soon.'

I had barely cleared the door, when I heard it close and lock behind me.

I was unnerved by this little exchange. I wondered what the Yorks' future would be like.

I went to the lawyer's office, and I cleaned, but I was absorbed in my thoughts the whole time and hardly remember doing it afterward. I was recalled to my self when I nodded to his secretary on my way out the door. Now I had to drive two miles out of town to Mrs Rossiter's. I had forgotten my earplugs, damn it.

Today was Durwood's biweekly bath. Durwood is Mrs Rossiter's old cocker spaniel, and Mrs Rossiter likes him to smell good, which is not a normal state for Durwood. When Mrs Rossiter had fallen out with the local pet groomer, she'd been in a quandary, since Durwood doesn't travel by car well enough to handle a drive to Montrose. She'd been explaining her problem at her church-circle meeting, and God bless Mrs Hofstettler, she'd chimed in to say she was sure Lily Bard could bathe that little dog.

Durwood isn't a bad dog, but bathing him is a hard job, and drying him is worse, to say nothing of cleaning the bathroom afterward. As I went to Mrs Rossiter's front door, my rubber apron under my arm, I thought for the twentieth time that the worst thing of all was Mrs Rossiter, who always regards Durwood's bath as a monologue opportunity, with me cast as the listener. I'd done everything in my not-inconsiderable power to quell the woman. It hadn't worked. And I didn't have my earplugs.

Mrs Rossiter was off and running (at the mouth) the minute she came to the door. She told me I'd been beaten up by that drunk Norvel Whitbread, that the SCC people were saying it was because I'd made Norvel angry at church, though why that would make it okay for Norvel to hide in my yard and jump out at me, she couldn't figure.

When I'd filled Mrs Rossiter's guest bathtub and set the shampoo handily within reach and pulled on my gloves, she told me that I lived next to Pardon Albee, who'd been murdered a week ago, and she'd heard I was seeing that strong young man who ran the health club, and did I know that he was still married to that cute little gal who worked at the SCC Day Care? Did I know that someone had left a rat on that gal's table, and written a dirty word in spray paint on her door?

I was only surprised Mrs Rossiter didn't tell me I'd been raped in Memphis a few years ago.

By now I was soaping down the shivering Durwood. Letting Mrs Rossiter's words run over me like water, I rubbed the lather gently through the dog's coat, wondering at the omission.

So far no one, *no one*, except for members of the Shakespeare Police Department, had mentioned Memphis to me or even looked at me as if they'd heard something. I simply couldn't believe that Tom David Meiklejohn, for instance, wouldn't want to share the sensational details with his drinking buddies – for that matter, wouldn't he enjoy even more giving the gory details to Thea?

I mulled this over while Mrs Rossiter, perched on the closed toilet so she wouldn't miss a minute of my mute company, ran down the scale of gossip to arrive at her own blood pressure, which was always a prime topic.

I interrupted her once to ask her to turn on the ceiling heat lamp so Durwood could dry faster, and once again to ask her to pass me a towel that had fallen from its rack. By the time I'd gotten the dog dry and he'd pranced off with his owner to get a treat in the kitchen, I had arrived at the only possible reason the Shakespeare police force hadn't talked: Claude had threatened them with dismissal if they did. That was what he'd meant when he'd told me he was taking steps to minimize the damage he'd caused.

I shook gentle scouring powder into the fiberglass tub, having pulled the rubber mat off the bottom to pop into the wash pile on my way out. I scrubbed the tub slowly, turning this idea over in my mind. Though I rummaged through my brain, I could come up with no other solution that fit the facts.

After I'd cleaned up, Mrs Rossiter handed me a twenty-dollar bill, and I nodded, my hand on the doorknob.

'See you in two weeks, won't we, Durwood?' she said, looking down at the sweet-smelling Durwood. He looked as if he hoped not, but he wagged his tail, since she seemed to expect it.

The rest of the day was a slump time for me. I would see Marshall that night in class, and for the first time since I'd come to Shakespeare, I was not looking forward to it. I was grateful to Claude Friedrich for trying to make up for his error, but I didn't want to be. I couldn't be sure what his motive was. The stop at the Yorks' had upset me, not that I was bothered that a piece of trash like Harley Don Murrell was dead, but I hated seeing the Yorks in such a state.

There was nothing I could do about any of this.

I brooded my way through my last job, went home to get my gi, still dragging my feet. I even considered skipping class, a first. I couldn't quite bring myself to do that: It seemed like cowardice.

But I deliberately waited till the last minute to go, so I wouldn't have to talk to Marshall before class began.

I had a definite feeling of deflation when I bowed and straightened and realized Marshall was not in the room. He'd been afraid to face me, too. Oddly enough, this made me feel good, proud.

'You leading class tonight?' I asked Raphael, the only student who has been there longer than I.

'That's what the man told me,' he said, pleased under his offhandedness. 'You gonna be okay? Your ribs? I heard you put that guy in the emergency room. Way to go, Lily!'

To my amazement, the other class members strolled up for their turn at congratulating me. I saw that from their point of view, my short skirmish with Norvel had validated what they were doing in the class, the time and pain they were expending to learn how to defend themselves. Janet Shook actually patted me on the shoulder. It was an effort to keep still. I took my place in line – first, tonight, since Raphael was facing us – in a daze. Whatever I had expected, this wasn't it.

Carlton was there again. Most people faltered after the second time, so I saw his attendance as a good sign. He wasn't quite as sore, I could tell by the way he moved, and he was stretching better. It wouldn't be long before he'd be able to do things that would amaze him. Raphael called us to attention, we bowed, and once again we began our uncomfortable routine.

Sit-ups reawakened the pain in my side, and I had to stop after thirty.

'Slacker,' said Raphael, and Janet laughed. I told myself they were teasing, and made myself smile. Carlton came over and extended a hand to help me up, and, surprising even myself, I took it.

'Seriously, Lily, don't hurt yourself worse. Marshall told me to be sure and watch you don't overdo it,' Raphael said as we drifted back in after our water break. I ducked my head to hide my expression and went back to my place, but when I faced forward for his next command, I saw Raphael looking at me with some speculation. We practiced some restraint moves, nothing I hadn't learned already. Everyone pretended to be scared to be my partner.

'So, woman of steel, when's your next match?' Carlton asked as we pulled on our shoes. He, Raphael, and Janet were the only ones left in the big room.

I actually laughed.

'You know, Norvel's already out on bail,' I said, not knowing how to respond.

'Bet he won't be coming around you anymore,' Janet said dryly. I figured she was still there because she was maneuvering to leave at the same time Carlton did, hoping for some significant exchange about meeting for a drink, maybe.

'Better not,' I said sincerely. There was a little silence. They exchanged glances.

'Did you enjoy it, Lily?' Raphael asked suddenly. 'I mean, here we practice all the time, spar all the time, have aches and pains that make my wife ask why I'm doing this. And me, big man, I've never been in a fight since I got out of junior high. But you, woman, you've done it. So how did it feel?'

'I'll tell you,' I said after I'd thought for a moment. 'It was scary and exciting and I could have hurt him real bad if the police hadn't shown up so quick.'

'They pull you and Norvel apart?' Janet asked.

'No, I had him on the ground – bleeding. He was whipped. But I would have hurt him more.' Raphael and Carlton exchanged uneasy looks. 'It was the adrenaline,' I tried to explain. 'I had beaten a real man in a real fight, but he scared me, coming at me like that, unexpected. And since I was scared, I was mad. I was so mad at him for scaring me, I wanted to hurt him even worse.' Admitting I'd been frightened wasn't too easy.

Raphael and Carlton were thinking over what I'd said, but Janet was after something else. 'So it did work, all this training,' she said, leaning forward to stare in my face. 'You reacted just like you would in class, no freeze moment, the training kicked in.' I could tell what she was scared of – not too hard to figure out.

And there was a short answer. 'Yes, the training kicked in.'

She nodded, a short, sharp bob of the head that signified confirmation of a deeply held hope. Then she smiled, a cold smile that made this shortish, ordinary woman something formidable. It was my turn to lean forward, and for once deliberately I looked someone else straight in the eyes, searching hers for what I suspected. I found it. I gave my own little nod. We were fellow survivors.

But we weren't going to talk about it. I wanted to avoid a girlish mutual emotional bath at all costs. It was something I couldn't bear. So I grabbed my stuff and mumbled something about going home to get cleaned up, said I was hungry.

I started thinking about Pardon's shirt on the way home. I've done laundry. I know the way clothes look when they've been washed hundreds of times. Pardon's shirt was a cheap shirt to begin with and he'd worn it and washed it repeatedly for years. It had been almost thin enough to read through. I remembered in my flashlight's beam seeing the ripped chest pocket. The threads had been frayed. I did not doubt that some of those threads remained at the site of Pardon's death, which had probably occurred in his apartment. More of them had to be at the place where his body had been stored. And where were his keys?

I prepared a baked potato and vegetables when I got home, but I hardly tasted the meal. That body had been hidden on the street I considered my turf. My cart had been used to haul Pardon to the dump site. Now that my mind was unclouded by thoughts of Marshall – or at least mostly unclouded – it began to run around the track of speculation about Pardon's death.

Suddenly, the parking garage popped into my mind. Something about it had sparked an uneasiness; something not as it was supposed to be? A memory jogged by something I'd seen there?

It bothered me while I washed my dishes, bothered me while I showered. I wasn't going to sleep. I put on black spandex shorts and a black sports bra, then pulled a red UA sweatshirt over that. Black socks and black cross-trainers completed my outfit. I punched in Claude's number, sure that if I heard his voice, I'd know what I wanted to tell him. But his answering machine came on. I don't leave messages on machines. I paced up and down my hall. I tried his number again.

Finally, I had to get out. Dark night. Cool air on my bare legs. Walking. It was a relief to be outside, to be silent, to be moving. I passed Thea's house without so much as a glance. And then I passed Marshall's. His car wasn't there. I walked on. I heard someone else coming on Indian Way and glided behind some azaleas. Joel McCorkindale ran by, wearing sweats, Nikes, and a determined expression. I waited till the sound of his running feet faded into the night before I stepped back out on the street.

The wind was blowing, making the new leaves rustle together, a sound almost like the sea.

I walked faster and faster, until I, too, was running down the middle of the street in silent Shakespeare, seeing no one, wondering if I was invisible.

I entered the arboretum from the far side, plunging into the trees and stopping to catch my breath in their concealment.

It came to me what I had to do. I had to go back to the garage. Looking at it would be better than visualizing. I would remember what had been niggling at me if I stood there long enough.

It was maybe eleven-forty-five when I walked silently up the north side of the apartment driveway. I hugged the brick wall so anyone glancing out a window would not see me. I checked the lights. Mrs Hofstettler's was out – no surprise there. A dim glow lit up the Yorks' bedroom window; maybe one of them was reading in bed. I had a hard time imagining that. Maybe a night-light? Norvel's second-floor apartment was dark, as was Marcus's.

As long as I was doing a bed check, I circled the building.

Of course Pardon's rooms were dark, and the O'Hagens'. Tom would be at work and Jenny would have to be in bed at this hour. Upstairs, Deedra's lights were out. She was in bed either solo or duo. There was a light in Claude's bathroom window, so I walked around front to check his bedroom window. It was lit.

I didn't want to go in the building. I squatted and patted the ground around me until I found a rock the size of my thumbnail. I threw it at his window. It made quite a sound. I flattened myself against the wall again in case someone other than Claude had heard the noise. But no one came to see what it was, not even Claude.

All right, then, I'd remember on my own.

And suddenly, I did.

I'd have to go in the building after all. I moved around to the back door, taking a terrible chance. I pulled the key no one had thought to take away from me, the key to the back door, from my bra. I unlocked the door as quietly as it could be done, then went in. The stairs creak less by the wall, so I went up them quietly and carefully, one foot in front of the other. I passed Claude's door and went to Deedra's, decorated with a little grapevine wreath wrapped with purple ribbon and dried flowers. I knocked quietly.

The door opened so quickly, I was sure Deedra had been lying on the floor right inside it, with company. In the light falling through from the hall, I could see a male leg, and since it was dark, I deduced that Marcus Jefferson had succumbed to temptation once again.

Deedra looked very pissed off, and I couldn't blame her, but I didn't have time for it.

'Tell me again what you told me – about when you came home from work early to give Pardon the rent check.'

'I swear to God you are the weirdest cleaning woman in Arkansas,' Deedra said.

'Talk to me. For once, I want to listen.'

'Will you go away right after? No more questions?'

'Probably.'

'Okay. I came home from work. I ran upstairs to get the check Mama had given me. I took it down to Pardon's. The door was a little open. He was lying on the couch, his back to the door. The area rug was all rumpled and the couch was crooked. I said his name, I said it a lot, but he didn't move. I figured he'd maybe had a drink and passed out or he was taking a hell of a nap, so I just put the check on his desk, to the left of the door. This what you want?'

I beckoned to her to keep on.

'So . . . so then, I . . . well, I went back and got in my car. I had to go back to work even though I just had a few minutes left. You wouldn't believe how ticky Celie Schiller is . . .'

'Lower your voice and speed up,' I suggested quietly.

'My maid tells me what to do,' she told the air. 'Incredible.'

But she looked in my face and went on. 'And then I got in my car . . . and I backed out of my place, and put it in drive to go out, and I had to go out careful because of the Yorks' stupid camper . . .'

I held a finger to my lips. Her voice was rising.

'That's what I wanted,' I whispered.

'Oh, don't want to hear about the run in my hose that day?' she asked with killing sarcasm, then shut the door firmly in my face.

I ran my fingers through my hair and gripped two handfuls of it. I stood there thinking, my eyes closed, still facing Deedra's door. I took a few steps down the hall and tapped Claude's door with one finger. I couldn't risk more.

No answer. I turned the handle. Locked, of course.

I went back down the stairs quietly. Even if I'd been standing in the bottom hall, I wouldn't have heard me.

I didn't know why I was so tense, why my mission seemed so urgent. But I never ignore the back of my neck, and the skin of it was crawling. There was tension in air. In the silent building, the air was humming with it. I opened the door with a feeling of relief to be getting out, and I eased through the opening as silently as I could manage. I re-locked the door behind me.

Going from the lighted hall to the relative gloom of the parking area cost me some vision, and I stood still to let my eyes adjust. Pardon had installed one all-night security light in the middle of the garage, and it lit up that immediate area like stage lighting. But the illumination didn't extend to the end stalls. I skirted the edge of the light and drifted to the outside wall of the garage. For maybe five minutes, I stood in the darkness, listening. I shifted my foot, and something clinked.

Slowly, I crouched down in the weeds that had found life

against the wall of the garage, sprouting through cracks in the pavement. I patted the ground gently. My fingers found a familiar shape, traced it. I tried to pick up what I'd found all in one piece, so it wouldn't jingle. I held it up close to my face. Pardon Albee's key ring. I had nowhere to put it; there were at least fifteen keys on the metal circle. The safest place was where they'd been, so I gently laid them back in the weeds, where they'd been since the day he died.

Nothing moved. I didn't hear anything but the faint sound of a car cruising by in the street. Even that died away. But as quiet as it was, I knew there were people near. I could feel the hair standing up on the nape of my neck. So I slowly rose to my feet, nearly moved away to the safety of my house, wondered if I would make it.

I extended my hand to the knob on the camper. It was in the camper that Pardon's body had been concealed; if any evidence remained, it would be in that little space.

The Yorks hadn't been due home until night. But they'd come home earlier, the day Pardon had died. I knew it.

And then I turned the knob. The door popped open with a click, and just as I took in a breath of triumph, a huge shape launched itself at me from the black interior.

I didn't have a chance to defend myself. In ferocious silence, I was being beaten, and I needed all my breath to fend off the blows, to keep the fists from killing me. I knew only one person was there, but it was a person possessed of a demon, a man who seemed to have more than two hands.

I had to fight back or I would die, but the frequency and pain of the blows left me scant brainpower. I formed a fist and struck the first thing I could see, some ribs, not an effective blow, but a start, a gesture. I was weakening and soon I would be down on the ground, and it would be all over if I fell. It was almost a miracle I'd managed to keep on my feet as long as this.

Then I caught a glimpse of exposed neck and drove the edge of my hand in as hard as I could. My attacker gave a grunt and faltered, and I thrust-kicked with all my strength, not really caring where it landed as long as it sank into him. He staggered, and I could take a deep breath, and then a voice behind me said, 'Stop right there.'

Who? Who should stop? My attacker was in no doubt, and he threw himself at the source of the command, again moving so quickly and with so much determination that the speaker and I were unprepared.

The struggle came into the light, moving toward the center of the parking area, and I could see T. L. York and Claude rolling on the ground, struggling for a gun that I thought must be in Claude's hand. Their hands and legs were so confused and I was so dazed by the suddenness of all this that for a second I stood staring blankly, as if I had no stake in the outcome. I was weak enough to be shaking, but I had to move, to help – whom?

'Lily!' Claude said, in what he maybe intended as a shout, and that decided me. Only the innocent one would want my help.

I circled them, looking for my chance. It came, when T. L. rolled on top of Claude, still gripping both Claude's wrists. I leaped in to straddle them, grabbed T. L. by his hair with one hand and cupped his chin with the other, and pulled back hard, almost hearing the faint echo of Marshall's voice adjuring me to be careful practicing this in class, since a wrong move could cause serious injury.

Well, this was serious-injury time. I twisted his head and pulled up. You have to follow your head. The rest of his body had to come up, too, or his neck would break. With a howl, he let go of Claude and raked backward, trying to get me off him, but I had my fingers sunk in his still-thick hair. In agony, he reared back, but my legs were locked on either side of him, I was gripping him with my knees, and the only way he could get rid of me was to do what he did next – fall backward on top of me. I wrapped my legs around him as he left the ground and heaved back, and I never loosened my grip on his head. I began squeezing with my strong legs, my ankles crossed over his gut, and he rolled from side to side trying to dislodge me.

'Hold still, goddamn it!' said a voice I could hardly recognize as

Claude's, and again I didn't know if he meant me or T. L. I didn't have a lot of options, since I couldn't breathe and I could tell only my own rage was keeping me attached to him.

Then the gun went off. It was deafening. T. L. screamed, and since my grip had loosened at the shock of the sound, he could roll off me and continue to scream. Suddenly, I could breathe. I didn't feel like getting up, though. It was enough to lie on the filthy concrete and look up at the moths circling in the light.

Chapter Eleven

I wasn't in the hospital, but I was under house arrest.

The chief of police had confined me to my own home for a week. He had coaxed Mrs Hofstettler into calling all my clients and explaining (as if they hadn't heard) that I'd been a little hurt and had to recuperate. I told Mrs Hofstettler, via Claude, to tell them I didn't expect to get paid, since I wasn't going to work. I don't know if she passed the message along. Everyone sent me a check but the Winthrops, which figured. However, Bobo came by to bring me a fruit basket he said was from his mother. I was sure he'd bought it himself.

Marshall really had gone out of town; he wasn't just avoiding me. He called me from Memphis to tell me his father had had a heart attack and he and the rest of his family were just circling the hospital room in a holding pattern, waiting to see what would happen. I assured him several times that I would be all right, and after I'd detailed my wounds to him and explained what I was doing for their treatment, he seemed satisfied I would live. He called me every other day. I was stunned to receive flowers with his name on the card. He was eloquently silent when I told him Claude was with me one night when he called.

Mrs Rossiter brought the damn dog by to see me. Claude told her I was asleep.

Carrie Thrush paid me a house call.

'You should be in the hospital,' she said sternly.

'No,' I said. 'My insurance won't cover enough of it.' She didn't say any more after that, since she wouldn't question me about my finances, but all the medicine she gave me was in sample boxes.

Claude came every day. He had gone with me in the ambulance to the hospital, following the one carrying T. L.

He had shot T. L. in the leg.

'I wanted to hit him in the head with the pistol butt,' he said when we were waiting for the doctor in a white cubicle that night. I was glad to listen to him talking, so I wouldn't moan and disgrace myself. 'I've never shot anyone before – at least to actually hit them.'

'Um-hum,' I said, concentrating fiercely on his voice.

'But I was sure I would hit you instead, and I didn't want to beat up my ally.'

'Good.'

'So I had to shoot him.' His big hand came up to touch my shoulder, stroke it. That hurt like hell. But I didn't say anything.

'Why were you there?' I asked after a long pause.

'I'd been staking out the camper for the last week.'

'Oh, for God's sake,' I said, thinking that all my inspiration had been for nothing. Claude had been there mentally before me.

'No, I thought that someone else had killed Pardon, not T. L. I thought the Yorks didn't want to tell anybody Pardon's body had been in their camper, but I didn't think they had put him there.'

'The curtains,' I said.

'Curtains? What curtains?'

But by then the doctor had come in and told Claude he had to step outside. It was the emergency room doctor, who'd just finished sending T. L. up to the operating room. His eyebrows flew up when he saw my scars, but for once I didn't care.

'Your X rays,' he said.

'Mmm?'

'You have no broken bones,' he said, as if that was the most amazing thing he'd ever heard. 'But many of your muscles are badly strained. You are very thoroughly bruised. But I can tell you're a workout buff; underneath all that, you're physically fit. Normally, I'd put you in the hospital, just for a night or two, just as a precaution. What do you think?' He observed me closely from behind glasses that reflected the glaring overhead light. His ponytail was caught up neatly in an elastic band at the nape of his neck.

'Home,' I said.

'Anyone there to take care of you?'

'I am,' rumbled Claude from outside the curtain.

I opened my mouth to protest, but the doctor said, 'Well, if you have someone to help . . . Believe me, you're not going to be able to get to the bathroom without help for a few days.'

I stared at him, dismayed.

'You have some healing injuries. You seem to be prone to get into trouble,' the doctor observed, sticking his pen behind his ear.

I heard Claude snort.

I had a couple of emergency room pain pills, and Carrie came by and supplemented. Claude proved to be an unexpectedly good nurse. His big hands were gentle. He knew about the scars beforehand from the Memphis police report, which was good, because there was no way I could conceal them from someone who helped me with a sponge bath. He also helped me hobble to the toilet, and he changed my sheets. The food I'd frozen ahead came in very handy, since I couldn't stand long enough to cook, and when I was by myself, I could take my time getting to the kitchen to heat it up.

A couple of times, Claude brought carryout and we ate together, the first time in my bedroom – he improvised a bed tray – and the second time, I was able to sit at the table, though it exhausted me.

The swelling was almost gone and I had evolved from black and blue to sickly shades of green and yellow when we finally talked about the Yorks.

'How did you come to be watching?' I asked him. I felt good. I'd just taken a pain pill, I was clean and my sheets were clean, and I'd managed to brush my hair. I lay there neatly, my hands resting by my sides, a little sleepy and relaxed. That was as good as it got, that week.

'I went over everyone's statement several times. I drew up a timetable, and a list of alibis; it was just like a TV special,' he said, his legs extended comfortably in front of him, his fingers laced across his belly. He'd hauled the armchair into my bedroom.

'Marcus was my hottest suspect for a long time,' he continued. 'But he just couldn't have left work – too many witnesses. Deedra, too. She was gone from work for maybe thirty minutes, and she was out on a date while Pardon's body was being dumped. After you told me exactly when that was,' and he shot me a mildly reproachful look, 'I could eliminate her. Marie Hofstettler is just too old and infirm. Norvel was a possibility, and Tom O'Hagen. But Tom was at work when Pardon was killed, and Jenny was working at the country club on decorations for the spring dance . . . lots of witnesses. She couldn't have killed Pardon.

'And I didn't think it was you, at least not after a few days.'

'Why?' The pill was taking effect, and I was only mildly interested in the answer.

'Maybe because the only secret you'd kill for is what happened to you in Memphis. And when I let it slip, you didn't try to kill me.'

I was faintly amused. I looked off in a corner.

'So that left Norvel,' I said quietly.

'Unless the Yorks had come home early.'

'I would have picked Norvel.'

'I couldn't decide. In a way, it seemed too smart for Norvel to think of. But in a way, it seemed exactly like Norvel, drunk. Wavering between one hidey-hole and the next. Moving Pardon here. Moving him there. We looked in every apartment in the building, in one way or another.'

I wasn't going to ask questions.

'No traces of the body anywhere. He'd bled a little from the mouth. No hairs, and the only fibers on the body were from a cotton blend, deep red and bright gold and blue.'

'Alvah's curtains,' I murmured.

'I didn't know about Alvah's curtains,' Claude rumbled. 'But I didn't see anything in anyone else's apartment that came close to matching those.'

I remembered him walking through my house the first time

he'd come in. He'd been looking for something that would ring a bell.

'We went all over the parking stalls, trying to find one that could have been used for the body. No luck there. I saw you looking that day, and I wondered what you were up to.'

'Saw me from where?'

'Pardon's apartment. I'd been sitting in it some days and every night, watching people go in and out and do their curious things, and trying to get some idea of where to take this.'

I was definitely feeling dimmer.

'We'd searched the garbage the day Pardon's body was found.'

I smiled to myself.

'We'd looked in every apartment. We'd kept a watch on the movements of everyone for a day or two, then only on Norvel and the Yorks.'

'Not a close enough watch on Norvel.'

'Goddamn it, Lily, he goes out walking, we don't know he's got a ski mask stuffed in his pocket. He must have stuck the broom handle by the fence earlier in the day. I never saw him with it.'

'But that was how you were able to get there so fast. You were awake. Did you pull your shirt off on purpose?'

'Yeah,' he confessed, looking embarrassed. 'I thought it would look more like I'd been awakened by you yelling.'

'So, you were watching the Yorks and Norvel.'

'I'd caught Deedra's reference to the camper, too. She might have gotten confused. She pulls in and out of the parking lot every day. But she sounded sure. I couldn't grill her without even her getting the drift, but the more I thought about it, the more possible I thought the Yorks' presence was. I called the Creek County courthouse. Harley Don Murrell's trial was over in time for the Yorks to have driven home. I checked with their daughter over there, real casually, and she said they'd left at one, right after lunch, too upset to stay any longer. Alvah and T. L. had said they'd stopped at the Hillside flea market and walked around a little to stretch their legs, but if that wasn't true, they could have gotten here before three.'

'They did. Alvah had watered the plant in the kitchen. It was wet when I went to water it at three,' I said. 'Her bedroom blinds were open. Those were the things she did when she first came home. And her living room curtains were down. I didn't notice that day, but I did notice on Wednesday. I thought Alvah had started spring cleaning, but T. L. wrapped the body in them.' That, I had figured out all by myself.

Claude stretched his long arms above his head and lapsed back into his former position. 'Alvah told me today that when they got back to Shakespeare, she went in the apartment with her suitcase and left T. L. unloading the rest of the stuff. She watered the plant and opened the blinds.' He tipped an imaginary hat to me.

'Outside, she could hear voices. Their door was open, and so was Pardon's; T. L. had stopped by to pay the rent. Pardon had found out about the trial and the verdict from his friend in Creek County, but instead of consoling the Yorks over the difficulty of living through a trial like that, Pardon chose to quote what Murrell's wife had said about the Yorks' granddaughter. And after the worst day of his life, T. L. just couldn't take it. T. L. and Pardon exchanged words, and he hit Pardon in the mouth. Pardon jumped back and bumped into the couch. It was like running from a hostile dog. T. L. went after him. He was going to hit Pardon in the jaw, but Pardon turned and slipped, and he hit Pardon in the neck with his fist, as hard as he could. It crushed Pardon's throat.'

'And they put him in the camper,' I said.

'Yep. T. L. ran into his apartment, past Alvah, ripped down the curtains without asking her, and ran back in to Pardon's place. Alvah followed. They loaded Pardon into the camper, wrapped in the curtains – his keys fell out then – and they drove around with him for a little while. They were completely panicked. They couldn't decide what to do. The Yorks had never broken the law in their lives. They were going to dump him by a back road, to make it seem he hadn't been killed by an apartment resident. But they realized they could establish an alibi, since no one had seen them return, if Pardon's body was found closer to the apartments to make that alibi valid.

'While they were driving around with Pardon's body, Tom went to Pardon's apartment to pay his rent. Door unlocked, no Pardon. Then the Yorks returned, pulled right up to the back door, opened the camper door, stowed Pardon back in his apartment.'

'How come they didn't hear Deedra knock on his door?' I asked.

'Alvah got nauseated,' Claude said, looking down at his hands. 'She had to run in her place to the toilet and T. L. went with her. While Alvah was being sick, Deedra left for work. They never knew she'd seen the camper – lucky for Deedra. When Alvah was better, they drove away again. They didn't think about disposing of the curtains he'd been wrapped in. They didn't think about the threads from his torn pocket getting left in the camper. They didn't think about people trying to pay their rent, not finding Pardon in his place. And they couldn't lock the door to Pardon's apartment because they had to get back in, and they couldn't find Pardon's keys.

'They evidently drove around in a daze, and just came home when they'd originally intended to, between seven and eight at night. They put the rest of their gear into their place. They'd been talking, of course, and they'd decided Pardon had to be found somewhere close to his apartment, someplace he could've walked, but also someplace he could have chanced across a mugger. The arboretum was the logical place, maybe the only sane choice the Yorks made. T. L. remembered your garbage-can cart. He'd seen it sitting by the curb on garbage days and always kind of coveted it . . . So he waited, thinking no one in Shakespeare would be up that late. And he was nearly right.'

'When did you decide it wasn't Norvel?'

'When I saw T. L. come out of the camper at you.' He smiled at me, making fun of himself. 'I'd thought maybe Norvel had just used the camper to stow Pardon's body and that the Yorks were so afraid of looking guilty that they were covering that up. I didn't want it to be the Yorks.'

'I knew it was the Yorks,' I said calmly. 'Because of the curtains.'

'You figured it out that way?'

'If Alvah's curtains were missing, there had to be a reason. And only T. L. would grab curtains down from their hooks. If Alvah had known what he was doing, she would have run and gotten a sheet or tablecloth that I wouldn't've missed. But I missed the curtains,' I said drowsily, 'and I knew someone had watered the plant.'

'Why . . . Lily, why did you go to the camper?'

'I wanted to see what was in it,' I said, and let my eyes close.

'Oh, yeah,' I said thickly, hauling my lids up again. 'How come you didn't know T. L. was in there?'

'I did,' he said, trying not to sound angry with me. 'I was waiting for him to come out with some evidence. He couldn't destroy it in the camper; he would've had to take it into the apartment. I couldn't get a warrant to search the camper. I didn't have enough evidence.'

' 'Kay. My mind's at rest.'

'One more thing.'

'Mmm?'

'What about the handcuffs on the Drinkwaters' steps, Lily? What about the dead rat?'

'Oh, that was Thea. I was pretty sure as soon as Marshall told me what her secret life was like. And I knew for sure after I realized you'd threatened everyone who worked for you with death if they talked about what happened to me. But Tom David had already told his honey bunch. He didn't let her tell anyone else. But she knew, and she wanted to torment me. Once I figured that out, I didn't worry about it anymore. I can handle ole Thea.'

I rolled an eye at Claude.

'Secret life?' he said hopefully. 'Thea Sedaka has a secret life?'

'Maybe tell you sometime,' I said.

'I hear Marshall's coming back tomorrow, Lily,' Claude said when I was almost drifting off. 'What are you going to do?'

'Go to sleep,' I mumbled, and did.

Shakespeare's Champion

This book is dedicated to my newsletter group,
the Femmes Fatale
(http://members.aol.com/femmesweb),
who make me laugh
more than I have since I left college.

Prologue

The man lying on the padded bench had been working out for two hours and he was drenched with sweat. His short blond hair was matted at his forehead, and his sharply etched body glistened. His hacked-off sweatshirt and shorts, originally blue but now faded, showed dark rings under the arms. It was October, but he had a glowing tan. He was exactly five feet ten inches and he weighed one hundred seventy-four pounds, both facts being of crucial importance to his regimen.

The other members of the Body Time gym had gone home an hour ago when the gym officially closed, leaving this dedicated and privileged being, Del Packard, to his solitary calling. After the others had gone, Del's spotter arrived, wearing ancient black sweatpants and an old gray sweatshirt with the sleeves scooted up.

Del had let the spotter in with his own key, on loan from gym owner Marshall Sedaka. Del had talked Marshall into issuing him a key so Del could work out every free minute he could beg from his job. The competition was only a month away.

'I think I'm going to make it this time,' Del said. He was resting between sets. The weighted bar lay in its rack above his head. 'I was second last year, but I hadn't put in the hours I have this year. And I've practiced my posing every day. I've gotten rid of every hair on my body, and if you think Lindy has stood that without complaining, you can think again.'

His spotter laughed. 'Want another dime?'

'Yeah,' said Del. 'I want to do ten reps, okay? Only help me if I'm hurting.'

The spotter added a ten-pound disc to each end of the bar. It already held a total of two hundred and seventy pounds.

Del tightened the wrist straps of his lifting gloves, flexed his fingers. But he delayed for a moment longer, saying, 'You been to that Marvel's Gym? It's the biggest place I ever seen.'

'No.' Del's companion also adjusted his black leather gloves. Lifting gloves stop at the first knuckle and have padded palms. Del's spotter had forgotten to bring his, he'd explained, and had pulled a pair of regular gloves out of the lost-and-found box. Now, the spotter casually pulled down the sleeves of his sweatshirt.

'I don't mind telling you, last year I was pretty nervous. There was guys in that middleweight division pumped up like tanks, been in training since they could walk. And their outfits! And here was me, ole country boy. But I did all right.' Del smiled proudly. 'This year I'll do better. No one from Shakespeare but me is entered this year. Marshall tried to get Lily Bard – you know her? blond? don't talk much? – to enter in the women's novice division, or the open, but she said she wasn't about to spend eight months pumping up to stand in front of a bunch of people she didn't know, all greased up like a pig. Well, that's one point of view. I look on it as an honor to represent Shakespeare at the Marvel Gym competition. Lily's got great chest and arm development, but she's pretty weird.'

Del lay back on the bench and looked up at the face of his spotter, who was bent over him, gloved hands resting casually on the bar. His spotter lifted his eyebrows in query.

'You remember, I was kind of worried after we had that conversation last week?' Del asked.

'Yep,' the spotter said with a dash of impatience in his voice.

'Well, Mr Winthrop says everything is okay. Just not to talk about it to anyone.'

'That's a relief. You gonna lift this, or just look at it?'

Del nodded his blond head sharply. 'Okay, I'm ready. After this set, I'm quitting for the night. I'm dead beat.'

The spotter smiled down at him. With a grunt, the spotter lifted the bar, now weighted with two hundred ninety pounds. He moved the bar into position above Del's open hands and began lowering it.

Just as Del's fingers were about to close around the bar, the spotter pulled it toward himself a little, till it was right over Del's neck. With great control, the spotter positioned it exactly over Del's Adam's apple.

Just as Del opened his mouth to ask what the hell was going on, the spotter dropped the bar.

Del's hands scrabbled convulsively at the weight crushing his neck for a few seconds, hard enough to make his fingers bleed, but his companion squatted down and held either side of the bar, the gloves and sweatshirt protecting him from Del's fingers.

Very shortly, Del lay still.

The spotter carefully examined his gloves. In the overhead light, they looked fine. He threw them back in the lost-and-found bin. Del had left his gym key on the counter, and the spotter used it to unlock the front door. Halfway out the door, he paused. His knees were shaking. He hadn't any idea of what to do with the key, and no one had thought to tell him. If he put it back in Del's pocket, he'd have to leave the door unlocked. Would that look suspicious? But if he took it with him to relock the door from the outside, wouldn't that tell the police that Del had had someone with him? This whole assignment was more terrible and perplexing than he'd imagined. But he could handle it, he reassured himself. The boss had said so. He was loyal and he was strong.

Hesitantly, the spotter rethreaded his steps between the pieces of equipment. With his face compressed into an expression of disgust, he tucked the key in Del's shorts pocket and rubbed the enclosing material around the key. He backed away from the still figure on the bench, then walked out hastily, almost running. He automatically flicked the light switch down on his way out. Glancing from side to side, the spotter finally broke and ran to the dark corner of the parking lot where his pickup was waiting, fairly well concealed by a few wax myrtles.

On his way home, he suddenly wondered if he could now get a date with Lindy Roland.

Chapter One

I grumbled to myself as I slid out of my Skylark, Marshall's keys clinking in my hand. Since I made my living doing favors for people, it hardly seemed fair to be doing a favor for free this early in the morning.

But this fall a flu epidemic was scything its way through Shakespeare. It had crept into the Body Time gym enclosed in the body of my friend Raphael Roundtree. Raphael had coughed and sneezed in karate class after working out in the weights room, neatly distributing the virus among almost all the Body Time clientele, with the exception of the aerobics class.

And me. Viruses don't seem to be able to abide in my body.

When I'd dropped by Marshall Sedaka's rented house even earlier that morning, Marshall had been at that stage of the flu where his greatest desire was to be left alone to his misery. So fit and healthy that he took sickness as an insult, Marshall was a terrible patient; and he was vain enough to hate my seeing him throw up. So he'd thrust the keys to Body Time into my hand, slammed the door, and yelled from behind it, 'Go open! Tanya's coming after her first class if I can't get anyone else!'

I'd been left with my mouth hanging open and a handful of keys.

It was my day to work at the Drinkwaters' house. I had to be there between 8:00 and 8:15, when the Drinkwaters left for work. It was now 7:00. Tanya, a student at the nearby Montrose branch of the University of Arkansas, might get out of her first class at 9:00. That would put her arrival time at somewhere around 9:40.

But Marshall was sometimes my lover and also sometimes my workout partner; and he was always my sensei, my karate instructor.

I'd blown air out of my mouth to make the curls at my forehead fluff, and driven out to Body Time. I'd decided I'd just unlock the gym and leave. The same people came every morning, and they could be trusted to work out alone. Most days, I was one of them.

Marshall's almost incoherent appeal for help had come when I had been dressing to leave for the gym, as a matter of fact, and I was already in my sweats. I could go to work at the Drinkwaters' as I was, though I hated beginning my earning day without having showered and put on makeup.

I don't like breaks in my routine. My job depends on the clock. Two and a half hours at the Drinkwaters' house, a ten- or fifteen-minute gap, another house; that's my day and my income.

Body Time is in a somewhat isolated position on the bypass that swerves around Shakespeare, allowing speedier access from the south to the university at Montrose. Marshall's gym has a large graveled parking lot and big plate-glass windows at the front, which are covered by Venetian blinds lowered at six on winter afternoons, four in the summer. There was already a car in the parking lot, a battered Camaro. I expected to see some impatient enthusiast waiting in its front seat, but the car was empty. I walked over, cast a cursory look over the car's clean interior. It told me nothing. I shrugged, and crunched across the gravel in the chilly, pale early morning light, fumbling through Marshall's keys. As I sorted through them to find the one marked *FD* for front door, another vehicle pulled up beside mine. Bobo Winthrop, eighteen and chock-full of hormones, emerged from his fully equipped Jeep.

I clean for Bobo's mother Beanie. I have always liked Bobo despite the fact that he is beautiful, smart enough to scrape by, and has everything he has ever expressed a wish for. Somehow Bobo had charmed his way into Marshall's good graces, probably by working out on as demanding a schedule as Marshall himself. When Bobo had decided to start college in nearby Montrose, Marshall had finally agreed to hire the boy to work a few hours a week at Body Time.

Since Bobo isn't hurting for money, I can only figure his job motivation is getting to ogle many women of all ages in form-fitting outfits and getting to see all his friends, who naturally all have memberships in Body Time.

Bobo was running his fingers through his floppy fair hair by way of grooming. He said groggily, 'Whatcha doin', Lily?'

'Trying to find the right key,' I said, with a certain edge to my voice.

'This is it.' A long finger attached to a huge hand nudged one key out of the cluster. Bobo gave a jaw-cracking yawn.

'Thanks.' I put the key in the lock, but as I did I felt the door move a little.

'It's unlocked,' I said, hearing my voice come out sharp. I was now really uneasy. The back of my neck began to prickle.

'Del's already here. That's his car,' Bobo said calmly. 'But he's supposed to lock the front door when he's here by himself. Marshall's gonna be mad.'

The gloom in the big room was pronounced. Shades still closed, all lights off.

'He must be in the tanning bed,' Bobo said, and kept going across the room as I flipped on the central panel of lights with one hand. I reached for the ringing phone with the other.

'Body Time,' I said sharply, my eyes ranging from side to side. Something smelled wrong.

'I was able to get Bobo after you left,' Marshall said weakly. 'He can stay, Lily. I don't want you to miss work. Oops. Gotta . . .' He slammed down the phone.

I'd almost told Marshall something was wrong. But that would have been pointless, worrying him until I found out what was making the skin of my neck crawl.

I'd only switched on the central panel of lights, so the sides of the big room were still dark. Bobo had begun turning on lights and opening doors in the rear of the building. So I was by myself when I noticed the man lying on the bench in the far left corner.

I didn't for one minute think he was asleep, not with the barbell across his neck. His arms were dangling awkwardly, his legs spraddled. There was a stain. There were lots of stains.

I was scrabbling at the switch plate behind me, trying not to take my eyes off that still figure, when Bobo came from the hall that led to Marshall's office, the tanning beds, and the karate and aerobics room.

'Hey, Lily, you like Natural Morning Zap Tea? I didn't see Del, but I found this bag in Marshall's office . . .'

My fingers located the light switch for the left side of the room, and as Bobo looked to see what I was staring at, I flicked it up.

'Aw, shit,' said Bobo. We both stared at what was lying on the bench. We could see it all too clearly now.

Bobo scuttled sideways until he was behind me, looking over the top of my head. He put his hands on my shoulders, more to keep me firmly between him and It than to comfort me. 'Aw. . . shit,' he said again, gulping ominously. Just at that moment, Bobo came down hard on the 'boy' side of eighteen.

I had already encountered two nauseated males and it wasn't even seven o'clock.

'I've got to go check,' I said, 'If you're going to throw up, go outside.'

'Check what? He's dead as a doornail,' said Bobo, his big hands anchoring me firmly on his side of the service counter.

'Who is it, you reckon? Del?' Possibly I was stalling.

'Yeah, from the clothes. That's what Mr Packard was wearing last night.'

'You left him here by himself?' I asked as I began walking over to the body on the bench.

'He was doing chest when I left. He had his own key, to lock up. Marshall had told me that was okay. And Mr Packard said he had a spotter coming,' Bobo said defensively. 'I had a date, and it was closing time.' Bobo's voice got stronger and angrier as he saw he was going to have to justify leaving Del alone in the gym. At least he didn't sound nauseated anymore.

I finally got to the corner. It had been a long journey. Before I got there, I took a deep breath, held it, and bent over to check

Del's wrist. I had never touched Del alive, and I didn't want to do it now that he was dead, but if there was any chance there was a spark of life left . . .

His skin felt strange, rubbery, or it might have been my imagination. The smell was not my imagination, nor was the lack of pulse. To make absolutely sure, I held my big watch in front of Del's nostrils. There were trails of dried blood running from them. I bit my lip hard, forced myself to hold still a moment. When I pulled my arm back to my side, the watch face was clear. I found myself backing up for the first two feet, as if it would be irreverent or dangerous to turn my back on poor Del Packard. I hadn't been scared of him when I'd been able to talk to him. It was absurd to be nervous around him now. But I had to tell myself that several times.

I picked up the phone again and punched in some numbers. I looked up at Bobo while I waited for the ring. He was staring at the body in the corner with a horrified fascination. Perhaps this was the first dead person he'd ever seen. I reached over and patted the back of his big hand, lying on the counter. He turned it over and clutched my fingers.

'Umhum,' rumbled a deep voice at the other end of the line.

'Claude,' I said.

'Lily' he said, warm and relaxed.

'I'm at Body Time.' I gave him a minute to switch gears.

'Okay,' Claude said cautiously. I could hear a creaking of bedsprings as the big policeman sat up in bed.

Maybe if I took this step by step it wouldn't be so bad? I glanced over at the still figure on the bench.

No way to ease up to this. I'd just plunge right in.

'Del Packard is here, and he got squashed,' I said.

I did make it to my first job on time, but I was still in my workout sweats, and still barefaced. So I was uncomfortable, and disinclined to do more than nod by way of greeting Helen and Mel Drinkwater. They weren't chatty people either, and Helen didn't like to see me work; she just liked seeing the results. She'd been giving me hard looks, since September when I'd been sucked into a notorious brawl in the Burger Tycoon parking lot – but she hadn't said anything, and she hadn't fired me.

I'd decided that she'd passed the point of most concern. Her pleasure in a clean house had outweighed her misgivings about my character.

Today the Drinkwaters went out their kitchen door at a pretty sharp clip, each sliding into a car to begin his/her own workday, and I was able to start my usual routine.

Helen Drinkwater doesn't want to pay me to do a total cleaning job on the whole house, which is a turn-of-the-century two-storey. She pays me for two and a half hours, long enough to change the sheets, do the bathrooms and kitchen, dust, gather up the trash, and vacuum. I do a quick pickup first because it makes everything easier. The Drinkwaters are not messy, but their grandchildren live just down the street, and they are. I patrolled the house for scattered toys and put them all in the basket Helen keeps by the fireplace. Then I pulled on rubber gloves and trotted up to the main bathroom, to start scrubbing and dusting my way through the house. No pets, and the Drinkwaters washed and hung up their clothes and did their own dishes. By the time I rewound the cord on the vacuum cleaner, the house was looking very good. I pocketed my check on the way out. Helen always leaves it on the kitchen counter with the salt shaker on top of it, as if some internal wind would blow it away otherwise. This time she'd anchored down a note, too. 'We need to pick a Wednesday for you to do the downstairs windows,' said Helen's spiky handwriting.

Wednesday is the morning I reserve for unusual jobs, like helping with someone's spring cleaning, or doing windows, or occasionally mowing a yard. I looked at the calendar by the phone, picked two Wednesdays that would do, and wrote both dates on the bottom of the note with a question mark.

I deposited the check in the bank on my way home for lunch. Claude was walking up my driveway when I arrived.

Chief of Police Claude Friedrich lives next door to me, in the Shakespeare Garden Apartments. My small house is a little downhill from the apartments, and separated from the tenants' parking lot by a high fence. As I unlocked my front door, I felt Claude's big hand rubbing my shoulder. He likes to touch me, but I have put off any more intimate relationship with the chief; so his touches have to have a locker-room context.

'How was it after I left?' I asked, walking through the living room to the kitchen. Claude was right behind me, and when I turned to look up at him he wrapped his arms around me. I felt the tickle of his mustache against my face as his lips drifted across my cheek to fasten on a more promising target. Claude was my good friend but he wanted to be my lover, too.

'Claude, let me go.'

'Lily, when are you going to let me spend the night?' he asked quietly, no begging or whining in his voice because Claude is not a begging or whining man.

I turned sharply so my face was to the refrigerator. I could feel the muscles in my neck and shoulders tighten. I made myself hold still. Claude's hands dropped to his sides. I got out some leftover dishes and opened the microwave, moving slowly, trying not to show my agitation with jerky gestures.

When the microwave was humming, I turned to face Claude, looking up at his face. Claude is in his midforties, ten years or more older than I, and he has graying brown hair and a permanent tan. After years of working in dark corners of Little Rock and dark places in people's hearts, Claude has a few wrinkles, deep and decisive wrinkles, and a massive calm that must be his way of keeping sane.

'Do you want me?' he asked me now.

I hated being backed into a corner. And there wasn't a simple answer to the question.

He touched my hair with gentle fingers.

'Claude.' I enjoyed saying his name, unlovely as it was. I wanted to lay my hands on each side of his face and return his kiss. I wanted him to walk out and never come back. I wanted him not to want me. I had liked having a friend.

'You know I'm just used to living my own life,' was what I said.

'Is it Sedaka?'

Oh, *hell*. I hated this. Marshall and I had been dating and bedding for months. Under Claude's scrutiny, I grew even more tense. Without my conscious direction, my hand crept under the neck of my sweatshirt, rubbing the scars.

'Don't, Lily.' Claude's voice was gentle, but very firm. 'I know what happened to you, and it doesn't make me feel anything except admiration that you lived through it. If you care about Sedaka I'll never say another word. From my point of view, you and I've been happy in the times we've spent together, and I'd like an extension.'

'And exclusive rights?' I met his eyes steadily. Claude would never share a woman.

'And exclusive rights,' he admitted calmly. 'Till we see how it goes.'

'I'll think,' I forced myself to say. 'Now, let's eat. I have to go back to work.'

Claude eyed me for a long moment, then nodded. He got the tea from the refrigerator and poured us each a glass, put sugar in his, and set the table. I put a bowl of fruit between our places, got out the whole-wheat bread and a cutting board for the reheated meat loaf. As we ate, we were quiet, and I liked that. As Claude was slicing an apple for himself and I was peeling a banana, he broke that comfortable silence.

'We sent Del Packard's body to Little Rock,' he told me.

'What do you think?' I was relieved at the change of topic.

'It's hard to say what might have happened,' Claude rumbled. He had the most comforting voice, like distant thunder.

'Well, he dropped the bar on himself – didn't he?' I hadn't been particularly friendly with Del, but it wasn't bearable to think of him struggling to get the bar back up to the rack, failing, all by himself.

'Why was he there alone, Lily? Sedaka was so sick I couldn't figure out what he was telling me.'

'Del was training for the championships at Marvel Gym in Little Rock.'

'The poster, right?'

I nodded. Taped to one of the many mirrors lining the walls at Body Time, there was a poster giving the specifics of the event, with a picture of last year's winners. 'Del competed last year, in the men's middleweight division, novice class. He came in second.'

'How big a deal is this?'

'To a novice bodybuilder, pretty big. Del had never been in a competition before he got second place at Marvel Gym. If he'd won this year – and Marshall thought he had a chance – Del could've gone on to another competition, and another, until he entered one of the nationals.'

Claude shook his big head in amazement at the prospect. 'Is "posing" like the swimsuit part of Miss America?'

'Yes, but he'd be wearing a lot less. A monokini, like a glorified jockstrap. And he'd have removed his body hair . . .'

Claude looked a little disgusted. 'I wondered about that. I noticed.'

'He'd been working on his tan. And he'd grease up for the competition.'

Claude raised his eyebrows interrogatively.

'I don't know what they use.' I was getting tired of this conversation. But Claude was circling his hand in a gesture that meant 'Amplify'.

'You have a series of poses you go through, to emphasize the muscle groups.' I rose to give Claude a demonstration. I turned my body a little sideways to him, fisted my hand, arched my arms in pumped-up curves. I gave him the blank eyes and small smile that said, 'Look how superior my body is. Don't you wish you were me?'

Claude made a face. 'What's the point?'

'Just like a beauty contest, Claude.' I resumed my seat at the table. 'Except the focus is on muscular development.'

'I saw the poster of last year's winners. That woman was like nothing I've ever seen,' Claude said, wrinkling his nose.

'Marshall wanted me to enter.'

'You'd do that?' he asked, horrified. 'That gal looked like a small pumped-up man with boobs slapped on.'

I shrugged. 'I don't want to spend the time training. It takes months to get ready for a competition. Plus, I'd have to camouflage all the scars, which I think would be impossible. But that was what Del wanted to do, train and compete. Develop himself to his full potential, was the way he put it.' I'd watched Del stare at one of his muscles for a good five minutes, wrapped up in his own reflection to the exclusion of the other people in the gym.

'I think I could have lifted what he had on the bar,' Claude said, a question in his voice. He rinsed off the plates and put them in the dishwasher. 'It came to two hundred ninety pounds.'

I thought Claude was flattering himself, though I didn't say so out loud. Claude seemed to have a fair body, but he did not exercise and hadn't as long as I'd known him. 'Bodybuilding isn't exactly like competitive weight lifting,' I said. 'Training for a competition, some people use somewhat lower weights and lots of reps, rather than really heavy weights and a few reps. That was probably Del's highest weight.'

'Reps?' Claude said cautiously.

'Repetitions.'

'Would he be lifting so much by himself? Del wasn't that big a man.'

'That's what I don't understand,' I admitted, retying my New Balances. 'Del was so careful of himself. He wouldn't risk pulling a muscle or getting any injury this close to the competition. Surely he had a spotter. He told Bobo he was expecting someone.'

'What's a spotter?' demanded Claude.

'A spotter is a buddy,' I said, having to define a term so familiar to me I'd forgotten a time I hadn't known it. 'A workout partner. If you don't have someone to spot for you, you would have to ask whoever was working at the gym . . .' I could tell from Claude's frown that I wasn't being precise. 'It's someone who stands there while you're doing the hardest part of your workout. That person is there to act as your safety net: hand you the weights, or the bar, take them when you've finished your set, cheer you on, grab your wrists if they start to weaken.'

'So you won't drop the weights on yourself.'

'Exactly. And to help you do those last few you need to finish your set.'

'Example.'

'Like if I was doing forty-fives, and that was my top capability or close to it, I'd lie down on the bench holding the dumbbells, and the spotter would stand or kneel at my head, and when I was pushing the weights up, if my arms started to shake, the spotter would grab my wrists and help me keep them steady.'

'Forty-fives?'

'Two forty-five-pound dumbbells. Some people lift using the bar and adding weights, some people use different-weighted dumbbells. I happen to prefer dumbbells. Del liked the bar. He thought he got better chest development.'

Claude looked at me thoughtfully. 'You're telling me you can lift ninety pounds with your hands?'

'No,' I said, surprised.

Claude looked relieved.

'I can lift a hundred ten or a hundred twenty.'

'You.'

'Sure.'

'Isn't that a lot? For a woman?'

'In Shakespeare it is,' I said. 'At one of the bigger city gyms, probably not, You'd have a bigger pool of weight trainers.'

'So how much would a man serious about training be able to do?'

'A man about Del's build, under six feet, about one hundred seventy? After intense training, I guess he'd be able to lift maybe three hundred twenty pounds, more or less. So you can see strength wasn't Del's sole goal, though he was very strong. He wanted exceptional muscular development, for the look of it. I just like to be strong.'

'Hmmm.' Claude thought about the difference. 'So you knew Del?'

'Sure. I saw him almost every morning at Body Time. We weren't particularly friendly.' I was wiping off the table, since I had to go to work in ten minutes.

'Why not?'

I thought about it while I rinsed out the dishrag. I wrung it and folded it neatly and draped it over the divider between my sinks. I stepped across the hall to the bathroom, washed my hands and face, and slapped on a little makeup for my self-respect. Claude leaned against the kitchen doorframe to watch. He was waiting for an answer.

'Just . . . nothing in common. He was from here, had lots of family, dated a hometown girl. He didn't like blacks, he didn't like the Notre Dame football team, he didn't like big words.' That was as close as I could come to explaining.

'You think enjoying living in a small town is wrong?'

I hadn't meant this to be an analysis of my worldview.

'No, not at all. Del was a good guy in some ways.' I looked at my face, put on some lipstick, shrugged at my reflection. Makeup didn't change the face underneath it, but somehow I always felt better when I'd used it. I washed my hands and turned to look at Claude. 'He was harmless.' Right away I wondered what I meant. But I was too taken aback by the expression on Claude's face to think it through right then.

Claude said, 'I'll tell you something strange, Lily. There weren't any fingerprints on that bar where there should have been. There should have been lots, where a man would normally grip the bar. Del's should have been on top. But there weren't any. There were just smears. And you know what, Lily? I don't think you'd put on your makeup in front of me if you had any serious interest in me.'

He stopped at the front door to deliver his parting shot. 'And, I'd like to know, if Del Packard was in the gym by himself, how he turned out the lights after he died.'

It was a day that had started out worst and moved up to merely rotten.

I was cleaning in a spirit of anger, and the results were not harmonious. I dropped papers, got paper cuts when I picked them up, slammed the toilet lid down so hard that a box of Kleenex plummeted from a flimsy rattan shelf in the travel agent's bathroom, vacuumed up a few pushpins at the base of the bulletin board, and developed a full-blown hatred for the poster of a couple on the deck of a cruise ship because they looked so simple. They looked like they could say, 'Gee, we really get along well. Let's go to bed together!' and it would actually work.

I was glad this was my last job of the day. I locked the door behind me with a sigh of relief.

On my way home, I detoured to Marshall's dumpy rented house. He'd offered me a key when we began 'seeing' each other, but I had refused. So he had to stagger to the door to let me in, and stagger right back to the ancient plaid couch he'd scrounged from a friend when he'd separated from his wife. I put his Body Time key ring on the equally dilapidated coffee table, and went to sit on the floor near him. Marshall was sprawled full length and obviously felt lousy. But he wasn't groaning, and his fever was down, I thought as I touched his forehead.

'Can you eat yet?' I asked, not knowing what else I could do for him.

'Maybe some toast,' he said in a pitiful voice that sounded very odd issuing from his extremely muscular throat. Marshall is one-quarter Chinese. He has skin that's just between pink and ivory, and his eyes and hair are dark. His eyes have a bit of a slant, just a hint. Other than that, he's Caucasian, but since he's a martial arts teacher he enjoys emphasizing the Oriental fraction of his heritage.

'Please,' he added, even more pitifully, and I laughed.

'Mean,' he said.

I got up and found his whole-wheat bread and waved a butter knife over it, toasted it dry, and brought it to him with some water.

He sat up and ate every crumb.

'You're going to live.' I took the plate from him and carried it to the sink. I would coddle him to the extent of loading his dish-washer, I decided.

Afterward I returned to sit by the couch. He'd slid down to his original position. He took my hand.

'I guess I will live,' he admitted, 'though for a few hours I didn't want to. And finding out about Del, God! Who would have thought Del would be dumb enough to drop a weight on his neck?'

'I don't think he did.' I told Marshall about the lack of finger-prints on the bar, about the lights that should have been on.

'You think the spotter dropped the bar on Del by accident and then panicked?'

I shrugged.

'Hey, you don't think someone killed Del on purpose? Who would do that?'

'I'm not a doctor, so I don't know if this is possible . . . but if you felt a crushing weight on your neck and you knew you would die if it stayed there, and you were a grown healthy man, wouldn't you fight to heave it off?'

'If I wasn't killed instantly, I'd try as hard as I could,' Marshall said grimly. 'If you're saying someone held the bar down, who would be cruel enough to do that?'

I shrugged again. In my opinion, any number of people had that capacity for cruelty, even if they hadn't discovered it in them-selves yet, and I told Marshall that. I just couldn't understand why anyone would indulge that cruelty by killing harmless, thick-headed Del Packard.

'You're cold sometimes, you know?' Marshall had said that more than once lately. I looked at him sharply. This cold woman had gotten her butt out at six in the morning to open his business.

He went on. 'Maybe Del was seeing someone else's wife – that got Len Elgin killed – or maybe Lindy got mad at his training so much.'

'Del was too self-involved to go to the trouble of sneaking around,' I said. 'And if you think Lindy Roland can lift fifty pounds, let alone close to three hundred, you better find another job.'

'That's right, the one who dropped the weight had to be able to lift it first,' Marshall said thoughtfully. 'Who do we know that can lift that much?'

'Almost anyone we know that works out regularly could lift that. Especially the men. Maybe I could, if I had to.' But I said the last part doubtfully. It would take a mighty surge of adrenaline.

'Yeah, but you wouldn't kill Del.'

I could kill a man – I had killed a man – but I didn't think I could do it unprovoked. I began mentally reviewing the list of regular weight lifters at Body Time.

'I can think of at least twelve and I've only been trying for a minute or two,' I said.

'Me, too,' Marshall said, and sighed. 'Aside from feeling sorry for Del and his folks and Lindy, this isn't going to be good for business.'

'Who's cleaning up the mess?' I asked.

'Would you . . .'

'No.'

'Maybe the cleaning service from Montrose?'

'Phone them,' I said.

He looked at me accusingly. 'You're being cold about this.'

I felt a surge of irritation. There was that accusation again.

Marshall wanted me to yoke myself with him and his interests as though we were a permanent couple.

I wasn't willing.

I shifted my shoulders under my T-shirt, rolling the muscles in an effort to relax. I reminded myself once again that Marshall was ill. I slid my hand from his.

'Marshall,' I said, keeping my voice quiet and even, 'if you wanted warm-fuzzy you came to the wrong woman.'

He laid his head back against his pillow and laughed. I made myself think of his having thrown up all night and some of the morning. I made myself remember an especially good time we'd had in that bed I could glimpse through his open bedroom door. There were several to choose from.

He'd been my sensei, my karate teacher, for four years now. We'd become friends. Then Marshall had left his terror of a wife, Thea. After that we'd shared a bed from time to time, and some good hours of companionship. Marshall was capable of moments of great compassion and sensitivity.

But as our relationship progressed, I'd discovered Marshall expected me to change, and swiftly; expected all my edges to be rounded off by that lust, companionship, compassion, and sensitivity . . . all my peculiarities to be solved by the fact that I had a steady guy.

Since having a steady guy, having Marshall, was nice in many ways, I found myself wishing it worked that way. But it didn't.

As I said a brief good-bye and left for home, I felt gloomy and restless. I'd rebuffed Claude, who was a proud man; now I was considering parting from Marshall. I couldn't read my own signals, but I could tell it was time for a change.

During the week after Del Packard's death, my life went according to routine once more.

I didn't catch the flu.

A woman who specialized in cleaning up crime scenes drove to the gym from Little Rock. She expunged the mess Del's passing had left. The gym reopened and Marshall resumed running it and teaching karate. He rearranged the workout equipment and mixed the bench Del had died on in with the others, so no one could say it was haunted, or try to reenact the crime.

I went to karate class, and I worked out. But I went to my home alone instead of to Marshall's after karate, contrary to my recent practice. Though Marshall looked a little angry and a little hurt as I wished him a good evening, he also looked a little relieved. He didn't ask me to explain myself, which was a pleasant surprise.

I didn't see Claude Friedrich. It took me a couple of days to register that I wasn't running into him and he wasn't dropping in

for lunch, and after that it took me a couple more to decide that
this was by design, his design. I missed Claude's company, but I
didn't miss the pressure of his desire.

And I lost clients. Tom and Jenny O'Hagen, who'd lived next
door to me in the Shakespeare Garden Apartments, moved to
Illinois to manage a larger Bippy's. I wasn't too concerned at the
opening in my schedule. I had a standby list. I began calling. The
first two potential clients fobbed me off with a lame excuse, and I
could feel the worry start somewhere in my gut. Ever since the
Burger Tycoon parking lot fight, I'd been concerned that my
clientele would drop off.

The third family had found another maid, so I crossed them off.
The woman who answered at the fourth number said she and her
husband had decided to get divorced, and she would be doing her
own cleaning. Another X. The fifth name on the list was Mookie
Preston. After puzzling over the entry, I remembered that when
Ms Preston had called me a couple of months before, she'd said
she'd just moved to Shakespeare. When I called her, she sounded
delighted to hear that I could work for her on Friday mornings.
She was renting a house, and she wanted longer than the hour and
a half I'd given the O'Hagen apartment.

'Why don't I work from ten to twelve on Fridays?' I was trying
to imagine why a young single woman would need me for that
long.

'We'll see,' said the rich fruity voice. 'I'm a little messy.'

I'd never laid eyes on Mookie Preston, but she sounded . . .
eccentric. As long as her checks were good, I didn't care if she
raised catfish in the bathtub and wore a Barney the Dinosaur
costume.

When I went to Body Time Thursday morning, I found Bobo
sitting behind the counter to the left of the entrance. He looked as
dispirited as an eighteen-year-old can look. I pitched my gym bag
into an empty plastic cubicle, one of fifteen stacked against the
east wall, after extracting my weight-lifting gloves. They were
looking very shabby, and I knew I'd have to have a new pair soon;
another item for my already tight budget. I began to pull them on,

eyeing Bobo as I circled my wrists with the straps and Velcroed them tightly. Bobo stared back. He was even sitting depressed: shoulders sagging, hands idle on the counter, head sagging on his neck.

'What?' I asked.

'They've questioned me twice now, Lily,' he said.

'Why?'

'I guess the detective thinks I had something to do with Del getting killed.' He took a gulp of a repulsive-looking protein mixture that was the craze among the younger workout crowd. I wouldn't have touched it with a ten-foot pole.

'How come?'

'Del worked for my dad.'

Among his many financial pies, Bobo's father, Howell Winthrop, Jr., owned the local sports/exercise equipment/marine supplies store. Del had worked there, mostly in the exercise equipment and exercise clothing department, though he'd had to know enough about hunting and fishing to sell all the other products Winthrop Sporting Goods carried. Del himself had told me all about it at excruciating length when I'd been buying my punching bag.

'So do a lot of people in town,' I observed.

Bobo looked at me blankly.

'Work for your dad.'

Bobo grinned. It was like the sun coming out from behind a cloud. He was really a lovely boy.

'Yeah, but Mr Jinks seems to think that I decided Del knew something that would ruin Dad's business, so either I thought of killing him or Dad told me to.'

'Because you were the last one to see him here?' Dedford Jinks is a detective on the little Shakespeare police force.

Bobo nodded. 'Someone told the chief, who told Mr Jinks, that when people didn't bring their own spotters, they asked the staff to spot for them. Which, naturally, would be me.' He silently held out his plastic cup of goop. With a shudder, I shook my head.

I struggled with my guilt. It was I who had mentioned to

Claude that sometimes a member of the staff was asked to fill in as spotter.

'I didn't know Mr Packard very well.' said the golden boy. 'But really, I don't think he could have found out anything illegal my dad was doing. This may not be respectful, especially now that Mr Packard's dead, but I never thought he was that smart, and if he knew something Dad was doing that was wrong, I think he'd just feel like he didn't really understand. Or he'd go talk to Dad about it.'

I thought Bobo was exactly right.

'You look nice, Lily,' Bobo said, changing the subject so abruptly that it took a minute for his words to sink in.

'Oh. Thanks.' I was wearing a teal-colored T-shirt and sweat-pants, new and unstained but strictly Wal-Mart.

'Why don't you wear something like that?' Bobo pointed to the sportswear rack that Marshall kept stocked with expensive exer-cise clothing. The garment that had caught Bobo's eye was pale pink and blue swirled in a tie-dye pattern, cut low over the boobs and high in the legs, meant to be worn over coordinating tights.

I snorted. 'Right.'

'You'd look pretty. You've got the body for it,' he said self-consciously. 'I'd like to watch your back when you're doing lat pull-downs.'

'Thank you,' I said stiffly. 'But stuff like that just isn't my style.'

I went over to say hello to Raphael. He'd recovered from his flu, but he had something on his mind. His greeting was not the usual happy roar.

'What?'

'You askin' me what?' he said, rubbing the back of his head. Raphael kept his hair clipped so short that the passage of his mahogany hand made no change in the tight black curls. 'I tell you what, Lily.' His voice got louder than it should have been, and I knew immediately that I had spoken to him at the wrong moment.

'You're a good woman, Lily, but this place is not friendly to blacks.'

'Marshall—' I began. I was about to say Marshall was not a racist or some such thing, but I got interrupted.

'I know Marshall is not a bigot. But there are too many others here who are. I can't come to a place where I'm not welcome as a black man.'

I'd never heard Raphael speak so seriously and angrily in the four years I'd known him. He was glaring at two men who were working out together on the other side of the room. They paused, stared at him for a minute, then went back to their activity. One of them was Darcy Orchard, a massively built man with long, thinning beige hair and acne-scarred cheeks, a broad Slavic face and legs like trees. I didn't know the other man.

As I was trying to think what to say to Raphael, he just picked up his gym bag and walked out. I looked over at Darcy. He had his back turned, and his companion was lifting the bar. Everyone in the gym seemed to be looking somewhere else.

As I worked my way through my routine (today was legs and shoulders day) I tried not to brood about the little incident. I hated to think I might feel obliged to quit the gym, too. It meant so much to me, the daily workout. If I had to, could I buy my own gym equipment? No, not on my budget, not having already paid my annual fee here. I had to save so much each month, against the rainy day that would surely come. I already suspected Marshall discounted my Body Time membership.

Other users of the gym trickled in and began their workout after waving a hand or calling hello to each other and to me. This was the only group of which I could call myself a member, except for my karate class. Until a few minutes ago, Raphael had been one of us. This fellowship of sweat had a wildly fluctuating membership as people made resolutions and broke them, lasting on an average three weeks into their exercise program. There was a hard-core group of members like me who came nearly every day, and we had gradually gotten to know each other. More or less.

Del Packard had been one of this group.

All the regulars except Del were here today: Janet Shook, who was also in my karate class, a short chunky woman with dark brown hair and eyes who'd had a crush on Marshall ever since I'd met her; Brian Gruber, silver-haired and attractive, the president of a mattress manufacturing plant; Jerri Sizemore, former wife of Dr John Sizemore, a local dentist; and Darcy Orchard, who worked at the sporting goods store, as Del had. Darcy usually worked out with Jim Box, another store employee, but today Jim was absent – probably home with the flu; he'd been sneezing yesterday. I wondered who Darcy's new partner was. Eventually Darcy's companion, whom I dimly recognized as someone I'd seen around the Shakespeare Garden Apartments, left. But Darcy lingered on.

Darcy was on the calf extension machine, which was my next station, so I watched as he did his second set. He had the pin pushed in at the two-hundred-pound mark, and as I waited he adjusted the shoulder pressure. Darcy, who was about six feet tall, had the rippling pectorals and ridged biceps of a workout fanatic. I thought there might be an ounce of subcutaneous fat on his body. He was wearing one of the ripped-up sweatshirts – arms chopped off, neck binding torn out – that were the mark of the committed, and his sweatpants were probably the same ones he'd worn in high school.

'Be through in a minute,' he panted, doing a set of twelve. He stepped down and walked around for a minute, relaxing the calf muscles that were taking such a beating. Darcy gathered himself, moved the pin down two more notches to add forty more pounds to his load, and stepped up on the narrow bar, his toes bearing his weight. Down went his heels, then up, for twelve more reps. 'Ow!' he said, getting off. 'Ow!' Staring at the floor with a scowl, Darcy relaxed the protesting muscles in his legs. 'Let me just burn out now,' he said, and moved the pin up to a more reasonable weight. He stepped back on the ledge and did twenty-four reps very rapidly, until the grimace of concentration on his face became a rictus of pain.

All together this took only minutes, and I was glad of the rest.

'How you doing, Lily?' Darcy asked, walking in place to work off the strain. He grabbed up a beige towel and patted his acne-pitted cheeks with it.

'Fine.' I wondered if he'd say anything about Raphael's exit. But Darcy had something else on his mind.

'Hear you found ole Del.' His small brown eyes scanned my face.

'Yeah.'

'Del was a good guy,' Darcy said slowly. It was a kind of elegy. 'Del was always smiling. That guy that was here with me a minute ago, that's the guy Howell hired to replace him. He's a big change.'

'Local fella?' I asked politely, as I adjusted the shoulder bars down for my five feet, five inches.

'Nope, from Little Rock, I think. He's one tough son of a bitch, 'scuse my language.'

I moved the pin up to eighty pounds. I stepped onto a narrow ledge, came up under the padded shoulder bars to take the weight, and dropped my heels down. I pushed up twenty times, very quick reps.

I stepped down to walk it off and shift the pin to a higher weight.

'You dating anybody now, Lily? I heard you and Marshall weren't such an item anymore.'

I looked up in surprise. Darcy was still there. Though Darcy had a wonderful body, it was the only thing about him that I found remotely interesting, and that wasn't enough basis for an evening together. Darcy's conversation bored me, and something about him made me wary. I never ignore feelings like that.

'I don't want to,' I said.

He smiled a little, like someone who was sure he'd misunderstood. 'Don't want to . . . ?' he asked.

'Date anyone.'

'Whoa, Lily! A fine woman like you doesn't want a man to take her out?'

'As of now, right.' I stepped up, took the hundred pounds on my shoulders, and did another set of twenty. The last five were something of a challenge.

'How come? You like women instead?' Darcy was sneering, as though he felt obliged to look contemptuous when lesbianism was mentioned.

'No. I'm going to finish here now.'

Darcy smiled again, even more uncertainly, though I'd been as civil as I was able. He couldn't seem to believe that any woman wouldn't want to date; specifically, date him. But after a moment of waiting for me to take back my dismissal, he stalked over to the Roman chair, his narrow lips pressed together firmly in anger.

As I moved the pin to one hundred twenty pounds, once again I wondered whom Del might have asked to spot for him. Del would have trusted anyone in the room. Even Janet and I were just about strong enough to help him with some of the lower (but still formidable) weights that Del used for his bodybuilding. Janet was nearly as strong as I in the chest and arms, and had an edge on me in the legs since she taught two aerobics classes a day in addition to working at the Kids' Clubs, which provided community-sponsored after-school care for kids.

After I finished my calf workout, I drifted over to Janet, who was doing abdominal crunches. Sweat had darkened her short brown hair to a black fringe around her square little face.

'One hundred ten,' she gasped, as I stood over her. I nodded, and waited.

'One twenty-five,' she said after a moment, relaxing in a heap. Her eyes shut.

'Janet,' I said, after a respectful moment of silence.

'Umm?'

'Del ever ask you to spot for him?'

Janet's brown eyes flew open. They fixed on my face with some amusement. 'Him? He didn't think a woman could carry her own groceries, much less spot for him.'

'He'd seen female bodybuilders at those competitions. For that matter, he'd watched us work out many a morning.'

Janet made a rude noise. 'Yeah, but we're freaks to him,' she said, resentment in her voice. 'Well, we were,' she amended, more neutrally. 'He judged all women by that Lindy he went with, and Lindy couldn't cut a ham without an electric knife.'

I laughed.

Janet looked up at me with some surprise. 'That's good to hear, you laughing. You don't do that too much' she observed.

I shrugged.

'Now that you're over here,' she said, sitting up and patting her face with her towel, 'I've been wanting to ask you something.'

I sat on the closest bench and waited.

'Are you and Marshall a locked-in thing?'

I'd been expecting Janet to ask me to spot her, or to go over the fine points of the latest kata we'd learned in karate class.

Everyone wanted to know about my love life today.

I kind of liked Janet, so answering her would be harder than answering Darcy. Saying no meant Marshall was open game for any woman who wanted a shot at him; I was abdicating all claim to him. Saying yes committed me to Marshall for the foreseeable future.

'No,' I said, and went to do my last set.

On her way to the changing room, Janet stopped. 'Are you mad at me?' she asked.

I was a little surprised. 'No,' I said.

But I was really surprised when Janet laughed.

'Oh, Lily,' she said, shaking her head from side to side. 'You're so weird.' She said that as if being 'weird' was a cute little personality quirk of mine, like insisting my panties match my shoes or always wearing green on Mondays.

I left Body Time, vaguely dissatisfied with my workout session. I'd had my first personal conversation with Darcy Orchard, and I hoped it would be my last. I had confirmed that Janet Shook lusted after Marshall Sedaka; not exactly stop-the-press news. I had confirmed that Del almost certainly wouldn't have asked a woman to spot for him. And I'd found out that Raphael felt he was getting a cold reception at a business he'd paid to patronize.

As I drove home, I tried to trace the reason for my dissatisfaction. Why did I think I should have gotten more out of the morning than a good workout? After all, it was as little my business what had happened in Body Time the night Del died as it was Janet's business whether or not Marshall and I were committed to each other.

I hadn't particularly liked Del. Why did I care whether he'd died accidentally or on purpose?

I'd told Claude that Del had been harmless. As I showered, for the first time I really considered Del Packard.

He hadn't made any of the jocular comments about my strength I occasionally got from other men. Del had been mildly pleased to see me when I was in front of him, hadn't missed me when I was gone, would have been glad to help me do anything I'd have asked him to help me with, was overwhelmingly proud of being Shakespeare's champion, would cheerfully have gone on doing his Del Packard thing the rest of his life . . . if his life had been allowed to run its natural course.

He loved his mama and daddy, sent his girlfriend Lindy flowers, performed his job adequately, and went his own way without bothering a soul. All he'd wanted with any passion was to be a champion again, this time a number-one champion.

If Del's spotter had killed Del through carelessness, he should come forward. If he had murdered Del out of malice, that, too, should be paid for.

I toweled my hair dry and put on my makeup, still turning over the questions about Del's death to discover the source of my feeling I had a personal stake in the answers.

The police were working to discover how Del had met his death, and that should be enough to satisfy me. I certainly hadn't felt any urge to seek personal knowledge after the beating death of Darnell Glass early in the fall, or the shooting of Len Elgin weeks afterward, both of which cases remained unsolved.

An answer came to me as I was getting in the car to go to my first job. I cared about Del's death for two more reasons. Firstly, Bobo Winthrop was implicated, partly because of something I'd told Claude. Secondly, I was upset because Del had been killed *in the gym*, one of the few places I felt at home. So I cared about Del's death, and I cared about payment for it.

Chapter Two

As the plain days passed, I missed Claude more and more.

He'd taken care of me a few months before when I'd been hurt. He'd helped me take a sink bath, he'd helped me dress, he'd helped me get back in bed. It had seemed quite natural to put on my makeup in front of him, an act he'd construed as indicating a lack of interest in him as a man.

I'd figured he'd seen the worst. The makeup had not been for him, but for the rest of the world.

The only true thing I found hiding in my psyche was that I missed Claude, missed his dropping over to share my lunch, missed his occasional appearance at my doorstep with Chinese takeout or a video he'd rented.

And another true thing was that I didn't miss a dating relationship with Marshall. In fact, it felt good to slip back into comradeship and the teacher/student relationship we'd shared before. I found that disturbing.

I'd seen Del Packard's sweetheart, Lindy Roland, on the street today. Lindy was a strapping girl, with big brown hair and a ready smile. But when I'd seen her, Lindy's eyes had been red and her whole body seemed to sag. At Del's funeral, according to the grapevine at Body Time, Lindy had gone to pieces. Now, there was Del, under the ground at Sweet Rest Cemetery, and here was Lindy, alone and lonely.

After my solitary supper that night, after the dishes were washed and everything neat, I paced the house.

I took another shower and washed off all my makeup. I made sure I was shaved smooth and my eyebrows were plucked, and I put on all the usual lotions and a tiny dab of perfume.

I stood in my bedroom, naked and irresolute. I looked in my

closet, knowing before I looked what I would see: blue jeans, T-shirts, sweats. A couple of dresses and a suit from my former life. Even thinking about a seduction seemed incredibly stupid as I saw how ill-equipped I was for one.

Suddenly I jettisoned the idea. It felt wrong. Claude deserved someone more – malleable, someone with a silk teddy and a Sunday dress.

I valued control over my life more than anything. With Marshall, and now with Claude, I was not willing to relinquish that control, to bind my life to either of theirs. Neither of them was necessary enough to me for me to take that frightening leap. This was a bitter acknowledgment.

Angry at myself, at Claude, I pulled on dark clothes and went out to walk. I wouldn't sleep much tonight. The light in Claude's window was on, a glance up at his apartment told me. If I'd found it in myself, I would be up there sharing that light with him, and he would be happy . . . at least for a little while.

I drifted through Shakespeare, merging with the night. In a while, I began to feel the chill and the wet. After shivering in my jacket for a few blocks, I was on my way home when I saw I had company.

On the other side of the street, walking as silently and darkly as I, went a man I didn't know, a man with long black hair. In the silence we turned our heads to look at each other. Neither of us smiled or spoke. I was not frightened or angry. In seconds we were past each other, continuing on our ways in the chilly sodden night. I'd seen him before, I reflected; where? It came to me that he was the man who'd been working out with Darcy Orchard the day Jim Box had been out with the flu.

I went home to work out with my punching bag, which hangs from the ceiling in the middle of my empty extra bedroom. I kicked kogen geri, a snapping kick, until my instep burned. Then mae geri, the thrusting kick, until my legs ached. Then I just punched the bag, over and over, making it swing; no art, just power expended.

I slumped down to the floor and dried my face with the pink towel I kept hanging from a hook by the door.

Now, after I showered, I would probably sleep.

As I pulled up my covers and turned on my right side, I wondered where the man was, what he was doing, why he had been walking the night.

I felt too draggy to go to Body Time the next morning, even though I was due to do chest and biceps, my favorites. I forced myself to do fifty pushups and leg lifts as compensation. While I was on the floor, I had to notice that my baseboards needed dusting, and after I patted my face with the pink towel, I used it to do the job. I pitched the towel in the wash basket and went through my usual morning preparation.

My first job on Fridays was Deedra Dean's apartment in the building right next door, which coincidentally was upstairs by Chief of Police Claude Friedrich's. At the request of a local lawyer who represented the estate of Pardon Albee, I had been cleaning the public parts of the apartment building until Pardon's heir made some other arrangement. So I noticed all the mud the tenants had tracked in after the recent rain, and decided I'd have to work in an extra vacuuming before its regular late-Saturday cleaning. Unclipping my work keys from my belt, I went up the stairs quickly.

But Deedra's dead bolt was on. She was still home. She'd be late for work again. I pocketed my key and knocked. There was a kind of scuffling noise on the other side of the door, then a sharp exchange between Deedra and someone else, an exchange I couldn't decipher.

I went on alert. Not because Deedra had company; that was no surprise. Deedra believes in the joy of indiscriminate giving. But scuffling, harsh words, these weren't things she was used to. As Deedra yanked open the door and stepped back, I saw that her guest was her stepfather, Jerrell Knopp. Jerrell had married 'up' when he wed the widowed, well-to-do Lacey Dean. Jerrell was attractive – lean, gray-haired, with dazzling blue eyes – and he treated his wife with courtesy and tenderness, if the little inter-action I'd observed was the norm. But Jerrell had a mean side, and Deedra was bearing the brunt of it now. She had a bright red mark on her arm as if Jerrell had been holding her with a squeezing grip. He wasn't too pleased she'd let me in. Tough.

'The chief is right on the other side of this wall,' I lied. Claude was sure to be at work by now. 'He can be here in a split second.' I looked from the red mark to Jerrell. I'd cross him if I had to, but I didn't look forward to it.

'This here's a family talk, Lily Bard. You just butt out,' Jerrell said, very firmly. I thought it would make me feel pretty good to hit him.

'This is Deedra's apartment. I think she gets some say in who stays and who goes.' I was always hoping Deedra would show some backbone – or some sense – and I was always disappointed. This morning was no exception.

'You better start in my bedroom,' Deedra said in a small voice. There were tears on her face. 'I'll be all right, Lily.'

I gave her stepfather a warning look and carried my caddy of cleaning materials into Deedra's bedroom. It had a dismal view of the parking lot, and beyond that the embankment and the railroad track, and a bit of the Winthrop lumber-and-hardware business that backed onto the other side of the track. The most interesting thing about the view this morning was Deedra's beautiful red Taurus in the parking lot, halfway out of its stall. Someone had taken a can of white spray paint and carefully scripted, *'She fucks niggers'* on the hood.

I felt sick and old.

Deedra had apparently pulled out of her parking spot before she saw the writing. Then, I supposed, she'd run inside to call Mom, but Stepdad had come instead.

A tide of rage and fear rolled over me. My primary rage was directed at the bastards who'd ruined Deedra's car, and most likely her life. The story would be all over town in no time, and there wouldn't be any discreet lid on it, like there was on Deedra's bad reputation.

And then, less to my credit, I was angry with Deedra. She *had* been sleeping – from time to time – with Marcus Jefferson, who also lived in the apartment building, across the hall from Claude. And she'd told me it wasn't for any noble reason, such as love, or even a bizarre reason, such as a desire to cement race relations. She was screwing him for the fun of it.

You couldn't do that in Shakespeare unless you stood willing to pay the price. Deedra had received the bill.

I pointedly crossed through the living room a couple of times as Jerrell and Deedra continued their encounter. I couldn't call it a dialogue, since what one said made no difference to what the other responded. Jerrell was bawling Deedra out, up one side and down the other, for dragging herself (and her mother) through the mud, for polluting herself, for exposing all of them to the glare of gossip and the threat of danger.

'You know what happened to that black boy not two months ago?' Jerrell said hoarsely. 'You want something like that to happen to you? Or to that man you're going to bed with?'

I was polishing the mirror over Deedra's nine-drawer dresser when Jerrell said that, and I saw my reflection in the mirror. I looked sick. He was referring to Darnell Glass, who'd been beaten to death by person or persons unknown. I'd known Darnell Glass.

'But, Jerrell, I didn't do it!' Deedra persisted in stonewalling. 'I don't know where anyone would get that idea!'

'Girl, everyone but your mother knows you're just a whore that don't take money,' Jerrell said brutally. 'Lacey would kill herself if she knew black hands had been on your body.'

I made a face into the mirror as I dusted the top of the dresser. I dropped a pair of earrings into Deedra's earring box.

'I didn't do it!' Deedra moaned.

Childlike in many ways, Deedra believed that if you denied something often enough, it actually hadn't happened. 'Deedra, unless you change your ways right now, I mean this minute, worse things than that paint job are going to happen to you, and I won't be able to stop them from happening,' Jerrell said.

'What do you mean?' Deedra asked, sobbing. 'What could be worse?'

Childlike and stupid.

'There's lots worse things than a little bit of white paint,' Jerrell said grimly, but with a somewhat milder voice. 'There's people in this town that take a situation like yours so seriously, you wouldn't believe it.'

He was threatening her.

Contrarily enough, I was all for it. As much as I now found I disliked Jerrell Knopp, any method that would scare Deedra into dropping her risky lifestyle was okay with me. The woman (and she was a woman in her twenties, though she often seemed much younger) would either contract HIV or another disease, or bring home someone who would brutalize her, if she didn't alter her ways.

'Now,' Jerrell was winding down, 'I've already called the car place to get your paint redone. Just drive it down there. Donnie'll give you a lift to work, I'll drop by to take you home, and your car'll be done in a couple of days.'

'I can't drive it down there,' Deedra whined. 'I'd die.'

'You may die if you don't stay away from black men,' he said, and there was stark warning in his voice. Jerrell wasn't just theorizing. He knew something.

I felt the hair on my neck stand up. I stepped into the living room, my dust cloth in my hand. Jerrell and I had a good ole look at each other.

'Would you drive my car to the paint shop?' Deedra asked, that little-girl look on her face that said she knew she was asking a lot, but it would be too much for *her* to do that thing.

'No,' I said briefly, and went back to work.

I don't know how Deedra and Jerrell settled it. I buckled down to cleaning, thinking hard thoughts about everyone involved, including Marcus Jefferson. I was willing to bet Marcus was running scared by now. He worked at the same factory as Jerrell Knopp, and if he hadn't seen Deedra's car when he left for work that morning, someone at the factory would let him know about it. I figured Marcus was going to be anxious, if not out-and-out terrified.

My oldest client, Marie Hofstettler, had told me it had been seven decades since Shakespeare had suffered a racially motivated lynching. If I'd been Marcus Jefferson, those seven decades would have seemed like yesterday.

Deedra and Jerrell cleared out without speaking to me, which was just fine. I finished my work in peace, or in the little peace they'd left behind them. The apartment still echoed with various gradations of anger and fear. It seemed to me that currents of bad feeling were drifting like smog through Shakespeare. My little adopted town had generally been quiet and predictable and pokey. I liked it like that. I loaded my arsenal of cleaning aids back into my car, trying to stave away a gnawing worry.

My new client, Mookie Preston, was next on my schedule, and I was able to feel a little more cheerful as I drove to her house.

I'd never worked on Sycamore Street before. It was lined with small white houses with neatly raked yards, in a neighborhood that had sprung up in the fifties, a neighborhood generally considered a starting-out point for newly-weds or an ending-up point for seniors.

The house Mookie Preston rented was in the middle of the block and indistinguishable from the others. A green Toyota was parked in the driveway. It had an Illinois plate. If the car was any indicator of the condition of the house, Mookie Preston needed me. Badly. The Toyota was dusty and mud-streaked on the outside and littered with papers and fast-food debris on the inside.

I knocked briskly on the back door, and the same rich, fruity voice I'd heard on the phone called, 'Coming, coming!'

After a minute or so the back door opened and the woman on the other side of the screen door stood staring at me. She didn't speak. We examined each other.

Mookie Preston was younger than me, putting her somewhere in her midtwenties. She had very coarse, straight reddish hair skinned back into a ponytail, golden freckled skin, and big, dark brown eyes. Her face was round, and her teeth were perfect and white. If she was wearing any makeup, I couldn't see it.

And despite the fact that she was pretty, very pretty, and smiling in the friendliest way possible, this woman had thrown me off balance.

If her fading smile was any indication, she was feeling the same way about me.

'You're Lily Bard?' she said cautiously.

'I am.'

Slowly, she pushed open the screen door. She extended a plump golden hand. I shook it.

She stepped aside and I went in the house.

She began dithering around the filthy little kitchen. 'I should have been expecting you but I got caught up in my work,' she said over her shoulder, stacking plates by the sink in an effort to pretend she'd actually been engaged in doing so when I knocked.

'What do you do?'

'I'm a genealogist,' she said, her face turned away, which I thought was a lucky thing.

'Umm,' I said, which was the most noncommittal noise I could manage. 'You don't have to clean up for me. I'm the cleaning woman.'

She looked down at the plate in her hand as if she hadn't realized what she was doing, and very carefully deposited it on the drain board. 'Right.'

'What did you want me to do?' I asked.

'Okay.' That calmed her, as I'd intended. 'I want you to change my sheets – the clean ones are in the bathroom closet – and dust the house, and vacuum. There's only one bathroom, and it's in pretty bad shape. Clean the sink and tub, and wipe the kitchen counters. Mop the linoleum floors.'

'Okay. Anything else?'

'Not that I can think of right now.'

We discussed my pay, and my hours. She thought the house might take me until twelve-thirty to get in shape, and if the kitchen was any indication I agreed it would. I got to the

Winthrops' at one, usually, so that didn't leave me much leeway. I figured I could stop by my house and grab a piece of fruit on my way to the Winthrops'.

I examined the house first, to plan my work. Mookie had retreated to the living room at the front of the house, which she had turned into a workroom. There was an old couch, an old chair, an old television, and a huge desk. She hadn't hung any curtains, and the blinds on the big windows were coated with dust. The wastebasket was overflowing, and cups from various fast-food places dotted the desk, the arm of the couch, the floor. I kept my face blank. I've learned to do that.

As Mookie sat down at her computer, I wandered down the hall (filthy baseboards, fingerprints on the paint) to the bigger bedroom. I wrinkled my nose. The sheets certainly did need changing, and the bed had probably never been made since the sheets had been put on. There was a thick layer of dust on every surface – every surface that wasn't already covered with something else, like paperbacks, makeup, snack wrappers, tissues, jewelry, hairbows and brushes, receipts. I could feel that little contraction between my brows that meant I was perturbed. Then I examined the bathroom, and I shook my head in disbelief.

The second bedroom was almost empty, only luggage and a few boxes strewn about the floor . . . at random.

Now I wondered if the allotted time would be enough.

I went out to my car to get my supplies, wondering how far I could get. I'd start with the bathroom, for sure . . . then the bedroom.

Cleaning is work that doesn't occupy your whole mind, which is something I occasionally enjoy. I was half-smiling to myself as I began scrubbing the bathtub. I'd expected Mookie Preston to be completely white, and she'd expected me to be black. We'd both been astonished.

In a better world, we wouldn't have even noticed that we were of different races – maybe if we'd even met each other in a big city, we would just have celebrated our ethnic diversity. But it wasn't a better world, at least not here and now. Not in Shake-speare. Not lately.

My astonishment about my new employer faded as I con-centrated on the task at hand. After some determined scrubbing and mopping, I had the bathroom looking very respectable. I gave it a sharp nod and turned to start work in the bedroom. To my surprise, Mookie Preston was standing right behind me.

'I'm sorry I startled you,' she said, looking rather shocked herself as my hands fisted.

I relaxed with an effort. 'I didn't hear you,' I admitted, not happy at all about that.

'It looks great,' she said, looking past me into the small room. 'Wow, the mirror especially.'

Yeah, you could see your reflection now. 'Good,' I said.

'Listen, are you put off by my being mixed race?'

'What you are is none of my business.' Why did people always want to talk about every little thing? Even before a gang had held me down and drawn pictures on my chest with a knife, I hadn't been one for chatter.

'I didn't know you were going to be white.'

'Yeah.'

'So, can we make this work?' she persisted.

'I am working,' I said, trying to make a point, and began to strip the sheets off her bed. What I wanted Mookie Preston to get out of this was that if I'd seriously objected to her parentage, I would've hopped back in my Skylark and gone home to try the next name on my standby list.

Whether she got the point or not, I don't know. After waiting for me to say something else, she drifted back to her computer, to my relief.

She left once, to go to the grocery store. Other than that one period of peace, my new employer was in constant motion, jumping up to go to the toilet, drifting down the hall to get a drink from the refrigerator, always making some passing remark. Apparently, Mookie Preston was one of those people who can't be still when someone else is working. When she told me for the third time she was leaving for the grocery, I decided it would be a good opportunity to clean the office area without her hovering presence.

At a closer examination of the nearly bare, dusty room, I realized the strips of paper fixed to the walls were genealogical charts. Some of them were printed really fancy with Gothic lettering, and some of them were dull-looking computer readouts. I shrugged. Not my thing, but harmless. There were a few books arranged on the old student standby of boards and cement blocks; three of them were about a woman named Sally Hemmings. I'd have to look her up at the library. There were stacks of software boxes, bearing titles like *Family Tree Maker* and *Family Origins*. I saw a list of Web sites taped beside the computer, and a list of phone numbers to places like the Family History Library and the Hidden Child Foundation.

But the more I dusted and straightened and vacuumed, the more questions I had about this woman. She'd been living here for at least five weeks, if she'd called me to get on my list right after she'd moved into this house. Why would a young woman like Mookie Preston move to a small southern town if she had no friends or relations in place here? If Mookie Preston was only a genealogical researcher, I was a sweet young thing.

She was gone a long time, which was fine with me. By the time she was toting in her plastic bags of Diet Pepsi and Healthy Choice microwave meals, I had the house looking much better. It would take a couple more sessions to finish clearing up the backlog of dirt and scrub down to a regular weekly accumulation, but I'd made a fighting start.

She looked around with her mouth a little open, stiff reddish hair brushing her shoulders as her head turned.

'This is really great,' she said, and she meant it, but she wasn't as enthusiastic about cleanliness as she was pretending to be. 'Can you come every week?'

I nodded.

'How do you prefer to be paid?' she asked, and we talked about that for a while.

'You work for a lot of the local upper crust, I bet?' she asked me, just when I thought she had about finished chattering. 'Like the Winthrops, and the Elgins?'

I regarded her steadily. 'I work for lots of different kinds of people,' I said. I turned to go, and this time Mookie Preston didn't detain me.

As I was assembling cheese, crackers, and fruit for a quick lunch in my own – thank God, spotless and silent – kitchen, the doorbell rang. I glanced out my living room window before answering the door. A pink van was parked in my driveway, with FANCY FLOWERS painted on the side.

It was surely the first time that particular vehicle had been to my place.

I opened the door, ready to tell the delivery person that she needed the apartment building next door, and the perky young woman on my doorstep said, 'Miss Bard?'

'Yes?'

'These are for you.'

'These' were a beautiful arrangement of pink roses, baby's breath, greenery, and white carnations.

'Are you sure?' I said doubtfully.

' "Lily Bard, Ten Track Street," ' the woman read from the back of the envelope, her smile fading a bit.

'Thank you.' I took the bowl and turned away, shutting the door behind me with one foot. I hadn't gotten flowers in . . . well, I just couldn't remember. Carefully, I set the bowl on my kitchen table and pulled the gift envelope out of the prolonged plastic holder. I noticed it had been licked and shut rather carefully, and after I extracted the card and read it, I appreciated the discretion. '*I miss you. Claude*', it read, in a slanted, sprawling hand.

I searched inside myself for a reaction and found I had no idea how to feel. I touched a pink rose with one fingertip. Though I wear plastic gloves when I work, my hands still get rough, and I was anxious I would damage the delicate smoothness of the flower. Next I touched a white ball of baby's breath. I slowly positioned the bowl in the exact middle of the table, and reached up a hand to wipe my cheeks.

I fought an impulse to call the florist and send some flowers right back to him, to show him how he'd touched me. But Claude wanted this to be a purely masculine gesture, and I would let it be.

When I left to bring order into the Winthrops' chaos, I could feel a faint smile on my face.

Luck continued with me – up to a point – that afternoon. Since the weather was clear, I parked in front of the Winthrop house on the street. I only used the garage when it was snowing or raining, because my car had an apparently incurable oil leak and I didn't want to spot the immaculate Winthrop garage floor. I'd driven by the garage, which opened onto a side street, and seen it was empty. Good. None of the Winthrops were home.

Beanie, a lean, attractive woman somewhere in her midforties, was likely to be playing tennis or doing volunteer work. Howell Winthrop, Jr., would be at Winthrop Sporting Goods or Winthrop Lumber and Home Supply, or even at Winthrop Oil. Amber Jean and Howell Three (that was what the family called him) were in junior high and high school. Bobo was at work at Body Time, or attending classes in the U of A extension thirty-five minutes away in Montrose. Though the Winthrops were very wealthy, no Winthrop child would consider going anywhere but the University of Arkansas, and my only surprise was that Bobo was going to the Montrose campus rather than the mother ship up north in Fayetteville. The razorback hog, symbol of the University of Arkansas, featured prominently in the Winthrops' design scheme.

On Fridays, I dusted, mopped, and vacuumed. I'd already done the laundry, ironing, and bathrooms on my first visit of the week on Tuesday morning. The Winthrop kids had gotten pretty good about washing any clothing item they just had to have between my visits, but they'd never learned to pick up their rooms properly. Beanie was pretty neat with her things, and Howell wasn't home enough to make a mess.

I paused in my dusting to examine the portrait of Beanie and Howell Jr. that had been their most recent anniversary present to each other. I could count on the fingers of one hand the number of times I'd seen Howell at home during the three years I'd worked for the family. He was balding, pleasantly good-looking, and perhaps twenty pounds over-weight. The artist had concealed that nicely. Howell was the same age as his wife, but not working quite as hard at concealing it. He spent a lot of time at the even more impressive home of his parents, Howell Sr. and Arnita, the uncrowned king and queen of Shakespeare. Howell Sr., though nominally retired, still had a say in every Winthrop enterprise, and the Seniors still led a very active role in the social and political life of the town. *They* had a full-time black housemaid, Callie Gandy.

As if thinking of Howell Jr. had conjured him up, I heard a key in the lock and he came in from the carport. Following behind him was the man who'd been out walking last night.

Now that I saw him in the daylight, I was sure he was also the man who'd been working out with Darcy Orchard the day Raphael had left Body Time.

The two men were each carrying a long, heavy black bag with a shoulder strap.

Howell stopped in his tracks. His face reddened, and he was obviously flustered.

'I'm sorry to disturb you at your work,' he said. 'I didn't see your car.'

'I parked in front.' Howell must have pulled into the garage from the side street.

'We won't get in your way,' he said.

My eyes narrowed. 'Okay,' I said cautiously. It was his house.

I looked past Howell at his companion. I was close enough to see his eyes. They were hazel. He was wearing a poly-filled vest, deep green, with a Winthrop Sporting Goods sweatshirt under it. The Winthrop sweats and tees, worn by all employees, were dark red with gold and white lettering. The man was eyeing me as intently as I was looking at him.

He didn't look like I would expect a friend of Howell's to look.

This man was far too dangerous. I recognized that, but I also knew that I was not afraid of him, I nearly forgot Howell was there until he cleared his throat, said, 'Well, we'll be . . .' and walked into the living room to cross to his study. With a backward glance, the man in the red sweatshirt followed him, and the study door closed behind him. I was left to finish dusting the living room and bedroom, all the while trying to figure out what was going on. It crossed my mind that Howell might be gay, but when I recalled Black Ponytail's eyes, I jettisoned the idea.

I had to cross the living room one more time, and I saw that the door to Howell's study was still shut. At least, I thought with obscure relief, I'd already dusted and vacuumed Howell's study. It was one of my favorite rooms in the house. Its walls were paneled, with bookcases galore. A leather chair was flanked by a reading lamp, Ducks Unlimited prints were hanging on the walls, and a very important-looking desk that was hell to polish stood before the bay window with its window seat.

I didn't want to look nosy, so I worked hard and fast trying to finish and get out of there before they emerged, but I didn't make it. The study door opened and out they came, just as I was mopping the kitchen. They were empty-handed.

Howell and the stranger stood in the middle of the floor making footprints I'd have to mop over. I was wearing yellow plastic gloves, my nose was surely shiny, and I was wearing my oldest jeans and an equally ancient T-shirt. All I wanted was for them to leave, and all Howell wanted was to obscure the oddity of the situation by making conversation.

'I hear you're the one who found poor Del?' Howell was asking sympathetically.

'Yes.'

'You're going with Marshall Sedaka, I hear? You have a key to Body Time?'

'No,' I said firmly, without being sure which question I was answering. 'I opened that morning for Marshall as a favor. He was sick.'

'My son admires you a great deal. He mentions you often.'

'I like Bobo,' I said, trying to keep my voice very small and even.

'There was no indication that anyone was with him when the accident occurred?'

I stood perplexed, unable to follow. Then I made the leap. All the intervening conversation had just been waffling. Howell wanted to know about the death of Del Packard.

I wondered what 'indication' Howell imagined there might have been. Footprints on the indoor/outdoor carpet? A mono-grammed handkerchief clutched in Del's fingers?

'Excuse me, Howell, I have to finish here and get to my next job,' I said abruptly, and rinsed out my mop. Though it took him a second, the man who signed so many local paychecks took the hint and hurried out the kitchen door. His companion lingered a moment behind him, long enough for me to meet his eyes when I looked up to see if they'd gone. I kept my gaze down until I heard the car start up in the carport.

After conscientiously mopping up their footprints, I wrung the mop and put it outside the back door to dry. With some relief, I locked the Winthrop house behind me and got into my car.

The Winthrops had irritated me, interested me, been a source of thought and observation for me for four years. But they had never been mysterious. Howell's sudden swerve from the straight-and-narrow of predictability made me anxious, and his association with the night-walking stranger with the black ponytail baffled me.

I discovered I had feelings ranging from tolerant to fond for the members of the Winthrop family. I had worked for them long enough to absorb a sense of their lives, to feel a certain loyalty to them.

Discovering this did not make me especially happy.

Chapter Three

Driving home from my last job of the day, I became acutely aware of how tired I was. I'd had little sleep the night before, I'd had a full working day, and I'd observed a lot of puzzling behavior.

But Claude's personal car, a burgundy Buick, was parked in front of my house. On the whole, I was glad to see it.

His window was rolled down, and I could hear his radio playing 'All Things Considered', the public-radio news program. Claude was slumped down in the driver's seat, his eyes closed. I wondered how long he had been waiting, since someone had stuck a blue sheet of paper under his windshield wiper. I could feel a smile somewhere inside me as I pulled into my carport and turned off the ignition. I'd missed him.

I walked quietly down the drive. I bent to his ear.

'Hey, hotshot,' I whispered.

He smiled before his eyes flew open.

'Lily,' he said, as if he enjoyed saying it. His hand went up to smooth his mustache, now more salt-and-pepper than brown.

'You going to sit out here or you going to come in?'

'In, now that you're here to offer.'

As Claude emerged from his Buick, I pulled the blue flyer from under his passenger-side wiper. I figured it was an ad for the new pizza place. I glanced at the heading idly.

'Claude,' I said.

He'd been retucking his shirttail. 'Yep?'

'Look.'

He took the sheet of blue paper from me, studied the dark print for a moment.

'Shit,' he said disgustedly. 'This is exactly what Shakespeare needs.'

'Yes indeed.'

TAKE BACK YOUR OWN, the headline read. In smaller print, the text read:

The white male is an endangered species. Due to government interference, white males cannot get the jobs they want or defend their families. ACT NOW!! BEFORE IT'S TOO LATE!!! Join us in this struggle. We'll be calling you. TAKE BACK YOUR OWN. We've been shoved enough. PUSH BACK!

'No address or phone number,' Claude observed.

'Dr Sizemore got one, too.' I remembered the color, though naturally I hadn't extracted the sheet from the dentist's garbage can.

Claude shrugged his heavy shoulders. 'No law against it, stupid as it seems.'

Northern Arkansas had hosted several white supremacist organizations over the past few decades. I wondered if this was an offshoot of one of them, one that had migrated south.

Everywhere I went, in the grocery, in the doctor's office, the rare occasions I worked at one of the churches, people all complained about not having enough time, having too much to do in the time they had available. It seemed to me after reading 'Take Back Your Own' that some people just weren't busy enough.

I crumpled the thing in my hand, turned and went up the stepping stones to my front door, my keys already out and ready to turn in both locks. Claude stretched. It was a large stretch for a large man.

He followed me in. I tensed, thinking he'd try to kiss me again, but he just began a rambling monologue about the trouble he was having scheduling enough cars on the streets during Halloween, when the fun tended to get too rowdy.

I was occupied in emptying my pockets onto the kitchen

counter, a soothing little ritual. I don't carry a purse when I'm working – it's just one more thing to tote in and out.

'Thank you for the flowers,' I said, my back still to him.

'It was my pleasure.'

'The flowers,' I began, and then stopped to take another deep breath. 'They are very pretty. And I liked the card,' I added, after another moment.

'Can I give you a hug?' he asked cautiously.

'Better not,' I said, trying to sound matter-of-fact.

On the card, he'd written that he missed my company. Of course, that wasn't true. Claude might enjoy my conversation, but his fundamental goal was getting me in bed. I sighed. So what else was new on the man/woman front?

I was more convinced than ever that intimacy wasn't a good idea for either of us.

I didn't say so, not just then; and that wasn't normal for me. But that evening, I wanted a friend. I wanted the company of a person I liked, to sit with me and drink coffee at my table. Though I knew it would prolong Claude's expectations, I temporarily bought into the illusion that it was only my companionship he wanted.

We did have coffee and a piece of fruit together, and a casual sort of conversation; but maybe because I was being in some sense deceptive, the warmth I'd hoped to feel didn't come.

Claude objected when I changed for karate class, but I never miss it if I can help it. I promised him that when I returned we'd go to dinner in Montrose, and I invited him to stay at my place and watch the football game on my TV while I was gone, since it had a bigger screen than his little portable. As I got in my car, I had a weary conviction that I should have told him to go on home.

I strode through the main room at Body Time, trying to look forward to the stress-reducing workout I was about to get. But mostly I felt . . . not very pleased with myself.

Though I'd been in there many times since Del had died, I always glanced at the corner where Del's body had rested on the bench. A smaller copy of Del's second-place trophy from the Marvel Gym competition the year before was still in its prominent position in the display case by the drinks cooler, since the gym where a winner trained was always recognized along with the winner.

I stopped to admire the shiny cup on its wooden stand, read the engraving. In the glass front of the display case, I could see the reflection of other potential champions as they went through their evening routines. I moved my hand up and down slightly to make sure I was there, too.

I shook my head at my reflection and continued down the hall to the open double doors of the aerobics/karate room. I bowed in the doorway to show respect, and entered. Janet Shook was already in her gi, its snowy whiteness setting off her dark hair and eyes. She was holding on to the barre, practicing side kicks. Marshall was talking to Carlton Cockroft, my next-door neighbor and my accountant, whom I hadn't seen in at least a week. There was a new woman limbering up, a woman with very long blond hair and a deep sun-bed tan. She was wearing a gi with a brown belt, and I regarded her with respect.

Raphael, who hadn't set foot in Body Time since the morning he'd left in a huff, was practicing the eight-point blocking system with Bobo Winthrop. I was glad to see Raphael, glad that whatever had eaten at him had eased up. As I watched the two spar, I noticed for the first time that Bobo was as tall as Raphael. I had to stop thinking of him as a boy.

'Yee-hah, Lily,' Bobo called cheerfully. I hadn't thought Bobo's naturally sunny nature would keep him down for long, and it was reassuring to see him smile and look less troubled. He and Raphael finished, and Bobo walked over to me as I finished tying my obi. I had time to think that Bobo looked like an all-American action hero in his white gi, when he simply reached over to place a large hand on each side of my waist, squatted slightly, and picked me up.

I had not been handled like that since I'd become an adult, and the sensation of being lifted and held up in the air abruptly returned me to childhood. I found myself laughing, looking down at Bobo, who was grinning up at me. Over his shoulder, I glimpsed the black-haired stranger, standing in the hall. His eyes were on me, and he was smiling a little as he patted his face with a towel.

Marshall, nodding at Black Ponytail, shut the double doors.

Bobo put me down.

I made a mock strike to his throat and he blocked me too late.

'Would've gotten you,' I warned him. 'You're stronger, but I'm quicker.'

Bobo was grinning at the success of his horseplay, and before I could move away, he gripped my wrists with his strong hands. As I stepped closer to him, I turned my palms up, bringing my hands up against his thumbs, and was free. I pantomimed chopping him in the neck with the sides of my hands. Then I patted him on his big shoulder and stepped away before he had any more ideas.

'Someday I'll get you,' Bobo called after me, shaking his finger.

'You get Lily, you're going to be sorry,' Raphael remarked. 'This gal can eat you for breakfast.'

Bobo turned dark red. I realized he'd read a double entendre into Raphael's remark. I turned away to hide my grin.

'Line up!' Marshall said sternly.

The blond woman was the highest-ranking student present. She took her place first in line. My belt is green, with one brown stripe. I took a deep breath, warned myself against unworthy feelings, and prepared myself to be pleasant.

'Kiotske,' Marshall said. We snapped to attention, our heels together.

'Rei.' We bowed to him, and he to us.

We worked through the familiar pain of three minutes in the shiko dachi position – pretty much like sitting on air – and calisthenics. Marshall was in a tough mood tonight. I didn't want to be petty enough to think he was giving us extra work because he was trying to impress the new class member; but he extended our sit-ups to one hundred. So we also did a hundred leg lifts and a hundred push-ups.

I was paired with the new woman, instead of Janet, for sit-ups. Her legs, hooked with mine, felt like bands of iron. She wasn't breathing heavily after eighty reps, though the next twenty were a little work. She broke into a light sweat after leg lifts, and was breathing a little hard after a hundred push-ups. But she had the energy to smile at me as she rose to her feet. I turned slightly to Raphael and gave him a look. He wiggled his eyebrows at me. We were impressed.

'Sanchin dachi blocking posture for jodan uki,' Marshall instructed. 'Komite!'

We assumed the correct position, right foot sweeping inward and forward, stopping when its heel was parallel with the toes of the left foot. I watched the blond out of the corner of my eye, wondering if she was from another discipline. She was, but she was also a quick study; watching Marshall intently, she swept her right foot in the correct half-arc and turned her toes in at a forty-five-degree angle to her body, her knees flexed slightly. Her left hand moved into chamber by her ribs, and her right formed a fist, as her right arm bent so that the fist faced her body at shoulder height.

As we went through kihon, practicing our strikes and blocks, I found myself distracted by my new neighbor. I made a determined effort to block her out of my consciousness. From then on, I felt more comfortable, and class went better. Marshall paired me with Carlton for practice. Between breaking free from each other and restraining each other, Carlton and I exchanged neighborhood news. He'd heard we were going to get new streetlights, and that the ownership of the empty lot at the corner – which I'd always thought was waste ground – had been decided among the five children of an elderly lady who'd passed away four years ago. What the new owner would do with the area, which would certainly be a challenge to fit a house on, Carlton hadn't yet discovered.

As I used one finger to jab the pressure point in Carlton's upper forearm, the one that made his knees crumple, he told me that he'd found a sheet of blue paper on his car when he'd come out to get his mail that afternoon. 'Nuts,' he commented.

I hoped everyone would dismiss the flyer so thoroughly. Then Carlton took his turn and pressed too hard, and from my position on the floor I looked up at him with my eyebrows raised.

When we had been dismissed, the blond drifted over to Marshall. Her hair flowed down to her butt, thick and straight, and though the youthful style didn't exactly match her apparent age, the effect was definitely enough to attract lots of attention. Janet was scowling as she sat on the floor to tie her shoes.

I was ready to go, having grabbed my gym bag and keys, when Marshall beckoned me over.

'Lily' he said, with a broad smile, 'this is Becca Whitley, Pardon's niece.'

Pardon Albee, the owner of the apartment building next to my house, had passed away the previous spring. Becca Whitley had taken her own sweet time in coming to check out her inheritance. One of the tenants in the apartment house, Marie Hofstettler, a very old woman who was one of my favorite clients, had told me the same lawyer who'd hired me to clean the halls had been collecting the rent for the past few months. And Deedra had told me that when her lease had expired her rent had gone up.

'I know I've been slow to get to Shakespeare to see to settling Uncle Pardon's estate,' the blond said, chiming in on my thoughts in a way that focused my wandering attention firmly. I looked at her directly for the first time. She was narrow-faced, with strong but scaled-down features. The deep tan was freckled. Her eyes were a bright I-wear-blue-contacts sapphire, and heavily made up. She also wore candy-pink lipstick and lined her lips with a darker shade. The effect stopped short of vampiric; but it was definitely predatory.

Becca Whitley was saying, 'I had a divorce to settle in Dallas, and an apartment to clean out.'

'So you're moving to Shakespeare?' I asked, hardly able to conceal my amazement. I took in her long mane of Lady Clairol hair, and the cone-shaped breasts bulging at her gi, and thought she would surely stir the local roosters up. Marshall was strutting around practically wiggling his crest and crowing. No wonder tonight he'd spared me most of those wounded looks he'd been casting me the past two weeks. I had to repress an impulse to snort.

'I think I'll just live in Uncle Pardon's apartment, at least for now,' Becca Whitley was saying. 'It's so convenient.'

'I hope Shakespeare isn't too quiet for you after such a big city,' I said. I realized that when I thought about Marshall's interest in Becca Whitley, the pang I felt was very small, almost negligible, which was only right.

'Oh, I've lived in Austin, which is really just a big town,' Becca said. 'But the past few months I've been in Dallas, and I couldn't stand the traffic and the pressure. See, I just got divorced, and I need a new life for myself.'

'Any children?' Janet asked hopefully. She'd come up behind me.

'Not a one,' our newest Shakespearean responded happily. 'Just too busy, I guess.'

Marshall was trying to conceal his relief just as hard as Janet was trying to conceal her chagrin.

'I've been cleaning the apartment halls since Pardon died,' I said. 'Do you want me to keep on, or have you made other plans?'

'I expect I'll be doing it,' Becca said.

I nodded and gathered my things together. The extra money had been pleasant, but working late on Saturday hadn't.

Our sensei was still telling Becca how much we wanted her to come back to class as Janet and I bowed at the door on our way out.

'Screw her,' Janet said quietly and viciously after we'd reached the parking lot.

It seemed to me it wouldn't be too long before Marshall tried to do just that, and Carlton, longtime most eligible bachelor in Shakespeare, had seemed interested, too.

I liked Janet pretty well, and I could see she was chagrined at the sexy and striking Becca Whitley's appearance and Marshall's obvious approval. Janet had been waiting for Marshall to notice her for a couple of years.

'She'll never last in Shakespeare,' I told the disappointed woman. I was surprised to hear my own voice.

'Thanks, Lily,' Janet said, sounding equally surprised. 'We'll have to wait and see.' To my amazement, she gave me a half-hug before unlocking her Trooper.

When I came in through the kitchen door, I could hear my television. Claude was parked in the double recliner watching a football game. He looked unnervingly at home. He waved a casual hand when I called 'Hello,' so I didn't hurry as I showered and dressed. When I emerged, once again made up and polished, Claude was in the kitchen drinking a glass of iced tea.

'What do you think of your new landlady?' I asked.

'The Whitley woman? Looks like a raccoon, don't she, with all that eye makeup?' he said lazily.

I smiled. 'Ready to eat?' I asked.

Soon we were driving toward Montrose, the nearest large town. It lay west and slightly north of Shakespeare, and it was the retail hub for many small towns like Shakespeare. Montrose, which boasted a population of around forty thousand year-round, more during college sessions, was where Shakespeareans went when they didn't want to make the somewhat longer northeast drive to Little Rock.

I'd never been enthusiastic about Montrose, a town which could have been dropped anywhere in the United States without its visitors knowing the difference. Montrose had no character; it had shopping. There were all the usual fast-food places and all the usual chain stores, and a five-screen movieplex, and a Wal-Mart Super Center. In my view, the main attractions of Montrose were its superior library, its one good independent bookstore, and perhaps four fairly good nonchain restaurants. And a couple of decent chain ones.

In the months I'd been seeing Marshall, I'd spent more time in Montrose than I had in the four years I'd lived in Shakespeare. Evenings at home had little charm for Marshall.

We'd tried every restaurant, sat through Jackie Chan and Steven Seagal movies, visited every sporting goods store to compare their prices to Winthrops', and done our weekly shopping at the Super Center.

This evening, Claude suggested a movie. I almost agreed out of courtesy. But remembering the uncomfortable hours with Marshall, I admitted, 'I really don't like going to the movies.'

'That so?'

'I don't like sitting with a lot of strangers in the dark, having to listen to them shift around and rattle paper and talk. I'd rather wait until it comes out on video and see it at home.'

'Okay,' he said. 'What would you like to do?'

'I want to eat at El Paso Grande and go to the bookstore,' I said.

Silence. I looked over at him out of the corners of my eyes.

'What about Catch the Wave and the bookstore?' he countered.

'Done,' I said, relieved. 'You don't like Tex-Mex?'

'Ate there last week when I had to come to Montrose to the courthouse.'

As we waited on our order in the seafood restaurant, Claude said, 'I think Darnell Glass's mother is going to bring a civil suit against the Shakespeare Police Department.'

'Against the department?' I asked sharply. 'That's unfair. It should be against Tom David.' Tom David Meicklejohn, one of Claude's patrolmen, had long been on my black list, and after the Darnell Glass incident, he'd moved to the number-one spot.

Suddenly, I wondered if this was the real reason for the flowers, the evening out: this conversation.

'Her lawyer's also naming Todd Picard. You think you could remember the timing just once more?'

I nodded, but I heaved an internal sigh. I was reluctant to recall the warm black night of The Fight. I'd been interviewed and interviewed about The Fight: That's what all the Shakespeareans called it. It had taken place in the parking lot of Burger Tycoon, a locally owned hamburger place that competed valiantly with Burger King and McDonald's, which were both down Main Street a piece.

I'd only come in on the crisis, but I'd read and heard enough later to flesh out what I'd actually seen.

Darnell Glass was sitting in his car in the Burger Tycoon parking lot, talking to his girlfriend. Bob Hodding, trying to pull into the adjacent parking space, hit Glass's rear bumper. Hodding was white, sixteen years old, a student at Shakespeare High School. Glass was eighteen and in his freshman year at UA Montrose. He had just made the first payment on his first car. Not too surprisingly, when he heard the unmistakable grinding crunch of the two bumpers tangling, Glass was enraged. He jumped out of his car, waving his hands and shouting.

Hodding was instantly on the offensive, since he knew the reputation of the young man whose car he'd just hit. Darnell Glass had attended the Shakespeare schools until he enrolled in college, and had a reputation as a bright and promising young man. But he was also known to be aggressive and hair-trigger sensitive in his dealings with white peers.

Bob Hodding had been raised with a Confederate flag flying in front of his house. He remembered Glass overreacting to situations at the high school. He wasn't afraid, since he had three of his buddies in his car, and he wasn't about to apologize in front of them, or admit his driving had been less than adequate.

A couple of witnesses told Claude later, privately, that Hodding pushed every emotional button he possibly could to further enrage Darnell Glass, including a jibe about Glass's mother, a junior high school teacher and well-known activist.

It was no surprise to anyone when Glass went ballistic.

And that was where I came in. I hadn't ever met Darnell Glass or Bob Hodding, but I was there when The Fight began.

So were two policemen.

I'd just pulled into the parking space on the other side of Glass's, having picked that night of all nights to buy a hamburger instead of cooking for myself, an event so rare it later seemed to me that a cosmic joke had placed me at the punch line. It was a very warm evening in early September; of course, in Shakespeare we have to mow our yards until well into November.

I was wearing my usual T-shirt and baggy jeans, and I'd just finished work. I was tired. I just wanted to get my carry-out food and watch an old movie on television, maybe read a chapter or two of the thriller I'd checked out of the library.

Off-duty Shakespeare patrol officer Todd Picard was in Burger Tycoon picking up his family's supper. On-duty patrol officer Tom David Meicklejohn had pulled in to get a Coke. But I didn't know there were two serving officers of the law present.

Not that their presence had made any difference. Though, of course, it should have.

I'd seen wiry Darnell wisely get in the first punch, and I saw the taller, more muscular Bob Hodding gag and double over, and then I watched his friends swarm over Darnell like angry bees.

If I'd had a gun or a whistle, maybe the sudden noise would have halted them, but I only had my fists. These were strong high school boys full of adrenaline and I had my work cut out for me. Not wanting to seriously hurt the little bastards made my job more difficult: I could drop them fairly easily if I was inclined to cause some lasting damage. Since Bob Hodding was temporarily out of the picture, puking his guts out in the crepe myrtles lining the parking lot, I concentrated on his buddies.

I moved up behind the tallest boy, who was raining punches on Darnell Glass. First I pinched a pressure point in the upper shoulder of the boy, who was standing between the other attackers, with my right hand. With my left, I pressed a point in his upper arm. The boy shrieked. Though he began to crumple, he still provided me with cover from the black-haired kid on my right, who was swinging blindly at me, but standing legs a-spraddle. . . someone who'd never fought in the street. I kicked him in the balls, just a glancing blow, a pretty neat kogen geri.

That took care of him.

The boy I'd disposed of first finally hit the ground wailing. He tried to scramble back, out of the way, to figure out what had happened.

From the corner of my eye I finally noticed the patrol car. I saw Deputy Tom David Meicklejohn climb out of it. He did nothing but smile his mean redneck smile and extend his arms to bar spectators from joining in the brawl. A man in civilian clothes, a bag and a cardboard tray with five cups in holders bogging him down, was yelling at Tom David. I later learned this was off-duty officer Todd Picard.

Meanwhile, the third boy grasped Darnell around the waist and tried to lift him off his feet, a wrestling move. Losing patience and temper, I hook-kicked him behind his knee, and of course his legs folded. But the parking lot sloped, and he brought Darnell down with him. Darnell rolled rapidly to the side. I slipped on a wrapper on the pavement and hit the ground myself, and the boy's flailing foot, shod in a boot, caught me painfully right at the joint of my right hip. I rolled away and jumped to my feet before the pain could get its teeth into me. When the wrestler struggled to his knees, I pulled his arm up behind him. 'I'll break it if you move,' I said. Most people recognize absolute sincerity. He didn't move.

Being on the ground is most often bad in a fight, but Darnell, though bleeding in several places on his face and badly bruised, had not lost his spirit. Bob Hodding, slightly recovered from the punch to the stomach and frantic with rage, staggered toward Darnell for another try. Darnell kicked up at Bob, who staggered back into the arms of a Marine who happened to be on leave and visiting his family. This huge young man, right out of basic training, stepped around Tom David to grip Bob Hodding with a hold like handcuffs and give him some sound, if unprintable, advice.

I stood panting, scanning the group for another adversary. I was feeling pain in my lip, and I noticed a few spots of bright blood staining my gray T-shirt; an elbow had caught me in the mouth somewhere along the way. I straightened up, evaluated the remaining fight left in the boy I was restraining, decided it was practically nil. The Marine, whose name I never learned, caught my eye and gave me an approving nod.

'Sorry I didn't get out here earlier' he said. 'That Tae Kwon Do?'

'Goju. For close fighting.'

'My drill sergeant would love you,' he said.

I tried to scrape together a smile.

At that point a noise like a siren went off a few feet away.

It was coming from the mouth of Darnell Glass's girlfriend, Tee Lee Blaine. She'd watched the fight from inside the car. Now she scrambled out to help Darnell rise. She was floundering through a spectrum of emotions, from fear for her own safety and Darnell's, to anger over the dent in the car, to rage that Darnell had been ganged up on. She knew each of the white boys by name, and she gave each of them a few new ones.

I caught Tom David Meicklejohn's eye. I wanted powerfully to kick him.

He smiled at me. 'Keeping back the crowd,' he said succinctly. By then, Todd Picard had deposited the food in his car and was standing by Tom David's patrol vehicle. Todd looked ashamed. I'd finally recognized him, and if I'd had the energy I'd have slapped him. I expected no better from Tom David, but Todd could have given me a hand.

For the first time, I realized there was quite a crowd. Burger Tycoon is on Main Street (Shakespeare's not too imaginative about street names) and the restaurant had been full. It was true that if Tom David had not kept the crowd back the incident could have turned into a full-fledged riot; but he had allowed most of this to happen, as I saw it.

Suddenly the hip that had taken the kick began to throb. I'd run out of adrenaline. I eased myself down into a sitting position and leaned my head back against the car.

'Lily! You okay?' a voice called from the crowd, and I saw my neighbor. Carlton, neatly groomed as always, was accompanied by a bosomy brunette with a headful of curls. I remember thinking about his companion for longer than the topic deserved, trying to recall where the woman worked.

It had been nice to have someone ask about my welfare. I was feeling distinctly flat and a little shaky.

'I'll be fine,' I said. I closed my eyes. I would have to get up in a minute. I couldn't sit here looking hurt.

Then Claude was bending over me, saying, 'Lily! Lily! Are you hurt?'

'Sure,' I said angrily. I opened my eyes. 'Having to do your cops' jobs for them. Help me up.'

Claude extended his hand and I gripped it. He straightened and pulled, and I came up. Maybe not gracefully, but at least I was steady on my feet once I got there.

Darnell Glass was standing by that time, too, but leaning heavily against his car, Tee Lee supporting him on his other side. The Marine let go of his captive, and the white boys were getting into Tom David's patrol car.

'You have a problem with your officer there,' I told Claude.

'I have more problems than that right now,' he answered quietly, and I observed that the crowd was restless, and hot words were being exchanged among a few young men in the parking lot.

'Get in my car,' he said. 'I'll get the boy and the girl.'

So we all took a ride down to the police station. The rest of the evening was completely miserable. The white boys were all juveniles. Their parents descended in a cloud of buzzing, like angry African bees. One father snapped at me that he ought to sue me for hurting his boy – the one I'd kicked in the groin – and I used his prejudice against him. 'I would love to tell the court how a woman beat up your boy and two others,' I said. 'Especially when they were ganging up on one young man by himself.' I heard no more comments about suing.

Until now. And I wasn't the target of the lawsuit.

As our waitress left, Claude spread his napkin in his lap and speared a shrimp. 'Tom David was there and did nothing,' he said, just a hint of question in his voice. 'Todd was there and did nothing.'

I raised my brows. 'That's right,' I said. 'Do you doubt it?'

He shot a look at me from under his heavy brows. 'Tom David says he had to keep the other people from joining in. Todd says he was afraid he wouldn't be recognized as an off-duty officer and would be seen as joining the brawl.'

'Of course they're going to say that, and there may even be some trace of truth to it. But they also let two other people do their job, me and the Marine. Tom David, for sure, wanted Darnell Glass to get beat up. At the very least, Todd didn't care if that happened.'

Claude avoided my eyes, clearly unhappy with the idea that a member of his force would let violence go unchecked, even though to my certain knowledge, Claude bore no love whatsoever for Tom David Meicklejohn.

'And Darnell struck the first blow,' he said, again in the tone of one confirming an unpleasant truth.

'Yes. It was a good one.'

'You never met any of those boys beforehand,' Claude said.

'No.'

'Then why so partisan?'

I stared over at him, my fork suspended midway to my mouth with a bit of flounder impaled on the tines. 'I didn't care until they all jumped him,' I said after a moment's thought. 'I would have done the same if Darnell had been white and the other guys black.' I thought about it. Yes, that was true. Then the familiar tide of anger surged up. 'Of course, as it turned out, I might have saved my strength and let them go on and stomp him.'

A dull red flush crept up Claude's face. He believed I was accusing him of something. But I wasn't, at least not consciously.

Darnell Glass hadn't lived long after that evening in the Burger Tycoon parking lot.

Four weeks later, he'd been beaten to death in a clearing in the woods north of town.

No one had been arrested for the crime.

'If the rumors are true and Mrs Glass does bring a suit, you're sure to be called as witness.' Claude felt obliged to point that out to me, and he wasn't happy about it, any more than I was.

'I wish we hadn't started talking about this,' I said, knowing it was futile to say. 'If you're really worried about the future of your police department, thinking it'll rest on my testimony . . . I can't change or shade what I saw. You may not want to be around me.' This wasn't the right place. I said it too bluntly. And I felt a funny pang when the words left my mouth.

'Is that what you want?' Claude said. His voice was very quiet.

Truth time. 'I want to see you if you're going to be my friend, but I don't see us becoming lovers. I don't think that's right for us.'

'And if I do?' I could see the distance growing in his eyes.

'Claude, I feel comfortable when I'm in your company, but if we have sex that'll be ruined. I don't think we can carry this to another dimension.'

'Lily, I'll always like you,' he said after a long pause. 'But I'm at the age and disposition where I'm thinking, I can't be in law enforcement forever. I want a wife, and a home, and someone to go camping with, someone to decorate the Christmas tree with. That was what I was thinking might happen with you. As I hear it, you're telling me it's not gonna.'

God, I hated explaining my emotions.

'I can't see my way to that, Claude. I just can't make that leap with you. And if I use up your time trying, you might miss something better.'

'Nothing can be better, Lily. I may find something different, something good. But nothing better.'

'So,' I said quietly. 'Here we are in Montrose, have to drive home, have to be with each other. We should have done this in Shakespeare, huh? Then you could go over to your apartment and I could lock my door and we could lick our wounds.'

'I wish I could believe that you have wounds to lick, Lily,' he said. 'Let's go look at some books.'

*

Of course after the restaurant discussion, the bookstore wasn't much fun.

I read biographies, mostly; maybe I'm hoping I'll find the key to make my life lighter by finding out how someone else managed. Or maybe I loved company in my miserable past; I could always find a tougher life than mine. But not tonight.

I found myself thinking not about Claude and myself, but about Darnell Glass.

I glanced at the true crime books, which I cannot stomach any more than I can watch the news on television.

No one would ever write a book about Darnell Glass.

A beating death in Arkansas, especially the beating death of a black male, was not newsworthy, unless whoever'd killed Darnell got arrested and generated some lurid publicity – if the murderer was one of the local ministers maybe, or if Darnell's death was the first escapade of a flamboyant serial killer.

I had managed to make my way through the newspaper account. The Shakespeare paper did its best to defuse tense situations, but even its brief references to the young man's long list of injuries made my stomach lurch.

Darnell Glass had suffered a broken jaw, five broken ribs, multiple arm fractures, and the blow that had mercifully killed him, a crushing strike to the skull. He had suffered massive internal injuries consistent with a determined beating.

He'd died surrounded by enemies – in rage, in terror, in disbelief – in an unremarkable clearing in the piney woods.

No one deserved that. Well, I had to amend that thought. I could think of a few people I wouldn't weep over if they met an identical end. But Darnell Glass, though no saint, was a very smart young man with no criminal record, whose worst crime (apparently) was a bad temper.

'Let's go,' I said to Claude, and he looked surprised at the shortness of my tone.

All the way back home I kept silent, which Claude perhaps interpreted as regret. Or sulking. Anyway, he gave me a brusque cheek peck on the doorstep that had a sort of chilly finality to it. It seemed to me, watching his broad back retreat, that I'd never see him again. I went inside and looked at the flowers, still beautiful and sweet. I wondered if Claude regretted sending them now. I almost pulled them from the vase to throw away. But that would have been silly, wasteful.

As I prepared for bed, thankful to be alone, I wondered if Marshall's charge was true. Was I a cold woman?

I could never see myself as cold; self-protective, maybe, but not cold. It seemed to me that underneath the surface, I was always on fire.

I tossed and turned, tried relaxation techniques.

I got up to walk. It was chilly outside now, midnight in late October, and it was windy; before morning it would rain again. I wore a T-shirt, a sweatshirt, sweatpants, and Nikes, all dark shades: I was in a hateful mood, and didn't want anyone to see me. The streetlights at each corner of my street, Track Street, were dispensing their usual feeble nimbus. Claude's window was dark, as was every window in the apartment building; an early night for tenants old and new. The Shakespeare Combined Church, or SCC as the members called it, was dark except for some security lights. There was very little movement in the town, period. Shakespeare rises early and goes to bed early, except for the men and women who work the late shift at one or two of the fast-food places, and the people who work nights at the mattress factory or the chicken processing plant, which run round the clock.

I went as far as the lower-middle-class neighborhood in which Darnell Glass had grown up, one of Shakespeare's few mixed-race areas. I passed the little house Glass's mother, Lanette, had bought when she moved back to Shakespeare from Chicago. It, too, was dark and silent. None of these homes had garages or porte cocheres, so it was easy to see Lanette Glass was not at home.

But I found out where she was.

She was at Mookie Preston's house.

While I'd been thinking about my curious cleaning stint at Mookie's that day, I'd drifted in that direction without conscious thought. So I was opposite the house when Lanette Glass emerged. I wasn't close enough to see her expression, which the deep shadows of the streetlight behind her would have made difficult anyway, but from the way she walked – shoulders hunched, head shaking slightly from side to side, purse clasped hard against her side – Lanette Glass was a woman in trouble, and a troubled woman.

More and more I wondered about the purposes of the mysterious Mookie Preston.

As a cold breeze stirred my hair, I felt some of its chill creep down my spine. Something was brewing in Shakespeare, something sick and dangerous. I'd always felt comfortable about the state of race relations in my adopted town. There were still taboos, plenty of them, probably several of which I wasn't even conscious. But there were also blacks in managerial positions, blacks who owned comfortable homes. Several clubs and one church were integrated. The public school system seemed to be functioning with little friction, and Lanette Glass was only one of many black teachers.

The habits and prejudices of over a century weren't going to vanish overnight, or even in thirty years; and I'd always felt that progress, quiet and slow, was being made.

I wondered now if I'd been in a fool's paradise. I had assumed that my approval of this change was shared by most people of both races, and I still thought so. But something evil was slithering through Shakespeare, had been for months.

Perhaps three weeks after Darnell Glass had been killed, Len Elgin had been found shot dead in his Ford pickup, on a little-traveled country road just within the city limits. Len, a prosperous white farmer in his fifties, was a genial and intelligent man, a pillar of his church, father of four, and an avid reader and hunter. Len had been a personal friend of Claude's. Failure to solve Len's murder had been eating at Claude, and the rumors that spread like wildfire had made handling Len Elgin's death investigation even more delicate.

One school of thought had Elgin being killed in retaliation for the death of Darnell Glass. Of course the guilty parties, in this version, would be black extremists, even as Glass's death was ascribed to white extremists.

Another rumor had it as fact that Len was being unfaithful to his wife, Mary Lee, with the wife of another farmer. According to this rumor, the murderer was either Mary Lee, the other farmer (who was named Booth Moore), or Moore's wife Erica. Those who accused Erica were assuming that Len had terminated their relationship.

Somehow the fight – The Fight – in the Burger Tycoon parking lot had triggered all this.

We were all losing our sense of community; we were sub-dividing into groups not only by race but by the degree of our intensity of feeling about that race. I thought about the ugly scrawl on Deedra's car. I thought about Tom David Meicklejohn's scarcely concealed glee that September night in the parking lot. I remembered glimpsing, through the windows of the limousine following the hearse, Mary Lee Elgin's face as the funeral cortege passed by. And then, banal in its wrongheadedness, but no less vicious for its banality, the sheet of blue paper under Claude's windshield wiper.

Surely it was stretching credulity to think that Del Packard's death in the gym was totally unrelated to the deaths of Darnell Glass and Len Elgin. How could three men be done to death in a town the size of Shakespeare in a space of two months and the killings all be mysterious? If Darnell Glass had been knifed behind a local bar during a fight over a girl, if Len Elgin had been shot in Erica Moore's bed, if Del had been in the habit of lifting alone and maybe had some undiagnosed physical weakness . . .

I was making another circuit by the apartments. I looked up at Claude's window, thinking sadly about the man inside. Would I change my mind about what I'd said, given another chance? I was genuinely fond of Claude, and grateful to him, and he had a lot on his shoulders.

But that was his chosen job. And Darnell Glass's death had taken place in the country, so that investigation was Sheriff Marty

Schuster's headache. I didn't know too much about the sheriff, except that he was good at politicking and was a Vietnam veteran. I wondered if Schuster could calm the rising storm that was rattling Shakespeare's windows.

I had to walk another hour before I could sleep.

Chapter Four

I woke up and looked out at sheets of rain, a chilly autumnal gray rain. I'd slept a little late since I'd had such a hard time getting to bed the night before. I'd have to hurry to make it to Body Time. Before I dressed, I poured myself a cup of coffee and drank it at the kitchen table, the morning paper unopened beside me. I had a lot to think about.

I worked out without talking to anyone. I drove home feeling a lot better.

I showered, dressed, put on my makeup, and fluffed my hair.

I wondered if the black-haired man had been out walking in the night, too.

As my car lurched slowly along the driveway that led to the back of the small Shakespeare Clinic, an uninspiring yellow brick office structure dating from the early sixties, I was betting that Carrie Thrush would be working today.

Sure enough, Carrie's aging white Subaru was in its usual place behind the building. I used my key and called 'Hi!' down the hall. Carrie's clinic was depressing. The walls were painted an uninspiring tan and the floors were covered with a pitted brown linoleum. There wasn't enough money yet for renovation. The doctor had massive debts to pay off.

Carrie's answer came floating back, and I stepped into the doorway of her office. The best thing you could say about Carrie's office was that it was large enough. She did a lot of scut work herself, to save money to pay back the loans that had gotten her through med school. The doctor was in black denims and a rust-red sweater. Carrie is short, rounded, pale, and serious, and she hasn't had a date in the two years since she's come to Shakespeare.

For one thing, she's all too likely to be interrupted in any free time she might manage. Then, too, men are intimidated by Carrie's calm intelligence and competence. At least that was what I figured.

'Anything interesting happen this week?' she asked, as if she wanted to take her mind off the heap of paper. She shoved her brown chin-length hair behind her ears, resettled her glasses on her snub nose. Her beautiful brown eyes were magnified many times by the lenses.

'Becca Whitley, the niece, is living in Pardon's apartment.' I said, after some thought. 'The man who's taken Del Packard's place at Winthrop Sporting is living in Norvel Whitbread's old apartment. And Marcus Jefferson moved out in a hurry after the Deedra Dean car-painting incident.' I'd seen the U-Haul trailer attached to Marcus's car the morning before.

'That was probably a good move,' Carrie said. 'Sad though that state of affairs is.'

I tried to think of other items of interest. 'I ate out in Montrose with the chief of police,' I told her. Carrie hungered for something frivolous after being a sober, God-like decision-maker all week.

'Is that the niece everyone was talking about, the one he left everything to?' Carrie had fastened on the first item. But she would get around to all of them.

I nodded.

'What's she like?'

'She's got long blond hair, she wears heavy makeup, she works out and takes karate, and she probably features in the wet dreams of half the guys she meets.'

'Smart?'

'Don't know.'

'Has she rented out Marcus's apartment yet? A lab tech at the hospital is looking for a place to live.' Shakespeare had a tiny hospital, perpetually in danger of being closed.

'I don't think the dust has had time to settle on the windowsill yet. Tell the lab tech to get on down there and knock on the apartment to the rear right.'

'So what's with the chief? He show you his nightstick?'

I smiled. Carrie had a ribald sense of humor. 'He wants to, but I don't think it's a good idea.'

'He's been hanging around you for months like a faithful hound, Lily. Cut him loose or give in.'

I was reminded yet again of how much people in a small town knew about you even when you tried to keep your life private.

'He's cut loose as of last night,' I said. 'I just enjoy his company. He knows that.'

'Do you think you can be comfortable with him now?'

I thought of a quick answer and a longer truer one. I sat down in one of the two patient chairs and said, 'It was possible until Claude started talking about the Darnell Glass lawsuit.'

'Yeah, I hear Mrs Glass is talking to a lawyer from Little Rock about bringing a suit. You'd be a witness, huh?'

'I reckon.'

'Tom David Meicklejohn is such a jerk.'

'But he's Claude's jerk. She'd be suing the Shakespeare Police Department, not just Tom David or Todd.'

Carrie shook her head. 'Rough waters ahead. Think you and Claude can weather it as friends?'

I shrugged.

Carrie's smile was wry. 'It's uphill work being your confidant, Bard.'

I sat silent for a minute. 'I expect that's from being Victim of the Year after I got raped. Too many people I talked to, people I'd known all my life, turned around and told everything I said to the press.'

Carrie looked at me, her mouth slightly open in surprise. 'Gosh,' she said finally.

'Got to work.' I got up and pulled on my yellow rubber gloves, prepared to tackle the patients' bathroom first, since it was always the nastiest.

When I left the room, Carrie was bending over her paperwork with a little smile on her lips.

*

Another favorite woman of mine was Marie Hofstettler, and I was sorry to see today was not one of her 'limber' days. When I used my key to enter her ground-floor apartment, I could see at a glance that she wasn't in her usual chair. Marie had been living in the Shakespeare Garden Apartments, next door to me, for years. Her son, Chuck, who lives in Memphis, pays me to clean once a week and take Mrs Hofstettler wherever she wants to go on Saturdays.

'Mrs Hofstettler,' I called. I didn't want to scare her. Lately, she'd been forgetting when I was due to come.

'Lily.' Her voice was very faint.

I hurried back to her bedroom. Marie Hofstettler was propped up, her long silky white hair in an untidy braid trailing over one shoulder. Somehow she seemed smaller to me, and her myriad wrinkles looked deeper, chiseled into her fine skin. Her color was bad, both pale and gray-tinged.

She looked like she was dying. The effort of calling out to me had clearly exhausted her. She gasped for breath. I picked up the phone on the bedside table, jammed between a framed picture of her great-grandchild and a box of Kleenex.

'Don't call,' Marie managed to say.

'You have to go to the hospital,' I said.

'Want to stay here,' she whispered.

'I know, and I'm sorry. But I can't . . .' My voice trailed off as I realized I'd been about to say 'be responsible for your death.' I cleared my throat. I thought about her courage in the face of the pain she'd endured for years, from arthritis and a bad heart.

'Don't,' she said, and she was begging.

As I knelt by the bed and held Mrs Hofstettler's hand, I thought of all the people in this apartment building I'd seen come and go from its eight units. Pardon Albee had died, the O'Hagens had moved, the Yorks were gone, and Norvel Whitbread was in jail for forging a check: this, out of the tenants that had been in the Garden Apartments this time last year. And now Marie Hofstettler.

*

She was gone in an hour.

When I judged the end was near, and I knew she no longer heard me, I called Carrie.

'I'm at Marie Hofstettler's,' I said. I heard paper shuffling around on Carrie's desk.

'What's up?' Carrie knew something was wrong by my voice.

'She's leaving us,' I said very quietly.

'I'm on my way.'

'She wants you to drive slow.'

A silence. 'I hear you,' Carrie said. 'But you have to call nine-one-one to cover your ass.'

I put down the phone with the one hand I had free. I'd been holding Marie's thin bony fingers with the other. When I focused on Marie's face, she sighed, and then her soul left her body. I gave a sigh of my own.

I punched in 911. 'I've been here cleaning Marie Hofstettler's apartment,' I said. 'I left the room for a while to clean the bathroom and when I checked back on her, she was . . . I think she's dead.'

Then I had to move quickly. I grabbed some glass cleaner to give the bathroom a very quick once-over. I left the spray bottle and some paper towels by the sink and I stuck the bowl brush in the toilet, hastily pouring some blue cleanser in the water.

Carrie Thrush knocked on the door, and she was barely bending over Marie when the EMTs got there.

As I let them in, the door across the hall and to the back opened, and Becca Whitley looked out. She was dressed to kill, in tailored red slacks and a black sweater.

'The old lady?' she asked me.

I nodded.

'She having a crisis?'

'She died.'

'Should I call someone?'

'Yes. Her son, Chuck. The phone number is right here.' While Carrie and the EMTs consulted over Mrs Hofstettler and then loaded her onto a gurney, I fetched the pad of telephone numbers the old lady had kept by the living room phone, and handed it to Becca Whitley.

I was relieved beyond words to be spared calling Chuck, not only because I didn't like him but because I was feeling guilt. As Marie was wheeled out to the ambulance, I thought of the things I should have done; I should have called Carrie, or 911, immediately, called Marie's best friend – the older Mrs Winthrop, Arnita – and then talked Marie into wanting to go on. But Marie had been in more and more pain, more and more dependent, the past few months. There'd been many days I'd had to dress her, and times I wasn't scheduled to come and found later she'd stayed in bed all day because she couldn't do otherwise. She'd refused her son's proposal to move her to a nursing home, she'd refused to have a nurse in the apartment, and she'd made up her own mind when to let go.

Suddenly I realized how much I would miss Mrs Hofstettler, and the impact of witnessing her death hit me broadside. I sat down on the stairs up to the second floor's four apartments, sat down and felt the wetness on my cheeks.

'I got Chuck's wife,' Becca said. She was in her stocking feet, I noticed, trying to figure out how she'd crept up on me. 'She didn't exactly sound torn up.'

I didn't look up at her.

'They wrote her off a few years ago,' I said flatly.

'You're not in her will, are you?' Becca asked me, her voice calm.

'I hope not.' And then I did look up at her, and she stared back at me with her contact-blue eyes, and after a minute she nodded and went back into her place.

I was scared to finish my work in Mrs Hofstettler's apartment without permission. If anyone came asking me questions about her death, I didn't want my staying to clean afterward to look suspicious, as though I was clearing away evidence or stealing valuables. So I locked the door behind me, and turned my key over to Becca, who took it without comment.

As her own door closed behind me, I heard another one above me slam shut. I looked up the stairs. Down came the man who'd rented Norvel Whitbread's apartment, the man who'd come into the Winthrops' with Howell the day before. He was maybe my age, I now conjectured, about five foot ten, with a prominent straight nose, straight black brows over those hazel eyes. Again, his hair was pulled back in a ponytail. He had narrow, finely chiseled lips and a strong chin. There was a thin scar, slightly puckered, running from the hairline by his right eye down to his jaw. He was wearing an ancient leather jacket, dark green flannel shirt, and jeans.

I was able to take all this in so minutely because he stopped at the bottom of the stairs and looked at me for a long moment.

'You've been crying,' he said finally. 'You all right?'

'I don't cry,' I said furiously and absurdly. I met his eyes. It seemed to me I was full of fear; it seemed to me I could feel something inside me cracking.

He raised his straight brows, stared for an instant longer, and then went past me, out the back door to the tenants' parking area. The door didn't sigh shut for a long moment. I could see that he sat in his car for a beat or two before he pulled out of his space and drove away.

Mrs Hofstettler's funeral was Monday, quick work even for Shakespeare. She'd planned the service two years before; I remembered the Episcopal priest, a tiny man almost as old as Marie, coming by to talk to her about it.

I hadn't entered a church in years, so I had a long struggle with myself. I'd already said good-bye to Marie, but it came to me very strongly that she would have wanted me to be at the funeral.

Stiffly, reluctantly, I called two of my Monday afternoon regulars to reschedule. I brushed and pressed my long-stored, expensive black suit (which I'd retained from my former life as being all-purpose). I'd bought a pair of pantyhose, and now I wriggled into the nasty things. Grimacing with distaste, I slid my feet into high-heeled black pumps. Two of my scars were visible, thin and white, because of the square neckline of the suit. I was so pale that the scars weren't conspicuous, I decided; anyway, there was nothing to be done about it. I wasn't about to buy another dress. This one still fit, but not exactly the way it used to. Working out so consistently had resculpted my body.

The black suit seemed dreary unadorned, so I put my grandmother's diamond earrings in my ears, and added her diamond bar pin to the ensemble. I still had a good black purse; like the suit, it was a relic of my former life.

Shakespeare police always escort local funerals, and one of the cars is always stationed at the church. I hadn't anticipated this, especially that the police car attending to the church traffic would be manned by Claude. He watched me get out of my Skylark, and stood drop-jawed as I came down the sidewalk to enter the church.

'Lily, you look beautiful,' he said, unflatteringly amazed. 'I've never seen you dressed up before.'

I shot him a glance and passed in to the warm dimness of tiny Saint Stephen's. The dark old Episcopal church was absolutely jam-packed with friends and connections from Marie Hofstettler's long life; her contemporaries, their children, other members of the church, volunteers from her favorite charity. Only two pews had been marked off at the front for the family. Chuck, now in his late fifties, was Mrs Hofstettler's only living child.

It was obvious what sitting room there was left should be saved for the older people who formed the majority of the mourners. I stood at the back, bowing my head as the coffin was brought in draped with the heavy church pall, staring at the sparse hair on the back of Chuck Hofstettler's head as he followed behind the coffin. He was looking at the embroidered pall with a kind of grieved fascination. To me, the container and its contents were uninteresting. The essential Marie was elsewhere. The casket was only there to provide a focus for grief and meditation, the way a flag provided a focus for patriotic upswelling.

Marie's best friend, Arnita Winthrop, was seated near the front of the church with her husband, Howell Sr., her son, and his wife.

Old Mr Winthrop was holding his wife's hand. Somehow I found that touching. Beanie, chic as always, had lightened her hair a couple of shades, I noticed. Beanie and Howell Jr. were not holding hands.

The unfamiliar service progressed slowly. Without a prayer book, I was at a loss. There were quite a few of us standing, and more people crowded in even after the service began. It took at least five minutes for me to realize who was a little behind me. As if some inner radar had blipped, I turned my head slightly to see the man who'd come down the apartment building stairs the day Marie died, Howell's mysterious friend.

He was as duded up as I was. He was wearing a suit with a vest, a navy-blue pinstripe. Instead of Nikes, he was shod in gleaming wing tips. His shirt was white and his tie was a conservative navy, green, and gold stripe. The black ponytail and the puckered scar contrasted oddly with the banker's costume.

As I located him, he turned his head to look at me. Our eyes met. I looked forward again. What was he doing here? Was he some long-ago army buddy of Howell's? Was he Howell's bodyguard? Why would Howell Winthrop need a bodyguard?

When the interminable service was over, I left the church as quickly as I could. I refused to look around me. I climbed back into my car and went home to change and go to work. Even for Marie, I wasn't going out to the cemetery.

When I went in to Body Time the next morning, Darcy Orchard greeted me with, 'Is it true you're working for a nigger?'

'What?' I realized I hadn't heard that word in years. I hadn't missed it.

'You working for that gal who rented the house on Sycamore?'

'Yes.'

'She's gotta be half black, Lily.'

'OK.'

'What's she doing here in Shakespeare, she told you?'

'No.'

'Lily, it's not my business, but it don't look right, a white woman cleaning for a black.'

'You're right. It's none of your business.'

'I'll say this for you, Lily,' Darcy said slowly. 'You know how to keep your mouth shut.'

I turned to stare at Darcy. I'd been doing lat pull-downs, and I didn't rise, just swiveled on the narrow seat. I looked at him thoroughly, from magnificent physique to acne-marked cheeks, and I looked beyond him at his shadow, Jim Box, a darker, leaner version of Darcy.

'Yes,' I said finally. 'I do.'

I wondered what Darcy's reaction would be if I told him that the last time I'd cleaned at Mookie Preston's house, I'd found a rifle under her bed, along with a bundle of targets. Nearly every target was neatly drilled through the middle.

The next day I stayed at Body Time longer than I usually do. I keep Wednesday mornings open for cleaning emergencies, and the only thing I had scheduled was my semiannual turnout of Beanie Winthrop's walk-in closet.

Bobo was working that morning, and once again he seemed depressed. Jim and Darcy were attacking triceps work with determination. They both gave me curt hellos before diving back into their schedule. I nodded back as I stretched.

Jerri Sizemore fluttered her fingers at me. I decided it must be the effect of my new outfit. I'd unbent enough to buy a pair of calf-length blue spandex workout pants and matching sports bra, but I'd mitigated the bare effect by pulling on an old cutoff T-shirt.

I finished my regular routine and decided to try some chin-ups, just to see if I could. I'd turned to face the wall instead of the room, because the T-shirt came up when I raised my arms, exposing a stretch of scarred ribs. I'd pulled over a stool to help me grip the high bar initially, but after that I'd shoved it away with a dangling foot so I wouldn't be tempted to cheat.

The first chin-up went fairly well, and the second and third. I watched myself in the mirror on the wall, noticing with irritation that the T-shirt certainly did expose a lot of skin. I should never have listened to Bobo's flattery.

By the fourth rep, I wouldn't have cared if the shirt fell off, I was in so much pain. But I'd promised myself I'd do at least seven. I shut my eyes to concentrate. I whined out loud when I'd achieved the fifth, and dangled from the bar, despairing of finishing my set. I was taken by surprise when big hands gripped me at the hipbones and pushed up, providing just enough boost to enable me to finish the sixth chin-up. I lowered myself, growled, 'One more,' and began to pull up again. The hands gave a trifle more boost, enabling me to accomplish the seventh.

'Done,' I said wearily. 'Thanks, Bobo.' The big hands began lowering me to the stool he'd shoved back into position.

'You're welcome,' said a voice that wasn't Bobo's. After a moment, his hands fell away, leaving an impression of heat on my stomach and hips.

I pivoted on the stool. My spotter had been the black-haired man. He was wearing a chopped-off gray sweatshirt and red sweatpants. He hadn't shaved that morning.

He walked away, and began doing lunges on the other side of the room. Picking an exercise almost at random, I hooked my feet under the bar on the lat pull-down machine and did stomach crunches, my arms crossed over my chest. I kept an eye on the stranger as he did leg presses. After he'd warmed up, he pulled off his sweatshirt to reveal a red tank top and a lot of shoulder. I turned my back.

As I was leaving, I almost asked Bobo if he knew the man's name. Then I thought, I'll be damned if I ask anybody anything, least of all Bobo. I gathered my gym bag and my jacket and started to the door.

Marshall entered as I reached it. He threw his arm around my shoulders. I leaned away from him, startled, but he pulled me close and hugged me.

'Sorry about Marie Hofstettler' Marshall said gently. 'I know you cared about her.'

I was embarrassed at mistaking his intention, and his concern and tenderness reminded me of the reasons I'd hooked up with him initially. But I wanted him to let go. 'Thanks,' I said stiffly.

The black-haired man was looking at us, as he stood with Jim and Darcy, who were chattering away. It seemed to me now that something about him was familiar, an echo of long ago, from the darkest time in my life. I couldn't quite track the trace of the memory back to its origins.

'How's your hip been?' Marshall asked professionally.

'A little stiff,' I confessed. The kick that I'd taken in The Fight had proved to be a more troublesome injury than I'd guessed at the time. Standing on my left foot, I swung my right leg back and forth to show Marshall my range of motion. He crouched before me, watching my leg move. He told me to raise my leg sideways, like a male dog about to pee, the position the karate class assumed for side kicks. It was very uncomfortable. Marshall talked about my hip for maybe five more minutes, with other people contributing opinions and remedies like I'd asked for them.

None from the black-haired man, though he drew close to listen to the discussion, which ranged from my hip to The Fight to Lanette Glass's civil suit to some upcoming meeting at one of the black churches.

While I showered and dressed, I thought how strange it was that this black-haired man was cropping up everywhere.

It could be a coincidence. Or maybe I was just being paranoid. He could have his eye on someone else other than me; maybe Becca Whitley? Or maybe (I brightened) the finances of the Shakespeare Combined Church had attracted the interest of some government agency? The church pastor, Brother Joel McCorkindale, had always alerted that sense in me that detected craziness, twistedness, in other people. Maybe Mr Black Ponytail was after the good brother.

Then why the secret tryst with Howell? The black bags? I hadn't opened the window seat when I'd been cleaning the day before, because I hadn't any business in Howell's study.

Of course, I could be attributing all sorts of things to a regular working guy, who also liked to keep fit, and go to funerals of old women he didn't know, and have secret meetings with his employer.

What with Mookie Preston, Becca Whitley, and this scarred man with his long black hair, in no time at all I was going to lose my standing as the most exotic imported resident of Shakespeare.

It was a chilly day, almost visible-breath temperature. Though I don't like to work in long sleeves, I pulled on an old turtleneck I wore when it was too cold to do without. I'd bought it before I started muscle-building, and it was tight in the neck, the shoulders, the chest, the upper arms . . . I shook my head at my reflection in the mirror. I looked as obvious as Becca Whitley. I'd throw it out after I wore it today, but it certainly would do to clean Beanie's closet. I pulled on my baggy jeans and some old Converse high-tops, and after checking my mirror one more time to verify that my hair was curling and fluffy and my makeup was smooth and unobtrusive – evaluating Becca's cosmetics had made me more aware of the dangers of overdoing it – I went out to my car.

It wouldn't start.

'Son of a *bitch*,' I said, and a few more things. I raised the hood. One of the legacies of my gentle upbringing is that I don't know shit about cars. And since I became ungentle, I have been too busy making a living to learn. I stalked back into my house and called the only mechanic I trusted in Shakespeare.

The phone was picked up to a mind-numbing blast of rap music.

'Cedric?'

'Who you want?'

'Cedric?'

'I'll get him.'

'Hello? Who wants Big Cedric?'

'Cedric, this is Lily Bard.'

'Lily, what can I do for you this fine cold day?'

'You can come find out what's wrong with my car. It was running smooth this morning. Now it won't start.'

'I won't insult you by asking if you got gas in it.'

'I'm glad you're not going to insult me.'

'Okay, I tell you what. I got this car up on the rack I got to finish with, then I come by. You gonna be there?'

'No, I got a job. I can walk to it. I'll leave the keys in the car.'

'Okay, we'll get this problem taken care of.'

'Thank you, Cedric.'

The phone went down without further ado. I sighed at the thought of the expense of fixing the car – again – on a tight budget like mine, detached the car keys from my ring and put them in the ignition, and started walking to the Winthrops'.

Nothing in Shakespeare is really far away from anything else. But it was a considerable hike to the Winthrops' neighborhood in the northern part of town, especially in the cold.

At least it wasn't raining.

I reminded myself of that frequently. I promised myself something extra good for lunch, maybe a whole peanut butter-and-jelly sandwich with my homemade soup. I deserved another treat, too. Maybe a new pair of boots? Nope, couldn't do that if I had to pay for the car repairs . . .

Finally, about nine-thirty, I got to the Winthrops', the jewel of the most opulent new neighborhood in Shakespeare. This neighborhood, not coincidentally, was farthest away from the southwestern black area and my own slightly-less-southern patch to the east.

The Winthrop lot was a corner lot. Today I used the kitchen door at the back of the garage, which was a wing on the side of the house opening onto Blanche Street, since I didn't have my oil-spotting car. The front door of the house faced Amanda Street. To compensate for the small trees in front (this was a new sub-division) the landscaper had made the backyard a veritable jungle enclosed by a wooden privacy fence. There were several gates in the privacy fence, always kept carefully locked by the Winthrops so neighborhood children wouldn't trespass for a dip in the pool or a game of hide-and-seek. The Winthrop house backed up to an equally large home that had employed the same landscape planner, so in the greener seasons their block resembled the tropical bird enclosure at a good zoo. There was a narrow alley in between the back gates of the two houses. It ran the length of the block and allowed passage for the Shakespeare garbage trucks and the lawn service that maintained almost every lawn in the neighborhood.

I stepped into the Winthrop kitchen, for once feeling positively happy to be there. The kitchen was dim and warm, wonderfully warm. For a couple of minutes I stood under a vent, enjoying the rush of heated air, restoring my circulation. I pulled off my old red Lands End squall jacket and hung it on one of the chairs at the round table where the family ate most of their meals. I strolled out of the kitchen, still rubbing my hands together, to the huge family room, stylishly carpeted in hunter green and decorated in taupe, burgundy, and gold. I picked up a couch pillow and fluffed it, replacing it automatically in the correct corner of the couch, which could easily seat four.

Still trying to reach a normal temperature, I stood staring out the sliding glass doors. The backyard looked melancholy in the late autumn, the foliage thinned out and the high fence depressingly obvious. The gray pool cover was spotted with puddles of rainwater. The warm colors of the big room were more pleasant, and I roamed around it picking up odds and ends as I stretched chilled muscles.

The pleasure of being warm made me feel like singing. I'd only rediscovered my voice recently; it was as though for years I'd forgotten I had the ability. At first the memories had wrenched at me – I remembered singing at weddings as a teenager, remembered church solos . . . remembered what my life once was. But I'd gotten past that. I began humming.

Though it wasn't my regular cleaning day, from habit I walked through the whole house, as I always did when I came in. Upstairs, Bobo's room was picked up and the bedspread was actually pulled straight. No such epiphany had inspired Amber Jean and Howell Three, but then they'd never been as sloppy as Bobo. The two upstairs bathrooms were more or less straight. Downstairs, Beanie always made the king-size bed in the huge master bedroom, and she was meticulous about hanging up her clothes because she had paid a lot for them. Beanie's family had a great regard for money.

I began singing 'The First Time Ever I Saw Your Face' as I went to the 'cleaning stuff' closet in the kitchen to select what I'd need: dust cloths, the vacuum cleaner, glass cleaner and rags, shoe polish.

Twice a year, for extra pay of course, I performed this odd little service for Beanie. I took everything out of her huge walk-in closet, every single thing. Then I cleaned the closet, reorganized her clothes, and checked to make sure all her shoes were polished and ready to wear. Any clothes that needed mending or were missing buttons I put to one side for Beanie's attention, or rather her seamstress's.

I had sung my way to the end of the ballad when I took all my cleaning paraphernalia into the big dark bedroom – Beanie kept the drapes drawn – and dumped it on the floor to one side of Beanie's closet. I opened the mirrored door and reached inside to switch on the light.

Someone grabbed my wrist and yanked me in.

I fought immediately, because Marshall had taught me not to hesitate; if you hesitate, if you falter, you've already lost psychological ground. In fact, I almost went crazy and lost all my training, but hung on by a little rag of intelligence. I formed a good fist and hit with my free left hand, striking for anything I could hit. I couldn't place my assailant exactly, had no idea who had grabbed me.

My blows made contact with flesh, I thought a cheek. He grunted but didn't lessen his formidable grip on my right wrist, and it was only with an effort that I kept the left hand free. I knew it was a man from the sound of the grunt, so I went for his balls, but he twisted to one side and evaded my fingers. He'd been wanting to catch that free hand, and this he finally did; bad news for me. I tried breaking loose by stepping into him and bringing my hands, palms up, against his thumbs, the same move that had worked against Bobo; once I was free, I would slap him over the ears or gouge his eyes, I wasn't particular, I would kill him or hurt him however I could.

The move didn't work because he'd been expecting it. His hands slid down from my wrists to hold me right below the elbows. I slammed my head forward to break his nose but got his chest instead. As I threw my head back up I heard his teeth click together, so I'd clipped his chin, but that wasn't enough to effect any major damage. I tried for the groin again with my knee and this time managed to make some contact because I got the grunt again. Elated, I tried to bring him down by hooking my leg between his legs and kicking the back of his knee. This was incredibly stupid on my part, because I succeeded. I brought him down right on top of me.

He pinned me to the floor with his body, his strong hands gripping my arms to my sides, his legs weighting mine. I lost my mind. I bit him on the ear.

'Goddamn! Stop it!' He never lessened his grip, which was what I was working for, but brought his forehead down on mine, using my own trick against me. He hadn't used full force, not by a long shot, but I gasped with pain and felt tears form in my eyes.

He moved his head down to my ear, so his cheek was against mine, an oddly intimate contact. I heaved and bucked against him, but I could feel the weakness in my movements. 'Listen,' he hissed. And then as I opened my mouth to scream, hoping to throw him off guard for a second, he said the one thing that could have achieved a truce.

'They're breaking in,' he whispered. 'For God's sake, just shut up and be still. They'll kill us both.'

I know how to shut up and I know how to be still, though I couldn't stop quivering. My eyes finally adjusted to the near-darkness of the closet, and by the faint light coming in through the partly open door, I saw that the man on top of me was Mr Black Ponytail.

After a second, I wasn't too surprised.

Those eyes were not focused on me, but staring out the closet door as the man listened to the faint sounds that were just now penetrating my tangled state of fear and rage.

He bent back so his mouth was by my ear, his newly shaven cheek again resting against mine. 'It's gonna take them a while. They don't know shit about breaking and entering,' he said in a voice so low it seemed to come from somewhere inside my own head. 'Now, who the fuck are you?'

Through clenched teeth I said, 'I am the fucking *maid*.' Every muscle in my body was tensed, and the shivering would not stop no matter how I willed myself to be still. I began to make myself relax, knowing that if I didn't, I would remain weak and disadvantaged.

'That's better. We're on the same side,' whispered the man as he felt my body soften and still beneath him.

'Who are you?' I asked him.

'I,' he told my ear, 'am the fucking *detective*.' He shifted on top of me. He wasn't as calm or cool as he was trying to sound. His body was reacting to its proximity with mine, and he was getting uncomfortable. 'If I let you go, are you gonna give me any trouble? They're much more dangerous than I am.'

I thought about it. I had no idea if he really was a detective. And whose detective? FBI? Private? ATF? The Shakespeare police force? Winthrop County?

I heard glass shattering.

'They're in,' he breathed into my ear. 'Listen, the game plan has changed.'

'Huh,' I said contemptuously and almost inaudibly. I hated sports metaphors. I felt much better almost immediately. Angry is better than scared or confused.

'They'll kill us if we're caught,' he told me again. His lips, so close to my ear, suddenly made me want to shiver again in a completely different way. His body was talking to mine at great length, no matter what his mouth was saying.

'Now, what I want you to do, when they're all in the house,' he whispered breathlessly, 'is start screaming. I'm going out the front door, circling around to the alley to get their license plate number, identify the car, so I can try to find where they go after this.'

I wondered what his original plan had been. This one seemed awful haphazard. His hands, instead of gripping my arms, were rubbing them slowly.

'They'll know it was me and come after me.'

'If you're never in their sight, they won't believe you saw them,' he breathed. 'Give me three minutes, then scream.'

'No,' I said very softly. 'I'll turn on the vacuum cleaner.'

I sensed a certain amount of exasperation rolling off Mr Ponytail. 'OK,' he agreed. 'Whatever.'

Then he slid off me, and rose to his feet. He held out his hand and I took it without thinking. He pulled me up as easily as he'd helped me do chin-ups that morning. He gave me a sharp nod to indicate the clock was running, and then he was gone, easing himself out of the closet, through Beanie's bedroom, and presumably down the little hall that led to the foyer of the house. His exit was much more subtle than the burglars' entrance.

I peered at my big-faced man's watch, actually timing the self-proclaimed detective, trying not to wonder why I was doing what he said. At two and a half minutes, I risked stepping out of the closet. I could hear the intruders clearly now. Once they'd gotten into the house, they'd abandoned all attempts at silence.

After plugging in the vacuum cleaner, I suddenly began belting out 'Whistle While You Work'. Without waiting to assess the reaction, I stepped on the 'On' button and the vacuum cleaner roared to life. I was careful to keep my back to the bedroom door as I began industriously vacuuming, because I could see in Beanie's dressing table mirror if I was being stalked. I caught a shadow swooping across the mirror, but its owner was in the act of departure. I'd spooked them.

When I felt sure they were gone, I turned off the vacuum cleaner. Watchfully, I once again toured the Winthrop house. One of the sliding glass doors leading to the pool area was broken. Looking across the covered pool, I saw one of the wooden gates standing ajar. The Winthrops needed a full-fledged security system, I thought severely. Then I realized I would have to clean up all the glass, and I found myself irrationally peeved.

Also, I had to call the police.

There was no way around it.

Should I tell them about Black Ponytail? If it weren't for Claude, I'd lie in a jiffy. All my contacts with the police had been painful. But I trusted Claude. I should tell him the truth. But what could I tell him?

I was fairly sure Howell Jr. must have admitted Black Ponytail to the house or given him the keys. My doubts about their relationship recurred. But no matter what that relationship was, it seemed to me I'd be violating whatever loyalty I was supposed to have to the Winthrop family if I told the police Black Ponytail had been already concealed in the house, anticipating this very break-in.

This was knotty.

I called the police station and reported the break-in, and had a few moments to think hard.

The safest thing was a straight break-in. I don't know nothin', boss.

It helped immensely that Claude didn't come. Dedford Jinks, the detective who'd so frightened Bobo, and two patrolmen responded to my call. Claude was in a meeting with the county judge and the mayor and had not been told about the incident, I gathered from listening to the patrolmen.

Dedford was a good ole guy with a beer gut hanging over a worn belt buckle he'd won in his calf-roping days. He had thin graying hair, a thin compressed mouth, and a ruddy complexion. Dedford was nobody's fool.

My story was this: I'd heard little noises, but thought that a member of the family had come in. From then on, I told the truth: I'd plugged in the vacuum and turned it on, I'd heard a big commotion, I hadn't seen anyone.

After they'd checked out the backyard and found a gate unlocked, and many footprints in the flower beds, the police said I could go.

'I have to clean up,' I said, gesturing to the glass on the Winthrops' thick hunter-green carpet. They'd gathered up the biggest pieces for fingerprint testing, but there were lots of fragments.

'Oh,' said one of the patrolmen, disconcerted. 'Well, OK.'

Then Howell burst into the house, moving faster than I'd ever seen him move. His face was red.

'My God, Lily, are you all right?' He actually took one of my hands and held it. I reclaimed it. This was strange. I could feel the policemen looking at each other.

'Yes, Howell, I'm fine.'

'They didn't hurt you?'

I gestured wide with my hands to draw his notice to my uninjured body.

'But the bruise on your forehead?'

I touched my face carefully. Sure enough, my forehead was tender and puffy. Thanks, Mr Ponytail. I hoped his ear hurt.

'I guess I ran into the doorframe,' I said. 'I got pretty excited.'

'Well, sure. But one of the men didn't . . .'

'No.'

'I had no idea you were going to be here today,' Howell said, taking his snowy white handkerchief out of his pocket and patting his face with it. 'I am so glad you weren't harmed.'

'I came to do your wife's closet. It's just a twice-a-year thing,' I explained. For me, I was talking too much. I hoped no one would notice. I was rattled. I knew now that Howell was directly involved in this day's peculiar doings. At least it was Howell who had let Ponytail in, so he had been here legitimately. I guessed Howell was now wondering where the hell his man was and what part he'd played in this fiasco.

'I'll just clean up this mess and go,' I suggested again.

'No, no, you need to go home after this,' Howell exclaimed, his handsome, fleshy face creased with anxiety. 'I'll be glad to clean it up.'

Definite glances between all police personnel within earshot. Shit.

'But I'd like to . . .' I let my sentence trail off as Dedford raised an eyebrow in my direction. If I insisted longer, so would Howell, drawing more attention to his unusual preoccupation with my condition. He was obviously guiltstricken. If he kept this up, everyone present would figure something strange was going on, and they might think it was more than Howell having an affair with his maid, which was bad enough.

'Where's your car?' Howell asked suddenly.

'It wouldn't start this morning,' I said wearily, by now tired of explaining myself. 'I walked.'

'Oh my God, all that way! I'm sure one of these boys will be glad to give you a ride home!'

One of the 'boys', the older paunchier one with a disbelieving mouth, said he sure would be glad to do that.

So I got delivered to my house in style. My car was still in my carport, but with a sheet of yellow legal paper stuck under the windshield. It read, '*I fixed it. You owe me $68.23.*' It was a lot more direct and honest than the blue sheets that were suddenly papering the town. I turned to the patrolman, who was waiting to see me enter my house safely. 'Do you know anything about those flyers that are turning up under everyone's windshield wipers?'

'I know they ain't no ordinance against it,' he replied, and his face closed like a fist. 'Likewise they ain't no ordinance against the blacks meeting to talk about it, which they aim to do tonight.'

'Where?'

'The meeting? At the Golgotha A.M.E. Church on Castle Road. We got to maintain a presence, case there's any trouble.'

'That's good,' I said, and after thanking the man for giving me a ride home (and being willing to part with information without asking any questions) I sat in my recliner and thought.

Chapter Five

I don't know what I expected of the rest of the day. I think I expected the man in the closet to pop up any minute; to tell me what had happened when he left, to ask me if he'd hurt me in our struggle, to explain himself.

After seeing him everywhere I turned, now he was nowhere. I passed through being worried, to being angry, and back through worried. I made my feelings cool down, concentrated on chilling them; I told myself the fear and rage engendered by our silent struggle in Beanie Winthrop's walk-in closet – what a location – had nudged me past some internal boundary marker.

Out of sheer restlessness, that night I attended the meeting at Golgotha A.M.E. Church. I found it with a little difficulty since it was in the center of the largest black residential area in Shakespeare, which I seldom had reason to visit. The church itself, redbrick and larger than I expected, was set up on a knoll, with cracked concrete steps bordered by a handrail leading up to the main doors. It was on a corner lot, and there was a big streetlight shining down those steps. Golgotha was so centrally located that I saw many people walking to the meeting despite the gusty cold wind.

I also saw two police cars on the way there. One was driven by Todd Picard, who gave me an unhappy nod. It was easy to tell that every time he saw me, I reminded him of something he wanted to forget. I felt the same way about him.

I went up the steps of the church at a fast clip, anxious to get out of the wind. It seemed to me I'd been cold all day. There were double doors at the top of the steps, and inside those, a large foyer with two coatracks, a table spread with lots of free literature on Planned Parenthood and Alcoholics Anonymous and the practice of daily prayer, and the doors to two rooms, one on each side, that I guessed were vesting rooms or perhaps served for choir practice. Ahead, there were two sets of doors into the body of the church. I picked the right set of doors and followed the flow of people into the sanctuary. There was a long center set of pews and a shorter set on each side, with wide aisles in between, the same conformation I'd seen in many churches. I picked a long central pew at random, and scooted toward the center to give later arrivals easy access.

The meeting was scheduled to begin at seven, and surprisingly enough it did. The high attendance on a cold school night was a measure of how strong feeling was running in the African-American community. Mine was not the only white face in view. The Catholic sisters who ran a preschool for disadvantaged children were seated some distance away, and Claude was there: a good public relations move, I thought. He gave me a curt nod. Sheriff Marty Schuster was sitting beside Claude on the dais. To my surprise, he was a small wizened man you would've thought couldn't arrest a possum. But his appearance was deceiving; I'd heard more than once that Sheriff Schuster had cracked his share of skulls. Schuster's secret, Jim Box had told me one morning, was to always strike first and hardest.

Claude and Marty Schuster shared the platform with a man I supposed was the church's pastor, a short, square man with great dignity and angry eyes. He was holding a Bible.

Another light face caught my eye. Mookie Preston was there, too, sitting by herself. When Lanette Glass came in, the two women exchanged a long look before Lanette sat by another teacher.

I saw Cedric, my mechanic, and Raphael Roundtree, who was sitting with his wife. Cedric gave me a surprised smile and wave, but Raphael's greeting was subdued. His wife just stared.

The meeting went like many community meetings with an ill-defined goal. It opened with a prayer so fervent that I half expected God to touch everyone's heart with love and understanding on the spot. If He did, the results were not immediate.

Everyone had something to say, and wanted to say it simultaneously. They were all angry about the blue pieces of paper, and
wanted to know what the chief of police and the sheriff were
doing about them. At tedious length, the lawmen explained that
they couldn't do anything about them; the handouts were not
obscene, did not contain a clear and overt incitement to violence.
Of course, this was not a satisfactory response to most of the
people in the church.

At least three people were trying to speak when Lanette Glass
stood up. There was silence, gradually; a deep silence.

'My son is dead,' Lanette said. Her glasses caught the harsh
fluorescent light and winked. Darnell's mother was probably still
in her forties, with a pleasant round figure and a pretty round face.
She was wearing a brown, cream, and black pantsuit. She looked
very sad, very angry.

'You may talk about "we don't know this" and "we can't guess
that," but we all know good and well that Darnell was murdered
by the same men that are passing around this paper.'

'We can't know that, Mrs Glass,' Marty Schuster said helplessly.
'I sympathize with your grief, and your son's is one of the three
homicides the city and county police are working on – believe me,
we're working on it, we want to find out what happened to your
son – but we can't go haring off and accuse people who don't
even have an identity.'

'I can,' she said unanswerably. 'I can also say what everyone
here is thinking, blacks and probably whites, too: that if Darnell
hadn't been killed, Len Elgin would not have died, and maybe Del
Packard, too. And I want to know what we, the black community,
are supposed to do about these rumors of armed militia in our
town, armed white men who hate us.'

I awaited a reply with interest. An armed militia? The problem
was, just about every white man – and black – in town was
already armed. Guns were not exactly scarce in this area, where
lots of citizens felt you were wise to carry a weapon if you
traveled to Little Rock. You could buy arms at Winthrop Sporting
Goods, if you wanted a top-of-the-line piece. You could buy a gun

at Wal-Mart, or at the pawnshop, or just about anywhere in Shakespeare. So the 'armed' part wasn't exactly a shocker, but the 'militia' part was.

I wasn't too surprised when Claude and Marty Schuster protested ignorance of any knowledge of an armed militia in our fair city.

The meeting was effectively over, but no one wanted to admit it. Everyone had had his or her say, and no solution had been reached, because a solution to this problem was simply unreachable. A few die-hards were still trying to get the lawmen to make some kind of statement committing the law to eradicating the group apparently inciting white Shakespeareans to some kind of action against dark Shakespeareans, but Marty and Claude refused to be pinned.

People rose and began to shuffle toward the two exits: I saw Marty Schuster, Claude, and the minister go toward the aisle on my left. I stood admiring the carved pulpit, at the end of the aisle to the right, before I stepped into the aisle. I had zipped up my coat and was pulling on my black leather gloves when I felt a hand on my arm. I turned to meet the magnified eyes of Lanette Glass.

'Thank you for helping my son,' she said. She looked at me unwaveringly, but her eyes suddenly swam in tears.

'I wasn't able to help when it counted,' I said.

'You can't blame yourself,' she said gently. 'You can't count the times I've cried since he died, thinking I could somehow have warned him, somehow rescued him. I could have gone out for milk myself, instead of asking him to run to the store. That was when they got him, you know, in the parking lot . . . at least that was where his car was found.'

His new car, still with its crumpled fender.

'But you, you fought for him,' Lanette said quietly. 'You bled for him.'

'Don't make me better than I am,' I said flatly. 'You're a brave woman, Mrs Glass.'

'Don't you make me any better than I am,' Lanette Glass said quietly. 'I thanked the black Marine the day after the fight. I never thanked you until tonight.'

I looked down at the floor, at my hands, at anything but Lanette Glass's large brown eyes; and when I looked up, she had gone.

The crowd continued to exit slowly. People were talking, shaking their heads, pulling on their own coats and scarves and gloves. I moved along with them, thinking my own thoughts. I pushed up my sleeve to check my watch: It was 8:15. Through the open doors ahead of me, I could see that the crowd was thick in the church's foyer. People were hesitating before stepping out into the cold. There were about three people between me and the sanctuary doors, and there were at least six people behind me.

The stout woman on my left turned to me to say something. I never found out what it was. The bomb went off.

I can't remember if I knew what had happened right away or not. When I try, my head hurts. But I must have turned. Somehow I had a sense of the pulpit disintegrating.

I was pushed from behind by a powerful wind and I saw the head of the woman beside me separate from her body as a collection plate clove through her neck. I was sprayed with her blood as her body crumpled and her head and I went flying forward. My thick coat and scarf helped absorb some pressure. So did the bodies of the people behind me. The wooden pews also blocked some of the blast, but they splintered, of course, and those splinters were deadly . . . some of them were as big as spears, just as lethal.

The roar deafened me and in silence I flew through the air. All this happened at the same time, too much to catalog . . . the woman's head flew with me, we flew together into kingdom come.

I was lying halfway on my right side, on something lumpy. Something else was lying on me. I was soaking wet. There were cold winds blowing in the church, and flames were flickering here and there. I was in hell. I watched the flames and wondered why I was so cold. Then I realized if I turned my head a little, I could see the stars, though I was in a building. This was remarkable; I should tell someone. The lights were out, but I could see a little. I could smell smoke, too, and the sharp smell of blood, and even worse things. And there was a heavy chemical smell overlaying everything, an odor that was completely new to me.

My situation isn't good, I thought. I need to move. I want to go home. Take a shower.

I tried to sit up. I couldn't hear a thing. That made my state even more surrealistic. With some senses so drenched with input and others totally deprived, it was easy to convince myself I was in a nightmare. I lost my place for a few minutes, I think. Then I reoriented, after a fashion. Someone was near me, I could tell, I could feel movement but not hear it. I turned painfully onto my back, put my hands on whatever was lying on my chest, and shoved. It moved. I tried to sit up, fell back. That hurt. A face appeared through the gloom in front of me. It was the face of Lanette Glass. She was talking, I could tell, because her mouth was moving.

At last she seemed to realize that she wasn't getting through. She moved her lips slowly. I decided she was saying, 'Where – is – Mookie?'

I remembered who Mookie was, and I remembered seeing her earlier. She had been on the other side of the church – that was where I was, in the Golgotha A.M.E. Church – and I'd glanced across at Mookie as she'd passed from the sanctuary into the foyer.

'Can you hear me?' I asked Lanette. I couldn't hear myself. It was overwhelmingly strange. I thought of going to the dentist, not being able to feel your own lips after he filled a tooth. I went off course, for a minute. Lanette shook me. She was nodding frantically. It took me another moment to realize she was letting me know she could hear me. That was great! I smiled. 'Mookie is on the other side of the church,' I said. 'In the foyer.'

Lanette vanished.

I wondered if I could stand up and go to a warm place and shower. I tried to roll onto my knees; I pushed against the thing underneath me, to flip from my back to my stomach. When I'd gotten that done, I saw the lump underneath me was the body of a girl, about ten or twelve years old. Her hair was elaborately decorated with beads. There was a sharp splinter protruding from her neck. Her eyes were blank. I closed my mind to that. I pulled up on a bench upended and aslant, propped against another bench. I wondered at the multitude of benches. Then I thought, church. Pews.

I stood erect. Everything swung around me, and I had to hold on to the back of the pew, actually a leg, since it was upside down. I suspected that all the flashing I could see meant I was losing my vision; but it was blue flashing. I was looking through the sanctuary doors to the foyer, through the foyer door to the outside; all the doors were open. No. The doors weren't there anymore. Maybe I was seeing police cars? Surely, in an emergency like this, they would help?

I wondered how I might get out of this place. Though the electricity had gone out, there was that big streetlight right outside, and its light was coming through the holes in the roof. There were flames in several spots around me, though I couldn't hear them crackle.

I remembered I was strong. I remembered I should be helping. Well, there was no helping the girl beneath me. I had helped Lanette by telling her where Mookie had been the last time I'd seen her. And look at what happened. Lanette had left. Maybe I should just fend for myself, huh?

But then I thought of Claude. I should find him and help him. It seemed to me it was my turn.

I took a shuffling step, now that I had a purpose. My left leg hurt very badly, but that was hardly a big surprise. Didn't make it hurt any the less, though. I looked down unwillingly, and saw there was a cut in my leg, a very long slicing cut down the side of my thigh. I was terrified I'd see another splinter protruding, but I didn't. I was bleeding, though. Understatement.

I took another step, over something I didn't want to identify. I could feel my throat moving and I knew I was making sounds, though I couldn't hear them, which was fine. They were better unheard. The beams of the streetlight that came through the roof had a surrealistic air because of the dust, which swam and floated in their light.

I stepped carefully through debris where there had been order just minutes before; the dead and dying and terribly injured where there had been whole clean living people. My leg collapsed once. I got back up. I could see other people moving. One man had gotten to his knees as I neared him. I held out my hand. He looked at it as if he'd never seen a hand. His eyes followed the line of my arm up to my face. He flinched when he looked at me. I figured I looked pretty bad. He didn't look so great himself. He was covered with dust, and he had blood flowing from a deep cut in his arm. He'd lost the sleeve of his coat. He took my hand. I pulled. He came up. I nodded to him and went on.

I found Claude in the far aisle of the church, where I'd last seen him talking to the sheriff and the minister. I'd been closer to the bomb on the east side of the church, but the sheriff and the minister were dead. One of the big bar-shaped lighting fixtures had fallen from the ceiling and hit them square. They'd been much the same height. Claude must have been a step ahead of them. His legs were under the long heavy bar and he was lying on his stomach. His hands and arms and the back of his head were covered with white powder and debris and dark red blood. He was motionless.

I touched his neck, couldn't remember why I was doing that, and began to push the long lighting fixture that was pinning his legs. It was very heavy. I was in terrible pain, and wanted desperately to lie down. But I felt there was something wrong about that, something bad, and I had to keep on pushing and pulling at the light fixture.

I finally got it off Claude's legs. He was stirring, heaving up on his arms. I made a connection in my mind between the flashing blue light and Claude. I saw a group of lights swinging around catching millions of dust motes, thought it was in my head. But I gradually worked out that these were flashlights in the hands of rescuers.

It seemed to me they would want to move the most seriously injured first; at the same time, I had to admit, I really wanted to go home and shower. Maybe an ambulance would drop me off at home. I was sure sticky and smelly, and I was so sleepy. Maybe Claude and I could drive together, since we lived side by side. I knelt down by him and leaned over to look in his face. He was in agony, his eyes wide. When he saw me, his lips began moving. I smiled at him and shook my head, to show I couldn't hear. His lips drew back from his teeth, and I knew that Claude was screaming.

Oh, I had to get up again, I realized wearily. I made it, but I was pretty sick of trying to walk. I shuffled a few steps, saw an upright figure ahead of me in the uncertain gloom. He swung around, and my eyes dazzled in the sudden blast of the flashlight. It was Todd Picard, and he was talking to me.

'I can't hear,' I said. He ran the flashlight up and down my length, and when I could see his face in its glow again, he looked sick.

'I know where Claude is,' I said. 'You need him, right?'

He illuminated himself with the flash. 'Where – is – he?' Todd mouthed. I took his free hand and pulled, and he followed me.

I pointed down at Claude.

Todd turned in another direction, and I could see his hand go up to his mouth, his lips moving; he was screaming for help. Claude was still alive; his fingers were moving. I bent down to pat him reassuringly, and I just fell over. I didn't get back up.

I don't remember being loaded onto the stretcher, but I do remember the jolt of being carried. I remember the brilliance of the lights of the emergency room. I remember Carrie, all in white, looking so clean and calm, and I remember her trying to ask me questions. I kept shaking my head, I couldn't hear anything.

'Deaf,' I said finally, and her lips stopped moving. People were busy around me; there was near-chaos in the hospital corridor. Since I wasn't the most seriously injured, I had to wait my turn, and that was fine, except I couldn't have any pain medication until Carrie had looked me over.

I blanked in and out, waking to see people moving up and down the hall, gurneys rolling past, all the doctors in town and most all the medical personnel of any kind.

And then, very oddly, I felt fingers on my wrist. Someone was taking my pulse, and while that was not so extraordinary, I knew I had to open my eyes. With an effort, I did. The detective was bending over me. He was so clean.

I could not hear much, I found, but I could hear a little, and I could lip-read.

'Is your head hurt?' he asked.

'I don't know,' I said slowly, every word an effort. 'My leg is.'

He looked down. 'They'll have to stitch it up,' he told me, and he looked very angry. 'Who can I call for you? Someone should be here with you.'

'No one,' I said. It was an effort to talk.

'There's blood all over your face.'

'The woman next to me was . . .' I couldn't think of *decapitated*. 'Her head came off,' I said, and closed my eyes again.

When I opened them some time later, he was gone.

I hardly woke up when Carrie stitched on me, and it was a surprise to find myself in the X-ray room. Other than these travels, I was out in the hall all night, which was fine. All the rooms were filled with the more seriously injured. And I could tell by the constant flow of ambulance personnel that some people were being sent to Montrose or Little Rock. Carrie came by and shook me awake every so often to check my eyes, and the nurses took my pulse and blood pressure, and I wanted most of all to be left alone. Hospitals are not places for being left alone.

The next time I opened my eyes, it was daylight. I could see a pale watery morning through the glass doors of the emergency room. A man in a suit was standing by my gurney. He was looking down at me. He, too, was looking a little squeamish. I was really tired of people looking at me that way.

'How do you feel, Miss Bard?' he asked, and I could hear him, though his voice was oddly beelike.

'I don't know. I don't know what happened to me.'

'A bomb went off,' he said. 'In Golgotha Church.'

'Right.' I accepted that as the truth, but it was the first time I had thought of the word *bomb*. Bomb, man-made. Someone had actually done that on purpose.

'I'm John Bellingham. I'm with the FBI.' He showed me some identification, but my brain was too scrambled for it to make sense.

I absorbed that, trying to make sense of it. I thought that since Claude and the sheriff were down, the FBI had been called in to keep the peace. Then I cleared up a little. Church bombing. Civil rights. FBI.

'OK.'

'Can you describe what happened last night?'

'The church blew up as we were leaving.'

'Why did you attend the meeting, Miss Bard?'

'I didn't like the blue sheets.'

He looked at me as if I were insane.

'Blue sheets . . .'

'The papers,' I said, beginning to be angry. 'The blue sheets of paper they were putting under everyone's windshield wipers.'

'Are you a civil rights activist, Miss Bard?'

'No.'

'You have friends in the black community?'

I wondered if Raphael would consider himself my friend. I decided, yes.

'Raphael Roundtree,' I said carefully.

He seemed to be writing that down.

'Can you find out if he's okay?' I asked. 'And Claude, is Claude alive?'

'Claude . . .'

'The police chief,' I said. I couldn't remember Claude's last name, and that made me feel very odd.

'Yes, he's alive. Can you describe in your own words what happened in the church?'

I said slowly, 'The meeting went long. I looked at my watch. It was eight-fifteen when I was leaving, walking down the aisle.'

He definitely wrote that down.

'Do you still have your watch on?' he asked.

'You can look and see,' I said indifferently. I didn't want to move. He pulled the sheet down and looked at my arm.

'It's here,' he said. He pulled out his handkerchief, wet it with his tongue, and scrubbed at my wrist. I realized he was cleaning the watch face. 'Sorry,' he apologized, and when he pocketed the handkerchief again I could see it was stained.

He bent over me, trying to read the watch without shifting me.

'Hey, it's still ticking along,' he said cheerfully. He checked it against his own watch. 'And right on time. So, it was eight-fifteen, and you were leaving . . . ?'

'The woman next to me was about to say something,' I said. 'And then her head wasn't there.'

He looked serious and subdued, but he had no idea what it had been like: though when I thought about it, I had little idea myself. I could not remember exactly . . . I could see the shiny edge of the collection plate. So I told John Bellingham about the collection plate. I recalled Lanette Glass speaking to me, and I mentioned that, and I remembered helping the man up, and I knew I'd journeyed across the church to find Claude. But I refused to recall what I'd seen on that journey, and to this day I do not want to remember.

I told John Bellingham about finding Claude, about leading Todd to him.

'Was it you that moved the fixture off his legs?' the agent asked.

'I believe so,' I said slowly.

'You're one strong lady.' He asked me more questions, lots more, about whom I'd seen, white people in particular of course, and where I'd been sitting . . . ta da ta da ta da.

'Find out about Claude,' I told him, wearying of the conversation.

Instead, he sent me Carrie.

She was so tired her face had a gray cast. Her white coat was filthy now, and her glasses smeared with fingerprints. I was glad to see her.

'You have a long cut on your leg. Some stitches and some butterfly bandages are holding it together. You have a slight concussion. You have bruising all across your back, including your butt. A splinter evidently grazed your scalp, one reason you looked so horrendous when they brought you in, and another splinter took off a little of your earlobe. You won't miss it. You have dozens of abrasions, none of them serious, all of them painful. I can't believe it, but you have no broken bones. How's your hearing?'

'Everything sounds buzzy,' I said with an effort.

'Yeah, I can imagine. It'll get better.'

'So I can go home?'

'As soon as we're sure about the concussion. Probably in a few hours.'

'Are you gonna charge me for a room since I was out in the hall all night?'

Carrie laughed. 'Nope.'

'Good. You know I don't have much insurance.'

'Yeah.'

Carrie had arranged for me to be in the hall. I felt a surge of gratitude. 'What about Claude?' I asked.

Her face grew more serious. 'He's got a badly broken leg, broken in two places,' she began. 'Like you, he has a concussion, and he's temporarily deaf. He has a serious cut on one arm, and his kidneys are bruised.'

'He's going to be okay?'

'Yes,' she said, 'but it's going to take a long time.'

'Did you treat my friend Raphael Roundtree, by chance?'

'Nope, or I did but I don't remember the name, which is entirely possible.' Carrie yawned, and I could tell how exhausted she was. 'But I'll look for him.'

'Thanks.'

A nurse came a few minutes later to tell me Raphael had been treated and released the night before.

A few hours later, a hospital volunteer gave me a ride back to my car, still parked a couple of blocks away from the ruin of

Golgotha Church. She was civil enough, but I could tell she thought I'd mostly deserved what happened to me because I'd gone to a meeting in a black church. I was not surprised at her attitude, and I didn't care a whole lot. My coat was in a wastebasket at the hospital because the back of it was shredded, and the hospital gave me a huge ancient jacket of sweatsuit material, with a hood, which I was grateful to wrap around me. I knew I looked pretty disreputable. Bits of my shoes were missing and my blue jeans had been cut off to treat my leg. I was wearing even older sweatpants.

The wound was in my left leg, which was fortunate, because it meant I could drive. It was painful to walk – hell, it was painful to move – and I wanted to be home locked inside my own place so bad that I could just barely endure the process of getting there.

I parked my car in my own carport and unlocked my own kitchen door with a relief so great I could almost taste it. My bed was waiting for me, with clean sheets and firm pillows and no one shaking me awake to check my pupils, but I could not get into it as filthy as I was.

When I looked into my bathroom mirror, I was amazed that anyone had been able to endure looking at me. Though I'd been swabbed at some, the hospital had been so flooded with injuries that cleaning up the victims had had low priority. I had speckles of blood all over my face and clotting my hair, my neck had a dried river where my ear had bled, my shirt and bra were splotched in blood and smelled to high heaven of all kinds of things, and my shoes would have to go. It took a long long time to get all this off me. I threw the remains of my clothes and shoes into a plastic bag, set it outside the kitchen door, and hobbled laboriously to the bathroom to sponge myself. It was impossible to get in the bathtub, and my stitches were supposed to be kept dry, too. I stood on a towel by my sink, and soaped with one washrag and rinsed with another, until I looked and smelled more like my own self. I even did that to my hair; all I can say of my hair after that is that it was clean. I dabbed more antiseptic ointment on the scalp wound. I threw away the earring still in my right ear – the left earring had been removed in the hospital when they'd treated my ear, and I had no idea where it was and cared less. I did look at my left ear to make sure I could still wear a pair of pierced earrings. I could, but I needed to grow my hair longer to cover the place about midway down the edge of my earlobe where there was, and would always be, a notch.

Finally – barely able to walk, full of medicine, and still oddly numb emotionally – I was able to lower myself into my bed. I flipped the volume of the telephone ring to its lowest setting, but left it on the hook. I didn't want anyone breaking in to see if I'd died. Then I lay back very very carefully and let the darkness come.

I had to miss two and a half days of work, and I had Sunday as a free day anyway. I should have stayed home Monday (and maybe Tuesday), too, but I knew I had to pay the hospital for the emergency room visit, and Carrie for treatment. I always cleaned for Carrie to pay her, but I didn't want my debt to mount too high.

That Monday, it was much easier to clean for the clients who weren't present when I got to work. Otherwise, they tried to send me home.

Bobo had come by the evening of the day I went home.

'How'd you find out?' I asked.

'That new guy said you might need some help.'

I was too exhausted to ask questions, and I was too depressed to care.

Bobo came every day after that, too. He brought in my mail and my paper, and made me sandwiches so thick they were almost impossible to chew. Carrie ran by one evening, but I felt guilty because she looked so tired. The hospital was still full.

'How many dead?' I asked, lying back in my recliner.

She was in the blue wing-back chair. 'So far, five,' she said. 'If it had gone off five minutes later, there would maybe have been no fatalities and few injuries. Five minutes earlier, and the death toll would have been very high.'

'Who died?' I asked.

Carrie fetched the local paper and read me the names. I hadn't personally known any of them, and I was glad of that.

I asked about Claude, and she told me he was better. But she didn't sound comfortable about his progress. 'And I'm worried about him going home by himself, anyway. He lives upstairs.'

'Move all his stuff to the empty downstairs apartment,' I said wearily. 'They're just alike. Tell all the officers they have to show up and help. Don't ask Claude if that's what he wants. Just get it done.'

Carrie looked at me with some amazement. 'All right,' she said slowly.

Carrie had suggested I use a cane for a few days until the swelling and pain in my leg subsided, and I was glad to have the one she loaned me. Marshall came the same evening after she'd left, and he was horrified to see me hobble. He brought three movies he'd taped off HBO for me to watch, and a take-out meal from a local restaurant. I was glad for both. Thinking and standing were not things I wanted to do. When Marshall left, I noticed that he walked next door to the apartments. I figured he was going to see Becca Whitley. I didn't care.

To my amazement, Janet Shook dropped by about lunchtime on Sunday. I'd never seen Janet in a dress before, but she'd been to church and was all decked out in a deep blue dress that looked very nice. She had made me a pot of stew and a loaf of bread, and while she was there she helped me shave my legs and wash my hair properly, two problems that had been bothering me to the point of distraction.

When I went back to work Monday, I can't say I did a good job, but I did my best: That would have to do. I would do extra things, I promised myself, to atone for leaving some chores not well accomplished this time.

I tried all day to save some energy, and at the end of it I drove to the hospital. I was really hurting by then, but I knew if I went home first and took a pain pill I wouldn't persuade myself to go back out. I was looking forward to taking the strongest ones, the ones Carrie had said to take if I knew I wasn't going anywhere.

I had some flowers in a bud vase in my right hand, and my cane in my left, so I was glad the doors were automatic. I made my way to Claude's room, resting here and there. I couldn't knock with both hands occupied, so I called out through the partially open door, 'Claude? Can I come in?'

'Lily? Sure.' At least he seemed to be hearing better.

I butted the door open with my head and hobbled in.

'Damn, girl, I better move over and let you in with me,' he said wearily.

I was shocked when I had a good look at Claude. His face was not its normal healthy color, and his hair was spiky. He was shaven, at least. His right leg and his right arm were engulfed in bandages and casts. He had visibly lost weight.

To my horror, I felt tears crawling down my cheeks.

'Didn't know I looked that bad,' Claude murmured.

'I just thought . . . when I saw you that night . . . I thought you were gone.'

'I hear you did me a favor.'

'You've done plenty for me.'

'Let's call us even, then. No more rescuing each other.'

'Sounds good.'

I sank into the chair by the bed. I felt like hell.

Carrie trotted in then, moving fast as always, her professional face on.

'Two-for-one visit,' she remarked. 'I just came to check in on you, Claude, before I leave for the day.'

Claude smiled at her. Carrie suddenly looked more like a woman than a doctor. I felt extra.

'I ain't feeling as bad as yesterday,' Claude rumbled. 'You get on out of here and get some rest, or you'll end up looking as ragged as Lily. And she hasn't been at work all day.'

'Yes, I have.'

They both looked at me like I was the biggest fool they'd ever encountered. I could feel my face hardening defensively.

'Lily, you'll end up back in bed if you don't rest,' Carrie said, keeping her voice even though it obviously cost her a great deal of self-control.

'I've got to go,' I said, hauling myself up with an effort I didn't want to show. I had counted on sitting longer before I walked back out to my car.

I hobbled out, trying not to limp, failing, getting angry and sad.

For the first time in years, as I stood at the front doors of the hospital and looked at how far away my car was parked, I wanted someone to make my life easier. I had even thought of calling my parents and asking for help, but I hadn't asked them for anything for so long that I'd gotten out of the habit. They would have come, I knew. But they'd have had to book a room at the motel on the bypass, they'd have looked at everything in my house and gotten a close-up of my life. It seemed more trouble, finally, than the help was worth. And I knew from their letters that my sister Serena was heavily involved in engagement parties and showers; the wedding would be just after Christmas. Serena would resent me even more than she already did if I horned in on her spotlight.

Well, this was too close to wallowing in self-pity. I jerked my shoulders straight. I set my eyes on my car, I gripped the cane and started walking.

Two nights later I got an unexpected summons.

The phone rang when I'd finally gotten warm and comfortable, curled up in my double recliner watching TV, covered by an afghan my grandmother had crocheted for me. When the shrill of the bell jolted me into awareness, I realized I hadn't registered anything I was supposed to be watching. I stretched out a hand to lift the receiver.

'Miss Bard?' An old voice, an empress's voice.

'Yes.'

'This is Arnita Winthrop. I wonder if you could come by the house. I would surely like to talk to you.'

'When did you have in mind?'

'Well, young woman, would now be inconvenient for you? I

know you're a working woman, and I'm sure you're mighty tired by the evening . . .'

I was still dressed. I hadn't taken a pain pill. Tonight would be as good a time as any. Though I could tell my body was healing, since the night of the explosion I'd been gripped by an apathy that I could not shake. It seemed a great deal of trouble to get out again, but that was no good reason to refuse.

'I can come now. Could you tell me what this is about? Are you thinking of replacing your maid?'

'Oh, no. Our Callie is part of our family, Miss Bard. No, there's something I need to give you.'

'All right. I'll come.'

'Oh, wonderful! You know where we live? The white house on Partridge Road?'

'Yes, ma'am.'

'We'll see you in a few minutes, then.'

I hung up. After powdering my nose I got my better coat from the closet, the one with no stains or holes, and buttons instead of a zipper. It was all I had left. I was tired, so I took the cane, though I'd managed that day without it.

In a few minutes, I was a little out of town but still within the city limits at the white house on Partridge Road. *House* was a belittling term to apply to the senior Winthrops' dwelling. *Mansion* or *estate* would be more accurate. I turned onto the semi-circular drive that swept opulently through a huge front yard. The drive was illuminated by lampposts stationed at intervals on either side of the paved surface. Pools of water from an afternoon shower glistened with reflected light.

I went up the shallow front steps as quickly as I could. The wind was biting through my coat and jeans. I limped across the stone flags of the front portico, too cold to even think about standing back to admire the facade of the house. I punched the doorbell.

Mrs Winthrop opened the door herself. I had to look down at her. I judged Arnita Winthrop to be in her midseventies. She was beautifully turned out in chestnut brown, which made the rich white of her hair glow. She was lightly made up, and her nails were manicured and coated in clear polish. Her earrings would have paid six months' electric bills for my house. She was absolutely charming.

'Come in, come in, it's freezing out there!' As I stepped past her into the glowing warmth of the entrance hall, she took my hand and clasped it lightly and briefly.

'I'm so glad to meet you at last,' she said with a smile. She glanced at my cane and courteously did not mention it.

Her southern accent, laced with the flat vowels of southern Arkansas, was the thickest I'd heard in years. It made everything she said sound warm and homey.

'Marie talked about you all the time,' Mrs Winthrop continued. 'You were so helpful to her, and she thought so highly of you.'

'I liked her.'

'Here, let me take your coat.' To my discomfort, Mrs Winthrop eased the coat off my shoulders and hung it in a convenient closet. 'Now, come on in the family room. My husband and son are in there, having a drink.'

The family room, predictably, was as large as the ground floor of the Shakespeare Garden Apartments. I had never seen a room that amounted to an investment. There were animal heads on the dark paneling, which had never been on sale at Home Depot. The colors in the upholstery and wallpaper were deep and rich. On top of the wall-to-wall was a rug that I could have stared at for hours, its pattern was so intricate and beautiful.

The two men in the room weren't nearly as appealing.

Howell Winthrop, Sr., was a little rat terrier of a man, with thin gray hair and a thin sharp face and an alert expression. He was wearing a suit and tie, and looked as if that was his casual wear. I thought he was older than his wife, perhaps eighty. Howell Jr. looked much less at ease than his father; in fact, he looked terrible.

'Honey, this is Lily Bard,' Arnita Winthrop said as if her husband should be happy to hear it. At least her equal in manners, he tried to look delighted I'd come, and he and his son both rose without hesitation.

'Pleased to meet you, young lady,' the older man said, and I could hear his age in his voice. 'I've heard a lot of nice things about you.' But his tone said 'interesting stories' rather than 'nice things.'

Howell Jr. and I nodded at each other. I hadn't seen Howell since the day of the break-in. He was giving me the strangest, most intense look. I could see he was trying to transfer some thought directly to my brain.

This was becoming more complex by the second. Now, what might he want me to say, or not say? And why? Could I manage to care?

'Lily and I will just go into the other room for a minute,' Arnita Winthrop excused us. Underneath her courtesy and the mask of her expensive turnout, I realized the older woman was anxious. Very anxious. That made three of us.

Her husband looked cool as a cucumber.

'Now, sugar, wait a minute,' Howell Sr. said, with the greatest good nature. 'You can't just whisk the prettiest woman I've seen in ages out of the room before I have a chance to get a good look at her.'

'Oh, you!' said Arnita with an excellent imitation of perfect good humor. She relaxed visibly. 'Sit down, then, Miss Bard.' She set an example by easing into the couch opposite the two men, who were in higher wing chairs. I had to comply or look like a clod.

I was sorry I'd come. I wanted to go home.

'Miss Bard, weren't you in the church during the explosion, *and* at my son's house at the time of this very mysterious break-in?'

My senses went on full alert. The older Winthrop knew full well I had been there.

'Yes.'

He waited a second for me to say more, saw I wasn't going to.

'Oh my goodness,' Arnita murmured. 'I know you were scared to death.'

I cocked an eyebrow.

Howell Jr.'s forehead was beaded with sweat.

I didn't want to talk about the church. 'Actually, I didn't know anyone was breaking into the house until he left. I probably scared him more than he scared me.' I hoped making the burglar singular would make me sound more ignorant. Howell Jr. looked off at a stag's head, but I could read relief in his posture. I'd given the correct response.

Looking at the three other people in the room, I had the strangest feeling: It seemed so unlikely that I was in this house, in their company. It was like falling down the rabbit's hole in *Alice in Wonderland*. I wondered if I was suffering some strange aftereffect of the explosion.

Howell Sr. found my last remark quite amusing. 'You got any idea what they were after, young lady? You even know if they were niggers or whites?'

I was used to taking people in their context, but I felt my back stiffen and probably my face, too. I felt Howell Sr.'s tone was contemptuous and hectoring. But if I'd been tempted to upbraid the old man, that temptation passed from me when I saw the anxiety in my hostess's face.

'No,' I said.

'My goodness, a woman of few words, ain't that unusual,' Howell Sr. cackled. But his faded blue eyes were not amused. The oldest living Winthrop was used to more respect.

'A break-in in broad daylight,' Arnita said, shaking her head at the evils of the modern world. 'I can't think what was going through their minds.'

'Oh, Mama,' said her son, 'they could have taken the VCRs and the camcorder and even the television sets and gotten enough money to buy drugs for days.'

'I guess you're right.' Arnita shook her head in dismay. 'The world's just not getting any better.'

It seemed a strange point to make with me, but perhaps the older Winthrops were the only two people in Shakespeare who didn't know my history.

'Honey, Miss Bard knows how bad the world is,' her husband said, his voice sad. 'Her past, and this terrible bombing . . .'

'Oh, my dear! Forgive me, I would never want to—'

'It's all right,' I said, unable to keep the weariness from my voice.

'How's your leg, Miss Bard?' the old man asked. He sounded just as tired as I was. 'And I understand you lost part of your ear?'

'Not the important part,' I said. 'And my leg is better.'

All the Winthrops made commiserating noises.

Arnita seized the ensuing pause to tell her husband and son firmly that she and I had something to discuss, and I heaved myself to my feet to follow her erect back down a hall to a smaller room that appeared to be Arnita's own little sitting room. It was decorated in off-white, beige, and peach, and all the furniture was scaled down for Arnita Winthrop's small body.

Again I was ensconced on a comfortable sofa, again Arnita sat, too, and she got down to business.

'Lily, if I may call you that, I have something of Marie's to give you.'

I digested that in silence. Marie hadn't had much at all, and I'd assumed Chuck would be handling whatever little odds and ends of business Marie had left to be completed. I nodded at Arnita to indicate she could continue when she chose.

'You came by on days you weren't supposed to work at Marie's.'

I looked off. That was no one's concern.

'She appreciated it more than you will realize until you get old yourself, Lily.'

'I liked her.' I looked at an oil painting of the three Winthrop grandchildren. Somehow it felt even odder seeing Bobo's young face in these unfamiliar surroundings. Amber Jean looked more like her mother in the picture than she did in the flesh. Howell Three looked gangly and charming.

'Of course, Marie was always conscious that she didn't have much, and Chuck was helping her live in a tolerable way.'

'As he damn well ought to,' I said flatly.

Our eyes met. 'We certainly agree on that,' Arnita said, her voice dry. I almost found myself liking her. 'The point is, Marie couldn't leave you money to thank you for your kindness to her, so she told me she wanted you to have this little ring. No strings. You can sell it or wear it, whatever.'

Arnita Winthrop held out a shabby brown velvet ring box. I took it, opened it. Inside was a ring so pretty and feminine that I smiled involuntarily. It was designed to look like a flower, the petals formed of pinkish opals, the center a pearl circled by tiny diamond chips. There were two leaves, suggested by two dark green stones, which of course were not real emeralds.

'It's a pretty little thing, isn't it?' my hostess said gently.

'Oh, yes,' I said. But even as I spoke, it was occurring to me that I didn't remember seeing the worn velvet box among Marie's things, and I'd been familiar with her belongings for years. I could tell my smile was fading. Marie could have concealed it somewhere clever, I supposed, but still . . .

'What's the matter?' Arnita leaned forward to look at my face, her own deeply concerned.

'Nothing,' I said, quite automatically hiding my worry. 'I'm glad to have it to remember her by, if you're sure that's what she wanted.' I hesitated. 'I can't recollect ever seeing Marie wear this ring.'

'She didn't, for years, thought it looked too young for an old wrinkled woman like the ones we'd turned into,' said Arnita, with a comic grimace.

'Thanks,' I said, there being nothing else to do that I could think of. I stood and pulled my car keys out of my pocket.

Arnita looked a bit startled.

'Well, good night,' I said, seeing I'd been too abrupt.

'Good night, Lily.' The older woman rose, pushing a little on the arms of her chair. 'Let me see you out and get your coat.'

I protested, but she was adamant about fulfilling the forms of courtesy. She opened the beautiful doors to the family room so I was obliged to say good-bye to Howells Sr. and Jr. I hadn't brought a purse so the ring box was in my hand. Howell Jr.'s eyes registered it, and suddenly he turned white.

Then his eyes met mine, and he looked as though he were going to be sick. I was bewildered, and I am sure I looked it.

What was wrong with these people?

I said the minimum courtesy demanded, and I left the room, taking my coat from Arnita at the door. She saw me to the porch and stood there while I climbed into my car. She waved, called out admonitions to drive carefully on the wet streets, thanked me for coming, hoped she would see me again soon. At last she closed her doors behind her.

I shook my head as I turned my keys in the ignition, switched on my headlights. Then my head jerked, following a movement I'd caught out of the corner of my eye. I was out of the car as quickly as I could manage, staring through the dark shapes of the bushes lining the drive, trying to figure out what I'd just seen. I wasn't about to run from the lamplight illuminating the drive into that outer darkness, and I wasn't really sure that I'd seen an actual living thing. Maybe it had been shadows shifting as I turned on my lights. Maybe it had been a dog or cat. As I began to ease down the drive, I scanned the shrubbery for movement, but I saw nothing, nothing at all.

My summons and visit to the Winthrop mansion had been peculiar and strangely off-kilter, and I was tempted to think over the problems this family obviously had. But getting involved in the internecine squabbles of the most powerful family in the county was no way to earn a living. Head low, go forward; I needed to go home and write that a hundred times.

I had a bad feeling. I was already enmeshed in more trouble than I could imagine.

The next day was so normal it was a relief. Though I couldn't stop myself from looking side to side when I was out driving from one job to another, at least I didn't have that jumpy feeling that something – or someone – was about to leap out in front of me in challenge.

The assorted minor bruises on my face and arms had faded to a dusty eggplant shade, and the worst ones on my back were at least less painful. My leg felt much better. The cut on my scalp was almost healed and the notch in my ear was somewhat less disgusting.

I had no appetite for lunch, so after eating a piece of fruit at home I decided to go make a necessary purchase, one I'd been putting off for a few days. My workout gloves were falling apart at the seams, literally. Maybe if I got new gloves, I would go back to Body Time. I hadn't worked out or been to karate since the explosion. I knew I was hardly up to my former routine, but I could be doing abdominal crunches or some biceps work. All my energy seemed to be absorbed in just making my body get through the movements of life, and sometimes I swear I had to remind myself to breathe, it felt like so much trouble. New gloves, a little treat, might set me back on my former track.

Since my street is the bottom stroke of a U-shaped dead end, I had to take a circuitous route to Winthrop Sporting Goods. If I'd wanted to walk up the hill and cross the railroad tracks behind my house, I'd have reached the chain-link fence enclosing the huge back lot of Winthrop Lumber and Supply, which abutted directly onto the equally huge fenced back lot of the sporting goods store. But the fences and the rough ground made walking impractical, especially in my weakened state, so I had to make a ten-minute drive that routed me through a portion of downtown Shakespeare, then off to the right on Finley.

I had too much time to think as I drove, and was scowling when I walked in the front door of Winthrop Sporting Goods. Darcy Orchard looked up, flushed nearly the color of the red store sweatshirt, and flinched in exaggerated terror as I came in.

'You better smile, girl!' he called. 'You gonna crack any mirror if you walk by.'

I looked around me. I was always staggered by the sheer size and complexity of Winthrop's. The building had been remodeled inside any number of times, until now it consisted of a huge central cavern with specialty rooms lining the walls on either side of the store. There was a room for rifles, and one for bows – bow hunting is very popular in Shakespeare. There was a room over on the left wall just for fishing paraphernalia, and another for camping accessories. There was at least an acre of open yard out back for Jet Skis, boats, deer stands, and four-wheelers.

But the main room was full of everything else. There were high racks of camouflage gear in every conceivable shade of green and brown, in sizes down to infant sleepers. There were hunting caps, and insulated socks, and special gloves, and thermoses, and coolers. Life vests screamed in neon orange, deer corn was piled in fifty-pound bags, and oars were arranged in upright racks. There was a display of bottles containing fluids that made you smell like raccoon pee or a doe in heat or a skunk.

There were other clothes for every sport, even a small section for skiing outfits, since the wealthy of Shakespeare went to Colorado when the snow was deep. Every time I came to Winthrop's, it was to be amazed all over again that a place this size could thrive in a town as small as Shakespeare. But the surrounding area was known for its hunting, and sportsmen came from all over the region to the numerous hunting camps in the deep woods. Engaged couples were known to keep a list of desirable gifts hanging behind the counter. Whole families came from Little Rock to shop at Winthrop Sporting Goods, and there had been a rumor Howell Jr. was going to start sending out a catalog.

I realized as I looked around that the Winthrops must be incredibly rich, on paper at least. I'd seen the evidence in the size of the houses the family lived in, their clothes and jewelry and toys. But seeing the vastness of the store, thinking of the huge lumber and home supply store right next to this place, remembering all the fences I'd seen across areas containing working oil wells marked WINTHROP OIL, NO ENTRANCE, the amount of money the family must have in the bank just winded me.

Well, I didn't want it. All I wanted was gloves.

I would have to safari into the camouflage jungle to reach the little area I wanted, a far hike to the rear if I remembered the store layout correctly. Darcy Orchard seemed to feel I wanted his company, and when he found out what I needed he led me down the narrow middle aisle and veered to the left. I lifted a

hand to Jim Box, who was explaining to a teenager why he needed
a gun case that would float. The young woman who worked in
boating accessories came up and gave me a half-hug and asked
about my leg, and one of the men who'd worked in the store for
over twenty years – his sweatshirt said so – patted me on the back
in the friendliest way, though I hadn't a clue who he was. These
were nice people, and their kindness and their courtesy in not
asking questions reminded me of why I'd liked Shakespeare in the
first place.

'You can meet the new guy, if you haven't already. He's 'bout
as mean as you,' Darcy said in that jocular tone some men reserve
for insults they don't want you to take them up on. I suddenly
remembered who the new man was, suddenly and for the first
time realized . . . Just as a jolt of alarm went through me, I made
myself pay attention to Darcy.

Darcy's voice had been offhand, but something in his tone had
made the hair on my neck stand up. 'You sure turn up in funny
places,' he said now. 'You in the Winthrop house when it's not
your day to work, you in the church when everyone going to that
meeting is black.'

'Did your wife tell you everything she was going to do, Darcy?'

I recalled he been married for six years or so, though he'd been
divorced as long as I'd known him.

'My wife had more plans than the Pentagon,' Darcy said grimly,
but he seemed to relax.

We rounded a corner consisting of men's jumpsuits (very
popular in Shakespeare) which led us into the small open area
devoted to workout equipment and workout clothes.

Reading the instructions for an abdominal exerciser gadget,
with a skeptical sideways pull to his lips, was the detective, Black
Pony tail. I'd just figured out who I was going to see, but he didn't
have any warning. I admired the calm with which he took me in.
His hands tightened on the brochure, but that was the only
outward sign that we weren't seeing each other for the first time.

'Lily, this is Jared Fletcher,' Darcy said. 'He's got those abs of
steel, don't you, Jared?'

His name wasn't Jared. I knew him now. He'd had the same skeptical look in the newspaper photos. I could feel my breath shorten.

'Jared, this is Lily, the toughest woman in Shakespeare.' Darcy completed the introduction with relish. 'You two ought to hit it off great.'

Even Darcy seemed to realize there was something tense in the ensuing silence.

'You two already know each other?' he asked, his beige head turning from me to 'Jared' and back again.

'I've seen Lily at the gym,' the new man said easily. 'But we've never actually met.'

'Oh, sure.' Darcy's face cleared. 'I'll leave you two to it, then. Jared, Miss Lily here needs herself some new gloves. Might oughta sell her some body armor, too, since she seems to always be in the wrong place at the wrong time.'

'What size?' the dark man asked as Darcy reluctantly went back to his work area.

I held out my hand. 'What do you think?' I asked, meeting his eyes.

He took my hand with his right and stepped closer to me. This area of the store seemed isolated and silent, suddenly, though I knew there were people just through the dense racks of clothes. His other hand reached up to touch the bruise on my forehead. Among my other injuries, the place he'd bopped me had paled into insignificance.

'Sorry,' he said. He was so close I was afraid he could hear my pulse. I laid my finger on his wrist. I felt his blood leap. The apathy that had lain on my shoulders like a fog seemed to be lifting.

'Gloves,' I reminded him. My voice was scratchy.

'Right,' he said, stepping away. He looked around him like the new employee he was. 'Jared' hadn't had much time to get acclimated.

'There,' I pointed. 'Women's mediums?'

'We have some in black,' he said.

'Black is okay.'

He pulled down a plastic container and popped it open. 'You better try them on.'

Again I held out my hand, and he wriggled the glove over my fingers, wrapping the strap around my wrist and Velcroing it snugly. I flexed my fingers, made a fist, looked at him. He smiled, and deep arcs appeared on each side of his mouth. The smile changed him totally, threw me off balance.

'Don't hit me here. Save it for later,' he murmured. 'You're quite a fighter.' I remembered I'd bitten him on the ear. I looked at it. It looked better than mine.

It had been a long time since I'd met someone new. It had been even longer since I'd met someone who apparently didn't know who I was.

'Lived here long?' he asked, as if we'd just seen each other for the first time and he was introducing a standard conversational gambit. I looked down at the glove on my right hand, considered the fit.

'Over four years,' I said, holding out my left hand.

'And you have your own maid service?'

'I clean houses and run errands,' I said a little sharply. 'I work by myself.'

His fingers stroked my hand as he pulled the other glove on.

'Do you think they're too tight?' I asked, pantomiming a *seiken zuki* strike to get the feel of the glove. I was able to curl my fingers more easily than I'd thought. I practiced a hammer fist strike. I'd looked at the price tag. The gloves were very expensive, and I'd better be sure they suited me. I picked up one of the twenty-pound barbells, gripped it, raised it over my head. It was a very unpleasant surprise to find it felt heavy.

'They'll loosen a little. Lily is a pretty name.'

I shot him a look.

He looked back steadily. 'I know you live next to my apartment building. But if I wanted to call you, how are you listed in the phone book?'

As if he couldn't ask Howell. Or anyone else in town, for that matter. I put down the barbell very gently. I'd enjoyed a few minutes of feeling normal.

'Bard,' I said. 'My name is Lily Bard.' I knew he would remember.

Because I didn't want to see the look on his face, I took the package the gloves had come in from his suddenly still hands, walked out of the area stripping off the gloves. I paid for them at the front counter, exchanging a few idle words with Al Ferrar, a big, friendly redheaded man whose fingers seemed too large to punch the cash register keys. The hunting bows were behind him, and I stared at them as he rang up the purchase. The arrowheads hung in bubble containers on the wall behind him some so wickedly sharp, like four razors joined together, that I could hardly believe the user wouldn't be frightened to fit them on the shafts. When Al handed me the plastic bag with the gloves in it, I stared at him blankly for a minute and then left the store.

I stood looking up into the sky when I'd reached my car, lost in the gray emptiness of an overcast November day. Wet leaves had piled up in the lower parts of the parking lot. It was going to rain again that evening, the weatherman had predicted. I heard footsteps behind me. The apathy washed back over me, a wave that pulled me under. I was so tired I could scarcely move. I wished the coming scene to be over and done with, wished I could go somewhere else while it was accomplished.

'Why'd you run out like that?'

'You'd better go back to your area, or you'll blow your cover.'

'I'm working,' he said harshly.

'Night and day. At the store and elsewhere, Jack.'

There was a moment of silence.

'Look at me, dammit.'

It would have seemed too affected not to, so I stopped looking at the bleak sky and looked instead at Jack Leeds's bleak face.

'I get a hard-on every time I see you,' he said.

'Try sending me roses. It's a little more subtle.'

He gazed off at a corner of the asphalt. He'd come out without a jacket. I was meanly glad to see him shiver.

'OK. I'll start over,' he said through gritted teeth. 'You know I'm working, and you know what I am.'

He waited for me to nod. To get it over with, I did.

'I am not seeing anyone right now. I've been divorced twice, but you may remember that from the papers.'

I leaned against my car, feeling far away, glad to be there.

With the speed of a snake, he ran his hand under my jacket and T-shirt, placing it flat on my ribs. I gasped and flinched, but his hand stayed there, warm and firm.

'Move your hand,' I said, my voice ragged.

'Got your attention. Listen to me. This job in Shakespeare will come to an end. I want to see you then.'

I shivered, standing stock-still, rigid, taken by surprise. His fingers moved against my skin, touching the scars gently. A silver pickup pulled into the space two vehicles away and the driver gave us a curious look. I chopped down on Jack Leeds's wrist, knocking his hand from its intimate lodgment.

'I have to go to work, Jared,' I said numbly, and got in my car and backed up, avoiding looking at him again.

Carrie was coming to supper tonight and I thought about what I'd fix, not one of my usual frozen-ahead dishes that I prepared on Sundays to carry me through the week. Maybe fettuccine with ham . . . or chili would be good, on such a chilly gray day, but I didn't have enough time to let it simmer.

Keeping my thoughts to a simple minimum, I managed my afternoon well. It was a relief to go home, to allow myself ten minutes in my favorite chair reading a news magazine. Then I set to work, tossing a salad, preparing the fettuccine, heating some garlic bread, chopping the ham. When Carrie knocked on the front door, I was ready.

'Those morons at the hospital!' she said, sliding out of her coat, tossing her gloves on the table.

'Hello to you, too '

'You'd think they could see the handwriting on the wall. Everyone else can.' The tiny Shakespeare Hospital was in perpetual crisis trying to maintain its accreditation, with no adequate budget to supply its lacks, which were legion.

I let Carrie bear the brunt of the conversation, which she seemed quite willing to do. There were few people Carrie could talk to, as a woman and a doctor and an outlander from northern Arkansas. I knew from previous talks with Carrie that she had gotten a loan to attend medical school. The terms of the loan stipulated that she had to go to somewhere other doctors didn't want to go and stay there for four years; and other doctors didn't want to go to Shakespeare. Carrie was one of four local GPs, who all made a decent living, but for more specialized medical care Shakespeareans had to travel to Montrose, or in dire need, Little Rock.

'Where'd you get the ring?' Carrie asked suddenly.

I'd been feeling a warm hand on my skin. It took me a second to reorient.

'The older Mrs Winthrop says Marie Hofstettler left me this,' I told Carrie.

'It's a pretty ring,' she said. 'Can I see it?'

I slid the ring off and handed it to Carrie. I thought of my strange visit to the Winthrop house the night before, the pallor of Howell Winthrop's face as he saw the ring box in my hand.

Some things that were supposed to be free actually came mighty expensive. I wondered if this little ring was one of them.

Then I wondered why that thought had crossed my mind.

I took the ring back from Carrie and slid it on my right hand, then took it back off and dropped it in my pocket. Carrie raised her thick dark brows, but didn't say anything.

We washed the dishes, talking in a companionable way of whatever crossed our minds: the price of milk, the vagaries of dealing with the public, the onset of hunting season (which would have a certain impact on Carrie's job *and* mine, since hunting engendered both injuries and dirt galore), and the recuperation of Claude, which continued at too slow a pace to suit him, and, I suspected, Carrie. She told me she'd gotten the green light to move Claude from an upstairs to a downstairs apartment, but that he wanted to be on the scene to direct the move, so a date hadn't been set yet.

When Carrie left, it was a little later than usual, and I was worn out. I took a quick shower, put on my favorite blue nightgown, laid out my clothes for the next morning. I went through my nightly routine of checking the locks at the windows and doors. I felt more relaxed, more content. Tomorrow might be a regular day.

Chapter Six

My heart was hammering. The bad time was back again. I sat up in bed, gasping, my nightgown damp against my breasts. I'd been sweating in my sleep. Horrible dreams, old dreams, the worst: the chains, the shack, the rhythmic thud of the iron headboard against the wall.

Something had wakened me, something besides the dream; or maybe something had sparked the dream. I scrambled out of bed and pulled on the white chenille robe I keep draped across the footboard. As I tied the sash tightly around my waist, I glanced at my digital clock. One-thirty. I heard a sound: a quick, light rapping at my back door.

I crept out of my bedroom. It's next to that door. I put my ear against the wood. A voice on the other side of the door was saying something over and over, and as my hand reached for the switch, I realized the voice was saying, 'Don't turn on the light! For God's sake, don't turn on the light!'

'Who is it?' I asked, my ear pressed to the meeting of door and frame so I could hear better.

'Jack, it's Jack. Let me in, they're after me!'

I heard the desperation in his voice. I pushed the dead bolt back and opened the door. A dark form hurtled past me and crashed on the hall floor as I slammed the door shut and relocked it.

I knelt beside him. The faint radiance provided by the nightlight burning behind the nearly shut bathroom door was almost useless. His breathing was ragged and loud; no point in asking him questions. I moved my fingers up Jack's legs first: wet boots, damp blue jeans – it was raining again. My hands moved higher, running over his butt and crotch; then I felt his chest, his back, under his padded waterproof vest.

The detective rolled to his right side. He groaned when my fingers found the sticky patch on his left shoulder, I flinched, too, but I made my hand return to the wound. There was a hole in the vest. I probed further. There was a big hole in the vest, and the shirt underneath was ripped. It seemed plain enough that Jack Leeds had been shot high in the shoulder.

'I need to look at this in some light,' I said. His breathing seemed closer to normal. He was shaking now, from cold and perhaps relief.

'If you turn on a light, they'll know I woke you. They're gonna knock on your door any minute.' He took a deep breath, let it out slowly, trying for control. He made a little sound through clenched teeth.

I'd have to turn on the outside light, then. I thought about Jack's wet boots and the little roof over the back porch.

'Crawl into the first door on your left,' I said. I hurried into the kitchen, glad my leg was so much better. I washed my hands in the dark. I filled a saucepan with water. Returning to the back door, I edged it open and listened; not a sound beyond the cool patter of the rain. I opened the door wider. The security light in the parking lot to the rear of the apartment building also benefited my backyard, at least a little. I could see the dark wet footprints Jack had left on the boards. I poured water over the porch and steps, wiping out the marks of his entrance. I could only hope 'they' (whoever they were) wouldn't be observant enough to wonder why my sheltered porch was soaking wet.

Shutting and locking the door again, I automatically placed the inverted pan in the kitchen drainer. I stood in the middle of the room, thinking furiously. No, there was nothing more I could do. Jack had surely left tracks on the wet ground, but it was beyond my power to obliterate them.

I padded silently into my bedroom. 'Where are you?' I whispered. This was like playing hide-and-seek, in a scary kind of way.

'By the bed, on the rug,' he said. 'Don't want to mess up your sheets or your floor.'

I appreciated the consideration. 'How'd you get here? To the house?' I asked, ashamed of the anxious undertone I could hear in my own voice.

'Over the fence, from the back lot of the lumber place. But I went further down to the vacant lot at the corner, then cut back here on the pavement. I started to come to your front door, but then I figured they might have a car cruising the neighborhood by now, if they've stopped to think. So I went up your driveway, around your carport, and took the stepping stones to the back door.' He paused. 'Oh, shit, the porch! Footprints!'

'I took care of it.'

I could sense his movement as he turned to stare in my direction. But all he said was 'Good.' His eyes closed, I thought, and he shifted positions painfully.

My eyes had done some adjusting, enough to make him out. He hadn't cut all his hair off, as it had looked at first. He was wearing a black knit watch cap and he'd tucked all his hair up under it. I eased it off. Of course the cap hadn't done anything to keep his head dry. The released strands spread in rat's tails across the white bedside rug.

He opened his eyes and regarded me steadily. I found myself running my fingers through my hair to fluff it out. Ridiculous. I couldn't postpone dealing with the wound any longer.

'Let's get your vest off,' I said, trying to sound matter-of-fact. I scooted closer. 'Hold out your hand. I'll help you sit up.'

Jack had better night vision than I did. His hand was on mine instantly. I gripped and pulled, automatically giving the 'Huh!' of heavy exertion. I leaned him against the side of the bed and un-zipped the vest. I pulled it down his right arm first. I eased it across his back, leaning almost against his chest to accomplish the maneuver. I smelled the wet of his vest and his shirtsleeves, and the scent of his skin, the faintest trace of some aftershave. Then I scuttled over to his left side, held up his left arm with one hand while I tugged at the vest with the other. He gave a deep groan, and I sucked my breath in sympathetically. But I didn't stop. The vest wasn't actually stuck; it was the movement of his arm and shoulder that was causing him pain.

His flannel shirt, now, *that* was stuck. I fetched my heavy kitchen scissors and began to cut through the thick material. This proved impossible and dangerous in the darkness. I left to push the bathroom door wide open. I'd worried about the nightlight, but I figured a nightlight in a bathroom was no big wonder, and it was my habit. Suddenly switching it off might be even more suspicious.

With the slightly improved visibility I could just see enough to cut off the shirt without hurting Jack worse. He was leaning back against the bed with his eyes closed.

I wanted to call Carrie, but her arrival would be a dead give-away. Jack was still shivering, but it didn't seem to be as teeth-chattering a tremor as before.

There was a single loud knock at the back door. Jack's eyes flew open and stared into mine, only a few inches away.

'They won't come in,' I promised. I looked down at my robe. It was streaked with dirt and damp and blood. I unbelted it and draped it over Jack, wiping my hands on its hem. I went into the hall and up to the back door, as noisily as I could.

'Who is it?' I asked loudly. 'I'm going to call the police!'

'Lily, hey! It's Darcy!'

'Darcy Orchard, what the hell are you doing knocking at my door in the middle of the night? Go away!'

'Lily, we just want to make sure you're all right. Someone broke in over at the store.'

'So?'

'He took off running across the back lot. He scaled the fence and went into the lumber yard lot. We think he climbed out and came across the tracks.'

'So?'

'Let us lay eyes on you, Lily. We gotta be sure you're not being held hostage.'

That was clever.

'I'm not letting you in my house in the middle of the night,' I said baldly, figuring that would be congruent with my history and

character. And it was the simple truth. They would not come into
my house.

'No, that's fine, honey. We just want to see you're okay.' Darcy
did a good job of sounding concerned.

I switched on the light above the back door, which I'd been
hoping to avoid in case Jack had left traces I hadn't anticipated. I
stuck my head out the door and glared at Darcy up on my back
porch and the group of men in my backyard. Darcy wasn't dressed
for the weather; he looked exactly like he'd run out the door in
whatever he had on. His thinning hair was plastered to his head.
His pale eyes glistened in the porch light. Darcy was enjoying
himself.

I swept my eyes over the four bundled figures clustered together behind him, enduring the light rain and chill wind. I was
trying to gather in a look at the posts supporting the little porch
roof while I was at it.

Dammit all to hell. Jack had left a bloody handprint on one of
them; but it was on the inside toward me, thank God.

To make sure their attention didn't wander, I stepped out on
the tiny porch in my nightgown, and five pairs of eyes bugged out.

I heard a reverent 'Wow,' which Darcy instantly suppressed by
turning to glare at the offender. Despite the fact that all the men
had pulled up their collars and pulled down their hats, I could
recognize the exclamation had come from the boy who worked
at the loading dock of the lumber supply house. I wondered
how they'd picked Darcy to be the one who got his name on the
record, so to speak.

'See, I'm fine,' I said, not having to work at sounding furious.
'I'm under no duress, and I could walk away from this house right
now if I wanted to freeze. How come all of you are out in the rain
chasing a burglar, anyway? Don't you have an alarm system that
calls the police?'

As I'd hoped, going on the offense made them begin to back
away.

'We were having a little . . .' Darcy paused, clearly unsure how
to end the sentence.

'Inventory,' said one of the men. His voice was oddly muffled since he was trying to keep his face buried in his collar. I was pretty sure it was Jim Box, Darcy's work out buddy and coworker. Jim had always thought quicker than Darcy, but without the panache. Behind him, a figure crouched with a hood covering most of his features, but I would recognize that thin, mean mouth anywhere. Tom David Meicklejohn, in mufti. Hmmm.

'Right, we have to do pre-Christmas inventory,' Darcy said, relieved. 'Takes all night. We'd turned off the alarm because we were going in and out.'

'Um-hmm,' I said, neutrally. As I'd anticipated, they began to back off even more quickly, though still keeping their eyes on my nightgown. I decided to burn it.

'Aren't you going to go wake up Carlton, too?' I demanded, jerking my head toward Carlton's little house, almost identical to mine. 'Maybe *he's* a hostage.'

The bedraggled group began to herd toward Carlton's house, where I'd noticed a light burning in the bedroom. I figured Carlton had company and would give them as warm a reception as I had. I slammed my back door shut, turned the locks as loudly as I could, and switched off the porch light quickly, hoping they would fall in a puddle in the sudden darkness.

Fools. Dangerous fools.

It made me sick that I had exposed myself to them. I crossed my arms over my chest, tried to feel warmer.

I went into my bedroom and padded past Jack to get to the window. Opening the shades a trifle, I peered out. Yes, Carlton was standing at his back door now, in an attractive velour bathrobe and nothing else, looked like. He was very angry.

Even as I watched, he slammed his own back door and switched out his light. I'd closed my eyes the second before, so when I thought my vision had adjusted, I peered into the darkness again. I could make out vague shapes, trailing back across my yard and up the steep embankment to the railroad tracks. They'd given up the chase.

'They've gone,' I said.

'Good,' Jack said. His voice was a little steadier, but hoarse with suppressed pain. I shut the shades again, tightly, and loosened the tiebacks on the curtains so they fell shut, too. Instead of switching on the overhead light, I used the bedside lamp. I knelt down by Jack again. His eyes had closed against the sudden light. I stared at him for a long moment. I was thinking that I'd better have put my money on the right horse, or the consequences would be too drastic to imagine.

I sat back on my heels. The shoulder wound was the only injury Jack had. It had stopped bleeding. It looked awful. I didn't have any experience treating bullet wounds, but it seemed that the bullet had plowed through the top of Jack's shoulder; and since the bleeding had stopped, I knew it hadn't severed a major blood line.

So infection had to be the biggest danger. I'd have to clean the wound. Unless . . .

'Is there any chance of me taking you to the hospital?' I asked.

He shot me a look that said the question had been as futile as I'd feared. 'I'll get back to my place,' Jack said. He began trying to push himself up from the floor with his uninjured arm.

'Oh, sure.' I was scared of treating the wound, so my voice came out harsh.

'Obviously, this is too much of a risk for you,' he said, in an I'm-trying-to-be-patient voice.

Quelling my impulse to haul him to his feet, twist his good arm behind his back, and propel him into the nearest wall, I inhaled a calming breath. I let it out evenly, with control.

'You don't get to tell me what risks I'm prepared to assume,' I said.

'I can go back to Little Rock, but you live here.'

'I appreciate your pointing that out to me. Give me your hand.' I was going through my own set of shakes. Stepping outside in my nightgown had chilled me to the bone in all kinds of ways.

Jack reached out with his good hand, and I planted my feet, gripped the hand firmly, and pulled up. His face twisted as he rose to his feet. Standing, he was taller than me, his physical presence dominating. I decided I preferred him on the floor. No. I felt more comfortable with him on the floor.

'You're freezing!' he said, and stretched out his good arm as if he would gather me to him. My white bathrobe fell off him and crumpled in a dirty heap. The remains of his shirt hung in rags around his shoulders.

'We're going into the bathroom to work on your wound,' I told him, trying to sound confident. 'Can you walk?'

He could, and was sitting on the toilet seat in a few seconds. I got out all my first-aid equipment. I had some sterile water, and some bandages containing powdered antibiotic, and a tube of antibiotic ointment. I had a lot of gauze and some tape. The Lily Bard MASH unit for wounded detectives.

The sterile water was even in a squirt bottle.

I worked the rest of the shirt off Jack, tried not to be distracted by his resulting bareness, and draped him with my oldest towels. I swept his half-dry hair over onto his sound shoulder. I assumed nurses and doctors learned how to detach themselves from touching people so intimately; I had not. This felt very personal to me.

'I'm going to clean the wound,' I said.

'Yeah.'

I lifted the plastic squeeze bottle. 'So, did you recognize the men after you?' I asked. I squirted sterile water onto the bloody furrow. Jack turned whiter, and dark stubble stood out sharply on his lean cheeks. 'Answer me, Jack Leeds,' I said sharply.

'Not all of them.' His voice more of a gasp.

'Of course there was Darcy.' I squirted again, this time from the back. I thought of tiny fragments of shirt, or microscopic bits of the vest, that might be embedded in this tear in Jack's flesh. I felt dreadfully responsible.

'Uh-huh.' His eyes closed. I kept going with the lavage.

'Who was another one, Jack?'

'The kid, the one with the pimples, works on the loading dock at the lumber and home supply place.'

I patted the area dry with the cleanest whitest washcloth I had. I examined it. It looked clean, but how did I know? I wasn't used to cleaning on a microscopic scale. I squirted.

'And the guy with the big belly, the one who looks like a good heart-attack risk, I've seen him.'

'That was Cleve Ragland, works down at the mattress factory,' I murmured. 'Cleve's been arrested for drunken driving at least twice, got a kid in jail for attempted rape.'

Squirt, wipe.

'The other guy,' Jack gasped, 'isn't he a cop?'

'Uh-huh, Tom David Meicklejohn – in plain clothes. He kept to the back like it was possible for me to mistake him,' I said, hoping the plowed track of the wound was clean enough. At least Jack's eyes were open again, though he wasn't looking at my face.

'And then there was Jim, works in the gun department, works out with Darcy. Another coworker.' I patted again.

It looked dry. It looked clean. I leaned even closer to inspect it, and nodded in satisfaction. I hoped I hadn't hurt Jack too much. He had a very strange expression on his face.

'Lean forward,' I told him, I spread the antiseptic ointment on the wound. I put an antiseptic pad on the shoulder, with a strip of surgical tape to hold it in place.

'Lean back.' I padded the wound with sterile gauze in case he bled again, and unrolled surgical tape to secure the gauze. Jack's face relaxed while I did this, and I felt proud of myself. I turned and began to search the bathroom cabinet for a pain reliever. While my back was to him, Jack's finger traced the curve of my hip.

I stood still, not believing it.

'Are you crazy?' I said. 'You just got shot!'

'Lily, all that got me through that bandaging was your breast wobbling about three inches from my face.'

I couldn't think of anything to say.

'Did I hear you step out in front of them in your nightgown?' he asked.

I nodded.

'No wonder they were all quiet. Not a one will be able to sleep tonight.'

'You'd left a handprint on one of the posts.'

'You did a damn fine job of distracting.'

'I hated doing that. Don't talk like it was easy.'

'I hope I know better.'

'We need to get your wet clothes off so you can come get in bed.'

'I thought you'd never say it.'

I noticed that he wasn't any longer mentioning going home. And he'd never suggested we call the police, though in view of Tom David's presence, that had probably been wise. I shook out a pill, handed him a glass of water. He swallowed it and leaned back, his eyes closed.

I pulled off Jack's boots and socks, wiping off his wet cold feet with a hot washcloth and drying them vigorously with a towel. But I left him to remove his own jeans. I went outside one more time, to clean the bloody handprint from the post. That had been niggling at me.

It was still raining. Any other traces Jack had left would surely be obliterated.

I'd turned down the bed, and by the time I came in the room, Jack had managed to climb in and cover up. On my side. His chest was bare and it occurred to me he was most likely bare all the way down.

I'd given him one of the pain pills Carrie had left me a few months before when my ribs had been bruised. It had knocked Jack Leeds clean out, as I'd expected.

I yanked the blue nightgown off and stuffed it in the trash can. I pulled a pink one out of my dresser drawer. It was almost as pretty; I buy good nightgowns. I put the bloodstained bathrobe into my washer and set it to wash on cold; as an after-thought, I threw in Jack's damp jeans, socks, and underwear, which he'd left in a heap on the bathroom floor. Hot water would have been better for his stuff, but I couldn't stay awake for two loads. While the clothes churned through the shortest cycle, I straightened up the bathroom and set out a toothbrush, still in its wrapper. I rechecked all the locks. Then I put the washed clothes in the dryer.

When all the lights were out, I slid into bed on the wrong side. The night was silent except for the friendly sound of the tumbling dryer and the detective breathing heavily beside me, and I slept.

I opened my eyes about five-thirty, later than I usually get up. To see my clock, I had to raise myself to peer over the dark mound that was Jack. I thought I'd heard him go into the bathroom, heard the water running, but he seemed to be asleep again. I could barely discern the outline of his features. The bedclothes had fallen down, and I could see his exposed shoulder because of the white of the bandage. I covered him back up, very carefully, not wanting to wake him. His loose hair had fallen over his face. Gently, as delicately as I could manage, I brushed it back.

The rain was drumming on the roof again, loud enough to penetrate the comforting drone of the central heating. I made my own trip to the bathroom, rinsed out my mouth. I snuggled back down into bed, turned away from my sleeping companion. I sank into a half-doze, random thoughts floating through my head.

It was Friday. Not a good day to start back to Body Time, considering my interrupted night. Nor a good day to resume karate. But I had to work today . . . Deedra, the peculiar Mookie Preston, the Winthrops, another afternoon appointment . . . I waited expectantly, but I couldn't summon the surge of purpose I needed to feel at the onset of the working day.

What I felt instead was a surge of hormones. Jack Leeds had woken me the night before, beating on my door. Now he was waking me in an altogether different way. Jack was stroking my back and hips. I sighed, hardly knowing if it was one of exasperation or sheer desire. But I certainly didn't feel apathetic any longer.

I knew he could tell I was awake. When I didn't speak, he scooted closer, fitting his body to mine. His hand circled around, cupped a breast, resumed the rhythmical stroking. I had to bite my lip to keep silent.

'What happened to "after this job is over"?' I asked finally, and my voice was more like a gasp.

'Waking up in a warm bed with a beautiful woman on a rainy day in winter' – and while he was speaking his hand never stopped – 'has overcome my business instincts.' His voice was breathy and low. His mouth began to deliver little sucking kisses to my neck, and I shivered. He began to ease up the pink nightgown. It was now or never. What did I want? My body was about to take over from my brain.

I turned toward him, putting up a hand to press against his chest and hold him at a little distance – I think – but at that moment his fingers slid between my legs and instead I wrapped my arm around his neck and pulled him close for a kiss. It was so dark and private in my room, like a quiet cave. After a while, his mouth descended to cover my nipple through the nightgown. I reached down to touch him. He was swollen and ready. It was his turn to do a little moaning.

'Do you have . . . ?' he asked.

I reached across him to grope in the night-table drawer for protection.

Jack began to whisper to me, telling me about what we were going to do and how it was going to feel. His hands never stopped.

'Now,' I said.

'Wait a little.'

I waited as long as I could. I was shaking. 'Now.'

And then he was in me. I arched against him, found his rhythm. My pleasure was instant, and I cried out his name.

'Again,' he said in my ear, and kept on going. I tried to keep pace, once again matched him. I began urging him on, gripping him with my inner muscles, digging my nails into his hips. At last he made an incoherent sound and climaxed, and I did, too.

He collapsed on top of me and I put both my arms around him for the first time. I ran my hands over his back and bottom, feeling skin and muscles, planes and curves. He nuzzled my neck gently for a minute, withdrew from me, and rolled onto his back. The white gauze was spotted with red.

'Your shoulder!' I raised up on an elbow to look. My bedroom was getting a little lighter; the dark and secret cave had opened to the world.

'I don't care,' he said, shaking his head from side to side on the pillow. 'Someone could come in here and shoot me again, and right this moment I wouldn't care. I tried to stay away from you, tried not to think about you . . . if they hadn't been so close, I wouldn't have come here, but I can't be sorry. Jesus God, Lily, that was absolutely – wonderful. No other woman . . . God, that was sensational.'

I was shattered myself. Even more than by the physical sensations Jack had given me, I was a little frightened by the urge I had to touch him, hold him, bathe myself in him. In self-defense, I thought of all the women he'd had.

'Who are you thinking about?' He opened his eyes and stared at me. 'Oh, Karen.' I was frightened that he knew so much about me that he would read my face that way. His own eyes lost their glow, flattened, when he said the name Karen.

Jack Leeds had become a household reference right about the time Lily Bard had, in the same state, Tennessee; and in the same city, Memphis. While my name became linked with that of the crime committed against me ('Lily Bard, victim of a brutal rape and mutilation'), Jack's was always followed by the trailer, 'alleged lover of Karen Kingsland'.

Karen Kingsland, from her newspaper photos a sweet-faced brunette, had been sleeping with Jack for four months when catastrophe wiped out three lives. She was twenty-six years old, earning her master's degree in education from the University of Memphis. She was also the wife of another cop.

One Thursday morning, Walter Kingsland, Karen's husband, got an anonymous letter at work. A uniformed officer for ten years, he was about to go on patrol. Opening the letter, laughing about receiving it, in front of many of his friends, Walter read that

Karen and Jack were having sex, and having it often. The letter, which Walter dropped to the floor as he left, was quite detailed. A friend of Jack's called Jack instantly, but he was not as quick as Walter. No one called Karen.

Walter drove home like a maniac, arriving just as Karen was leaving for class. He barricaded himself and his wife in the bedroom of their east Memphis home. Jack came in through the front door moments later, hoping to end the situation quickly and privately somehow. He had not been thinking well. He stood at the door of the bedroom and listened to Walter plead with his wife to say Jack had raped her, or that it was all a malicious lie on the part of some enemy.

By that time, the modest Kingsland home was surrounded by cops. The phone rang and rang, and finally Jack picked it up in the living room and described the situation to his coworkers and superiors. There was not going to be any private or amicable solution, and it would be fortunate if all three involved made it through alive. Jack wanted to offer himself as hostage in exchange for Karen. His superiors, on the advice of the hostage negotiation team, turned him down. Then Jack revealed to them what Walter did not know yet, what Karen had only told Jack the day before: Karen Kingsland was pregnant.

At that point, it would have been hard to find anyone in the Memphis Police Department who wasn't, at the very least, disgusted with Jack Leeds.

From the living room, Jack could hear Karen scream in pain.

He yelled through the door that Walter should exchange his wife for Jack, since torturing a woman was nothing a real man would do.

This time Walter agreed to swap his wife for his wife's lover.

Without consulting anyone, Jack agreed.

Walter yelled that he'd bring Karen to the back door. Jack should be standing on the sundeck, weaponless. Walter would push Karen out and Jack would come in.

Detective Jack Leeds went outside, took off his jacket, his shoes and socks, his shirt, so Walter Kingsland could tell Jack wasn't carrying a concealed weapon. And sure enough, out of the bedroom came Walter and Karen. From inside the kitchen, Walter yelled to Jack to turn around, so Walter could make sure there wasn't a gun stuck in the back of Jack's slacks.

Then Walter appeared, framed in the open back door holding Karen by one of her arms, his gun to her head. Now there was tape over her mouth, and her eyes were crazed. She was missing the little finger of her right hand, and blood was pouring out of the wound.

'Come closer,' Kingsland said. 'Then I'll let her go.'

Jack had stepped closer, his eyes on his lover.

Walter Kingsland shot Karen through the head and shoved her out on top of Jack.

And this part, media hounds, was on videotape. Jack's yell of horror, Walter Kingsland's screaming, 'You want her so bad, you got her!' Walter's taking aim at Jack, now covered with Karen's blood and brains, trying to rise: a dozen bullets cutting Walter down, bullets fired unwillingly by men that knew him, men that knew Walter Kingsland for high-strung, hot-tempered, possessive; but also as brave, good-natured, and resourceful.

Jack had been a plainclothes detective, often working undercover. He had a stellar work record. He had a rotten personal life. He drank, he smoked, he'd already been divorced twice. He was envied, but not liked; decorated, but not altogether trusted. And after that day in the Kingslands' backyard, he was no longer a Memphis cop. Like me, he sank to the bottom to avoid the light of the public eye.

This was the chronicle of the man I was in bed with.

'I guess we'll have to talk about that sometime,' he said with a sigh, and his face looked immeasurably older than it had been. 'And what happened to you.' His finger traced the worst scar, the one circling my right breast.

I lay close to him, put my arm over his chest, 'No,' I said. 'We don't have to.'

'The funny thing is,' he said quietly, 'Karen wrote that letter herself.'

'Oh, no.'

'She did.' After all this time, there was still pained wonder in his voice. 'It was from her typewriter. She wanted Walter to know. I'll never understand why. Maybe she wanted more attention from him. Maybe she wanted him to initiate a divorce. Maybe she wanted us to fight over her. I thought I knew her, thought I loved her. But I won't ever know why she did that.'

I thought of things I could say, even things I wanted to say, but none of them could repair the damage I'd recalled to his mind. Nothing could ever make up for what Karen Kingsland had done to Jack, what he had done to himself. Nothing could ever get back Jack's job, his reputation. And I knew nothing would ever erase the memory of Karen's head exploding in front of his eyes.

And nothing could ever erase what had happened to me a couple of months afterward: the abduction, the rape, the cutting, the man I'd shot. I felt the urge to make some good memories.

I swung my leg over him, straddled him, bent to kiss him, smoothed his long black hair against the white lace-trimmed pillowcase. I was not ashamed of my scars with Jack Leeds. He had a full set of his own. I told him, close to his ear, that I was about to take him inside me again. I told him how it would feel. I could hear him draw his breath, and soon I could feel his excitement. My own heart was pounding.

It was even better this time.

'Why housecleaning?' He asked later.

'I knew how to do it, and I could do it by myself.' That was the short answer, and true enough, as far as it went. 'Why detective? What kind are you, anyway?'

'Private. Based in Little Rock. I knew how to do it, and I could do it by myself.' He smiled at me, a small smile, but there. 'After a two-year apprenticeship with another detective, that is. There was another ex-cop from Memphis working there. I knew him a little.'

So Jack must be working for the Winthrops.

'I have to get dressed. I have an appointment,' I said, trying not to sound sad or regretful. So my departure wouldn't seem too abrupt – cold, as Marshall would have said – I gave Jack a kiss before I swung out of bed. Somehow, the farther away from him I moved, the more I became conscious of my scars. I saw his eyes on them, seeing them for the first time in one frame, so to speak. I stood still, letting him look. But it was very hard, and my fists clenched.

'I'd kill them all for you if I could,' he said.

'At least I killed one,' I said. Our eyes met. He nodded.

I took a wonderful hot shower and shaved my legs and washed my hair and put on my makeup, restraining an urge to laugh out loud.

And I thought: Nothing. I will ask for *nothing*.

Jack had found his surviving clothes in the dryer and pulled them on. I eyed him thoughtfully, and rummaged in my drawers for one of those promotional T-shirts that are all one size. I'd gotten it when I'd donated blood. It had swallowed me, but it fit him, rather snugly; but it covered the bandage and his goose bumps. He winced as he maneuvered his left arm into its sleeve. I had the old jacket the hospital had pulled from its rummage closet, the one I'd worn home the day after the explosion. It fit, too.

He'd perked some coffee while I was showering, and he'd made an effort to pull the bedding straight.

'Normally I do better, but with my shoulder . . .' He apologized as I came into the bedroom to get my socks and sneakers.

'It's all right,' I said briefly, and sat on the little chair in the corner to pull my socks on. I'd put on two T-shirts, which works better for me in cold weather than a sweatshirt – long sleeves are just a nuisance with housework. The edge of the pink tee peeked from under the sky blue of my outer shirt; happy colors. I'd picked pink socks, too. And my favorite pink and white high-tops. I was the brightest maid in Shakespeare. To hell with the cold and rain.

'Aren't you going to ask me? About what I was doing last night?' he said. He was sitting on the end of the bed, looking braced for an attack.

I finished tying one bow, put my right foot on the floor, lifted my left. 'I guess not,' I said. 'I'm reckoning it has something to do with guns, the Winthrop clan, and maybe Del Packard's murder. But I don't know. Better not tell me, unless you need someplace to run to when the bad guys are chasing you.'

I'd meant that lightly, but Jack thought I was telling him he should explain his business to me since he'd taken shelter in my home; that he owed me, since he'd 'used' me. I could see his face harden, see the distance opening.

'I mean that literally,' I told him. 'Better not tell me, unless they're after you.'

'What will you do, Lily,' he asked, putting his arms around me as I stood, 'what will you do, when they come after me?'

I smiled. 'I'll fight,' I said.

Chapter Seven

Getting Jack to his apartment, though it was just a few yards away, was quite a challenge. At least it was his day off, and his shoulder would have a chance to rest before he had to show up at Winthrop Sporting Goods. It would have looked better if he could have worked out at Body Time this morning, but it was beyond even someone as determined as Jack Leeds. He was hurting.

I gave him my last hoarded pain pill to take when he got home. He stowed it in his pocket. Then, when nothing was passing on Track Street, he ducked out my kitchen door and into my car. I backed out and drove out of my driveway and into the Garden Apartments driveway, going all the way to the rear parking area. When I was closest to the door, so close it would be hard to see from the rear windows of the top apartments, Jack jumped out and went inside. I pulled into Marcus Jefferson's former space and followed him in, to provide myself with a reason for entering the apartment parking lot. Even to me, this seemed a bit overly careful, but Jack had just given me a look to reinforce his admonishment that 'these people' were very dangerous.

So I climbed the stairs to work in Deedra's apartment, which was absolutely normal and gave me a bona fide reason to enter the building at this hour. I carried my caddy of cleaning materials up the stairs, expecting Jack would already be in his apartment and trying to get his clothes off to bathe, without upsetting his wound. I'd offered to help, but he wanted my day to run absolutely normally.

Far from being empty, the landing was full of men and suspicion. Darcy and the bullish Cleve Ragland were waiting in front of Jack's door. They were having a face-off with Jack, who was standing with his keys in his hand.

'. . . don't have to tell anyone where I spend the night,' Jack was saying, and there was a cold edge to his voice that meant business.

He hadn't wanted us to be publicly associated. For that matter, neither had I. I should unlock Deedra's apartment and trot back downstairs to get my mop leaving Jack to stonewall his way through this. That was what he'd want me to do.

'Hey again, Lily,' Darcy said, surprise evident in his voice. He looked bright-eyed and bushy-tailed, but Cleve was showing signs of wear and tear. He hadn't shaved, and maybe had slept in his clothes.

'You keep long hours, Darcy,' I replied, depositing my caddy at Deedra's door and joining the little group. Jack glared at me.

'We just come by here to see if Jared was all right,' Darcy said, and his flat blue eyes swung back to Jack. 'We rung him last night after the robbery and got no answer.'

'And I was telling you,' Jack said just as coldly, 'that what I do on my time off is my business.'

I approached Jack from his left, put my arm around him, blocking the wounded side in case they tried clapping him on the shoulder.

'Our business,' I corrected him, looking steadily at Darcy.

'Whoo-ee,' Darcy said, sticking his hands in his own jean pockets as if he didn't know what to do with them. His heavy coat bulged up in semicircles around his tucked hands.

Cleve glanced from me to Jack and back again, and said, 'Reckon ole Jared got lucky.'

Immediately the tension eased. Jack slowly looped his arm around me. His fingers bit into my shoulder.

'Well, you were being a gentleman,' Darcy said approvingly.

'Now you got your question answered, can I get in my apartment?' Jack said, making an effort to sound amiable. But I could hear the anger pulsing in his voice.

'Sure, man. We're going this very minute,' said Darcy, a broad grin on his face that I wanted to wipe right off. I promised myself I would if I got half a chance.

Jack stepped between Darcy and Cleve, put his key in the lock, and turned it as they started down the stairs, He automatically stood back to let me enter first, then shut the door behind us. Jack relocked it and went over to the window to see if his 'friends' really left.

Then he swung around to face me, his anger open now and misdirected at me.

'We talked about this,' he began. 'No one was going to connect us.'

'Okay, I'm gone,' I said shortly, and started for the door.

'Talk to me,' he demanded.

I sighed. 'How else could you have gotten out of that?' I asked.

'Well, I . . . could have told them I'd driven to Little Rock to see my girlfriend.'

'And when they said, "Then why was your car parked here all night?"'

Frustrated, Jack brought his fist down on a little desk by the window. 'Dammit, I won't have it!'

I shrugged. No point in all this now. If he was going to act like a jerk, I'd go downstairs and get my mop. I had to work.

When I was on the top stair, he caught me. His good hand clamped down on my shoulder like iron. I stopped dead. I turned very slowly and said to him in my sincerest voice, 'How about saying, "Thanks, Lily, for bailing me out, even though you had to stand there and be leered at for the second time in twelve hours"?'

Jack turned whiter around the mouth than he had been, and his hand dropped from my shoulder.

'And don't you ever, ever restrain me again,' I told him, my eyes staring directly into his.

I turned, and with a sick feeling in the pit of my stomach, I went down the stairs. When I came up with the mop, I stood on the landing for a second, listening. His apartment was silent. I went into Deedra's to work.

So much drama, so early in the morning, left me exhausted. I scarcely registered the unusual order in Deedra's apartment; it was as if she was trying to show she'd changed her social habits by keeping her apartment neater. As I put away her clean underwear, I noted the absence of the pile of naughty pictures of herself she had kept underneath her bras. I expected to feel good about Deedra's changed lifestyle, but instead, I could barely manage to finish my cleaning.

As I dumped the last waste can into a plastic bag, I admitted to myself that even more than tired, I felt sad. It would have been a pleasant treat to have had a morning to think of Jack in the relaxed warmth of good sex, in the glow of – what could I call it? Happiness. But, thanks to his pride – as I saw it – we'd ended on a sour note.

There was a pile of pierced earrings on Deedra's dresser, and I decided to just sit there and pair them up. For a minute or two that was simple and satisfying; after all, they match or they don't. But my restless mind began wandering again.

A pretend robbery during a mysterious meeting at Winthrop Sporting Goods, in the middle of a most inclement night. The blue flyers that had caused so much trouble. The long, heavy black bags that the Winthrop house had been burgled to get – where were they now? The three unsolved murders in tiny Shakespeare. The out-of-place Mookie Preston. The bombing. I couldn't make sense of all the pieces at one time, but the shape of it was wrong. This was no group of fanatics with a coherent manifesto at work; it all seemed very sloppy. For the first time, I considered what Carrie had said about the timing of the bombing. If the goal had been to kill lots of black people, the explosion had come too late. If the goal had been to 'merely' terrorize the black community, the explosion had come too early. The deaths in the church had enraged the African-American people of Shakespeare. Whoever had planted the bomb did not represent white supremacy, but white stupidity.

As I locked Deedra's apartment – scorning to even cross the landing and listen at Jack's door – and descended the stairs to drive to Mookie Preston's modest rental, I thought about the unexpected, normally concealed aspects of the people around me, the part I was seeing the past few days. It was like seeing their skeleton beneath their outer flesh.

Bluff, hearty good ole boy Darcy Orchard, for example: I'd worked out with Darcy for years, and seen only the good-natured sportsman. But last night I'd seen him tracking a man, at the head of a pack of hunters. Beneath his yard-dog exterior, Darcy was a wolf.

I'd always known that about Tom David Meicklejohn. He was naturally cruel and sly, naturally an able and remorseless hunter. He was reliable in what he undertook, whether good or bad. But Darcy had kept this facet of his character buried, and something or someone had unearthed it and used it.

For the first time, I allowed myself to imagine what would have happened if the pack had caught Jack.

And I found myself almost sure they would have killed him.

I began work at Mookie's house in a grim mood. Of course her place couldn't be as dirty as it had been the first time I'd cleaned it, but every week she did a grand job of retrashing it. I scrubbed the bathroom in silence, trying to ignore the little questions and comments she tossed to me as she passed by the open door.

Mookie showed me her cuts from the bombing. They'd been caused by flying splinters, and they were healing well. She inquired after my leg. Would the woman never shut up and settle down to her work?

Once I got the bathroom decent again, I moved into the bedroom. This old house had big rooms and high ceilings, and Mookie's low modern bed and chest of drawers looked out of place. The bare wooden floors made a bit of an echo, footsteps clacking unnaturally loud. Maybe she liked the noise, maybe it kept her company.

'You know,' Mookie said, making one of her abrupt appearances, 'they haven't got a clue who planted that bomb.' She'd been reading the papers. I hadn't.

'Is that right?' I asked. I really didn't want to talk.

'The device that started the explosion was a wristwatch, like the one you've got on,' Mookie said. She was very angry, very intense. I'd had enough angry and intense already today. 'All the chemicals in the bomb were things you could order from any chemical supply house. All you'd have to do is not order everything from one place, so they won't get suspicious.'

'I wouldn't know,' I said pointedly.

'It's in books you can check out of the library here!' she said, her hands flying up in a gesture of complete exasperation, 'It's in books you can buy at the bookstore in Montrose!'

'So it's probably almost as easy to make a bomb as it is to buy a rifle,' I said, my voice calm and even.

The rifle was not under her bed any longer.

'A rifle's legal.'

'Sure.' I was careful not to turn and look her in the eyes. I didn't want any kind of confrontation. That, too, I'd had enough of already today.

After I changed the sheets and dusted the bedroom, I looked around for an empty bag to dump the contents of the plastic garbage pail, which was full of soiled tissues, balls of hair, and gum wrappers. There, next to a Reebok shoe box, was a dark red plastic bag, and it bore the distinctive logo of Winthrop Sporting Goods.

I tried to persuade myself that there was nothing odd about this. People did mostly buy their sports shoes at Winthrop's, because the store carried a great selection and would special-order what they didn't have in stock.

But I'd seen another red plastic bag the week before. And I remembered seeing yet another crammed into the kitchen garbage. Mookie was going to Winthrop's very frequently.

Slowly I dumped the garbage pail into the bag and went to the bathroom to empty another one. Mookie barely glanced at me as I cleared the one by her desk. Her coarse reddish hair was braided today, and she was wearing wind-suit pants and a turtle-neck. She was tapping computer keys with great energy. The same charts were taped to the wall behind her. There was a pile of library books on the desk, studded with slips of paper marking pages she wanted to refer to.

'How does a genealogist work?' I asked.

For once, she'd been engrossed in what she was doing, and she took a minute to focus on my question.

'Mostly by computer these days,' she answered. 'Which is great for me. I do work for a company that advertises in small specialty magazines, or regional mags, like *Southern Living*. We trace your ancestry for you if you give us some basic information. The Mormons, oddly enough, have the best records; I think they believe they can baptize their ancestors and get them into heaven that way, or something. Then there are country records, and so on.

'Did you want your folks traced?' she asked me now, a hint of amusement in the set of her mouth.

'I know who my family is,' I said, and spoke the truth, for my mother's idea of a great Christmas present was a family tree ready-framed for my wall. For all I knew, she'd hired Mookie Preston's company to do the research.

'Then you're lucky. Most Americans can only name as far back as their great-grandparents. They're shaky after that.'

I tried to think of myself as lucky.

I failed.

I wanted to sit in the battered armchair in front of her desk and ask her what I really needed to know. Why was she here? What trouble was she getting into? Would I come to work next week and find her dead, for sticking her nose into a hornet's nest and getting stung?

Mookie laughed uneasily. 'You're looking at me funny, Lily.'

Bits of information slid around in my head and rearranged into a pattern. Lanette had come looking for Mookie secretly one night. Mookie had moved to town right after Darnell Glass had been killed. Mookie had an Illinois license plate. Lanette had returned to Shakespeare after living in Chicago for a time. I studied the round line of Mookie's cheeks and the strong column of her neck, and then I knew why she seemed familiar.

I gave Mookie a brisk nod and went back to work on the kitchen. Mookie was Darnell's half-sister. But there seemed no point in talking to Mookie about it: Strictly speaking, it wasn't my business, and Mookie knew better than anyone who she was and what she had to mourn. I wondered whose idea it had been to keep silent. Had Mookie wanted to do some kind of undercover work on the murder of her brother, or had Lanette been unwilling to admit to the town that she'd had a liaison with a white man?

I wondered if Lanette had left for Chicago pregnant.

I wondered if the father was still alive, still here in Shakespeare. I wondered if he and Mookie had talked.

The rifle, black and brown and deadly, had spooked me. I hadn't seen loose firearms in anyone's house since I began cleaning. I'd polished my share of gun cabinets, but I'd never found one unsecured and its contents easily available; which didn't mean the guns hadn't been there, in night tables and closets, just that they hadn't been quite so . . . accessible. I felt I hadn't been meant to see the rifle, that Mookie's carelessness had been a mistake. I had no idea what Arkansas gun laws were, since I'd never wanted to carry a gun myself. Maybe the rifle was locked in Mookie's car trunk.

I remembered the targets. If they were typical of Mookie's marksmanship, she was a good shot.

I thought of the pack of men who'd been after Jack. Darcy knew Mookie's name and address. I thought of him thinking the same thoughts about Mookie that I'd been thinking.

I gathered up my things and told Mookie I was leaving. She was coming outside to check her mailbox at the same time, and after she'd paid me we walked down the driveway together. I thought hard about what to say, if to speak at all.

Almost too late, I made up my mind. 'You should go,' I said. Her back was to me. I already had one foot in the car.

She twisted halfway around, paused for a moment. 'Would you?' She asked.

I considered it. 'No,' I said finally.

'There, then.' She collected her mail and passed me again on her way back into that half-empty echoing house. She acted as though I wasn't there.

*

When I got home that night, all the sleeplessness of the night before and the emotional strain of the day hit me in the face. It would have done me good to go to karate, blow off some tension. But I was so miserable I couldn't bring myself to dress for it. Waves of black depression rolled over me as I sat at my bare kitchen table. I thought I'd left death behind me when I'd found this little town, picked it off the map because it was called Shakespeare and my name was Bard – as good a reason as any to settle somewhere, I'd figured at the time. I'd tried so many places after I'd gotten out of the hospital; from my parents' home to Jackson, Mississippi, to Waverly, Tennessee . . . waitressed, cleaned, washed hair in a salon, anything I could leave behind me when I walked out the door at the end of the workday.

Then I'd found Shakespeare, and Shakespeare needed a maid.

When Pardon Albee had died, it had been a small thing, an individual thing. But this that was happening now, this craziness . . . it was generated by a pack mentality, something particularly terrifying and enraging to me. I'd experienced men in packs.

I thought of Jack Leeds, who would never be part of any pack. He'd get over being mad at me . . . or he wouldn't. It was out of my hands. I would not go to him, no matter how many grieved girlfriends and widows passed through my mind. Sometimes I hated chemistry, which could play such tricks with your good sense, your promises to yourself.

When the knock came at the front door, I glanced at the clock on the wall. I'd been sitting and staring for an hour. My injured hip hurt when I rose, having been in the same position for so long.

I looked through the peephole. Bobo was on my doorstep, and he looked anxious. I let him in. He was wearing a brown coat over his gi.

'Hey, how are you?' he asked. 'I missed you at karate. Marshall did, too.' He added that hastily, as though I would accuse him of hogging all the missing that was going around.

If it had been anyone but Bobo, I wouldn't have opened the

door I'd known him since he was just beginning to shave; he'd sometimes been arrogant, sometimes too big for his britches, but he had always been sweet. I wondered how this boy had gotten to be my friend.

'Have you been crying, Lily?' he asked now.

I reached up to touch my cheek. Yes, I had been.

'It doesn't matter,' I said, wanting him to not notice, to drop it.

'Yes, it does,' he said. 'You're always beating yourself up, Lily. It does matter.' Amazingly, Bobo pulled a clean handkerchief from his coat pocket, and wiped my cheeks with gentle fingers.

This was not the way conversations with Bobo usually went. Usually he told me how his classes were going, or we talked about a new throw Marshall had taught us, or the boy Amber Jean was dating.

'Bobo,' I began uneasily, puzzled. I was trying to think how to proceed when Bobo acted instead, decisively. He gathered me up and kissed me hard, with an unnerving degree of expertise. For a few shocked seconds I stood quietly accepting this intimacy, feeling the warmth of his mouth against mine, the hard pressure of his body, before my internal alarm system went off. I slid my hands up and pressed gently against his chest. He instantly released me. I looked into his face, and saw a man who desired me.

'I'm so sorry, Bobo,' I said. 'I hope I'm always your friend.' It was a dreary thing to say, but I meant it.

Not that pushing him away was effortless: It was all too easy to envision welcoming Bobo – young, vigorous, strong, handsome, endearing – into my bed. I'd been hoping to wipe out bad memories with good ones; Bobo and I could certainly give each other a few. Even now I felt the pull of temptation, as I saw his face close around the pain.

'I – have someone else,' I told him. And I hated the fact that what I said was true.

'Marshall?' he breathed.

'No. It's not important who it is, Bobo.' I made another effort. 'You have no idea how tempted and flattered I am.' The unevenness of my voice gave witness to that. I saw the pride return to his face as he heard the truth in what I was saying.

'I've cared about you for a long time,' he said.

'Thank you.' I never meant anything as much. 'That makes me proud.'

Amazingly, after he'd opened the door to leave, he turned and lifted my hand and kissed it.

I watched his Jeep pull away.

'Touching scene,' Jack Leeds said acerbically.

He stepped out of the shadows in the carport and walked across the little patch of lawn to my front door. He stood inches away, his arms crossed over his chest, a sneer on his face.

I could truly almost feel my heart sinking. I thought of closing the door and locking it in his face. I wasn't up to another scene.

'Did you give him the time of his life, Lily? Golden boy, no past to slow him down?'

I felt something snap in me. I'd been pushed beyond some limit. He could read it in my eyes, and I saw him start to uncross his arms in sudden alarm, but I struck him as hard as I could in the solar plexus. He made a sound and began to double over. I folded my arm, aimed the point of my elbow at the base of his skull. I pulled it at the very last instant, because it was a killing blow. But I had pulled the blow too soon, because he could launch himself at me. He knocked me back inside my front door onto the carpet. He kicked the door shut behind him.

This was the second time Jack had had me pinned. I wasn't going to have it. I struck his hurt shoulder, and over he went, and then I was on top. I had his jacket gripped with one hand while my other twisted his knit shirt, tightening the neck band, my knuckles digging into his throat while he made a gagging noise.

'Oh yes, Jack, this is love, all right,' I said in a trembling voice that I hardly recognized. I rolled off him and sat with my back to him, my hands over my face, waiting for him to hit me or leave.

After a long time I risked a look at him. He was still lying on his back, his eyes fixed on me. He was visibly shaken, and I was glad to see it. He beckoned me with an inward curl of his fingers. I shook my head violently.

After another long time I heard him move. He sat behind me, his legs spread, and pulled me back against him. His arms crossed in front of me, holding me to him, but gently. Gradually I calmed, stopped shaking.

'We're okay, Lily,' he said. 'We're okay.'

'Can this poor sense of timing be why you have such a – checkered career – as a lover?' I asked.

'I – am – sorry,' he said between clenched teeth.

'That helps.'

'Really sorry.'

'Good.'

'Can I—?'

'What? What do you want to do, Jack?'

He told me.

I told him he could try.

Later, in the quiet of my bed, he began to talk about something else. And all the pieces began to fall into place.

'Howell Winthrop, Jr., hired me,' he said. We were lying facing each other. 'He told me a week ago not to trust you.'

I could feel my eyes open wide as I absorbed all this.

'You saw the men last night. You have to have figured it out.'

'I guess Darcy is involved. All the others?'

'Yes, and a few more. Not the whole town, not even a sizable proportion of the white males. Just a few mental misfits who think their dicks are on the line. They think their manhood is tied up in keeping blacks, and women for that matter, in their place.'

'So they meet at Winthrop's Sporting Goods.'

'The group evolved that way. Most of them are passing through there to buy things pretty often anyway, so it just happened. Ninety-eight percent of the people that patronize Winthrop's are just regular nice people, but the two percent . . . Howell didn't know anything about it until he noticed that guns were being bought through the store accounts that didn't show up in the store. And it wasn't even Howell that noticed it.'

'Oh no.' I thought for a moment. 'It was Del.'

'Yeah, Del Packard. He went to Howell. Howell told him not to tell anyone else. But he must have.'

'Poor Del. Who killed him?'

'I don't know yet. I don't know if Del knew more than he told Howell, or if they were just scared of him telling it to the police – maybe they even asked Del to join them and he refused – but one of them took Del out.'

'Surely not all the Winthrop employees are in on it?' So many people worked at Winthrop's, at least twenty men and four or five women who did office work. Added to the staff of the Winthrop-owned lumber and home supply business right next door . . . and there was Winthrop Oil . . .

'No, not by a long shot. Only three or four men at the Sporting Goods place, that I've been able to make sure of. And a couple, maybe three men from the place next door. Plus a few guys who just joined in, like Tom David and the one you told me was Cleve Ragland. The day they came to steal back the bags at the Winthrops' house, they were in Cleve Ragland's car.'

Since Jack was in a tell-all mood, I decided I would ask as many questions as I could.

'What was in the black bags?'

'Guns. And rifles. For the past four years Jim Box has been the man who ordered for the store. Someone got the bright idea for Jim to order a little more than he thought Winthrop's could sell. Then they were going to stage a robbery and list those arms as stolen, which is why that excuse popped into their minds so quickly last night, I guess. They'd figured if they set up a robbery, no one could blame the store – Howell – if the guns were used for illegal stuff. Instead of walking out with one weapon at a time, they began stockpiling what they wanted in the storeroom at the back of the store in two black bags, waiting for the right moment to stage the break-in. They should've gone on and moved their pile after Del died, but we're not talking big brains here.'

'Then you and Howell took the bags.'

'Yeah, everyone in on it was gone to lunch, so we loaded them into Howell's car and drove out to his house.' He kissed me. 'The day I saw you there. You had the strangest expression on your face.'

'I couldn't figure you two out. I was thinking you and Howell were maybe – thataway.'

Jack laughed out loud. 'Beanie's safe.'

'Why did you put them in Howell's house?'

'We wanted to see who'd come after them. We knew by then who on Howell's payroll was involved, but not the names of the rest of the group. I also figured lying concealed in Howell's house would be safer than hiding at the store every night, waiting for the staged burglary to take place. So Howell told Darcy about this strange cache of arms he'd found in the store, how he thought he'd keep them at his house until he decided whether he should call the police or not.'

'Wasn't that just a little more dangerous for Howell and his family?' I asked, trying to keep my voice even.

'Well, I knew the day they were going to try. And Howell has this conviction they won't hurt him or his family. He has this weird sense of – like he owes them, because they work for him. He doesn't even seem to want to turn them in when he finds out who it is . . . and he wants to know exactly. It's strange. He doesn't want anyone falsely accused, and I can respect that. But it's like there's something he's not telling me.'

I should have listened to that sentence harder, mulled over it like I mulled over so many things. But I was still trying to understand Jack and Howell's plan of action. So far, frankly, it didn't seem that much better than the thieves'. 'So you hid out in Beanie's closet. To wait and see who came to call.'

'Yeah. And you came in, I knew who you were the minute you hit me, but I didn't know your name.'

'You hadn't heard the men talk?'

'I'd heard people mention Lily, but I didn't know that was you.

You didn't look like any maid I'd ever seen, or any karate expert, either. Or any weight lifter.'

'What did I look like?' I asked, very close to his face.

'Like the most exciting woman I'd ever seen.'

Every now and then, Jack said exactly the right thing.

He whispered, 'I wanted to touch you. I just wanted to lay my hands on you.' He demonstrated. 'When Howell heard about the bomb he called me and told me to go down to the hospital to verify how many hurt and dead there were. He knew it would seem strange if he did it. He's sure one of his employees set the bomb, and he wanted to know if one of them had been brought in hurt. He thought maybe they'd hang around to see the explosion, get caught in it. So I went down to the hospital. It was eerie. I just walked in, and strolled through the halls looking. No one stopped me, or asked me what my business was there. The idea was a good one, but it didn't pan out. No one associated with the group was brought in injured. But I saw you on the gurney.'

'You were at the hospital! I thought it was a dream.'

'It was me. I wanted to stay, but I knew that would look strange.'

'You asked me if there was anyone you could call for me.'

'I wanted someone to come take care of you. And I wanted to know if there was anyone ahead of me. Everyone had told me you were with Marshall. I felt he was pretty formidable competition. If you'd asked me to call him . . .'

'What would you have done?'

'I would have called him. But I would have tried to find some way to pry you loose when you were feeling better.'

We didn't talk for a while.

I got up to get a drink, came back.

'Why do you think Howell doesn't trust me?' I asked. That stung me. I had kept faith with the Winthrop family over and above the demands of my paycheck.

'I don't know. When I was asking him who had keys to the house, as a matter of routine, he said, "The maid," and he said you'd worked for him for four years and he was sure you were absolutely reliable. But then, about a week ago, he called me into his office first thing in the morning to tell me to avoid you, that he thought you were in on something.'

He kissed me to show me how little he'd listened.

'I can't think of what I've done to earn Howell's mistrust.' I stowed that away to think of later. 'What's their goal in stockpiling all these weapons?'

'From what I've pieced together, their goal is to start a white supremacist militia group here, using Cleve Ragland's hunting camp as a training base. They want to be a big-time organization rather than a few bastards who grouse and murder children in bombings.'

'Have you heard anything about Darnell Glass?' I asked.

Jack lay back, pushed his hair back with his fingers. 'It's strange,' he said finally. 'It's like there were two things going on. After meeting most of the men who are involved in this, at least I think I've met most of them, what I've been impressed with most is their stupidity. Keeping the arms they were stealing at the store: dumb. Trying to steal them back from Howell's house: dumb. Spray-painting Deedra's car, and that was the boy who works at the loading dock at the Home Supply store – I actually saw him do it – there again, dumb. I think Deedra snubbed him when she went in the store to get a new curtain rod, so he got her back. Then the bomb. The day after the bomb went off, when they'd heard Claude Friedrich and you were hurt and Sheriff Schuster was killed – they were all hangdog as hell. I think it bothered them about the little girl, too. You know why that all happened? The bomb didn't go off at the right time. That I did overhear, directly, Jim and Darcy venting their guilt. They were trying to shift the blame to the victims – you shouldn't have been there in the first place. Sheriff Schuster shouldn't have gotten out faster. The little girl should have been home doing her homework. Crap like that.'

'They killed those people out of incompetence.' I closed my eyes. I remembered the scene inside the church.

'There are groups that like to kill as many black people as they can, Lily, and don't care what age they get. These guys, no . . . they hadn't ever built a bomb before and they got it wrong.'

'How'd they get it in the church before the meeting?'

'The church is unlocked during the day. Jim just chanced it, best as I can piece it out.'

I felt sick.

'But Darnell, they haven't said anything about him?'

'No, but your name has come up a bunch of times.'

'Wait.' The most important question of all hadn't even occurred to me until now. Jack was new at the store. Why would they trust him to keep silent? 'How can you overhear all this?'

'Lily, I put a bug in the employee lounge.'

'Is that legal?'

'Well . . .'

'Hmmm.'

'It's not exactly true to say they haven't talked about Darnell's murder,' Jack said, perhaps to distract me from wondering about how much illegality he'd put up with. 'They all feel like he got what was coming to him. Don't ask me to explain their thinking, because that's impossible. And then they mention you, because I gather that was a real brawl. Did you have to pitch in?' He turned me to face him and looked me in the eyes. His own eyes were serious. I ran my finger down his cheek, down his scar, traced his neck to his collarbone.

'Don't think I haven't had regrets that the whole thing happened, that I happened to be there, even. I'm no activist. I want to be left alone. But I was there, and he was outnumbered, and those boys would've beat the shit out of him.'

Jack absorbed that, accepted it. 'But you see, from their point of view,' he said, very quietly, 'you defended Darnell, and you were there at Howell's when they came to reclaim the rifles, and you were in the church when it blew up. That's too many coincidences for them, no matter that you were minding your own business in every instance.'

'Do they think I'm you? Do they think I'm some kind of detective?'

'They think you like black people too much and they do think you might have something to do with their not being able to get the guns back. Then I spend the night with you on the very night they're trying to find out who was spying on them. So they wonder about you, a lot. At the same time, it seems like they have a weird kind of respect for you.'

'How did they come to chase you last night?'

'I was hidden in a sort of niche I'd made. If you think the customer part of the store is overwhelming, you should see the back of the store. Someone could live back there for a week and no one would ever know. Anyway, I knew they were going to be meeting after hours in the storeroom, and it's not bugged. I wanted to know what they were planning.'

'How'd they know you were there?'

'You're going to laugh,' he said gloomily, and I had a feeling I really wasn't. 'The boy, Paulie, who works at the Home Supply store, brought his dog with him. He's real proud of that dog, talks about it all the time. It cost some ungodly amount. A bluetick hound, I think. The dog sniffed me, started barking. It seemed smarter to run for it than to wait until they came to investigate.'

I was right. I wasn't laughing. 'They would have killed you.'

'I know it.' He lay staring at my ceiling, thinking about that real hard. 'I don't think all of them were in on Darnell's murder, but they would have killed me last night because they were all together and they were scared.'

'Do you think they're suspicious now?'

'Maybe. I got a phone call today from Jim. He said he'd heard from Darcy that I was courting Lily Bard. He suggested I'd be better off with some more traditional girl.'

'Courting, huh? That what this is?'

'Damn if I know. But I like it, whatever we call it.'

'And I'm a girl,' I said thoughtfully. 'A nontraditional girl.'

'Screw tradition, in that case,' Jack murmured.

'So what are you going to do next?'

'I'm going to keep on like I have been, as long as I can.

Collecting the tape every night, listening to it, copying it, phoning Howell with any information I can glean. Waiting for him to decide what he's going to do; after all, he's my boss.' Jack put his arms around me. 'Lilly, I get stubborn and mad and do the wrong thing sometimes. If I was really a great detective, I'd tell you I can't see you until this is over. Maybe I'm putting you in even more danger than you're already in. But maybe somehow, since they still believe my cover, I'm giving you a little credence with them. If a bad boy like me is interested in you, you can't be a snitch, they figure – I hope. But I just don't know.'

He sat up, swung his legs over the side of the bed. I was treated to a view of his bare back and bottom. I enjoyed it very much. I traced his spine with my finger, and he arched his back. 'You can tell,' he said, not looking at me, 'that I have a real problem with impulsiveness.'

'You're kidding,' I said, deadpan.

'Let's not joke about this, OK. I came to your house when I was wounded, brought you under more suspicion, maybe. Put you in danger. I made love to you on impulse. I can't regret that. I'd stay in bed with you for a year if I could. But I was impulsive starting that affair with Karen, and she died.' He turned a little to meet my eyes. 'I can't let my thoughtlessness put you in danger, like it did her.'

'I don't guess you'll be able to stop it. And I'm not Karen Kingsland.' There was a certain edge in my voice.

'Lily, listen to me! I know you're strong, I know you think of yourself as a tough woman, but this is not just one opponent who fights fair. This is a pack, and they would kill you . . . and maybe not straightaway.'

I stared at him. Somehow I had lost pleasure in the view.

'You're saying – stop me if I get this wrong, Jack – you're saying that I only think of myself as tough, I'm really not . . . that I can only win if my opponents fight fair . . . that Darcy and Jim and Tom David would rape me if they had the chance. Gosh, why would that occur to me?'

'I know you're getting mad,' he said, turning around and

looking down at me. 'And I probably deserve it, but I just can't let anything happen to you. You just can't be involved in this in any way, any longer.'

'You'll just stop by when you have a minute to fuck? Insult my other guests?'

His sculpted lips tightened. He was beginning to get mad, too.

'No. I shouldn't have said anything about Bobo being here. I had no right. And I told you I was sorry. Hey, I never said anything about the cop sending you flowers, and they were still sitting on your kitchen table with the card stuck in them.'

'Which, of course, you had a perfect right to read.'

'Lily, I'm a *detective*. Of course I read it.'

I gripped my head with my hands. I shook it to clear it.

'Go,' I said. 'I can't deal with you right now.'

'We're doing this again,' he said helplessly.

'No, *you* are.' I meant it. 'You screw my brains out after telling me we shouldn't be publicly involved. Okay, I admit, I screwed you right back, and I publicly involved us – to save your ass. You spill your guts to me – on impulse – tell me my employer doesn't trust me, tell me I may or may not be in serious danger, and then tell me not to involve myself in the resolution of this mess.'

'Put that way, I admit, it doesn't sound like I'm doing the right thing by you.'

'Gosh, no kidding.'

'Why do we get so – so – crossways? I'm trying to do the right thing! I don't want you to get hurt!'

'I know,' I said. I sighed. 'You need to go on now. Come back and talk to me – somewhere public – when you decide what your current policy is.'

He stood. His face was full of conflict. He held out his hand.

'Kiss me,' he said. 'I can't leave like this. This is something real we have.'

Almost unwillingly, I held out my hand, and he pulled me up to kneel on the bed. He bent over and kissed me hard on the mouth. I felt the heat begin to slide through me again. I pulled back.

'Yeah. It's real,' he said, and dressed. He dropped a kiss on my head before he went out the door.

Chapter Eight

Carrie wasn't at the clinic that morning. It was the first time in a long time she hadn't been there on a Saturday. I hadn't realized how much I'd counted on seeing her until I pulled into the lot behind the clinic and found it empty.

She'd left me a note taped to the patients' bathroom door, since she knew I cleaned that first.

Lily – I'm following your suggestion. Today the entire off-duty police department is moving Claude downstairs to the O'Hagens' old apartment. Becca Whitley's putting in a ramp at the back door! Knew you would want to know.

I was a little disconcerted by Carrie's taking charge of Claude. I'd been to see him in the hospital a couple more times, and I realized now that both times he'd talked about Carrie. Maybe the reason I hadn't worried about the problems of Claude's homecoming was that I'd absorbed the clues that someone else was doing it for me? Well, well, well. Carrie and Claude. It sounded nice.

I got the clinic cleaned, though I felt lonely without Carrie. As I started work at my next client's, I brooded about what Jack had told me. It gnawed at me that Howell didn't trust me. I am very reliable, I keep my mouth shut, and I'm honest. My reputation as a cleaning woman depends on those qualities.

I struggled to recall all the contacts I'd had with Howell recently, trying to pick out one that would explain his sudden lack of faith in me.

By the time I was through for the day, I'd decided to make a call.

After checking the phone book and the map, I drove again into the black area of Shakespeare which surrounded Golgotha Church. I felt a wave of nausea when I passed the damaged structure, now bathed in bright winter sunshine. The cold wind rippled a large sheet of plastic over the hole in the roof, and temporary front doors had been hung. A junked pile of splintered pews lay outside in the grass. A whiff of burning still lingered in the air. Men were at work inside and out. A white man was among them, and after a careful look I recognized the Catholic priest from Montrose. Then I saw another white face: Brian Gruber, the mattress factory executive. And redheaded Al from Winthrop's Sporting Goods. I felt a little better after that.

My business lay a block or two away, in one of the few brick homes in the area. Tidy and tiny, it sat within a four-foot chain-link fence, with a 'Beware of the Dog' notice. The shutters and eaves were painted golden yellow to contrast with the brown bricks. I scanned the yard, didn't see the dog to beware of. I lifted the gate latch, and a big tan short-eared dog of unfortunate parentage tore around the house. He woofed and he growled, and he ran from side to side right within the fence.

A small black woman came to the front door, she was trim and tidy like the house, and she had picked rose red to wear today, her day off. At her appearance, the dog instantly silenced, waiting to see what the woman's attitude would be.

'What you want?' she called. She was neither welcoming nor repelling.

'If you're Callie Gandy, I need to talk to you. I'm Lily Bard.'

'I know who you are. What do we have to talk about?'

'This.' I held up the shabby brown velvet ring box.

'What you doing with Mrs Winthrop's ring?'

Bingo. Just as I had suspected, this had never been Marie Hofstettler's ring.

'Miss Gandy, I really want to talk.'

'Miss Bard, I'm not aiming to be rude, but you are only trouble and I don't need any more of that than I have.'

I had already learned what I needed to know.

'All right. Good-bye.'

She didn't answer. She and the tan dog watched me with poker-faced stillness while I returned to my car and buckled up. She closed her door then, and I drove home with even more to think about.

That afternoon I went to the grocery, cleaned my own house, and made some banana nut bread for Claude. He liked it for breakfast. It seemed very sweet, very personal to know that about a friend. That was what I'd missed most, without ever knowing it, in my wandering years and my first years in Shakespeare: the little details, the intimacy, of friendship.

I retrieved one of my homemade individual entrées from the freezer. Claude liked lasagna, I remembered. Feeling like a small-town paradigm of neighborliness, I walked over to the apartments.

The move was complete, apparently, and some of Claude's cops were still there drinking a beer by way of thank-you. Claude was on his old couch, his bad leg propped up on an ottoman. The door was open, so I just stepped in, self-conscious at having an audience.

'Lily, are you a sight for sore eyes!' Claude boomed, and I noticed he looked better than he had since his injury. 'Come on in and have a brew.'

I glanced around at the men lounging in the living room. I nodded at Dedford Jinks, whom I hadn't seen since the Winthrop break-in, and Todd Picard. He seemed a little more relaxed in my presence than he had been in weeks past. Tom David was sitting on the floor, his long legs crossed at the ankle, a Michelob bottle in his hand. His bright mean eyes scanned me, and his mouth curved in a nasty smile.

Judas, I thought, drinking Claude's beer when you knew he was going to be in that church. Could you have kept that child from dying?

My face must have become very unpleasant, because Tom David looked startled then defensive. His smile faltered, then increased in wattage.

'Hoo hoo, it's Miss Bard, tore herself away from her new love long enough to pay you a visit, Claude!'

Claude just smiled, perhaps because Carrie came out of the kitchen at that moment. Carrie was wearing leggings and a University of Arkansas sweatshirt, and she looked – for once – carefree. Her glasses were propped on top of her head, and her eyes were round and brown and warm.

Tom David was taken aback when he realized no one was going to pick up on his cue. Dedford Jinks, the detective, ran a hand over his own thinning hair and gave Tom David a look of sheer irritation.

I smiled at Carrie, bobbed my head to Dedford and a patrolman I didn't know, a tall black man with a bandage on his arm. I looked at him carefully. I'd helped him up in the church. He recognized me, too. We exchanged nods.

I told Claude, 'I figured you wouldn't be baking anytime soon, so I brought you some bread.'

'Would that by any chance be banana nut? I can smell it from here.'

I nodded. 'Some lasagna, too,' I muttered. I wished everyone would look somewhere else.

'Lily, you are sure sweet,' Claude declared. 'Without Carrie helping me move and you cooking for me, I'd have to rely on pizza delivery.'

'Oh, of course, no one else in town will bring you meals,' Carrie said sarcastically. And she was right to take Claude's words with a grain of salt. He'd be inundated with food within days, if not hours.

'Where should I put this?' I asked Carrie, tacitly acknowledging her place in the apartment.

She looked a little surprised, then pleased.

'Come help me unpack the kitchen, if you have a minute,' she invited. She could tell I was uncomfortable. I followed her from the room gladly, giving Claude a gentle pat on the shoulder as I passed him.

Carrie and I were a little old for girlish confidences, but I felt obliged to say something. 'This what it looks like?' I asked, keeping my voice low.

She shrugged, trying to look noncommittal, but a little smile curved her lips.

'Good,' I said. 'Now, where you think he wants these spices?'

'I'm trying to put everything where he had it in the apartment upstairs,' Carrie said. 'I don't want him to feel like a stranger in his own kitchen. I tried to remember. I even drew a diagram. But it got a little hectic up there with the men coming in and out.'

'Spices were here, I believe,' I said, opening the cabinet right by the stove. I was hoping Carrie wouldn't take this wrong, and she didn't, being above all a sensible woman.

Luckily, Becca Whitley (I assumed) had given the apartment a thorough cleaning after the O'Hagens moved out. All we had to do was put things in what we considered a logical place. After Carrie and I had worked a while, we took a break and had a Coke. Leaning against the counters in companionable weariness, we exchanged smiles.

'They carried everything down without a problem, but I guess the unpacking is woman's work,' Carrie said wryly. She lowered her voice. 'What's this Tom David was trying to start trouble with?' We could still hear men's voices in the living room, but we didn't know who'd gone and who'd come in.

'I'm . . .' To my horror, I could feel myself turning red, and I had to look off into the distance.

'Are you all right?' Carrie asked. She got her doctor look on.

'Yes.' I took a breath. 'I'm seeing the new man at Winthrop's Sporting Goods.' For an awful minute I could not remember Jack's cover name. 'Jared Fletcher.'

'The one who lives here in the apartments? The one with the lips and the hair?'

I nodded, grinning at this description.

'How'd you meet him?'

'I went in to buy some weight-lifting gloves,' I said, sifting through the weeks past to find something believable.

'That's romantic,' Carrie said.

I looked at her sharply to see if she was teasing me, but she was dead serious.

'Didn't I see him at the hospital the night of the bombing?' she said doubtfully.

Now, that was before I'd officially met Jack. But Carrie didn't know that, didn't know when I'd bought my new gloves. This was so complicated. I hated telling lies, especially to one of my few friends.

'Yes,' I said.

'He came to see about you?'

I nodded, figuring that was a little better than trying to sort partial truth from fiction.

'Oh, wow,' Carrie said, all dewy-eyed.

As if on cue, I heard a familiar voice from the living room.

'Hey, I hear you deserted us upstairs. There must be a secret benefit to living down here!' Jack said heartily.

Claude's response was less audible, but I heard the word 'beer' clearly.

'I just may do that,' Jack answered. 'I've been working all day and I could use some liquid refreshment. Speaking of which, I picked up this bottle for your housewarming.'

'Thank you, neighbor,' Claude said, more audibly. He must have turned his head toward a moving Jack. 'You'll have to come share it with me when I open it.'

Jack appeared in the kitchen doorway, wearing his red sweat-shirt with the Winthrop logo and his leather jacket. He betrayed his surprise at finding me there only by a widening of his eyes.

'Lily,' he said, and kissed me on the cheek. His hand groped for mine, squeezed it hard for a moment, released it. 'The chief says you have some loose beer in here.'

I pointed at the refrigerator. Carrie beamed at Jack and extended a hand.

'I'm so glad to meet you. I'm Carrie Thrush.'

'The good doctor Thrush. I've heard great things about you,' Jack said. 'I'm Jared Fletcher. New man in town.' He was smiling genuinely. He set a bottle of bourbon on the counter, Claude's homecoming gift, and opened the refrigerator to extract a beer.

'You'll have to bring Lily down for supper some night. Maybe she and I can collaborate on cooking and you and Claude can evaluate the result,' Carrie said cheerfully.

'Tom David told on us, Jared,' I said, trying to speak lightly. But I haven't done that in a long time, and it came out sounding very unnatural. Carrie swung a look in my direction, then back to Jack.

'That would be great, Carrie,' Jack said smoothly. He looked at me to tell me he'd gotten my message: the little cabal was having conversations about us.

'Lily brought Claude some bread and some lasagna,' Carrie said, pushing my praiseworthy aspects.

'Did you, baby?' Jack looked at me, and if there was a flash of heat in his eyes, there was none in his voice.

Baby? I was trying to imagine double-dating with Carrie and Claude. I was trying to imagine everything being straightforward, Jack really working at Winthrop's Sporting Goods, having no other agenda than making a living. I would just be a maid, and he would just sell workout equipment . . . We'd date, go out on real dates, during which no one would get shot. We'd never hit each other, or even want to.

'Claude took care of me when I got hurt last spring,' I said, suddenly feeling very tired. I didn't owe Jack an explanation, but I needed to say something.

'You got hurt . . .' Jack began, his eyes narrowing.

'Old story. Go out there and have your beer, *sugar*,' I said dismissively, and gave him what I hoped was a loverlike shove to the uninjured shoulder. He righted himself after a tense second and stalked into the living room.

'Did I catch some undercurrent there?' Carrie asked.

'Yeah, well, nothing's easy,' I muttered.

'Not with you, anyway,' she said, but her voice was gentle.

'Actually, in this case, it's him,' I told her grimly.

'Hmmm. You think this is going to work out?'

'Who knows?' I said, exasperated. 'Let's get this kitchen done.'

'It hardly seems right for you to work so hard, Lily. You spend all week cleaning and arranging other people's things. Why don't you go sit out there and have some down time?'

With Claude and Jack and Tom David? 'Not on your life,' I told her, and finished placing pots and pans in the cabinet.

We worked on the bedroom next, sliding all the drawers back into their correct position, rearranging the clothes in the closet. I polished all the furniture after I found the cleaning supplies, and I quickly stowed away the bathroom things while Carrie set Claude's desk to rights in the second bedroom.

Then I was through, and I knew it was time for me to leave. Carrie would have to be helping Claude do personal things, I supposed; he would be tired.

He was, in fact, asleep on the couch. All the men had left except Jack, who had opened a box of books and was shelving them in the low bookcase. He'd gathered up all the beer bottles and put them in a plastic garbage bag. He half-turned as he heard my steps, smiled at me, and pushed a dictionary into place. It all seemed so pleasant and normal. I didn't know what attitude to take. He'd severed our connection until this episode was over. But we were alone in the room except for the sleeping policeman.

I knelt by him, and he turned and kissed me, his hand going to the back of my neck. It was a kiss that started out to be short and ended up to be long.

'Damn,' he breathed, moving back from me.

'Gotta go,' I said very quietly, not wanting to disturb the sleeper.

'Yeah, me, too,' he whispered, standing and stretching. 'I need to listen to today's tape.' He patted his jacket pocket.

'Jack,' I said in his ear, 'if Howell won't call the law, you have to. You'll get in awful trouble.' It was an idea that had consumed any extra minute I'd had during the day. I darted a glance at 'the law', sound asleep on the couch. 'Promise me,' I whispered. I looked straight into his hazel eyes.

'Are you scared?' he breathed.

I nodded. 'For you,' I told him.

He stared at me. 'I'll talk to Howell tomorrow,' he said.

I smiled at him, rubbed my knuckles against his cheek in a caress. ''Bye,' I whispered, and tiptoed out Claude's door.

I pulled on my coat in the hall, zipping the front and pulling my hood up. It was really cold, biting cold; the temperature would be well below freezing tonight. I wouldn't be able to walk even if I needed to. But after extracting Jack's promise I felt very relaxed. It might not take me too long to sleep.

Just to make sure, I walked the four streets around the arboretum twice, very briskly, and then took the trails through the trees. When I emerged onto Track Street, it was full dark. My feet were feeling numb and my hands were chilled despite my gloves.

I was halfway across the street, angling to my house, when a Jeep rounded the corner at a high speed and screeched to a halt a foot away from my right leg.

'Where've you been, Lily?' Bobo was hatless and frantic, his brown coat unbuttoned. There was no trace of the ardent young man who had kissed me the night before.

'Helping Claude move downstairs. Walking.'

'I've been looking for you everywhere. Get inside your house and don't go out tonight.'

His face, almost on a level with mine because of the height of the Jeep, was white and strained. No eighteen-year-old should look like that. Bobo was scared and angry and desperate.

'What's going to happen?'

'You've been too many places, Lily. Some people don't understand.' He wanted to say more. His teeth bared from his inner tension. He was on the verge of screaming.

'Tell me,' I said, as calmly as I could manage. I snatched off a glove and laid my hand over his. But instead of soothing him, my touch seemed to spark even more inner storms. He yanked away from me as if I'd poked him with a cattle prod. From between clenched teeth, he said, '*Stay in!*' He roared off as fast as he'd come, as recklessly.

My own anxiety level jumped off the scale. What could have

happened so suddenly? I looked up at the facade of the apartment building. Claude's new windows were dark. Deedra's, above him, were also out. But Jack's lights were on, at least some of them. His living room window was faintly illuminated.

I stood in the middle of the street in the freezing cold and tried to make my brain work.

Without deciding it consciously, I began to run – not toward my house but toward the apartments. Once I was inside the hall, hurrying past Claude's door, I tried to walk quietly. I went up the stairs like a snake, swift and silent. I tried Jack's door. It was unlocked and open an inch. A ball of fear settled in my stomach.

I slipped inside. No one in the living room, lit only by the dim light reaching it from the kitchen. Jack's leather jacket was tossed on the couch. Further down the hall, the overhead light in the spare bedroom glared through its open door. I listened, closing my eyes to listen more intently. I felt the hair stand up on my neck. Silence.

I'd only been in here once, so I picked my way through Jack's sparse furniture very carefully.

No one in the kitchen, either.

I was biting my lip to keep from making a sound when I stood in the doorway of the guest bedroom. There was a card table holding a tape player, a pad of paper, and a pencil. There was a Dr Pepper can on the table. The folding chair that had been in front of the table was lying on its side. I touched my fingers to the Dr Pepper can. It was still cold. A red light indicated the tape player was on, but the tape compartment was open and empty. I ran back to the living room and fumbled through the pockets of the leather jacket. They were empty, too.

'They've got Jack,' I said to no one.

I covered my eyes to think more intently. Claude was downstairs unable to get around on his own. At least some portion of his police force was corrupt. Sheriff Schuster was dead and I didn't know any of his people. Maybe the sheriff's department, too, contained one or two men who at least sympathized with the Take Back Your Own group.

What if I couldn't save Jack by myself? Whom could I call?

Carrie was a noncombatant. Raphael had a wife and family, and without putting it to myself clearly in words, I knew a black man's involvement would escalate whatever was happening into a war.

If I went in and was captured, too, who would help?

Then I thought of someone.

I remembered the number and punched it in on Jack's phone.

'Mookie,' I said when she answered. 'I need you to come. Bring the rifle.'

'Where?'

'Winthrop's. They've got – my man.' I was beyond trying to explain who Jack was. 'He's a detective. He's been taping them.'

'Where'll I meet you?' She sounded cool.

'Let's go in over the back fence. I live right behind the Home Supply store.'

'I know. I'm coming.' She put her phone down.

This was the woman I'd cautioned about leaving town yesterday, and now I was urging her to put herself into danger on my say-so. But I didn't have time to worry about irony. I ran down the stairs, leaving Jack's door wide open. It wouldn't hurt for someone else to become alarmed. I ran to my place, let myself in. I pulled off my coat, found a heavy dark sweat-shirt, and yanked it down over my T-shirts. I found Jack's forgotten watch cap. I pulled it over my light hair. No gloves, I needed my hands. I untied my high-tops and pulled on dark boots, laced then tight. I would have darkened my face if I could have thought of something to do it with. I came out of my front door as Mookie pulled in. She leaped out of the car with the rifle in one hand.

'What's your weapon?' she asked.

I raised my hands.

'Cool,' she said, and we began to run for the tracks without further conversation. From the high point of the railroad, we surveyed the back lot of the Sporting Goods store. There were

lights on in the store. The back lot was always lit, but there were
pools of darkness, too.

'Let's go,' my companion said. She seemed quite happy and
relaxed. She required not one word of explanation, which was
refreshing, since I wasn't sure I could manage anything coherent.
We jogged down the embankment. I was about to take a run at
the fence and accept the barbed wire at the top, but Mookie pulled
wire cutters from a pocket in her dark jumpsuit. This was no
fashion model garment, but a padded, heavy, dark workman's
jumpsuit with many pockets. Mookie had a knit cap pulled over
her hair, too. She went to work with the wire cutters, while I
looked around us for any signs of detection.

Nothing moved but us.

Finally the opening was large enough and we scrambled
through it, Mookie first. Again, nothing happened. We moved
into a pool of darkness and crouched there behind a gleaming new
four-wheeler. Mookie pointed at our next goal, a boat. We had to
cross through some light, but made the boat safely. We waited.

In this run-and-wait fashion we worked our way from the rear
of the lot to the back of the store. There was a customer door at
ground level and a loading dock with a set of four steps going up
to it. From the dock there was an employee door leading inside to
the huge storeroom. The customer door was dark. I was willing
to bet it was heavily locked.

They'd left someone on guard at the loading bay door. It was
the pimply boy from the Home Supply store, and he was shifting
from foot to foot in the cold, which I no longer felt. He had a rifle,
too. Mookie whispered, 'Can you take him out silently?'

I nodded. I'd never attacked anyone like this, someone who
hadn't attacked me first, but before that thought could lodge
firmly in my consciousness and weaken me, I focused on his rifle.
If he had it, I had to assume he was willing to use it.

The boy turned to peer through the window in the employee
door, and sneezed. Under cover of that noise, I leaped silently up
the steps, came up behind him, snaked my arms around him to

grip the rifle, and pulled it up against his throat. He struggled against me but I was determined to silence him.

He weakened. He grew limp. Mookie helped me lower him to the concrete platform. She pulled a scarf from one of her pockets and tied it around his mouth and bound his hands behind him with another. She took his rifle and held it out to me. I shook my head. She placed it down against the base of the loading dock, out of sight. She evidently thought he was alive and worth binding, so I didn't ask. I didn't want to know now if I'd killed him.

I wondered if they'd come to check on him. I stood sideways to the little head-high window reinforced with diamond-patterned wire, and looked through into the lighted storeroom. I could just see movement past a wall of boxes and racks, but I couldn't tell what was happening.

'Cover inside,' I whispered to Mookie. 'Go left when we go in.'

She nodded. I took a deep breath, turned the knob, praying that it would not make a noise. To me, the twist of the metal was loud as cymbals, but no one appeared at the gap in boxes to investigate. I pulled the door open and Mookie went in low, rifle at the ready. No one shot her. No one shouted. I went in after a second, dropped to a squat right inside the door, letting it ease shut against me.

Mookie was crouched behind a chest-deep pile of stenciled boxes. An array of huge metal shelves, all labeled and aligned, loomed ahead of us. To our right, across the aisle left open for passage to the back door, was a rack of camouflage jumpsuits in the colder, grayer, green and black of winter camo. There were more rows of shelves in front of the rack.

I could hear voices now, the raucous laughter of men high on their testosterone. In the middle of the laughter there was a cut-off yelp. Jack.

I was ready to kill now. I worked my hands, getting the stiffness and cold out of them. Mookie eyed me with some doubt.

'Which man is yours?' she asked almost inaudibly.

'The one who yelled,' I told her. Her eyes widened. 'He's got long black hair.' She would need to know which one was Jack.

'We'll work our way up there, see what happens,' she breathed.

That was as good a plan as any. We ducked around the boxes and concealed ourselves behind the next row of shelves. We could see through the gaps in the stacked goods. Darcy was there, Jim was there, and Cleve Ragland, Tom David Meicklejohn. About who I'd expected. There was at least one person I couldn't see; I noticed the men turn to their right a few times, addressing a remark to whoever sat there.

They were torturing Jack.

As we worked our way to the front of the storage area, I saw more and more. I saw too much. Jack was tied to a chair, a wooden one on rollers. His arms were tied to the chair arms. He had the beginning of a black eye, and a cut on one cheek, maybe from when they'd grabbed him in his apartment. They'd taken off his shirt. They'd pulled the bandage off his bullet wound. Darcy had a hunting knife, and Cleve had devised his own little implement by heating an arrowhead with a lighter and putting it on Jack's skin. Jim Box looked nauseated. Tom David was watching, and though he did not look sick, he did not look happy, either. His eyes flickered toward whoever was seated out of sight, and back to Jack.

Darcy turned away from cutting Jack right under the nipple. The knife glistened with blood. I would kill him first, I thought, so consumed by the thought that I could not reason, could not plan what I should do. I had forgotten Mookie's existence until she nudged me. She pointed a slim finger to a man sitting on his haunches in the shadow of a shelving unit, a man I hadn't seen before, and I thought I would vomit. I recognized the pale floppy hair instantly. Bobo. Darcy said something to him.

Bobo raised his face to look at Darcy, and I saw tears on his face.

'I gotta ask you, boy, where you went just a while ago,' Darcy said genially. He raised the knife so the light caught the part of the blade that was not red. Bobo stood up. His shoulders squared.

'I'm hoping you didn't betray your family by telling anyone what we'd caught here,' Darcy said, waiting for Bobo to answer.

When the silence dragged on, everyone turned to look at Bobo, even Jim Box. Jack was taking advantage of the respite by closing his eyes. I saw his hands working under the tight cord around his wrists. He was biting his lower lip. There were a dozen cuts and burns on his chest, and they'd reopened the bullet wound. Streaks of blood clotted his chest hair.

'Did you go tell that blond bitch?' Darcy asked, quietly. 'You tell that gal her little bedmate was in trouble here?'

Bobo didn't speak. He stared at Darcy, his blue eyes narrowed with turmoil. Something hardened in his face as I watched.

'I hope she does come looking,' Cleve said suddenly. 'We get to reenact her worst nightmare.'

Darcy looked at Cleve in some surprise. Then he realized what Cleve meant. He laughed, his head thrown back, the overhead light scouring his face of any sign of humanity.

Jack's eyes were open now, all right. He was looking at Cleve with a brand new nightmare for Cleve in his eyes. Cleve looked down, flinched. Then he seemed to recall that he was in charge.

'We can give her a real good time right here,' he told Jack. 'You can watch, Bobo. Learn how it's done.'

Tom David's eyes were slitted in distaste. He was looking at his coconspirators as if he'd just learned something about them that he didn't like. Bobo's face said he couldn't believe what he'd heard. He was waiting for some other explanation of the words to occur to him.

'This is going to be a pleasure,' Mookie said in my ear. She pulled a knife from one of her pockets, handed it to me.

'I cover you, you cut him free,' she said. 'We get out the best way we can.'

I nodded.

'Or maybe I'll kill them all,' she said, to herself.

'They killed Darnell?'

'Yeah, I do believe. My mother got some calls after Darnell's death, anonymous, nasty, really explicit about Darnell's injuries. They came from this store. She has caller ID,' Mookie whispered.

'Dumb shitasses didn't even think about a black woman having caller ID. Get ready.'

She stepped out then, her rifle up at her shoulder.

'Okay, assholes,' she said. 'Down on the floor.'

They all froze, Darcy in the act of bending over to put the knife to Jack's chest again; Cleve had the arrow in one hand, the lighter in the other. Beyond them, Tom David was still leaning against the wall, his arms crossed on his chest. Jim Box was beside him. Bobo, who'd been close to the door into the store, turned and stepped through it, and the clunk as the heavy door closed behind him made Cleve jump.

In that flicker of time, Darcy threw the knife at Mookie and dived to his right. Mookie fired and ducked to her right. Her bullet hit Jim Box, who'd been beyond Darcy; I glimpsed a red flower blossoming on his chest. And the knife missed her, but got me. I felt the sudden cold where my shirt sliced open, felt the pressure, but I was running for Jack. Cleve charged me, his thick chest and heavy chin making him look like an angry bull. I stepped aside as he came to me, and I extended my arm. It caught him in the throat. His head stayed still, but his feet kept on going. When the rest of his body didn't follow, they flew up in the air, and down he went. His head thudded against the concrete floor. And I heard the clunk of the door again. Someone else had fled into the store.

I knelt by the chair, cutting at the cords binding Jack. I was awkward about it, but Mookie's knife was sharp. I heard a rush of feet, light and quick, and then the *paw!* of the rifle. Mookie passing by, doing God knows what damage. I thought I heard the door again.

I could pay attention to nothing else while I was using the knife, and when I'd sawed through the second set of bonds and I could look up, everything had changed.

I saw no one, at least no one moving.

Cleve was down for good. I felt a flash of satisfaction. Jim Box had vanished, but there were drops of blood on the floor where he'd been standing. I saw there was a chair in the shadows, across from Jack's. It was empty.

Jack whispered, 'Help me up.'

I jumped to my feet, held out my hands. To my horror, I could not meet Jack's eyes; that seemed worse, much worse, than what I'd done to Cleve Ragland. Jack made an awful sound of pain as he pulled himself up on me. There was a discarded brown coat, Bobo's, lying on a nearby shelf. I grabbed it. I had in mind fleeing through the rear door, trying to make it through the back lot and hole in the fence to my house, calling – someone. Fleetingly, I thought of the FBI men, who might still be at the motel where they'd been camped since the bombing.

'Put this on,' I said urgently, holding out the coat to Jack. I was thinking of the bitter cold, Jack's wounds, shock, God knows what.

I kept lookout while Jack tried to manage, but in the end I had to help him. I was so intent on maneuvering Jack's left arm into the sleeve that I did not know anyone was behind me until Jack's face gave me a second's warning. Just as Jack began to move, something slammed against my shoulder. I shrieked involuntarily, knocked to my right, off my feet. I slammed my head into the shelves and fell to the floor hard enough to knock the breath from my lungs. I couldn't move. I stared up at the bright lights of the storeroom, high above me. I could see tall dark Jim Box, his shirt soaked with blood. He gripped an oar, holding it like a baseball bat, and he was swinging it back. He was going to hit me in the head, and there wasn't a damn thing I could do about it.

Jack went mad. He launched himself at Jim, wrenched the oar from him, and slammed it into Jim's head. Jim went over like a felled tree, without a sound. Jack stood over him, his blood-spattered chest heaving, wanting Jim to move, wanting to strike again.

But Jim didn't move.

With a rush the air came back into my lungs. I moaned, not only from pain but from black despair. We were both hurt now, weak. How many more were in the building? Where was Mookie? Had they killed her?

Jack stood over me with the oar. Gradually some of the madness seeped from his face and he crouched beside me.

'Can you get up?' he whispered. I saw the finger marks on his throat for the first time. They'd choked him, enough to almost cost him his voice. I wanted to tell him no, I couldn't move, but found myself nodding instead. That was a mistake. Pain rocketed through my head. I had to lie still a moment, before I rolled over on my stomach, pushed up to my knees. My arm, sliced by Darcy's knife, was bleeding. I touched my hair, which felt – funny. There was blood on my hand when I took it down. I'd hit a shelf with my head when I'd gone sideways, I remembered slowly. Maybe I had a concussion. As if to confirm that suspicion, I vomited. When the spasm was over, I felt like I would welcome dying. But Jack needed me to get up.

I gripped the nearest upright, a corner bar for the shelves, and tried to gain my feet while Jack stayed alert for another attack. Finally I was standing, though I could feel myself swaying from side to side; or maybe I was still and the warehouse was swaying? Earthquake?

'You're really hurt,' Jack rasped, and I could hear a little fear even in his strained voice.

I felt weak and shaken. I was letting him down.

'Go,' I said.

'Right,' he whispered, the sarcasm diminished by his voice level.

'You can move. I'm not sure I can,' I faltered. I hated the wavering of my voice. 'They won't kill me. How many more are there?'

'Two in the store, and the old man.'

What old man?

'Bobo won't hurt me,' I reassured Jack, thinking he was counting Bobo as one of the adversaries.

'No, I don't think he will. I think he didn't know any of this. I hope to God he's calling the police.'

That was funny. Speaking of old men, it sure looked to me as if

Howell Sr., uncrowned king of Shakespeare, was standing right over there by the door.

'Look,' I said to Jack, amazed.

Jack turned, and old Mr Winthrop raised a hand. To my bewilderment, it held a gun. I opened my mouth to yell something, I don't know what, when two strong arms wrapped around the old man and lifted him from the floor.

'No, Grandfather,' Bobo said. The expression on the wizened old rat terrier's face had to be seen to be believed. Howell Sr. struggled and wriggled in his grandson's grasp, but it was a futile effort. If I'd had any inclination toward humor, it would have been funny. Bobo walked through the storeroom and out onto the loading dock carrying the old man, who called him names I'd never heard an elderly person use.

Bobo's face was tragic. He didn't look at me, at Jack. He was alone with the bitterest betrayal of his short life.

I didn't care where he was taking his grandfather, because the measure of that betrayal was unfolding itself to me. Howell Sr. had used his own son's business as a cover for his little hate group. Howell Sr. was the reason his son, Jack's employer, had kept secrets from Jack. Howell must have suspected his father's involvement from the first. So he hadn't contacted police, or ATF agents, or the FBI. He'd hired Jack.

And here we were, thanks to old man Winthrop, bleeding and maybe dying in a damn storeroom.

'Where's Mookie?' I asked Jack. 'The woman with the rifle.'

'She went in the store after Darcy,' Jack whispered. The jacket hung open over his bare bloody chest. He'd laid down the oar in favor of Mookie's knife, the knife I'd used to slash his bonds.

'Tom David,' I said.

Jack was puzzled for a minute. Then his face cleared. 'I don't know. He may be in the store, too.'

'Naw, I'm here,' said a taut voice from a few feet away. 'I'm out of the fight.'

I staggered over in the direction of the voice despite Jack's telling me not to. I didn't seem to have much control over my actions. Tom David was lying on the floor to the right of the door. The left leg of his jeans was soaked with red. Now I knew where Mookie's second shot had gone. The policeman's face was absolutely white. His eyes shone brilliant blue.

'I am sorry,' he said.

I stared down at him.

'You can call the police, it'll be safe. I'm the only one.'

I nodded, and nearly threw up again.

'I don't hold with what they did to Jared, and I wouldn't have hurt you he said wearily, and closed his eyes.

'Did you kill Darnell?' I asked.

He opened his eyes at that. 'I was there.'

'Who did it?'

'Darcy and Jim. The old man. Paulie who works over there,' and he moved his head infinitesimally in the direction of the Home Supply store. 'Len. Bay Hodding, Bob's dad. He ain't here tonight. Wedding anniversary.' And Tom David grinned a horrible grin. Those blue eyes were now not so bright. 'Who cares, anyway? Nigger. Now, Del Packard . . . that was Darcy. I regret it.' And his face relaxed. Looking down at the pool of blood beneath my feet, I thought Tom David Meicklejohn had closed his mean eyes forever.

But the policeman's final testimony had taken valuable time, and in that time things once again had happened without my awareness or participation.

I was alone.

The bright storeroom, with its long stretches of shelves and dark shadows, was empty except for the silent bodies of the fallen and dead. I felt like an actor onstage after the play is over.

Then, from the store, I heard a scream.

I shuffled toward the door. The clear pane set at eye level had gone dark. The store lights had been shut off. As my hand closed around the knob, I realized that when I opened it, I would be silhouetted against the storeroom lights. I switched them off. Then I opened the door and propelled myself through it, and seconds later heard the distinctive *clunk!* of its falling shut.

There was a whoosh of sound over my head, a heavy impact. Then silence. I reached up cautiously. A hunting arrow protruded from the wooden doorframe. My skin crawled. Darcy was an avid bow-hunter. He and Jim had discussed it morning after morning this fall.

I had to get away from the door. He'd be coming. I pulled myself forward on my elbows, trying to hug the floor as closely as possible. It was all too easy, and I cursed myself for a fool in thinking my venturing into this trap could help anyone.

I tried to summon up the floor plan, see it in my head. I felt hopeless when I thought of how familiar it was to Darcy.

'I got your yellow friend,' he called to me. 'She's de-ad. Got an arrow in her he-ad.' He was singing. He was having a good time.

I didn't believe it. Mookie had screamed; at least, I was almost certain it had been her. You can't scream if an arrow goes through your head. But I knew my reasoning, like my sense of balance and my judgment, was very shaky just now. If only I knew where Jack was, I thought, I'd just curl up somewhere and go to sleep. That sounded good. I laid my head on the rough indoor-outdoor carpet and began to drift.

'I'm com-ing,' Darcy crooned. Darcy, who had beaten a young man to death for being black. Darcy, who had crushed his friend's throat.

He sounded so close I knew I shouldn't move. I didn't feel sleepy anymore. I felt close to death. I thought of the hightech bows I'd seen dangling from the ceiling on my trips to the store, the ones that looked so lethal they would've scared Robin Hood . . . Wow, was I drifting . . .

A foot fell on the carpet an inch from my face. His next step would be on me. Act or *die*.

Galvanized, I shrieked and scrambled up, grabbing what I could, hoping for an arm. I locked my arms and legs around Darcy Orchard like a lover, holding him as tightly as I'd ever held Jack or Marshall, squeezing till tears ran from my eyes. I was riding his back.

He was so big and strong, and not wounded. He didn't go

down even with my full weight wrapped around him. I'd scared the shit out of him, and it took him seconds to recover, but only seconds. He heaved and bucked, and I heard the clatter of something falling, and I thought it might be the bow. But he had an arrow in his hand, and he began stabbing backward with it, though not with the full force or range of his arm since I embraced him. He jabbed my thigh the first time, and he could tell where to go after that, and he scored my ribs a dozen times. Scars on scars, I thought through the terrible pain. I wanted to let go. But it seemed I couldn't, couldn't get the message to my fingers to relax. Death grip, I thought. Death grip.

The lights came on. The glare seemed to shoot a lance through my eyes, made me so sick I nearly fainted, but I was shocked into alertness by something so awful I could only believe it because it was this night, this bloody night. Behind one of the counters that held a display of knives, I glimpsed Mookie fixed to the wall by an arrow through her chest. Her head sagged to one side and her eyes were open.

Then past Darcy's shoulder I saw someone running toward us, toward Darcy and me locked in our little dance. It was Jack, with a rifle in his hands. We were too close, he couldn't shoot, I thought. As if we had one mind Jack reversed the rifle and clubbed Darcy in the head with the stock. Darcy howled and lurched, wanting to go for Jack, but I would not let go, would not would not would not . . .

Blackness.

'Wake up, honey. I have to check you.'

No.

'Open your eyes, Lily. It's me, Carrie.'

No.

'Lily!'

I slitted my eyes.

'That's better.'

Blinding light.

'Don't moan. It's just – necessary.'

Back to sleep. Nice period of darkness and silence.

Then, 'Wake up, Lily!'

The next day was agony. My head ached, a condition that bore no more relationship to a normal headache than a stomachache bore to appendicitis. My ribs were notched and gouged and the skin above them a bloody mess stitched together like a crazy quilt. The wound in my thigh, though not serious, added its own note to my symphony of pain, as did the slice in my arm.

I was in a private room, courtesy of Howell Winthrop, Jr., Carrie told me when I demanded to go home. When I realized someone else was paying for it, I decided to rest while I could. He was paying for Jack's room next door, too. Jack came in during that horrible morning, when even the medication that made me mentally dull could not smother the hurt.

When I saw him in the doorway, tears began oozing from the corners of my eyes, running down the side of my face to soak my pillow.

'I didn't mean to have that effect on you,' he said. His voice was husky, but stronger.

I raised a hand, and he shuffled slowly to the bed and wrapped his own around it. His hand felt warm and hard and steady.

'You should sit,' I said, and my own voice sounded distant and thick.

'Got you drugged, huh?'

'Yes.' Nodding hurt more than speaking. 'How'd they get you, Jack?'

'They found the bug,' he said simply. 'Jim spilled a Coke in the lounge, and in the process of mopping up the mess, he found it. Jim called old Mr Winthrop. He advised them to watch from concealment and see who came to extract the tape; and that was me. They had to consult with each other for a while. They decided they could find out who hired me if they put me through the wringer. Cleve and Jim thought all along it was Howell, but the others voted for something federal. They thought Mookie was federal, too. They thought about going to get her, bring her along to join the party. Said she'd been in the store too much to be natural. Lucky for me they didn't. Why did you think of calling her? Who the hell is she?'

I tried to explain Mookie to him without revealing any of her secrets. I am not sure I managed, but Jack knew I worked for her, that she had a personal stake in uncovering our fledgling white supremacy group, and that I had known she could shoot. Jack held my hand for some time, rubbing it gently as he thought, and then suddenly he said, 'When he knocked you down, when you hit the shelf and the floor – and I swear to God, Lily, you bounced – I thought he'd killed you.'

'You went crazy,' I observed.

He smiled a little. 'Yes, I did. When you could stand, and you could walk – sort of – I knew you'd be okay. Probably. And after a look at Tom David, I knew he wasn't a threat to you . . .'

'So you left.'

'Hunting.' He was not apologetic. He'd had to pursue the man who had degraded him. I, of all people, could understand that.

'Who's dead?' Carrie had refused to talk about it.

'Tom David. Jim Box.'

'That's all?'

'I wanted Darcy to die, but I didn't hit him that final time that would have settled it. His jaw is broken, though. The cops were there by then, for one thing.' Jack sank into the chair, and thoughtfully punched the button to lower my bed so I could see him more easily.

'How come?'

'Bobo called them, when he went into the store after all the shooting started. And he was trying to find his grandfather. The old man had armed himself, and Bobo managed to track him down just in time.'

I remembered Bobo's face as he'd lifted his grandfather and carried him off. A few more tears oozed down my face. I wanted to know what would happen to old Mr Winthrop, but it could wait. Roasting in hell came to mind as fitting. 'Mookie's alive?' I had belatedly realized her name was not on the dead list.

Jack closed his eyes. 'She's just hanging on. She wants to talk to you.'

'Oh, no.' I felt so washed out, and washed up, I couldn't stand the thought of one more confession. 'She's really not going to make it?'

'The arrow went right through. You saw.'

'I was hoping I made it up.' I looked away, at the curtained window.

Jack kept holding my hand, waiting for me to make up my mind.

'So Cleve didn't die?' I was stalling.

'He has a fractured skull. Much worse than your concussion.'

'Not possible. Okay, get a nurse or two to load me in a chair.'

After a lip-biting interval, I was being pushed into Mookie's room. There were blinking machines, and a constant low hum, and Mookie was hooked into more tubes than I had ever imagined a human being could be. Her color was ashen, and her lips had lost color. Lanette was in the corner of the room, her hands over her face, rocking back and forth in a straight chair. Her firstborn child was dying, and she had already lost her second.

The nurse went to stand out of earshot, and I raised my hand, with great effort, to touch Mookie Preston, that odd and lonely and brave woman.

'Mookie, I'm here – Lily,' I said.

'Lily. You lived,' she said very slowly, and her eyes never opened.

'Thanks to you.' If I had gone in there by myself, I would have died horribly and slowly. By asking her to go with me, I had set her death in motion.

'Don't be sorry,' she said. Her voice was slow, and soft, but the words were distinct. 'I got to kill some of them, the ones that killed my brother.'

I sighed softly. I had been thinking, while in my haze of pain and drugs. 'Did you kill someone else?' I whispered.

'Yes.' She dragged out the word painfully.

'Len Elgin?'

'Yes.'

'He was involved in Darnell's death.'

'Yes. I talked to him before I shot him. He was my . . . father.'

I should not remind Mookie of Len Elgin. I should say something else to Mookie Preston, something good. She was on her way to meet her Maker, and I could not send her out thinking of the deaths she had caused.

She spoke again. Her eyes opened and fastened on mine. 'Don't tell.'

I understood after a moment, even through the drugs. 'Don't tell about Len,' I said, to be sure.

'Don't tell,' she repeated.

This was my punishment for leading this woman to her death. I would know the truth, but could not reveal it. No matter what happened to Len Elgin's extramarital lover, Erica Moore, and her husband Booth. No matter what suspicions attached to Mary Lee Elgin.

'I won't tell,' I said, accepting it. I was so doped up it seemed logical and appropriate.

'Mama,' she said.

'Lanette,' I called, and she leaped up from her chair and came to the bed. I motioned to the nurse who was waiting in the doorway, and she came to take me back to my room.

I think Mookie died before I got there.

After three days, I went home. The doctor herself drove me.

This homecoming-from-the-hospital routine – the stale house, the life untouched while I was gone – was getting old. I didn't want to get hurt anymore. I didn't want pain. I needed to work, to have order, to have emotional quiet.

What I had was pain and phone calls from Jack.

He'd had to talk to many many people: local, state, federal. Most of that I had been spared because of my concussion, the second I'd had in a month, but I'd had my share of interviews. Some questions I just hadn't been able to answer. Like: Why had I called Mookie Preston? The answer, because I thought she could help me kill the men who had Jack, just wasn't palatable. So I had lied, just a little. I said that I'd called Mookie when I discovered Jack was gone – I figured they could find that out somehow from the phone company – and that she'd agreed to accompany me to Winthrop Sporting Goods because I was so distraught. Yes, I knew what Jack was doing, so I suspected where he'd been taken and who had taken him.

I never said that Mookie had brought the rifle or the knife, and I think they all assumed both weapons came from the store stock. When it was found the bullets that had killed Tom David (and ultimately Jim) had come from the same weapon that had killed Len Elgin months ago, the official line of reasoning seemed to be that someone from the store's little cadre of bad boys had been responsible for shooting Len. A motivation for this assassination was never uncovered, but it was assumed that somehow he had thwarted one of their plans or uncovered evidence that implicated one of them in the death of Darnell.

So Len Elgin came out looking better in death than he'd been in life, and I never opened my mouth, The police knew, from all of us, that Mookie had shot men in the store; but since they all supposed she'd found and loaded the weapon when she got there, Mookie, too, emerged from the inquiry looking posthumously brave and resourceful – as, indeed, she had been.

The Winthrops pulled up the drawbridge and weathered the siege. Howell Winthrop, Sr., was arrested and promptly made bail, and he was denying all involvement in the bombing and in the deaths of Darnell Glass, Len Elgin, and Del Packard. He was admitting he'd been present during Jack's torture, but alleging he'd thought Jack was a renegade white supremacist. No one believed him, but that was what he was saying. Bobo transferred to a college in Florida (Marshall told me), and Amber Jean and Howell Three just left school and went on a vacation with Beanie in an unspecified location.

Howell called me one afternoon before I left the hospital, and we had a brief, horribly uncomfortable conversation. He assured me that he would pay for every ache and pain I endured for the next few years, and I assured him just as earnestly that this hospitalization and the ensuing pharmacy bills were the only ones I would appreciate him paying.

'Your mother can have her ring back,' I said.

'She'll never want it,' he answered.

'She told me it was Marie Hofstettler's bequest to me.' I wanted to be sure Howell knew I had not taken the ring as some kind of bribe, which is what he had assumed when he saw the brown velvet box – which he knew to be his mother's – in my hand. 'Why did your parents want me to come to their house?'

'I can't talk about that,' he said stiffly. 'But Bobo told me I had to tell you he knew nothing.'

I am sure we were both glad to hang up. I thought about that strange evening on Partridge Road, the big white house, the tiny old people. I hoped Arnita Winthrop had not known about her husband then, had really been the gracious woman she had seemed. Maybe she had reasoned I deserved something tangible for being Marie's friend; maybe that was why she'd given me an old ring of her own, passed it off as a posthumous gift. Maybe her husband had had a curiosity to see me, had asked her to think of a way to get me to the house so he could look me over. The running figure that night had been Jack, he'd finally told me. Jack had been asked to watch the comings and goings at the Partridge Road house whenever he could. He'd been at Marie's funeral to get a good look at the older Winthrops, since there was no casual way for him to meet them.

Jack made the papers, state and national. He was something of a hero for a while. It was good for his business. He got all kinds of inquiries, and as soon as he could manage physically, he left for Little Rock. I had a feeling it was a relief to get a little distance between himself and the place and time of his ordeal. He'd been overpowered, bound, and tortured; he had managed to regain some measure of maleness, of wholeness, back by conquering Jim and Darcy. But I knew the bad nights he'd have, the self-doubts. Who could know better?

As the days passed, I began to have the dreary conviction he would write me off as part of that time. Sometimes I was anguished and sometimes I was angry, but I could not return to my former detachment.

I had been back at work for three weeks, back to working out at Body Time for one week, when I came home to find Jack's car in the driveway. He had flowers – a bigger arrangement than Claude had sent me, of course – and a present festooned with a huge pink net bow.

I felt a rush of joy at the sight of him. Suddenly I didn't know what to say to him, after weeks of imagining this moment. I pointed to the flowers. 'For me?'

'Jeez,' he said, shaking his head and smiling. 'If you are still the Lily Bard who sucker-punched me right here in this doorway, these are indeed for you.'

'Want me to do it again? Just to verify my identity?'

'No, thank you, ma'am.'

I unlocked the door and he followed me in. I took the flowers from him and headed down the hall with them.

'Where you taking those?' he asked, with some interest.

'My bedroom.'

'So . . . are you planning on letting me join you in admiring them?'

'I expect so, depending on your good behavior this evening. I'm assuming you brought a doctor's note, to prove that you're up to such vigorous . . . activity.'

'We are so playful this evening, Miss Bard. We are so relaxed and – normal-date-like.'

'It's a stretch,' I said. 'But I'm up to it.'

Shakespeare's Christmas

Chapter One

My situation was as surreal as one of those slomo nightmares Hollywood uses to pad B movies.

I was sitting in the bed of a moving Dodge Ram pickup. I was enthroned on a wobbly plastic lawn chair, thinly disguised by a red plush couch throw edged with fringe. A crowd lined both sides of the street, waving and yelling. From time to time, I dipped my hand into the white plastic bucket settled on my lap, coming up with a fistful of candy to pitch to the spectators.

Though I was clothed, which I understand is not the case in many dreams, my clothes were hardly typical. I was wearing a red Santa hat with a big white ball on the end, bright new green sweats, and I had a disgusting artificial holly corsage pinned to my chest. I was trying to smile.

Spotting a familiar face in the crowd, a face pasted with an unconcealed smirk, I pitched the next peppermint with deliberate accuracy. It smacked my neighbor, Carlton Cockroft, right in the middle of the chest, wiping off that smirk for at least a second.

The pickup paused, continuing a familiar and irritating pattern that had begun minutes after the parade had started lurching down Main Street. One of the bands ahead of us had stopped to blare out a Christmas song, and I had to smile and wave at the same damn people over and over until the song was finished.

My face hurt.

At least in the green sweats, with a layer of thermal underwear underneath, I was fairly warm, which was more than I could say for the girls who had enthusiastically agreed to ride on the Body Time float directly ahead. They also were wearing Santa hats, but below the hats they wore only scanty exercise outfits, since at their age making an impact was more important than staying comfortable and healthy.

'How you doing back there?' Raphael Roundtree called, leaning out of the pickup window to give me an inquiring glance.

I glared back at him. Raphael was wearing a coat, scarf, and gloves, and the heat in the cab of the truck was turned on full blast. His round brown face looked plain old smug.

'Just fine,' I said ferociously.

'Lily, Lily, Lily,' he said, shaking his head. 'Slap that smile back on, girl. You're gonna scare customers away, rather than pick some up.'

I cast my gaze to heaven to indicate I was asking for patience. But instead of a clear gray sky, I found myself staring at tacky fake greenery strung across the street. Everywhere I looked, the trappings of the season had taken over. Shakespeare doesn't have a lot of money for Christmas decorations, so I'd seen the same ones every holiday in the four-plus years I'd spent in this little Arkansas town. Every alternate streetlight had a big candle suspended on a curved 'candleholder'. The other streetlights sported bells.

The town's seasonal centerpiece (since the manger scene had to be removed) was a huge Christmas tree on the courthouse lawn; the churches sponsored a big public party to decorate it. In consequence, it looked very homey rather than elegant – typical of Shakespeare, come to think of it. Once we passed the court-house, the parade would be nearly over.

There was a little tree in the pickup bed with me, but it was artificial. I'd decorated it with gold stiffened ribbon, gold ornaments, and gold and white artificial flowers. A discreet sign attached to it read, TREE DECORATING DONE BY APPOINTMENT BUSINESSES AND HOMES. This new service I was providing was definitely designed for people who'd opted for elegance.

The banners on the sides of the pickup read, SHAKESPEARE'S CLEANING AND ERRANDS, followed by my phone number. Since Carlton, my accountant, had advised it so strongly, I had finally made myself a business. Carlton further advised me to begin to establish a public presence, very much against my own inclinations.

So here I was in the damn Christmas parade.

'Smile!' called Janet Shook, who was marching in place right behind the pickup. She made a face at me, then turned to the forty or so kids following her and said, 'Okay, kids! Let's Shakespear-ecise!' The children, amazingly, did not throw up, maybe because none of them was over ten. They all attended the town-sponsored 'Safe After School' program that employed Janet, and they seemed happy to obey her. They all began to do jumping jacks.

I envied them. Despite my insulation, sitting still was taking its toll. Though Shakespeare has very mild winters as a rule, today was the coldest temperature for Christmas parade day in seven years, the local radio station had informed us.

Janet's kids looked red-cheeked and sparkly eyed, and so did Janet. The jumping jacks had turned into a kind of dance. At least, I guessed it was. I am not exactly tuned in to popular culture.

I was still stretching my lips up to smile at the surrounding faces, but it was a real strain. Relief overwhelmed me as the truck began moving again. I started tossing candy and waving.

This was hell. But unlike hell, it was finite. Eventually, the candy bucket was empty and the parade had reached its endpoint, the parking lot of Superette Grocery. Raphael and his oldest son helped me take the tree back to the travel agent's office for whom I'd decorated it, and they carted the plastic chair back to their own backyard. I'd thanked Raphael and paid him for his gas and time, though he'd protested.

'It was worth it just to see you smile that long. Your face is gonna be sore tomorrow,' Raphael said gleefully.

What became of the red plush throw I don't know and don't want to know.

Jack was not exactly sympathetic when he called me from Little Rock that night. In fact, he laughed.

'Did anyone film this parade?' he asked, gasping with the end convulsions of his mirth.

'I hope not.'

'Come on, Lily, loosen up,' he said. I could still hear the humor in his voice. 'What are you doing this holiday?'

This seemed like a touchy question to me. Jack Leeds and I had been seeing each other for about seven weeks. We were too new to take it for granted that we'd be spending Christmas together, and too unsure to have had any frank discussion about making arrangements.

'I have to go home,' I said flatly. 'To Bartley.'

A long silence.

'How do you feel about that?' Jack asked cautiously.

I steeled myself to be honest. Frank. Open. 'I have to go to my sister Varena's wedding. I'm a bridesmaid.'

Now he didn't laugh.

'How long has it been since you saw your folks?' he asked.

It was strange that I didn't know the answer. 'I guess maybe . . . six months? Eight? I met them in Little Rock one day . . . around Easter. It's years since I've seen Varena.'

'And you don't want to go now?'

'No,' I said, relieved to be able to speak the truth. When I'd been arranging my week off work, after my employers got over the shock of my asking, they'd been almost universally delighted to hear that I was going to my sister's wedding. They couldn't tell me fast enough that it was fine for me to miss a week. They'd asked about my sister's age (twenty-eight, younger than me by three years), her fiancé (a pharmacist, widowed, with a little daughter), and what I was going to wear in the wedding. (I didn't know. I'd sent Varena some money and my size when she said she'd settled on bridesmaids' dresses, but I hadn't seen her selection.)

'So when can I see you?' Jack asked.

I felt a warm trickle of relief. I was never sure what was going to happen next with us. It seemed possible to me that someday Jack wouldn't call at all.

'I'll be in Bartley all the week before Christmas,' I said. 'I was planning on getting back to my house by Christmas Day.'

'Miss having Christmas at home?' I could feel Jack's surprise echoing over the telephone line.

'I will be home – here – for Christmas,' I said sharply. 'What about you?'

'I don't have any plans. My brother and his wife asked me, but they didn't sound real sincere, if you know what I mean.' Jack's parents had both died within the past four years.

'You want to come here?' My face tensed with anxiety as I waited to hear his answer.

'Sure,' he said, and his voice was so gentle I knew he could tell how much it had cost me to ask. 'Will you put up mistletoe? Everywhere?'

'Maybe,' I said, trying not to sound as relieved as I was, or as happy as I felt. I bit my lip, suppressing a lot of things. 'Do you want to have a real Christmas dinner?'

'Turkey?' he said hopefully. 'Cornbread dressing?'

'I can do that.'

'Cranberry sauce?'

'English peas?'

'Spinach Madeleine,' I countered.

'Sounds good. What can I bring?'

'Wine.' I seldom drank alcohol, but I thought with Jack around a drink or two might be all right.

'OK. If you think of anything else, give me a call. I've got some work to finish up here within the next week, then I have a meeting about a job I might take on. So I may not get down there until Christmas.'

'Actually, I have a lot to do right now, too. Everyone's trying to get extra cleaning done, giving Christmas parties, putting up trees in their offices.'

It was just over three weeks until Christmas. That was a long time to spend without seeing Jack. Even though I knew I was going to be working hard the entire period, since I counted going home to the wedding as a sort of subcategory of work, I felt a sharp pang at the thought of three weeks' separation.

'That seems like a long time,' he said suddenly.

'Yes.'

Having admitted that, both of us backed hastily away.

'Well, I'll be calling you,' Jack said briskly.

He'd be sprawled on the couch in his apartment in Little Rock as he talked on the phone. His thick dark hair would be pulled back in a ponytail. The cold weather would have made the scar on his face stand out, thin and white, a little puckered where it began at the hairline close to his right eye. If Jack had met with a client today, he'd be wearing nice slacks and a sports coat, wing tips, a dress shirt, and a tie. If he'd been working surveillance, or doing the computer work that increasingly formed the bulk of a private detective's routine, he'd be in jeans and a sweater.

'What are you wearing?' I asked suddenly.

'I thought I was supposed to ask you that.' He sounded amused, again.

I kept a stubborn silence.

'Oh, OK. I'm wearing – you want me to start with the bottom or the top? – Reeboks, white athletic socks, navy blue sweatpants, Jockeys, and a Marvel Gym T-shirt. I just got home from working out.'

'Dress up at Christmas.'

'A suit?'

'Oh, maybe you don't have to go that far. But nice.'

'OK,' he said cautiously.

Christmas this year was on a Friday. I had only two Saturday clients at the moment, and neither of them would be open the day after Christmas. Maybe I could get them done on Christmas morning, before Jack got here.

'Bring clothes for two days,' I said. 'We can have Friday afternoon and Saturday and Sunday.' I suddenly realized I'd *assumed*, and I took a sharp breath. 'That is, if you can stay that long. If you want to.'

'Oh, yes,' he said. His voice sounded rougher, darker. 'Yes, I want to.'

'Are you smiling?'

'You could say so,' he affirmed. 'All over.'

I smiled a little myself. 'OK, see you then.'

'Where'd you say your family was? Bartley, right? I was talking to a friend of mine about that a couple of nights ago.'

It felt strange to know he had talked about me. 'Yes, Bartley. It's in the Delta, a little north and a lot east of Little Rock.'

'Hmmm. It'll be OK, seeing your family. You can tell me all about it.'

'OK.' That did sound good, realizing I could talk about it afterward, that I wouldn't come home to silence and emptiness, drag through days and days rehashing the tensions in my family.

Instead of saying this to Jack, I said, 'Good-bye.'

I heard him respond as I laid the receiver down. We always had a hard time ending conversations.

There are two towns in Arkansas named Montrose. The next day, I drove to the one that had shopping.

Since I no longer worked for the Winthrops, I had more free time on my hands than I could afford: that was the only reason I'd listened when Carlton had proposed the Christmas parade appearance. Until more people opted for my services, I had just about two free mornings a week. This free morning, I'd gone to Body Time for my workout (it was triceps day), come home to shower and dress, and stopped by the office of the little Shakespeare paper to place an ad in the classifieds ('Give your wife her secret Christmas wish – a maid').

And now here I was, involuntarily listening – once again – to taped Christmas carols, surrounded by people who were shopping with some air of excitement and anticipation. I was about to do what I like least to do: spend money when I had little coming in, and spend that money on clothing.

In what I thought of as my previous life, the life I'd led in Memphis as scheduler for a large cleaning service, I'd been quite a dresser. In that life, I'd had long brown hair, and lifting two twenty-pound dumbbells had made my arms tremble. I'd also been naive beyond belief. I had believed that all women were sisters under the skin, and that underneath all the crap, men were basically decent and honest.

I made an involuntary sound of disgust at the memory, and the white-haired lady sitting on the bench a yard away said, 'Yes, it is a little overwhelming after a month and more, isn't it?'

I turned to look at her. Short and stout, she had chosen to wear a Christmas sweatshirt with reindeer on it and green slacks. Her shoes could have been advertised as 'comfort-plus walkers.' She smiled at me. She was alone like I was, and she had more to say.

'They start the selling season so early, and the stores put up the decorations almost before they clear the Halloween stuff away! Takes you right out of the mood, doesn't it!'

'Yes,' I agreed. I swung back to glance in the window, seeing my reflection . . . checking. Yes, I was Lily, the newer version, short blond hair, muscles like hard elastic bands, wary and alert. Strangers generally tended to address their remarks to someone else.

'It's a shame about Christmas,' I told the old woman and walked away.

I pulled the list out of my purse. It would never be shorter unless I could mark something off by making a purchase. My mother had very carefully written down all the social events included in my sister's prewedding buildup and starred all the ones I was absolutely required to attend. She had included notes on what I should wear, in case I'd forgotten what was appropriate for Bartley society.

Unspoken in the letter, though I could read the words in invisible ink, was the plea that I honor my sister by wearing suitable clothes and making an effort to be 'social'.

I was a grown woman, thirty-one. I was not childish enough, or crazy enough, to cause Varena and my parents distress by inappropriate clothing and behavior.

But as I went into the best department store in the mall, as I stared over the racks and racks of clothing, I found myself completely at a loss. There were too many choices for a woman who'd simplified her life down to the bone. A saleswoman asked if she could help me, and I shook my head.

This paralysis was humiliating. I prodded my brain. I could do this. I should get . . .

'Lily,' said a warm, deep voice.

I followed it up, and up, to the face of my friend Bobo Winthrop. Bobo's face had lost the element of boy that had made it sweet. He was a nineteen-year-old man.

Without a thought, I put my arms around him. The last time I'd seen Bobo, he'd been involved in a family tragedy that had torn the Winthrop clan in two. He'd transferred to a college out of state, somewhere in Florida. He looked as if he'd made the most of it. He was tan, had apparently lost a little weight.

He hugged me back even more eagerly. Then as I leaned back to look at him again, he kissed me, but he was wise enough to break it off before it became an issue.

'Are you out of school for the holidays?' I asked.

'Yes, and after that I'll start back here at U of A.' The University of Arkansas had a large campus at Montrose, though some of the Shakespeare kids preferred the biggest establishment in Fayette-ville, or the Little Rock branch.

We looked at each other, in silent agreement not to discuss the reasons Bobo had left the state for a while.

'What are you doing today, Lily? Not at work?'

'No,' I answered shortly, hoping he wouldn't ask me to spell out the fact that his mother no longer employed me, and as a result, I'd lost a couple of other clients.

He gave me a look that I could only characterize as assessing. 'And you're here shopping?'

'My sister's getting married. I have to go home for the wedding and the prewedding parties.'

'So, you're here to get something to wear.' Bobo eyed me a minute more. 'And you don't like to shop.'

'Right,' I said disconsolately.

'Got to go to a shower?'

'I have a list,' I told him, aware of how bleak my voice sounded.

'Let's see.'

I handed him the sheet of stationery.

'A shower . . . two showers. A dinner. Then the rehearsal dinner. The wedding. You'll be a bridesmaid?'

I nodded.

'So she's got your dress for that?'

I nodded again.

'So, what do you need?'

'I have a nice black suit,' I said.

Bobo looked expectantly at me.

'That's it.'

'Oh, wow, Lily,' he said, suddenly sounding his age. 'Do you ever have *shopping* to do.'

That evening I spread out my purchases on the bed. I'd had to use my charge card, but everything I'd gotten I could use for a long time.

A pair of well-cut black slacks. For one shower, I'd wear them with a gold satin vest and an off-white silk blouse. For the second, I'd wear them with an electric blue silk shell and a black jacket. I could wear the shoes that went with the black suit, or a pair of blue leather pumps that had been on sale. I could wear my good black suit to the rehearsal dinner. For the dinner party I had a white dress, sleeveless, that I could wear in the winter with the black jacket, in the summer by itself. I had the correct under-pinnings for each outfit, and I had bought a pair of gold hoop earrings and a big gold free-form pin. I already had diamond earrings and a diamond bar pin my grandmother had left me.

This was all thanks to Bobo's advice.

'You must have read some of Amber Jean's girls' magazines,' I had accused him. Bobo had a younger sister.

'Nah. That's the only shopping wisdom I have to offer. "Everything has to match or coordinate". I guess I learned it from my mom. She has whole sections of clothes that can be mixed and matched.'

I should have remembered that. I used to clean out Beanie Winthrop's closet twice a year.

'Are you living at home?' I had asked when he'd turned to go. I was a little hesitant about asking Bobo any questions that might pertain to his family, so strained was the Winthrop situation.

'No. I have an apartment here. On Chert Avenue. I just moved in, to be ready for the spring semester.' Bobo had flushed, for the first time looking awkward. 'I'm trying to spend some time at home, so my folks don't feel too . . . ditched.' He'd run his fingers through his floppy blond hair. 'How've you been doing? You still seeing that private detective?'

'Yeah.'

'Still working out?' he'd added hastily, getting off dangerous ground.

I'd nodded.

He'd hugged me again and gone about whatever his errand was, leaving me to a saleswoman named Marianna. She'd homed in on us when Bobo had joined me, and now that he had left, she was stuck with me.

After I'd gotten over the sticker shock, it felt almost good to have new clothes. I cut off the tags and hung all the new things in the closet in the guest bedroom, spacing the hangers so the clothes wouldn't wrinkle. Days afterward, I found myself looking at them from time to time, opening the door suspiciously as if my new garments might have gone back to the store.

I'd always been very careful with makeup, with my hair; I keep my legs shaved as smooth as a baby's bottom. I like to know what I look like; I like to control it. But I don't want people to turn to look at me, I don't want people to notice me. The jeans and sweats I wore to clean houses, to bathe dogs, to fill some shut-in's grocery list, acted as camouflage. Practical, cheap, camouflage.

People would look at me when I wore my new clothes.

Made uneasy by all these changes, by the prospect of going back to Bartley, I plunged myself into what work I had. I still cleaned

Carrie Thrush's office every Saturday, and Carrie had mentioned she wanted me to come more often, but I had to be sure it wasn't because she thought I was hurting financially. Pity shouldn't have any part in a business arrangement, or a friendship.

I had the Drinkwaters' house, and the travel agent's office, and Dr Sizemore's office. I still cleaned Deedra Dean's apartment, and I was working more hours for Mrs Rossiter, who had broken her arm while she was walking Durwood, her old cocker spaniel. But it wasn't enough.

I did get the job of decorating two more office Christmas trees, and I did a good job on one and an outstanding job on the other, which was a very visible advertisement since it stood in the Chamber of Commerce office. I used birds and fruit for that one, and the warm, hushed colors and carefully concealed lights made the tree a little more peaceful than some of the others I saw around town.

I'd quit taking the Little Rock newspaper to cut back on expenses until my client list built up. So I was in Dr Sizemore's office, on a Tuesday afternoon, when I saw the creased section from one of the Sunday editions. I scooped it up to dump into the recycle bin, and my gaze happened to land on the headline 'Unsolved Crimes Mean No Happy Holiday'. The paper was dated two days after Thanksgiving, which told me that one of the office staff had stuffed it somewhere and then unearthed it in her pre-Christmas cleaning.

I sank down onto the edge of one of the waiting room chairs to read the first three paragraphs.

In the yearly effort to pack as many holiday-related stories as possible into the paper, the *Arkansas Democrat Gazette* had interviewed the families of people who had been murdered (if the murder was unsolved) or abducted (if the abductee hadn't been found).

I wouldn't have continued to read the article, since it's just the kind of thing that brings back too many bad memories, if it hadn't been for the picture of the baby.

The cutline under the picture read, 'Summer Dawn Macklesby

at the time of her disappearance. Summer has been missing for almost eight years.'

She was a tiny infant in the picture, perhaps a week old. She had a little lace bow attached somehow to a scanty strand of hair.

Though I knew it would make me miserable, I found myself searching for the child's name again, in the column of text. It jumped out at me about halfway through the story, past the mother of three who'd been gunned down at an automated teller on Christmas Eve and the engaged convenience store clerk raped and knifed to death on her Thanksgiving birthday.

'Eight years ago this week, Summer Dawn Macklesby was snatched from her infant seat on her parents' enclosed front porch in suburban Conway,' the sentence began. 'Teresa Macklesby, preparing for a shopping expedition, left her infant daughter on the porch while she stepped back into the house to retrieve a package she intended to mail before Christmas. While she was in the house, the telephone rang, and though Macklesby is sure she was absent from the porch no longer than five minutes, by the time she returned Summer Dawn had vanished.'

I closed my eyes. I folded the paper so I couldn't read the rest of the story and carried it to the recycle bin and dumped it in as if it were contaminated with the grief and agony implied in that one partial story.

That night I had to walk.

Some nights sleep played a cheap trick on me and hid. Those nights, no matter how tired I was, no matter what energy I needed for the day to come, I had to walk. Though these episodes were less frequent than even a year ago, they still occurred perhaps once every two weeks.

Sometimes I made sure nobody saw me. Sometimes I strode down the middle of the street. My thoughts were seldom pleasant on walking nights, and yet my mind could not be at peace any more than my body.

I haven't ever understood it.

After all, as I often tell myself, the Bad Thing has already happened. I do not need to fear anymore.

Doesn't everyone wait for the Bad Thing? Every woman I've ever known does. Maybe men have a Bad Thing, too, and they don't admit it. A woman's Bad Thing, of course, is being abducted, raped, and knifed; left bleeding, an object of revulsion and pity to those who find her, be she dead or alive.

Well, that had happened to me.

Since I had never been a mother, I had never had to imagine any other disasters. But tonight I thought maybe there was a Worse Thing. The Worse Thing would be years of imagining that child's bones lying in the mud in some ditch, or your child alive and being molested methodically by some monster.

Not knowing.

Thanks to that glimpse of newspaper, I was imagining that now.

I hoped Summer Dawn Macklesby was dead. I hoped she had died within an hour of her abduction. I hoped for that hour she had been unconscious. As I walked and walked in the cold night, that seemed to me to be the best-case scenario.

Of course, it was possible that some loving couple who desperately wanted a little girl had just picked up Summer Dawn and had bought her everything her heart desired and enrolled her in an excellent school and were doing a great job of raising her.

But I didn't believe that stories like Summer Dawn Macklesby's could have a happy ending, just like I didn't believe that all people are basically good. I didn't believe that God gave you compensation for your griefs. I didn't believe that when one door closes, another opens.

I believed that was crap.

I was going to miss some karate classes while I was in Bartley. And the gym would be closed for Christmas Eve, Christmas, and the day after. Maybe I could do calisthenics in my room to compensate? And my sore shoulder could use a rest. So as I packed my bag to leave, I tried not to grumble any more than I already had. I had to make this visit, had to do it with grace.

As I drove to Bartley, which was about a three-hour journey

east and a little north from Shakespeare, I tried to drum up some sort of pleasurable anticipation about the coming visit.

It would have been more straightforward if I hated my parents. I loved them.

It was in no way their fault that my abduction, rape, and mutilation had made such a media roar that my life, and theirs, had changed even more than was inevitable.

And it was in no way their fault that no one I'd grown up with seemed to be able to treat me as a normal person, after that second, public, rape in the spotlight of the press and the TV cameras.

Nor was it my parents' fault that my boyfriend of two years had quit seeing me after the press turned their attention away from him.

None of it was their fault – or mine – but it had permanently altered the relationships between us. My mother and father couldn't look at me without thinking of what had happened to me. They couldn't talk to me without it coloring the most commonplace conversation. My only sibling, Varena, who had always been more relaxed and elastic than I had, had never been able to understand why I didn't recover more swiftly and get on with my life as it had been before; and my parents didn't know how to get in contact with the woman I'd become.

Weary of scrambling through this emotional equivalent of a hamster exercise wheel, I was nearly glad to see the outskirts of Bartley – the poor rickety homes and marginal businesses that blotch the approach to most small towns.

Then I was rolling past the filling station where my parents gassed their cars; past the dry cleaner where Mother took their coats; past the Presbyterian church they'd attended all their lives, where they'd been baptized, married, christened their daughters, from which they would be buried.

I turned down the familiar street. On the next block, the house I grew up in was wearing its winter coat. The rosebushes had been trimmed back. The smooth grass of the big yard was pale after the frost. The house sat in the middle of the large lot, surrounded by my father's rose beds. A huge Christmas wreath made from twined grapevines and little gold toy trumpets hung on the front door, and the decorated tree was visible in the big picture window in the living room. Mom and Dad had repainted the house when Varena and Dill got engaged, so it was gleaming white for the wedding festivities.

I parked to the side of the driveway on a concrete apron my parents had poured when Varena and I began driving. We'd had friends over all the time, and my folks got tired of their own vehicles getting blocked in.

I eased out of my car and looked at the house for a long moment, stretching my legs after the drive. It had seemed so big when I'd lived in it. I had always felt so lucky to grow up in this house.

Now I saw a fairly typical built-in-the-fifties house, with a double garage, a living room, a den, a big kitchen, a dining room, and three bedrooms, two baths.

There was a workroom at the back of the garage for my father – not that he ever did anything in it, but men needed a workroom. Just like there was a sewing machine in the corner of my parents' bedroom, because a woman ought to have a sewing machine – not that my mother ever sewed more than a ripped seam. And we Bards had a full complement of family silver – not that we ever ate with it. Someday, in the course of time, Varena and I would divide that silver between us, and the care of it would be on our shoulders; that heavy, ornate silver that was too fine and too much trouble to use.

I got my suitcase and my hanging bag out of the backseat and went up to the front door. My feet felt heavier with every step.

I was home.

Varena answered the door, and we gave each other a quick look of assessment and a tentative hug.

Varena was looking good.

I had been the prettier when we were girls. My eyes are bluer, my nose is straighter, my lips are fuller. But that doesn't have much meaning for me anymore. I think it still matters very much to Varena. Her hair is long and naturally a redder brown than mine had been. She wears blue contacts, which intensify her eye color to an almost bizarre extent. Her nose turns up a little, and she is about two inches shorter, with bigger breasts and a bigger bottom.

'How is the wedding process?' I asked.

She widened her eyes and made her hands tremble. On edge.

Beyond her, I could see the tables that had been set up to accommodate the presents.

'Wow,' I said, shaking my head in acknowledgment of the sight. There were three long tables (I was sure my folks had borrowed them from the church) draped in gleaming white tablecloths, and every inch was covered with consumer goods. Wineglasses, cloth napkins and tablecloths, china, silver – more silver – vases, letter openers, picture albums, knives and cutting boards, toasters, blankets . . .

'People are being so sweet,' Varena said, and I could tell that was her stock response; not that she didn't mean it, but I was sure she'd said that over and over and over to visitors.

'Well, no one's ever had to spend anything on us, have they?' I observed, raising my eyebrows. Neither Varena or I had ever been married, unlike some in our high school circles who'd been divorced twice by now.

My mother came into the living room from the den. She was pale, but then she always is, like me. Varena likes to tan, and my father does inevitably; he'd rather be out working in the yard than almost anything.

'Oh, sugar!' my mother said and folded me to her. My mother is shorter than me, bone-thin, and her hair is such a faded blond it's almost white. Her eyes are blue like every member of our family's, but their color seems to have faded in the past five or six years. She's never had to wear glasses, her hearing is excellent, and she beat breast cancer ten years ago. She doesn't wear clothes that are at all trendy or fashionable, but she never looks frumpy, either.

The months, the years, seemed to dissolve. It felt like I'd seen them yesterday.

'Where's Dad?' I asked.

'He's gone down to the church to get another table,' Varena explained, trying not to smile too broadly. My mother suppressed the curve of her own lips.

'Is he rolling in this wedding stuff?'

'You know it,' Varena said. 'He just loves it. He's been waiting for this for years.'

'This'll be the wedding of the decade in Bartley,' I said.

'Well,' Varena began, as we all started down the hall to my old room, 'if Mrs Kingery can get here, it may be.' Her voice sounded a little whiny, a bit flat, as though this worry or complaint were so longstanding she'd worn out the emotion behind it.

'Dill's mother may not come?' I asked, incredulous. 'So, she's really old and sick . . . or what?'

My mother sighed. 'We can't quite decide what the problem is,' she explained. She stared off into the distance for a moment, as if the clue to Varena's future mother-in-law's behavior was written on the lawn outside the window.

Varena had taken my hanging bag and opened the closet to hook the hangers over the rod. I put my suitcase on the triple dresser that had been my pride and joy at age sixteen. Varena looked back at me over her shoulder.

'I think,' she said, 'that maybe Mrs Kingery was just so crazy about Dill's first wife that she hates to see her replaced. You know, with Anna being their child, and all.'

'Seems to me like she'd be glad that Anna's going to have such a good stepmother,' I said, though in truth, I'd never thought what kind of stepmother Varena would make.

'That would be the sensible attitude.' My mother sighed. 'I just don't know, and you can't ask point-blank.'

I could. But I knew they wouldn't want me to.

'She'll have to come to the rehearsal, right?'

My mother and sister looked anxiously at each other.

'We think she will,' Varena said. 'But Dill can't seem to tell me what that woman will do.'

Dill (Dillard) Kingery's mother was still in Dill's hometown, which I thought was Pine Bluff.

'How long have you been dating Dill?' I asked.

'Seven years,' Varena said, smiling brightly. This, too, was obviously a question that had been asked many times since Varena and Dill had announced their engagement.

'Dill is older than you?'

'Yeah, he's even older than you,' my sister said.

Some things never change.

We heard my father's yell from the front door. 'One a you come help me with this damn thing?' he bellowed.

I got there first.

My father, who is stocky and short and bald as an eight ball, had hauled the long table out of the bed of his pickup to the front door and definitely needed help getting it up the steps.

'Hey, pigeon,' he said, his smile radiant.

I figured that would fade soon enough, so I hugged him while I could. Then I lifted the front of the table, which he'd propped against the iron railing that bordered the steps up to the front door.

'You sure that's not too heavy for you?' Dad fussed. He had always had the delusion that the attack I'd endured somehow had made me weak internally, that I was now frail in some invisible manner. The fact that I could bench-press 120 pounds, sometimes more, had no influence on this delusion.

'I'm fine,' I said.

He picked up the rear of the table, which was the kind with metal legs that fold underneath for easy carrying. With a little maneuvering, we got it up the steps and into the living room. While I held the table on its side, he pulled out the metal legs and locked them into place. We swung the table upright. The whole time he worried out loud about me doing too much, straining myself.

I began to get that tight, hot feeling behind my eyes.

My mother appeared in the nick of time with yet another spotless white tablecloth. Without speaking she shook it out. I took the loose end, and together we spread it evenly over the table. My father talked the whole time, about the number of wedding presents Varena and Dill had gotten, about the number of wedding invitations they'd sent, about the acceptances they'd received, about the reception . . .

I eyed him covertly while we transferred some of the crowded presents to the new table. Dad didn't look good. His face seemed redder than it should have been, his legs seemed to be giving him pain, and his hands shook a little. I knew he'd been diagnosed with high blood pressure and arthritis.

There was an awkward pause, once we'd gotten our little task accomplished.

'Ride over to my apartment with me and see the dress,' Varena offered.

'OK.'

We got in Varena's car for the short drive over to her apartment, which was a small yellow cottage to the side of a big old yellow house where Emory and Meredith Osborn lived with their little girl and a new baby, Varena explained.

'When the Osborns bought this house from old Mrs Smitherton – she had to go into Dogwood Manor, did I tell you? – I was worried they'd raise the rent, but they didn't. I like them both, not that I see them that much. The little girl is cute, always got a bow in her hair. She plays with Anna sometimes. Meredith keeps Anna and the O'Sheas' little girl after school, now and then.'

I thought I remembered that the O'Sheas were the Presbyterian minister and his wife. They'd come after I'd begun living in Shakespeare.

Varena was chattering away, as if she could hardly wait to fill me in on all the details of her life. Or as if she were uncomfortable with me.

We pulled into the driveway and passed the larger house to park in front of Varena's place. It was a copy of the house in miniature, done in pale yellow siding with dark green shutters and white trim.

A little girl was playing in the yard, a thin child with long brown hair. Sure enough, a perky red-and-green bow was clipped right above her bangs. On this cold day, she was wearing a sweatsuit topped by a coat and earmuffs, but still she looked chilly. She waved as Varena got out of her car.

'Hey, Miss Varena,' she called politely. She held a ball in her hands. When I got out of the passenger's door, she stared at me with curiosity.

'Eve, this is my sister, Lily.' Varena turned to me. 'Eve has a sister, too, a new one.'

'What's her name?' I asked, since that seemed indicated. I am very uneasy around children.

'Jane Lilith,' Eve mumbled.

'That's pretty,' I said, because I couldn't think of anything else to say.

'Is your sister taking a nap right now?' Varena asked.

'Yeah, and my mom too,' the girl said forlornly.

'Come in and see my dress,' Varena invited.

Eve really brightened up. Varena seemed to have a way with children. We trailed into the little front room of the house and followed Varena back to her bedroom. The closet door was open, and the wedding dress, swathed in plastic, was hanging on a special hanger that fitted over the top of the door.

Well, it was white and it was a wedding dress.

'It's beautiful,' I said instantly. I am not stupid.

Eve was awestruck. 'Oooo,' she said breathlessly.

Varena laughed, and as I looked at my sister, I saw how warm and responsive her face was, how good-natured she looked. 'I'm glad you like it,' she said and went on talking to the child in an easy way that was totally beyond me.

'Can you pick me up so I can see the scarf?' Eve asked Varena.

I looked where the child was pointing. The veil, yards and yards of it, attached to an elaborate sort of tiara, was in a separate bag attached to the one holding the dress.

'Oh, honey, you're too big for me to pick up,' Varena said, shaking her head. I could feel my eyebrows crawl up. Was it possible Varena couldn't lift this girl? I assessed the child. Seventy-five pounds, tops. I squatted, wrapped my arms around her hips, and lifted.

Eve squealed with surprise and delight. She turned to look down at me.

'Can you see?' I asked.

Eve examined the veil, admired the glittering sequined tiara, and went all dreamy-eyed for a minute or two.

'You can put me down now,' she said eventually, and I gently lowered her to the floor. The girl turned to give me a long stare of evaluation.

'You're really strong,' she said admiringly. 'I bet nobody messes with you.'

I could practically taste Varena's sudden silence.

'No,' I told the little girl. 'Nobody messes with me now.'

Eve's narrow face turned thoughtful. She thanked Varena for showing her the dress and veil in a perfectly polite way, but she seemed almost abstracted as she said she'd better be getting home.

Varena saw Eve out. 'Oh, Dill's here!' she exclaimed in a happy voice. I stared at the frothy white construction of the dress for a moment more before I followed Varena to the living room.

I'd known Dill Kingery since he moved to Bartley. He'd just begun dating Varena when the whole eruption in my life had occurred. He'd been a great solace to my sister during that time, when the whole family had needed all the help we could get.

They'd continued dating ever since. It had been a long engagement, long enough for Varena to bear a good amount of teasing from her coworkers at the tiny Bartley hospital.

Looking at Dill now, I wondered why he'd dragged his feet. I didn't think he'd been beating other women off with a stick. Dill was perfectly nice and perfectly pleasant, but you wouldn't turn to look at him twice on the street. My sister's fiancé had thinning sandy hair, attractive brown eyes, wire-rimmed glasses, and a happy smile. His daughter, Anna, was another skinny little eight-year-old, with thick, shoulder-length brown hair that was lighter than her father's. Anna had her dad's eyes and smile. Anna's mother had died when Anna was about eighteen months old, Dill had told us, in a car accident.

I watched while Anna hugged Varena. She was about to run to play with Eve when Dill stopped her. 'Say hi to your aunt Lily,' he said firmly.

'Hey, Aunt Lily,' Anna said and gave me a casual wave of the hand, which I returned. 'Can I play with Eve now, Daddy?'

'OK, sweetie,' Dill said, and the two girls clattered outside while Dill turned to me to give me a hug. I had to endure it, so I did, but I'm not a casual toucher. And I hadn't quite adjusted to being 'Aunt Lily'.

Dill asked me the usual questions you ask of someone you haven't seen in awhile, and I managed to answer civilly. I was tensing up already, and nothing had happened to make me so. What was wrong with me? I stared out the front window while Dill and my sister talked over the plans for the evening. Tonight, I gathered, Dill was attending his bachelor dinner, while Varena and I and Mother were going to a wedding shower.

As I watched the two little girls playing on the front lawn, heaving the beach ball back and forth between them and running a lot, I tried to recall playing with Varena like that. Surely we had? But I couldn't dredge up a single recollection.

Without asking me, Dill told Varena he'd run me home so she could start getting ready. I looked at my watch. If Varena needed three hours to get ready for a party, she needed help, in my opinion. But Varena seemed pleased with Dill's offer, so I went outside to stand by Dill's Bronco. A tiny, thin woman had come outside of the bigger house to call to Eve.

'Hey,' she said when she noticed me.

'Hello,' I said.

Eve came running up, Anna in tow.

'This is Varena's sister, Mama,' she said. 'She came for the wedding. Miss Varena showed me her dress, and Miss Lily picked me up so I could see the veil. You wouldn't believe how strong Miss Lily is! I bet she can lift a horse!'

'Oh, my goodness,' said Eve's mama, her thin face transformed by a sweet smile. 'I better say hello, then. I'm Eve's mother, as I'm sure you figured. Meredith Osborn.'

'Hello again,' I said. 'Lily Bard.' This woman had just had a baby, according to Varena, but she looked no larger than a child herself. Losing 'baby weight' was not going to be a problem for Meredith Osborn. I didn't think Meredith Osborn was over thirty-one, my age, and she might be even younger.

'Can you pick us both up, Miss Lily?' Eve asked, and my niece-to-be suddenly looked much more interested in me.

'I think so,' I said and bent my knees. 'One on either side, now!'

The girls each picked a side, and I hooked my arms around them and stood, making sure I was steady. The girls were squealing with excitement. 'Hold still,' I reminded them, and they stopped the thrashing that I had worried would topple us all over onto the driveway.

'We're queens of the world,' Anna shouted extravagantly, sweeping her arm to indicate her turf. 'Look at how high up we are!'

Dill had been talking to Varena in the doorway, but now he glanced over to find out what Anna was doing. His face looked almost comical with surprise when he saw the girls.

With the anxious smile of someone who is trying not to panic, he strode over. 'Better get down, sweetie! You're a big load for Miss Lily.'

'They're both small,' I said mildly and surrendered Anna to her dad. I swung Eve in front of me and set her down gently. She grinned up at me. Her mother was looking at her with that smile of love women get when they look at their kids. A little mewling sound came from the house. 'I hear your sister crying,' Meredith Osborn said wearily. 'We better go in and see. Good-bye, Miss Bard, nice to meet you.'

I nodded at Meredith and gave Eve a little smile. Her brown eyes, peering up at me, looked enormous. She grinned at me, a smile stretching from one ear to another, and dashed in after her mother.

Anna and her father were already in the Bronco, so I climbed in, too. Dill chatted all the way back to my parents' home, but I half tuned him out. I had already talked to more people today than I normally spoke to in three or four days in Shakespeare. I was out of the habit of chitchat.

I got out at my folks' with a nod to Dill and Anna and strode into the house. My mother was fluttering around the kitchen, trying to get something ready for us to eat before we went to the shower. My dad was in the bathroom getting ready for the bachelor dinner.

My mother was worried that some of Dill's friends might get carried away and have a stripper perform at the party. I shrugged. My father wouldn't be mortally offended.

'It's your dad's blood pressure I'm really worried about,' Mom said with a half smile. 'If a naked woman popped out of a cake, no telling what might happen!'

I poured iced tea and set the glasses on the table. 'It doesn't seem too likely that anyone will do that,' I said, because she was looking for reassurance. 'Dill's not a kid, and it's not his first marriage. I don't think any of his local friends are likely to get that carried away.' I sat down at my place.

'You're right,' Mom said with some relief. 'You always have such good sense, Lily.'

Not always.

'Are you . . . seeing anyone . . . now, honey?' Mom asked gently.

I stared up at her as she hovered over the table, plates in her hands. I almost said no automatically,

'Yes.'

The fleeting look of sheer relief and pleasure that flashed across my mother's pale, narrow face was so intense I felt like taking back my yes. I was feeling my way with Jack every hour we were together, and to have our relationship classified as a standard dating situation made me horribly anxious.

'Can you tell me a little about him?' Mom's voice was calm, her hands steady as she set the plates down at our places. She sat down across from me and began to stir sugar into her tea.

I had no idea what to say.

'Oh, that's all right, I don't want to intrude on your privacy,' she said after a moment, flustered.

'No,' I said just as quickly. It seemed awful to me that we were so leery of each other's every word and silence. 'No, that's . . . no, it's OK. He . . .' I pictured Jack, and a tide of longing swept over me, so intense and painful that it took my breath away. After it ebbed, I said, 'He's a private detective. He lives in Little Rock. He's thirty-five.'

My mother put her sandwich down on her plate and began smiling. 'That's wonderful, honey. What's his name? Has he been married before?'

'Yes. His name is Jack Leeds.'

'Any kids?'

'No.'

'That's easier.'

'Yes.'

'Though I know little Anna so well now, at first when Dill and Varena began dating . . . Anna was so little, not even toilet trained, and Dill's mother didn't seem to want to come to take care of Anna, though she was a cute little toddler . . .'

'That worried you?'

'Yes,' she admitted, nodding her faded blond head. 'Yes, it did. I didn't know if Varena could handle it. She never enjoyed baby-sitting very much, and she never talked about having babies, like most girls do. But she and Anna seemed to take to each other just fine. Sometimes she gets fed up with Anna's little tricks, and sometimes Anna reminds Varena that she isn't her real mother, but for the most part they get along great.'

'Dill wasn't in the car wreck that killed his wife?'

'No, it was a one-car accident. Evidently, Judy, his wife, had just dropped off Anna at a sitter's.'

'That was before Dill moved here?'

'Yes, just a few months before. He'd been living up northwest of Little Rock. He says he felt he just couldn't bear to raise Anna there, every day having to pass the spot where his wife died.'

'So he moves to a town where he doesn't know a soul, where he doesn't have any family to help him raise Anna.' I spoke before I thought.

My mother gave me a sharp look. 'And we're mighty glad he did,' she said firmly. 'The pharmacy here was up for sale, and it's been wonderful to have it open, so we have a choice.' There was a chain pharmacy in Bartley, too.

'Of course,' I said, to keep the peace.

We finished our meal in silence. My father stomped through on his way out the kitchen door to his car, grousing the whole time about not fitting in at a bachelor dinner. We could tell he was really gleeful about being invited. He had a wrapped present tucked under his arm, and when I asked what it was, his face turned even redder. He pulled on his topcoat and slammed the back door behind him without answering.

'I suspect he bought one of those nasty gag gifts,' Mom said with a little smile as she listened to Father back out of the driveway.

I loved getting surprised by my mother. 'I'll do the dishes while you get ready,' I said.

'You need to try on your bridesmaid dress!' she said abruptly as she was rising to leave the kitchen.

'Right now?'

'What if we need to take it up?'

'Oh . . . all right.' This was not a moment I'd anticipated with any pleasure. Bridesmaids' dresses are notorious for being un-usable, and I'd paid for this one as a good bridesmaid should. But I hadn't seen it yet. I had a horrible, wincing moment of picturing the dress as red velvet with fake fur trim to suit the Christmas motif.

I should have had more trust in Varena. The dress, which was hanging in my bedroom closet swathed in plastic like Varena's own dress, was deep burgundy velvet, with a band of matching satin ribbon sewed under the breasts. In back, where the edges of the ribbon came together, there was a matching bow – but it was detachable. The dress had a high neckline but was cut low in the back. My sister didn't want her bridesmaids demure, that was for sure.

'Try it on,' Mother urged. I could tell she wouldn't be happy until I did. With my back to her, I pulled off my shirt and wriggled out of my shoes and jeans. But I had to turn to face her to get the dress, which she'd been divesting of its plastic bag.

Every time, the impact of my scars hit her in the heart. She took a deep, ragged breath and handed me the dress, and I got it over my head as quickly as possible. I turned so she could zip me, and together we looked at it in the mirror. Both our pairs of eyes went immediately to the neckline. Perfect. Nothing showed. Thank you, Varena.

'It looks beautiful,' Mother said stoutly. 'Stand up straight, now.' (As if I slouched.) The dress did fit well, and who doesn't love the feel of velvet?

'What kind of flowers are we carrying?'

'The bridesmaids' bouquets are going to be long sprays of glads and some other stuff,' Mother said, who strictly left the gardening to my father. 'You're the maid of honor, you know.'

Varena hadn't seen me in three years.

This wasn't just a wedding, then. This was a full-scale family reconciliation.

I was willing, but I didn't know if I was able. Plus, I hadn't been to a wedding in a long time.

'Do I have to do anything special?'

'You have to carry the ring Varena's giving Dill. You have to take her bouquet while she's saying her vows.' Mom smiled at me, and her washed-blue eyes crinkled around the corners of her eyelids. When my mother smiled, her whole face smiled with her. 'You're lucky she didn't pick a dress with a ten-foot train, because you'd have to turn it around for her before she leaves the church.'

I thought I could remember the ring and the bouquet.

'I'll have to thank her for the honor,' I said, and Mom's face sagged for just a minute. She thought I was being sarcastic.

'I mean it,' I told her, and I could almost feel her relax.

Had I been so frightening, so unpredictable, so rude?

When I'd worked my way carefully out of the dress, and pulled my T-shirt back on, I patted my mother gently on the shoulder as she made sure the dress was absolutely even on its padded hanger.

She smiled fleetingly at me, and then we went back to the kitchen to clean up.

Chapter Two

I wore the off-white blouse, gold vest, and black pants to the shower. I buttoned the blouse all the way up to the neck. My makeup was light and perfect, and my hair fluffed out in the right way. I looked fine, I decided, appropriate. I worked on relaxing, buckled into the backseat of my mother's car.

We picked up Varena on the way. This was at least her second shower, but she was as excited and pleased as though celebrating her forthcoming marriage was an original idea.

We drove across town to the home of the shower hostess, Margie Lipscom. Margie was another nurse at the little Bartley hospital, which was always threatened with closing or being closed. Margie was married to one of the more prominent lawyers in Bartley, which was actually not saying much. Bartley is a Delta town, and in this phase of its existence, that means poor.

It meant that at least seventy percent of the town's population was on welfare.

When I'd been growing up, it had just meant that Bartley was flat. You don't know what flat is until you've lived in the Delta.

I missed the low, rolling hills around Shakespeare. I missed the ratty Christmas decorations. I missed my house. I missed my gym.

I would have given anything to be selfish enough to jump in my car and drive home.

I took slow, deep breaths, like I did before I attempted to lift a weight that was a real challenge. Like I did before we sparred in karate class.

Mom drove past Bartley's dilapidated motel, and I glanced into its U of rooms. There was a car parked there – that, in itself, was nearly amazing – and it looked like . . . my heart began to stutter in an uncomfortable way.

I shook my head. Couldn't be.

We parked on the street in front of the white-painted brick house all lit up like a birthday cake. There was a white-and-silver paper wedding bell fixed to the front door. A stout redhead stood just within the foyer . . . Margie Lipscom. I'd known her as a plump brunette.

My mother got patted, my sister got hugged, and I was greeted with a shriek.

'Oh, *Lily!* Girl, you look beautiful!' Margie exclaimed. She grabbed me and embraced me. I endured it. Margie was my age, had never been a particular friend of mine; she had grown closer to my sister when they began working together. Margie had always been a hooter and a hugger. She was going to fuss extra over me now, because she felt sorry for me.

'Isn't she even prettier, Frieda?' Margie said to my mother. Overcompensating for her discomfort.

'Lily has always been lovely,' my mother said calmly.

'Well, let's go see everyone!' Margie grabbed my hand and led me into the living room. I was biting the inside of my mouth. I was having a little flutter of panic and anger, the sort of nervous spasm I hadn't had in a long time. A long, long time.

I found a smile and fixed it on my face.

After I'd nodded to everyone and said, 'Tell you later,' in answer to almost every query, I was able to sit in a straight chair that had been crammed into a corner of the crowded living room. After that, all I had to do was aim a pleasant look in the direction of the loudest speaker, and I was fine.

This was a lingerie shower, and I'd gotten Varena a present when I'd shopped for myself in Montrose. She hadn't expected a gift from me, hadn't noticed me bring it into the house. She looked up at me in surprise when she read the card on the front. I may have imagined it, but she looked a little apprehensive.

My gift was a nightgown, full-length, with spaghetti straps and lace panels – sheer lace panels – over the breasts. It was black. It was beautiful. It was really, really sexy. As Varena was ripping off the paper, I was suddenly convinced I'd made a terrible mistake.

The most daring garment Varena had received so far was a tiger-print teddy, and there had been some red faces over that.

When Varena shook out the gown and held it up, there was a moment of silence, during which I decided I might as well sneak out the back way. Then Varena said, 'Wow. *This* is for the wedding night.' And there was a chorus of 'Oooo' and 'Oh, boy!'

'Lily, this is beautiful,' Varena said directly. 'And I bet Dill's gonna thank you, too!'

There was a chorus of laughter, and then the next gift was passed to my sister to open.

I relaxed and coasted on autopilot for the rest of the evening.

During the punch and cakes, the talk turned to Bartley's purse snatcher. This seemed an urban sort of crime for Bartley, so I paid attention. Margie was saying, 'And he stole Diane's purse right off her arm and ran off with it!'

'Did she get a good look at him?' the minister's wife asked. Lou O'Shea was a buxom brunette with a ski-jump nose and intelligent eyes. I'd never met her before. I hadn't been to church, in Bartley or anywhere else, in years.

'Just a black guy, medium height,' Margie said. 'Could be a hundred people.'

'She's all right?' my mother asked.

'Well, he knocked her down to the sidewalk, so she had some scrapes and bruises. It could've been a lot worse.'

After a second's thoughtful pause, a few eyes slid in my direction. I was the worse it could have been.

But I was used to that. I kept my face blank, and the little moment passed. A purse snatching did not seem as remarkable as it would have a few years ago. Now, with gang presence and drugs in every tiny town up and down the interstate and all in between, what happened to Diane Dykeman, a sales clerk at one of the local clothing stores, didn't seem so bad. She seemed lucky to be unhurt, rather than unfortunate to have her purse snatched at all.

After a tedious two and a half hours we drove home, taking a different route this time since we were giving a lift to Lou O'Shea, whose husband had dropped her off on his way to a meeting. The Presbyterian manse was a large redbrick home that matched the adjacent church. I half listened to the backseat conversation between Varena and Lou, enough to gather that Lou, like Meredith Osborn, had an eight-year-old girl and another, younger child. When we pulled into the driveway, Lou seemed reluctant to get out.

'I'm afraid it doesn't make Krista any fonder of Luke, him crying so much,' Lou told us with a heavy sigh. 'She's not too enthusiastic about her little brother right now.'

'Krista is Anna's age, they play together a lot,' Varena reminded me.

'It'll all straighten out,' my mother said in her soothing way. 'Sooner or later you'll find out why Luke cries all night, and he'll stop. And then Krista will forget all about it. She's a smart little girl, Lou.'

'You're right,' Lou said instantly, back on her mettle as a minister's wife. 'Thanks for the lift. I'll see you-all tomorrow afternoon!'

When we were driving away, Varena said, 'Lou'll be coming to the rehearsal dinner tomorrow night.'

'Isn't it traditional to have the rehearsal dinner the night before the wedding?' I didn't want to sound critical, but I was faintly curious.

'Yes. Dill had originally scheduled it for that night,' Mother said. I was being subtly reminded that the groom's family had the responsibility for the rehearsal dinner. 'But Sarah May's was already booked for the two evenings before the wedding! So we just moved it to three nights, and the couple giving the supper for Dill and Varena rescheduled it to the night before the wedding, bless them.'

I nodded, hardly paying attention. I was absolutely confident I would be told what to do, when. I found myself wanting to be alone so badly I could taste it. When we got to Varena's, I unloaded the shower presents with great dispatch, and at my folks' house, I said a brief goodnight to Mom before heading for my room.

My father hadn't yet gotten home from the bachelor party. I hoped he wasn't drinking and smoking cigars. His blood pressure would soar.

I sat in the little chair in my room and read for a long time, a biography I'd brought with me. Then I hooked my feet under the bed and did sit-ups, I dropped and did pushups, and I did eighty leg lifts. After that, it was time for a relaxing shower. I noticed that my father had come in at some point and turned out the remaining lights.

But even after the hot shower, I felt itchy. I couldn't walk in Bartley. People would talk about my family. The police weren't used to me. They might stop me – if I saw any. The Bartley police force was not large.

I pushed the temptation away and forced myself to climb in the bed. I worked three crossword puzzles in a book I found in the bedside table drawer. Somehow, trying to think of a five-letter word meaning an earth-covered Indian dwelling did the trick. Finally, I was able to draw a curtain on a very long day.

Unfortunately, the next was more of the same.

Before noon, I decided that everyone in my family should have had to go to work until an hour before the wedding.

My father had taken two weeks' vacation from the electric company. Since my mother was a housewife, she was always at work – but still in the house, constantly thinking of things that just had to be done. Varena had just taken three weeks' leave from her job at the hospital, and even Dill was often leaving the drugstore to his normally part-time assistant, a young mother who was also a pharmacist.

More presents arrived, to be unwrapped and admired and entered on the list. More thank-you notes had to be written. The two other bridesmaids had to stop by and admire and check on last-minute plans. The minister, Jess O'Shea, came in for a minute to verify a couple of things. He had smooth dark blond hair and was quietly good-looking in a blocky, square-jawed way: I hoped he was as good as he was handsome, because I'd always imagined that ministers were prime targets for neurotic – or just hopeful – members of their congregation.

His little girl was in tow. Chunky Krista, whose hair was the same dark brown as her mother's but not as perfectly smooth, was sleepy-eyed and cross with her baby brother's nocturnal activity, just as Lou had predicted. Krista was in a whiny mood.

'Luke cried all night,' she said sullenly when someone asked her for the third time where her brother was.

'Oh, Krista!' one of the other bridesmaids said disapprovingly. Varena's lifelong best friend, Tootsie Monahan, was blond and round-faced and low on brain cells. 'How can you say that about a little kid like Luke? Toddlers are so cute.'

I saw Krista's face flush. Tootsie was pushing the old guilt button hard. I'd been leaning against the wall in the living room. I shoved off and maneuvered myself closer to the little girl.

'Varena cried all night when she was baby,' I told Krista very quietly.

Krista looked up at me unbelievingly. Her round hazel eyes, definitely her best feature, fastened on me with every appearance of skepticism. 'Did not,' she said tentatively.

'Did too.' I nodded firmly and drifted into the kitchen, where I managed to sneak Krista some sort of carbonated drink that she really enjoyed. She probably wasn't supposed to have it. Then I wandered around the house, from time to time retreating to my room and shutting the door for ten minutes. (That was the length of time, I'd found from trial and error, before someone missed me and came to see how I was, what I was doing.)

Varena popped her head in my door about 12:45 to ask me if I'd go with her to the doctor's. 'I need to go in to pick up my birth-control pill prescription, but I want Dr LeMay to check my ears. The right one is feeling a little achy, and I'm scared it'll be a full-blown infection by the wedding day. Binnie said come on in, he'd see me before the afternoon patients stacked up.'

One of the perks of being a nurse was the quick in-and-out you got at the local doctors' offices, Varena had told me years ago. As long as I could remember, Varena had suffered from allergies, which frequently caused ear infections. She had always developed them at the most inconvenient times. Like four days before her wedding.

I followed her out to her car with a sense of release. 'I know you need to get out of the house,' Varena said, giving me a little sideways glance. We pulled out of the driveway and began the short hop to Dr LeMay's office.

'Is it that obvious?'

'Only to someone who knows you,' Varena said ruefully. 'Yes, Lily, it's like seeing a tiger in a cage at the zoo. Back and forth, back and forth, giving all the people who walk by that ferocious stare.'

'Surely not that bad,' I said anxiously. 'I don't want to upset them.'

'I know you don't. And I'm glad to see you caring.'

'I never stopped.'

'You could have fooled me.'

'I just didn't have the extra . . .' Staying sane had taken all the energy I had. Trying to reassure other people had been simply impossible.

'I think I understand, finally,' Varena said. 'I'm sorry I brought it up. Mom and Dad know, better than me, that you care about them.'

I was being forgiven for something I hadn't done, or at least had done only in Varena's opinion. But she was making an effort. I would make an effort, too.

Dr LeMay was still based in the same little building in which he'd practiced medicine his entire career, all forty years of it. He must be nearing retirement age, his nurse Binnie Armstrong, too. They'd been a team for twenty-five years, I figured.

Varena pulled into one of the angled parking spots, and we went down the narrow sidewalk to the front door. A matching door, the one that had been labeled 'Blacks Only' at the beginning of Dr LeMay's practice, had been replaced by a picture window. In the past five years, a set of bars had been installed across the vulnerable glass. Kind of wrapped up Bartley's history in a nut-shell, I decided.

The door had been painted blue to match the eaves, but the paint had already chipped to show a long-familiar shade of green underneath. I twisted the knob and pushed, stepping in ahead of Varena.

The little building was oddly silent. No phones ringing, no copier running, no radio playing, no piped-in music.

I turned to look at my sister. Something was wrong. But Varena's gaze slid away from mine. She wasn't going to admit it, yet.

'Binnie!' she called too cheerfully. 'Lily and I are here! Come see her.' She stared at the closed door on the other side of the waiting room, the door leading back to the examining rooms and offices. The glass that enclosed the receptionist's cubicle remained empty.

We heard a faint, terrible sound. It was the sound of someone dying. I had heard it before.

I took six steps across the waiting room and opened the second door. The familiar hall, with three rooms to the right and three rooms to the left, was now floored with imitation wood-pattern linoleum instead of the speckled beige pattern I remembered, I thought incongruously.

Then I noticed the advancing rivulet of blood, the only move-ment in the hall. I traced it, not really wanting to find the source, but in that small space it was all too obvious. A woman in a once-white uniform lay in the doorway of the middle room on the right.

'Binnie,' screamed Varena, her hands flying up to her face. But then my sister remembered that she was a nurse, and she was instantly on her knees by the bloody woman. It was hard to discern the contours of Binnie Armstrong's face and head, she was so bludgeoned. It was from her throat the noise had come.

While Varena knelt by her, trying to take her pulse, Binnie Armstrong died. I watched her whole body relax in final abandonment.

I glanced in the door to the right, the one to the receptionist's little office. Clean and empty. I looked in the room to the left, an examining room. Clean and empty. I moved carefully down the hall, while my sister did CPR on the dead nurse, and I cautiously craned around the door of the next room on the left, another examining room. Empty. The doorway Binnie lay in led to the tiny lab and storage room. I stepped carefully past my sister and found Dr LeMay in the last room to the right, his office.

'Varena,' I said sharply.

Varena looked up, dabbled with blood from the corpse.

'Binnie's dead, Varena.' I nodded in the direction of the office. 'Come check Dr LeMay.'

Varena leaped to her feet and took a couple of steps to stare in the door. Then she was moving to the other side of the desk to take his pulse but shaking her head as she went.

'He was killed at his desk,' she said, as though that made it worse.

Dr LeMay's white hair was clotted with blood. It was pooled on the desk where his head lay. His glasses were askew, ugly black-framed trifocals, and I wanted so badly to set them square on his face – as if, when I did, he would see again. I had known Dr LeMay my whole life. He had delivered me.

Varena touched his hand, which was resting on the desk. I noticed in a stunned, slow way that it was absolutely clean. He had not had a chance to fight back. The first blow had been a devastating one. The room was full of paper, files and claim forms and team physicals . . . most of it now spotted with blood.

'He's gone,' Varena whispered, not that there had been any doubt.

'We need to get out of here,' I said, my voice loud and sharp in the little room with its awful sights and smells.

And we stared at each other, our eyes widening with a sudden shared terror.

I jerked my head toward the front door, and Varena scooted past me. She ran out while I waited to see if anything moved.

I was the only live person in the office.

I followed Varena out.

She was already across the street at the State Farm Insurance office, pulling open the glass door and lifting the receiver off the phone on the receptionist's desk. That stout and permed lady, wearing a bright red blouse and a Christmas corsage, was looking up at Varena as if she were speaking Navaho into the telephone. Within two minutes a police car pulled up in front of Dr LeMay's office, and a tall, thin black man got out.

'You the one called in?' he asked.

'My sister, in the office over there.' I nodded toward the plate-glass window, through which Varena could be seen sitting in the client's chair, sobbing. The woman with the corsage was bending over her, offering Varena some tissues.

'I'm Detective Brainerd,' the man said reassuringly, as though I'd indicated I'd thought he might be an imposter. 'Did you go in the building here?'

'Yes.'

'Did you see Dr LeMay and his nurse?'

'Yes.'

'And they're dead.'

'Yes.'

'Is there anyone else in the building?'

'No.'

'So, is there a gas leak, or was there a fire smoldering, maybe smoke inhalation . . . ?'

'They were both beaten.' My gaze skimmed the top of the old, old gum trees lining the street. 'To death.'

'Okay, now. I'll tell you what we're going to do here.'

He was extremely nervous, and I didn't blame him one bit.

'You're gonna stay right here, ma'am, while I go in there and take a look. Don't go anywhere, now.'

'No.'

I waited by the police car, the cold gray day pinching my face and hands.

This is a world of carnage and cruelty: I had momentarily put that aside in the false security of my hometown, in the optimistic atmosphere of my sister's marriage.

I began to detach from the scene, to float away, escaping this town, this building, these dead. It had been a long time since I'd retreated like this, gone to the remote place where I was not responsible for feeling.

A young woman was standing in front of me in a paramedic's uniform.

'Ma'am? Ma'am? Are you all right?' Her dark, anxious face peered into mine, her black hair stiff, smooth, and shoulder length under a cap with a caduceus patch on it.

'Yes.'

'Officer Brainerd said you had seen the bodies.'

I nodded.

'Are you . . . maybe you better come sit down over here, ma'am.'.

My eyes followed her pointing finger to the rear of the ambulance.

'No, thanks,' I said politely. 'My sister is over there in the State Farm office, though. She might need help.'

'I think you may need a little help yourself, ma'am,' the woman said earnestly, loudly, as though I was retarded, as though I couldn't tell the difference between clinical shock and just being numb.

'No.' I said it as finally and definitely as I knew how. I waited. I heard her muttering to someone else, but she did leave me alone after that. Varena came to stand beside me. Her eyes were red, and her makeup was streaked.

'Let's go home,' she said.

'The policeman told me to wait.'

'Oh.'

Just then the same policeman, Brainerd, came striding out of the doctor's office. He'd gotten over his fit of nerves, and he'd seen the worst. He was focused, ready to go to work. He asked us a lot of questions, keeping us out in the cold for half an hour when we'd told him the sum of our knowledge in one minute.

Finally, we buckled up in Varena's car. As she started back to our parents' house, I switched Varena's heater to full blast. I glanced over at my sister. Her face was blanched by the cold, her eyes red from crying with her contacts in. She'd pulled her hair back this morning in a ponytail, with a bright red scarf tied over the elastic band. The scarf still looked crisp and cheerful, though Varena had wilted. Varena's eyes met mine while we were waiting our turn at a four-way stop. She said, 'The drug cabinet was closed and full.'

'I saw.' Dr LeMay had always kept the samples, and his supplies, in the same cabinet in the lab, a glass-front old-fashioned one. Since I'd been his patient as a child, that cabinet had stood in the same place with the same sort of contents. It would have surprised me profoundly if Dr LeMay had ever kept anything very street-desirable . . . he'd have antibiotics, antihistamines, skin ointments, that kind of thing, I thought vaguely. Maybe painkillers.

Like Varena, I'd seen past Binnie's body that the cabinet door was shut and everything in the room was orderly. It didn't seem likely that the same person who would commit such messy murders would leave the drug cabinet so neat if he'd searched it.

'I don't know what to make of that,' I told Varena. She shook her head. She didn't, either. I stared out of the window at the familiar passing scenery, wishing I was anywhere but in Bartley.

'Lily, are you all right?' Varena asked, her voice curiously hesitant.

'Sure, are you?' I sounded more abrupt than I'd intended.

'I have to be, don't I? The wedding rehearsal is tonight, and I don't see how we can call it off. Plus, I've seen worse, frankly. It's just it being Dr LeMay and Binnie that gave me such a wallop.'

My sister sounded simply matter-of-fact. It hit me forcefully that Varena, as a nurse, had seen more blood and pain and awfulness than I see in a lifetime. She was practical. After overcoming the initial shock, she was tough. She pulled into our parents' driveway and switched off the ignition.

'You're right. You can't call it off. People die all the time, Varena, and you can't derail your wedding because of it.'

We were just the Practical Sisters.

'Right,' she said, looking at me oddly. 'We have to go in and tell Mom and Dad.'

I stared at the house in front of us as if I had never seen it.

'Yes. Let's go.'

But it was Varena who got out of the car first. And it was Varena who told my parents the bad news, in a grave, firm voice that somehow implied that any emotional display would be in bad taste.

Chapter Three

The rehearsal was scheduled for six o'clock, and we arrived at the Presbyterian church on the dot. Tootsie Monahan was already there, her hair in long curly strands like a show poodle's, talking and laughing with Dill and his best man. It was apparent that no one was going to talk about the death of the doctor and his nurse, unless they went into a corner and whispered. Everyone was struggling to keep this a joyous occasion, or at the very least to hold the emotional level above grim.

I was introduced to Berry Duff, Dill's former college roommate and present best man, with some significance. After all, we were both single and in the same age group. The barely unspoken hope was that something might happen.

Berry Duff was very tall, with thinning dark hair, wide dark eyes, and an enviable olive complexion. He was a farmer in Mississippi, had been divorced for about three years, and, I was given to understand, the embodiment of all things desirable: well-to-do, solid, religious, divorced without child custody. Dill managed to cram a surprising amount of that information into his introduction, and after a few minutes' conversation with Berry, I learned the rest.

Berry seemed like a nice guy, and it was pleasant to stand with him while we waited for the players to assemble. I was not much of a person for small talk, and Berry didn't seem to mind, which was refreshing. He took his time poking around conversationally for some common ground, found it in dislike of movie theaters and love of weight lifting, which he'd enjoyed in college.

I was wearing the white dress with the black jacket. At the last minute my mother had insisted I needed some color besides my lipstick, a point I was willing to concede. She'd put a filmy scarf in autumn reds and golds around my neck and anchored it with the gold pin I'd brought.

'You look very nice,' Dill said, on one of his pass-bys. He and Varena seemed to be awfully nervous and were inventing errands to send them pacing around the small church. We were all hovering near the front, since the back was in darkness beyond the pews. The door close to the pulpit, opening into a hall leading past the minister's study, gave a pneumatic hiss as people came and went. The heavier door beyond the big open area at the back of the church thudded from time to time as the members of the wedding party assembled.

Finally, everyone was there. Varena; Tootsie; me; the other bridesmaid, Janna Russell; my mother and father; Jess and Lou O'Shea, the one in his capacity as minister and the other in her capacity as church organist; Dill; Berry Duff; Dill's unmarried younger brother Jay; a cousin of Dill's, Matthew Kingery; the florist who'd been hired to supply the wedding flowers, who would double as wedding director; and miracle of miracles, Dill's mother, Lula. Watching the relief spread over Varena's face as the old woman stomped in on Jay's arm made me want to take Lula Kingery aside and have a few sharp words with her.

I watched the woman closely while the florist was giving the assembled group some directions. It didn't take long to conclude that Dill's mother was a few bricks short of a load. She was inappropriately dressed (a short-sleeved floral housedress with a hole in it, high heels with rhinestone buckles), which was in itself no clear signal of mental derangement, but when you added the ensemble to her out-of-the-ballpark questions ('Do I have to walk down the aisle too?') and her constant hand and eye movement, the sum total was significant.

Well. So Dill's family had a skeleton too.

Notch one up for my family. At least I could pretty much be relied on to do the right thing, if I actually made an appearance. Dill's mom was definitely a loose cannon.

Varena was handling Mrs Kingery with amazing tact and kindness. So were my parents. I felt a proprietary swell of pride at my folks' goodness and had to resume my conversation with Berry Duff to cover the rush of emotion.

After even more last-minute toing and froing, the rehearsal began. Patsy Green, the florist, gathered us together and gave us our marching orders. We took our positions to walk through the ceremonial paces.

Getting the cues straight from Lou O'Shea on the organ, an usher escorted Mrs Kingery to her place at the front of the church. Then my mother was guided to her front pew on the other side.

While I clustered with the other bridesmaids at the back of the church, Jess O'Shea came in from the hall that ran in front of his office to the church sanctuary. He went to the top of the steps in front of the altar and stood there smiling. Dill entered the sanctuary from the same door, accompanied by Berry, who grinned at me. Patsy Green issued last-minute instructions. 'Hold the book at this angle. Walk *smoothly* and *slowly*.'

I always walk smoothly.

She reminded me to smile.

Jay Kingery came in from the hall, and Janna started down the aisle. Then the groomsman, cousin Matthew, took his place, and Tootsie did her long walk. I set off on cue, with Patsy Green hissing 'Smile!' at my back.

Then the pièce de résistance. Varena came down the aisle on my father's arm, and she looked flushed and happy. So did Dad. Dill was beaming like a fool at his bride. Berry raised an eyebrow at me, and I felt my mouth twitch in response.

'That went well!' Patsy Green called from the back of the church. She began walking toward us, and we all turned to listen to her comments. I wasn't at all surprised it had fallen into place, since almost everyone in the party was old enough to have played a role in a score of weddings and been a major participant in a daunting number.

My attention drifted, and I began looking around the church, the one I'd attended every Sunday as a child. The walls always seemed newly painted a brilliant white, and the carpet was always replaced with the same deep green as the cushions on the pews.

The high ceiling always made me think *up* – space, infinity, the omnipotent unknown.

I heard a little cough and brought my gaze down from the infinite to stare into the pews. Someone was in the shadows at the back of the church. My heart started pounding in an uncomfortable way. Before I had formed a thought, I began to walk down the steps and the long strip of green carpet. I didn't even feel my feet moving.

He stood up and moved to the door.

At the moment I reached him, he opened the door for me, and we stepped out into the cold night. In one move, he pulled me to him and kissed me.

'Jack,' I said when I could breathe, 'Jack.'

My hands went under his suit coat to touch his back through his striped shirt.

He kissed me again. His hands tightened on me, pressed me harder against his body.

'Glad to see me,' I observed after a while. My breathing was not even.

'Yeah,' he said hoarsely.

I pulled away a little to look at him. 'You're wearing a tie.'

'I knew you'd be dressed up. I had to look as nice as you.'

'You a psychic detective?'

'Just a damn good one.'

'Umhum. What are you doing in Bartley?'

'You don't think I'm here just to see you?'

'No.'

'You're almost wrong.'

'Almost?' I felt a mixture of relief and disappointment.

'Yes, ma'am. Last week, I was clearing off my desk so I could come down here to lend you some moral support – or maybe morale support – when I got a call from an old friend of mine.'

'And?'

'Can I tell you later? Say, at my motel room?'

'That *was* your car I saw! How long have you been here?' For a moment I wondered if Jack had revealed his presence just because he'd figured I'd identify his car sooner or later, in a town the size of Bartley.

'Since yesterday. Later? God, you look good,' he said, and his mouth traveled down my neck. His fingers pulled the scarf away from my neck. Despite the cold, I began to have that warmth that meant I was just as glad to see him, especially after the horrors of the day.

'OK, I'll come by to hear your story, but it'll have to be after the rehearsal dinner,' I said firmly. I gasped a second later. 'No, Jack. This is my sister's wedding. This is a have-to.'

'I admire a woman who sticks to her principles.' His voice was low and rough.

'Will you come in and meet my family?'

'That's why I'm wearing the suit.'

I looked up at him with some suspicion. Jack is a little older than I am and four inches taller. In the security lights of the church parking lot, I could see that he had his black hair brushed back into a neat ponytail, as usual. He has a beautiful thin, prominent nose, and his lips are thin and sculpted. Jack used to be a Memphis policeman, until he left the force after his involvement in an unsavory and bloody scandal.

He's got lips, he knows how to use 'em, I thought, almost intoxicated by his presence. Only Jack could get me in the mood to paraphrase an old ZZ Top song.

'Let's go do the right thing, before I try something here in the parking lot,' he suggested.

I stared at him and turned to walk back in the church. Somehow, I expected him to vanish between the door and the altar, but he followed me in and down the aisle, flanking me when we reached the clustered wedding party. Naturally enough, they were all staring our way. I could feel my face harden. I hate explaining myself.

And Jack stepped up beside me, put his arm around me, and said, 'You must be Lily's mother! I'm Jack Leeds, Lily's . . .'

I waited with some interest while Jack, normally a smooth talker, floundered at the end of the sentence.

'Boyfriend,' he finished, with a certain inaccuracy.

'Frieda Bard,' my mother said, looking a little stunned. 'This is my husband, Gerald.'

'Mr Bard,' Jack said respectfully, 'glad to meet you.'

My father pumped Jack's hand, beaming like someone who's just found Ed McMahon and a camera crew on his doorstep. Even the ponytail and the scar on Jack's right cheek didn't diminish my father's smile. Jack's suit was expensive, a very muted brown plaid that brought out the color of his hazel eyes. His shoes were polished. He looked prosperous, healthy, clean shaven, and I looked happy. That was enough for my dad, at least for the moment.

'And you must be Varena.' Jack turned to my sister.

When would everyone stop looking like deer caught in head-lights? You'd think I was a damn leper, they were so amazed I had a man. Jack actually kissed Varena, a quick light one on the forehead. 'Kiss the bride for luck,' he said, with that sudden, brilliant smile that was so winning.

Dill recovered quickest.

'I'm about to join the family,' he told Jack. 'I'm Dill Kingery.'

'Pleased to meet you.' The shake again.

And it went on from there, with me not saying a word. Jack glad-handed the men and gave the women a flash of clean, earnest sexuality. Even off-kilter Mrs Kingery beamed at him in a dazed way. 'You're trouble on the hoof, and I know it,' she said firmly.

Everyone froze in horror, but Jack laughed with genuine amusement. The moment passed, and I saw Dill close his eyes in relief.

'I'll take off, since you're in the middle of your special occasion,' Jack told the group generally, with no hint of a hint in his voice. 'I just wanted to meet Lily's folks.'

'Please,' Dill said instantly, 'we'd really enjoy your joining us for the rehearsal dinner.'

Jack did the polite thing and declined, mentioning the import-ant family occasion and the fact that he had arrived unannounced.

Dill repeated his invitation. Social Ping-Pong.

When Varena joined in, Jack allowed himself to be persuaded.

He retired to sit at the back of the church. My eyes followed him every inch of the way.

We walked through the ceremony again. I went through my paces on autopilot. Patsy Green reminded me again to smile. This time she sounded a little sharper.

I was thinking hard during the rest of the rehearsal, but I couldn't come to any conclusion. Could it possibly be true that Jack was here for me? He had admitted he had another reason, but he'd said he was coming here anyway. If that was true . . .

But it was too painful to believe.

Jack had already been here when Dr LeMay and Binnie Armstrong were done to death. So his arrival couldn't be connected with the double murder.

'Looks like I'm too late on the scene,' Berry said to me in a pleasant way after Patsy Green and the O'Sheas agreed we had the procedure down pat. We were just outside the church doors.

'That's so flattering of you,' I said with a genuine smile. For once, I had said the right thing. He smiled back at me.

'Lily!' Jack called. He was holding open the passenger door of his car. I couldn't imagine why.

'Excuse me,' I told Berry and strolled over. 'Since when,' I muttered, conscious of my voice carrying in the cold clear air, 'have you found it necessary to hold doors for me?'

Jack looked wounded. 'Darlin', I'm your slave.' He seemed to be imitating Berry's Delta accent.

'Don't be an ass,' I whispered. 'Seeing you is so good. Don't ruin it.'

He stared down at me as I swung my legs into his car. The taut muscles around his mouth relaxed. 'All right,' he said and shut the door.

We backed up to follow the other cars out of the parking lot.

'You found the doctor today,' he said.

'Yes. How did you know?'

'I brought my police scanner. Are you OK?'

'Yes.'

'How much do you know about Dill Kingery?' he asked. I felt as though he'd punched me in the stomach. I had to sit silent to gather breath, my panic was so complete and sudden. 'Is something wrong with him?' I asked finally, my voice coming out not so much angry as scared. Varena's face smiling up at Dill came into my mind, the long engagement, the relationship Varena had worked so hard to build up with Dill's daughter, Varena's cheerful acceptance of crazy Mrs Kingery . . .

'Probably nothing. Just tell me.'

'He's a pharmacist. He's a widower. He's a father. He pays his bills on time. His mother is crazy.'

'That's the old biddy who said I was trouble?'

'Yes.' She was right.

'The first wife's been dead how long?'

'Six or seven years. Anna doesn't remember her.'

'And Jess O'Shea? The preacher?'

I looked over at Jack as we passed a streetlight. His expression was tense, almost angry. That made two of us. 'I don't know anything about him. I've met his wife and little girl. They have a boy, too.'

'He coming to the rehearsal dinner?'

'The minister usually does. Yes, I heard them say they'd gotten a sitter.'

I wanted to hit Jack, a not uncommon situation.

We pulled into Sarah May's Restaurant parking lot. Jack parked a little away from the other cars.

'I can't believe you've upset me this much in five minutes,' I said, hearing my own voice coming out distant and cold. And shaking.

He stared through the windshield at the restaurant windows. They were edged with flickering Christmas lights. The glow flashed across his face. *Damn* blinking lights. After what felt like a very long time, Jack turned to me. He took my left hand with his right.

'Lily, when I explain what I'm working on, you'll forgive me,' he said, with a kind of painful sincerity I was forced to respect. He sat holding my hand, making no move to open his door, waiting for me to extend him . . . trust? Advance absolution? I felt as if he'd opened a cavity in my chest and turned a spotlight on it.

I nodded sharply, opened my door, and got out. We met in front of the car. He took my hand again, and we went into Sarah May's.

Sarah Cawthorne, half of the Sarah May of the name, showed us to the private room that Dill had reserved for the party. Of course, all of us but Jack and Mrs Kingery had been in it many times, since it was one of two places in Bartley you could dine out privately. I saw that it had been recently carpeted and wallpapered in the apparently perpetually popular hunter green and burgundy, and the artificial Christmas tree in the corner had been decorated with burgundy and off-white lace and matching ribbons. This tree was lit, too, of course, draped with the small clear lights, and thank God they didn't blink.

The tables had Christmas centerpieces in the same colors, and the place mats were cloth and so were the napkins. (This was very swank for Bartley.) The U-shaped banquet arrangement hadn't changed, though, and as we all drifted to our seats I realized that Jack was maneuvering us toward the O'Sheas. He was steering me unobtrusively with his hand on my back, and I was reminded of a puppet sitting on a ventriloquist's knee, the controlling hand hidden in a hole in the puppet's back. Jack caught my look, and his hand dropped away.

Dill was already standing behind a chair with my sister on one side and his mother on the other, so only Jess O'Shea was available as a target.

Jack managed to slot us between the O'Sheas. I was between the two men, and to Jack's right was Lou. Across the table from us was Patsy Green, squired by one of the ushers, a banker who played golf with Dill, I remembered.

The salads were served almost immediately, and Dill properly asked Jess to say grace. Of course, Jess obliged. Next to me, Jack bowed his head and shut his eyes, but his hand found mine and his fingers wrapped tightly around mine. He brought my hand to his mouth and kissed it – I could feel his warm lips, the hint of teeth – then deposited the hand back in my lap and relaxed his grip. When Jess said, 'Amen,' Jack let go and spread his napkin on his lap as though the little moment had been a dream.

I glanced up and down the table to see if anyone had noticed, and the only eyes that met mine were my mother's. She looked as though she were half embarrassed by the sexuality of the gesture . . . but pleased by the emotional wallop of it.

I had no idea what my own face looked like. A salad was placed in front of me, and I stared down blindly at it. When the waitress asked me what dressing I wanted, I answered her at random, and she dolloped my lettuce and tomato with a bright orange substance.

Jack began gently questioning Lou about her life. He was so good at it that few civilians would have suspected he had a hidden agenda. I tried not to speculate on the nature of that agenda.

I turned to Jess, who was having a little trouble with a jar of bacon bits. After the nicely decorated room, plunking the jar of bits down on the table reminded me firmly we were in Bartley. I held out my hand with a give-me curve of the fingers.

Somewhat surprised, Jess handed me the jar. I gripped it firmly, inhaled. I twisted as I exhaled. The lid came off. I handed the jar to him.

When I looked up in his face, there was a kind of dubious amusement on it.

Dubious was OK. Amusement wasn't.

'You're very strong,' he observed.

'Yes,' I said. I took a bite of salad, then remembered that Jack needed to know more about this man.

'Did you grow up in a town bigger than Bartley?' I asked.

'Oh, not bigger at all,' he said genially. 'Ocolona, Mississippi. My folks still live there.'

'And your wife, is she from Mississippi also?'

I hated this.

'Yes, but from Pass Christian. We met in college at Ole Miss.'

'And then you went to seminary?'

'Yes, four years at Westminister Theological Seminary in Philadelphia. Lou and I just had to put our trust in the Lord. It was a long separation. In fact, after the first two years, I missed being away from her so much, we got married. She held any job she could get in the area while I worked to graduate. She played the organ at churches, she played the piano for parties. She even worked at a fast-food place, God bless her.' Jess's square, handsome face relaxed and warmed as he talked about his wife. I felt acutely uncomfortable.

The salad dressing was thick as sour cream, and sweet. I shoved the most heavily laden lettuce to one side and tried to eat the rest. I couldn't just sit there and question him.

'And you,' he began the conversational return, 'what's your occupation?'

Someone who didn't know my life history?

'I'm a house cleaner, and I run errands for people. I decorate Christmas trees for businesses. I take old ladies grocery shopping.'

'A girl Friday, though I guess "girl" is politically incorrect now.' He gave the strained smile of a conservative paying lip service to liberality.

'Yes,' I said.

'And you live in Arkansas?'

'Yes.' I prodded myself mentally. 'Shakespeare.'

'Any bigger than Bartley?'

'Yes.'

He eyed me with a determined smile. 'And have you lived there long?'

'Over four years now. I bought a house.' There, that was contributing to the conversation. What did Jack want to know about this man?

'What do you do in your spare time?'

'I work out. Lifting weights. And I take karate.' And now I see Jack. The thought sent a warm rush through my pelvis. I remembered his lips against my hand.

'And your friend Mr Leeds? Does he live in Shakespeare?'

'No, Jack lives in Little Rock.'

'He works there, too?'

Did Jack want it known what he did?

'His job takes him different places,' I said neutrally. 'Did Lou have Luke – isn't that your little boy's name? – here in the Shakespeare hospital?' People really like to talk about their child-birth experiences.

'Yes, right here at the hospital. We were a little worried . . . there are some emergencies this hospital can't handle. But Lou is healthy, and indications were that the baby was healthy, so we decided it would be better to show our faith in the local people. And it was just a great experience.'

Lucky for you and Luke and Lou, I thought. 'And Krista?' I asked, thinking this meal would never end. We hadn't even gotten our entrees. 'Did you have her here? No, she's at least eight, and you've been here only three years, I believe?'

'Right. No, we moved here from Philadelphia with Krista.' But something about the way he said it was odd.

'She was born at one of the big hospitals there? That must have been a very different experience from having your little boy here.'

He said, 'Are you older than Varena?'

Whoa. Change of subject. And a clumsy one. Anyone could tell I was older than Varena.

'Yes.'

'You must have traveled around some in your life, too,' the minister observed. The strip lights above the table winked off his blond hair, about ten shades darker than mine and certainly more natural. 'You've been in Shakespeare for about four years . . . did you ever live here, in Bartley, after you got out of college?'

'I lived in Memphis, after I graduated from college,' I said, knowing that would probably cue his memory. Someone had to have told him the story, since he'd been living here more than three years. My history was part of town folklore, just like Mrs Fontenot shooting her equally married lover on the courthouse lawn in 1931.

'Memphis,' he repeated, suddenly looking a little uneasy.

'Yes, I worked for a big housecleaning service there as a scheduler and supervisor,' I said deliberately.

That flipped his memory switch. I saw his pleasant, bland face grow rigid, trying to restrain his dismay at his faux pas.

'Of course, that was years ago, now,' I said, easing him off the horns of the dilemma.

'Yes, a long time,' he said. He looked sorry for me for a minute, then said tactfully, 'I haven't had a chance to ask Dill where he and Varena plan to go on their honeymoon.'

I nodded dismissively and turned to Jack just at the instant he turned to me. Our eyes met, and he smiled that smile that altered his whole face, deep arcs appearing from his nose to his lips. Instead of the tough reserve of his defense-against-the-world face, he looked infectiously happy.

I leaned over so my lips almost touched his ear. 'I have an early Christmas present for you,' I said very softly.

His eyes flared wide in surmise.

'You'll like it very much,' I promised, breathing the words.

During the rest of the meal, whenever Jack wasn't engaged in talking to Lou O'Shea or charming my mother, he was giving me little glances full of speculation.

We left soon after the dessert plates were cleared away. Jack seemed torn between talking to Dill and Varena and rushing me back to his hotel. I made it as difficult for him as I possibly could. As we stood making conversation with Dill, I held his hand and made circles on his palm with my thumb, very gently, very lightly.

After a few seconds, he dropped my hand to grip my arm almost painfully.

'Good-bye, Frieda, Gerald,' he said to my parents, after he'd thanked Dill for inviting him. My mother and father beamed happily at him. 'I'll be bringing Lily home later. We have some catching up to do.'

I could see my father's mouth open to ask where this 'catching up' would take place, and I saw my mother's elbow connect with his ribs, a gentle reminder to my father that I was nearly thirty-two. So Dad kept his smile in place, but it was weaker.

Waving at everyone, smiling hard, we got out the door and hurried through the freezing air to scramble into Jack's car. We had scarcely shut the doors when Jack put his fingers under my chin and turned my face to his. His mouth covered mine in a long, breathless kiss. His hands began reacquainting themselves with my topography.

'The others'll be coming out in a minute,' I reminded him.

Jack said something really vile and turned on his engine. We drove to the motel in silence, Jack keeping both hands on the wheel and his eyes straight ahead.

'This place is horrible,' he warned me, unlocking the door and pushing it open. He reached in past me to switch on a light.

I pulled the drapes shut all the way and turned to him, sliding out of my black jacket as I turned. He was wrapped around me before I had my arm out of the second sleeve. We undressed in stages, interrupted by the long making out that Jack loved. He was fumbling in his suitcase with one hand for those little square foil packages, when I said, 'Christmas present.'

He raised his eyebrows.

'I got an implant. You don't have to use anything.'

'Oh, Lily,' he breathed, closing his eyes to savor the moment. He looked like a Boy Scout who'd just been given the ingredients for S'mores. I wondered when he would work out the other implications of my gift. Then Jack slid on top of me, and I quit caring.

We were wrapped in the bed together an hour later, having finally pulled down the spread and the blanket and the sheets. The sheets, at least, looked clean. One of Jack's legs was thrown across mine, securing me.

'Why are you here?' I asked. This was when Jack liked to talk.

'Lily,' he said slowly, taking pleasure in saying it. 'I was going to come to see you here. I did think you might need me, or at least that seeing me might help.' One long finger traced my spine as I lay facing him, my face tucked in the hollow of his neck. To my horror, I could feel my nose clog up and my eyes fill. I kept my face turned down. A tear trickled down my cheek, and since I was on my side it ran into the curve of one nostril and then underneath. So elegant.

'And then Roy called me. You remember Roy?'

I nodded, so he could feel my head move.

I recalled Roy Costimiglia as a short, stout man with thinning gray hair, probably in his late fifties. You could pass him six times on the street and never remember you'd seen him before. Roy was the detective with whom Jack had served his two-year apprenticeship.

'Roy and I had talked over supper one night when Roy's wife was out of town, so he knew I was seeing a woman who had originally come from Bartley. He called because he'd been given one more lead to run down in a case he's had for four years.'

I surreptitiously wiped my face with a bit of sheet.

'What case is that?' My voice did not sound too wobbly.

'Summer Dawn Macklesby.' Jack's voice was as bleak and grim as I'd ever heard it. 'You remember the baby girl who was kidnapped?'

And I felt cold all over again.

'I read just a little of the update story in the paper.'

'So did a lot of people, and one of them reacted pretty strangely. The last paragraph of the article mentioned that Roy has been working for the Macklesby family for the past few years. Through Roy, the Macklesbys had run down every lead, checked every piece of information, every rumor, that's come to them for the past four and a half years . . . ever since they felt the police had more or less given up on the case. The Macklesbys hoped there would be some response to the story, and that's why they consented to do it. They're really nice people. I've met them. Of course, they've kind of disintegrated since she's been gone . . . the baby.'

Jack kissed my cheek, and his arms tightened around me. He knew I had been crying. He was not going to talk about it.

'What response was there to the story? A phone call?'

'This.' Jack sat up on the side of the bed. He unlocked his briefcase and pulled out two pieces of paper. The first was a copy of the same article I'd seen in the newspaper, with the sad picture of the Macklesbys now and the old picture of the baby in her infant seat. The Macklesbys looked as though something had chewed them up and spit them out: Teresa Macklesby, especially, was haggard with eyes that had seen hell. Her husband, Simon's, face was almost taut with restraint, and the hand that rested on his knee was clenched in a fist.

The second piece of paper was a picture from the local elementary school memory book, last year's edition; 'The Bartley Banner' was printed, with the date, across the top of the page, page 23. The picture at the top of the page, below the heading, was an enlarged black-and-white snapshot of three little girls playing on a slide. The one flying down, her long hair trailing behind her, was Eve Osborn. The girl waiting her turn at the top of the slide was Krista O'Shea, looking much happier than I'd seen her. The child climbing the ladder had turned to smile at the camera, and my breath caught in my throat.

The caption read, 'These second graders enjoy the new play-ground equipment donated in March by Bartley Tractor and Tire Company and Choctaw County Welding.'

'This was paper-clipped to the article from the paper,' Jack said. 'It was in a mailing envelope postmarked Bartley. Someone here in town thinks one of these little girls is Summer Dawn Macklesby.'

'Oh, no.'

His finger brushed the third child's face. 'Dill's girl? Anna Kingery?'

I nodded, covered my own face with my hands.

'Sweetheart, I have to do this.'

'Why did you come instead of Roy?'

'Because Roy had a heart attack two days ago. He called me from his hospital bed.'

Chapter Four

'Is he going to be ok?'

'I don't know,' Jack said. He was sad, and angry, too, though I wasn't sure where the anger came in. Maybe his own helplessness. 'All those years of eating wrong and not exercising . . . but the main thing is, he just has a bad heart.'

I sat up, too, and put my arms around Jack. For a moment he accepted the comfort. He rested his head on my shoulder, his arms encircling me. I'd taken the band off his ponytail, and his long black hair fell soft against my skin. But then he raised his head and looked at me, our faces inches apart.

'I have to do this, Lily. For Roy. He took me in and trained me. If it was anyone but him, any case but one involving a child, I'd turn it down since it concerns someone close to you . . . but this I have to do.' Even if Anna Kingery turned out to be Summer Dawn Macklesby, even if Varena's life was ruined. I looked back at him, the pain in my heart so complicated I could not think how to express it.

'If he did that,' Jack said, so intent on me he had read my silent thoughts, 'you couldn't let her marry him anyway.'

I nodded, still trying to accommodate this sharp pang. For all the years we'd spent apart, for all our estrangement, Varena was my sister, and we were the only people in the world who shared, who would remember, our common family life.

'This has to be resolved before the wedding,' I said.

'Two days? Three?'

I actually had to think. 'Three.'

'Shit,' Jack said.

'What do you have?' I pulled, away from him, and his head

began to lower to my breasts, as if drawn by a magnet. I grabbed his ears. 'Jack, we have to finish talking.'

'Then you'll have to cover up.' He got his bathrobe out of the tiny closet and tossed it to me. It was the one he carried when he traveled, a thin, red, silky one, and I belted it around me.

'That's not much better,' he said after a thorough look. 'But it'll have to do.' He pulled on a T-shirt and some Jockeys. He set his briefcase on the bed, and because it was cold in that bleak motel room, we both crawled back under the covers, sitting with our backs propped against the wall.

Jack put on his reading glasses, little half-lens ones that made him even sexier. I didn't know how long he'd used them, but he'd only recently begun wearing them in front of me. This was the first time I hadn't appreciated the effect.

'First, to find out who the little girls were, Roy hired Aunt Betty.'

'Who?'

'You haven't met Aunt Betty yet. She's another PI, lives in Little Rock. She's amazing. In her fifties, hair dyed a medium brown, looks respectable to the core. She looks like everybody's Aunt Betty. Her real name is Elizabeth Fry. People tell her the most amazing things, because she looks like . . . well, their aunt! And damn, that woman can listen!'

'Why'd Roy send her instead of you?'

'Well, surprise, but in some situations I don't blend in like Aunt Betty does. I was good for the Shakespeare job since I look just like someone who'd work in a sporting goods store, but I don't look like I could go around a small town asking for the names of little girls and get away with it. Right?'

I tried not to laugh. That was certainly true.

'So that's the kind of job Aunt Betty's perfect for. She found out who prints the most school memory books in the state, went to them, told them she was from a private school and she was looking for a printer. The guy gave her all kinds of samples to show her parents committee.'

Jack seemed to want me to acknowledge Aunt Betty's clever-ness, so I nodded.

'Then,' he continued, 'Betty comes down to Bartley, goes in to see the elementary school principal, shows her all the samples of memory books she has, and tells the principal she works for a printing company that can give them a competitive bid on the next memory book.'

'And?'

'Then she asks to see this year's Bartley memory book, notices the slide picture, asks the principal who the photographer was, maybe her company might be able to use him for extra work. Betty figured the shot was good enough to justify the lie.'

I shook my head. Betty must be persuasive and totally re-spectable and nonthreatening. I'd known the elementary school principal, Beryl Trotter, for fifteen years, and she was not a fool.

'How does it help, having the whole book?' I asked.

'If worst had come to worst, we would have looked at all the faces in the class section until we had them matched, so we could get their names. Or Betty would have called on the man who took the picture and coasted the conversation along until he told her who the girls were. But, as it happened, Mrs Trotter asked Betty to have a cup of coffee, and Betty found out everything from Mrs Trotter.'

'The names of the girls? Their parents? Everything?'

'Yep.'

This was a little frightening.

'So, once we had the names of the parents, we were able to do some background on the O'Sheas, since he's a minister and they have several professional directories that give little biographies. Dill, too, because the pharmacists have a state association. Chock full of information. The Osborns were harder. Aunt Betty had to go to Makepeace Furniture, pretend she'd just moved in and was shopping for a new table. It was risky. But she managed to talk to Emory, find out a few things about him, and get out without having to give a local address or mention any local relatives whom he could check up on.'

'So then you knew the names of the girls and their parents, and some facts about their parents.'

'Yep. Then we got busy on the computers, and then I started traveling.'

I felt overwhelmed. I'd never talked to Jack in any depth about what he did. I'd never fully realized that one of the qualifications for a successful private detective is the ability to lie convincingly and at the drop of a hat. I pulled away from Jack a little. He took some papers from his briefcase.

'This is a computer-enhanced drawing of Summer Dawn as she may look now,' he said, apparently not conscious of my unhappiness. 'Of course, we have photographs of her only as an infant. Who knows how accurate this is?'

I looked at the picture. It looked like someone, all right, but it could have been any of the girls. I decided that the drawing looked most like Krista O'Shea, because it depicted Summer Dawn still plump-cheeked, like the baby snapshot the newspaper had printed.

'I thought these were supposed to be really accurate,' I said. 'Does it look so anonymous because she was a baby when she vanished?'

'Partly. And as it happens, none of the pictures of Summer Dawn was really good to use for this. The Macklesbys took fewer pictures of her than of their other two children because Summer Dawn was the third child, and the third child just doesn't get photographed as much as number one and number two. The picture that appeared in the newspaper was really the best one the parents had. They had an appointment to get Summer's picture made the week she disappeared.'

I didn't want to think about that. I shuffled the top drawing, looked at the other three. The second was of the same face but framed by long, straight hair. In the third, a somewhat thinner-cheeked version of Summer Dawn was topped with short, wavy hair. There was a fourth, with medium-length hair and glasses.

'One of her sisters is nearsighted,' Jack explained.

Eight years.

'She has sisters?' I kept my voice level. At least I tried.

'Yeah. Two. They're fourteen and sixteen, now. Teenagers, with posters on their walls of musicians I've never listened to. Closets full of clothes. Boyfriends. And a little sister they don't remember at all.'

'The Macklesbys must have money.' Hiring a private detective for all those years would be expensive, and paying for the extra services of Aunt Betty and Jack.

'They're well-off. Simon Macklesby reacted to the kidnapping by throwing himself into his work. He's a partner in an office supplies business that's taken off since offices became computerized. No matter how much money they've got, the Macklesbys were lucky they went to Roy instead of to someone who would really soak them. There were months when he didn't have anything to show them, no work to do. Some guys . . . and some women . . . would've made things up to pad the file.'

It was a relief to find that Roy was as honest as I'd always thought him, after Jack's obvious admiration at Aunt Betty's creative lying. There was a separation, thank God, between lying on the job and relating to people in real life.

'What do you *know*?' I asked him, my fear finally showing in my voice.

'I know that the O'Shea girl is adopted, at least that's what the O'Sheas' neighbors in Philadelphia recall.'

I remembered the slight change in Jess O'Shea's face when I'd asked him how the big-city hospital had been different from the tiny one in Bartley.

'You've been to Pennsylvania?'

'Their Philadelphia neighbors were seminary students like Jess, so naturally they've scattered. I've used other PIs in Florida, Kentucky, and Indiana. According to the people who'd talk to us, the O'Sheas arranged to adopt the baby girl of the sister of another seminary student. The O'Sheas had gotten a pretty discouraging work-up from a fertility specialist in Philadelphia. The sister had to give the baby up because she was in late-stage AIDS. Her family wouldn't take the baby because they believed the baby might be carrying the disease. It didn't matter that the baby had tested negative. In fact, the couple in Tennessee, the one I interviewed myself, are still convinced the little girl might have been "carrying" AIDS, despite the testing the doctors did.'

I shook my head. 'How do you get people to tell you this?'

'I'm persuasive, in case you hadn't noticed.' Jack ran his hand down my leg and leered at me. Then he sobered.

'So why are the O'Sheas still on your list?'

'One, Krista O'Shea is in the picture that Roy got. Two, what if this isn't the same girl they adopted?'

'What?'

'What if the tests were wrong? What if that child was born with AIDS, or died from some other cause? What if Lou O'Shea abducted Summer Dawn to take her place? What if the O'Sheas bought her?'

'That seems so far-fetched. They were up in Philadelphia for at least a few months after they adopted Krista. Summer Dawn was abducted in Conway, right?'

'Yes. But the O'Sheas have cousins living in the Conway area, cousins they visited when Jess finished the seminary. The dates coincide. So I can't rule them out. It's circumstantially possible. If they bought Summer Dawn from someone who abducted her, they would know that was illegal. They maybe pretended the baby was the one they'd adopted.'

'What about Anna?' I asked sharply.

'Judy Kingery, Dill's first wife, was mentally ill.'

I'd resumed studying the pictures. I turned to stare at Jack.

'Her auto accident was almost certainly suicide.' His clear hazel eyes peered at me over his reading glasses.

'Oh, poor Dill.' No wonder he'd taken his time dating Varena. He would be extra cautious after a hellish marriage like that, yoked to a woman with so many problems after his upbringing by a woman who was not exactly compos mentis.

'We can't be sure the wife didn't do something crazy. Maybe she killed their own baby and stole Summer Dawn as compensation. The Kingerys were living in Conway at the time the baby was taken. Maybe Judy Kingery snatched Summer Dawn and gave Dill some incredibly persuasive story.'

'You're saying . . . it might be possible that Dill didn't know?'

Jack shrugged. 'It's possible,' he said but not with any great conviction.

I blew out a deep breath of tension. 'OK, Eve Osborn.'

'The Osborns moved here from a little town on the interstate about ten miles from Conway. He's worked at furniture stores since he got out of junior college. Meredith Osborn didn't make it through a whole year of college before she married him. Emory Ted Osborn . . .' Jack was peering through his glasses at a page of notes. 'Emory sells furniture and appliances at Makepeace Furniture Center. Oh, I told you that when I told you Betty went to meet him there.'

Makepeace Furniture Center was Bartley's best. It sold only upscale furniture and appliances, and it was located on the town square, having gradually crept through two or three buildings on one side.

'Emory have any criminal record?'

Jack shook his head. 'None of these people do.'

'Surely there's something that excludes Eve Osborn?'

'You know her?'

'Yes, I do. The Osborns own the little place my sister lives in. It's right in back of their house.'

'I've driven by. I didn't realize your sister rented the cottage.'

'Did you know that Meredith Osborn babysits both Anna and Krista from time to time? I met the mother and the little girl, Eve, when I was at Varena's a couple of days ago.'

'What did you think?'

'There's a new baby, a girl. Mrs Osborn is about as big as some twelve-year-olds, and she seems nice enough. Eve is a . . . well, a little girl, maybe a little shy. Real thin, like her mother. I haven't met Emory.'

'He's small, too, thin and blond. He's got that really fair coloring, light blue eyes, invisible eyelashes. Looks like he still doesn't have to shave. Very reserved. Smiles a lot.'

'So, where was Eve born?'

'That's why she can't be eliminated. Eve was a home birth,' Jack said, both eyebrows raised as far as they could go. 'Emory delivered her. He'd had some paramedic training. The baby evidently came too fast for them to get to the hospital.'

'Meredith had the baby at her house?' Though I knew historically that women had been having their babies at home far longer than they'd had them in hospitals, the idea jarred me.

'Yep.' Jack's face expressed such distaste that I found myself hoping Jack was never trapped in a stalled elevator with a pregnant woman.

We stayed snuggled in the bed and each other's warmth a while more, talking ourselves in circles. I could not make this go away, and I could not stop Jack from investigating, even if I thought that right . . . which I didn't. I had tremendous pity for the anguished parents who had been wanting their child for so many years, and I had pity for my sister, whose life might be ruined in the three days before her wedding. There didn't seem to be anything I could do to affect the outcome of Jack's investigation.

It had been a long day.

I thought of the scene in the doctor's office, the devastation that had visited the two aging workhorses in their old office.

Wrapping my arms around my knees, I told Jack about Dr LeMay and Mrs Armstrong. He listened with close attention and asked me a lot more questions than I could answer.

'Do you think this could be connected with what you're investigating?' I asked.

'I don't see how.' He took off his glasses, put them on the night table. 'But it does seem like quite a coincidence that they're killed this week, just when I come on the scene, just when there's a new development in the Macklesby case. I've tried to be very discreet, but sooner or later in a town this size, everyone's gonna know why I'm here. You're providing me with cover right now, but it won't last if I ask the wrong questions.'

I looked at Jack's watch then and slid out of the bed. The room felt even colder after I'd been warmed by Jack. I wanted more than anything to lie beside him tonight, but I couldn't.

'I have to get back,' I said, pulling on my clothes and trying to make them look as neat and straight as they had been earlier.

Jack got out of bed, too, but not as rapidly.

'I guess you have to,' he said with an attempt at wistfulness.

'You know I have to go to their house tonight,' I said, but not harshly. He'd pulled his slacks on by then. I was putting on my jacket when he began kissing me again. I tried to push him away when he made his first pass, but at his second, I put my arms around him.

'I know that you having gotten the implant, me not using a condom anymore, means you know I'm sleeping only with you,' he told me.

It meant something else, too. 'Ah . . . it means I'm not sleeping with anyone else, either,' I reminded him.

After a moment of pregnant silence, he squeezed me so tightly I could not breathe, and he made an inarticulate noise. Suddenly I knew we were feeling exactly the same thing – just for a second, a flash, but it was a flash so bright it blinded me.

Then we had to bounce away from each other, frightened by the intimacy. Jack swung away to put on his shirt; I sat down to slide my feet into my shoes. I ran my fingers through my hair, took care of a button I'd skipped.

We were silent on the ride to my house, the bitter cold biting into our bones. When we pulled into the driveway I saw one light burning on the dimmest setting, in the living room. Jack leaned over to give me a quick kiss, and I was out of the car in a wink, running across the frosty lawn to the front door.

I locked the door behind me and went to the picture window. Looking out the small triangle unobscured by the Christmas tree, I saw Jack's car back out and start back to the motel. The sheets of his bed would smell like me.

Once in my room, where my mother had left a lamp on, I slowly undressed. It was too late to shower; it might wake my parents, if they weren't in their room lying awake to make sure I was home safe, like they'd done when I was a teenager. There was no counting the sleepless nights I'd given them.

Fleetingly, I thought about Teresa and Simon Macklesby. How many good nights' rest had they managed in the eight years since their daughter had vanished?

The murders of the doctor and his nurse, the strain of the wedding rehearsal, and the shock of all Jack had told me should have kept me awake. But being with Jack had drained the tension from me. Even if we hadn't had sex, I thought with some surprise, I would have felt better. I crawled in my bed, turned on my side, slid my hand under the pillow, and was immediately asleep.

The next day I had showered and dressed before I came out to have some coffee and breakfast. I'd done some situps and leg lifts in my room so I wouldn't feel like a slug the rest of the day. My parents were both at the table, sections of newspaper propped up, when I got a mug from the cabinet.

'Good morning,' my mother said with a smile.

My father grunted and nodded.

'How was your date last night?' Mother ventured when I was sitting with them.

'Fine,' I said. My toast popped up, and I put it on a plate.

Dad peered over his glasses at me. 'Got home late,' he observed.

'Yes.'

'How long you been dating this man? Your mother says you told her he was a private detective? Isn't that kind of dangerous?'

I answered the safest question. 'I've been dating him for a few weeks.'

'You think he might be serious?'

'Sometimes.'

My father regarded me with some exasperation. 'Now, what does that mean?'

'I think it means she doesn't want to answer any more questions, Gerald,' Mother said. She rubbed the bridge of her nose with her thumb and forefinger, hiding a little smile.

'A father needs to know about men who are seeing his girl,' my father said.

'This girl is almost thirty-two,' I reminded him, trying to keep my voice gentle.

He shook his head. 'I don't believe it. Why, that would make me *old*, gosh dog it!'

We all laughed as the little touchy moment passed.

Dad got up to shave, following his nearly invariable morning routine. He stuck his head back in the door just as I bit into my toast. 'Can you make any kind of living as a detective?' he asked, then hurried away before I could either laugh or throw my toast at him.

'The paper says,' my mother began when I'd finished my coffee, 'that Dave LeMay and Binnie Armstrong were killed right before you and Varena found them.'

'I thought so,' I said after a pause.

'You touched them?'

'Varena did. She's the nurse,' I said, reminding my mother that I was not the only one present when awful things happened.

'That's true,' my mother said slowly, as one who has received a revelation of which she's half proud, half dismayed. 'She has to deal with things like that all the time.'

'That bad or worse.' Once upon a time, Varena had given me a graphic description of a motorcycle rider who'd stretched out his arm at the wrong moment and come into the hospital without it. A passerby had had the presence of mind to wrap it in the blanket his dog sat on when it rode in the car and bring it into the hospital. I had seen bad things . . . maybe just as bad . . . but I didn't think I could have dealt calmly with that. Varena had been excited – not by the crisis but by her team's effective response.

Evidently she didn't talk about some aspects of being a nurse, at least to our mother.

'I never quite pictured her job that way.' Mother looked thoughtful, as if she were seeing her younger daughter in a different light.

I read the comics for a minute or two, Ann Landers, the

horoscopes, the scrambled words, the 'find the errors' drawing. I never had time to do this at home. Thank God.

'What's on the agenda today?' I asked, without feeling one bit excited. The pleasure of Jack's presence in town had faded, to be replaced by the gnawing anxiety of his suspicions.

'Oh, there's the shower at Grace's in the afternoon, but this morning we have to go to Corbett's to pick up a few things they called us about.'

Corbett's was the town's premier gift shop. Every bride with any claim to class went to Corbett's to register her china and silver patterns, and also to indicate a range of acceptable colors that would look good in the bride's future kitchen and bath. Corbett's also carried small appliances, pricey kitchenware, and sheets and table linens. Many brides left an all-encompassing list at Corbett's. Varena and I had always called it the 'I want it' list.

Two hours later – two dragging, boring hours later – we were in Varena's car, parallel parking on Bartley's town square. The old post office crumbled on one side, while the courthouse, in the center on a manicured lawn, was festooned with Christmas decorations. Unlike Shakespeare, Bartley was holding on to its manger scene, though I had never found plastic figures in a wooden shed exactly spiritual. Carols blared endlessly from the speakers located around the square, and all the merchants had lined their store windows with twinkling colored lights and artificial snow.

If there was a true religious emotion to be felt about Christmas, I had been too numbed by all this claptrap to feel it for the past three years.

I was glad to see Varena click the 'lock' button on her key-ring control, and the car gave its little *honk!* to show it had received her command. Naturally we all looked at the car as it made the sound, a senseless but natural reaction, and I almost didn't see the running man until too late.

He was coming for us out of nowhere, his hand already outstretched to grab my mother's purse, which she was clutching loosely under her right arm.

With a positive rush of pleasure, I planted my left foot, came up with my right knee, and flicked my foot out to catch him in the jaw. In real life (as opposed to movies) high kicks are risky and energy draining. The knee and the groin are much more reliable targets. But this was my chance to land a high kick, and I took it. Thanks to hours and hours of practice, my instep smacked his jaw correctly, and he staggered. I got him again on the way down, though it was not as effective an impact. It hastened his fall rather than damaging him further.

He managed to land on his knees, and I seized his right arm and twisted it sharply behind him. He screamed and hit the pavement, and I kept his arm behind and up at an angle I knew to be extremely painful. I was on his right, out of reach of his left hand if he could manage to lever himself up to grab for my ankle.

'I'll break your arm if you move,' I told him sincerely.

He believed me. He lay on the sidewalk, panting for breath – sobbing for breath, really.

I glanced up to see my mother and sister staring not at their assailant but at me, with stunned amazement making their faces foolish.

'Call the police,' I prompted them.

Varena kind of jumped and ran into Corbett's. She was doing a lot of police calling these days. The Bard sisters were on a roll.

The man I'd downed was short, stocky, black. He had on a ragged coat, and he smelled. I figured this was probably the same man who'd taken Diane Dykeman's purse a couple of days ago.

'Let me up, bitch,' he said now, having gathered enough breath to speak.

'Be polite,' I said, my voice harsh. I gave his arm a yank upward, and he screamed.

'Oh, Lily,' my mother gasped. 'Oh, honey. Do you have to . . . ?' Her voice trailed off as I looked up to meet her eyes.

'Yes,' I said. 'I have to.'

A siren went off right behind me. The patrol officer must have been two blocks away when he got the call from the dispatcher, so he put on his siren. It nearly made me lose my grip. The car had 'Bartley Police Department' printed in an arc over the Bartley town symbol, some complicated mishmash involving cotton and tractors. Under the symbol, the word 'Chief' was centered in large letters.

'What we got here?' called the man in the uniform as he bounded up on the sidewalk. He had brown hair and a neat mustache. He was lean except for a curious potbelly, like a five-month pregnancy. He looked at the man on the sidewalk, at my grip on his arm.

'Hey, Lily,' he said, after assessing all this. 'What you got here?'

'Chandler?' I said, peering up at his face. 'Chandler McAdoo?'

'In the flesh,' he drawled. 'You caught you a purse snatcher?'

'So it seems.'

'Hi, Miz Bard,' Chandler said, nodding at my mother, who nodded back automatically. I looked up at her shocked face, thinking as I did so that nothing could make her feel better for a little bit. Being the victim of a random crime was a shocking experience.

Chandler McAdoo had been my lab partner in high school, one memorable semester. We had done the frog thing together. I had been holding the knife – or the scalpel? I couldn't remember – and I had been on the verge of going silly-girl squeamish, when Chandler had looked me straight in the eye and told me I was a weak and useless critter if I couldn't cut one little hole in a dead frog.

He was right, I had figured, and I had cut.

That wasn't the only thing Chandler McAdoo had dared me to do, but it was the only dare I'd taken.

Chandler bent over now with his handcuffs, and with a practiced move, he had my prisoner cuffed before the man knew what was happening. I rose, with a courteous assist from Chief Chandler, and while I was telling him what had happened, he hauled the cuffed man to his feet and propelled the prisoner toward the squad car.

He listened, made a call on his radio.

I stared at every move he made, unable to square this man, this police chief with his severe haircut and cool eyes, with the boy who'd gotten drunk with me on Rebel Yell.

'Where you think he came from?' Chandler asked, as if it weren't too important. My mother had been coaxed inside the store by Varena and the sales clerks.

'Must have been there,' I decided, pointing at the alley running between Corbett's and the furniture store. 'That's the only place he could've been hiding unseen.' It was a narrow alley, and if he'd been just a few feet inside it, he would have been invisible. 'Where was Diane Dykeman when her purse was snatched?'

Chandler cocked an eye at me. 'She was over by Dill's pharmacy, two blocks away,' he said. 'The snatcher dodged back in the alley, and we couldn't track him. I don't see how we could have missed this guy, but I guess he could have hidden until we'd checked the alley behind the store. There are more little niches and hidey-holes in this downtown area than you can shake a stick at.'

I nodded. Since the downtown area of Bartley was more than a hundred and fifty years old, during which time the Square businesses had flourished and gone broke in cycles, I could well believe it.

'You stay put.' Chandler said and strode down the alley. I sighed and stayed put. I glanced at my watch once or twice. He was gone for seven minutes.

'I think he's been sleeping back there,' Chandler said when he reemerged onto the sidewalk. Suddenly my high school buddy was galvanized, and there wasn't any languid small-town-cop air about him anymore. 'I didn't find Diane's purse, but there're some refrigerator cartons and a nest of rags.'

Chandler had that saving-the-punchline air. He bent into his car and used the radio again.

'I just called Brainerd, who answered the call on the murder cases,' he told me after he straightened. 'Come look.'

I followed Chandler down the alley. We arrived at the T junction, where this little alley joined the larger one running behind the buildings on the west of the square. There was a refrigerator carton tucked into a niche behind some bushes that had made their precarious lives in the cracks in the rough pavement. Chandler pointed, and I followed his finger to see a length of rusty pipe close to but not visible from the carton, as I figured it. The pipe had been placed on a broken drain that had formerly run from the top of the flat-roofed furniture store to the gutter, and the placement rendered it all but invisible if it had not been stained at one end. The pipe, more than two feet long and about two inches in diameter, was darker at one end than the other.

'Bloodstains?' Chandler said. 'Dave LeMay, I'm thinking.'

I stared at the pipe again and understood.

The same man who might have beaten to death the doctor and his nurse had come that close to my *mother*. For a savage second, I wished I had kicked him harder and longer. I could have broken his arm, or his skull so easily while I had him down on the sidewalk. I stared out of the alley. I could just glimpse the man's profile as he sat in Chandler's car. That face was vacant. Nobody home.

'You go on in the store, Lily,' Chandler said, maybe reading my face too easily. 'Your mama might need you right now, Varena too. We'll talk later.'

I spun on my heel and strode down the alley to the street, to enter the glass-paned front door of Corbett's. A bell attached to the door tinkled, and the little crowd around my mother shifted to absorb me.

There was a couch positioned opposite the Bride's Area, where all the local brides' and grooms' selections of china and silverware were displayed. Mother was sitting on that sofa, Varena beside her explaining what had happened.

Another police car pulled to the curb outside, spurring more activity. Amid all the bustle, the telephoning, and the concern on the faces of the women around her, my mother gradually recovered her color and composure. When she knew Mom was okay, Varena took me aside and gripped my arm.

'Way to go, Sis,' she said.

I shrugged.

'You did good.'

I almost shrugged again and looked away. But instead I ventured a smile.

And Varena smiled back.

'Hey, I hate to interrupt this sister-sister talk,' Chandler said, sticking his head in the shop door, 'but I gotta take statements from you three.'

So we all went down to the little Bartley police station, one block away, to make our statements. What had happened had been so quick and simple, really just a matter of a few seconds, that it didn't take long. As we left, Chandler reminded us to stop by the station the next day to sign our statements.

Chandler motioned me to remain. I obediently lagged behind. I looked curiously at him. He didn't, wouldn't meet my eyes.

'They ever catch 'em, Lily?'

The back of my neck prickled and tightened. 'No,' I said.

'Damn.' And back into his tiny office he strode, all the equipment he wore on his belt making every step a statement of certainty. I took a deep breath and hurried to catch up with Mom and Varena.

We still had to go back to Corbett's Gift Shop. The women in my family weren't going to let a little thing like an attempted theft deter them from their appointed rounds. So we slid back into our little wedding groove. Varena got the basket full of presents she'd come to pick up, Mother accepted compliments on Varena's impending marriage, I was patted on the back (though somewhat gingerly) for stopping the purse snatcher, and when my adrenaline jolt finally expired . . . I was back to being bored.

We drove home to open and record the presents. While Mother and Varena told Daddy about our unexpectedly exciting shopping expedition, I wandered into the living room and stared out the front window. I switched on the Christmas tree lights, found that they blinked, shut them off.

I wondered what Jack was doing.

I found myself thinking about the homeless man I'd kicked. I thought of the redness of his eyes, the stubble on his face, his dishevelment, his smell. Would Dr LeMay have remained seated behind his desk if such a man had come into his office? I didn't think so.

And Dr LeMay must have died first. If he'd heard Binnie Armstrong speaking to an unknown man, Binnie being attacked, he would *never* have been caught sitting. He would have been up and around the desk, struggling, despite his age. He had been a proud man, a man's man.

If that sad specimen had made his way into the doctor's office when it was officially closed, Dr LeMay would have shown him the door, or told him to make an appointment, or called the police, or referred him to the emergency room doctor who drove out from Pine Bluff every day. Dave LeMay would have dealt with the homeless man any number of ways.

But he wouldn't have stayed behind his desk.

The intruder would have had the pipe in his hands. He hadn't come upon a rusty pipe in the doctor's office. And if the intruder had entered with the pipe, he had *intended* to kill Dr LeMay and Mrs Armstrong.

I shook my head as I stared out the living room window. I was not a law enforcement officer or any kind of detective, but several things about the homeless-man-as-murderer scenario just didn't make sense. And the more I thought about it, the fishier it seemed: If the homeless man had killed Dr LeMay and Mrs Armstrong, why hadn't he robbed the place? Could the horror of what he'd done have driven him out before he accomplished his purpose?

If he was innocent, how had the murder weapon – what Chandler McAdoo seemed to think was the murder weapon – come to be in the alley? If this man was clever enough to hide Diane Dykeman's purse, which he almost certainly had stolen, why hadn't he been clever enough to get rid of the evidence of a much more serious crime?

I'll tell you what I'd do, I thought. If I wanted to commit a murder and pin it on a throwaway person, I'd put the murder weapon right by a homeless man, moreover a black homeless man . . . someone with no local ties, no likely alibi, and already reported to be a purse snatcher.

That's what I'd do.

The back door to the doctor's office had been locked, I recalled. So the murderer had come in the front, as Varena and I had. He had walked past the doorway of the room in which Mrs Armstrong was working, and she had *not been alarmed*. Binnie Armstrong had been lying in the doorway, so she had calmly continued whatever she had been doing in the little lab.

So. The murderer – carrying the pipe – walks into the office, which is officially closed. The murderer passes Binnie Armstrong, who stays right where she is. Then the murderer had gone into Dr LeMay's office, looked at the old man on the other side of the piled desk, spoken to him. Though the killer had had a length of pipe in one hand, *still* the doctor hadn't been alarmed.

I felt goosebumps shiver down my arms.

Without warning – since Dr LeMay was still in his chair, which was still pushed right up to the desk – the murderer had lifted the pipe and hit Dr LeMay over the head, kept hitting him, until he was just tissue. Then the killer had stepped out into the hall, and while Binnie was hurrying from the lab to investigate the awful sounds she'd heard, he hit her, too . . . until she was on the verge of death.

Then he'd stepped out the front door and gotten into his vehicle . . . but surely he must have been covered in blood?

I frowned. Here was a snag. Even the most angelic of white men could not step out in front of the doctor's office in the day-time with blood-soaked clothing, carrying a bloody pipe.

'Lily?' My mother's voice. 'Lily?'

'Yes?'

'I thought we'd have an early lunch, since the shower is this afternoon.'

'OK.' I tried to control the lurch of my stomach at the thought of food.

'It's on the table. I've called you twice.'

'Oh. Sorry.' As I reluctantly dipped my spoon into my mother's homemade beef soup, I tried to get back on my train of thought, but it had rolled out of the station.

Here we all were, sitting around the kitchen table, just as we had for so many years.

Suddenly, this scene seemed overwhelmingly bleak. *Here we still were*, the four of us.

'Excuse me, I have to walk,' I said, pushing away from the table. The three of them looked up at me, a familiar dismay dragging at their mouths. But the compulsion had gotten so strong that I could no longer play my part.

I threw on my coat, pulled on gloves as I left the house.

The first block was bliss. Even in the freezing cold, even in the face of the sharp wind, I was by myself. At least the sun was shining in its watery winter way, and the clear colors of the pines and holly bushes against the pale blue sky made my eyes blink with pleasure. The branches of the hardwood trees looked like a bleak version of lace. Our neighbor's big brown dog barked and trailed my progress for the length of his yard, but he stopped at that and gave me no more trouble. I remembered I had to nod when cars went past, but in Bartley that was not so frequent, even at lunchtime.

I turned a corner to put the wind behind me, and in time I passed the Presbyterian church and the manse, where the O'Sheas lived. I wondered if the toddler, Luke, was letting Lou sleep. But I couldn't think about the O'Sheas without thinking of the picture that Roy Costimiglia had received in the mail.

Whoever sent that picture obviously knew which girl was the abducted Summer Dawn Macklesby. That particular picture, attached to that particular article, sent to the Macklesbys' PI, was intended to lead Roy Costimiglia to one conclusion. Why hadn't the anonymous sender gone one step further and circled the child's face? Why the ambiguity?

That was a real puzzle.

Of course . . . if you could figure out who'd sent it . . . you could find out why. Maybe.

Great piece of detection, Lily, I told myself scornfully, and walked even faster. A brown mailing envelope that could be bought at any Wal-Mart, a picture from a yearbook that hundreds of students had purchased . . . well, one copy would be missing that page now. Page 23, I remembered, from looking so hard at the one in Jack's briefcase.

Of course, the whole thing was really Jack's problem. Furthermore, it was a problem Jack was being paid to solve.

But I needed to know the answer before Varena married Dill Kingery. And the fact was evident that, though Jack was a trained and dogged detective, I was the one on the inside track, here in Bartley.

So I tried to imagine some way I could help Jack, some information I could discover for him.

I couldn't think of a damn thing I could do.

But maybe something would come to me.

The harder and longer I walked, the better I felt. I was breathing easier: The claustrophobia induced by family closeness was loosening its knot.

I glanced at my watch and stopped dead in my tracks.

It was time for Varena's shower.

Luckily, I had been meandering around in my parents' neighborhood, so I was only four blocks away from their house. I set out quickly, arriving at the front door within minutes. They'd left it unlocked, which was a relief. I dashed to my bedroom, skinned out of my jeans and sweater, and pulled on my black pants-blue blouse-black jacket combination. I checked the shower location and dashed out the door.

I was only ten minutes late.

This was a kitchen shower at the home of Mother's best friend, Grace Parks. Grace lived on a street of large homes, and hers was one of the largest. She had daily help, I remembered, and I cast a professional eye over the house as I entered.

You wouldn't catch Grace looking relieved to see me, but the lines bracketing her generous mouth did relax when I came in. She gave me a ritual hug and a pat on the shoulder that was just a little too forceful, as she told me my mother and sister were in the living room waiting for me. I'd always like Grace, who would be blond until the day she died. Grace seemed indestructible. Her brown eyes were always made up, her curvy figure had never sagged (at least on the surface), and she wore magnificent jewelry quite routinely.

She slid me into a chair she'd saved right by my mother and answered a question from one of the assembled guests even as she was putting the pencil and notepad in my hands. I stared at it blankly for a moment until I realized I'd been assigned the task of recording the gifts and givers.

I gave Mom a cautious smile, and she cautiously smiled back. Varena gave me a compound look, irritation and relief mixed in equal parts. 'Sorry,' I said quietly.

'You made it,' my mother said, her voice calm and matter-of-fact.

I nodded at the circle of women in Grace's huge living room, recognizing most of them from the shower two days ago. These people would be just as relieved as Varena to have the wedding over with. More people seemed to have been invited to this shower; maybe since Grace had such a large home, she'd told Varena to expand the basic guest list.

Because I'd been thinking of their daughters, I particularly noticed Meredith Osborn and Lou O'Shea. Mrs Kingery was sitting on the other side of Varena, which was a relief. It seemed unfair to me that Dill should have such a nerve-wracking mother after his wife had been unstable enough to kill herself. I could see why he'd be attracted to Varena, who had always seemed to be one of the most stable and balanced people I'd ever known.

It was the first time I'd realized that. It's strange how you can know someone all your life and still not spell out her strong and weak points to yourself.

This shower had a kitchen theme. All the guests had been asked to include their favorite recipe with their gift. As we began the grand opening, I got busy. My handwriting is not elegant, but it is clear, and I tried to do a thorough job. Some boxes were stuffed with little things rather than a single gift, like a set of dish towels.

Diane Dykeman (she of the snatched purse) had given Varena a
set of measuring spoons and measuring cups, a little scale, and
a chart of weight equivalencies, and I had to use my most
microscopic writing to enter everything.

This was really an excellent job to have, I decided, because I
didn't have to talk to anyone. The story about me kicking the
purse snatcher wasn't town currency yet, and Mother and Varena
were avoiding the subject. But I was pretty sure it would begin to
make the rounds when time came for refreshments.

When that moment arrived – when all the gifts had been
opened and Grace Parks had vanished for a significant time – she
reappeared at my elbow and asked me to pour the punch.

It occurred to me that Grace understood me pretty well. I gave
her an assessing look as I took my place at one end of her massive
oval dining table, polished to a gleaming shine, bisected by a
Christmas runner and covered with the usual shower food: nuts,
cake, finger sandwiches, mints, snack mix.

'You're like me,' Grace said. She gave me a direct look. 'You
like to be busy more than you like to sit and listen.'

It had never crossed my mind that I was in any way like the
elegant Grace Parks. I nodded and began to fill my ladle for the
first one around the table – Varena, of course, the honoree.

I had to do no more than say 'Punch?' after that and smile and
nod.

After a long time, it was over, and once again we loaded gifts
into the car, thanked Grace profusely, and drove home to unload.

After I'd changed back to jeans and the sweater, Varena asked
me if I'd go to her cottage with her to help pack. She'd been
moving her things slowly into Dill's house over the past month,
beginning with the things she needed least.

Of course I agreed, relieved both at the prospect of being busy
and of being helpful. We had a quick sandwich and went over to
the cottage, with a few stops along the way. Dill, Varena told me,
was spending some quality time with Anna, who'd been showing
signs of being overwhelmed by all the wedding excitement.

'I've reached the point where all I can do here at my place is sleep,' she told me, after she'd put her sweats on. 'But I kept the lease up until the end of December, because I really didn't want to move back in with the folks.' I nodded. I could see that once she did that, she and Dill would have lost whatever privacy they had. Or did Varena just want to ensure she had a break from our parents?

'What do you have left to pack?'

Varena began to open closets, showing me what she hadn't managed to empty out before now.

We'd stopped behind some stores to collect boxes. Downtown had been empty, now that most of the businesses were closed. It was fully dark at six o'clock this time of year, and the night was very cold. The cottage seemed warm and homey in contrast to the blackness outside.

I was assigned to pack the tiny closet by the front door, which contained things like extra lightbulbs, extension cords, batteries, and the vacuum cleaner. As I began to pack them in a sturdy box, Varena started wrapping some pots and pans with newspaper. We worked in comfortable silence for a little while.

Varena had just asked me if I wanted some instant hot chocolate when we heard the sound of someone walking outside the cottage.

The scare we'd had that morning must have made us jumpy. Both of us raised our heads like deer hearing the sound of the hunter's boots. Peripherally, I saw Varena turn to me, but I shook my head slightly to make her keep silent.

Then someone kicked the front door.

Varena shrieked.

'Who is it?' I called, standing to one side of the door.

'Jack,' he yelled. 'Let me in!'

I caught my breath in a rattling gasp, frightened and furious at being so. I yanked the door open, ready to let him know how much I appreciated being jolted like that. The words died in my throat when I opened the door. Jack was carrying Meredith Osborn. She was covered in blood.

Behind me I heard Varena pick up the phone, punch in 911. She spoke tersely to whoever answered.

Jack was haggard with shock. Some of Meredith Osborn's blood was smeared on him. He was breathing raggedly. Though she was a small woman, he'd been carrying her as a dead weight.

Varena picked up a sheet she'd just folded and flung it over the couch in one movement, and Jack gladly laid the little woman down. When he'd deposited his burden he stood for a moment with his arms still curved. Then with a groan he straightened them, his shoulders moving unconsciously in an effort to relax strained muscles.

Varena was already on her knees beside the couch, her hands on her landlady's wrist. She was shaking her head.

'She's got a pulse, but it's . . .' Varena shook her head again. 'She's been lying outside.' The dying woman's face was ice-white, and the cold was rolling off the tiny body, eddying through the warm room.

We heard the sound of the ambulance in the distance.

Meredith Osborn opened her eyes. They fixed on mine.

Someone had struck her across her face, and her lips were cracked, had bled. Underneath the blood, they were blue, to match the tinge of her fingernails.

Her mouth opened. 'The children,' she whispered.

'Don't worry,' Varena said instantly. 'They're fine.'

Meredith Osborn turned her gaze from my face to Varena's. Her mouth moved again. She tried as hard as she could to tell Varena something.

Instead, she died.

Chapter Five

I held on to Jack. He held on to me. We'd seen people die – bad people, violent people, people who had the misfortune to be in the wrong place at the wrong time. This young woman, newly a mother, beaten and left in the freezing air, was something else again.

It was Varena who ran over to the Osborn house to see if the children were there, Varena who discovered that the house was empty and silent. And, twenty minutes later, it was Varena who saw the car with Emory Osborn, Eve, and the baby Jane pull into the driveway, to be met with the news that would change their lives forever.

Lanky Detective Brainerd was on duty again, or still on duty, and he eyed me dubiously, even after we explained what had happened.

'What were you doing here?' he asked Jack directly. 'I don't believe you're from here, sir.'

'No, sir, I'm not. I'm here to visit Lily, and I'm staying at the Delta Motel.' Jack let go of me and stepped closer to Brainerd.

I kept my gaze on the floor. I didn't know if Jack was making a mistake or not, keeping his business in Bartley a secret.

'How'd you know Miss Bard was here?'

'Her car is here,' Jack said.

It was true, we'd come in my car. Mother had taken Varena to the wedding shower, so I'd given her a ride from their place over to the cottage.

After her burst of energy, Varena was slumped in an armchair, staring into space.

'So you stopped here to see Miss Bard . . . ?'

'And when I got out of the car, I thought I heard a noise from behind the big house,' Jack said calmly. 'So I thought I'd check it out before I alarmed Lily and Varena.'

'You found Mrs Osborn.'

'Yes. She was lying between the back of the house and their garage.'

'Did she speak to you?'

'No.'

'She said nothing?'

'No. She didn't seem to know I'd picked her up.'

'But she spoke when she was lying on the couch?'

'Yes,' I said.

Jack and Detective Brainerd turned simultaneously.

'And what did she say?' the policeman asked.

'She said, 'The children.''

'And that's all?'

'That's all.'

Brainerd looked thoughtful, as well he might.

What had Meredith Osborn meant? Had the last thoughts of the dying woman simply been dwelling on the children she was leaving behind? Or did those words mean more? Were her two children in danger? Or was she thinking of the three girls in the picture?

Whoever had sent the picture to Jack's friend Roy had started a deadly train of events.

After the ambulance removed Meredith's body, I stared out the side window of Varena's cottage, watching the police search the backyard where she had lain bleeding and freezing.

I was full of anger.

The death of Meredith Osborn had not even had the mercy of being fast. Dave LeMay and Binnie Armstrong had had only moments to fear death – and those were dreadful moments, I fully appreciated that, believe me. But lying in your own backyard, unable to summon help, feeling your own end creeping through you . . . I closed my eyes, felt myself shudder. I knew something about hours of fear, about being certain your death was imminent and unavoidable. I had been spared, finally. Meredith Osborn had not.

Jack put an arm around my shoulder.

'I want to go away,' I whispered.

I couldn't, and we both knew it.

'Excuse me,' I said at a more conversational volume, hearing my voice's coldness. 'I'm being silly.'

Jack sighed. 'I wish I could go away, too.'

'What killed her?'

'Not a gun. Knife wounds, I think.'

I shivered. I hated knives.

'Did we bring this here with us, Jack?' I whispered.

'No,' he said. 'This was here before we came. But it won't be here when I leave.' When Jack got his teeth into something, he didn't let go, even when he was biting the wrong part.

'Tomorrow,' I told him, quietly. 'Tomorrow we'll talk.'

'Yes.'

I was taking Varena home to spend the night. She couldn't sleep in this cottage. She was ready, standing staring out the side window at the lit backyard, the figures moving around it. So I tried to walk out the door. But after I'd stepped away from Jack I reached back to grip his wrist. I couldn't seem to let go. I looked down at my feet, struggling with myself.

'Lily?' Under the questioning tone, his voice was hoarse.

I bit my lip, hard.

'I'm gone,' I said, letting go of him. 'I'll see you in the morning, at eight. At the motel.' I glanced at his face.

He nodded.

'Lock her cottage when the police let you go, OK?'

Varena didn't seem to hear us. She stood like a statue at that window, her overnight bag on the floor beside her.

'Sure,' he said, still looking intently at me.

'Then I'll see you tomorrow,' I said and turned my back on him and walked out, beckoning to my sister to follow.

I have done so many hard things, but that was one of the hardest.

★

It was only nine by the time we got to my parents' house, but it felt like midnight. I didn't want to see anyone or talk to anyone, and yet somehow my parents had to be told, had to be talked to. Luckily for me, Varena had regained her balance by the time she saw my mother, and though she cried a little, she managed to relate the horrible death of Meredith Osborn.

'Should I just cancel the wedding?' she asked tearfully.

I knew my mother would talk her out of it. I really couldn't bear to be with people right now. I went to my room and shut the door firmly. My father came to stand outside in the hall; I knew his footsteps.

'Are you okay, pumpkin?' he called.

'Yes.'

'Do you want to be alone?'

I clenched my fists until even my short fingernails bit into my palms. 'Yes, please.'

'OK.' Off he went, God bless him.

I lay on the hard bed, hands clasped across my stomach, and thought.

I could not imagine how I could find out any more information about the three girls who might be Summer Dawn. But I was convinced that Meredith Osborn's death had come about because she knew which girl was not who she seemed to be. I tried to picture Lou O'Shea or the Reverend O'Shea attacking Meredith in the freezing cold of her backyard, but I just could not. Still less could I imagine mild Dill Kingery stabbing Meredith into silence. Dill's mother was certainly off-base, but I'd never seen any tendency to violence. Mrs Kingery just seemed daffy.

I thought of Meredith Osborn taking care of Krista O'Shea and Anna Kingery. What could she have seen – or heard – that would lead her to think she knew that one of the girls had been born with a different identity?

I'd never had a baby, so I didn't know what happened bureaucratically when you gave birth. Some hospitals, I knew, took little footprints – I'd seen them framed on the walls of the

Althaus family when I cleaned for them. And of course there was the birth certificate. And pictures. A lot of hospitals took pictures, for the parents. To me, all babies pretty much looked the same, red and scrunch-faced, or brown and scrunch-faced. That some had hair and some didn't was the only obvious distinction I could see.

I had learned, also from the much-birthed Carol Althaus, that the fingerprints police or volunteers sometimes took at mall booths were not helpful because often they were of poor quality. I didn't know if that was true, but it sounded reasonable. I was willing to bet the same reasons would render any existing baby footprints of Summer Dawn unusable.

So fingerprints and footprints were a no go. DNA testing could prove Summer Dawn's identity, I was sure, but of course you had to know whom to test. I couldn't see Jack demanding that the three girls undergo DNA testing. Well, I could see him demanding it, but I could also see all three sets of parents turning him down cold.

I stared at the ceiling until I realized my mind was going through the same cycle of thought, over and over, and it was no more productive than it had been the first time I'd gone through it.

I remembered, as I was undressing and pulling on a nightgown, that when Jack had first come to my bed, the next morning I'd made myself a promise: never to ask Jack for anything.

I was having a hard time keeping that promise.

As I lay once again on the bed I'd slept in as a virgin, I had to remind myself over and over that there was a corollary to that promise: not to offer what was not asked for.

I heard my sister next door in her old room, going through the same motions I'd gone through. I was sure she was hurting, sure she was suffering doubly since this blood and gore was happening at the time that was supposed to be the happiest in her life.

I felt helpless.

It was the most galling feeling in the world.

*

I was up and out of the house the next morning before my parents were stirring. I couldn't wait for eight o'clock. I rose, took a hasty shower, and yanked on ordinary clothes, not much caring what they were as long as they were warm.

I started my car with a little difficulty and drove through the frosty streets. There were a few more cars at the motel, so my knock at Jack's door was quiet.

He opened it after just a second, and I stepped inside. Jack closed the door quickly behind me, shirtless and shivering in the gust of cold air that entered with me.

What I had been going to do, planning to do, was sit in one of the two comfortable vinyl-covered chairs while Jack sat in the other and discuss his plans and how I could help.

What happened was, the minute the door was closed we were on each other like hungry wolves. When I touched him, my hands were pleased with everything they encountered. When I kissed him, I wanted him instantly. I was shaking so hard with wanting him that I couldn't get my clothes off, and he pulled my sweatshirt over my head and yanked down my jeans and underwear, helping me step out of them, pulling me to the bed into his nest of residual warmth.

Afterward, we lay with our arms around each other. I didn't care that my left arm was going to sleep, he didn't seem to mind that there wasn't an altogether comfortable place for his right leg.

He whispered my name in my ear. I smoothed his hair, tangled and loose, back from his face. I ran my fingers over the stubble on his chin. There were words in my mouth that I would not say. I clamped my teeth over them and continued to touch him. That stupid, fragile, ludicrous swelling in my chest had to remain contained.

His hands were occupied, too, and after a few minutes we made love again, not as frantically. There was nothing I wanted so much as to stay in that sorry motel bed, as long as Jack was in it.

I was dressing (again) after another quick shower. 'What are you going to do next?' I asked, hearing the reluctance in my voice.

'Find out which of the little girls had seen Dr LeMay recently.'

'I figured that had something to do with it. After all, the homeless man was in jail when Meredith Osborn was killed.'

'She wasn't beaten like the doctor and his nurse.' Jack had been brushing his hair back into its ponytail. Now he gave me a curious look. He was wearing a long-sleeved polo shirt striped rust and brown, and the scar that ran down his cheek to his jaw seemed whiter in contrast. He ran a belt through the loops on his khakis. 'Might have been a different killer.'

'Umhum,' I said skeptically. 'All of a sudden, Bartley is full of brutal murders. And you're trying to find a missing child. This is just coincidence.'

He gave me the look that I'd learned meant he was up to something: It was a sideways look, a quick flash of the eyes, to gauge my mood.

'The homeless man's name is Christopher Darby Sims.'

'OK, I'll bite. How'd you know that?'

'I have a connection here at the police department.'

I wondered uneasily if this was one of those good ole boy things, or if Jack meant he'd bribed a cop. Or perhaps both.

'So, can this connection look through the doctor's records?'

'I can't ask that much. I'm feeling my way. Are you still squeamish about frogs?' Jack asked, a little smile turning up the corners of his mouth.

'Chandler McAdoo.'

Jack lifted a corner of the curtain, peered out at the bleak day and the depressing motel court. 'I stopped by the police station yesterday. Once I mentioned your name and hinted pretty strongly that we were tight, Chandler began to talk to me. He's given me some fascinating stories about your teen years.' He tried not to grin too broadly.

As long as Chandler hadn't told him about the later years. 'I can't even remember what I was like then,' I said. And I was speaking the literal truth. 'I can remember some of the things we got up to,' I said, smiling a little, tentatively. 'But I can't for the life of me recall what I felt. Too much water under the bridge, I guess.' It was like I could see a silent movie of my life without hearing sound or feeling emotion. I shrugged. What was gone, was gone.

'I'm memorizing some stories,' Jack warned me. 'And when you least expect it . . .'

I tightened my shoelaces, still smiling, and kissed Jack good-bye. 'Call me when you know something or want me to do something,' I told him. I felt the smile slide right off my mouth. 'I want this over.'

Jack nodded. 'I do, too,' he said, his voice even. 'And then I never want to see Teresa and Simon Macklesby again.'

I looked up at him, reading his face. I touched his cheek with my fingers. 'You can do this,' I said.

'Yeah, I should be able to,' he told me, his voice bleak and empty.

'What's your program for the morning?' I asked.

'I'm helping Dill put a floor in his attic.'

'What?'

'I just happened to be in the pharmacy yesterday afternoon and we were talking, and he told me that was what he was going to be doing this morning, no matter how cold it was. He wanted to get the job finished before the wedding. So I said I didn't have anything to do since you were wrapped up in wedding plans, and I'd be glad to lend him a hand.'

'And ask him a few questions while you're at it?'

'Possibly.' Jack smiled at me, that charming smile that coaxed so much information out of citizens.

I drove home, trying to think my way through a maze.

My family was up, Varena shaky but much better. They'd had a conference while I was gone and made up their minds to go through with the wedding no matter what. I was glad I'd missed that one, glad the decision had been made without me. If Varena had postponed her wedding, it would have made the time frame easier, but I had a concern I hadn't shared with Jack.

I was afraid – if the murderer of Dr LeMay, Mrs Armstrong, and Meredith Osborn was the same person – that this criminal was getting frantic. And a person frantically trying to conceal a crime was likely to kill the strongest link between him and the crime.

In this case, that would be Summer Dawn Macklesby.

On one level, it didn't seem likely that whoever'd gone to such extreme lengths to conceal the original crime – the abduction – would even consider killing the girl. But on another level, it seemed obvious, even likely.

I knew nothing that could help solve this crime. What did I know how to do? I knew how to clean and how to fight.

I also knew where people were most likely to hide things. Cleaning had certainly taught me that. Objects could be mislaid anywhere (though I had a mental list of places I checked first, when employers asked me to keep my eyes open for some missing item) but hidden . . . that was a different matter.

So? I asked myself sarcastically. How was that going to help?

'Could you, sweetheart?' my mother was saying.

'What?' I asked, my voice sharp and quick. She'd startled me.

'I'm sorry,' my mother said, her voice making it clear I should be saying that to her. 'I asked if you would mind going over to Varena's place and finishing her packing?'

I wasn't sure why I was being asked to do this. Was Varena too scared to be there by herself? And it wasn't supposed to bother me? But maybe I'd been woolgathering while they'd spelled it out.

Varena certainly looked as if she needed sleep and a holiday. And this, right before the happiest time of her life.

'Of course,' I said. 'What about the wedding dress?'

'Oh, my heavens!' Mother exclaimed. 'We've got to get that out right away!' Mother's pale face flushed. Somehow, the wedding dress was at risk in that apartment. Galvanized by this sudden urgency, Mother shooed me into my car and bundled herself up in record time.

She followed me over to Varena's and took the dress home personally, carrying it from the cottage to the car as though it were the crown and scepter of royalty.

I was left alone in Varena's place, an oddly unsettling feeling. It was like surreptitiously going through her drawers. I shrugged. I was here to do a job. That thought was very normal, very steadying, after all we'd seen lately.

I counted boxes, moved the ones already full out to my car trunk after labeling them with Varena's black marker. 'Martha Stewart, that's me,' I muttered and folded out the flaps on another box, placing it by the nearest closet. This was a little double closet with sliding doors in Varena's tiny hall. It held only a few linens and towels. I guessed Varena had already moved the others.

Just as I'd picked up the first handful, trying to restrain myself from shaking the sheets out and refolding them, there was a knock on the door. I looked through Varena's peephole. The knocker was a blond man, small, fair, with red-rimmed blue eyes. He looked mild and sad. I was sure I knew who it was.

'Emory Osborn,' he said, when I opened the door. I shook his hand. His was that soft boneless handshake some men give a woman, as though they're scared if they squeeze with all their masculine power they'll break her delicate fingers. It felt like shaking hands with the Pillsbury Dough Boy. This was something Jess O'Shea and Emory Osborn had in common.

'Come in,' I said. After all, he owned the cottage.

Emory Osborn stepped over the threshold. The widower was maybe 5′7″, not much taller than I. He was very fair and blue-eyed, handsome on a small scale, and he had the most flawless skin I'd ever seen on a man. Right at the moment, it was pink from the cold.

'I'm sorry for your loss,' I told him.

He looked directly at me then. 'You were here in the cottage last night?'

'Yes, I was.'

'You saw her?'

'Yes.'

'She was alive.'

I shifted uneasily. 'Yes,' I told him reluctantly.

'Did she speak?'

'She asked after the children.'

'The children?'

'That's all.'

His eyes closed, and for one awful moment I thought he was going to cry.

'Have a seat,' I said abruptly. I startled him into sitting down in the nearest chair, an armchair that must be Varena's favorite from the way she'd positioned it.

'Let me get you some hot chocolate.' I went into the kitchen without waiting for an answer. I knew there would be some since Varena'd offered it to me the night before. There it was, on the counter where she'd set it, along with two mugs. Luckily, the microwave was built in, so I was able to heat the water in it. I stirred in the powder. It wasn't very good, but it was hot and sweet, and he looked in need of both sugar and warmth.

'Where are the children?' I asked as I put his mug on the small oak table by the chair.

'They're with church members,' he said. His voice was rich but not big.

'So, what can I do for you?' It didn't seem that he would say anything else unless I prompted him.

'I wanted to see where she died.'

This was very nearly intolerable. 'There, on the couch,' I said brusquely.

He stared. 'There aren't any stains,' he told me.

'Varena slung a sheet over it.' This was beyond strange. The back of my neck began to prickle. I wasn't going to sit knee to knee with him – I'd been perched on the ottoman that matched the chair – and point out where Meredith's head had been, what spot her feet had touched.

'Before your friend put Meredith down?'

'Yes.' I jumped up to pull a fitted sheet from the closet. Giving way to an almost irresistible compulsion, I refolded it, and knew I'd straighten all the rest, too. The hell with Varena's finer feelings.

'And he is—?'

'My friend.' I could hear my voice get flatter and harder.

'You're angry with me, I'm afraid,' he said wearily. And sure enough, he was weeping, tears were running down his cheeks. He blotted them automatically with a well-used handkerchief.

'You shouldn't put yourself through this.' My tone was still not the one a nice woman would use to a widower. I meant he shouldn't put *me* through it.

'I feel like God's abandoned me and the kids. I'm heartbroken,' and I reflected I'd never actually heard anyone use that word out loud, 'and my faith has left me,' he finished, without taking a breath. He put his face in his hands.

Oh, man. I didn't want to hear this. I didn't want to be here.

Through the uncurtained window, I saw a car pull in behind mine in the cottage's narrow driveway. Jess O'Shea got out and began his way to the door, his head bowed. A minister – just the person to deal with a lapse of faith and recent bereavement. I opened the door before he had a chance to knock.

'Jess,' I said. Even I could hear the naked relief in my voice. 'Emory Osborn is here, and he is really, really . . .' I stood there, nodding significantly, unable to pin down exactly what Emory Osborn was.

Jess O'Shea seemed to be taking in my drift. He stepped around me and over to the smaller man, claiming my former seat on the ottoman. He took Emory's hands in his.

I tried to block out the two men's voices as I continued the job of packing, despite the feeling I should leave while Emory talked with his minister. But Emory had the option of going to his own house if he wanted complete privacy. If I looked at it practically, he'd known I was here and come in the cottage anyway . . .

Jess and Emory were praying together now, the fervent expression on Emory's face the only one I could see. Jess's back was bent and his hands clasped in front of his face. The two fair heads were close together.

Then Dill stepped in, looking at the two men praying, at me folding, trying to keep my eyes to myself. He looked startled and not too happy at this tableau.

All three dads in the same room. Except that one of them was probably not really a father at all but a thief who had stolen his fatherhood.

Dill turned to me, his whole face a question. I shrugged.

'Where's Varena?' he whispered.

'At our folks'',' I whispered. 'You go over there. You two need to talk about what's going to happen. And aren't you supposed to be meeting Jack at your place?' I gave him a little push with my hand, and he took a step back before he recovered his footing. Possibly I'd pushed a little harder than I'd planned.

After Dill obediently got in his car and left, I finished refolding and found I had packed all the remaining items in the linen closet. I checked the bathroom cabinet. It held only a few things, which I also boxed.

When I turned around, Jess O'Shea was right behind me. My arms tensed immediately and my hands fisted.

'Sorry, did I surprise you?' he asked, with apparent innocence.

'Yes.'

'I think Emory is feeling a little better. We're going over to his house. Thanks for comforting him.'

I couldn't recall any comforting I'd done; it must have been in the eye of the comfortee. I made a noncommittal sound.

'I'm so glad you've returned to reconcile with your family,' Jess said, all in a rush. 'I know this has meant so much to them.'

This was his business? I raised my eyebrows.

He reddened when I didn't speak. 'I guess it's a professional hazard, giving out emotional pats on the back,' he said finally. 'I apologize.'

I nodded. 'How is Krista?' I asked.

'She's fine,' he said, surprised. 'It's a little hard to get her to understand that her friend's mother is gone, she seems not to see it as a reality yet. That can be a blessing, you know. I think we'll be keeping Eve for a while until Emory can cope a little better. Maybe the baby, too, if Lou thinks she can handle it.'

'Didn't Lou tell me she'd taken Krista to the doctor last week?' I asked.

If Jess noticed the contrast between my lack of response to his observations about my family and my willingness to chatter about his child, he didn't comment on it. Parents almost always seem willing to believe other people are as fascinated with their children as they are.

'No,' he said, obviously searching his memory. 'Krista hasn't even had a cold since we started her on her allergy shots last summer.' His face lightened. 'Before that, we were in to Dr LeMay's every week, it seemed like! My goodness, this is so much better. Lou gives Krista the shots herself.'

I nodded and began opening cabinets in the kitchen. Jess took the hint and left, pulling on his heavy coat as he walked across the yard. Evidently he wasn't going to stay at Emory's long.

After he left I wrote a note on a pad I found under Varena's phone. I hopped in my car and drove to the motel. As I'd expected, Jack's car wasn't there. I pulled up in front of his room. I squatted and slid the note under his door.

It said, 'Krista O'Shea didn't go to the doctor recently.' I didn't sign it. Who else would be leaving Jack a note?

On my way back to Varena's, I scavenged alleys, for more boxes. I was particularly interested in the alley behind the gift store and furniture store.

It was clean, for an alley, and I even scored a couple of very decent boxes before I began my search. There was a Dumpster back there; I was sure the police had been through it, since it was suspiciously empty. The appliance carton Christopher Sims had been using for shelter was gone, too, maybe appropriated by the police.

I looked down the alley in both directions. Main Street was on one end, and anyone driving east would be able to glance down the alley and catch a glimpse of whoever was in it, unless that person was in the niche where Sims's box had been located.

To the south end of the alley was a quiet street with small businesses in older houses and a few remaining homes still occupied by one family apiece. That street, Macon, saw quite a lot of foot traffic: the square's parking space was severely limited,

so downtown shoppers were always looking for a spot within
walking distance.

It sure would be easy to catch a glimpse of Christopher Darby
Sims while he squatted in this alley. It sure would be tempting to
capitalize on the presence of a homeless black in Bartley. It would
be no trouble at all to slip through the alley with, say, a length of
bloody pipe. Deposit it behind a handy box.

The back door of the furniture store opened. A woman about
my age came out, looking cautiously at me.

'Hi,' she called. She was clearly waiting for me to account for
my presence.

'I'm collecting boxes for my sister's move,' I told her, gesturing
toward my car with its open trunk.

'Oh,' she said, relief written on her face in big bold letters. 'I
hate to seem suspicious, but we had a . . . Lily?'

'Maude? Mary Maude?' I was looking at her just as incredulously.

She came down the back steps of the building in a rush and
threw her arms around me. I staggered back under her weight.
Mary Maude was still pretty and always would be, but she was
considerably rounder than she had been in high school. I made
myself hug her back. 'Mary Maude Plummer,' I said tentatively,
patting her plump shoulder very gently.

'Well, it was Mary Maude Baumgartner for about five years,
and now it's back to Plummer,' she told me, sniffing a little. Mary
Maude had always been emotional. I had a clenched feeling
around my heart. I had a lot of memories of this woman.

'You never called me,' she said now, looking up at me. She
meant, after the rape. I could never get away from it here.

'I never called anyone,' I said. I had to tell Mary Maude the
truth. 'I couldn't face doing it. I had too hard a time.'

Her eyes filled with tears. 'But I've always loved you.'

Always right to the emotional truth, no matter how uncomfortable. Could this be why I'd never called Mary Maude after my Bad
Time? We'd let go of each other, taken a step back.

I remembered another important truth. 'I love you too,' I said.

'But I couldn't stand to be around people who were always thinking about what had happened to me. I couldn't do it'

She nodded. Her red hair, almost to her shoulders, turned under in a neat curve all the way around, and she had heavy gold earrings in her pierced ears. 'I think I can understand that. I've been all these years forgiving you for refusing my comfort.'

'Are we all right?'

'Yeah,' she said, smiling up at me. 'We're all right, now.'

We both gave a little laugh, half happy, half embarrassed.

'So, you're getting boxes for Varena?'

'Yeah. She's getting her stuff out of the cottage. The wedding's day after tomorrow. And after the murder last night . . .'

'Oh, right, that's the place Varena rented! You know, the husband, Emory, works right here, with me.' And Mary Maude pointed at the door from which she'd issued. 'He's the sweetest guy.'

He would certainly have been aware of Christopher Sims's presence in the alley in back of the store.

'So, I guess you knew this guy was living back here, the purse snatcher?'

'Well, we'd caught glimpses. Just in the two days before the police got him. Wait . . . my God, Lily, was that you who kicked him?'

I nodded.

'Wow, girl, what have you done with yourself?' She eyed me up and down.

'Taken karate for a few years, worked out some.'

'I can tell! You were so brave, too!'

'So you knew Sims was back here?'

'Huh? Oh, yeah. But we weren't sure what to do about it. We've never had any problem like that, and we were trying to decide what the safe thing to do was, and what the Christian thing to do was. It's tough when that might not be the same thing! We got Jess O'Shea down here to talk to the man, try to see where he wanted a bus ticket to, you know? Or if he was sick. Or hungry.'

So Jess had actually met the man.

'What did Jess say?'

'He said this Sims guy told him he was just fine right where he was, he had been getting handouts from some people in the, you know, black community, and he was just going to stay in the alley until God guided him somewhere else.'

'Somewhere where they had more purses?'

'Could be.' Mary Maude laughed. 'I hear Diane positively identified him. He told Diane at the police station that he was an angel and was trying to point out to Diane the hazards of possessing too many worldly goods.'

'That's original.'

'Yeah, give him points for a talent for fiction, anyway.'

'He say anything about the murders?' Since Mary Maude apparently had such access to the local gossip pipeline, I thought I might as well tap in.

'No. Isn't that a little strange? You'd think on one hand he'd be too deranged to understand that the murders are so much more serious, and yet he's saying that he never saw the pipe until the police found it stuffed behind his box, you know, the one where he was sleeping.'

I noticed that Mary Maude had come to check me out without a coat on, and she was shivering in her expensive white blouse and sweater-vest embroidered in holly and Christmas ornaments. Our reunion had its own background sound track, as the loudspeakers positioned around the square continued to blare out Christmas music.

'How do you stand it?' I asked, nodding my head toward the noise in the square.

'The carols? Oh, after a while you just tune them out,' she said wearily. 'They just leach the spirit out of me.'

'Maybe that's what made the purse snatcher deranged,' I offered, and she burst into laughter. Mary Maude had always laughed easily, charmingly, making it impossible not at least to smile along with her.

She hugged me again, made me promise to call her when I came back to town after the wedding, and scampered back into the store, her body shaking with the cold. I stood looking after her for a minute. Then I threw a couple more boxes into the car and drove carefully out of the alley.

Within a block of turning out onto the side street, Macon, I passed Dill's pharmacy.

I had a lot to think about.

I would have given almost anything to have had my punching bag.

I returned to Varena's place and packed everything I could find. Every half hour or so, I straightened up and looked out the window. There were lots of visitors at the Osborn house: women dropping off food, mostly. Emory appeared in the yard from time to time, walking restlessly, and a couple of times he was crying. Once he drove off in his car, returning in less than an hour. But he didn't knock on the cottage door again, to my great relief.

I had carefully folded Varena's remaining clothes and placed them in suitcases, since I didn't know what she'd planned on taking on the honeymoon. Most of her clothes were already at Dill's.

Finally, by three o'clock, all Varena's belongings were packed. I moved all the boxes into my car, except for a short stack by the front door that just couldn't fit. And of course, there was the remaining furniture, but that wasn't my problem.

I began cleaning the apartment.

It felt surprisingly good to have something to clean. Varena, while not a slob, was no compulsive housekeeper, and there was plenty to do. I was also actively enjoying the break from my family and the alone time.

As I was running the vacuum, I heard a heavy knock on the door. I jumped. I hadn't heard a car pull up, but then I wouldn't have over the drone of the machine.

I opened the door. Jack was there, and he was angry.

'What?' I asked.

He pushed past me. 'My room at the motel got broken into.' He was furious. 'Someone came in through the bathroom window. It looks out on a field. No one saw.'

'Anything taken?'

'No. Whoever it was rummaged through everything, broke the lock on my briefcase.'

I had an ominous sinking somewhere in the region of my stomach. 'Did you find my note?'

'What?' He stared at me, anger giving way to something else.

'I left you a note.' I sat down abruptly on the ottoman. 'I left you a note,' I repeated stupidly. 'About Krista O'Shea.'

'You signed it?'

'No.'

'What did it say?'

'That she hadn't been to the doctor in weeks.'

Jack's eyes flickered from item to item in the clean room, as he thought about what I'd told him.

'Did you call the police?' I asked.

'They were there when I pulled in. Mr Patel, the manager, had called. He had seen the window was broken when he went to put the garbage out behind the building.'

'What did you tell them?'

'The truth. That my things had been gone through but nothing had been stolen. I hadn't left any money in my room. I never do. And I don't carry valuable things with me.'

Jack felt angry and sick because his space, however temporary, had been invaded, and his things had been riffled. I understand that feeling all too well. But Jack would never talk about it in those terms, because he was a man.

'So now someone knows exactly why I'm here in Bartley.' He'd cover that violated feeling with practical considerations.

'That person also knows I have an accomplice,' he continued.

That was one way to put it.

Suddenly I stood, walked over to the window. I was crackling with restless energy. Trouble was coming, and every nerve in my body was warning me to get in my car and go home to Shakespeare.

But *I couldn't go*. My *family* kept me here.

No, that wasn't completely true. I could have brought myself to leave my family if I felt threatened enough. *Jack* kept me here.

Without a thought in my head, I made a fist and would have driven it into the window if Jack hadn't caught my arm.

I rounded on him, crazy with jolts of feeling that I wouldn't identify. Instead of striking him, I ran my arm around his neck and drew him ferociously to me. The stresses and strains on me were almost intolerable.

Jack, understandably surprised, made a questioning noise but then shut up. He let go of the arm he was gripping and tentatively put his own arms around me. We stood silently for what seemed like a long time.

'So,' he said, 'you want to talk about whatever this is that's got you so upset? Have you run out of tolerance for being in your parents' house? Has your sister made you mad? Or . . . have you found out something else about her fiancé?'

I pushed away from him and began to pace the room.

'I have some ideas,' I said.

His dark brows flew up. I should've kept my mouth shut. I didn't want to have the whole conversation: I'd tell him I would get in the houses, he'd tell me it was his job, blah blah blah. Why not skip the whole thing?

'Lily, I'm going to get mad at you,' Jack said with a sort of fatalistic certainty.

'You can't do the things I can do. What's your next step now?' I challenged him. 'Is there one more thing you can find out here?'

Sure enough, he was looking angry already. He stuck his hands in the pockets of his leather jacket and glanced around for something handy to kick. Finding nothing, he too began pacing. We shifted around the room as if we were sword fighters waiting for our opponent to give us an opening.

'Ask the chief if I can go in and look at those files at Dr LeMay's,' he suggested defiantly.

'It'll never happen.' I knew Chandler: He would go only so far.

'Find whatever the murderer was wearing when he killed the doctor and the nurse and Meredith Osborn.'

So Jack had decided, as I had, that the killer had worn some covering garment over his clothes.

'It's not gonna be in the house,' I told him.

'You think not?'

'I know not. When people hide something like that, they want it to be close but not as personally close as their own house.'

'You're thinking carport, garage?'

I nodded. 'Or car. But you know as well as I do that'll put you in a terrible position legally. Before you do that, isn't there anything else you can try?'

'I'd hoped to get something from Dill. He's a nice guy, but he just won't talk about his first marriage. At least his attic has a good floored section now.' Jack gave a short laugh. 'I thought about going back to reinterview the couple that lived next door to Meredith and Emory when they had their first child,' Jack said reluctantly. 'I've been reviewing what they said, and I think I see a hole in their account.'

'Where do they live?'

'The pod link town north of Little Rock where the Osborns lived before they came here. You know . . . the one not far from Conway.'

'What was the hole?'

'Not so much a hole, as . . . something the woman said just didn't make sense. She said that Meredith told her the baby coming was the saddest day of her life. And Meredith told her that the home birth had been terrible.'

That could be significant or just plain nothing more than what it was, the outpourings of a woman who'd just experienced childbirth for the first time.

'She had the second baby in the hospital,' I observed. 'At least, I assume so; I think someone would have mentioned it before now if she'd had Jane Lilith at home.' But I made a mental note to check.

'Why would Meredith have to die?' Jack said. 'Why Meredith?' He wasn't talking to me, not really. He was staring out the front window, his hands still in his pockets. Seen in profile, he looked stern and frightening. If I mentally lopped off his ponytail, I could see how he'd looked as a cop. I would not have been afraid of being beaten if I'd been arrested by him, I thought, but I would have known I'd be a fool to try to escape.

'She babysat the other two girls,' I offered.

Jack nodded. 'So she knew them all physically. She'd have an opportunity, sooner or later, to see each girl naked. But the Macklesby baby didn't have any distinguishing physical marks.'

'So who do you think sent you the picture?'

'I think it was Meredith Osborn.' He turned from the window to look at me directly. 'I think she sent it because she wanted to right some great wrong. And I think that's why she was killed.'

'What were you really doing the night she died?'

'I was on my way to ask her some questions,' he said. 'I'd driven past the Bartley Grill and I saw her husband and the kids inside. The baby was on the table in one of those carriers, and he and Eve were chattering away. So I knew Meredith was home by herself, and I thought she might know more about the picture.'

'Why?'

'Roy had brushed the picture and the envelope for fingerprints. There weren't any on the picture – it had been wiped – but there was one on the envelope, on the tape used to seal the flap. It was a clear print, very small. You'd told me how little Meredith was. Did you ever notice how tiny her hands were?'

I never had.

'I'd hoped to get some fingerprints of hers to compare. I planned on ringing the doorbell, telling her that I was a detective in town on a job as well as being your boyfriend. I was going to hand her a photo, ask her to identify it. When she said she didn't know the subject, I would put the photo in a bag and later test it for fingerprints.'

If I were in the Osborn house I could find something I could almost bet would have her fingerprints on it. I could also check to see if Eve's memory book was missing a page.

'But I don't want you getting into this. You saw how she died,'

Jack said brutally. I looked up sharply. He was standing right in front of me.

'I can tell when you're going to do something; you get this stubborn clench to your jaw,' he continued. 'What's in your head, Lily?'

'Cleaning,' I said.

'Cleaning what?'

'Cleaning the Osborn house, and the Kingery house.'

He thought that over. 'This isn't your case,' he said.

'I want us out of here by Christmas.'

'Me too,' he said fervently.

'Well, then,' I said, concluding our discussion.

'Did I just say something I didn't know I said?'

'We agree on getting this done by Christmas.'

Jack gave me a dark look. 'So, I'm driving out of here,' he said abruptly. 'I'll call you. Don't do anything that could put you in danger.'

'Drive careful,' I told him. He gave me an unloving peck on the cheek, another suspicious look, and, without further ado, he left. I watched through the uncurtained window as Jack fastened his seat belt and backed out of the driveway.

Then I went over to the widower and offered to clean his house.

Chapter Six

Since Emory was so fine-boned and fair, the swollen red eyes made him look rabbity. Those eyes hardly seemed to register my identity. He was completely preoccupied, eaten up from the inside out.

'Ah, yes? What can I do for you?' he asked me, his voice coming from a great interior distance.

'I've come to clean your house.'

'What?'

'That's what I do for a living, clean. This is what I can offer you in your time of trouble.'

He was still bewildered. I was unhappy with myself, so it was more difficult to keep my impatience under wraps.

'My sister . . .' he faltered. 'She'll be coming tomorrow.'

'Then you need the house clean for her arrival.'

He stared some more. I stared right back. Behind him, down a dark hall, I saw Eve creep out of an open doorway. She looked like a little ghost of herself.

'Miss Lily,' she said. 'Thanks for coming.'

It was what she'd heard her father say to callers all day, and her attempt to be adult gave my heart a little pang. I also wondered what Eve was doing at home, when I'd thought she was with the O'Sheas.

Emory finally stood aside so I could enter, but he still seemed uncertain. I glanced at my watch, letting him know how valuable I thought my time was, and that shook him from his lethargy.

'This is so kind of you, Miss . . . Bard,' he said. 'Is there anything we need to . . . ?'

'I expect Eve can show me where things are.' I am no grief

counselor. I don't know squat about children. But it's always better to be busy.

'That would be good,' Emory said vaguely. 'So I'll . . .' and he just wandered off. 'Oh, Eve,' he said over his shoulder, 'remember your company manners. Stay with Miss Bard.'

Eve looked a little resentful, but she replied, 'Yes, Daddy.'

The girl and I looked at each other carefully. 'Where's the baby?' I asked.

'She's at the O'Sheas' house. I was there for a while, too, but Daddy said I needed to come home.'

'All right, then. Where is the kitchen?'

Her lips curved in an incredulous smile. Surely everyone knew where the kitchen was! But Eve was polite, and she guided me to the back of the house and to the right.

'Where's all the cleaning stuff?' I asked. I set my purse down on the kitchen counter, shrugged off my coat, and hung it on one of the kitchen chairs.

Eve opened a cupboard in the adjacent washroom. I could see that the laundry basket was full of clothes.

'Maybe you better show me the house before I start.'

So the little girl showed me her home. It was a large older house, with high ceilings and dark hardwood paneling and floors that needed work. I noticed the register of a floor furnace. I hadn't seen one of those in years. A Christmas tree decorated with religious symbols stood in the living room, the family's only communal room. The sofa, coffee table, and chair combo was maple with upholstery of a muted brown plaid. Clean but hideous.

Emory was slumped in the chair, his hand wrapped around a cold mug that had held coffee. I knew it was cold because I could see the ring around the middle. He'd had a drink after it had been sitting a spell. He didn't acknowledge our passage through the room. I wondered if I'd have to dust him like a piece of furniture.

The master bedroom was tidy, but the furniture needed polishing. Eve's room . . . well, her bed had been made haphazardly, but the floor was littered with Barbies and coloring books. The baby's room was neatest, since the baby couldn't walk yet. The diaper pail needed emptying. The bathroom needed a complete scrubbing. The kitchen was not too bad.

'Where are the sheets?' I asked.

Eve said, 'Mama's are in there.' She pointed to the double closet in the master bedroom.

I stripped down the double bed, carried the dirty sheets to the washroom, started a load of wash. Back in the bedroom, I opened the closet door.

'There's Mama's stool,' Eve said helpfully. 'She always needs it to get things down from the closet shelf.'

I was at least six inches taller than Meredith Osborn had been, and I could easily reach the shelf. But if I wanted to look at what was behind the sheets, the stool would be handy.

I stepped up, lifted the set of sheets, and scanned the contents of the closet shelf. Another blanket for the bed, a box marked 'Shoe Polish,' a cheap metal box for files and important papers. Then, under a pile of purses, I spotted a box marked 'Eve.' After I'd snapped the clean sheets on the bed, I sent Eve out of the room to fetch a dustcloth and the furniture polish.

I lifted down the box and opened it. I had to clench my teeth to make myself examine its contents. My sense of invasion was overwhelming.

In the box were faded 'Welcome, Baby' cards, the kind family and friends send a couple when they have a child. I quickly riffled through them. They were only what they seemed. Also in the box was a little rattle and a baby outfit. It was soft knit, yellow, with little green giraffes scattered over it, the usual snap crotch and long sleeves. It had been folded carefully. Eve's coming home from the hospital outfit, maybe. But Eve had been born at home, I remembered. Well, then, Meredith's favorite of all Eve's baby clothes. My mother had some of mine and Varena's still packed away in our attic.

I closed the box and popped it back into position. By the time

Eve returned, I had the flowered bedspread smoothed flat and taut across the bed and the blanket folded at the foot.

Together, we polished and dusted. Eve naturally didn't do things the most efficient way, since she was a grieving eight-year-old child. I am rigid about the way I like housework done and not used to working with anyone, but I managed it.

I'd had a pang of worry about Eve handling her mother's belongings, but Eve seemed to do that so matter-of-factly that I wondered if she didn't yet comprehend that her mother would not be returning.

In the course of cleaning that room I made sure I examined every nook and cranny. Short of going through the chest of drawers and the drawers in the night tables, I saw what there was to see in that bedroom: under the bed, the corners of the closet, the backs and bottoms of almost every single piece of furniture. Later, when I began to put the laundry away, I even caught glimpses of what was in the drawers. Just the usual stuff, as far as I could tell.

One drawer of the little desk in the corner was stacked with medical bills related to Meredith's pregnancy. At a glance, it had been a difficult one. I hoped the furniture store had a group policy.

'Shake the can, Eve,' I reminded her, and she shook the yellow aerosol can of furniture polish. 'Now, spray.'

She carefully sent a stream of polish onto the bare top of the desk. I swabbed with a cloth, over and over, then put the letter rack, mug full of pens and pencils, and box containing stamps and return address labels back in their former positions. When Eve excused herself to use the bathroom, I gritted my teeth and did something that disgusted me: I picked up Meredith Osborn's hairbrush, which could reasonably be assumed to have her fingerprints on it, wrapped it in a discarded plastic cleaner's bag, and stepped through to the kitchen and shoved it in my purse.

I was back in the Osborns' bedroom, tamping the stack of papers so the edges were square and neat, when Eve came back.

'Those are Mama's bills,' she said importantly. 'We always pay our bills.'

'Of course.' I gathered the cleaning things and handed some of them to Eve. 'We've finished here.'

As we began to work on Eve's room, I could tell that the little girl was getting bored, after the novelty of helping me work wore thin.

'Where'd you eat last night?' I asked casually.

'We went to the restaurant,' she said. 'I got a milkshake. Jane slept the whole time. It was great.'

'Your dad was with you,' I observed.

'Yeah, he wanted to give Mama a night off,' Eve said approvingly. Then the ending of that night off hit her in the face, and I saw her pleasure in the little memory of the milkshake crumple. I could not ask her any more questions about last night.

'Why don't you find your last school memory book and show me who your friends are?' I suggested, as I got her clean sheets out of her little closet and began to remake her single bed.

'Oh, sure!' Eve said enthusiastically. She began to rummage through the low bookcase that was filled with children's books and knickknacks. Nothing in the bookcase seemed to be in any particular order, and I wasn't too surprised when Eve told me she couldn't come up with her most recent memory book. She fetched one from two years ago instead and had an excellent time telling me the name of every child in every picture. I was required only to smile and nod, and every now and then I said, 'Really?' As casually as I could manage it, I went through the books in the bookcase myself. The past year's memory book wasn't there.

Eve relaxed perceptibly as she looked at the pictures of her friends and acquaintances.

'Did you go to the doctor last week, Eve?' I asked casually.

'Why do you want to know that?' she asked.

I was floored. It hadn't occurred to me that a child would ask me why I wanted to know.

'I just wondered what doctor you went to.'

'Doctor LeMay.' Her brown eyes looked huge as she thought about her answer. 'He's dead, too,' she said wearily, as if the whole world was dying around her. To Eve, it must have felt so.

I could not think of a natural, painless way to ask again, and I just couldn't put the girl through any more grief. To my surprise, Eve volunteered, 'Mama went with me.'

'She did?' I tried to keep my voice as noncommittal as possible.

'Yep. She liked Dr LeMay, Miss Binnie, too.'

I nodded, lifting a stack of coloring books and shaking them into an orderly rectangle.

'It hurt, but it was over before too long,' Eve said, obviously quoting someone.

'What was over?' I asked.

'They took my blood,' Eve said importantly.

'Yuck.'

'Yeah, it hurt,' said the girl, shaking her head just like a middle-aged woman, philosophically. 'But some things hurt, and you just gotta handle it.'

I nodded. This was a lot of stoical philosophy from a third grader.

'I was losing weight, and my mama thought something might be wrong,' Eve explained.

'So, what was wrong?'

'I don't know.' Eve looked down at her feet. 'She never said.'

I nodded as if that were quite usual. But what Eve had told me worried me, worried me badly. What if something really was wrong physically with the child? Surely her father knew about it, about the visit and the blood test? What if Eve were anemic or had some worse disease?

She looked healthy enough to me, but I was certainly willing to concede that I was hardly a competent judge. Eve was thin and pale, yes, but not abnormally so. Her hair shone and her teeth looked sound and clean, she smelled good and she stood like she was comfortable, and she was able to meet my eyes: The absence of any of these conditions is reason to worry, their presence reassuring. So why wasn't I relaxing?

We moved on to the baby's room, Eve shadowing my every step. From time to time the doorbell rang, and I would hear Emory drift through the house to answer it, but the callers never stayed long. Faced with Emory's naked grief, it would be hard to stand and chat.

After I'd finished the baby's room and the bathroom, I entered the kitchen to find that food was accumulating faster than Emory could store it. He was standing there with a plastic bowl in his hands, a bowl wrapped in the rose-colored plastic wrap that was so popular locally. I opened the refrigerator and evaluated the situation.

'Hmmm,' I said. I began removing everything. Emory put the bowl down and helped. All the little odds and ends of leftovers went into the garbage, the dishes they'd been in went in the sink, and I wiped down the bottom shelf where there'd been a little spillage.

'Do you have a list?' I asked Emory.

He seemed to come out of his trance. 'A list?' he asked, as if he'd never heard the word.

'You need to keep a list of who brings what food in what dish. Do you have a piece of paper handy?' That sister of Emory's needed to get here fast.

'Daddy, I've got notebook paper in my room!' Eve said and ran off to fetch it.

'I guess I knew that, but I forgot,' Emory said. He blinked his red eyes, seemed to wake up a little. When Eve dashed into the kitchen with several sheets of paper, he hugged her. She wriggled in his grasp.

'We have to start the list, Daddy!' She looked up at him sternly.

I thought that Eve had probably been hugged and patted enough for two lifetimes in the day just past.

She began the list herself, in shaky and idiosyncratic writing. I told her how to do it, and she perched on a stool at the counter, laboriously entering the food gifts on one side, the bringer on the other, and a star when there was a dish that had to be returned.

Galvanized by our activity, Emory began making calls from the telephone on the kitchen counter. I gathered from the snatches of conversation I overheard that he was calling the police department to find out when they thought Meredith's body could come back from its autopsy in Little Rock, making arrangements for the music at the funeral service, checking in at work, trying to start his life back into motion. He began writing his own list, in tiny, illegible writing. It was a list of things to do before the funeral, he told me in his quiet voice. I was glad to see him shake off his torpor.

It was getting late so I accelerated my work rate, sweeping and mopping and wiping down the kitchen counters with dispatch. I selected a few dishes for Emory and Eve's supper, leaving them on the counter with heating instructions. Emory was still talking on the phone, so I just drifted out of the room with Eve behind me. I pulled on my coat, pulled up the strap of my purse.

'Can you come back, Lily?' Eve asked. 'You know how to do everything.'

I looked down at her. I was betraying this child and her father, abusing their trust. Eve's admiration for me was painful.

'I can't come back tomorrow, no,' I said as gently as I was capable of. 'Varena's getting married the day after, and I still have a lot to do for that. But I'll try to see you again.'

'OK.' She took that in a soldierlike way, which I was beginning to understand was typical of Eve Osborn. 'And thank you for helping today,' Eve said, after a couple of gulps. Very much woman of the house.

'I figured cleaning would be more use than more food.'

'You were right,' she said soberly. 'The house looks so much nicer.'

'See ya,' I said. I bent to give her a little hug. I felt awkward. 'Take care of yourself.' What a stupid thing to tell a child, I castigated myself, but I had no idea what else to say.

Emory was standing by the front door. I felt like snarling. I had almost made it out without talking to him. 'I can't thank you enough for this,' he said, his sincerity painful and unwelcome.

'It was nothing.'

'No, no,' he insisted. 'It meant so much to us.' He was going to cry again.

Oh, hell. 'Good-bye,' I told him firmly and was out the door.

Glancing down at my watch again as I walked out to my car, I realized there was no way to get out of explaining to my folks where I'd been and what I'd been doing.

To compound my guilt, my parents thought I'd done a wonderful Christian thing, helping out Emory Osborn in his hour of travail. I had to let them think the best of me when I least deserved it.

I tried hard to pack my guilt into a smaller space in my heart. Reduced to the most basic terms, the Osborns now had a clean house in which to receive visitors. And I had a negative report for Jack. I hadn't discovered anything of note, except for Eve's trip to the doctor. Though I had stolen the brush.

When Varena emerged from her room, looking almost as weepy as Emory, I put the second part of my plan into effect.

'I'm in the cleaning mood,' I told her. 'How about me cleaning Dill's house, so it'll be nice for your first Christmas together?' Varena and Dill weren't leaving for their honeymoon until after Christmas, so they'd be together at home with Anna.

Somehow, since my mission was to save Varena grief, I didn't feel quite as guilty as I had when I'd told Emory I was going to clean his house. But I had a sour taste in my mouth, and I figured it was self-disgust.

'Thanks,' Varena said, surprise evident in her voice. 'That would really be a load off my mind. You're sure?'

'You know I need something to do,' I told her truthfully.

'Bless your heart,' Varena said with compassion, giving me a hug. Somehow, my sister's unwanted sympathy stiffened my resolve.

Then the doorbell rang, and it was some friends of my parents', just back from a trip to see the Christmas decorations at Pigeon

Forge. They were full of their trip and had brought a present for Dill and Varena. It was easy for me to slip off to my room after a proper greeting. I took a hot, hot shower and waited for Jack to call me.

He didn't. The phone rang off the wall that evening, the callers ranging from friends wanting to check on wedding plans, Dill asking for Varena, credit card companies wanting to extend new cards to my parents, and church members trying to arrange a meal for the Osborn family after the relatives had arrived for Meredith's funeral.

But no Jack.

Something was niggling at me, and I wanted to look at the pictures of Summer Dawn at eight. I wanted to ask Jack some questions. I wanted to look at his briefcase. That was the closest I could get to figuring out what was bothering me.

About eight-thirty, I called Chandler McAdoo. 'Let's go riding,' I said.

Chandler pulled into my parents' drive in his own vehicle, a Jeep. He was wearing a heavy red-and-white-plaid flannel shirt, a camo jacket, jeans, and Nikes.

My mother answered the door before I could get there.

'Chandler,' she said, sounding a little at sea. 'Did you need to ask us something about the other day?'

'No, ma'am. I'm here to pick up Lily.' He was wearing an Arkansas Travellers gimme cap, and the bill of it tilted as he nodded at me. I was putting on my coat.

'*This* brings back old times,' my mother said with a smile.

'See you in a while, Mom,' I said, zipping up my old red Squall jacket.

'Okay, sweetie. You two have a good time.'

I liked the Jeep. Chandler kept it spick-and-span, and I approved. Jack tended to distribute paperwork all over his car.

'So, where we going?' Chandler asked.

'It's too cold and we're too old for Frankel's Pond,' I said. 'What about the Heart of the Delta?'

'The Heart it is,' he said.

By the time we scooted into a booth at the home-owned diner we'd patronized all through high school, I was in the midst of being updated about Chandler's two stabs at marriage, the little boy he was so proud of (by Cindy, wife number two), and the current woman in his life – Tootsie Monahan, my least favorite of Varena's bridesmaids.

When we had glanced at the menu – which seemed almost eerily the same as it had been when I was sixteen, except for the prices – and had given the waitress our order (a hamburger with everything and fries for Chandler, a butterscotch milkshake for me), Chandler gave me a sharp, let's-get-down-to-it look.

'So what's the deal with this guy you've hooked up with?'

'Jack.'

'I know his damn name. What's his business here?'

Chandler and I stared at each other for a moment. I took a deep breath.

'He's tracing an . . .' I stopped dead. How could I do this? Where did my loyalty lie?

Chandler made a rotary movement with his hand, wanting me to spill it out.

Chandler had already told Jack several things, operating on his affection for me. But the actual physical effort of opening my mouth, telling him Jack's business, was almost impossible. I closed my eyes for a second, took a deep breath. 'A missing person,' I said.

He absorbed that.

'Okay, tell me.'

I hesitated. 'It's not my call.'

'What do you want from me, Lily?'

Chandler's face was infinitely older.

Oh, Jesus, I hated this.

'Tell me what people were doing when Meredith Osborn was killed. I don't know if that has anything to do with Jack's job, Chandler, and that's the truth. I was in that house, just a few feet away from her, and if there's anything I know it's how to fight.' I hadn't known how that bothered me until I said it. 'I didn't have a chance to lift a finger to help her. Just tell me about that evening.'

He could do that without violating any laws, I figured.

'What people were doing. What happened to Meredith.' Chandler appeared to be thinking, his eyes focused on the salt-shaker with its grains of rice showing yellower than the stark white of the salt.

I didn't know I'd been holding my breath until Chandler began talking. He folded his small hands in front of him, and his face took on a faintly stern, stiff set that I realized must be his professional demeanor.

'Mrs Osborn died, as far as I could tell by a visual exam, from multiple stab wounds to the chest,' he began. 'She'd been hit in the face, maybe to knock her on the ground so the stabbing would be easier. The attack took place in the backyard. It would have required only a minute or two. She wasn't able to move more than a yard after she was stabbed. Her wounds were very severe. Plus, the temperature was below freezing, and she didn't have a coat on.'

'But she did move that one yard.'

'Yes.'

'Toward Varena's little house.'

'Yes.'

I could feel my mouth compress in a hard line and my eyes narrow, in what my friend Marshall had once called my 'fist face'.

'What kind of knife?'

'Some kind of single-blade kitchen knife, looked like, but we have to wait on the autopsy to be sure. We haven't found any kind of knife.'

'Did you go in the Osborns' house?'

'Sure. We had to see if the killer was in there, and the back door was unlocked.'

'So someone had made a noise, or called Meredith out of the house . . . ?'

He shrugged. 'Something like that, we figure. She wasn't scared. She would have stayed in the house and locked the back door if she'd been scared. She could have called us. The phone was working, I checked. Instead, she went outside.'

Unspoken between us lay the inescapable conclusion that Meredith had seen someone she knew and trusted in the yard.

'When does Emory say he left the house?'

'About seven. He had the two little girls. He wanted to give his wife some time to herself, he said. She'd had a hard time with the baby's birth, wasn't getting her strength back, and so on.'

I raised my brows.

'Yes, the waitress confirms that Emory got to the restaurant about five after. It took about forty-five minutes for Emory and Eve to eat, and then the baby woke up and Emory gave her a bottle, burped her, the whole nine yards. So they left the restaurant maybe fifteen minutes after eight, Emory had some things to pick up at the Kmart, so he took the girls with him in there, and they got some vitamins and other junk . . . that brings us up to around eight-fifty, nine o'clock, somewhere in there.'

'Then he comes home.'

'Then he comes home,' Chandler agreed. 'He was mighty tore up. Turned white as a sheet.'

'You had already searched the house?'

'Yes, had to. Didn't find any evidence anyone but the family had been in it. Nothing suspicious in any way. No forced entry, no threatening messages on the answering machine, no sign of a struggle . . . a big zero.'

'Chandler . . .' I hesitated. But I could think of no other way to find out. 'Did you search his car?'

Chandler shifted in his seat. 'No. Do you think we should have?'

'Did you ask Eve if her dad had stopped back by the house for anything?'

'I did my best to ask her that. I had to be real careful how I put it, didn't want the girl to think we figured her dad had done it. She's just eight!' Chandler looked at me angrily, as if that were my doing.

'What did she say?' I asked, keeping my voice very quiet and level.

'She said they went to the restaurant. Period. Then to Kmart. Period.'

I nodded, looked away. 'Where was Jess O'Shea?' I asked.

I could feel the heat of Chandler's glare even though I was looking over at the chipped Formica counter.

'Dave asked Emory what church he went to, and when he said Presbyterian, we called Jess,' Chandler said slowly. 'Lou said he was over in his office counseling a member of the congregation.'

'Did you call over there?'

'Yes.'

'Get an answer?'

'Yes. But he said he couldn't come right that second.'

I wondered if Jess had actually come over to the Osborns' house that night. I couldn't remember if the scene between him and Emory the next day had given me a sense of an original encounter or a continuation of a dialogue begun the night before. I had been so embarrassed that I had tried to block out their conversation.

'Did he give a reason?'

'I just assumed he had to finish talking to whoever was there.'

The upshot was, Jess had been away from home and the police had not asked him to account for his time. There was no reason why they should, from their point of view.

Varena had told me Dill was going to spend the evening at home with Anna. I didn't think Dill was the kind of father who'd leave Anna in the house by herself, but he could have worked it out somehow, I guessed. I wondered if I could think of a way to ask questions that wouldn't make red flags go up in Varena's mind.

'Lily, if someone's safety is at stake, or if you have any idea at all who killed that poor woman, you are legally obliged to tell me. Morally, too,'

I looked into Chandler's round brown eyes. I'd known this man my whole life, been friends with him, off and on, that long.

When I'd come home to Bartley after my spectacular victimization and subsequent media bath, Chandler had been a constant
visitor. He'd been between marriages, and we had gone out to
eat together, ridden around together, spent time together so I
could get away from my family and their love that was just
choking me.

During that time, seven years ago, we had also shared a horribly embarrassing evening in the big pickup Chandler had been
driving then. But I was sure we both did our best not to remember that.

'I don't know the identity of anyone who is in danger,' I said
carefully. 'I don't know who killed Meredith.' That was absolutely
true.

'You should tell me everything you know,' Chandler said, his
voice so low and intent it was scary as a snake's rattle.

My hands, resting on the worn gray and pink Formica of the
table's surface, clenched into hard fists. My heels dug into the
wooden base of the booth, giving me launching power. A startled
look crossed Chandler's face, and he leaned away from me.

'What's in your mind?' he asked sharply, and he brushed his
empty plate to one side without taking his eyes off me, clearing
his own deck for action.

For once, I was anxious to explain myself. But I couldn't. I took
a couple of deep breaths, made myself relax.

'You love this man,' he said.

I started to shake my head side to side: no. But I said, 'Yes.'

'This is the one.'

I nodded, a jerky little up-and-down movement.

'And he doesn't . . . he can handle . . . what happened to you?'

'He doesn't mind the scars,' I said, my voice as light and
smooth as the changing scenery of a dream.

Chandler turned red. His eyes left mine, focused on the pattern
of the Formica.

'It's OK,' I told him, just above a whisper.

'Does he . . . does he know how lucky he is?' Chandler asked, not able to think of any other way of asking me if Jack loved me back.

'I don't know.'

'Lily, if you want me to have a serious talk with this joker, just say the word.' And he really meant it. I looked at Chandler with new eyes. This man would put himself through a humiliating conversation and not think twice about it.

'Will you make him go down on one knee and swear to forsake all others?' I was smiling a little, I couldn't help it.

'Damn straight.'

This, too, he meant.

'What a great guy you are,' I said. All the aggression leaked out of me, as if I was a balloon with a pinhole. 'You've been talking with Jack, haven't you?'

'He's an ex-cop, and no matter how his career ended,' and Chandler flushed uncomfortably since Jack had not exactly left the Memphis police force under creditable circumstances, 'Jack Leeds was a good detective and made some good arrests. I called the Memphis cops, talked to a friend of mine there, as soon as I realized who he was.'

That was interesting. Chandler had known Jack was in town probably before I did – and had checked up on him.

'Fact is, the only thing this guy knew against Jack was that he'd hooked up with a shady cleaning lady,' Chandler said with a grin.

I grinned back. All the tension was gone, and we were old friends together. Without asking, Chandler paid for my milkshake and his meal, and I slid out of the booth and into my coat.

When he dropped me off at home, Chandler gave me a kiss on the cheek. We hadn't said another word about Meredith Osborn, or Dr LeMay, or Jack. I knew Chandler had backed off only because he owed me, on some level: The last time we'd been together had been a terrible evening for both of us. Whatever the reason, I was grateful. But I knew that if Chandler thought I was concealing something that would contribute to solving the murders that had taken place in the town he was sworn to protect, he would come down on me like a ton of bricks.

We might be old friends, but we were both weighted down with adult burdens.

Jack didn't call.

That night I lay sleepless, my arms rigidly at my sides, watching the bars of moonlight striping the ceiling of my old room. It was the distillation of all the bad nights I'd had in the past seven years; except in my parents' house, I could not resort to my usual methods of escape and relief. Finally I got up, sat in the little slipper chair in the corner of the room, and turned on the lamp.

I'd finished my biography. Luckily I'd brought some paperbacks with me from Varena's, anticipating just such a night . . . not that I would have picked these books if I'd had much choice. The first was a book of advice on dealing with your stepchildren, and the second was a historical romance. Its cover featured a guy with an amazing physique. I stared at his bare, hairless chest with its immense pectorals, wondering if even my sensei's musculature would match this man's. I found it very unlikely that a sensible fighting man would wear his shirt halfway off his shoulders in that inconvenient and impractical way, and I thought it even sillier that his lady friend would choose to try to embrace him when he was leaning down from a horse. I calculated his weight, the angle of his upper body, and the pull she was exerting. I factored in the high wind blowing her hair out in a fan, and decided Lord Robert Dumaury was going to end up on the ground at Phillipetta Dunmore's feet within seconds, probably dislocating his shoulder in the process . . . and that's if he was lucky. I shook my head.

So I plowed through the advice, learning more about being a new mother to a growing not-your-own child than I ever wanted to know. This paperback showed serious signs of being read and reread. I hoped it would be of more use to Varena than Ms Dunmore's adventures with Pectoral Man.

I would have given anything for a good thick biography.

I got halfway through the book before sleep overcame me. I was still in the chair, the lamp still on, when I woke at seven to the sounds of my family stirring.

I felt exhausted, almost too tired to move.

I did some push-ups, tried some leg lifts. But my muscles felt slack and weak, as if I were recovering from major surgery. Slowly, I pulled on my sweats. I'd committed my morning to cleaning Dill's house. But instead of rising and getting into the bathroom, I sat back in the chair with my face covered by my hands.

Being involved in this child abduction felt so wrong, so bad, but for my family's sake I couldn't imagine what else I could do. With a sigh of sheer weariness, I hauled myself to my feet and opened the bedroom door to reenter my family's life.

It was like dipping your toes into a quiet pond, only to have a whirlpool suck you under.

Since this was the day before the wedding, Mother and Varena had every hour mapped out. Mother had to go to the local seamstress's house to pick up the dress she planned to wear tomorrow: It had required hemming. She had to drop in on the caterer to go over final arrangements for the reception. She and Varena had to take Anna to a friend's birthday party, and then to pick up Anna's flower girl dress, which was being shipped to the local Penney's catalog store after some delay. (Due to a last-minute growth spurt, Anna's fancy dress, bought months before, was now too tight in the shoulders, so Varena had had to scour catalogs for a quickly purchasable substitute.) Both Varena and my mother were determined that Anna should try the dress on instantly.

The list of errands grew longer and longer. I found myself tuning out after the first few items. Dill dropped Anna off to run errands with Varena and Mom, and Anna and I sat together at the kitchen table in the strange peace that lies at the eye of the storm.

'Is getting married always like this, Aunt Lily?' Anna asked wearily.

'No. You can just elope.'

'Elope? Like the animal?'

'It's like an antelope only in that you run fast. When you elope, the man and woman who are getting married get in the car and drive somewhere and get married where nobody knows them. Then they come home and tell their families.'

'I think that's what I'm gonna do,' Anna told me.

'No. Have a big wedding. Pay them back for all this,' I advised.

Anna grinned. 'I'll invite everyone in the whole town,' she said. 'And Little Rock, too!'

'That'll do it.' I nodded approvingly.

'Maybe in the whole world.'

'Even better.'

'Do you have a boyfriend, Aunt Lily?'

'Yes.'

'Does he write you notes?' Anna made a squeezed face, like she felt she was asking a stupid question, but she wanted to know the answer anyway.

'He calls me on the phone,' I said. 'Sometimes.'

'Does he . . .' Anna was rummaging in her brain for other things grown-up boyfriends might do. 'Does he send you flowers and candy?'

'He hasn't yet.'

'What does he do to show you he likes you?'

Couldn't share that with an eight-year-old. 'He hugs me,' I told her.

'Ewwww. Does he kiss you?'

'Yeah, sometimes.'

'Bobby Mitzer kissed me,' Anna said in a whisper.

'No kidding? Did you like it?'

'Ewwww.'

'Maybe he's just not the right guy,' I said, and we smiled at each other.

Then Mom and Varena told Anna they had been ready to go for minutes and inquired why she was still sitting at the table as if we had all day.

★

'You can manage at Dill's by yourself, can't you?' Varena asked anxiously. She'd returned from dropping Anna off at the party, complete with present. 'You sure don't have to do it if you don't want to.'

'I'll be fine,' I said, hearing my voice come out flat and cold. I'd enjoyed talking to Anna, but now I felt exhausted again.

Mother eyed me sharply. 'You didn't sleep well,' she said. 'Bad dreams again?' And she and Varena and my father stared at me with matching expressions of concern.

'I'm absolutely all right,' I said, trying to be civil, hating them thinking about the ordeal again. Was I being disgustingly self-pitying? It was just being *home*.

For the first time it occurred to me that if I'd been able to stay longer after the attack, if I'd toughed it out, they might have become used to me again, and they would have seen my life as a continuation, not a broken line. But I'd felt compelled to leave, and their clearest, most recent memory of me was of a woman in horrible pain of both kinds, plagued by nightmares waking and sleeping.

'I'll go clean now.' I pulled on my coat.

'Dill's at work checking his inventory,' Varena said. 'I don't know how long he'll be. We'll be picking Anna up and taking her straight to Penney's from the party. Then we'll come back here.' I nodded and went to get my purse.

Mother and Varena were still fine-tuning their agenda when I walked out the door. My father was working a crossword puzzle, a half smile on his face as he caught snatches of their discussion. He didn't loathe this wedding frenzy, as most men did or pretended to. He loved it. He was having a great time fussing about the cost of the reception, whether he needed to go to the church to borrow yet another table for the still-incoming gifts, whether Varena had written every single thank-you note promptly.

I touched Father's shoulder as I went by, and he reached up and captured my hand. After a second, he patted it gently and let me go.

Dill owned an undistinguished three-bedroom, three-bath

ranch-style in the newest section of Bartley. Varena had given me a key. It still felt strange to find a locked door in my little hometown. When I'd been growing up, no one had ever locked anything.

On the way to Dill's, I'd seen another homeless person, this one a white woman. She was gray-haired but sturdy looking, pedaling an ancient bicycle laden down with an assortment of strange items bound together with nylon rope.

The night before, my parents' friends had been talking about gang activity at the Bartley High School. Gangs! In the Arkansas Delta! In flat, remote, tiny, impoverished Bartley.

I guess in some corner of my mind, I'd expected Bartley would remain untouched by the currents of the world, would retain its small-town safety and assurance. Home had changed. I could go there again, but its character was permanently altered.

Abruptly, I was sick of myself and my problems. It was high time I got back to work.

I started, as I like to do, with a survey of the job to be done. Dill's house, which looked freshly painted and carpeted, was fairly straight and fairly clean – but, like the Osborns', it was showing signs of a few days of neglect. Varena wasn't the only one feeling the effects of prolonged wedding fever.

I had no guide here to show me where everything was. I wondered if Anna would have been as interesting a helper as Eve had been the day before.

That recalled me to the purpose of my cleaning offer. Before anything or anyone could interrupt me, I searched Anna's room for her memory book. As I searched, naturally I picked up her room, which was a real mess. I slung soiled clothes into the hamper, stacked school papers, tossed dolls into a clear Rubbermaid tub firmly labeled 'Dolls and doll clothes.'

I found the memory book under her bed. Page 23 was missing.

I rocked back on my haunches, feeling as though an adversary had socked me in the stomach.

'No,' I said out loud, hearing the misery in my own voice.

After a few minutes trying to think, I stuck the book in the rack on Anna's little desk and kept on cleaning. There was nothing else for me to do.

I had to face the fact that the page that had been sent to Roy Costimiglia and passed to Jack had almost certainly come from Anna's book. But, I told myself, that didn't have to mean Anna was Summer Dawn Macklesby.

The book being in Dill's house perhaps raised the odds that someone besides Meredith Osborn might have mailed the page to Roy Costimiglia. At least, that was what I thought. But I wished I'd found the book anywhere but here.

If Anna was the abducted child, Dill could be suffering from the terrible dichotomy of wanting to square things with Summer's family and wanting to keep his beloved daughter. What if his unstable wife had been the one to kidnap the Macklesby baby, and Dill had just now become aware of it? He'd raised Anna as his own for eight years.

And if Dill's first wife had abducted Summer Dawn, what had happened to their biological baby?

As I paired Anna's shoes and placed them on a rack in the closet, I saw a familiar blue cover peeking from behind a pair of rain boots. I frowned and squatted, reaching back in the closet and finally managing to slide a finger between the book and wall. I fished out the book and flipped it over to read the cover.

It was another copy of the memory book.

I opened it, hoping fervently that Anna had written her name in it. No name.

'Shit,' I said out loud. When I'd been young, and we'd gotten our yearbooks, or memory books, or whatever you wanted to call them, the first thing we'd done was write our names inside.

One of these books had to be Anna's. If Jack's basic assumption was correct, if the person who'd sent the memory book page to Roy Costimiglia wasn't a complete lunatic, then the other book belonged to either Eve or Krista, and it was someone very close to one of them who had sent the picture. Like someone in their house. A parent.

Dill was using the third bedroom as a study. There was a

framed picture of Dill holding a baby I presumed was Anna. The snapshot had obviously been taken in a hospital room, and Anna looked like a newborn. But to me all babies looked more or less the same, and the infant Dill was gazing at so lovingly could have been Anna, or it could have been another child. The baby was swaddled in a receiving blanket.

I cleaned, scrubbed, and worried at the problem. I straightened and dusted and vacuumed and polished and mopped, and the activity did me good. But I didn't solve anything.

When I went in Anna's room yet again to return a Barbie I'd found in the kitchen, I looked more closely at Anna's collection of framed snapshots. One was of a woman I was sure must be Dill's first wife, Anna's mother. She was buxom, like Varena; and like Varena her hair was brown, her eyes blue. Aside from those superficial similarities, she didn't look at all like my sister, really. I stared at the picture, trying to read the woman's character in this likeness. Was there something tense, something a little desperate, in the way she was clutching the little dog on her lap? Was her smile strained, insincere?

I shook my head. I would never have given the picture two thoughts if I hadn't known that the woman had eventually killed herself. So much despair, so well hidden. Dill had an unstable mother, had married an unstable wife. I was frightened that he could see something deep in Varena that we didn't suspect, some inner weakness, that attracted him or made him feel comfortable with her. But Varena seemed sane and sturdy to me, and I have a built-in Geiger counter for the ripples of instability in others.

It felt odd to see Varena's clothes hanging in half of Dill's closet, her china in his cabinets. She had really and truly moved into Dill's house. That intimacy bore in on me how much Varena would lose if Anna was someone else's daughter, for surely there would be the scandal to end all scandals . . . media coverage, intense and drenching. I shivered. I knew how that could affect your life.

The wedding was so close. One more day.

Very reluctantly, I reentered Dill's office and opened the filing cabinet. I had put on a pair of fresh rubber gloves, and I kept them on. That shows you how guilty I was feeling.

But this *had* to be done.

Dill was an orderly man, and I quickly found the file labeled simply 'Anna – Year One.' There was a separate file for each year of her life, containing drawings, pictures, and a page of cute things she'd said or done. The school-age files were crammed with report cards and test scores.

As far as I was concerned, Anna's first year was the most important. The file contained Anna's birth certificate, a record of her immunizations, her baby book, and some negatives in a white envelope marked 'Baby Is Born'. The handwriting wasn't Dill's. There was not a thing there that would prove Anna's identity one way or another. No blood type, no record of any distinguishing characteristic. A certificate from the hospital had Anna's baby footprints in black ink. I would ask Jack if the Macklesbys had similar prints of Summer Dawn's. If the contour of the foot was completely different from Anna's, surely that would mean something?

Blind alley. Dead end.

Suddenly I remembered the negatives marked 'Birth Pictures'. Where were the family photo albums?

I found them in a cabinet in the living room and blessed Dill for being orderly. They were labeled by year.

I yanked out the one marked with Anna's birth year. There were the pictures: a red infant in a doctor's arms, streaked with blood and other fluids, mouth open in a yell; the baby, now held by a masked and gowned Dill, the baby's round little bottom toward the camera – presumably this one had been taken by a nurse. In the corner of the picture, her face just visible, was the woman in the picture in Anna's room. Her mother, Judy.

And on the baby's bottom, a big brown birthmark.

This was proof, wasn't it? This was indisputably a delivery room picture, this was indisputably the baby born to Dill and his wife, Judy. And this baby, shown in a third picture cradled in the arms of the woman in the picture in Anna's room, was absolutely positively the original Anna Kingery.

The elation at finding something certain helped me through the pang of guilt I suffered as I extracted the key picture from the album. It, too, went in my purse, after I'd returned the photo album to its former position.

I finished my cleaning, surveyed the house, found it good. I put the garbage in the wheeled cans, swept the front and back steps. I was done. I went back in to put the broom away.

Dill was standing in the kitchen.

He had a pile of mail in his hands, was shuffling through it. When the broom hit the floor, Dill looked up sharply.

'Hi, Lily, this was mighty fine of you,' he said. He smiled at me, his bland and forgettable face beaming nothing but goodwill. 'Hey, did I scare you? I thought you heard me pull into the garage.'

He must have come in the back door while I was sweeping at the front.

Still tense all over, I bent to retrieve the broom, glad my face was hidden for a moment while I recovered.

'I saw Varena downtown,' he said, as I straightened and moved to the broom closet. 'I can't believe after all this waiting, it's finally going to be our wedding day tomorrow.'

I wrung out a dishrag I'd forgotten and draped it neatly over the sink divider. 'Lily, won't you turn to look at me?'

I turned to meet his eyes.

'Lily, I know you and I have never gotten close. But I don't have a sister, and I hope you'll be one to me.'

I was repelled. Emotional appeals were not the way to make a relationship happen.

'You don't know how hard it's always been for Varena.'

I raised my eyebrows. 'Excuse me?'

'Being your sister.'

I took a deep breath. I held my hand palm up. Explain?

'She would kill me if she knew I was saying this.' He shook his head at his own daring. 'She never felt as pretty as you, as smart as you.'

That didn't matter now. It hadn't mattered for more than a decade.

'Varena,' I began, and my voice sounded rusty, 'is a grown woman. We haven't been teenagers for years.'

'When you're a younger sister, apparently you have baggage you carry with you always. Varena thinks so, anyway. She always felt like an also-ran. With your parents. With your teachers. With your boyfriends.'

What crap was this? I gave Dill a cold stare.

'And when you got raped . . .'

I'll give him that, he went right on and said the word.

'. . . and all the focus was on you, and all you wanted was to get rid of it, I think in some way it gave Varena some . . . satisfaction.'

Which would have made her feel guilty.

'And of course, she began to feel guilty about that, about even feeling a particle of righteousness about your getting hurt.'

'Your point being?'

'You don't seem happy to be here. At the wedding. In the town. You don't seem happy for your sister.'

I couldn't quite see the connection between the two statements. Was I supposed to wag my tail since Varena was getting married . . . because she'd felt guilty when I got raped? I didn't have any active animosity toward Dill Kingery, so I tried to work through his thought.

I shook my head. I wasn't making any connections. 'Since Varena wants to marry you, I'm glad she is,' I said cautiously. I wasn't about to apologize for being who I was, what I had become.

Dill looked at me. He sighed. 'Well, that's as good as it's gonna get, I guess,' he said, with a tight little smile.

Guess so.

'What about you?' I asked. 'You married one unstable wife.

Your mother's not exactly predictable. I hope you see nothing like that in Varena.'

He threw back his head and laughed.

'You take the cake, you really do, Lily,' he said, shaking his head. He didn't seem to find that endearing. 'You don't say much, but you go for the throat when you decide to talk. I think that's what your parents have been dying to ask me for the past two years.'

I waited.

'No,' he said, quite seriously now. 'I see nothing like that in Varena. But that's why I dated her for so long. That's why our engagement went on forever. I had to be sure. For my sake, and especially for Anna's sake. I think Varena is the sanest woman I ever met.'

'Did your wife ever threaten to hurt Anna?'

He turned white as a sheet. I'd never seen anyone pale so fast. 'What – how—' He was spluttering.

'Before she killed herself, did she threaten to hurt Anna?'

It was like I was a cobra and he was a mouse.

'What have you heard?' he choked out.

'Just a guess. Did she try to hurt Anna?'

'Please go now,' he said finally. 'Lily, please go.'

I'd certainly handled that well. What a masterly interrogation! At least, I reflected, Dill and I had been equally unpleasant to each other, though I might have the edge since I'd talked about something new, something that wasn't common currency in Bartley – at least, judging by Dill's reaction.

I was willing to bet I wouldn't be invited to go on vacations with Dill and Varena.

It seemed possible that Dill's first wife had been capable – at least in Dill's estimation – of harming her baby. And page 23 was missing from a memory book that was most probably Anna's.

I understood what the word 'heartsick' meant. I tried to comfort myself with the thought of Anna's birthmark. At least I'd learned one fact.

As I backed out of Dill's driveway I discovered I didn't want to go home.

I began cruising aimlessly – shades of being a teenager, when 'riding around' had been a legitimate activity – and didn't know where I was going until I found myself parking at the town square.

I went into the furniture store, and a bell tinkled as the door swung shut. Mary Maude plummer was typing something into a computer at a desk behind a high counter in the middle of the store. Reading glasses perched at the end of her nose, and she was wearing her business face, competent and no-nonsense.

'Can I help you?' she asked and then looked up from the computer screen. 'Oh, Lily!' she said happily, her face changing from the inside out.

'Come go riding,' I suggested. 'I've got the car.'

'Your mom let you have it?' Mary Maude dissolved in giggles. She glanced around at the empty store. 'Maybe I can, really! Emory,' she called. Out of the shadows at the back of the store, Emory Osborn materialized like a thin, blond ghost.

'Hello, Miss Bard,' he said, his voice wispy.

'Emory, can you watch the store while I take my lunch hour?' Mary Maude asked in the gentle, earnest voice you use with slow children. 'Jerry and Sam should be back in just a minute.'

'Sure,' Emory said. He looked as if a good wind would whisk him away.

'Thanks.' Mary Maude fished her purse from some hidden spot under the counter.

When we were far enough away that Emory couldn't hear us, Mary Maude muttered, 'He should never have tried to come to work today. But his sister's here, and she's managing the home front, so I think he didn't have anything else to do.'

We went out the front door like two girls skipping school. I noticed how professional and groomed Mary Maude looked in her winter white suit, a sharp, unwelcome contrast to me in my sweats.

'I've been cleaning Dill's house,' I explained, suddenly self-conscious. I couldn't remember apologizing for my clothes, not for years.

'That's what you do for a living now?' Mary Maude asked as she buckled up.

'Yep,' I said flatly.

'Boy, did you ever think I'd end up selling furniture and you'd end up cleaning it?'

We shook our heads simultaneously.

'I'll bet you're tops at what you do,' Mary said, matter-of-factly.

I was surprised and oddly touched. 'I'll bet you sell a lot of furniture,' I offered and was even more surprised to find that I meant it.

'I do pretty well,' she answered, her voice offhand. She looked at me, and her face crinkled in a smile. 'You know, Lily, sometimes I just can't believe we grew up!'

That was never my problem. 'Sometimes I can't remember I was ever a teen,' I said.

'But here we are, alive, in good health, single but not without hope, and backed by family and friends,' Mary Maude said, almost chanting.

I raised my eyebrows.

'I have to practice counting my blessings all the time,' she explained, and I laughed. 'See, that didn't hurt,' she said.

We ate lunch at a fast-food place decorated with tinsel and lights and artificial snow. A Santa Claus robot nodded and waved from a plastic sleigh.

For a little while we just got used to each other. We talked about people we'd known and where they were now, how many times they'd been married and to whom. Mary Maude touched on her divorce and the baby she'd lost to crib death. We didn't need to talk about my past; it was too well known. But Mary asked me some questions about Shakespeare, about my daily life, and to my pleasure it was easy to answer.

She, too, asked if I was seeing someone special.

'Yes,' I said, trying not to stare down at my hands. 'A man from Little Rock, Jack Leeds.'

'Oh, is he the ponytail guy who showed up at the wedding rehearsal?'

'Yeah,' I said, not even trying to look up this time. 'How'd you know?' Why was I even asking, knowing the Bartley grapevine as I did?

'Lou O'Shea was in yesterday. She and Jess have a bed on layaway for Krista for Christmas.'

'They seem like a nice couple,' I said.

'Yeah, they are,' Mary Maude agreed, dipping a french fry in a puddle of ketchup. She'd made a trail of paper napkins to keep her winter white in a pristine state. 'They sure are having a hard time with that Krista since they had Luke.'

'That's what I hear. You reckon she feels unloved now that the little boy's here?'

'I suppose, though they were real open with her about her being adopted and telling her they loved her enough to pick her out. But I guess maybe she feels like Luke is really theirs, and she isn't.'

I said I hadn't realized that the O'Sheas were so open about Krista being adopted.

'Lou more than Jess,' Mary Maude commented. 'Lou has always been more out-front than her husband, but I guess he's had more practice at keeping secrets, him being a minister and all.'

Ministers do have to keep a lot of secrets. I hadn't thought of that before. I got up to get some more tea – and another napkin for Mary Maude.

'Lou tells me the man you're seeing is quite a looker,' Mary Maude said slyly, bringing the conversation back to the most interesting topic.

It had never occurred to me someone as conventional as Lou O'Shea would find him so. 'Yes.'

'Is he sweet to you?' Mary Maude sounded wistful.

This was everyone's day to want to know about Jack. First Anna, now Mary Maude. Weddings must bring it out in women. 'Sweet,' I said, trying the word on Jack to see how it fit. 'No. He's not sweet.'

Surprise hiked up Mary Maude's eyebrows. 'Not sweet! Well, then! Is he rich?'

'No,' I answered without hesitation.

'Then why are you seeing him?' Suddenly her cheeks got pinker, and she looked simultaneously delighted and embarrassed. 'Is he . . . ?'

'Yes,' I told her, trying not to look as self-conscious as I felt.

'Oh, girl,' said Mary Maude, shaking her head and giggling.

'Emory is single now,' I observed, trying to steer the conversation away from me and into a channel that might lead to some knowledge.

She didn't waste time looking shocked. 'Never in a million years,' Mary Maude told me as she consumed her last french fry.

'Why are you so sure about that?'

'Aside from the fact that now it would mean taking on a newborn baby and an eight-year-old girl, there's the man himself. I never met anyone as hard to read as Emory. He's polite as the day is long, he never uses bad language, he's . . . yes, he is . . . *sweet*. Old ladies just love him. But Emory's not a simple man, and he's not my idea of red-blooded.'

'Oh?'

'Not that I think he's gay,' Mary Maude protested hastily. 'It's just that, for example, we were outside the store watching the Harvest Festival parade, back in September, and all the beauty queens were coming by riding on the top of the convertibles, like we did?'

I'd completely forgotten that. Maybe that was why riding in the Shakespeare parade had plowed up my feelings so deeply?

'And Emory just wasn't interested. You know? You can tell when a man is appreciating women. And he wasn't. He enjoyed the floats and the bands. He loved the little girls, you know, Little Miss Pumpkin Patch, that kind of thing, and he told me he'd even thought of entering Eve, but his wife didn't like the idea. But those big gals in their sequin dresses and push-up bras didn't do a thing for Emory. No, I'm going to have to look farther than the furniture store to find someone to date.'

I made an indeterminate noise.

'Now, we were talking earlier about Lou and Jess O'Shea. They were watching that parade catty-corner to where I was standing, and believe me, honey! That Jess can enjoy grown-up women!'

'But he doesn't . . . ?'

'Oh, Lord, no! He is devoted to Lou. But he's not blind, either.' Mary Maude looked at her watch. 'Oh, girl! I have to get back.'

We tossed our litter into a can and walked out still talking. Well, Mary Maude was talking, and I was listening, but I was agreeable to listening. And when I dropped her off at Makepeace Furniture, I gave her a quick hug.

I couldn't think of anywhere to go but back to my parents' house.

I walked right into yet another crisis. The couples dinner in honor of Varena and Dill, which had been rescheduled at least twice, was once again endangered. The high school senior who had been booked to babysit Krista, her little brother Luke, and Anna had caught the flu.

According to Varena, who was sitting at the kitchen table with the tiny Bartley phone book open before her, she and Lou had called every adolescent known to babysit in Bartley, and all of them were either flu victims or already attending a teen Christmas party the Methodist church was giving.

This seemed to be a crisis I had no part in other than to look sympathetic. Then a solution to a couple of problems occurred to me, and I knew what I had to do.

Jack would owe me permanently, as far as I was concerned.

I tapped Varena on the shoulder. 'I'll do it,' I told her.

'What?' She'd been in the middle of a semihysterical outburst to my mother.

'I'll do it,' I repeated.

'You'll . . . babysit?'

'That's what I said.' I was feeling touchy at the sheer incredulity in my sister's voice.

'Have you *ever* kept kids before?'

'Do you need a babysitter or don't you?'

'Yes, it would be wonderful, but . . . are you sure you wouldn't mind? You've never been . . . I mean, you've always said that children weren't your . . . special thing.'

'I can do it.'

'Well! That would be – just great,' Varena said stoutly, obviously realizing she had to show no reservations, no matter what she felt.

Actually, I had kept the four Althaus kids one afternoon and evening when Jay Althaus had been in a car wreck and Carol had had to go to the hospital. Both sets of grandparents had been out of town. Carol had been a frantic, panicked, pathetic mother and wife by the time I answered her phone call.

So I knew how to change diapers and bathe a baby, and the oldest Althaus boy had showed me how to heat up a bottle. I might not be Mary Poppins, but all the children would be alive and fed and clean by the time the parents got home.

Varena was on the phone with Lou O'Shea, giving her the good news.

'She's glad to do it,' Varena was saying, still trying not to sound amazed. 'So Lily should be there about, what? Six? Will the kids have eaten? Oh, OK. And there'll be Anna, Krista, your little boy . . . oh, really? Oh, gosh. Let me ask her.'

Varena covered the receiver. She was making a big effort to look cheerful and unconcerned. 'Lily, Lou says they've agreed to keep the Osborn kids, too. At the time, they thought Shelley was coming with her boyfriend.' Shelley was the flu-ridden teenager.

I took a deep, cleansing breath, like I did in karate class before I began my kata. 'No problem,' I said.

'You're sure?'

I confined myself to a nod.

'That's not a problem, she says,' Varena said chirpily into the phone. 'Right, it'll only last three hours at the most, two more likely, and we'll be just a few blocks away.'.

Sounded like Lou was a little concerned at the prospect of my babysitting such a mob.

The doorbell rang, and my mother hustled into the living room to answer it. I heard her say, 'Hello, again!' with a kind of supercharged enthusiasm that alerted me. Sure enough, she led Jack into the kitchen with a pleased, proud air, as though she'd snagged him just when he was about to get away.

I found myself on my feet and going to him before I even knew I was moving. His arms slid around me and he gave me a kiss, but a kiss that said my parents were looking at him over my shoulder.

'Well, young man, it's nice to see you again. We'd begun to think we wouldn't get to lay eyes on you before you left town.' My father was being bluff and hearty.

Jack was wearing a blue-and-green-plaid flannel shirt and blue jeans, and his thick hair was brushed smoothly back, gathered at the nape of his neck with an elastic band. I patted his shoulder gently and stepped away from him.

'I saw a mighty lot of presents in the living room,' Jack said to my father. 'Looks like you-all are having a wedding.' He smiled, and those seductive deep lines suddenly appeared in parentheses from his nose to the corners of his thin, mobile mouth.

Mother, Father, and Varena laughed, as charmed by his smile as I was.

'As a matter of fact,' Jack went on, 'I hoped this would be appropriate.'

'Why, thank you,' Varena said, surprised and showing it, taking the shallow wrapped box Jack pulled out of one jacket pocket.

When I turned to watch Varena open the present, Jack's arm went around my waist and pulled me against him, my back to his chest. I could feel the corners of my mouth tug up, and I looked down at my hands, resting on the arms crossed below my breasts. I took a deep breath. I made an effort to focus on the box Varena was holding.

She lifted the lid. From the tissue, she extracted an antique silver cake server, a lovely piece with engraving. When Varena passed it around, I could see the curling script read 'V K 1889.'

'This is just beautiful,' Varena said, delighted and not a little stunned. 'However did you find it?'

'Sheer luck,' Jack said. He was pressed very firmly against my bottom, 'I just happened to be in an antiques store and it caught my eye.'

I could see the wheels turning in my mother's head. I knew she was thinking that this was a serious present. Such a gift announced that Jack planned to be seeing me for some time, since he was displaying such a great desire to please my family. My father's face lit up (way too obviously) as the same idea occurred to him.

I felt I was watching a tribal ritual unfold.

'I have to put this somewhere conspicuous, so everyone'll notice it,' Varena told Jack, plainly wanting him to realize she was very pleased indeed.

'I'm glad you like it,' he said.

And before you could say Jack Robinson, Jack Leeds was installed at my parents' kitchen table, a grilled cheese sandwich and bowl of soup in front of him, Varena and my mother waiting on him hand and foot.

After he'd eaten, Mother and Varena practically threw us out of the kitchen so I wouldn't have to help with the dishes. They were flabbergasted when Jack offered to wash. They turned him down with fatuous smiles, and by the time I climbed into Jack's car I was torn between laughter and exasperation.

'I think they approve of me,' Jack said with a straight face.

'Well, you *are* breathing.'

He laughed, but he stopped abruptly and looked at me with an expression I couldn't decipher. He started the engine.

'Where are we going? I have to be at the manse at six o'clock,' I reminded him. Mother and Varena had immediately told Jack I'd volunteered to keep the kids.

'We need to talk,' he said. We were silent on the ride to the motel, Jack grim and taciturn, I uneasily aware that I was not on the same page.

As we turned on the corner by the Presbyterian manse, I thought of Krista, Anna, and Eve.

And, oddly, I suddenly remembered spending nights with other girls when I was really young. I remembered how I'd carry a whole suitcase full of stuff with me for an overnight visit, every-thing and anything I thought we might want to play with, or look at, or gossip about.

Including a memory book.

Chapter Seven

Jack was staying in a different room, since the motel manager was having the bathroom window fixed from the break-in in the room he'd had before.

I was already on edge when we went in, and when Jack sat on one of the stuffed vinyl-covered armchairs, all my systems went on defense. I perched on the edge of the other chair and eyed him warily.

'I saw you last night,' he said without preamble.

'Where?'

He sighed. 'Out with your old boyfriend.'

I made my breathing slow, fighting the rage that swept through me. I gripped the armrests of the damn orange chair. 'You got back to town early, and you didn't call me. Did you come back on purpose to spy on me?'

His back stiffened. He was doing a little chair gripping of his own. 'Of course not, Lily! I missed you, and I finished what I was doing early, and I drove all afternoon to get back here. Then I saw you in that diner with the cop.'

'Were we kissing, Jack?'

'No.'

'Were we holding hands, Jack?'

'No.'

'Was I looking at him with love, Jack?'

'No.'

'Did he look happy, Jack?'

'No.' Jack bowed his head, rubbed his forehead with his fingertips.

'Let me tell you what happened the last time I went on a date with Chandler McAdoo, Jack.' I bent to his level until he had to look me in the eyes or be a coward. 'It was seven years ago, the bad time, and I had been back in Bartley for two months. Chandler and I went to the movies, and then we drove out to the lake, like we'd done when we were kids.'

Jack's hazel eyes didn't flinch, and he was listening. I knew it.

'So when we were at the lake, Chandler wanted to kiss me, and I wanted to feel like a real woman again, so I let him. I even enjoyed it . . . a little. And then it went a little farther, and he pulled my T-shirt up. Want to know what happened then, Jack? Chandler started crying. The scars were real fresh then, red. He cried when he saw my body. And that's the last I saw of Chandler for seven years.'

A heavy silence settled in the cold motel room.

'Pardon me,' Jack said finally. He was absolutely sincere, not mouthing a social catchall. 'Pardon me.'

'Jack, you never believed I was sneaking behind your back.'

'I didn't?' He looked a little angry and a little amused.

'You gave Varena her present before you even discussed last night with me,' I said. 'You knew all along we weren't . . . parting.' I had almost used the phrase 'breaking up', but it seemed too childish.

Abruptly, Jack's face went absolutely still, as if he'd had a revelation of some kind.

He turned his eyes to me. 'How could he cry?' Jack asked me. 'You are so beautiful.'

I was still speechless, but for another reason. Jack had never said anything remotely like this.

'Don't pity me,' I said softly.

'Lily, you said I never really doubted you. Now, I say, you know that pity is the last thing I feel for you.'

He lay with his chest to my back, one arm thrown around me. He was still awake, I could tell. I had another hour and a half, by my watch.

I didn't want to think about Summer Dawn. I didn't want to think about the dead people littering the path to her recovery.

I wanted to touch Jack. I wanted to twine my fingers in his hair. I wanted to understand his thoughts.

But he was a man with a job to do, and he wanted more than anything in the world to take Summer Dawn back to her parents. While he kept his arm around me and from time to time dropped a kiss on my neck, his thoughts had drifted away from me, and mine had to follow.

Reluctantly, I began to tell him what I'd found: the two memory books, one whole and one mutilated, in Anna Kingery's room; the absence of the same book at Eve Osborn's. I told him that Eve Osborn had been to the doctor recently, that I didn't yet know about Anna. I told him about Anna's mother . . . the woman we were assuming was Anna's mother. And I pulled the plastic-wrapped brush and the birth photo of Anna out of my purse and placed them by Jack's briefcase.

I rolled over to face him when I'd finished. I don't know what he saw in my face, but he said, 'Damn,' under his breath, and looked away from me.

'Have you learned anything?' I asked, to get that expression off his face.

'Like I said, my trip was pretty much of a washout,' he told me, but not as if he was upset about it. I guess private eyes encounter a lot of dead-end streets. 'But early this morning, I wandered into the police station and took Chandler and a guy named Roger out for coffee and doughnuts. Since I used to be a cop, and they wanted to prove that small-town cops can be just as sharp as city cops, they were pretty forthcoming.'

I stroked his hair away from his face and nodded to show him I was listening. I didn't want to tell him they'd have told him nothing if Chandler hadn't checked up on him and talked to me about him.

'They told me the pipe recovered in the alley was definitely the one used to kill the doctor and his nurse,' Jack said. 'And Christopher Sims's fingerprints were nowhere on it. The pipe has a rusty surface, and some cloth had been run over it. Whoever tried to clean it didn't do a good job. He left one partial. It doesn't match Sims's. He's still in custody for the purse snatching, but I don't think he'll be charged with the murder any time soon.'

'Is he making sense?'

'Not a lot. He told the police he'd had a lot of visitors in his new home, which I gather means the alley behind the stores. That location in the alley is close to every father in this case. Jess O'Shea came to visit Sims as a minister, Emory works in Makepeace Furniture, which backs onto that alley, and Kingery's pharmacy is a block away.'

'I noticed that.'

'Of course you did,' he said and bent to kiss me. My arms went around his neck, and the kiss lasted longer than he thought it was going to. 'I want you again,' he told me, his voice low and rough.

'I noticed that, too.' I pressed against him gently. 'But the wedding is tomorrow. Let me tell you about tonight. Since I'm going to babysit all the children – Eve, the baby, Krista, Luke, and Anna – at the O'Sheas' house, maybe I can learn something from the children, or from being in that house.'

'Where are all the parents going?'

'To a dinner. It's a couples thing, so I was glad to get out of it.'

'Who would they have paired you with?' Jack asked.

I realized for the first time that I was causing a hostess some seating problems. 'I don't know,' I admitted. 'I guess that friend of Dill's, Berry Duff.'

'Has he been by your folks' much?'

'No, I think he went right home after the rehearsal dinner. He'll come back into town today, if I remember right, and spend the night somewhere here in town. I guess here at the motel.'

'He admired you.'

'Sure, I'm everyone's dream girl,' I said, hearing the sharp edge in my voice, unable to stop it.

'Did you like him?'

What the hell was this? 'He's nice enough,' I said.

'You could be with him,' he said. His light hazel eyes fixed on mine. He didn't blink. 'He wouldn't drag you into things like this.'

'Hmmm,' I said thoughtfully, 'Berry is awful cute . . . and he has his own farm. Varena was telling me how beautiful his house is. It's part of the spring garden tour.'

For a second Jack's face was a real picture. Then he pounced on me. He pinned me by the shoulders and scooted his body sideways until it lay over mine.

'Are you teasing me, house cleaner?'

'What do you think, detective?'

'I think I've got you where I want you,' he said, and his mouth descended.

'Jack,' I said after a moment, 'I need to tell you something.'

'What?'

'Don't ever hold me down.'

Jack rolled off instantly, his hands up in a surrender position.

'It's just that you feel so good,' he said. 'And . . . sometimes I think if I don't weigh you down you'll just drift away.' He looked off to the side, then back at me. 'What the hell did that mean?' he asked, shaking his head at his own fancy.

I knew exactly what he meant.

'I have to go back to the house,' I said. 'I'll be at the O'Sheas' from about five-thirty on.' I swung myself up and sat with my back to him, since I had to begin getting my clothes out of the heap by the bed.

I felt his hand on my back, stroking. I shivered.

'What are you going to do?' I said over my shoulder, as I bent to retrieve my bra.

'Oh, I have an idea or two,' he said casually. He hooked the bra for me.

Jack was going to do something illegal.

'Like what?' I pulled my shirt over my head.

'Oh . . . I might get into the doctor's office tonight.'

'Who would let you in? You can't possibly be thinking of breaking in?'

'I think it won't be a problem,' he assured me.

'You know anything you learn that way isn't real evidence,' I said incredulously. 'I've watched enough TV to know that.'

'Can you think of another way for me to find out their blood types?'

'Blood types? I thought you said Summer Dawn hadn't had her blood typed? And are you sure the blood types would be in a file at Dr LeMay's office?'

'All three families went to him.'

'But how many kids need to have their blood taken?'

'You said Eve had. If I can eliminate at least one of them, that'll be good,' he argued. 'I realized that there were only a couple of blood types she could be. In fact, it was Chandler's discussion of your high school biology class that reminded me.'

'What blood type would Summer Dawn be?'

'Her mother's A and her father's O. So Summer has to be A or O.' Jack had been consulting a page from a sheaf of Xeroxed material.

'So if Anna and Eve are type B or AB, they can't be Summer Dawn. It would have to be Krista.'

'Right.'

'I hope it isn't Anna,' I said, sorry immediately I'd said it out loud and with that edge of desperation in my voice.

'I hope not, too, for your sister's sake,' Jack said briskly, and I was even sorrier I'd said anything. I could feel him shoving off my fear, reminding me he had a job to do that he was compelled to finish. I hated the necessity for the reminder. 'Here, here's your sock.'

'Jack, what if they're all A or O?' I took the sock from him and pulled it on. I had my shoe tied before he answered.

'I don't know. I'll think of something,' he said, but not with any hope in his voice. 'Maybe that's not the way to go. I'll call Aunt Betty and see if she's got any ideas. I'll be in and out, so try here if you need me. Something's gotta break tonight.'

Before I left my folks' house for the O'Sheas', I dialed a Shakespeare number to talk to my friend Carrie Thrush. As I'd hoped, she was still at her office, having seen her last patient just minutes before.

'How are you?'

'Fine,' she said, surprise in her voice. 'I'll be glad when flu season is over.'

'The house is okay?' Carrie had agreed to stop by once or twice, check to make sure the mail carrier had obeyed my 'stop mail' card. I hadn't thought it was much of an imposition, since she was dating Claude Friedrich, who lived in the apartment next door. In fact, I would have asked Claude himself to do it if he hadn't been still limping from a leg injury.

'Lily, your house is fine,' Carrie said, good-humored toleration in her low voice. 'How are you doing?'

'OK,' I said grudgingly.

'Well, we'll be glad to see you come home. Oh, you'll want to know this! Old Mr Winthrop died yesterday, out at his place. He had a massive heart attack at the supper table. Arnita said he just slumped over in the sweet potatoes. She called nine-one-one, but it was too late.'

I figured the whole Winthrop family had to be relieved that the old tyrant was dead, but it wouldn't be decent to admit it.

'That family has been through everything this year,' Carrie commented, not at all put off by my lack of response.

'I saw Bobo before I left,' I told her.

'His Jeep went by your house twice yesterday evening.'

'Hmmm.'

'He's carrying a big torch.'

I cleared my throat. 'Well, he'll meet a gal his own age who doesn't kowtow to him because he's a Winthrop. He's just nineteen.'

'Right.' Carrie sounded amused. 'Besides, you have your own private dick.' This was Carrie's little term for Jack. She thought it was really funny. She was definitely smiling on the other end of the line. 'How is your family?' she asked.

'This wedding has got everyone crazy.'

'And speaking of Jack, have you heard from him?'

'He – ahhh – he's here.'

'There? In Bartley?' Carry was startled and impressed.

'It's work,' I said hastily. 'He's got a job here.'

'Right. How coincidental!'

'True,' I told her warningly. 'He's working.'

'So you haven't seen him at all, I'm sure.'

'Oh, well . . . a couple of times.'

'He come by the house?'

'Yes. He did.'

'Met your parents,' she prompted.

'Well, OK, he did.'

'O – kay.' She drew out the word as if she'd proved a point. 'He coming back to Shakespeare with you?'

'Yes.'

'For Christmas?'

'Yes.'

'Way to go, Lily!'

'We'll see,' I said skeptically. 'And you? You'll be there?'

'Yes, I'm cooking and Claude is coming to my house. I was going to go to my folks', even though it's such a long drive, but when I found out Claude was going to be on his own, I told them I'd have to see them in the spring.'

'Moving fast, there.'

'Nothing to stop us, is there? He's in his forties and I'm in my midthirties.'

I said, 'No point taking it slow.'

'Damn straight!' Carrie's voice grew muffled as she told her nurse to call someone and give him his test results. Then her voice grew clearer. 'So you're coming home when?'

'The day after the wedding,' I said firmly. 'I can't stand it another minute.'

She laughed. 'See you then, Lily.'

'OK. Thanks for checking the house.'

'No problem.'

We said good-bye and hung up, both with a few things to think about.

I could tell that Carrie's relationship with Chief of Police

Claude Friedrich was flourishing. I hoped it would last. I'd liked both of them for months before they'd ever looked at each other.

I found myself wondering how Bobo was feeling about the death of his grandfather. I was sure he felt some grief, but it must be at least a little mixed with relief. Now Bobo and his parents would have some peace, some time to recoup. It was almost possible they would rehire me.

I dragged myself back to the here and now. It was nearly time for me to go to my babysitting stint. I would be in the O'Sheas' house; I could search it as I had the Kingery house and the Osborn house. I was staring at myself in the mirror in the bathroom, refluffing my hair and powdering my face, when I finally registered how miserable I looked.

Couldn't be helped.

In my room, I pulled on my Christmas sweatsuit, the one I'd worn in the parade. I guess I thought the bright color might make me seem more kid-friendly. I ate a bowl of leftover fruit salad, all that I could find in the refrigerator since everyone else in the house was going to the supper.

Dill's friend Berry Duff rang the doorbell while I was washing up, and I let him in. He smiled down at me.

'You look cheerful,' he remarked.

'I'm going to babysit.'

His face fell. 'Oh, I was looking forward to talking to you at the dinner.'

'Last-minute emergency. The babysitter came down with the flu and they couldn't find another one.'

'I hope it goes smoothly,' Berry said, rather doubtfully, I thought. 'I have kids of my own, and a handful at a time is kind of a rough evening.'

'How old are yours?' I asked politely.

'I got one who's nine, one who's in the tenth grade . . . let's see . . . Daniel's fifteen now. They're both good kids. I don't get to see them often enough.'

I remember that his wife had custody of the children. 'Do they live close enough for you to see them regularly?' I asked.

'Every other weekend,' he answered. He looked sad and angry. 'That's just not as good, nowhere near as good, as watching them grow up every day.' He folded himself into one of the kitchen chairs, and I returned to the sink to finish drying the dishes.

'But you know where they are,' I said, surprising even myself. 'You know that they're safe. You can pick up the phone and call them.'

Berry stared at me in understandable surprise. 'That's true,' he said slowly, feeling his way. 'I'm sure the situation could be worse. You're saying, if my wife ran off with them, went underground, like some spouses do to keep the other parent away from the kids? That would be horrible. I guess I'd just go crazy.' Berry mulled it over for a minute. 'I'd do anything to get them back, if that happened,' he concluded. He looked up at me. 'My God, girl, how did we get on this depressing topic? This is supposed to be a happy household! Wedding tomorrow!'

'Yes,' I said. 'Wedding tomorrow.' I had to be resolute. This was not a problem I could solve by hitting or kicking. I puzzled Berry further by patting his shoulder, before I pulled on my coat and called good-bye to my parents.

I thought there was something I'd forgotten to tell Jack today, something small but important. But I couldn't make it float to the surface of my mind.

The O'Sheas had plenty of room in the Presbyterian manse, since the preacher for whom the home had been built had been the father of five. Of course, that had been in 1938. Now the manse was an underinsulated money pit in need of complete rewiring, Lou told me within the first five minutes after my arrival. I could see that she had some legitimate gripes, because the long, narrow shape of the living area made it hard to group furniture, just for starters. And though there was a fireplace, and it was decorated for the season, the chimney needed so much repair that it wasn't functional.

The preacher's wife was encased in a sage green suit and black suede pumps. Her dark hair was carefully turned under all the way around in a smooth pageboy, and her ski-jump nose had been minimized by some subtle makeup. Lou was clearly looking forward to getting out of her house without the kids in tow, but just as clearly she was a little anxious about my keeping them. She was doing her best not to show her worry, but the third time she pointed out the list of emergency phone numbers right by the telephone, I had a very sharp answer practically tottering on the edge of my tongue.

Instead, of course, I took a cleansing breath and nodded. But there may have been something grim in the set of my mouth, because Lou did a double take and apologized profusely for being overprotective. To cut short her apologies, she bent to plug in the Christmas tree, which almost filled a quarter of the room.

The lights began to blink.

I clenched my teeth to keep from saying something Lou was sure to find unacceptable.

The manse seemed as commercial as any other house tricked out for the season, with long plastic candy canes propped on either side of the nonfunctional hearth, where fireplace tools would ordinarily stand. A silver garland was draped between the corners of the mantelpiece, and Lou had hung long plastic icicles from the garland.

Opposite the hearth was a central window before which the tree was positioned. However, under the tree, instead of presents there stood a nativity scene, with a wooden stable and a full complement of shepherds, Joseph and Mary, camels and cows, and the baby Jesus in a manger.

Handsome Jess strode into the room, wearing a dark suit enlivened by a fancy Christmas vest. He was carrying Meredith Osborn's baby, Jane, and Jane was not happy.

It was time for me to prove my worth. I steeled myself to hold out my arms, and he placed the shrieking Jane in them.

'Is she due for a bottle?' I yelled.

'No,' bellowed Jess, 'I just fed her.'

Then she needed burping. After eating came burping, then excreting, then sleeping. This was what I had learned about babies. I turned Jane so she was upright and pointed over my shoulder and began patting her gently with my right hand. Little red-faced thing . . . she was so tiny. Jane had wisps of curling blond hair here and there on her smooth head. Her eyes were squeezed shut with rage, but as soon as I turned her upright she seemed to be crying with less volume. Her little eyes opened and looked hazily at me.

'Hi,' I said, feeling I should talk to her.

The other children came piling into the room, Krista's little brother Luke was a cement block of a toddler, so square and heavy that he stomped rather than walked. He was dark-haired like Lou, but he would have the heavy-jawed good looks of his father.

The most amazing belch erupted from the baby. Her body relaxed against my shoulder, which suddenly felt wet.

'Oh, dear,' Lou said. 'Oh, Lily . . .'

'Should have slung a diaper over your shoulder.' Jess's advice was just a little too late.

I looked directly into the baby's eyes, and she made one of those little baby noises. Her tiny hands flailed the air.

'I'll hold her while you clean up,' Eve volunteered, while Krista said, 'Ewww! Look at the white stuff on Miss Lily's shoulder!'

'Sit in the chair,' I told Eve.

Eve settled herself in the nearest armchair, her legs crossed on the seat. I settled Eve's sister into her lap and checked to make sure that Eve was holding the baby correctly. She was.

Followed by the herd of kids, I went to the bathroom, got a washcloth out of the linen closet, and dampened it to rub the worst of the belched liquid off my shoulder. I didn't want to smell it all night. Krista kept up a running commentary the whole time, Anna seemed conflicted between being sympathetic toward her future aunt and rolling in the grossness of baby throw up like Krista, and Luke just stared while holding his left ear with his left hand and gripping the hair on the top of his head with his right, a posture that made him look like he was receiving signals from another planet.

I realized that Luke was probably stilt wearing diapers, too.

The O'Sheas called good-bye as they escaped from the houseful of children, and I tossed the washrag into the dirty clothes hamper and glanced at my watch. It was time to change Jane.

I settled Luke in the far end of the living room in front of the television, watching a Christmas cartoon and communicating with Mars. He chose to sit almost inside the branches of the Christmas tree. The blinking didn't seem to bother him.

The girls all followed me to the baby's room. Eve was proprietary because the baby was her sister, Krista was hoping to see poop so she could provide running commentary on its grossness, and Anna was still waiting to see which way the wind blew.

Grabbing a fresh disposable diaper, I placed the baby on the changing table and went through the laborious and complicated process of unsnapping the crotch of Jane's sleeper. Mentally reviewing how I'd changed the Althaus baby, I opened the pull tabs on the old diaper, lifted Jane by the legs, removed the soiled diaper, pulled a wipe from the box on the end of the changing table, cleaned the pertinent areas, and pushed the new diaper under Jane. I ran the front part between her tiny legs, pulled the adhesive tabs shut, and reinserted the baby into the sleeper, getting the snaps wrong only one time.

The three girls decided this was boring. I watched them troop through the door to go to Krista's room. They were so superficially similar, yet so different. All were eight years old, give or take a few months; all were within three inches of being the same height; they had brown hair and brown eyes. But Eve's hair was long and looked as if someone had taken a curling iron to it, and Eve was thin and pale. Krista, blocky and with higher color, had short, thick, darker hair and a more decisive demeanor. Her jaw jutted out like she was about to take it on the chin. Anna had shoulder-length light brown hair, a medium build, and a ready smile.

One of these three little girls was not who she thought she was. Her parents were not the people she had always identified as her parents. Her home was not really her home; she belonged elsewhere. She was not the oldest child in the family but the youngest. Everything in her life had been a lie.

I wondered what Jack was doing. I hoped whatever it was, he wouldn't get caught.

I carried the baby into the living room with me. Luke was still absorbed in the television, but he half turned as I entered and asked me for a snack.

With the attention to detail you have to have around kids, I put Jane in her infant seat, fastened the strap and buckle arrangement that prevented her from falling out, and fetched Luke a banana from the chaotic kitchen.

'I want chips. I don't like nanas,' he said.

I exhaled gently. 'If you eat your banana, I'll get you some chips,' I said as diplomatically as I am able. 'After supper. I'll be putting supper on the table in just a minute.'

'Miss Lily!' shrieked Eve. 'Come look at us!'

Ignoring Luke's continued complaints about bananas, I strode down the hall to the room that must be Krista's, judging from all the signs on the door warning Luke never to come in.

It didn't seem possible the girls could have done so much to themselves in such a short time. Both Krista and Anna were daubed with makeup and swathed in full dress-up regalia: net skirts, feathered hats, tiny high heels. Eve, sitting on Krista's bed, was much more modestly decked out, and she wore no makeup at all.

I looked at Krista's and Anna's lurid faces and had a flash of horror before I realized that if all this stuff had been in Krista's room, this must be an approved activity.

'You look . . . charming,' I said, having no idea what an acceptable response would be.

'I'm the prettiest!' Krista said insistently.

If the basis for selection was heavy makeup, Krista was right.

'Why don't you wear makeup, Miss Lily?' Eve asked.

The three girls crowded around and analyzed my face.

'She's got mascara on,' Anna decided.

'Red stuff? Rouge?' Krista was peering at my cheeks.

'Eye shadow,' Eve said triumphantly.

'More isn't always better,' I said, to deaf ears.

'If you wore a lot of makeup, you'd be beautiful, Aunt Lily,' Anna said surprisingly.

'Thank you, Anna. I'd better go see how the baby is.'

Luke had unsnapped the baby's sleeper and pulled it from her tiny feet. He was bending over her with a pair of tiny, sharp fingernail scissors.

'What are you doing, Luke?' I asked when I could draw my breath.

'I'm gonna help you out,' he said happily. 'I'm gonna cut baby Jane's toenails.'

I shuddered. 'I appreciate your wanting to help. But you have to wait for Jane's daddy to say whether or not he wants you to do that.' That seemed pretty diplomatic to me.

Luke insisted vehemently that Jane's long toenails were endangering her life and had to be trimmed now.

I began to dislike this child very seriously.

'Listen to me,' I said quietly, cutting right through all his justification.

Luke shut right up. He looked plenty scared.

Good.

'Don't touch the baby unless I ask you to,' I said. I thought I was making a simple declarative sentence, but possibly Luke was good at interpreting voice tone. He dropped the scissors. I picked them up and shoved them in my sweatpants pocket where I could be certain he wouldn't reclaim them.

I picked up the infant seat and took Jane into the kitchen with me to set out the children's meal. Lou had left canned funny-shaped pasta in sauce, which I wouldn't have fed to my dog, if I'd had one. I heated it, trying not to inhale. I spooned it into bowls, then cut squares of Jell-O and put them on plates, adding apple slices that Lou had already prepared. I poured milk.

The kids ran in and scooted into chairs the minute I called them, even Luke. Without prompting, they all bowed their heads and said the 'God is great' prayer in unison. I was caught flat-footed, halfway to the refrigerator to put the milk carton away.

The next fifty minutes were . . . trying.

I understand that close to Christmas children get excited. I realize that children in packs are more excitable than children separately. I have heard that having a sitter instead of parental supervision causes kids to push their limits, or rather, their sitter's. But I had to take several deep breaths as the kids rampaged through their supper. I perched on a stool, baby Jane in her infant seat on the kitchen counter beside me. Jane, at least, was asleep. A sleeping baby is a near-perfect thing.

As I wiped up slopped tomato sauce, put more sliced apples into Luke's bowl, stopped Krista from poking Anna with a spoon, I gradually became aware that Eve was quieter than the others. She had to make a visible effort to join in the hilarity.

Of course, her mother had just died.

So I kept a wary eye on Eve.

Far from planning to learn something that evening, I was beginning to hope merely to survive it. I'd thought I'd get a moment to look for family records. That was so clearly impossible, I was convinced I'd leave as ignorant as when I'd come.

Krista took care of the problem for me.

Reaching for the crackers I'd set in the center of the table, she knocked over her milk, which cascaded off the table into Anna's lap. Anna shrieked, called Krista a butthead, and darted a terrified glance at me. This was not approved language in the Kingery household, and since I was almost her aunt, I gave Anna the obligatory stern look.

'Do you have a change of pants here?' I asked.

'Yes ma'am,' said a subdued Anna.

'Krista, you wipe up the milk with this towel while I take Anna to change. I'll need to put those pants right in the washer.'

I picked up the baby in her infant seat and carried her with me down the hall, trying not to jostle her from her sleep. Anna hurried ahead of me, wanting to change and get back to her friends.

I could tell that Anna was not comfortable taking off her clothes with me in the room, but we'd done a little bonding that morning and she didn't want to hurt my feelings by asking me to leave. God knows I hated invading anyone's privacy, but I had to do it. After I found a safe spot on the floor for Jane, I picked up the room while Anna untied her shoes and divested herself of her socks, pants, and panties. I had my back to her, but I was facing a mirror when her panties came down, and since she had her back to me, I was able to see clearly the dark brown splotch of the birthmark on her hip.

I had to lean against the wall. A wave of relief almost bowled me over. Anna having that birthmark simply had to mean that Anna was the baby in the birth picture with her mother and Dill, their original and true child, and not Summer Dawn Macklesby.

I had something to be thankful for, after all.

I picked up the wet clothes, and Anna, having pulled on some dry ones, dashed out of the room to finish her supper.

I was about to pick up Jane when Eve came in. She stood, her arms behind her back, looking at her shoes. Something about the way she was standing put me on full alert.

'Miss Lily, you remember that day you came to our house and cleaned up?' she asked, as though it had been weeks before.

I stood stock still. I saw myself opening the box on the shelf . . .

'Wait,' I told her. 'I want to talk to you. Wait just one moment.'

The nearest telephone, and the one that was the most private, was the one in the master bedroom across the hall.

I looked through the phone book, found the number of Jack's motel. Please let him be there, please let him be there . . .

Mr Patel connected me to Jack's room. Jack answered on the second ring.

'Jack, open your briefcase,' I said.

Some assorted sounds over the end.

'OK, It's done.'

'The picture of the baby.'

'Summer Dawn? The one that was in the paper?'

'Yes, that one. What is the baby wearing?'

'One of those one-piece things.'

'Jack, what does it look like?'

'Ah, long arms and legs, snaps . . .'

'What is the *pattern*?'

'Oh. Little animals, looks like.'

I took a deep, deep breath. 'Jack, what kind of animal?'

'Giraffes,' he said, after a long, analytical pause.

'Oh God,' I said, scarcely conscious of what I was saying.

Eve came into the bedroom. She had picked up the baby and brought her with her. I looked at her white face, and I am sure I looked as stricken as I felt.

'Miss Lily,' she said, and her voice was limp and a little sad. 'My dad's at the door. He came to get us.'

'He's here,' I said into the phone and hung up.

I got on my knees in front of Eve. 'What were you going to tell me?' I asked. 'I was wrong to go use the phone when you were waiting to talk to me. Tell me now.'

My intensity was making her nervous, I could see, but it wasn't something I could turn off. At least she knew I was taking her seriously.

'He's here now, it's . . . I have to go home.'

'No, you need to tell me.' I said it as gently as I could, but firmly.

'You're strong,' she said slowly. Her eyes couldn't meet mine. 'My dad said my mom was weak. But you're not.'

'I'm strong.' I said it flatly, with as much assurance as I could pack into a statement.

'Maybe . . . you could tell him me and Jane need to spend the night here, like we were supposed to? So he won't take us home?'

She'd intended to tell me something else.

I wondered how much time I had before Emory came to find out what was keeping us.

'Why don't you want to go home?' I asked, as if we had all the time in the world.

'Maybe if he really wanted me to come, Jane could stay here

with you?' Eve asked, and suddenly tears were trembling in her
eyes. 'She's so little.'

'He won't get her.'

Eve looked almost giddy with relief.

'You don't want to go,' I said.

'Please, no,' she whispered.

'Then he won't get you.'

Telling a father he couldn't have his kids was not going to go
over well. I hoped Jack had found something, or Emory would
make that one wrong move.

He'd have to. He'd have to be provoked.

Time to take my gloves off.

'Stay here,' I told Eve. 'This may get kind of awful, but I'm not
letting anyone take you and Jane out of this house.'

Eve suddenly looked frightened by what she had unleashed,
realizing on some level that the monster was out of the closet
now, and nothing would make it go back in. She had taken her
life, and her sister's, in her own hands at the ripe old age of eight. I
am sure she was wishing she could take back her words, her
appeal.

'It's out of your hands now,' I said. 'This is grown-up stuff.'

She looked relieved, and then she did something that sent
shivers down my back: She picked up the baby in her carrier and
took her to a corner of the bedroom, pulling out the straight-
backed chair that blocked it, crouching down behind it with the
baby beside her.

'Throw Reverend O'Shea's bathrobe over the chair,' the little
voice suggested. 'He won't find us, maybe.'

I felt my whole body clench. I picked up the blue velour
bathrobe that Jess had left lying across the foot of the bed and
draped it over the chair.

'I'll be back in a minute,' I said and went down the hall to the
living room, Anna's milk-stained clothes still under my arm. I
tossed them into the washroom as I passed it. I was trying to keep
things as normal as I could. There were children here, in my care.

Emory was standing just inside the front door. He was wearing jeans and a short jacket. He'd pulled his gloves off and stuck them in a pocket. His blond hair was brushed smooth, and he looked as if he'd just shaved. It was like . . . I hesitated to say this, even to myself.

It was like he was here to pick up his date.

His guileless blue eyes met mine with no hesitation. Luke, Anna, and Krista were playing a video game at the other end of the room.

'Hey, Miss Bard.' He looked a little puzzled. 'I sent Eve back to tell you I'd decided the girls should spend the night at home, after all. I've imposed on the O'Sheas too much.'

I walked over to the television. I had to turn off the screen before the children would look at me. Krista and Luke were surprised and angry, though they were too well raised to say anything. But Anna somehow knew that something was wrong. She stared at me, her eyes as round as quarters, but she didn't ask any questions.

'You three go back and play in Krista's room,' I said. Luke opened his mouth to protest, took a second look at me, and jumped up to run back to his sister's room. Krista gave me a mutinous glare, but when Anna, casting several backward looks, followed Luke, Krista left too.

Emory had moved closer to the hall leading down to the bedrooms. He was leaning on the mantel, in fact. He'd pulled off his jacket. He was still smiling gently at the children as they passed him. I moved closer.

'The girls are going to stay here tonight,' I said.

His smile began to twitch around the edges. 'I can take my children when I want, Miss Bard,' he told me. 'I'd thought I needed time alone with my sister to plan the funeral service, but she had to go home to Little Rock tonight, so I want my girls to come home.'

'The girls are going to stay here tonight.'

'Eve!' he bellowed suddenly. 'Come out here right now!'

I heard the children in Krista's room fall silent.

'Stay where you are!' I called, hoping each and every one of them understood I meant it.

'How can you tell me I can't have my kids?' Emory looked almost tearful, not angry, but there was something in the way he was standing that kept me on the edge of wary.

Truth or dare. 'I can tell you that so easy, Emory,' I said. 'I know about you.'

Something scary flared in his expression for just a second. 'What the heck are you talking about?' he said, permitting himself to show a reasonable anger and disgust. 'I came to get my little girls! You can't keep my little girls if I want them!'

'Depends on what you want them for, you son of a bitch.'

It was the bad language that cracked Emory's facade.

He came at me then. He grabbed one of the plastic icicles suspended from the garland on the O'Sheas' mantel, and if I hadn't caught his wrist, it would have been embedded in my neck. I overbalanced while I was keeping the tip away from my throat, and over we went. As Emory and I hit the floor with a thud, I could hear the children begin to wail, but it seemed far away and unimportant just now. I'd fallen sideways, and my right hand was trapped.

Emory was small and looked frail, but he was stronger than I'd expected. I was gripping his forearm with my left hand, keeping the hard plastic away from my neck, knowing that if he succeeded in driving it in I would surely die. His other hand fastened around my neck, and I heard my own choking noises.

I wrenched my shoulder in a desperate effort to pull my right hand out from under my body. Finally it was free, and I found my pocket. I pulled out the nail scissors and sunk them into Emory's side.

He howled and yanked sideways, and somehow I lost the scissors. But now I had two free hands. With both of them I forced his right hand back, heaved myself against him, and over we rolled with me on top but with his left hand still digging into my throat. I pushed his right arm back and down, though his braced left arm kept me too far away to force it to the ground and

break it. I struggled to straddle him and finally managed it. By
now I was seeing a wash of gray strewn with spots instead of
living room furniture. I pushed up on my knees and then let my
weight fall down on him as hard as I could. The air whooshed out
of Emory's lungs then, and he was trying to gasp for oxygen, but I
thought maybe I would give out first. I raised up and collapsed on
him again, but like a snake he took advantage of my movement to
start to roll on his side, and since I was pushing his right arm in
that direction, I went, too, and now we were on the floor under
the Christmas tree, the tiny colored lights blinking, blinking.

I could see the lights blinking through the gray fog, and they
maddened me.

Abruptly, I let go of Emory's arm and snatched a loop of lights
from the tree branches. I swung the loop around Emory's neck,
but I wasn't able to switch hands to give myself a good cross pull.
He drove the tip of the plastic icicle into my throat.

The plastic tip was duller than a knife, and I am muscular, so it
still hadn't penetrated by the time the string of blinking lights
around Emory's neck began to take effect.

He took his left hand from my throat to claw at the lights, his
major error since I'd been right on the verge of checking out of
consciousness. I was able to roll my head to the side to minimize
the pressure of the icicle. I was doing much better until Emory,
scrabbling around with that left hand, seized the stable of the
manger scene and brought it down on my head.

I was out only a minute, but in that minute the room had emptied
and the house had grown silent. I rolled to my knees and pushed
up on the couch. I took an experimental step. Well, I could walk. I
didn't know how much more I was capable of doing, but I seized
the nearest thing I could strike with, one of the long plastic candy
canes that Lou had set on each side of the hearth, and I started
down the hall, pressing myself against the wall. I passed the
washroom on my left and a closet on my right. The next door on
my left was Krista's room. The door was open.

I cautiously looked around the door frame. The three children were sitting on Krista's bed, Anna and Krista with their arms around each other, Luke frantically sucking on his fingers and pulling his hair. Krista gave a little shriek when she saw me. I put my finger across my lips, and she nodded in a panicky way. But Anna's eyes were wide and staring as if she was trying to think of how to tell me something.

I wondered if they would trust me, the mean stranger they didn't know, or Emory, the sweet man they'd seen around for years.

'Did he find Eve?' I asked, in a voice just above a whisper.

'No, he didn't,' Emory said and stepped out from behind the door. He'd gone by the kitchen; I saw by the knife in his hand.

Anna screamed. I didn't blame her.

'Anna,' said Emory. 'Sweet little girls don't make noise.' Anna choked back another scream, scared to death he would get near her, and the resulting sound was terrifying. Emory glanced her way.

I stepped all the way into the room, raised the plastic candy cane, and brought it down on Emory's arm with all the fury I had in me.

'*I'm* not sweet,' I said.

He howled and dropped the knife. I put one foot on it and scooted it behind me with the toe of my shoe, just as Emory charged. The plastic candy cane must not have been very intimidating.

This time I was ready, and as he lunged toward me, I stepped to one side, stuck out one foot, and as he stumbled over it, I brought the candy cane down again on the back of his neck.

If the children hadn't been there I would have kicked him or broken one of his arms, to make sure I wouldn't have to deal with him again. But the children were there, Luke screaming and wailing with all the abandon of a two-year-old, and Anna and Krista both sobbing.

Would hitting him again be any more traumatic for them? I thought not and raised my foot.

But Chandler McAdoo said, 'No.'

All the fight went out of me in a gust. I let the red-and-white-striped plastic fall from my fingers to the carpet, told myself I should comfort the children. But I realized in a dim way that I was not at all comforting right now.

'Eve and Jane are behind the chair in the bedroom across the hall,' I said. I sounded exhausted, even to myself.

'I know,' Chandler said. 'Eve called nine-one-one.'

'Miss Lily?' called a tiny, shaky voice.

I made myself plod into the master bedroom. Eve's head popped up from behind the chair. I sat on the end of the bed.

'You can bring Jane out now,' I said. 'Thank you for calling the police. That was so smart, so brave.' Eve pushed the chair out and picked up the infant seat, though now it was almost too heavy for her thin arms.

Chandler shut the door.

It promptly came open again and Jack came in. He paused and looked me over. 'Anything broken?' he asked.

'No.' I shook my head and wondered for a second if I would be able to stop. It felt like pendulum set in motion. I rubbed my throat absently.

'Bruise,' said Jack. I watched him try to decide how to approach me and Eve.

With great effort, I lifted my hand and patted Eve on the head. Then I folded her in my arms as she began to cry.

I sat with Eve in my lap that night as she told the police what had been happening in the yellow house on Fulbright Street. Chandler was there, and Jack – and Lou O'Shea, since Jess had passionately wanted to be there as Eve's pastor, but Eve had shown a definite preference for Lou.

Daddy, it seemed, had started getting funny when it became apparent that the bills from Meredith's pregnancy and delivery were going to be substantial. He began to enjoy playing with his eight-year-old daughter.

'He always liked me to wear lipstick and makeup,' Eve said. 'He liked me to play dress up all the time.'

'What did your mom have to say about that, Eve?' Chandler asked in a neutral voice.

'She thought it was funny, at first.'

'When did things change?'

'About Thanksgiving, I guess.'

It was just after Thanksgiving that the article about unsolved crimes had appeared in the Little Rock paper. With the picture of the baby in the giraffe sleeper. The same baby sleeper that Meredith had kept all these years in a box on the closet shelf, as a memento of her baby's first days.

'Mama wasn't happy. She'd walk around the house and cry. She had a hard time taking care of Jane. She . . .' Eve's voice dropped almost to a whisper. 'She asked me funny questions.'

'About . . . ?' Chandler again.

'About did Daddy touch me funny.'

'Oh. What did you tell her?' Chandler sounded quiet and respectful of Eve, as if this was a very ordinary conversation. I had not known my old friend could be this way.

'No, he never touched me . . . there. But he liked to play Come Here Little Girl.'

My stomach heaved.

I won't go through it all, but the gist of it was that Emory liked to deck Eve in lipstick and rouge and call her over to him as if they were strangers and induce her to touch him through his pants.

'So what else happened?' Chandler asked after a moment.

'He and Mama had a fight. Mama said they had to talk about when I was born, and Daddy said he wouldn't, and Mama said . . . oh, I don't remember.'

Had Meredith asked him if Eve was their baby? Had she asked him if he was molesting the child?

'Then Mama or Daddy got my memory book and took a page out of it. I didn't see them do it, but when I got home one day, the page was missing, my favorite picture of me and Anna and Krista. It had been cut out real neat, so I think Mama did it. So the next time I spent the night with Anna, I took it over there with me, so Mama couldn't cut out any more pages.'

Jack and I met each other's eyes.

'Then Mama said I needed a blood test. So I went to Dr LeMay, and he and Miss Binnie took some blood and said they were going to test it, and I had sure been a good girl, and he gave me a piece of candy.

'Mama told me not to tell anyone, but Daddy saw the needle mark when he bathed me that night! But I didn't tell, I didn't!' Big tears rolled down Eve's cheeks.

'No one thinks you did anything wrong,' I said.

I hadn't realized how tense she was until she relaxed.

'So Daddy found out. I think he went looking and found the paper Mama got from the doctor.'

The lab results? A receipt for whatever Meredith had paid for the blood test?

'So the next night he said Mama needed a break and he was going to take us out.'

'And you got in the car, right?' Chandler asked.

'Yep, me and Jane. I was buckling her car seat when Daddy said he'd left his gloves. He opened the trunk and got something out and put it on, and he went in the house. After a few minutes he came back out with something under his arm, and he put it in the trunk and we went out to eat. When we got home . . .' Eve began to cry in earnest then.

Chandler slipped out with Emory's keys to open Emory's trunk. He came back in five minutes.

'I got some people looking and taking pictures,' he said quietly. 'Come on, sweetie, let's put you on a bed for a little while, so you can lie still.'

Lou, who had tears running down her face, held out her arms to Eve, and Eve allowed Lou to pick her up and carry her off.

'What was in the trunk?' Jack asked.

'A clear plastic raincoat with lots of stains and a single-edge kitchen knife.'

I shuddered.

Jack and Chandler began to have a very important talk.

Chandler called over to the men searching the house on

Fulbright Street. In about thirty minutes, thin Detective Brainerd brought a familiar shoe box into the bedroom at the manse.

Jack put on gloves, opened the box, and began to smile.

Dill and Varena had taken Anna home long before, and I could assume they'd made a report to my parents about where I was.

Jack dropped me at his motel room while he went to the jail to have a conversation with Emory Osborn.

When he returned, I was still lying on the bed staring at the ceiling. I still had my coat on. My throat hurt.

Without speaking, Jack consulted an address book he fished out of his briefcase. Then he picked up the phone, took a deep breath, and began dialing.

'Roy? How you doing? Yeah, I know what time it is. But I thought you should be the one to call Teresa and Simon. Tell them we got the little girl . . . of course I wouldn't kid about something like that. No, I don't want to call them, it's your case.' Jack held the phone away from his ear, and I could hear Roy Costimiglia shouting on the other end. When the sound had abated a little, Jack started talking, telling Roy as much as he could in a few sentences.

'No, I don't know . . . they better call their lawyer, have her come down before they come down. I think there's a lot of steps to go through, but Osborn actually admitted it. Yeah.' Jack eased back on the bed until he was lying beside me, his body snug against mine. 'He delivered his own baby at home, and the baby died. I think there's something kinda hinky about that, it was a baby boy . . . and he definitely likes little girls. Anyway, he felt guilty and he couldn't tell his wife. He gave her a strong painkiller he'd been taking for a back injury, she conked out, he began riding around trying to think of how to tell her the baby didn't make it. He lived right close to Conway, and he found himself just cruising through Conway at random, he says. Yeah, I don't know whether to buy that, either, especially in view . . . wait, let me finish.' Jack pulled off his shoes. 'He says he rode through the Macklesbys' neighborhood, recognized the house because he'd delivered a couch there about four months before. He liked Teresa, thought

she was pretty. Suddenly he remembered that Teresa had been
pregnant, wondered if she'd had the baby . . . he watched the
house for a while, says he was too distraught to go home and face
his wife. Suddenly, he got his chance to make everything better.
He saw Teresa come out onto the porch with the baby in her
carrier, stop, put her down, and go back in the house. She was
such a bad mother she didn't deserve a baby, he decided, and she
already had two, anyway. His wife didn't have one. He took
Summer Dawn home with him.'

Roy must have been talking again. I could feel my eyes grow
heavy now that Jack's warmth relaxed me. I turned on my side
facing him, my eyes closing just for a minute since he had the
bedside lamp on and the glare was unpleasant.

'He took Meredith to the doctor the next day, told the doctor
that he'd taken the baby to a pediatrician already. He couldn't
have their doctor examine the baby, because he figured that the
umbilical thingy was more healed than it would be on a one-day-
old baby.'

Roy talked for a minute. It was a distant buzz. I kept my eyes
shut.

'Yeah, he's confessed all the way. Says it was all his wife's fault
for having a baby that died and it being a boy, for interrupting his
fun with the little girl he'd so thoughtfully gotten for her, for
beginning to wonder where that little girl had come from when
she saw the photo in the paper . . . evidently, Meredith took the
little girl in for a blood test, found out she couldn't be her
daughter. But she loved her so much, she couldn't make up her
mind what to do. Emory found out about the blood test, decided
Meredith was a traitor, and killed her. He broke into my hotel
room, found the pages she'd mailed me . . . it made him feel
justified.'

Some more talk.

Then Jack asked, 'You gonna call them now or wait till the
morning?'

Sometime after that, I lost track of what Jack was saying.

'Baby?'

I blinked. 'What?'

'Baby, it's morning.'

'What?'

'You got to go home and get ready for the wedding, Lily.'

My eyes flew open. It was definitely daytime. In a panic, I glanced at the bedside clock. I exhaled a long sigh of relief when I saw it was only eight o'clock.

Jack was standing by the bed. He'd just gotten out of the shower.

Normally in the morning I jump out of bed and get moving, but I felt so groggy. Then I remembered the night before, and I knew where I was.

'Oh, I do have to get home, I hope they're not worried,' I said. 'I've been so good this whole visit, I've done everything right! I hate to blow it the last day.'

Jack laughed. It was a good sound.

I sat up. He'd taken my coat off some time during the night. I'd slept in my clothes, with no shower, and I needed to brush my teeth in the worst possible way. When Jack bent down to hug me, I backed off.

'No no no,' I said firmly. 'Not now. I'm disgusting.'

When Jack saw I meant it, he perched in one of the vinyl chairs. 'Want me to go get us some coffee?' he asked.

'Oh, bless you for thinking of it, but I better get to my folks' and let them see me.'

'Then I'll see you at the wedding.'

'Sure.' I reached out, stroked his arm. 'What were you doing last night?'

'While you were confronting the real kidnapper?' Jack looked at me darkly. 'Well, sweetheart, I was rear-ending your soon-to-be brother-in-law.'

'What?'

'I decided the only way to look inside the car trunks – which, if you'll remember, was your suggestion – was to have a little accident with the cars involved. It would be reasonable to look in the trunk after that. I figured if I hit them just right, the trunk would open anyway.'

'Did you hit Jess?'

'Yep.'

'And Dill, too?'

'I was about to. But I was thinking I'd get whiplash, so I'd decided just to out-and-out break into Emory's. Then I got your call. I got to the O'Sheas' house just as your ex-boyfriend was pulling up. He cuffed me.'

'He *what?*'

'I didn't want him going in ahead of me, so he cuffed me.'

I didn't know what to say. I was trying not to smile.

'I better go get cleaned up,' I told him. 'You'll be there?'

'I brought my suit,' he reminded me.

The only day it was possible for my parents not to cast me disapproving looks was Varena's wedding day. They were not excited that Jack had dropped me off in front of the house in broad daylight, with me wearing yesterday's clothes.

But in the melee of the wedding day – and the day before – it could be legitimately ignored.

I took a very long shower and brushed my teeth twice. To regain control of myself, I shaved my legs and armpits, plucked my eyebrows, spent ten or fifteen minutes putting on lotions and makeup.

It was only after I came into the kitchen in my bathrobe to drink some coffee that my mother spotted the bruise.

She put her own mug down with a clunk.

'Your neck, Lily.'

I looked in a little mirror in the hall outside the kitchen. My neck had a spectacular dark bruise.

'Emory,' I explained, for the first time noticing how hoarse my voice was. I touched the dark splotch. Sore. Very sore.

'It's OK,' I said, 'really. Just need to drink something hot.'

And that's all we said about the night before.

It was the best luck I ever had, that day being Varena's wedding day.

And the next morning, Christmas Day, I drove home to Shakespeare.

I thought during the drive: I thought what would become of the baby, Jane, whom Eve (I had to think of her as Eve Osborn) regarded as her sister. I wondered what would happen in the days to come, when the Macklesbys would finally get to put their arms around their daughter. I wondered when I'd have to go back to testify at Emory's trial. It gave me the cold shakes, thinking of going back to Bartley again, but I would feel more amenable when the time was closer, I hoped.

I didn't have to talk to anyone or listen to anyone for four whole hours.

The tatty outskirts of Shakespeare were so welcome to my eyes that I almost cried.

The decorations, the smoke coming out of the chimneys, the empty lawns and streets: Today was Christmas.

If my friend Dr Carrie Thrush had remembered, the turkey would be thawed and waiting to be put in the oven.

And Jack, having detoured to Little Rock to pick up some more clothes, was on his way.

The presents I'd bought him were wrapped and in my closet. The spinach Madeleine, the sweet potato casserole, and the cranberry sauce were in the freezer.

I shed the past as I pulled into my own driveway.

I would have a Shakespeare Christmas.

Shakespeare's Trollop

*This book is dedicated to my other family,
the people of St James Episcopal Church.
They are at liberty to be horrified by its contents.*

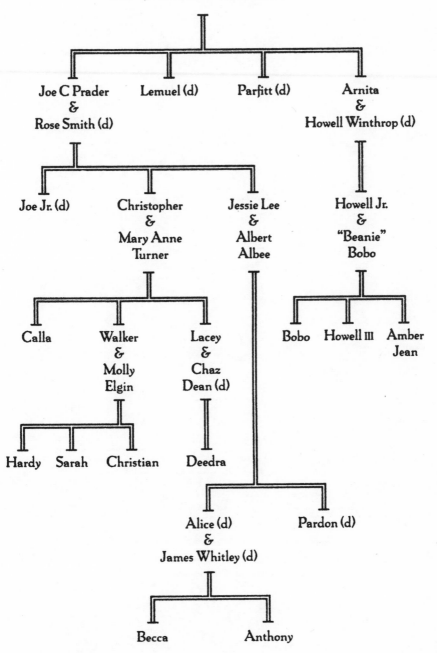

Jeremy Prader & Bessie Hewlett

Joe C Prader & Rose Smith (d) — Lemuel (d) — Parfitt (d) — Arnita & Howell Winthrop (d)

Joe Jr. (d) — Christopher & Mary Anne Turner — Jessie Lee & Albert Albee — Howell Jr. & "Beanie" Bobo

Calla — Walker & Molly Elgin — Lacey & Chaz Dean (d) — Bobo — Howell III — Amber Jean

Hardy — Sarah — Christian — Deedra

Alice (d) & James Whitley (d) — Pardon (d)

Becca — Anthony

Chapter One

By the time I opened my eyes and yawned that morning, *she* had been sitting in the car in the woods for seven hours. Of course, I didn't know that, didn't even know Deedra was missing. No one did.

If no one realizes a person is missing, is she gone?

While I brushed my teeth and drove to the gym, dew must have been glistening on the hood of her car. Since Deedra had been left leaning toward the open window on the driver's side, perhaps there was dew on her cheek, too.

As the people of Shakespeare read morning papers, showered, prepared school lunches for their children, and let their dogs out for a morning's commune with nature, Deedra was becoming part of nature herself – deconstructing, returning to her components. Later, when the sun warmed up the forest, there were flies. Her makeup looked ghastly, since the skin underlying it was changing color. Still she sat, unmoving, unmoved: life changing all around her, evolving constantly, and Deedra lifeless at its center, all her choices gone. The changes she would make from now on were involuntary.

One person in Shakespeare knew where Deedra was. One person knew that she was missing from her normal setting, in fact, missing from her life itself. And that person was waiting, waiting for some unlucky Arkansan – a hunter, a birdwatcher, a surveyor – to find Deedra, to set in motion the business of recording the circumstances of her permanent absence.

That unlucky citizen would be me.

If the dogwoods hadn't been blooming, I wouldn't have been looking at the trees. If I hadn't been looking at the trees, I wouldn't have seen the flash of red down the unmarked road to the right. Those little unmarked roads – more like tracks – are so common in rural Arkansas that they're not worth a second glance. Usually they lead to deer hunters' camps, or oil wells, or back into the property of someone who craves privacy *deeply*. But the dog-wood I glimpsed, perhaps twenty feet into the woods, was beautiful, its flowers glowing like pale butterflies among the dark branchless trunks of the slash pines. So I slowed down to look, and caught a glimpse of red down the track, and in so doing started the tiles falling in a certain pattern.

All the rest of my drive out to Mrs Rossiter's, and while I cleaned her pleasantly shabby house and bathed her reluctant spaniel, I thought about that flash of bright color. It hadn't been the brilliant carmine of a cardinal, or the soft purplish shade of an azalea, but a glossy metallic red, like the paint on a car.

In fact, it had been the exact shade of Deedra Dean's Taurus. There were lots of red cars in Shakespeare, and some of them were Tauruses. As I dusted Mrs Rossiter's den, I scorned myself for fretting about Deedra Dean, who was chronologically and biologically a woman. Deedra did not expect or require me to worry about her and I didn't need any more problems than I already had.

That afternoon, Mrs Rossiter provided a stream-of-consciousness commentary to my work. She, at least, was just as always: plump, sturdy, kind, curious, and centered on the old spaniel, Durwood. I wondered from time to time how Mr Rossiter had felt about this when he'd been alive. Maybe Mrs Rossiter had become so fixated on Durwood since her husband had died? I'd never known M. T. Rossiter, who had departed this world over four years ago, around the time I'd landed in Shakespeare. While I knelt in the bathroom, using the special rinse attachment to flush the shampoo out of Durwood's coat, I interrupted Mrs Rossiter's monologue on next month's Garden Club flower show to ask her what her husband had been like.

Since I'd stopped her midflow, it took Birdie Rossiter a moment to redirect the stream of conversation.

'Well . . . my husband . . . it's so strange you should ask, I was just thinking of him . . .'

Birdie Rossiter had always just been thinking of whatever topic you suggested.

'M. T. was a farmer.'

I nodded, to show I was listening. I'd spotted a flea in the water swirling down the drain and I was hoping Mrs Rossiter wouldn't see it. If she did, Durwood and I would have to go through various unpleasant processes.

'He farmed all his life, he came from a farming family. He never knew anything else but country. His mother actually chewed tobacco, Lily! Can you imagine? But she was a good woman, Miss Audie, with a good heart. When I married M. T. – I was just eighteen – Miss Audie told us to build a house wherever on their land we pleased. Wasn't that nice? So M. T. picked this site, and we spent a year working on the floor plan. And it turned out to be an ordinary old house, after all that planning!' Birdie laughed.

Under the fluorescent light of the bathroom, the threads of gray in the darkness of her hair shone so brightly they looked painted.

By the time Birdie had reached the point in her husband's biography where M. T. was asked to join the Gospellaires, a men's quartet at Mt. Olive Baptist, I had begun my next grocery list, at least in my head.

An hour later, I was saying good-bye, Mrs Rossiter's check tucked in the pocket of my blue jeans.

'See you next Monday afternoon,' she said, trying to sound offhand instead of lonely. 'We'll have our work cut out for us then, because it'll be the day before I have the prayer luncheon.'

I wondered if she would want me to put bows on Durwood's ears again, like I had the last time Birdie had hosted the prayer luncheon. The spaniel and I exchanged glances. Luckily for me, Durwood was the kind of dog who didn't hold a grudge. I nodded, grabbed up my caddy of cleaning products and rags, and retreated before Mrs Rossiter could think of something else to talk about. It was time to get to my next job, Camille Emerson's. I gave Durwood a farewell pat on the head as I opened the front door.

'He's looking good,' I offered. Durwood's poor health and bad eyesight were a never-ending worry to his owner. A few months before, he'd tripped Birdie with his leash and she'd broken her arm, but that hadn't lessened her attachment to the dog.

'I think he's good as gold,' Birdie told me, her voice firm. She stood on her front porch watching me as I put my supplies in the car and slid into the driver's seat. She laboriously squatted down by Durwood and made the dog raise his paw and wave good-bye to me. I lifted my hand: I knew from experience that she wouldn't stop Durwood's farewell until I responded.

As I thought about what I had to do next, I was almost tempted to turn off the engine and sit longer, listening to the ceaseless stream of Birdie Rossiter's talk. But I started the car, backed out of her driveway, and looked both ways several times before venturing out. There wasn't much traffic on Farm Hill Road, but what there was tended to be fast and careless.

I knew that when I drew opposite the unmarked road, I would stop on the narrow grassy shoulder. My window was open. When I cut my engine, the silence took over. I heard . . . nothing.

I got out and closed the door behind me. A breeze lifted my short, curly hair and made my T-shirt feel inadequate. I shivered. The tingling feeling at the back of my neck was warning me to drive off but sometimes, I guess, you just can't dodge the bullet.

My sneakers made small squeaky noises on the worn blacktop as I crossed the road. Deep in the woods to the west, I heard a bobwhite sound its cry. Not a car was in sight.

After a second's hesitation I entered the woods, following the unmarked road. It hardly deserved the name. It was really two bare tracks with grass growing up between them, some old gravel pressed down into the ground marking where the last load had been leveled years before. My progress was quiet, but not silent, and I slowed involuntarily. The path curved slightly to the right, and as I rounded that curve I saw the source of the flash of color.

It was a car – a Taurus – parked facing away from Farm Hill Road.

Someone was sitting in the front seat. I could see a head

outlined on the driver's side. I stopped dead in my tracks. My skin rose in goose bumps up and down my arms. If I'd been apprehensive before, now I was truly frightened. Somehow, that unexpected glimpse of another human being was more shocking than the discovery that a car was parked out here in the woods where it had no business parking.

'Hello?' I said quietly.

But the person in the front seat of the red Taurus did not move.

Suddenly I found I was too scared to say anything else. The woods seemed to close in around me. The silence had taken on an oppressive life of its own. 'Bob – *white!*' shrieked the bird, and I nearly leapt out of my skin.

I stood stock-still and fought a fierce internal battle. More than anything, I wanted to walk away from this car with its silent occupant – wanted to forget I'd ever been here.

I couldn't.

Despising my indecision, I marched up to the car and bent to look in.

For a moment I was distracted by her nakedness, by the bareness of breasts and thighs, by the alien protrusion between her legs. But when I looked into the face of the woman in the car, I had to bite my lower lip to keep from crying out. Deedra's eyes were halfway open, but they weren't returning my gaze.

I made myself acknowledge what I was seeing and smelling – the deadness of her – and then I let myself snap back up straight and move a step away from the car. I stood gasping until I felt steadier, thinking of what I should do next.

Another alien color, not natural to these greening woods, caught the corner of my eye and I began to look around me, trying not to move. In fact, I was hardly breathing in my effort to make no imprint on the scene around me.

The biggest patch of color was a cream-colored blouse tossed over a thorny vine that had woven itself between two trees. A few feet from that was a black skirt, cut narrow and short. It was on the ground, and it was as crumpled as the blouse. A pair of panty hose and – what was that? I leaned over to see more clearly, making an effort to satisfy my curiosity without moving my feet. Deedra's pearls. The panty hose and pearls were festooned over a low branch. I was missing the bra, which I eventually located hanging from a bush, and the shoes, which had been thrown separately some feet farther down the trail. Black leather pumps. That left the purse. I almost leaned over again to see if it was in the car, but instead I replayed the scene in my mind. The purse wasn't in the front seat of Deedra's car; she would've been carrying the little black leather shoulder-strap bag she usually used with the pumps. You don't work for someone as long as I'd worked for Deedra without knowing her clothes and her habits.

So I wouldn't have to decide what to do about this for a few more seconds, I looked hard for the purse, but I didn't spot it. Either it had been tossed farther than her clothes, or the person in the woods with her had taken it with him.

With Deedra it was always a 'him.'

I took a deep breath and braced myself, knowing what I had to do and admitting it to myself. I had to call the sheriff's department. I took one more look around, feeling the shock of the scene all over again, and patted my cheeks. But there were no tears.

Deedra was not someone you cried over, I realized as I walked swiftly out of the woods to the road. Deedra's was a shake-your-head death – not entirely unanticipated, within the realm of possibility. Since Deedra had been in her twenties, the mere fact that she was dead should have been shocking, but there again . . . it wasn't.

As I punched the number for the sheriff's department (the cell phone had been a Christmas surprise from Jack Leeds) I felt regret about my lack of amazement. The death of anyone young and healthy should be outrageous. But I knew, as I told the dispatcher where I was – right outside the Shakespeare city limit, in fact I could see the sign from where I stood – that very few people would truly be stunned about Deedra Dean being naked, violated, and dead in a car in the woods.

Of all the people in the world, I would be the last one to blame the victim for the crime. But it was simply undeniable that Deedra

had thrown herself into the victim pool with vigor, even eagerness. She must have considered her family's money and social
position life jacket enough.

After tossing the cell phone back into my car through the open
window, I leaned against the hood and wondered what situation
had led to Deedra's death. When a woman has many sexual
partners, the chance of her falling foul of one of them escalates,
and I was assuming that was what had happened. I mulled over
that assumption. If Deedra had worked in a factory that employed
mostly men, would she be more likely to die than a woman who
worked in a factory that employed mostly women? I had no idea. I
wondered if a promiscuous man was more likely to be murdered
than a chaste man.

I was actually happy to see the sheriff's car rounding the corner.
I hadn't met the new sheriff, though I'd seen her around town. As
Marta Schuster emerged from her official car, I crossed the road
once again.

We shook hands, and she gave me the silent eyes-up-and-down
evaluation that was supposed to prove to me that she was tough
and impartial.

I took the opportunity to scan her, too.

Marta's father, Marty Schuster, had been elected county sheriff
for many terms. When he'd died on the job last year, Marta had
been appointed to fill in the remainder of his term of office. Marty
had been a genuinely tough little bantamweight of a man, but his
wife must have been made of sterner and more majestic stuff.
Marta was a Valkyrie of a woman. She was robust, blond, and
very fair complexioned, like many people in this area. Shakespeare
had been founded by a literature-loving, homesick Englishman,
but in the late eighteen hundreds the little town had had an influx
of German immigrants.

The sheriff was small-bosomed and somewhat thickwaisted,
which the uniform blouse and skirt did nothing but accentuate.
Marta Schuster was somewhere in her mid-thirties, about my age.

'You're Lily Bard, who called in the death?'

'Yes.'

'The body is . . . ?'

'In there.' I pointed toward the little track.

Another sheriff's department car pulled in behind Marta Schuster's. The man who got out was tall, really tall, maybe six-four or more. I wondered if the sheriff's department had height restrictions, and if so how this man had gotten in. He looked like a brick wall in his uniform, and he was as fair-skinned as Marta, though his hair was dark – what there was of it. He was of the shaved-head school of law enforcement.

'Stay here,' Marta Schuster told me brusquely. She pointed to the bumper of her official vehicle. She went to the trunk, unlocked it, and pulled out a pair of sneakers. She slipped off her pumps and put on the sneakers. She wasn't happy about being in a skirt, I could tell; she hadn't known when she got to work that morning that she'd be called on to tromp around in the woods. The sheriff got a few more items out of her car and went to the edge of the trees. Marta Schuster was visibly bracing herself to remember every lesson she'd ever learned about homicide investigation.

I looked at my watch and tried not to sigh. It seemed likely that I would be late for Camille Emerson's.

When she'd finished preparing herself mentally, Marta made a gesture like ones I'd seen on TV in old westerns, where the head of the cavalry troop is ready to move out. You know, he raises his gloved hand and motions forward, without looking back. That was exactly the gesture Marta used, and the deputy obeyed it silently. I expected her to toss him a Milk Bone.

I was grabbing at any mental straw to avoid thinking of the body in the car, but I knew that I'd have to face it sooner or later. No matter what Deedra's life had been, or how I'd felt about her choices in that life, I discovered I was genuinely sorry that she was dead. And her mother! I winced when I thought of Lacey Dean Knopp's reaction to her only child's death. Lacey had always seemed oblivious of her daughter's activities, and I'd never known if that was self-protective or Deedra-protective. Either way, I kind of admired it.

My calm time ended when a third vehicle pulled over to the shoulder, this one a battered Subaru. A young man, blond and blocky, leapt from the driver's seat and looked around wildly. His eyes passed over me as if I were one of the trees. When the young man spotted the opening into the woods, he threw himself along the narrow shoulder like a novice skier hurls himself down a slope, apparently intending to dash down the road to the scene of Deedra's demise.

He was in civilian clothes, and I didn't know him. I was betting he had no business at the crime scene. But I wasn't the law. I let him pass, though I'd stopped leaning against the sheriff's car and uncrossed my arms. At that moment Marta Schuster came back into sight and yelled, 'No, Marlon!' The big deputy dogging her stepped around her neatly, grabbed the smaller man's shoulders, and held him fast. I'd seen the smaller man around the apartments, I recalled, and I realized for the first time that this boy was Marlon Schuster, Marta's brother. My stomach clenched at this bombshell of a complication.

'Marlon,' the sheriff said in a harsh voice. It would've stopped me. 'Marlon, get ahold of yourself.'

'Is it true? Is it her?'

From only five feet away, I could hardly avoid hearing this conversation.

Marta took a deep breath. 'Yes, it's Deedra,' she said, quite gently, and motioned to the deputy, who let go of the boy's arm.

To my amazement, the young man drew back that arm to swing at his sister. The deputy had turned to walk to his car, and Marta Schuster seemed too astounded to defend herself, so I covered the ground and seized his cocked right arm. The ungrateful fool swung around and went for me with his left. Well, I too had a free hand, and I struck him – *seiken*, a thrust – right in the solar plexus.

He made a sound like 'oof' as the air left him, and then went down on his knees. I released him and stepped away. He wouldn't be bothering anyone for a few minutes.

'Idiot,' the sheriff said, crouching down by him. The deputy was right by me, suddenly, his hand playing nervously around his gun. I wondered which of us he'd draw on. After a second his hand relaxed, and I did too.

'Where'd you learn that?' asked the deputy. I looked up at him. He had bitter-chocolate brown eyes.

'Karate class,' I said, throwing it away, not wanting to talk about it. Marshall Sedaka, my *sensei*, would be pleased.

'You're that woman,' the deputy said.

All of a sudden, I felt real tired. 'I'm Lily Bard,' I said, keeping my voice neutral. 'And if you all are through with me, I need to be getting to my next job.'

'Just tell me again how you happened to find her,' Marta Schuster said, leaving her brother to fend for himself. She looked sideways at her deputy. He nodded. They seemed to be good at nonverbal communication. She addressed me again. 'Then you can go, long as we know where to reach you.'

I gave her the Joe-Friday facts: Mrs Rossiter's phone number, my cell phone number, my home phone number, and where I'd be working this afternoon if I ever got to leave this stretch of road.

'And you knew the deceased how?' she asked again, as if that was a point she hadn't quite gotten straight in her head.

'I cleaned her place. I live next to her apartment building,' I said.

'How long had you worked for Deedra?'

The tall deputy had gone down the path with a camera after making sure that Marlon was off his tear. The sheriff's brother had recovered enough to haul himself up to the hood of his Subaru. He was sprawled over it, weeping, his head buried in his hands. His sister completely ignored him, though he was making a considerable amount of noise.

Two more deputies arrived in another squad car and emerged with rolls of crime-scene tape, and Marta Schuster interrupted me to give them directions.

'I worked for Deedra – though I'm sure her mother subsidized her – for over three years,' I said, when the sheriff turned her attention back to me. 'I cleaned Deedra's apartment once a week.'

'So, you were friendly with her?'

'No.' That didn't require any thought.

'Yet you knew her for more than three years,' Marta Schuster observed, pretending to be surprised.

I shrugged. 'She was most often gone to work while I was at her place.' Though sometimes she was still there; and sometimes the men would still be there, but the sheriff hadn't asked me about the men. She would, though.

While the sheriff gave more directions to her deputies, I had a little time to think. The pictures! I closed my eyes to contain my dismay.

One of the least explicable things about Deedra was her fondness for nude pictures of herself. She'd kept a little pile of them in her lingerie drawer for years. Every time I'd put her clean clothes away, I'd felt an uncomfortable stab of disapproval. Of all the things Deedra did to parade her vulnerability, this was the thing I found most distasteful.

I thought of those pictures lying out on a desk in the sheriff's office, being viewed by all and sundry. I felt a wave of regret, an almost overwhelming impulse to rush to Deedra's apartment ahead of the law, remove the pictures, and burn them.

Marlon Schuster slammed his hand against the hood of his car, and his sister, who was watching my face rather than his, jumped. I carefully avoided her eyes. Marlon needed to take his display of grief to another, more discreet, location.

'So, you have a key to the apartment?' Marty Schuster asked.

'I do,' I said promptly. 'And I'm going to give it to you now.' I abandoned any quixotic notion of shielding Deedra's true nature from the men and women examining her death. I was sure almost everyone in town had heard that Deedra was free with herself. But would they look for her killer as hard, once they'd seen those pictures? Would they keep their mouths shut, so rumors didn't reach Deedra's mother?

I pressed my lips together firmly. There was nothing I could do, I told myself sternly. Deedra was on her own. I'd set the investigation of her death in motion, but beyond that, I couldn't help her. The cost to myself would be too high.

So thinking, I worked her key off the ring and dropped it in the open palm of Sheriff Marta Schuster. A vague memory stirred, and I wondered if I knew of another key. Yes, I recalled, Deedra kept an emergency key in her stall in the apartment carport. As I opened my mouth to tell the sheriff about this key, she made a chopping gesture to cut off my comment. I shrugged. But I told myself that this was truly my only key, and that because I'd turned over this key, Deedra Dean was out of my life.

'I'll need a list of the people you've seen there,' Sheriff Schuster said sharply. She was aching to return to the crime scene, her face turning often to the woods.

I'd already begun to go back to my car. I didn't like being hushed with that chopping hand, it wasn't like I chattered. And I didn't like being ordered.

'I never saw anyone there,' I said, my back to the sheriff.

'You . . . in the years you cleaned her apartment, you never saw anyone else there?' Marta Schuster's tone let me know she was well aware of Deedra's reputation.

'Her stepfather was there one morning when Deedra was having car trouble.'

'And that's all?' Marta Schuster asked, openly disbelieving.

'That's all.' Marlon, of course, had been creeping out of there three or four days ago, but she knew about him already and it didn't seem the time to bring that up again.

'That's a little surprising.'

I half-turned, shrugging. 'You through with me?'

'No. I want you to meet me at the apartment in about two hours. Since you're familiar with Deedra's belongings, you can tell us if anything's missing or not. It would be better if Mrs Knopp didn't have to do it, I'm sure you agree.'

I felt trapped. There was nothing I could say besides, 'I'll be there.'

My involvement in the troubled life of Deedra Dean was not yet over.

Chapter Two

Camille Emerson would hate me later for not telling her my little news item, but I just didn't want to talk about Deedra's death. Camille was on her way out, anyway, a list clutched in her plump hand.

'I remembered to put the clean sheets out this time,' she said with a touch of pride. I nodded, not willing to give a grown woman a pat on the back for doing a simple thing like putting out clean sheets for me to change. Camille Emerson was cheerful and untidy. Though I didn't dislike her – in fact, I felt glad to work for her – Camille was trying to warm up our relationship into some kind of facsimile of friendship, and I found that as irritating as the employers who treated me like a slave.

'See you later!' Camille said finally, giving up on a response. After a second I said, 'Good-bye.' It was lucky I was in a mood to work hard, since the Emersons had made more than their usual mess since my last visit. There were only four of them (Camille, her husband, Cooper, their two boys) but each Emerson was determined to live in the center of chaos. After spending fifteen minutes one day trying to sort out the different sizes of sheets I needed, I'd suggested to Camille that she leave the clean sheets on each bed, ready for me to change. That was much better than extending my time there, since Mondays were always busy for me, and Camille had blanched at the thought of paying me more. We were both happy with the result; that is, when Camille remembered her part.

My cell phone rang while I was drying the newly scrubbed sink in the hall bathroom.

'Yes?' I said cautiously. I still wasn't used to carrying this phone.

'Hi.'

'Jack.' I could feel myself smiling. I grabbed my mop and cleaning materials in their caddy, awkwardly because of the telephone, and moved down the hall to the kitchen.

'Where are you?'

'Camille Emerson's.'

'Are you alone?'

'Yes.'

'I've got news.' Jack sounded half excited, half uneasy.

'What?'

'I'm catching a plane in an hour,'

'For?' He was supposed to be coming to stay with me tonight.

'I'm working on a fraud case. The main suspect left last night for Sacramento.'

I was even more miserable than I'd been after finding Deedra's body. I'd looked forward to Jack's visit so much. I'd even changed my sheets and come home from the gym early this morning to make sure my own little house was spanking clean. The disappointment bit into me.

'Lily?'

'I'm here.'

'I'm sorry.'

'You have to work,' I said, my voice flat and even. 'I'm just . . .' Angry, unhappy, empty; all of the above.

'I'm going to miss you, too.'

'Will you?' I asked, my voice as low as if there were someone there to hear me. 'Will you think of me when you're alone in your hotel room?'

He allowed as how he would.

We talked a little longer. Though I got satisfaction out of realizing that Jack really would regret he wasn't with me, the end result was the same; I wouldn't see him for a week, at the very least, and two weeks was more realistic.

After we hung up I realized I hadn't told him about finding Deedra dead. I wasn't going to phone him back. Our good-byes had been said. He'd met Deedra, but that was about the extent of his knowledge of her . . . as far as I knew. He'd lived across the hall from her before I'd met him, I recalled with a surge of uneasiness. But I channeled it aside, unwilling to worry about a faint possibility that Jack had enjoyed Deedra's offerings before he'd met me. I shrugged. I'd tell him about her death the next time we talked.

I tugged the crammed garbage bag out of the can, yanked the ties together in a knot, and braced myself as Camille Emerson staggered through the kitchen door, laden with grocery bags and goodwill.

I was late for my appointment with Marta Schuster, but I didn't care. I'd parked my car in my own carport before striding next door to the eight-unit apartment building, noticing as I threw open the big front door that there were two sheriff's department vehicles parked at the curb. I was in a bad mood, a truculent mood – not the best frame of mind for dealing with law-enforcement officials.

'Take a breath,' advised a cool, familiar, voice.

It was good advice, and I stopped to take it.

'Marta Schuster and her storm trooper are up there,' Becca Whitley went on, stepping from her apartment doorway at the back of the hall to stand by the foot of the stairs.

Becca Whitley was a wet dream about three years past its prime. She had very long blond hair, very bright blue eyes, strong (if miniature) features, and cone-shaped breasts thrusting out from an athletic body. Becca, who'd lived in Shakespeare for about five months, had inherited the apartment building from her uncle, Pardon Albee, and she lived in his old apartment.

I'd never thought Becca would last even this long in little Shakespeare; she'd told me she'd moved here from Dallas, and she seemed like a city kind of woman. I'd been sure she'd put the building up for sale and take off for some urban center. She'd surprised me by staying.

And she'd taken my place as the highest-ranking student in Marshall's class.

But there were moments I felt a connection to Becca, and this was one of them. We'd begun a tentative sort of friendship.

'How long have they been up there?' I asked.

'Hours.' Becca looked up the stairs as if, through the floors and doors, she could watch what the sheriff was so busy doing. 'Did they tell you to come?'

'Yes.'

'What about Marlon?'

'He was at the crime scene bawling his eyes out.'

'Ew.' Becca scrunched her nose in distaste. 'He's the one been seeing her so hot and heavy.'

I nodded. I wondered how well the sheriff would investigate her own brother.

'Do you have your key?' Becca asked.

'I gave it to them.'

'Good move,' she said. 'They got my copy of her key, too.'

I shifted from foot to foot. 'I better go up. I'm supposed to tell them if anything's missing.'

'See you tonight,' she called after me, and I lifted my hand in acknowledgment.

Deedra's apartment was the right rear, just above Becca's. It overlooked the paved rear parking lot, not an inspiring view. It held a carport divided into eight stalls, a Dumpster, and not much else. I wasn't sure who, besides Deedra, lived on the second floor now, but I'd known many of the people who'd passed through. Claude Friedrich, the chief of police and a friend of mine, had moved from the second floor to the first after a leg injury. I figured he and Deedra had been in the building the longest. Generally, the eight units of the so-called Shakespeare Garden Apartments stayed full because the units were a nice size and fairly reasonable. I was pretty sure Becca had gone up on the rent as the leases ran out, because I had a faint memory of Deedra complaining, but it hadn't been an outrageous increase.

I knocked on Deedra's door. The same tall officer answered, the guy who'd been at the crime scene. He filled up the doorway; after a long second, he stepped aside so I could enter. He was lucky looking at me was a free activity, or he would be broke by now.

'Sheriff's in there,' he said, pointing toward Deedra's bedroom. But instead of following his hint, I stood in the center of the living room and looked around. I'd been in to clean the past Friday, and today was Monday, so the place still looked good; Deedra was careless with herself, but she had always been fairly tidy with everything else.

The furniture seemed to be in the same spots, and all the cushions were straight. Her television and VCR were untouched; rows of videotapes sat neat and square on their little bookcase by the television. The brand-new CD player was on the stand by the television. All Deedra's magazines were in the neat stack I'd arranged a few days before, except for a new issue left open on the coffee table in front of the couch, where Deedra usually sat when she watched television. Her bills were piled in the shallow basket where she'd tossed them.

'Notice anything different?' The tall deputy was standing by the door and keeping quiet, a point in his favor.

I shook my head and resumed my examination.

'Emanuel,' he said suddenly.

Was this some kind of religious statement? My eyebrows drew in and I regarded him with some doubt.

'Clifton Emanuel.'

After a distinct pause, I understood. 'You're Clifton Emanuel,' I said tentatively. He nodded.

I didn't need to know his name, but he wanted me to know it. Maybe he was a celebrity freak, True Crime Division, Famous Victims Subsection. Like Sharon Tate, but alive.

Maybe he was just being polite.

I was relieved when the sheriff stuck her head out of Deedra's bedroom and jerked it back in a motion that told, me I'd better join her.

'Everything in the living room okay?' she asked.

'Yes.'

'What about this room?'

I stood at the foot of Deedra's bed and turned around slowly. Deedra had loved jewelry, and it was everywhere; necklaces, earrings, bracelets, an anklet or two. The impression was that the jewelry was strewn around, but if you looked closer, you would notice that the backs were on the earrings and the earrings were in pairs. The necklaces were lain straight and fastened so they wouldn't tangle. That was normal. Some of the drawers were not completely shut – there again, that was typical Deedra. The bed was made quite tidily; it was queen-size, with a high, carved headboard that dominated the room. I lifted the corner of the flowered bedspread and peered beneath it.

'Different sheets than I put on last Friday,' I said.

'Does that mean something?'

'Means someone slept in it with her since then.'

'Did she ever wash the sheets and put them right back on the bed?'

'She never washed anything, especially sheets. She had seven sets. I did her laundry.'

Marta Schuster looked startled. Then she looked disgusted. 'So if I count the sheet sets in the laundry hamper, I'll come up with the number of times she entertained since last Friday morning?'

I sighed, hating knowing these things about someone else, much less revealing them. But it was the nature of my job. 'Yes,' I said wearily.

'Did she have a video camera? I noticed all the tapes out there.'

'Yes, she did. She kept it up there, on the closet shelf.' I pointed, and Marta fetched. She opened the soft black case, removed the camera, turned it on, and opened the tape bay. Empty.

'Who paid you to clean this place?' she asked out of the blue.

'I thought we'd covered that. Her mother, Lacey, gave Deedra the money so she could afford me.'

'Deedra get along with her mother?'

'Yes.'

'What about her stepfather?'

I considered my answer. I'd heard a fight between the two so intense I'd considered intervening, maybe three or four months ago. I didn't like Jerrell Knopp. But it was one thing not to like him, another thing to tell the sheriff words he'd spoken in anger.

'They weren't close,' I said cautiously.

'Ever see them fight?'

I turned away, began putting Deedra's earrings into her special compartmented box.

'Stop,' the sheriff said sharply.

I dropped the pair I was holding as if they'd burst into flames. 'Sorry,' I said, shaking my head at my own error. 'It was automatic.' I hoped Marta Schuster stayed diverted.

'She always have this much jewelry lying around?'

'Yes.' I was relieved she'd asked a question so easily answered. I couldn't stop myself from glancing over at Deedra's chest of drawers, wondering if Marta Schuster had already found the pictures. I wondered whether mentioning them would help in some way.

'They're in my pocket,' she said quietly.

My eyes met hers. 'Good.'

'What do you know about her sex life?'

I could see that this was supposed to signal a tradeoff. My mouth twisted in distaste. 'Your brother was mighty interested in Deedra, from what I could see. Ask him.'

Marta Schuster's hard, square hand shot out and gripped my wrist. 'He's just the latest in her long string,' she said, her jaw as rigid as the grip of her hand. 'He's so new to her that he's dumb enough to be sorry she's dead.'

I looked down at her fingers and took slow breaths. I met her eyes again. 'Let go of me,' I told her in a very careful voice.

Keeping her eyes on my face, she did. Then she took a step away. But she said, 'I'm waiting.'

'You already know that Deedra was promiscuous. If a man was willing, she was, with very few exceptions.'

'Name some names.'

'No. It would take too long. Besides, they were almost always gone when I got here.' That was my first lie.

'What about the exceptions? She turn anyone down?'

I thought that over. 'That kid who worked at the loading dock over at Winthrop Lumber and Supply,' I said reluctantly.

'Danny Boyce? Yeah, he's out on parole now. Who else?'

'Dedford Jinks.'

'With the city police?' she asked, incredulity written all over her face. 'He must be in his fifties.'

'So he doesn't want sex?' What universe did Marta Schuster inhabit?

'He's married,' Marta protested. Then she flushed red. 'Forget I said that.'

I shrugged, tired of being in this room with this woman. 'He was separated from his wife. But Deedra didn't go with married men.'

The sheriff looked openly skeptical. 'Anyone else?'

I actually had a helpful memory. 'She'd had trouble with someone calling her.' Deedra had mentioned that to me the last time I'd cleaned the apartment, just this past Friday. She'd been running late for work, as she all too often did. 'Last Friday, she told me that she was getting calls at two or three in the morning. Really nasty calls from a guy . . . somehow disguising his voice, talking about sexual torture.'

I could see Deedra, sitting on the end of the very bed we stood by now, easing up her panty hose and sliding her narrow feet into brown low-heeled pumps. Deedra's head, crowned by its sexily tousled and newly red hair, had been bent to her task, but Deedra kept her head tucked quite a bit anyway to minimize her sharply receding chin, without a doubt her worst feature. She'd stood and scanned herself in the mirror, tugging at the top of the beige suit she thought appropriate for her job in the courthouse. A typical Deedra selection, the suit was just a bit too tight, a smidge too short, and a half-inch too low in the neckline.

Deedra had leaned over to peer into the mirror to apply her lipstick. Her dresser, with its triple mirror, was literally covered with bottles and plastic cases of makeup. Deedra was a virtuoso with foundation, rouge, and eye shadow. She'd had a real gift for it, for using cosmetics to make her look her very best with every outfit she wore. She'd studied the human face and the alterations and illusions a skilled applicator could effect.

I could still see how Deedra had looked as she'd half-turned to tell me what the caller had proposed to do to her; her lower lip a glossy peach and her upper lip bare, her clothes and hair and demeanor just a careful step away from floozy.

'Did she say who she thought he was, the man calling her?'

I shook my head. 'Can you check her phone records?' I asked.

'It'll take a while, but we'll get 'em,' Marta said.

Her deputy stuck his head into the room. 'I've finished searching the bathroom,' Emanuel said, his eyes scanning us curiously. 'What now?'

'Extra bedroom,' the sheriff said. 'And bag the sheets on the top of the washer.'

His head vanished.

'What about him?' I asked.

'What?' she said, as if she was about to get angry.

'Did he know Deedra?'

Her face changed, then, and I knew she was involved with Clifton Emanuel to some degree.

'I don't know,' she said. 'But I'll find out.'

Janet Shook aimed a kick at my stomach, and I arched back to dodge it. My hand shot out and gripped her ankle, and then I had her.

'Stop!' called a commanding voice. 'Okay, what are you going to do now, Janet?' our *sensei* continued. He was leaning against the mirrored wall, his arms folded across his chest.

We had frozen in position, Janet balancing easily on one foot, my fingers still circling her ankle. The seated class, looking like a strange nursery school in their loose white *gis*, studied the problem.

Janet looked grim. 'Land on my butt, looks like,' she conceded, after a moment's evaluation. I heard a couple of snorts of laughter.

'Lily, what would you do next, now that you're in control of the situation?' Marshall's faintly Asian face gave me no hint of the best answer.

'I'd keep going up on the ankle,' I told him, 'like so.' I lifted Janet's right foot another inch, and the knee of her supporting left leg began to buckle.

Marshall nodded briefly. He faced the other class members. Like the rest of us, Marshall was barefoot and wearing his *gi*. Its snowy whiteness, broken only by the black belt and the fist patch on his chest, emphasized the ivory of his skin. 'How could Janet have avoided this situation?' he asked the motley group sitting against the mirrored wall. 'Or having gotten into it, how can she get out?'

Raphael Roundtree, the largest and darkest man in the class, said, 'She should've drawn her kick back quicker.' I let go of Janet, though Marshall hadn't told me to, because she was beginning to have trouble keeping her balance. Janet looked relieved to have both feet on the floor, and she nodded to me by way of saying thanks.

'She shouldn't have kicked at all,' Becca Whitley rebutted.

'What should Janet have done instead?' Marshall asked her, a sweep of his hand inviting Becca to show us. She got up in one fluid movement. Becca often braided her hair for class – and she'd done so tonight – but she didn't lay off the makeup. Her toenails were bright scarlet, which for some reason struck me as improper for karate . . . though scarlet toenails didn't seem to bother Marshall, and it was his class.

Marshall Sedaka, our *sensei*, was also the owner of Body Time, where we were holding the class in the big aerobics room. I'd known Marshall for years. At one time, he'd been more to me than a friend. Now he straightened and moved closer to get a better view.

Janet moved away and Becca took her place, lifting and cocking her leg slowly so everyone could see what she meant to do.

'So,' she said, her narrow face intent, 'I kick, like so . . .' Her foot began moving toward my abdomen, as Janet's had. 'Then Lily takes a little hop back and her hand reaches for my ankle. That's what she did with Janet.'

I obliged, imitating my movements of moments ago.

'But,' continued Becca cheerfully, 'that was a feint. I snap it back and aim it higher this time,' Her leg floated back toward her, bent double at the knee, and lashed out again at my head. Becca was one of the few people in the class who could even attempt a head kick with any hope of success. 'See,' Becca pointed out, 'she's leaning to reach my ankle, so her head's a little lower than usual.'

I held still, with some effort, while Becca's foot with its bright nails flashed toward my face. Becca pulled the kick about an inch from my nose. I exhaled, I hoped silently. Becca winked at me.

'Good move, Becca,' Marshall said. 'But not an option open to many of the people in this class. Carlton, what would you do?'

Carlton was my next-door neighbor. He owned a little house almost identical to mine on Track Street, so if I stood facing my house, his would be on the right, and the Shakespeare Garden Apartments slightly uphill to my left. With his thick dark hair and large brown eyes, Carlton, single and self-supporting, was a real honeypot to Shakespeare's buzzing little hive of single women. Carlton went from one to the other, dating one for a month or two, then another; he wasn't as reckless as Deedra by a long shot, but he wasn't as careful as I was, either. In karate, Carlton was too slow and cautious, to his detriment. Maybe that caution, that deliberation, came from his being an accountant.

'I wouldn't kick at Lily at all,' Carlton said frankly, and Janet and Raphael laughed. 'I'm heavier than she is, and that's my only advantage with her. I'd try to strike her harder and hope that would take her out of the fight.'

'Come try.' Marshall returned to his spot against the wall.

With a marked reluctance, my neighbor scrambled to his feet and approached me slowly, while Becca folded gracefully to the floor with the rest of the students. I dropped into my fighting stance, knees slightly bent, one side turned toward Carlton.

'I'm supposed to stand and let him try to hit me?' I asked Marshall.

'No, give him some trouble,' Marshall directed, so Carlton and I began circling each other. I moved in a sort of smooth, sideways glide that kept me evenly balanced. My hands were up, fisted and ready. Carlton *was* a lot taller and heavier than I was, so I kept reminding myself not to discount him as an opponent. What I didn't allow for was the macho factor and Carlton's inexperience. Carlton was determined to best me, and inexperienced enough to gauge his strike wrong.

He struck at my ribs, *seiken*, with his left fist, and I blocked him, my right forearm coming up under his striking arm to deflect it upward. I didn't propel his arm sideways enough – definitely my mistake – so instead of his punch landing in the air to my right, as I'd intended, his momentum carried him forward and his fist smacked my jaw.

The next thing I knew, I was down on the mat and Carlton was leaning over me, looking absolutely horror-struck.

'Dammit, Lily, say something!' he said frantically, and then Marshall shoved him aside and took his place.

He peered at my eyes, asked me several interesting questions about what parts of my body I could move and how many fingers I could see, and then said, 'I think you're gonna be okay.'

'Can I stand up?' I asked peevishly. I was deeply chagrined at having been knocked down by Carlton Cockroft, of all people. The rest of the class was crowding around me, but since Marshall had said I was in no danger, I swore I could see some suppressed grins.

'Here,' Janet Shook said, her square little face both worried and amused. I gripped her outstretched hand and she braced her feet and pulled. With a little help from my own feet, I stood upright, and though everything looked funny for a second, I decided I was almost normal.

'Line up!' Marshall barked, and we took our places in line. I was sandwiched between Becca and Raphael.

'*Kiotske!*'

We put our heels together and stood to attention.

'*Rei!*'

We bowed.

'Class dismissed.'

Still feeling a tad shaky, I walked carefully over to my little pile of belongings, pulled off my sparring pads, and stowed them in my gym bag. I slid my feet into my sandals, thankful I didn't have to bend over to tie sneakers.

Janet joined me as I walked out to my old car.

'Are you really feeling all right?' she asked quietly.

My first impulse was to snarl at her, but instead I admitted, 'Not quite.' She relaxed, as if she'd expected the snarl and was pleasantly surprised at the admission.

I fumbled with unlocking my car, but finally got it right.

Janet said, 'I'm sorry about Deedra. I'm sorry you had to find her. It must have been awful.'

I tilted my head in a brief nod. 'I guess you and Deedra had known each other for a long time, both growing up here and all.'

Janet nodded, her thick brown hair swinging against each cheek. She'd let it grow to chin length, and wore bangs. It became her. 'Deedra was a little younger,' she said, leaning against my car. I threw my gym bag in to land on the passenger's seat, and propped myself against the open door. It was a beautiful night, clear and just a little cool. We wouldn't have many more evenings like this; summer practically pounces on spring in southern Arkansas.

'I was a year ahead of her in school,' Janet continued after a minute. 'I went to Sunday school with her at First Methodist. That was before they formed Shakespeare Combined Church, and way before Miss Lacey's first husband died and she married Jerrell Knopp and began going to SCC. My mom is still real good friends with Miss Lacey.'

'Was Deedra always . . . promiscuous?' I asked, since I seemed to be expected to keep the conversation going.

'No,' Janet said. 'Not always. It was her chin.'

And I understood. Her severely recessive chin was the only feature that had kept Deedra from real prettiness, the flaw that had kept her from being homecoming queen, head cheerleader, most prized girl to date – everything. It was easy to imagine Deedra gradually coming to feel that if she couldn't achieve those things, she could be remarkable in another way.

'Wonder why her parents didn't do anything about it?' I asked. 'Is there anything you can do about chins?'

'I don't know.' Janet shrugged. 'But I can tell you that Lacey has never believed in plastic surgery. She's real fundamentalist, you know. A great lady, but not a liberal bone in her body. That's why she took to Shakespeare Combined Church so well, when she married Jerrell and he wanted her to go to church with him.'

A tap on the jaw seemed to have much the same effect on me as a glass or two of wine. I felt disinclined to move, oddly content to be standing in a parking lot having an idle conversation with another human being.

'Jerrell and Deedra didn't get along so well,' I commented.

'No. Frankly, I've always wondered . . .' and Janet hesitated, her face compressing into an expression of both reluctance and distaste. 'Well, I've always wondered if he ever visited Deedra . . . you know? Before Lacey's husband died, before Jerrell ever imagined being able to marry Lacey?'

'Ugh,' I said. I turned this over in my mind for a minute. 'Oh, *yuck*.'

'Yeah, me too.' Our eyes met. We had matching expressions.

'I would think he would hate remembering that,' Janet said, slowly and carefully. 'I would think he'd hate wondering if Deedra would ever tell.'

After a long, thoughtful moment, I replied, 'Yes. I'd think he certainly would.'

Chapter Three

Lacey Knopp called me the next morning. I was about to leave for Joe C Prader's house when the phone rang. Hoping it was Jack, though the time difference made me fairly surely it wasn't, I said, 'Yes?'

'Lily, I need you to help me,' Lacey said. I hardly recognized her voice. She sounded like she'd been dragged over razor blades.

'How?'

'I need you to meet me at Deedra's tomorrow. I need help packing up the things in her apartment. Can you do that for me?'

I try to keep Wednesday mornings free for just such special projects. I wasn't more than a little surprised that Deedra's mother was in such a hurry to clear out Deedra's apartment. Many, many people react to grief with a furious flurry of activity. They figure if they don't hold still, it can't hit them.

'Yes, I can do that. What time?'

'Eight?'

'Sure.' I hesitated. 'I'm sorry,' I said.

'Thank you.' Lacey sounded shakier, suddenly. 'I'll see you tomorrow.'

I was so buried in thought that I took the wrong route to Mr Prader's, and had to turn around and go back.

Joe Christopher Prader was as old as God but as mean as the devil. Called 'Joe C' by all his family and cronies (those few still surviving), he'd been known for years for stalking around Shakespeare brandishing a cane at everyone who crossed his path, lamenting the passing of the better days, and bringing up old scandals at the most inopportune times.

Now Joe C's stalking-around days were pretty much done.

Some visits, I kind of enjoyed him. Others, I would have decked him gladly if he hadn't been so frail. More than once, I wondered if he was really as fragile as he seemed, or if maybe that show of frailty was a defense against just such impulses as mine.

Shakespeareans were inexplicably proud of having Joe C as a town character. His family was less thrilled. When his grand-daughter Calla had hired me, she'd begged me to work for at least a month before I quit. By that time, she hoped, I would be over the shock of him.

'If we could get him to move out of that old house,' Calla Prader had said despairingly. 'If we could get him into Shake-speare Manor . . . or if we could get him to agree to live-in help!'

Joe C was definitely not in the business of making life easier for anyone but himself, and that only when it suited him.

But I'd lasted my month, and was now into my third.

Joe C was up and dressed by the time I knocked on his door. He adamantly refused to let me have a key, so every week I had to wait for him to shuffle from his bedroom to the front door, which I tried to bear philosophically. After all, keeping his keys to himself was his right, and one I understood.

But I was sure he wouldn't give me a key simply out of meanness, rather than from principle. I'd noticed he came to the door especially slowly when the weather was bad, and I suspected he relished the idea of keeping me out in the rain or cold; any-way, keeping me at the mercy of Joe C Prader, all-powerful doorkeeper.

This morning he swung the door open after only a short delay. 'Well, here you are, then,' he said, amazed and disgusted by my persistence in arriving on time for my job.

'Here I am,' I agreed. I tried not to sigh too loudly when he turned to go ahead of me to his bedroom, where I usually started by stripping the bed. Joe C always had to lead the way, and he always went very, very slowly. But the man was a nonagenarian: What could I say? I looked around me at the remains of the grand house as I followed the old man. The Prader House, the only remaining home on one of the main commercial streets of Shake-speare, was a showplace that had seen better days. Built about

1890, the house had high ceilings, beautiful woodwork, restored but cranky plumbing, and an electrical system that had seen better decades. The upstairs, with its four bedrooms and huge bathroom, was closed off now, though Calla had told me that she cleaned it about twice a year. Joe C wasn't fit to go up stairs anymore.

'I'm all stopped up this week.' Joe C opened the conversation, which would not let up until I left the house. He lowered himself into the old red velvet chair in a corner of the large back bedroom.

'Allergies?' I said absently, stripping the bedding off the four-poster and pitching it into the hall, where I'd gather it up and take it to the washer. I shook out the bedspread and draped it over the footboard.

'Naw, I reckon I ate too much cheese. You know, it binds you.'

I exhaled slowly, calmly, as I stepped out into the hall to open the linen cupboard.

'Did you get Calla to get you some prunes?'

He cackled. I was one ahead of him. 'Yes, missy, I surely did, and ate them all. Today's the day.'

I wasn't in the best mood to put up with Joe C this morning. The charm of this particular town character was lost on me; maybe the sightseers the Chamber of Commerce was trying to attract would appreciate hearing colorful stories about Joe C's intestines. I couldn't imagine why any tourist would want to come to Shakespeare, since its only possible attraction would have been antebellum homes – if they hadn't been burned to the ground in the Late Unpleasantness, as Joe C's best friend, China Belle Lipscott, called the Civil War. So all Shakespeare could boast was, 'Yes, we're old, but we have nothing to show for it.'

Maybe Joe C could be propped on a bench on the square to amuse any soul who happened by. He could give a daily report on the state of his bowels.

'China Belle's daughter is dropping her off in a few minutes,' Joe C informed me. 'Is my tie crooked?'

I straightened from putting on the fitted sheet. I suspected he'd been eyeing my ass. 'You're okay,' I said unenthusiastically.

'China Belle's quite a gal,' he said, trying to leer.

'You creep,' I said. 'Mrs Lipscott is a perfectly nice woman who wouldn't go to bed with you if you owned the last mattress on earth. You stop talking dirty.'

'Oooh,' he said, in mock fear. 'Bully the old man, why dontcha. Come on, darlin', make old Joe C feel good again.'

That did it.

'Listen to me,' I said intently, squatting before him. He put his cane between us, I noticed, so he hadn't completely ruled out the fact that I might retaliate.

Good.

'You will not tell me about your body functions. Unless you're dripping blood, I don't care. You will not make sexual remarks.'

'Or what? You're going to hit me, a man in his nineties who walks with a cane?'

'Don't rule it out. Disgusting is disgusting.'

He eyed me malevolently. His brown eyes were almost hidden in the folds of skin that drooped all over him. 'Calla wouldn't pay you, you go to hit me,' he said in, defiance.

'It'd be worth losing the pay.'

He glared at me, resenting like hell his being old and powerless. I didn't blame him for that. I might feel exactly the same way if I reach his age. But there are some things I just won't put up with.

'Oh, all right,' he conceded. He looked into a corner of the room, not at me, and I rose and went back to making up the bed.

'You knew that gal that got killed, that Deedra?'

'Yes.'

'She was my great-granddaughter. She as loose as they say?'

'Yes,' I said, answering the second part of the question before the first had registered. Then I glared at him, shocked and angry.

'When I was a boy, it was Fannie Dooley,' Joe C said reminiscently, one gnarled hand rising to pat what was left of his hair. He was elaborately ignoring my anger. I'd seen a picture of Joe C when he was in his twenties: he'd had thick black hair, parted in the middle, and a straight, athletic body. He'd had a mouthful of healthy, if not straight, teeth. He'd started up a hardware store, and his sons had worked there with him until Joe Jr. had died early in World War II. After that, Joe C and his second son, Christopher, had kept Prader Hardware going for many more years. Joe C Prader had been a hard worker and man of consequence in Shakespeare. It must be his comparative helplessness that had made him so perverse and aggravating.

'Fannie Dooley?' I prompted. I was *not* going to gratify him by expressing my shock.

'Fannie was the town bad girl,' he explained. 'There's always one, isn't there? The girl from a good family, the kind that likes to do it, don't get paid?'

'Is there always one?'

'I think every small town's got one or two,' Joe C observed. 'Course it's bad when it's your own flesh and blood.'

'I guess so.' At my high school, a million years ago, it'd been Teresa Black. She'd moved to Little Rock and married four times since then. 'Deedra was your great-granddaughter?' I asked, surprised I'd never realized the connection.

'Sure was, darlin'. Every time she came around to see me, she was the picture of sweetness. I don't believe I ever would have guessed.'

'You're awful,' I said dispassionately. 'Someone's going to push you off your porch or beat you over the head.'

'They's always going to be bad girls,' he said, almost genially. 'Else, how's the good girls going to know they're good?'

I couldn't decide if that was really profound or just stupid. I shrugged and turned my back on the awful man, who told my back that he was going to get gussied up for his girlfriend.

By the time I'd worked my way through the ground floor of the old house, whose floors were none too level, Joe C and China Belle Lipscott were ensconced on the front porch in fairly comfortable padded wicker chairs, each with a glass of lemonade close to hand. They were having a round of 'What Is This World Coming To?' based on Deedra's murder. There may have been a town bad girl when they were growing up, but there'd also been plenty to eat for everyone, everyone had known their place, prices had been cheap, and almost no one had been murdered. Maybe the occasional black man had been hung without benefit of jury, maybe the occasional unwed mother had died from a botched abortion, and just possibly there'd been a round of lawlessness when oil had been discovered . . . but Joe C and China Belle chose to remember their childhood as perfect.

I found evidence (a filtered butt) that Joe C had once again been smoking. One of my little jobs was to tell Calla if I found traces of cigarettes, because Joe C had almost set the house afire once or twice by falling asleep with a cigarette in his hands. The second time that had happened, he'd been unconscious and his mattress smoldering when Calla had happened to drop by. Who could be smuggling the old man cigarettes? Someone who wanted him to enjoy one of his last pleasures, or someone who wanted him to die faster? I extricated the coffee mug he'd used as an ashtray from the depths of his closet and took it to the kitchen to wash.

I wondered if the old house was insured for much. Its location alone made it valuable, even if the structure itself was about to fall down around Joe C's ears. There were businesses now in the old homes on either side of the property, though the thick growth around the old place made them largely invisible from the front or back porch. The increased traffic due to the businesses (an antique store in one old home and a ladies' dress shop in the other) gratified Joe C no end, since he still knew everyone in town and related some nasty story about almost every person who drove by.

As I was putting my cleaning items away, Calla came in. She often timed her appearance so she'd arrive just as I was leaving, probably so she could check the job I'd done and vent her misery a little. Perhaps Calla thought that if she didn't keep an eye on me, I'd slack up on the job, since Joe C was certainly no critic of my work (unless he couldn't think of another way to rile me). Calla was a horse of a different color. Overworked (at least according to her) at her office job in the local mattress-manufacturing plant, perpetually harried, Calla was determined no one should cheat her any more than she'd already been cheated. She must have been a teenager once, must have laughed and dated boys, but it was hard to believe this pale, dark-haired woman had ever been anything but middle-aged and worried.

'How is he today?' she asked me in a low voice.

Since she'd passed her grandfather on her way in, and he was loudly in fine form, I didn't respond. 'He's been smoking again,' I said reluctantly, since I felt like a spy for telling on Joe C. At the same time, I didn't want him to burn up.

'Lily, who could be bringing him cigarettes?' Calla slapped the counter with a thin white hand. 'I've asked and asked, and no one will admit it. And yet, for someone who can't go to the store himself, he seems to have unlimited access to the things he's not supposed to have!'

'Who visits him?'

'Well, it's a complicated family.' Though it didn't seem complicated to me, as Calla began to explain it. I knew already that Joe C had had three children. The first was Joe Jr., who had died childless during World War II. The second boy, Christopher, had been the father of Calla, Walker, and Lacey. These three were the only surviving grandchildren of Joe C. Calla had never married. Walker, now living in North Carolina, had three teenage children, and Lacey had Deedra during her first marriage.

Calla's aunt (Joe C's third child), Jessie Lee Prader, had married Albert Albee. Jessie Lee and Albert had had two children, Alice (who'd married a James Whitley from Texas, moved there with him and had two children by him) and Pardon, who had been the owner of the Shakespeare Garden Apartments. When Pardon had died, he'd left the apartments to Alice Albee Whitley's children, Becca and Anthony, since the widowed Alice had herself died of cancer two years before.

The final complication was Joe C's sister, Arnita, who was much younger than Joe C. In the way of those times, the two babies their mother had had between them had died at birth or in infancy. Arnita married Howell Winthrop and they became the parents of Howell Winthrop, Jr., my former employer. Therefore, Joe C's sister was the grandmother of my young friend Bobo Winthrop and his brother, Howell III, and his sister, Amber Jean.

'So you, Becca Whitley and her brother, and the Winthrops are all related,' I concluded. Since I was cleaning the kitchen counter, I had been gainfully employed while listening to this long and fairly boring discourse.

Calla nodded. 'I was so glad when Becca moved here. I was crazy about Alice, and I hadn't gotten to see her in so many years.' Calla looked wistful, but her mood changed abruptly. 'Though you see who owns a whole building, who ended up in the mansion, and who's sitting in the house that's about to be zoned commercial,' she said sourly. Becca had the rent income, the Winthrops were wealthy from the lumber yard, the sporting goods store, and oil, while Calla's little house was sandwiched between an insurance office and small engine repair service.

There was no response to that. I was mostly indifferent to Calla, but I felt sorry for her some days. Other days, the resentment that was a cornerstone of her character grated at me, made me ornery.

'So, they all come around,' she said, staring out the kitchen window, the steam from her cup of fresh coffee rising in front of her face in a sinister way. I realized for the first time that the day had become overcast, that the darkness was reaching into the room. Like lawn furniture, Joe C and China Belle had to be brought in before they blew away or got wet.

'Great grandchildren – Becca Whitley, all painted up; Deedra, in her slutty dresses . . . Joe C just loved that. And the great-nieces and -nephews – Howell III, asking can he help by mowing the yard . . . like he'd ever mowed his own yard in his life.'

I hadn't realized Calla was quite this bitter. I turned around to look at the older woman, who almost seemed to be in a spell. I needed to go get the old people in, or else rouse Calla to do it. Thunder rumbled far away, and Calla's dark eyes scanned the sky outside, looking for the rain.

Finally she slid her gaze toward me, cold and remote.

'You can go,' she said, as distant as if I'd tried to claim relationship to Joe C myself.

I gathered my paraphernalia and left without another word,

leaving Calla to handle the business of relocating her grandfather and his girlfriend all by herself.

I wondered if Calla was glad of Deedra's death. Now there was one less person to come by, one less painted woman to titillate the old man and rob Calla of her possible inheritance.

Chapter Four

The sheriff was talking to Lacey Dean Knopp. Lacey, barely into her fifties, was a lovely blond woman with such an innocent face that almost everyone instantly wanted to give her his or her best manners, most conscientious opinion, hardest try. When I'd first met Lacey, the day she'd hired me to clean Deedra's apartment, that innocence had irritated me violently. But now, years later, I pitied Lacey all the more since she'd had farther to come to meet her grief.

The sheriff looked as though she'd slept only an hour or so for two nights in a row. Oh, her uniform was crisp and clean, her shoes were shiny, but her face had that crumpled, dusty look of sheets left too quick. I wondered how her brother Marlon was looking. If Marta Schuster had been thinking clearly, she'd deposited the grief-stricken young man away from public scrutiny.

'We're through in there,' she was telling Lacey, who nodded numbly in response. Marta gave me the thousand-yard stare when I leaned against the wall, waiting for Lacey to give me the word to enter.

'Lily Bard,' Marta said.

'Sheriff.'

'You're here for what reason?' Marta asked, her eyebrows going up. Her expression, as I perceived it, was disdainful.

'I asked Lily,' Lacey said. Her hands were gripping each other, and as I watched, Lacey drove the nails of her right hand into the skin on the back of her left hand. 'Lily's going to help me clean out my daughter's apartment,' Lacey went on. Her voice was dull and lifeless.

'Oh, she is,' the sheriff said, as though that was somehow significant.

I waited for her to move, and when she got tired of pondering, she stepped aside to let us in. But as I passed her, she tapped my shoulder. While Lacey stood stock-still in the living room, I hung back and looked at the sheriff inquiringly.

She peered past me to make sure Lacey was not listening. Then she leaned uncomfortably close and said, 'Clean out the box under the bed and the bottom drawer of the chest of drawers in the second bedroom.'

I understood after a second, and nodded.

Lacey hadn't registered any of this. As I closed the apartment door behind me, I saw that Lacey was staring around her as though she'd never seen her daughter's place before.

She caught my eyes. 'I never came up here much,' she said ruefully. 'I was so used to my house being "home", that's where I always felt Deedra belonged. I guess a mother always thinks her child is just playing at being a grown-up.'

I'd never felt so sorry for anyone. But feeling sorry for Lacey wasn't going to help her. She had plenty of pity available, if she wanted it. What she needed was practical help.

'Where did you want to start?' I asked. I could hardly march into the bedrooms to start looking for whatever Marta Schuster had wanted me to remove.

'Jerrell carried these up earlier,' she said, pointing at the pile of broken-down boxes and two rolls of trash bags. Then she stood silently again.

'Do you want to keep any of Deedra's things?' I asked, trying to prod her into giving me directions. 'For yourself?'

Lacey forced herself to answer. 'Some of the jewelry, maybe,' she said, in a fairly steady voice. 'None of the clothes; she wore a size smaller than I do.' Plus, Lacey Knopp wouldn't be caught dead in her daughter's just-this-side-of-tarty clothes. 'Could you use any of them?'

I took a moment so I wouldn't look like I was rejecting the offer without thinking it over. 'No, I'm too broad in the shoulders,' I said, which was on a par with Lacey claiming the clothes would be a size small. Then I thought of my bank account and I remembered I needed a winter coat. 'If there's a coat or a jacket that fits me, maybe I'd need that,' I said reluctantly, and Lacey looked almost grateful. 'So, where do you want the rest of the clothes to go?'

'SCC has a clothes closet for the needy,' Lacey said. 'I should take them there.' Shakespeare Combined Church was right down the street from the apartment building. It was the busiest church in Shakespeare, at the moment, having just added a new Sunday-school wing.

'Won't that bother you?'

'Seeing some poor woman go around in Deedra's old clothes?' She hesitated. 'No, I know Deedra would have wanted to help others.'

I was trying to remember someone Deedra had helped (other than by relieving sexual tension) during her life when Lacey added, 'All the kitchen things can go to the community relief fund. SCC doesn't keep anything but clothes.' The town of Shakespeare kept a few rooms at the old community center filled with odds and ends cleaned out from people's cabinets and attics: pots and pans, dishes, sheets, blankets, utensils. The purpose of this accumulation was to re-equip families who had met with a disaster. In our part of the country, 'disasters' generally translate as fires or tornadoes.

Again Lacey stood in silence for a few long moments.

'Where would you like me to begin?' I said as gently as I could.

'Her clothes, please. That would be hardest for me.' And Lacey turned and went into the kitchen with one of the boxes.

I admired her courage.

I got a box of my own, reassembled it, and went into the larger bedroom.

Everything had been searched, of course. I guess the police always hope to find a piece of paper with *Am meeting Joe Doe at 8:00. If evil befalls me, he is the guilty one* written on it. But I was pretty sure no one had found such a note, and I didn't find it either, though I conscientiously checked the pockets of each garment and the inside of every shoe as I packed boxes.

When I was sure Lacey was busy in the kitchen, I reached under Deedra's bed and slid out a box she'd stuffed under there. I'd only cleared under the bed a couple of times before, when Deedra (actually Lacey) had paid for a spring-cleaning. Then, Deedra had had plenty of warning to conceal this carved wooden box with its tight-fitting lid. I lifted it a little to look inside. After a long, comprehensive stare at the contents I slammed it shut and wondered where I could hide it from Lacey.

It had been years since I'd thought of myself as naive. But I discovered that not only could I still be shocked, but also I could say that whole areas of my life were unsophisticated.

I peeked again.

A couple of the sex toys in the box were easily identifiable, even to someone like me who'd never seen the like. But one or two baffled me. I knew their function was something I'd puzzle over in odd moments for some time to come, and the idea didn't make me happy. As I pushed the box back under the edge of the bedspread till I could think of a way to get it out of the apartment surreptitiously, I found myself wondering if Jack had ever used such items. I was embarrassed at the thought of asking him, to my astonishment. I hadn't realized there was anything we could say or do between us that would be embarrassing. Interesting.

I glanced out into the hall before I slipped into the guest bedroom. I opened the drawer the sheriff had designated, and discovered it was full of odds and ends like handcuffs, stained silk scarves, heavy cord . . . and movies.

'Oh, man,' I muttered as the titles registered. I could feel my face grow hot with shame. How could she have made herself so vulnerable? How could she have put herself at someone's mercy this way? It seemed to me that only a woman who'd never experienced sexual violence would think the imitation of it a turn-on. Maybe I was being naive about that, too, I thought gloomily.

I stuffed all the paraphernalia into a garbage bag, and deposited it under the bed with the carved box. Then I started packing clothes swiftly to make up for the lost time.

I resumed my task by opening the top drawer of Deedra's

lingerie chest. I wondered how pleased the women's group at Shakespeare Combined Church would be to get some of Deedra's exotic play clothes. Would the deserving poor be thrilled with a leopard-print thong and matching baby-doll nightie?

Soon I moved to the chest of drawers and more mundane items. As I folded everything neatly, I tried to keep all the categories together: slacks, spring dresses, T-shirts, shorts. I assumed Deedra had moved her out-of-season clothes to the closet of the second bedroom. That was where the jackets would be.

I was right. The second closet was just as packed as the first, but with fall and winter clothes. Most of her suits and dresses would be categorized as Professional – Slut Subsection. Deedra had loved dressing up for work. She'd liked her job, too; since she'd completed two mediocre years at junior college, Deedra had been a clerk in the county clerk's office. In Arkansas, the office of county clerk is an elected two-year position, quite often held by a woman. In Shakespeare's county, Hartsfield, a man, Choke Anson, had won the last election. My friend Claude Friedrich, the chief of police, thought Choke intended to use the office as an entrance to county politics, and thence to the state arena.

I was probably the least political person in Hartsfield County. In Arkansas, politics are a cross between a tabloid concoction and a brawl. Politicians in Arkansas are not afraid to be colorful, and they love to be folksy. Though my conscience would not permit me to skip voting, I often voted for the lesser of two evils. This past election, Choke Anson had been the lesser. I knew his opponent, Mary Elwood, having observed her at the SCC while I served the board meeting there. Mary Elwood was a stupid, ultraconservative homophobe who believed with absolute sincerity that she knew the will of God. She further believed that people who disagreed with her were not only wrong, but also evil. I'd figured Choke Anson simply couldn't be as bad. Now I wondered how Deedra had managed with a male superior.

'Did you pick a jacket?'

'What?' I was so startled I jumped.

Lacey brought another box into the room. 'Sorry, I didn't mean to scare you,' she said wearily. 'I was just hoping you'd found a jacket you could use. Deedra thought so highly of you, I know she'd like you to have whatever you could use.'

It was news to me that Deedra'd thought of me at all, much less that she'd had any particular regard for me. I would have been interested to hear that conversation, if it had ever taken place.

There was a forest-green thigh-length coat with a zip-out lining that would be very useful, and there was a leather jacket that I admired. The other coats and jackets were too fancy, or impractical, or looked too narrow in the shoulders. I didn't remember seeing Deedra wearing either of the ones I liked, so maybe they wouldn't be such reminders to her mother.

'These?' I asked, holding them up.

'Anything you want,' Lacey said, not even turning to look at my choices. I realized that she didn't want to know, didn't want to mark the clothes so when she saw me she wouldn't think of Deedra. I folded the garments and went back into Deedra's larger bedroom. There, I quickly placed the carved box into a re-assembled carton, and put the plastic bag of 'toys' in with it. I laid the two jackets on top, covering up the contraband. I wrote *Lily* on the top in Magic Marker, hoping that even if Lacey wondered why I'd put the jackets in a box instead of carrying them out over my arm, she'd be too preoccupied to ask.

We worked all morning, Lacey and I. Twice, Lacey went into the bathroom abruptly and I could hear her crying through the door. Since the apartment was so quiet, I had time to wonder why some friend of Lacey's wasn't helping her with this homely task. Surely this was the time when family and friends stepped in.

Then I noticed that Lacey was staring at a picture she'd pulled out of a drawer in the kitchen. I was in there only because the dust in the closet had made me thirsty.

Though I couldn't see the picture myself, Lacey's reaction told me what it was. I saw her expression of confusion, and then her cheeks turned red as she held it closer to her eyes as if she disbelieved what she was seeing. She chucked it in a trash bag with unnecessary force. Maybe, I thought, Lacey had had an inkling she would be finding items like this, and maybe she'd decided she couldn't risk any of her friends she saw socially having a peek at her daughter's playthings. Maybe Lacey was not quite as oblivious as she seemed.

I was glad I'd followed the sheriff's hints, glad I was the one to dispose of the items now in the box marked with my name. Lacey might happen upon a thing or two I'd missed, but there wasn't any point in grinding her face in her daughter's misbehavior.

I began to think better of Marta Schuster. She'd gotten rid of most of the pictures, so now they wouldn't be added to the local lore; and she'd warned me about the other stuff, so I'd had a chance to get it out of sight before Lacey had had to look at it. We couldn't block her from all knowledge, but we could dispose of a lot of the more graphic evidence.

By noon, when I had to go, we'd accomplished a lot. I'd emptied the closet and the chests in the larger bedroom, and made a beginning on the closet in the spare bedroom. Lacey had packed most of the kitchen items and some of the towels in the bathroom. I'd made five or six trips to the Dumpster in the parking lot.

A life couldn't be dismantled so quickly, but we'd made quite a start on Deedra's.

As I picked up the labeled box and my purse, Lacey asked me when I had more time to spare, and I realized that now I had Friday mornings open, since my client was dead.

'I can meet you here on Friday,' I said. 'Early as you want.'

'That would be great. Eight o'clock too early?'

I shook my head.

'I'll see you then,' Lacey said, 'and maybe before Friday I can have Jerrell come over with his truck and get some of these boxes delivered, so we'll have more room to work.'

She sounded detached, but I knew that couldn't be true. Numb was probably more accurate.

'Excuse me,' I began, and then I hesitated. 'When will the funeral be?'

'We're hoping to get her back here in time for a funeral on Saturday,' Lacey said.

As I carried the box down the stairs, I returned to a familiar worry. I'd have to get another regular client for Friday mornings. I'd had Deedra and the Winthrops on Friday; then the Winthrops had dropped me, and now Deedra was dead. My financial future was looking grimmer by the week.

I was supposed to meet my friend Carrie Thrush at her office; Carrie had said she'd bring a bag lunch for us both. I got in my car, stowing the box in the backseat. Minutes later, I glanced at my watch to find I was running a little late, because I had to find a business Dumpster on the other side of Shakespeare, one that wasn't too visible, and deposit the box of sex paraphernalia after removing the two jackets. I was certain no one saw me. By the time I turned in to Carrie's office, I assumed she'd be in her office, fussing over food growing cold.

But when I pulled down the small driveway marked STAFF PARKING ONLY, Carrie was standing in the little graveled lot behind her clinic, where she and her nurses parked their cars.

'Want to go somewhere with me?' Carrie's smile was stiff and self-conscious. She was wearing white, but it wasn't her lab coat, I realized after a second's scrutiny. She was wearing a white dress with a lacy white collar. I could feel my eyebrows draw together in a frown.

I didn't remember ever seeing Carrie in a dress, except at a funeral. Or a wedding.

'What?' I asked sharply.

'Go with me to the courthouse?'

'For?'

Her face scrunched up, causing her glasses to slide down her small nose.

Carrie had on makeup. And her hair wasn't pulled back behind her ears, as she usually wore it at work. It swung forward in shining brown wings.

'For?' I asked more insistently.

'Well . . . Claude and I are going to get married today.'

'At the courthouse?' I tried not to sound astonished, but she flushed.

'We have to do it before we lose our courage,' she said in a rush. 'We're both set in our ways, we both have everything we could need to start a household, and we both want to have just a couple of good friends at the ceremony. The marriage license list'll be out in the paper tomorrow and then everyone will know.' The legal notices always appeared in the local paper on Thursday afternoon.

'But . . .' I looked down at my working clothes, not exactly pristine after getting into closets and under beds at Deedra's.

'If you want to run home, we have a few minutes,' she said, glancing down at her watch. 'Not that I care what you wear, but if I know you, it'll bother you the whole time.'

'Yes, not being clean at a wedding does bother me,' I said shortly. 'Get in the car.'

I couldn't say why I felt a little angry, but I did. Maybe it was the surprise of it (I'm not fond of surprises) or maybe it was the switch in moods required of me: from death to marriage in a single day. I had become sure Claude Friedrich and Dr Carrie Thrush would get married, and I'd become sure it was a good idea. The difference in ages was substantial; Claude was probably forty-eight or so, and Carrie was about thirty-two. But I was confident their marriage would work, and I hadn't regretted turning down a chance to try intimacy with Claude myself. So why was I upset? I owed it to Carrie to be happy.

I made myself smile as Carrie ran on and on about why they'd made their decision, how her parents were going to take it, how soon they could get Claude's things moved into her small house.

'What about a honeymoon?' I asked, as I turned the key in the lock of my own little house, Carrie practically on my heels.

'That's going to have to wait for a month,' Carrie said. 'We'll take a long weekend starting today, from now until Monday night, but we're not going far. And Claude has to take his beeper with him.'

While Carrie alternated staring in the mirror and pacing the floor, I stripped off my cleaning clothes and pulled out my good black suit. No. Couldn't wear black to a wedding. I grasped the hanger holding my sleeveless white dress. No, couldn't wear white either.

But after a second's consideration, I realized I had to. I camouflaged it with my black jacket and a black belt, and I tucked a bright blue scarf into the neckline. I pulled up my thigh-highs, slid on my good black shoes, and replaced Carrie in front of the bathroom mirror to repowder and to fluff my short curly hair.

'I would have given you a wedding shower,' I said sourly, and met Carrie's eyes. After a little pause, we both began laughing, because that seemed such an unlikely scenario to both of us.

'Are you ready? You look pretty,' Carrie said, giving me a careful once-over.

'You too,' I said honestly. With her short-sleeved white dress, she was wearing brown pumps and carrying a brown purse. She looked fine, but not exactly festive. We got back into my car, and as we passed a florist, I pulled in to the curb.

'What?' Carrie asked anxiously. 'We're late.'

'Hold on a minute,' I said, and ran into the shop.

'I need a corsage,' I told the old woman that came to help me.

'An orchid?' she asked. 'Or some nice carnations?'

'Not carnations,' I told her. 'An orchid, with white net and a colored ribbon.'

This admirable woman didn't ask questions, she just went to work. In less than ten minutes, I was handing Carrie the orchid, netted in white and beribboned in green, and she tearfully pinned it to her dress.

'Now you really look like a bride,' I said, and the knot inside me eased.

'I wish Jack were here,' Carrie said politely, though she hadn't really had much of a chance to know him. 'Claude and I would have enjoyed him being with us.'

'He's still in California,' I told her. 'I don't know when he'll be back.'

'I hope you two . . .' but Carrie didn't finish that thought, and I was grateful.

The courthouse, which occupies a whole block downtown, is an old one, but recently renovated. Claude was waiting on the wheelchair ramp.

'He's wearing a suit,' I said, amazed almost beyond speech. I'd never seen Claude in anything but his uniform or blue jeans.

'Doesn't he look handsome?' Carrie's cheeks, normally on the sallow end of the spectrum, took on a becoming rose tint. In fact, she looked more twenty-five than thirty-two.

'Yes,' I said gently. 'He looks wonderful.'

Claude's brother, Charles, was with him, looking more uncomfortable than Claude did. Charles was more at home in overalls and a welder's cap than a suit. Shy and solitary by nature, Charles managed to make himself almost invisible even in this small town. I thought I could count on my fingers the number of times I'd seen Charles in the years I'd lived in Shakespeare.

He'd really made an effort today.

When Claude saw Carrie coming up the sidewalk, his face changed. I watched the hardness seep out of it, replaced by something more. He took her hand, and brought his other hand from behind him to present her with a bouquet.

'Oh, Claude,' she said, overcome with pleasure. 'You thought of this.'

Good. Much better than my corsage. Now Carrie looked truly bridelike.

'Claude, Charles,' I said, by way of greeting.

'Lily, thanks for coming. Let's go do it.'

If Claude had been any more nervous he would've made a hole in the sidewalk.

I spied Judge Hitchcock peering out of the door.

'Judge is waiting,' I said, and Claude and Carrie looked at each other, heaved a simultaneous sigh, and started toward the courthouse door. Charles and I were right behind.

After the brief ceremony, Claude and Carrie had eyes only for each other, though Carrie hugged Charles and me, and Claude shook our hands. He offered to buy us lunch, but with one voice we turned him down. Charles wanted to crawl back in his cave, wherever it was, and I was not in a festive mood after my morning's work, though I was making an effort to be cheerful for my friends' sakes.

Charles and I were glad to part, and as Carrie and her new husband drove away to their weekend prehoneymoon, I went back to my house, despising myself for my nasty mood, which I hoped I'd hidden well enough. Changing back into my working clothes, hanging my good outfit in the closet, and grabbing a piece of fruit for lunch, I was restless from the dark feeling inside me. As always, it translated into a need for action. It would have been a good day for me to be mugged, because I would have enjoyed hurting someone.

While I cleaned the tiny house of the very old Mrs Jepperson, while the round black woman who 'sat with' Mrs Jepperson every day did her best to catch me stealing something, I carried that core of anger within me, burning and painful.

It took me an hour to identify my anger as loneliness. It had been a long time since I'd felt lonely; I'm a person who enjoys being alone, and the past few years had afforded me plenty of that. For a long time, I hadn't made friends; I hadn't taken lovers. But this year had seen so many changes in me, and unfortunately, side by side with the willingness to have friends traveled the capacity for loneliness. I sighed as I put Mrs Jepperson's stained sheets in the washer to soak in bleach.

I was just plain old feeling sorry for myself. Even though I knew that, I didn't seem to be able to quench that resentful smoldering inside me.

I went to my next job, and then home, without being able to find a thought to still my inner restlessness. Jack, whose timing was often off, chose that moment to call me.

Every now and then Jack told me all about a case he was working on. But sometimes, especially in a case involving financial transactions and large sums of money, he kept his mouth shut, and this was one of those times. He missed me very much, he said. And I believed him. But I had unworthy thoughts, ideas that dismayed me; not their content, exactly, but the fact that *I* was having them. California, the home of tanned young hardbodies, I thought; Jack, the most passionate man I'd ever met, was in California. I wasn't jealous of a woman, but a *state*.

Not surprisingly, the conversation didn't go well. I was at my most clipped and inaccessible; Jack was frustrated and angry that I wasn't happier he'd called right in the middle of his busy day. I knew I was being impossible, without seeming to be able to stop it, and I believe he knew the same.

We needed to be together more. After we'd hung up, just barely managing not to snarl at each other, I made myself face the facts. One weekend every now and then wasn't enough. It took us hours to get re-accustomed to ourselves as a couple, together. After that we had a wonderful time, but then we had to go through the detachment process when Jack returned to Little Rock. His hours were unpredictable. My hours were generally regular. Only by living in the same town were we likely to see each other consistently enough to establish our relationship.

Your own life is plenty hard without complicating it with that of another. For a moment I wondered if we should stop trying. The idea was so painful that I had to admit to myself, all over again, that Jack was necessary to me.

I didn't want to call him back when I was so fraught. I couldn't predict what he would say, either. So what I ended up doing that evening was going into the empty guest bedroom and kicking the hell out of my punching bag.

Chapter Five

Thursday was biceps day in my personal schedule. Bicep curls may look impressive, but they're not my favorite exercise. And they're hard to do correctly. Most people swing the dumbbells up. Of course, the more swing you put in it, the less you're working your biceps. I've noticed that in every movie scene set in a gym, the characters are either doing bicep curls or bench presses. Usually the guy doing bicep curls is a jerk.

Just as I put the twenty-five-pound barbells back on the weight rack, Bobo Winthrop walked in with a girl. Bobo, though maybe twelve years younger than me, was my friend. I was glad to see him, and glad to see the girl accompanying him; for the past couple of years, even after all the trouble I'd had with his family, Bobo had been convinced that I was the woman for him. Now that Bobo divided his time between college in nearby Montrose and visits home to check on his ailing grandmother, visit his family, and do his laundry, I seldom got to visit with him. I realized I'd missed him, and that made me wary.

As I watched Bobo start working his way around the room, shaking hands and patting backs, I moved from free weights to the preacher bench. The short young woman in tow behind him kept smiling as Bobo, shoving his floppy blond hair out of his eyes, introduced her to the motley crew who inhabited the gym at this early hour. She had a good, easy, meet-and-greet style.

The early-morning people at Body Time ranged from Brian Gruber, an executive at a local mattress-manufacturing plant, to Jerri Sizemore, whose claim to fame was that she'd been married four times. As I put weights on the short curl bar at the preacher bench, I marked Bobo's progress with a touch of amusement. In his golden wake, he left smiles and some infusion of joie de vivre.

What did it feel like, I wondered, to be almost universally known and liked, to be attractive to almost everyone, to have the backing of a strong and influential family?

With a shock like a dash of ice water, it occurred to me that I had once been like that, when I'd been about Bobo's age: before I'd gone off to live in Memphis, before the media-saturated nightmare of my abduction and rape. I shook my head. Though I knew it was true, I found it was almost impossible to believe I had ever been that comfortable. Bobo had had some hard times himself, at least in the past year, yet his long look into darkness had only made his radiance stand out with greater relief.

I'd finished my first set with the curl bar and returned it to its rests by the time Bobo worked his way around to me.

'Lily!' His voice was full of pride. Was he showing me off to the girl, or the girl to me? His hand on my shoulder was warm and dry. 'This is Toni Holbrook,' he said. 'Toni, this is my friend Lily Bard.' The gaze of his dark blue eyes flicked back and forth between us.

I waited for my name to ring a bell with this girl – for the horrified fascination to creep into her gaze – but she was so young I guess she didn't remember the months when my name was in every newspaper. I relaxed and held out my hand to her. She stuck her fingers up against my palm instead of grasping my hand firmly. Almost always, the offenders who shake hands in this wishy-washy way are women. It felt like getting a handful of cannelloni.

'I'm so pleased to finally meet you,' she said with a sincere smile that made my teeth hurt. 'Bobo talks about you all the time.'

I flashed a glance at him. 'I used to clean for Bobo's mother,' I said, to put a different perspective on the conversation. I'll give her this, she didn't flinch.

'What you want on there, Lily?' Bobo asked. He waited at the disc rack.

'Another set of dimes,' I told him. He slid off two ten-pound discs, put one on each end of the bar, and then added clips to

secure them. We were comfortable working with weights together; Bobo's first job had been here at the gym, and he'd spotted
for me many a time. This morning, he took his position at the
front of the bar and I straddled the seat, leaning over the padded
rest, the backs of my hands toward the floor so I could grasp the
bar to curl up. I nodded when I was ready, and he helped me lift
the bar the first couple of inches. Then he let go, and I brought it
up myself, squeezing until the bar touched my chin. I finished my
ten reps without too much trouble, but I was glad when Bobo
helped me ease the bar down into the rack.

'Toni, are you here for the rest of the week?' I asked, making an
effort to be polite for Bobo's sake. He slid the clips off, raising his
blond eyebrows interrogatively. 'Dime again,' I said, and together
we prepared the bar.

'Yes, we'll go back to Montrose on Sunday afternoon,' Toni
said, with equal politeness and a tiny, clear emphasis on the *we*.
Her smooth black hair was cut just below chin-length, and looked
as if it always stayed brushed. It swung in a lively dance when she
moved her head. She had a sweet mouth and almond-shaped
brown eyes. 'I'm from DeQueen,' she added, when her first
sentence hung in the air for a second or two. I found I didn't care.

I nodded to show I was ready, and Bobo gave me a little boost
to get the bar off the stand. With a lot more difficulty, I completed
another set, making sure to breathe out as I lifted, in when I
lowered. My muscles began to tremble, I made the deep 'uh' that
accompanied my best effort, and Bobo did his job.

'Come on Lily, squeeze, you can do it,' he exhorted sternly, and
the bar touched my chin. 'Look at Lily's definition, Toni,' Bobo
said over his shoulder. Behind his back, Toni looked at me as if
she wished I'd vanish in a puff of smoke. But I was honor-bound
to complete the next two reps. When they were done, Bobo said,
'You can do another one. You've got it left in you.'

'I'm through, thanks,' I said firmly. I rose and removed the clips
that secured the weights. We began putting the discs back on the
rack.

Toni wandered over to the water fountain.

'I need to talk to you this weekend,' Bobo said quietly.

'Okay.' I hesitated. 'Saturday afternoon?'

He nodded. 'Your place?'

'All right.' I was doubtful about the wisdom of this, but I owed it to him to listen, whatever he wanted to say.

My forehead was beaded with sweat. Instead of searching out my towel, I lifted the hem of my T-shirt and dabbed at my forehead, ensuring Bobo saw the horrendous scars on my ribs.

I saw him gulp. I went on to my next exercise feeling obscurely vindicated. Though Bobo was handsome and wholesome as a loaf of good bread, and I had once or twice been tempted to take a bite, Toni was from his world. I intended to see he kept my age and bitter experience in his mind.

Janet was doing shoulders this morning, and I spotted for her while she worked on the Gravitron. Her knees on the small platform, the counterweight set at forty pounds so she wouldn't be lifting her whole body weight, Janet gripped the bars above her head and pulled up. She was working pretty hard the first few reps, and by number eight, I wandered over to hold her feet and push up gently to lighten the strain on her arms. When she'd finished number ten, Janet dangled from the bars, panting, and after a minute she slid her knees off the platform and stood on the uprights. Stepping off backward, she took a few more seconds to catch her breath and let the muscles of her shoulders recoup.

'Are you going to the funeral?' she asked. She moved the pin to the thirty-pound slot.

'I don't know.' I hated the thought of dressing up and going into the crowded Shakespeare Combined Church. 'Have you heard if the time's certain yet?'

'Last night, my mother was over at Lacey and Jerrell's when the funeral home called to say the coroner's office in Little Rock was sending the body back. Lacey said Saturday morning at eleven.'

I considered, scowling. I could probably finish work by eleven if I got up extra early and hurried. If I ever got around to getting my clients to sign a contract, I decided one of the clauses would be that I didn't have to go to their funerals.

'I guess I should,' I said reluctantly.

'Great!' Janet looked positively happy. 'If it's okay with you, I'll park at your house and we can walk to the funeral together.'

Making that little arrangement would never have occurred to me. 'Okay,' I said, struggling not to sound astonished or doubtful. Then I realized I had a bit of news I should share.

'Claude and Carrie got married,' I told her.

'You're . . . you're serious!' Janet faced me, astonished. 'When?'

'At the courthouse, yesterday.'

'Hey, Marshall!' Janet called to our *sensei*, who'd just come out of the office in the hallway between the weight room and the aerobics room where we held karate classes. Marshall turned, holding a glass of some grainy brown stuff he drank for breakfast. Marshall was wearing his normal uniform of T-shirt and muscle pants. He raised his black eyebrows to ask, What?

'Claude and Carrie got married, Lily says!'

This caused a general burst of comment among the others in the room. Brian Gruber quit doing stomach crunches and sat up on the bench, patting his face with his towel. Jeri yanked her cellular phone from her workout bag and called a friend she knew would be up and drinking her coffee. A couple of other people sauntered over to discuss this news. And I caught a blaze of some emotion on Bobo's face, some feeling I found didn't fit in any category of comfortable response to my trivial piece of gossip.

'How did you know?' Janet asked, and I discovered I was in the middle of a small group of sweaty and curious people.

'I was there,' I answered, surprised.

'You were a witness?'

I nodded.

'What did she wear?' Jerri asked, pushing her streaky blond hair away from her forehead.

'Where'd they go for their honeymoon?' asked Marlys Squire, a travel agent with four grandchildren.

'Where are they gonna live?' asked Brian Gruber, who'd been trying to sell his own house for five months.

For a moment, I thought of turning tail and simply walking away, but . . . maybe . . . it wasn't so bad, talking to these people, being part of a group.

But when I was driving away from the gym I felt the reaction; I'd let myself down, somehow, a corner of my brain warned. I'd opened myself, made it easy. Instead of sliding between those people, observing but not participating, I'd held still long enough to be pegged in place, laid myself open to interpretation by giving them a piece of my thoughts.

While I worked that day, I retreated into a deep silence, comforting and refreshing as an old bathrobe. But it wasn't as comfortable as it had been. It didn't seem, somehow, to fit anymore.

That evening I walked, the cool night covering me with its darkness. I saw Joel McCorkindale, the minister of the Shakespeare Combined Church, running his usual three miles, his charisma turned off for the evening. I observed that Doris Massey, whose husband had died the previous year, had resumed entertaining, since Charles Friedrich's truck was parked in front of her trailer. Clifton Emanuel, Marta Schuster's deputy, rolled by in a dark green Bronco. Two teenagers were breaking into the Bottle and Can Liquor Store, and I used my cell phone to call the police station before I melted into the night. No one saw me; I was invisible.

I was lonely.

Chapter Six

Jack called Friday morning just as I was leaving for my appointment with Lacey at Deedra's apartment.

'I'm on my way back,' he said. 'Maybe I can come down Sunday afternoon.'

I felt a flash of resentment. He'd drive down from Little Rock for the afternoon, we'd hop into bed, and he'd have to go back for work on Monday. I made myself admit that I had to work Monday, too, that even if he stayed in Shakespeare we wouldn't get to see each other that much. Seeing him a little was better than not seeing him at all . . . as of this moment.

'I'll see you then,' I said, but my pause had been perceptible and I knew I didn't sound happy enough.

There was a thoughtful silence on the other end of the line. Jack is not stupid, especially where I'm concerned.

'Something's wrong,' he said at last. 'Can we talk about it when I get there?'

'All right,' I said, trying to soften my voice. 'Goodbye.' And I hung up, taking care to be gentle with the telephone.

I was a little early. I propped myself against the wall by Deedra's apartment door and waited for Lacey. I was sullen and grim, and I knew that was unreasonable. When Lacey trudged up the stairs, I nodded a greeting, and she seemed just as content to leave it at that.

She'd succeeded in getting Jerrell to remove the boxes we'd packed the previous session, so the apartment looked a lot emptier. After a minimum of discussion, I began sorting through things in the small living room while Lacey boxed the linens.

I pitched all the magazines into a garbage bag and opened the drawer in the coffee table. I saw a roll of mints, a box of pens, some Post-It notes, and the instruction booklet that had come with Deedra's VCR. I patted the bottom of the drawer, then reached back in its depths. That netted me a coupon for a Healthy Choice microwave meal. I frowned, feeling the muscles around my mouth clamp in what would be wrinkles before too many years passed.

'It's gone,' I said.

Lacey said, 'What?'

I hadn't even heard her in the kitchen behind me. The service hatch was open.

'The *TV Guide*.'

'Maybe you threw it away Wednesday?'

'No,' I said positively.

'What possible difference could it make?' Lacey didn't sound dismissive, but she did sound puzzled.

I stood to face her. She was leaning, elbows on the kitchen counter, her golden-brown sweater already streaked with lint from the dryer. 'I don't know,' I said, and shrugged. 'But Deedra always, always kept the *TV Guide* in this drawer, because she marked the shows she wanted to tape.' I'd always found it interesting that someone with Deedra's limited intelligence was blessed with a knack for small appliances. She could set her VCR to tape her favorite shows in a matter of minutes. On nights she didn't have a date, Deedra had television. Even when Deedra was going to be in her apartment, if there was a man present, often she wouldn't watch her shows. She'd set up her VCR to record.

Every workday morning, Deedra slid in a tape to catch her favorite soaps, and sometimes *Oprah*. She used the Post-It notes to label her tapes; there was always a little yellow cloud of them in the living room wastebasket.

Oh, hell, what difference could a missing magazine make? Nothing else was missing – nothing that I'd yet discovered. If Deedra's purse was still missing (and I hadn't heard that it had been found) then the thief hadn't been after her keys for entry into her apartment, but had wanted something else in her purse.

I couldn't imagine what that object could be. And there wasn't anything of value missing from the apartment, only the stupid *TV Guide*. Oh, there might be some Kleenex missing. I hadn't counted those. Marta would probably ask me to.

While I'd been grumbling to myself, I'd been running my hands under the bright floral couch cushions, crouching to look underneath the little skirt that concealed the legs.

'It's just not here,' I concluded. Lacey had come into the living room. She was looking at me with a puzzled expression.

'Did you want it for something special?' she asked cautiously, obviously humoring me.

I felt like a fool. 'It's the only thing that's missing,' I explained. 'Marta Schuster asked me to tell her if I found anything gone missing, and the *TV Guide* is the only thing.'

'I just hardly see . . .' Lacey said doubtfully.

'Me too. But I guess I better call her.'

Marta Schuster was out of the office, so I talked to Deputy Emanuel. He promised to draw the absence of the magazine to Sheriff Schuster's attention. But the way he said it told me he thought I was crazy for reporting the missing *TV Guide*. And I couldn't blame him for his conclusion.

As I went back to my work, it occurred to me that only a maid would have noticed the absence of the *TV Guide*. And I had to admit to myself that I'd only noticed because once Deedra had left it on the couch and I'd put it on the kitchen counter: in the hatchway, though, so it was easily visible. But Deedra had had a fit, one of the very few she'd had while I'd cleaned for her. She'd told me in no uncertain terms that the *TV Guide* always, always went in the coffee-table drawer.

So a mad rapist molests Deedra, strangles her, parks her nude in her car out in the woods and . . . steals her *TV Guide*? *TV Guides* were readily available in at least five places in Shakespeare. Why would anyone need Deedra's? I snorted, and put the thought aside to work over some other time. But Deedra herself wouldn't leave my thoughts. That was only right, I admitted to myself reluctantly. I'd cleaned her apartment for four years; I knew many tiny details about her life that no one else knew. That's the thing with cleaning people's homes; you absorb a lot of information with that cleaning. There's nothing more revealing about people than the mess they leave for someone else. The only people who get to see a home unprepared and unguarded are a maid, a burglar, and a policeman.

I wondered which of the men Deedra had bedded had decided she had to die. Or had it been an impulse? Had she refused to perform some particular act, had she threatened to inform someone's wife that he was straying, had she clung too hard? Possible, all three scenarios, but not probable. As far as I knew there was nothing Deedra would refuse to do sexually, she'd steered clear of married men for the most part, and if she'd valued one bedmate over another I'd never known about it.

The sheriff's brother could've been different. He was attractive, and he'd certainly carried on like he was crazy about Deedra.

Deedra would sure have been an embarrassing sister-in-law for Marta Schuster. I was lying on the floor checking to make sure nothing else was underneath Deedra's couch when that unwelcome thought crossed my mind. I stayed down for a moment, turning the idea back and forth, chewing at it.

I nearly discarded it out of hand. Marta was tough enough to handle embarrassment. And from my reading of the situation, I felt Marlon had just begun his relationship with Deedra; there was no other way to explain his extravagant display of grief. He was young enough to have illusions, and maybe he'd dodged the talk about Deedra with enough agility to have hope she'd cleave only to him, to put a biblical spin on it.

Perhaps she would have. After all, Deedra hadn't been smart, but even Deedra must have seen that she couldn't go on as she had been. Right?

Maybe she'd never let herself think of the future. Maybe, once started on her course, she'd been content to just drift along? I felt a rush of contempt.

Then I wondered what I myself had been doing for the past six years.

As I rose to my knees and then to my feet, I argued to myself that I'd been learning to survive – to not go crazy – every single day since I'd been raped and knifed.

Standing in Deedra Dean's living room, listening to her mother working down the hall, I realized that I was no longer in danger of craziness, though I supposed I'd have fits of anxiety the rest of my days. I had made a life, I had earned my living, and I had bought a house of my own. I had insurance. I drove a car and paid taxes. I had mastered survival. For a long moment I stood staring through the hatchway into Deedra's fluorescently bright kitchen, thinking what a strange time and place it was to realize such a large thing.

And since I was in her apartment, I had to think of Deedra again. She'd been slaughtered before she'd had time to come through whatever was making her behave the way she did. Her body had been degraded – displayed naked, and violated. Though I had not let myself think of it before now, I had a mental picture of the Coca-Cola bottle protruding from Deedra's vagina. I wondered if she'd been alive when that had happened. I wondered if she'd had time to know.

I felt dizzy suddenly, almost sick, so I plopped down on the couch and stared at my hands. I'd gotten too wrapped up in my inner depiction of Deedra's last minutes. I was remembering the hours in the shack in the fields, the hours I'd spent chained to an old iron bedstead, waiting to die, almost longing for it. I thought of the sickness of the phone calls Deedra had been getting right before she was killed. There are men who should die, I thought.

'Lily? Are you all right?' Lacey leaned over me, her face concerned.

I yanked myself back to the moment. 'Yes,' I said stiffly. 'Thank you. I'm sorry.'

'You're sick?'

'I have an inner ear problem. I just got dizzy for a second,' I lied. It made me uncomfortable, lying, but it was easier on Lacey than the truth.

She went back to her task, casting an uneasy look back at me, and I began going through the tapes Deedra had had around the television, making sure there weren't any pornographic ones

mixed in with the ones marked ALL MY CHILDREN OR SALLY JESSY
ON THURSDAY. These tapes were all presumably still usable. I
figured I'd make sure there wasn't anything risqué on them, and
asked Lacey if I could use the tapes. As I expected, she agreed, and
I packed them in a box without finishing my evaluation. If I found
anything objectionable in the tapes, I could pitch them at home
more easily. Just another little cleanup job to complete.

We can't leave this world without leaving a lot of detritus
behind. We never go out as cleanly as we come in; and even
when we come in, there's the afterbirth.

I looked forward to karate that night more than I had in weeks. So
much reflection, so much unwelcome remembrance needed to
be worked out of my system. I liked to *do*, not reflect: I wanted
to kick some butt so badly I ached. That's not the right way to
approach the discipline, and that's not the correct mind frame for
martial arts. My body twanged with tension as I took my place in
line.

Attendance at the Friday-night classes tended to be a bit lighter
than at the Monday and Wednesday classes. Tonight there were
only ten people stretching at the barres along the wall. Bobo
bowed at the doorway and strolled into the room in a white tank
top and the pants-half of his *gi*. His girlfriend, Toni, had tagged
along. Bobo kicked off his sandals and got into line two people
down from me, pulling Toni in beside him. She was wearing black
shorts and a purple T-shirt, and she'd pinned her dark hair back
with an elastic band and a million hairpins. She was trying to look
comfortable.

As always, Becca was first in line. She'd stretched on her own
before class, smiling at Carlton when he wandered over to talk to
her, but not saying much herself. Raphael, usually on my left, was
at a dance; he and his wife were chaperoning his daughter's Spring
Fling at the high school. He'd told me he thought some of the
restraining moves Marshall had taught us might come in handy if
the boys went out in the parking lot to drink.

'You and Lacey 'bout done cleaning out Deedra's place?' Becca asked as we waited to be called to attention.

'We haven't finished yet. But a lot of boxes are gone. Just a little left to pack, and the big stuff can be moved out.'

She nodded, and was about to say something else when Marshall put on his hardest face and barked, '*Kiotske!*'

We came to attention and exchanged bows with him.

'Line up for sit-ups!'

Becca and I usually paired up, since we were much the same weight and height. I moved to stand facing her and checked to make sure everyone in my new line had a partner. Then Becca and I sat down facing each other, legs extended in front of us and slightly bent at the knees. Becca slid her feet between mine and turned them outward to hook under my calves. I turned my feet in to latch on to hers.

Marshall had motioned Bobo's girlfriend, Toni, to pair with Janet, who was much closer to Toni's size than Bobo. Bobo, in turn, had to make do with the only man approaching him in height and weight, Carlton. The two men of the world, I thought, and watched as Bobo and Carlton silently contended over who got to be 'outie' and who got to be 'innie'. Becca and I grinned at each other as Carlton slid his legs between Bobo's, who'd held out the longest.

'Put your hands under your butts, like this!' Marshall held up his hands so Toni could see. The index finger of his right hand touched the index finger of the left, and the opposing thumbs touched each other, but the matching pairs were spread as far apart as possible. 'Your tailbone should be in the open space. Let yourselves lie back, but don't touch the floor!' Marshall ordered, being specific since we had a visitor. He strolled down the line with his thumbs hooked in his obi. He examined himself in one of the mirrors that lined the wall, and smoothed his black hair with one ivory hand. Marshall's one-quarter-Asian blood was his favorite fraction, and he did everything he could to emphasize his otherness. He thought it made him more effective and attractive as a *sensei* and a gym owner if he looked exotic, or as exotic as southern Arkansas would tolerate. He was right.

Meanwhile, Becca and I tucked our hands under our respective butts and leaned back very slowly, mirroring each other, until our shoulders were about two inches from the floor. I was looking at the ceiling, concentrating on the crack I always used to focus my attention. With the pull from our linked legs providing an anchor, we would be able to maintain this excruciating position for an indeterminate time. I rolled my eyes sideways to check out what our *sensei* was doing. He was straightening his *gi*. Bobo, right beside me, met my eyes and shook his head slightly in mock despair. Carlton, beside Becca, had already broken into a sweat.

I made a tiny, derisive sound, just loud enough to carry to our *sensei*. Marshall was preening while we were hurting, and the weakest of us would be worn out by the time we started the exercise.

'On my count!' Marshall barked, and we all tensed. Carlton was trembling, and Toni, hooked to Janet, seemed totally unable to pull up off the floor, where her entire body was firmly settled. At least she was providing good ballast for her partner.

'One, two, three, four, five, six, seven, eight, nine, ten! One, two, three, four, five, six, seven, eight, nine, twenty! One, two . . .' With each count we tightened our abdominals, then relaxed them, our upper bodies rising perhaps six inches off the floor to relax down to two on the off count. Our row bobbed frantically to keep up, abdominals rigid with the effort of keeping our backs off the floor. I glanced to the right, checking my half of the row, since Marshall might ask me to correct their faults. Carlton and Toni were side by side on Becca's row, which pleased me. Bobo looked to his left just then, and our eyes met. He grinned at me. He thought this was great fun. He had to have found another dojo in Montrose, to be in such good shape. I shook my head in wry amazement, and turned my concentration back to my own work. I closed my eyes and kept up with the count, knowing Becca would never give up and go slack.

'Get your elbows off the floor!' Marshal admonished, and the two new boys at the end of the row gasped and obeyed. I scowled at the ceiling as I heard the thud of a head hitting the floor only seconds later. That was on my side, and it was one of the new boys. After a few halfhearted attempts to make his abdominals obey, he openly gave up, and he and Toni did fish imitations together, mouths open and gasping. Toni had lasted maybe the first set of ten. Obviously, Bobo hadn't met her in a gym.

Finally, only Bobo, Becca, and I were still going.

'One hundred!' Marshall said, and stopped. We three froze with our backs off the floor. I could hear Becca breathing loudly, and tried not to smile.

'Hold it!' commanded Marshall, and with an effort of will, I stayed up.

'Hold it!' he exhorted us. I began to tremble.

'Relax,' he said, and it was all I could do not to let myself collapse with the same embarrassing thud. I managed to detach my legs from Becca's and let my shoulders and back ease to the floor without any urgency. I hoped.

Ragged breathing filled the room. I turned to look at Bobo. He was beaming at me from a couple of feet away.

'How ya doing, Lily?' he gasped.

'I could have done thirty more,' I said with no conviction. He giggled weakly.

Marshall didn't tell us to put on sparring pads tonight. At least partly because of Toni's presence (even the students we called 'the new boys' had been coming a month) he decided to instruct us to practice breaking away. There were about four simple moves that each new class member had to learn. While the other people practiced more sophisticated maneuvers, I was set to teach these moves to Toni. She protested nervously several times that she was just visiting with Bobo – probably she would never come to class again. I just kept on instructing her. No one (least of all the timid Toni) would quite dare to just tell Marshall *no*. At least, no one I'd ever met.

My estimation of the girl rose as I worked with her. She gave it her best shot, though she was obviously uncomfortable with being in the class at all. I could like that determination – admire it, even.

'God, you're strong,' she said, trying not to sound angry, as I gripped her wrists and told her to practice the breaking-free method I'd just taught her.

'I've been working at this for years.'

'You're some kind of hero to Bobo,' she said, her eyes fixed on me to see how I'd react.

I had no idea how to respond to that. I wanted to ignore what Toni had said, but she refused to move when I took her wrist, playing my role of attacker. She just waited, her face turned up to mine.

'I'm not a hero in any sense,' I said curtly. 'Now, break free from my hold!'

I got out of there fast when class was over. Janet had left even faster after letting me know she had a date, so she wasn't there to chat with me on my way out, and the weight room was almost empty. I thought I heard Bobo call my name, but I kept marching forward. I'd see him tomorrow afternoon, anyway.

Chapter Seven

I was exhausted, but I couldn't sleep. There was no point in tearing up my bed tossing and turning any longer. In the darkness I slid into my jeans, black sports bra, an old black Nike T-shirt, and my sneakers. My keys and cell phone were always in the same place on my dresser; I pocketed them and slipped out the front door to begin walking.

There had been too many nights of this pointless activity, I reflected. Too many nights of striding through a silent town – for the past few years this particular silent town of Shakespeare. Before that, other towns in other states: Tennessee, Mississippi. My feet moved silently on the pavement as I covered ground.

I seldom felt the compulsion to walk when Jack stayed with me. If I was restless, I satisfied that restlessness in a more intimate way. Tonight I felt worn ragged, and old.

One of the town's night patrolmen, Gardner McClanahan, saluted me as he cruised slowly by. He knew better than to stop and talk. Though Claude would never have told me, I'd heard the town police called me the Night Walker, a pun on the title of an old TV show. Every patrol officer knew I'd anonymously called in at least five break-ins and three domestic situations, but we'd silently agreed to pretend they didn't know their tipster was me. After the previous year, they all knew about my past. I thought it very strange that they apparently respected me for it.

I didn't raise my hand to acknowledge Gardner, as I would some nights. I kept on moving.

Forty minutes later, I'd circled, doubled, gone to all four points of the compass, and still was only about six blocks from home. On Main, I was passing Joe C's house, thinking once again about its size and age, when I stopped in my tracks. Had that been a flicker of movement among the bushes in the yard of the Prader house? My hand dropped to the cell phone in my pocket, but there was no point calling the police if I'd been mistaken. I slunk into the yard myself, moving through the overgrown shrubbery as silently as I could.

Yes. Ahead of me, someone was moving. Someone all in black. Someone quiet and quick like me. The closest streetlight was half a block away and the yard was deep and shadowy.

It took me only seconds to realize that whoever this trespasser was, he was moving away from the house, not toward it. I wondered if he'd been trying the doors, hoping to enter and steal. I began making my way as quietly as I could through the jungle of Joe C's yard.

Then I smelled smoke. I froze in position, my head rotating to track from which direction the thick dark scent was pouring.

It was coming from the house. My skin began to crawl with apprehension. Not even attempting quiet movement, I pressed close enough to peer through the open curtains of Joe C's living room, the room I'd vacuumed just three days before. Now that I was out of the bushes, the streetlight gave me a little visibility. There were no lights on in the house, but I should have been able to see the outlines of the furniture. Instead, there was a dense movement inside the room. After a second, I realized the room was full of smoke; it was coiling against the windows, waiting to be let out. As I stared into the dark moving cloud, I saw the first dart of the flames.

I broke into a run, crashing through the overgrown crepe myrtles and camellias, around the house and up the shaky steps to Joe C's back door. I'd decided the back door was farthest from the fire. There was no time to waste trying to track the trespasser. As I pounded on the door to wake the old man, I pulled the phone out of my pocket and dialed 911.

I told the dispatcher what the situation was, and she answered, 'We'll be there in a minute, Lily,' which I'd probably find amusing another time. The smell of smoke was increasing by the second. I pocketed the phone and forced myself to touch the doorknob. It wasn't hot. Though I expected the door would be locked, it opened easily.

A cloud of darkness billowed out. With it came the terrible smell of things being consumed by fire. I was gasping with terror, knowing I had to try to reach Joe C.

I hesitated, shamefully, afraid of being trapped if I went in. I knew the door must be shut behind me to prevent cross breezes from fanning the flames. For a long second, I was awfully tempted to shut myself right back out on the porch. But that was just something I couldn't do. I took a deep breath of clean air. Then I entered the burning house and closed the opening to safety.

I started to switch on the lights, realized I shouldn't. In the choking gloom, I made my way across the kitchen to the familiar double sink, felt the dishcloth draped across the divider. I rinsed it out under cold water and held it across my mouth and nose as I tried to fumble my way out of the kitchen and across the hall to Joe C's bedroom.

I sucked in breath to call the old man, and that breath exploded out in a bout of coughing. I saw flames to my right, in the living room. Smoke, a deadly silent killer, filled the wide hall. I put one hand to the wall to orient myself, touching a picture of Joe C's mother I recalled was hanging about a yard to the left of the door to Joe C's bedroom. I could hear sirens now, but no coughing from anyone but me.

'Joe C!' I screamed, the intake of smoke causing me another coughing spasm. I might have heard something in reply. At least I imagined that I heard a faint answer after I gave a second call. The fire was in the living room, moving closer to the hall, licking at something it really liked. I could feel a sudden escalation in its energy, as if it had eaten a piece of candy. Maybe it had grabbed ahold of Joe C's antique rolltop desk, its wood dry and ready for the flame after a hundred and fifty years of use.

The door to Joe C's bedroom was closed. I didn't know if that was usual or not. I turned the knob, and it opened. I was having good luck with doors tonight, if nothing else.

'Joe C,' I called hoarsely. 'Where are you?' I stepped cautiously into the bedroom and shut the door behind me.

'Here,' came the feeble reply. 'I'm trying to open this damn winda.'

Since Joe C's bedroom and the kitchen were at the back of the house, away from the streetlight, between the smoke and the natural darkness I couldn't tell exactly where the old man was.

'Say something!' I began groping my way into the room, colliding with the bedpost as I shuffled forward. That gave me my bearings.'

Joe C said a few things, none of them repeatable.

Finally I reached him, hearing him begin to cough so violently that I knew he didn't have long to go if we stayed inside. I followed his hands up to the two locks on the window, and I took over the job of twisting them. The right one was easy, the left one very stiff. I wrestled with it, decided to break the glass in about one second if the lock didn't give.

'Damn, woman, get us out of here!' Joe C said urgently. 'The fire is at the door!' Then he was overwhelmed by another coughing spasm.

I glanced over my shoulder to see that the door appeared to be cracking, and the cracks had red edges. If I touched that doorknob now, my hands would burn.

As my whole body would if the damn window . . . there! The lock gave, I reached down to grip the handles, and I heaved up with all my strength. The window, which I had expected to resist, flew up, and I almost lost my footing. I stuck my hand outward to feel, and encountered a screen. Crap.

I took a step back, lifted my leg, and let it fly. The screen popped out of the window like a cork from a bottle, and I said, between bouts of a hacking cough, 'I'm going out first, and then I'm getting you over the sill, Joe C.'

He clung to me, still no more than part of the choking darkness, and I had to disengage his hands to swing my leg over the sill. Of course the bushes were thick underneath the window, and since the house was raised, the drop-off was at least a foot higher than I'd anticipated. I didn't land square on my feet, but careened sideways, grabbing at branches so I wouldn't end up on the ground. When my footing was stabilized, I turned and felt through the window until I had run my hands under both Joe C's armpits.

'Hold on to my shoulders!' I urged him, and his bony claws dug into my skin. I put my left foot somewhat back to keep me steady, and I heaved. Because of the high window, the angle was bad; I was too short to get a good purchase. I gradually worked Joe C about halfway out the window. He began hollering. I took two steps back and heaved again, my shoulders in agony from the strain. More of the old man appeared on my side of the window. I repeated the whole process. But now Joe C began yelling in earnest. I craned over his back to see that his left foot remained hooked to the sill in some mysterious way.

I had a moment of sheer panic. I could not think for the life of me – for *his* life – how I was going to extricate him. Luckily, I didn't have to solve the problem. There was commotion all around me now. I was never happier to see anyone in my life than the firefighter who pushed past me to unhook Joe C's left foot and bring it out to join the rest of him. I staggered back under Joe C's full weight, and instantly men were helping me to stand, whisking the old man over to an ambulance.

They tried to load me in, too, but I resisted. I'm no martyr, but I can only afford minimal insurance, and I could manage to stand and walk.

I sat on the tailgate of the fire chief's pickup while a couple of firefighters gave me oxygen, which felt sweet to my lungs. They checked me over; not a single burn. I reeked of smoke and didn't think I would ever breathe easily again, but those were minor considerations right now. At least six firefighters told me how lucky I was. They also mentioned that I should have waited for their help in extricating Joe C. I just nodded; I think we all knew that if I'd waited, Joe C wouldn't have had much of a chance.

When they were sure I was going to be all right, the two men who'd been tending to me went to help with the more exciting activity across the street. I didn't know if they'd be able to put out the fire before the first floor collapsed, but it was clear Joe C was not going to get his often-stated wish of dying in his own home.

Gradually, though the hubbub around me continued, I was able to think about something other than how afraid I'd been. I was able to think about what I'd seen.

'You feeling better?' demanded a nasal voice.

I nodded without looking up.

'Then you want to tell me how you came to be here?'

My questioner was Norman Farraclough, Claude's second in command. He was called 'Jump' Farraclough, the result of a story I'd never completely understood. I'd encountered Jump several times. He always seemed to be holding any judgment about me in reserve until he'd observed me a little longer. Actually, that was pretty much the same way I felt about him.

Jump was a late-night weight lifter, when his shift permitted. He often arrived at Body Time just when I was leaving karate class. The assistant police chief had a sharp hooked nose, a tiny mustache, and a pumped body that looked awkward in his blue uniform.

The fire chief, Frank Parrish, holding his helmet by one strap, came to stand by Jump, and they both looked down at me with expectant faces.

I explained very slowly how I'd come to be passing Joe C's house. Slowly, because not only was breathing still an act I wasn't taking for granted, but also I wanted to be sure I didn't make any error, any ambiguous statement, in what I was telling them. I told Jump and Frank about seeing someone in the yard, smelling the smoke, and finding the back door unlocked.

Jump's face remained expressionless, but Frank was openly troubled by my story.

'Was it a man or a woman?' he asked when I'd come to the end.

'Couldn't tell.'

'Which direction did he go in?'

'Towards the back of the yard, but there's no fence back there. He could've gone anywhere after that.'

'And that back door was unlocked?'

I sighed, tried to keep it inaudible. 'Yes.' It was the third time Frank had asked me.

'You work for Joe C, right?' Jump squatted down to my level to look me directly in the eyes. If this was supposed to be intimidating, it didn't work.

'Yes.'

'You and him get along?'

'He's a dirty old bastard,' I said.

And that shocked them, me saying out loud what everyone on God's green earth already knew.

'But you went in to the house to get him?'

'Obviously I did.' Though I was beginning to regret it.

'That lot is worth a right smart piece of change,' Frank observed to the night air.

I had no response to that. I wanted to shower, to get the stink of smoke off me. I never wanted to smell it again.

'I'm going home.' I stood and began walking.

'Whoa, just a minute!' Jump got into step beside me. 'Listen, lady, you ain't got no privileges now, with your buddy gone.'

'You're talking about your *boss*? The boss whose wedding I just attended? As his bride's *best friend*?' This behavior wasn't typical of me, but I was going to pull every string I could to get away from this fire, away from the old house and the smoke.

'Doesn't cut any ice with me,' Jump stated, but I didn't believe him.

'Your testosterone's showing,' I told him. He glanced down before he could stop himself. 'I saw a fire, I reported it like a good citizen, and I helped an old man escape death. You can make something suspicious out of that if you want, but I don't think it's gonna fly.' And I lengthened my stride, leaving him standing and staring after me with baffled irritation on his shadowed face.

Chapter 8

I slept late the next day. I must have punched down my alarm button without even knowing it, because when I finally checked the clock, I saw that I was supposed to be at my first Saturday morning cleaning job. I left my bed unmade, my breakfast uneaten, and arrived at Carrie's office barefaced and groggy. There was no one there to see me in any condition at all, so I accelerated my pace and got her office finished, then scooted over to the travel agent's.

I'd gotten my adrenaline pumping so effectively that I actually finished early. When I got home I collapsed at my kitchen table, trying to figure out what the rest of the day held. My Saturdays were usually spent grocery shopping and cleaning my own place. I tried to recall what else I had going.

Well, there was Deedra's funeral. Janet was coming by within the hour to accompany me to that. Then Bobo was coming over for some unstated purpose. And I still had to shop and clean since Jack was driving in tomorrow.

All I wanted to do was sleep, or rent a movie and sit in a silent lump on my double recliner to watch it. But I hoisted myself to my feet and went to the bathroom for a hot shower.

When Janet thumped on my front door forty-five minutes later, I was in my black suit, made up, with hose and pumps making me feel like a stranger to myself. I had just completed my makeup, and as I opened the door to her, I was pushing the back onto my left earring.

'Lily, you look good in black,' Janet said.

'Thanks. You're looking good yourself.' It was true; Janet was wearing a chestnut sheath with a brown-gold-green jacket, and it brought out the best in her coloring and figure.

It was time to go, so I grabbed my purse and locked the door on the way out.

'Oh, by the way,' Janet said, 'I told Becca we'd stop by the apartments and pick her up.'

I shrugged. Why anyone needed to be accompanied to a funeral was outside of my understanding, but I had no objection.

Becca came out of the big front doors of the Shakespeare Garden Apartments just as we walked up. She was wearing a dark blue dress with big white polka dots, and she'd put up her hair somehow under a navy blue straw hat. With her usual dramatic makeup, Becca looked as if she had a bit part in a film about charming Southern eccentrics.

'Hidey!' she said, all perky and upbeat. I stared at her. 'Sorry,' Becca told us after a second. 'I've got to sober down. I just got a real good piece of news, and I haven't got it out of my system.'

'Can we ask?' asked Janet. Her round brown eyes were almost protruding with curiosity.

'Well,' Becca said, looking as though she'd blush with pleasure if Revlon hadn't already done it for her, 'my brother is coming to see me.'

Janet and I exchanged significant glances. Becca had only mentioned her brother Anthony a time or two, and Janet had wondered aloud one time why the apartments had been left to Becca. Why not a fair split between sister and brother? I hadn't responded, because it was none of my business how Pardon Albee had left his estate, but I had had to admit to myself that singling out Becca had seemed a little unusual. Now we'd get to meet the brother, maybe discover why Becca had been so favored.

In a polite voice, Janet said, 'That's real nice.' We were too close to the church to keep the discussion open.

Distracted by Becca's surprising mood and news, I hadn't noticed that our small street was very nearly in a state of gridlock. Cars were parked on both sides of Track Street and around the corner, as far as I could see. Track Street is the base of three streets laid out like a U tipped on its left side. Estes Arboretum fills up the empty part of the U, and the Shakespeare Combined

Church is on the upper bar. It's a fundamentalist Christian church with a pastor, Joel McCorkindale, who can raise money like nobody's business. Joel is handsome and shiny, like a country-and-western star, with his razor-cut hair and perfect white teeth. He's added a mustache trimmed so precisely that it looks as though he could chop his meat with it.

The SCC, as the Shakespeareans call it, has added two wings in the past three years. There's a day care, a preschool, and a basketball gym for the teenagers. I was assuming they found time to have church on Sundays, sandwiched somewhere between Singles Hour, Teen Handbells, and classes like How to Please your Husband in a Christian Marriage. I've worked there from time to time, and the Reverend McCorkindale and I have had some interesting conversations.

The steeple bell was tolling heavily as we three strode up the gentle slope that leveled off in front of the church. The white hearse of Shields Funeral Home was lined up with its white limousine parallel to the curb directly in front of the church, and through the smoked windows of the limousine I could make out the family waiting to enter. Though I didn't want to stare at them, I couldn't seem to help it. Lacey looked stricken and hopeless. Jerrell looked resigned.

Janet, Becca, and I entered the main doors and were escorted by an usher to our seats. I made sure Becca went first so he grasped her arm instead of mine. The church was packed with pale people in dark clothes. The family pews, with the front one left empty for Lacey and Jerrell, were filled with all the cousins and aunts and uncles of the dead woman, and I picked out Bobo's bright hair beside the dark head of Calla Prader. I had forgotten that Deedra was Bobo's cousin.

The usher gestured us into the end of a pew about midway down the church. It was a good thing we'd come when we had, since it was the last place open that could accommodate three people. Janet glanced around the sanctuary with curiosity. Becca studied the program the usher had handed us. I wished I were somewhere else, anywhere. Jack would be here tomorrow and there was a lot I needed to do; I was worried about his visit, about the problems we faced. The scent of the banks of flowers filled the air of the church, already challenged by all these people, and my head began to ache.

Joel McCorkindale, in a black robe with even blacker velvet bands striping the sleeves, appeared at the front of the church after the organ had droned through several gloomy pieces. We all rose, and with due professional solemnity the team from the funeral home (one male Shields and one female Shields) wheeled the coffin down the aisle. After the casket came the pallbearers, two by two, each wearing a carnation in his lapel and walking slowly with eyes downcast. All the pallbearers were male, and as I scanned their faces I wondered how many of them had performed intimate acts with the body in the coffin preceding them. It was a grotesque thought. I wasn't proud of myself for entertaining it. Most of them were older men, men the age of Jerrell and Lacey, who were coming in at the pallbearers' heels.

Lacey was clinging to Jerrell, and he had to give her a lot of help just to make it to the front pew. As the couple went past the rest of the family, it occurred to me to wonder why Becca was sitting beside me instead of on the other side of the church. She was a cousin of Deedra's, too, though she'd had little chance to get to know her.

It had been a crowded week for the Prader/Dean/Winthrop/ Albee clan. I wondered how many of them were thinking of the burning of Joe C's house the night before instead of the murder of the woman in the casket.

A few more people slipped in at the back before the ushers closed the doors. The church was packed to capacity. Not only was Deedra too young to die, she had been murdered. So perhaps the curiosity factor had a part to play in this crowd.

Maybe because I was stifling – the press of people and the heavy scent of flowers almost overwhelmed me – I found myself wondering if my own funeral would have been as well attended if I'd died when I'd been abducted years before. It was all too easy to imagine my parents following the coffin in, and I could even be pretty sure who my pallbearers would have been . . .

I yanked myself back to the here-and-now. There was something sickly self-indulgent about reviewing my own funeral.

The ceremony continued about like I'd expected. We listened to two singers plow through two old standards, 'Amazing Grace' and 'What a Friend We Have in Jesus.' Since I can sing myself, the performances were interesting, but no more than that. No one here in Shakespeare knew that I used to sing at weddings and funerals in my little hometown, and that was just fine with me. I was better than the woman who sang 'Amazing Grace', but my range wasn't as good as the girl who performed second.

I sighed and recrossed my legs. Janet kept her gaze fixed properly on the singers, and Becca examined her cuticles and removed a fragment of thread from the setting of her diamond dinner ring.

I might have known Joel McCorkindale would not let the occasion pass with a simple eulogy, if he'd decided there was a point to be made. To no one's surprise, he based his sermon on the passage in Thessalonians where Paul warns us that the day of Lord will come like a thief in the night.

The preacher made more of a meal of it than I'd expected. His point was that someone had usurped God's rights in taking Deedra's life. I found myself growing stern and affronted. He was taking away the focus of the funeral from Deedra, who was actually the dead person, and focusing on the man who'd killed her.

To my alarm, the people in the congregation who were used to his style of preaching began to agree audibly with his points. Every now and then a man or a woman would raise hands above head and say, 'Amen! Praise the Lord!'

I turned my head slightly to check out Janet's reaction. Her eyes were about to pop out of her head, and she gave them a significant roll when she saw me match her own astonishment. I had never been in a church where it was the norm for the congregation to speak out loud, and by Janet's facial expression, neither had she. Becca, on the other hand, was smiling slightly, as if the whole thing was performance art staged for her benefit.

I could tell the men and women who ordinarily attended this church were very comfortable with this, this . . . audience participation. But I was horribly embarrassed, and when I saw Lacey leaning forward in her seat, hands clasped above her head, tears rolling down her face, I almost got up and left. I never talked to God myself, having gotten out of the inclination for faith after that summer in Memphis; but if I did have such a conversation, I knew it would be in private and no one around me would know. In fact, I promised myself that.

Janet and I were so glad when the service was over that it was all we could do not to bolt from the church. Becca seemed intrigued with the whole experience.

'Have you ever seen anything like that before?' she asked, but not in a voice low enough to suit me. We were still close to the other mourners, who were scattering to climb into their cars for the drive to the cemetery.

Janet shook her head silently.

'Who knows what'll happen at the grave site,' Becca said in happy anticipation.

'You'll have to catch a ride with Carlton,' I said, nodding toward my neighbor who was just coming out of the church. 'I'm going home.' I started down the sidewalk. Janet trotted after me.

'Hold up, Lily!' she said. 'I don't think I'll go to the cemetery either. That service kind of shook me up. I guess Methodists are too repressed for something that emotionally . . . open.'

' "Open",' I snarled, and kept on walking. 'I didn't like that.'

'You mean the church? The people?'

I nodded.

'Well, I wasn't raised that way either, but it seemed to make them feel better,' Janet commented cautiously. 'I don't know, it might have been kind of comforting.'

I shuddered.

'Listen, what are you going to do now?'

'Call the hospital.'

'About what?'

'Joe C.'

'Oh, yeah, he had a fire last night, didn't he?'

I nodded. 'See you later,' I told Janet. I forced myself to add, 'Thanks for going with me.'

Janet looked happier. 'You're welcome. Thanks for letting me use your driveway.' She got into her red Toyota and started it up, waving at me as she backed out.

The street was filled with cars pulling away from the curb, lining up to follow the hearse to the cemetery. As I stood in my front doorway, the street emptied of all its life like one of those time-lapse films. Only one Jeep remained parked farther up the street. I was alone with the trees in the arboretum across the street.

No, not quite alone. As I finally took a step back into my house I saw a man get out of the Jeep and begin to saunter down the street toward me.

It was Bobo, I realized with some astonishment, and remembered our appointment. As he walked, he was loosening his tie and pulling it off, stuffing it into the pocket of his dark suit. He loosened his collar button with two tan fingers, and raked back his blond hair.

Suddenly the postfuneral exaltation of being alive hit me. I felt the crackle of lightning about to strike. The man coming down the sidewalk toward me felt it too. He quickened his pace until he was actually hurrying, keeping all his attention focused on me. When he got to my door, without saying a word he wrapped me in his long arms and held me to him and kissed the hell out of me.

My brain said, *pull away!* But my body wasn't listening. My fingers were twining in Bobo's hair, my pelvis was pressed firmly against his, and I was kissing him back as hard as I could.

We were visible to any passersby.

That must have occurred to Bobo, too, because he pushed me a little and into my house we lurched and he spared a hand to press the door closed.

Bobo bit me on the neck and I growled and began grinding into him. The top of my suit was unbuttoned and his hand was inside, caressing me through my bra. Bobo ground right back, and my hands went under his suit coat to hold on to his butt, and our rhythm went on, and somehow he hit exactly the right spot and I saw stars. He groaned, and I felt the front of his pants grow wet.

Then there was only the sound of our panting.

'Floor,' Bobo suggested, and our knees gave way.

My living room isn't large and there isn't much floor space. I was sitting right next to the sprawled-out young man, and my blood was still humming through my veins.

But after only a few seconds, I was overwhelmed with the wrongness and stupidity of what I'd just done. And with someone I thought of as a friend. The day before Jack was returning.

All these years of trying so hard not to make a mistake had just gone down the drain.

'Lily,' said a voice gently. Bobo was propped up on his elbow next to me. His flushed face had returned to its normal coloring, his breathing was even. His big hand traveled an infinite distance to hold mine. 'Lily, don't feel sad.'

I was unable to speak. I wondered if Bobo was twenty-one yet. I told myself in the nastiest terms what a depraved moron I had been. I wanted to literally beat my head against the wall.

'It was the moment,' he said.

I took a deep breath. 'Yes,' I answered.

'Don't be so upset,' he repeated. 'I don't wanna be crude, Lily, but it was just a dry hump.'

I'd never heard the phrase before.

'You almost smiled, I saw your mouth twitch,' he told me, pleased.

I brushed his hair back from his forehead.

'Can we pretend it never happened?' My voice wasn't as shaky as I'd feared it would be.

'No, I don't think so. What it was, was fantastic. I've always had a thing about you.' He drew my hand to him, kissed it. 'But I never saw this coming. It was just funeral fever. You know – she's

dead, but we're alive. Sex is a great way to prove to yourself
you're alive.'

'You're being wise.'

'It's about time you got a break, let someone else do the wise
thing.'

'I do plenty of things that aren't so smart,' I said, unable to keep
the bitterness from my voice.

'Lily, this won't happen again, not ever. You're not gonna let it.
So let's be real honest with each other.'

I wasn't sure what that would entail. I waited for him to go on.

'There's no telling how many fantasies I've had about you since
you worked for my mother. When you know some beautiful,
mysterious woman is cleaning your room, it's just a sure thing
you're going to imagine . . . what if? My favorite one—'

'Please, no,' I said.

'Oh, all right.' He had the grace to look a little embarrassed.
'But the point of this is I *know* . . . I know it was just a fantasy,
that you're real, that we're not gonna have a relationship. I know
that you just like me as a . . . buddy.'

A little more than that, I thought ruefully. But I knew better
than to say it out loud. 'You don't really know me,' I said, as
gently as I was able.

'There's a lot I know about you that you won't admit about
yourself,' he retorted.

I didn't understand.

'You pull old men out of burning buildings. You saved Jack
Leeds's life and almost died in the act. You're willing, and brave
enough, to risk your life to save others.'

What a misconception! 'No, no, no,' I protested angrily. He
made a kind of dampening gesture, patting down the air with his
free hand. I sat up and reached over to the pile of folded laundry
on the chair, laundry I hadn't had a chance to put away today. I
passed him a hand towel, and he began dabbing at the front of his
pants, trying hard not to be embarrassed.

'You did those things. You are brave.' He sounded flat, and
final.

I didn't want to hear a booster speech from Bobo Winthrop. I was going to feel bad about what had just happened for a long, long time.

'And you're smart, and hardworking, and really, really, pretty.'

All of a sudden, tears stung the back of my eyelids. The final humiliation, I thought.

'You have to leave,' I said abruptly. I leaned over to kiss Bobo on his cheek. For the last – and only – time, I pulled him close and hugged him after we stood up.

'Now, you go, and we'll be okay in a week or two,' I told him, hoping that I was telling him the truth. He looked down at me very seriously, his handsome face so solemn I could scarcely bear it.

'I have to tell you something else,' Bobo insisted. 'Listen to me, Lily. I'm switching subjects here.'

I nodded, reluctantly, to show him I was waiting.

'That fire was set. The fire marshal came and told Calla this morning, and she called all of us in the family. Not Lacey, naturally, but all the others. Someone tried to kill Joe C, but you stopped them.'

I didn't listen to the renewed pat-on-the-back part of Bobo's speech. I was thinking about his opening sentence. I wasn't surprised by the news. In fact, I'd been taking it for granted that the person I'd seen in the yard of Joe C's house had actually started the fire. Trespasser + sudden fire = arson.

'How was it set?'

'A package of cigarettes. Not just one cigarette was lit, but a whole pack. They were left on the couch to smolder. But the flames ran away from the couch, didn't consume it, and the traces were still there.'

'How is Joe C?' I asked.

He looked surprised for a minute, as though he'd been expecting me to exclaim and ask a different question.

'Nothing can kill Joe C,' Bobo said, almost regretfully, pushing his hair back off his forehead. 'He's like a human cockroach. Hey, I saw that twitch again!'

I looked away.

'Lily, this isn't the end of the world.'

I saw I was hurting him, and I didn't want to. I didn't want to have done *any* of the things I'd done today.

And I was determined to stick to an impersonal topic.

'If Joe C had died, who would have inherited?' I asked.

Bobo turned red. 'I'm not supposed to know the answer to that, but I do,' he confessed. ''Cause I saw a copy of the will at Joe C's house. He had it stuck in the old rolltop desk. I've always loved that desk. Gee, I guess it's all burned up now. But I played with it since I was a little boy, you know, looking in the secret compartment that he'd shown me.'

'The will was there?' I prodded when memories seemed to wrap him up.

'Yes. The last time I went to see Joe C . . . last week, I guess it was . . . I was sitting with Toni in the living room while Aunt Calla was helping Joe C get his shoes on after his nap. He'd asked all of the greats to come over – grand children, nieces and nephews. Deedra, me, Amber and Howell Three, Becca. The other three live in North Carolina . . . So, I was showing Toni the little place you push to open the compartment. And there it was. I didn't mean anything by reading it, I promise.'

After a brief period of being his sex bunny, I was now back to being Bobo's wise woman who had to approve of his actions. I sighed.

'What did it say?'

'There was lots of lawyer language.' Bobo shrugged. 'But what I could tell, I guess, is that Great Uncle Joe C left one thing, one furniture item, to each of us Winthrop kids. So Amber and Howell Three and I could each pick something. I was hoping I'd get the desk. I was thinking I'd try to pick first. Now everything's burned or water damaged, I guess.' Bobo smiled his beautiful smile, amused at the confounding of his greed. 'Of course the main thing is the house. Joe C left proceeds from the sale of the house to his great-grandchildren. Walker's three kids, and Alice

Whitley's two, and Lacey's . . . oh, but . . .' His voice trailed away. 'But Deedra's dead,' Bobo resumed slowly.

I digested this slowly. I thought that whom Joe C'd included was just as interesting as who he'd left out. 'Nothing for Calla,' I pointed out. 'She's a granddaughter.'

Bobo actually looked horrified. 'But she's taken care of him all these years,' he said.

I remembered Bobo's grandfather. He'd only been a brother-in-law to Joe C, but they were from the same mold. I wondered what Shakespearean mothers had fed men-children in those days to make them so mean.

'Did anyone know this besides you?' I asked.

'Yeah. Well, I guess I don't know,' he muttered. He still seemed stunned at his great-uncle's mean-spiritedness. His thoughts must have followed the same trail mine had, because suddenly he said, 'What kind of people do I *come* from?'

'You come from your parents, and they're both nice people.' I had reservations about his mother, but this was no time to think about that. 'Your father is a nice man,' I said, and meant it. 'Your grandmother is a true lady.' That encompassed some less-than-desirable attributes as well as some great ones, but there again, I was always more clever at not saying things than saying them. Sometimes that was the better characteristic.

Bobo was looking a little less miserable.

'You're a good man.'

'You mean that?'

'You know I do.'

'That's the best thing you could've said to me.' He looked down at me soberly for a long minute before his smile cracked through the serious facade. 'Other than calling me your incredible stud and permanent sex slave.'

All of a sudden, I felt better. I could see that the brief sexual connection we'd had had faded out of existence and that our old friendship might replace it; that we might actually forget this past twenty minutes, or at least make a good enough pretense of it.

But Jack was still coming the next day, and any reprieve from self-loathing I'd felt was washed away in the flood of anguish the idea of seeing him caused me.

Bobo raised a hand to touch my hair, or caress my neck, but something in my face stopped him.

'Good-bye, Lily.'

'Good-bye,' I said steadily.

He opened the front door and buttoned his suit coat to cover, at least partially, the stain on the front of his pants. He half-turned when he was almost over the threshold.

'Do you think Calla could do that?' he asked, as though he were asking a student of the dark parts of the heart. 'You think she could do that to Joe C? Set the fire? The door was unlocked. She has keys.'

'I think she could want him to die if she knew about the will,' I told him honestly.

He was startled, but he took my word for it.

Shaking his head, he headed off down the street to find his Jeep and go home to his girlfriend and parents.

Then I was left alone with my own damn conscience.

Chapter Nine

I'd just put away my groceries when I heard a quiet knock on my front door.

Becca Whitley was there, still in brilliant makeup, though she'd changed into jeans and a T-shirt.

'You busy?' she asked.

'Come in,' I said, actually relieved to have someone else break into my thoughts.

Becca had been in my house only once before, so she didn't exactly relax once she was inside. 'Your boyfriend here this weekend?' she asked, standing in the middle of my tiny living room.

'Not until tomorrow. Would you like a drink?'

'Fruit juice or water,' she said. 'Whatever.'

I poured her a glass of pink grapefruit juice, and we sat in the living room.

'Have the police been by again?' I asked, since I couldn't think of anything else to say.

'Not for a couple of days. They ask you for a list of men she'd had up there?'

'Yes.'

'What'd you tell them?'

'That the men were gone before I got there in the morning.'

'Naughty, naughty.'

'What'd you tell them?'

'I gave them a list.'

I shrugged. I didn't expect everyone to do what I did.

'I hear that the sheriff's department has an automatic door that zips open and closed all day, so much traffic is going in and out.'

'You hear?' Someone's lips were awfully loose.

'Anna-Lise Puck.'

Anna-Lise was Becca's workout partner. She was also a civilian employee of the sheriff's department.

'Should she be talking about that?'

'No,' Becca said, 'But she enjoys being in the know so much that she just can't resist.'

I shook my head. Anna-Lise would find herself unemployed pretty soon. 'She better watch out,' I told Becca.

'She thinks she has job security.'

'Why?'

'Well, she was tight with the first Sheriff Schuster.' Becca shrugged. 'She figures the second Sheriff Schuster won't fire her because of that.'

We exchanged glances, and Becca grinned at me. Right.

'When I went to pick her up for lunch yesterday,' Becca told me, 'guess who I saw coming out of the door?'

I looked a question.

'Jerrell Knopp,' she said significantly. 'The stepfather himself.'

Poor Lacey. I wondered if she knew.

'And,' Becca continued, stepping on the word heavily, 'our esteemed neighbor Carlton.'

I was shocked. I had always figured Carlton as too fastidious for Deedra. I could feel my lips tighten in a small sneer. It just went to show.

'In fact,' Becca said, 'all the guys in our karate class have been in, including our esteemed *sensei*.'

'Raphael? Bobo?' Raphael was the most married man I'd ever met, and Bobo was Deedra's cousin.

'Yep, and the new guys. Plus a few men that haven't been to class in a long time.'

'But why?' Even Deedra couldn't have arranged a rendezvous with every single karate student.

Becca shrugged. 'I have no idea.'

Obviously, there was some reason, something that had been discovered during the investigation that had led to this. 'Are they bringing in the tae kwon do people?' I asked.

Becca looked pleased with me. 'Exactly what I asked Anna-

Lise,' she told me. 'Yes, all the martial arts guys in Shakespeare are visiting with the sheriff. Whether or not they are really known to have known our late neighbor.'

'That's quite a few men.' I hesitated, then went on. 'I just wonder if they'll ever find out who did kill her.'

'Lily, I want the police to solve this. You know one of the men she slept with did this to her.'

'Maybe.'

'They hauled out lots of sheets.'

'She had a drawerful of condoms.' Of course, I couldn't be sure she'd used them, but I thought fear of pregnancy would have prompted caution, if fear of disease didn't.

Becca stared at me, her eyes like bright blue marbles, while she thought that through. 'So, most likely there won't be semen stains on the sheets. So, no DNA to test and compare.' She'd crossed her legs, and her foot began to swing. 'There may not be DNA inside her, anyway. Hey, she ever go with women?'

I returned her stare with interest, trying not to look shocked. I was learning a lot about myself today. 'If she did, I never knew about it.'

'Now, don't get all tight-ass, Lily,' Becca said, seeing I wasn't happy with the conversation. 'You know, lots of women who went through what you did would be inclined that way after-wards. Maybe Deedra had run the gamut of men, wanted some-thing different.'

'And that would be equally no one else's business,' I said pointedly.

'Oh, you're no fun!' Becca recrossed her legs, picked up the morning newspaper, and tossed it down. 'Well, how's old Joe C?'

'I haven't called the hospital yet, but I hear he's still alive.'

'He's lucky you came along.' Her narrow face was utterly sober.

'Eventually someone would have called the fire department, and the firefighters would have gotten him out.'

'Well, I'm going to say thank you anyway, since Joe C is my great-grandfather.'

'Did you visit him often?'

'I hadn't been to Shakespeare since I was a little kid. But since Uncle Pardon died and I moved here, I've been by to see him maybe once every two weeks, something like that. That old rascal still likes short skirts and high heels, you know?'

'Yes, I know.'

'Kind of pathetic. But he's a peppy old bastard; I'll give him that. Still capable of launching into you in the wink of an eye, you give him cause. Rip you another asshole.'

'You specifically?'

'No, no. I was speaking in general. Not me.'

Was I supposed to ask who? I decided not to, out of sheer perversity. 'I understand you inherit, with the other great-grand-children,' I said instead, not knowing why I was commenting on what Bobo had told me.

'Yep, that's the way I hear it.' Becca was smiling broadly. 'But the old so-and-so isn't dead yet!' She seemed pleased to be related to such a tough bird. But then her face grew serious. 'What I really came here to tell you, Lily, is that you may be getting another visit from that woman sheriff.'

'Why?'

'Anna-Lise says all the karate women will come next. Because of the way Deedra died.'

'How did she die?'

'She was—.'

A heavy knock on the door interrupted this interesting bit of dialogue. 'Too late,' Becca said, almost blithely.

Before I could say anything, Becca just got up and went out my back door. I was left to answer the front with an increasingly bad feeling.

'Sheriff Schuster,' I said, and it was impossible for me to sound anything but grudging. This day had been too much for me already.

'Miss Bard,' she said crisply.

Marta stepped in with Deputy Emanuel on her heels. 'Please have a seat,' I said, my voice cool and insincere.

Of course, they did.

'The results of Deedra Dean's autopsy,' Marta Schuster said, 'were very interesting.'

I raised my hand, palm up. What?

'Though various things were done to her after death' – I couldn't help remembering the glint of glass between Deedra's thighs – 'she died of a single hard punch to the solar plexus.' The sheriff tapped her own solar plexus by way of visual aid.

I probably looked as stumped as I felt. I finally could think of nothing to say but, 'So . . . ?'

'It was a massive blow, and it stopped her heart. She didn't die from a fall or strangulation.'

I shook my head. I was still clueless. Whatever reaction Marta Schuster was expecting from me, she wasn't getting it, and it was making her angry.

'Of course, it might have been an accident,' Clifton Emanuel said suddenly, so we both looked at him. 'It might not have been intended to kill her. Someone might have just punched her, not knowing how hard they hit.'

Still I stared like a fool. I tried to understand the significance of his statement, which he had definitely delivered as though he was giving me the Big Clue.

'A hard punch,' I said blankly.

They waited, with twin expressions of expectancy, almost of gloating.

And the shoe dropped.

'Like a *karate* strike,' I said. 'So . . . you think . . . what do you think?'

'The pathologist said a person would have to be strong and probably trained in order to deliver such a blow.'

I felt the blood drain from my face. There was no defense against suspicion. There was no way to deny what they were simply thinking. I thought so many things at once that I had trouble sorting the ideas out. I recalled the people in my karate class, and scanned the faces in the line. Every one of the students who'd been in for more than a few months (as you can imagine, the class has a high attrition rate) had known Deedra. Raphael Roundtree had taught the math class Deedra took in high school, Carlton Cockroft had done her taxes, Bobo was her cousin, Marshall had seen Deedra trot in and out of Body Time's aerobics sessions. Though I could hardly believe it, each one could've slept with her, too.

And that was just the men. Janet had known Deedra for years, Becca was her landlady . . . and I worked for her.

I thought, *There goes my business.* I'd survived other scandals and upheavals in Shakespeare, and kept working, though not as busily as before. But if serious suspicion fell on me, I could kiss my livelihood good-bye. I would have to move. Again.

No one wants to be scared of her cleaning lady.

Schuster and Emanuel were still waiting for me to respond, and I couldn't summon a word to say. I stood. After a second of hesitation, they stood too. I walked to my door and opened it. I waited for them to leave.

They looked at each other questioningly, and then Schuster shrugged.

'We'll see you later,' she said coolly, and she preceded Emanuel down my two front steps.

'I don't think so,' I said, and closed the door behind them.

I sat with my hands on my knees and tried to think what to do. I could call a lawyer on Monday . . . who? Surely I knew a lawyer or two. Well, Carlton could recommend one. But I didn't want to do that, didn't want to spend the time and money to defend myself from a charge so unfounded. The sheriff's own brother was a more likely suspect than I. I figured that was why she was attaching more weight to the 'karate strike' theory than it maybe deserved. How could you characterize a blow? It was what it was. If you could call a stopped heart the result of a 'karate' blow, you might as well go on and say, 'This strike was delivered by a right-handed student who's taken *goju-ryo* karate for approximately three years from an Asian-born *sensei*.'

If an autopsy could show Deedra had been punched while she was standing, that would surely be important. There probably weren't that many men, and even fewer women, in Shakespeare who could deliver such a blow, or who would even realize such a blow could be fatal. But if Deedra had been punched while sitting or lying down – in either case resting against a hard surface – well, that feat could be performed by a much larger pool of people.

Just at the moment I couldn't quite visualize how such a sequence of events could have occurred, but it was possible. Among the many things the sheriff had neglected to mention was Deedra's artificial violation. Was that postmortem or ante-mortem?

When I thought about it, a *lot* depended on the answer to that question.

And why had she been left out in the woods? It was really bad for the case for my innocence that the place she'd been dumped was off a road I frequented. There were other homes and businesses out on Farm Hill Road, sure. There was a car repair shop not a quarter of a mile beyond Mrs Rossiter's house, and an antique/craft/flea market barn not a mile beyond that. That made me relax a little; the finger wasn't pointing so obviously at me.

Where had I been the night Deedra was killed? That would've been a Sunday. Last Sunday, though it seemed at least a month ago. Jack hadn't come that weekend; I'd done my usual chores on Saturday, the same list I was trying to complete this Saturday: two quick cleaning jobs, straightening my own house, shopping for groceries. I often followed that up by cooking for the coming week and freezing my meals. Yes, I recalled, I'd cooked Saturday night so I'd have a whole day on Sunday to do nothing much besides go work out, do some laundry, and finish a biography I'd checked out of the library.

And that had been exactly the program I'd followed on Sunday. No unexpected callers, no public appearances except the gym for an hour on Sunday afternoon. Janet and Becca had been there; I recalled speaking to both of them, I'd watched a rental movie on Sunday evening, and I'd finished the biography. No one had called. Typical Sunday evening for me.

What did all this boil down to?

I knew Deedra, and I took karate. I was somewhat familiar with the location where the body was found.

That was all.

And those same conditions applied to lots of other people.

No, I wouldn't let Sheriff Schuster get me panicked.

Not yet.

I'd automatically finished putting away my groceries, but I felt too unsettled to begin preparing my meals for the next week. It was almost suppertime, and the shadows of the tall trees in the arboretum across the street were making fringed patterns on the pavement. I tried to think of a reason to go out so I wouldn't be walking aimlessly. I decided to go see Joe C in the hospital. He didn't hear well over the telephone, anyway.

It was cool enough for a jacket. Track Street was quiet when I went out the front door. Carlton had mowed his grass for the first time, and the fresh smell released a puff of peace inside me – natural aromatherapy. That smell, when I was little, had meant home and Father and the proximity of summer. My troubles shifted, a bit; the burden was lighter.

A Bible verse flashed across my mind: 'My yoke is easy, and my burden is light.' The Book of Matthew, seemed like. I thought about that as I strode past Shakespeare Combined Church. After I'd been raped and scarred so horribly on my abdomen and chest, while the resulting terrible infection laid waste to my reproductive organs, my parents' minister had come to see me in the hospital. I'd sent him away. My parents had thought, maybe still thought, that I'd refused the consolation of religion because I was raging at fate. But it wasn't that I was asking, 'Why me?' That's futility. Why *not* me? Why should I be exempt from suffering because I was a believer?

What had enraged me to the point of transforming my life was the question of what would happen to the men who had done such terrible things to me. My hatred was so strong, so adamant, that it required all my emotional energy. I'd shut down the parts of me that wanted to reach out to others, to cry about the pain and the fear, to be horrified because I'd killed a man. I'd made my choice, the choice to live, but it wasn't always a comfortable choice. I was convinced it wasn't the godly choice.

Now, pausing at the four-way stop a block away from the modest Shakespeare hospital, I shook my head. I always ran up against the same wall when I thought of my situation then; chained to a bed in a rotting shack, waiting for the man who'd abducted me to come claim me again, and holding a gun with one bullet. I could have shot myself; God wouldn't have liked that. I could have shot my abductor, and did; killing him wasn't good, either. I'd never thought of a third option. But in the years since then, from time to time I'd thought I might have been better off using the bullet on myself.

At that moment, in that shack, the look on his face had been worth it.

'What else could I have done?' I whispered out loud as I threaded through the cars in the hospital parking lot.

I still had no answer. I wondered what Joel McCorkindale would think of to say. I knew I'd never ask him.

Visiting hours were almost over, but the volunteer at the front desk seemed quite happy to give me Joe C's room number. Our old hospital, always in danger of closing, had been expanded and updated to suit modern medicine, and the result was a maze hard to decipher even with a floor plan. But I found the right room. There were people standing out in the corridor, talking intently in low, hushed hospital voices; Bobo, his mother, Beanie, and Calla Prader. If I had learned the family tree correctly, Calla was a first cousin of Bobo's father, once removed.

I was not ready to see Bobo again and almost spun on my heel to walk away until they'd left, but Calla spied me and was on me before I could blink.

I don't expect much from people, but I did assume she was going to thank me for saving Joe C from the flames. Instead, Calla raised her hand to slap me in the face.

I don't allow that.

Before her hand could reach my cheek, I'd gripped her wrist and held her arm rigid. We froze in a tense tableau. Then the fury seemed to drain out of Calla, taking her energy with it. The rush of angry color left her face, and even her eyes went pale and empty. When I was sure the purpose had left her, I released her wrist, and her arm dropped, dangling down by her side as if her bones had gone soft.

I looked over Calla's shoulder at Beanie and raised my eyebrows. It seemed apparent to me that Calla had just now found out about Joe C's will, and I wondered once again where she'd been when the fire started.

'I'm so sorry,' Beanie said, mortified almost beyond speech. 'Our whole family owes you thanks, Lily.' And that must have choked her, considering the conversation we'd had when she'd terminated my employment. 'Calla is just . . . beside herself, aren't you, honey?'

Calla's eyes had never left my face.

'Did you know, too?' she asked me in a low voice.

I couldn't complete that sentence mentally. I shook my head at her.

'Did you know that he's left me nothing? Did you know, too? Everyone in town seems to know that but me.'

Normally I tell nothing but the truth, though I don't throw it around easily. But I could see that it was a good time to lie.

'No,' I said, in a voice just as low as hers. 'That makes him an old bastard, doesn't it?'

For all the violence of her feelings, that word shocked her back into herself.

Then she smiled. It wasn't a nice smile. It wasn't a middle-aged, church-going, rural-Arkansas-lady smile. Calla's smile was delighted and mean and just a wee bit triumphant.

'Old bastards,' she said clearly, 'have to cope for themselves, don't they?'

I smiled back. 'I guess they do.'

Calla Prader marched out of that hospital with a straight back and that happy, nasty smile still on her face.

Beanie stared after her, nonplussed. Beanie is in her midforties, an athletic, attractive woman whose most admirable trait is her love for her children.

'Thank you for handling that so well, Lily,' Beanie said uncertainly. She was wearing a beige and white linen dress, and against her tan skin and brunette hair, the dress looked wonderful. Bobo's mother's expensive exterior hid a selfish heart and a shallow intelligence, partially concealed by good manners.

I could feel Bobo hovering on my left, but could not bring myself to look up at his face.

'Thanks, Lily,' he echoed.

But his voice reminded his mother of his presence, and she turned on him like a snake about to strike.

'And *you*, young man,' she began, sounding happy to have found a focus for her excited feelings, '*You* were the one who let Calla know about the will.'

'I didn't know she was standing behind me,' Bobo said plaintively, sounding about fourteen. 'And anyway, now that we know, isn't it only honest to tell her?'

That stopped Beanie's anger like a dash of water; that question of morality, and the fact that she'd recollected that I was still standing there listening to all this family turmoil.

'Thank you for saving Uncle Joe C,' Beanie said more formally. 'The police tell me that you saw someone in his yard before the fire started?'

'Yes.'

'But you couldn't see who it was?'

'Too dark.'

'Probably some juvenile delinquent. These kids today will do anything, anything they see on television.'

I shrugged. Beanie had always reduced me to gestures and monosyllables.

'But it bothers me that it was cigarettes,' Beanie said, and then she sounded as if she were talking to a real person, me, instead of The Help.

I knew this from Bobo, but I had a feeling it wouldn't be wise

to reveal that. 'The fire was set with cigarettes?' That was expansive and unrevealing enough.

'Joe C says he didn't have any. Of course, the fire marshal
thought he might have set it himself, smoking in the living room.
But Joe C says no. Would you like to go in and talk to him?'

'Just to see how he's doing.'

'Bobo, take Lily in, please.' It might have been framed as a
question, but it was clearly a demand.

'Lily,' Bobo said, holding open the wide door to Joe C's room.
As I went by him, he lay his hand on my shoulder briefly, but I
kept right on walking and kept my eyes ahead.

Joe C looked like he was a thousand years old. With the
liveliness knocked out of him, he seemed like a pitiful old man.
Until he focused on me and snapped, 'You could have moved a
little faster, girl! I got my slippers scorched!'

I hadn't spelled it out to myself, but I suddenly realized that
now that Joe C didn't have a house, I didn't work for him. I felt
my lips curl up. I bent down to him. 'Maybe I should have just
walked on by,' I said very softly, but he heard every word. His
face told me.

Then I squirmed inwardly. Just as his trembling jaw had meant
me to. No matter how mean he was, Joe C was very old and very
frail, and he would not let me forget that, would trade on it as
much as he could. But I could walk away, and that was what I
chose to do.

I walked away from the old man, and from his great-nephew,
and I closed my heart against them both.

Chapter Ten

I was sickened by the world and the people in it, most of all by myself. I did something I hadn't done in years. I went home and went to bed without bathing or eating. I just stripped, brushed my teeth, pulled on a nightgown, and slid between my clean sheets.

The next thing I knew, I was peering at the bright numbers on the digital clock next to the bed. It was seven minutes after three. I wondered why I was awake.

Then I knew there was someone in the room with me.

My heart began that terrible pounding, but through its rhythm I heard the sounds of clothing being removed, the zipper of a gym bag, and it came to me that I was not attacking the intruder because on some level I had already recognized who was in my bedroom.

'Jack?'

'Lily,' he said, and slid under the covers with me. 'I took an earlier flight.'

My heart slowed down a little, to a rhythm that had more to do with another kind of excitement.

The smell of him, his skin and hair and deodorant and cologne and clothes, the combination of scents that said *Jack* filled my senses. I'd planned on making him wait to come down to Shakespeare, wait until I'd talked to him, told him I'd been unfaithful to him – sort of – so he could decide without seeing me whether or not to leave me for good. But in the private dark of my room, and because Jack was as necessary to me as water, I reached behind his head, my fingers clumsy with sleep, and worked the elastic band off his pony tail. I ran my fingers through his hair, dark and thick, separating it.

'Jack,' I said, my voice sad to my own ears, 'I have some things to tell you.'

'Not now, okay?' he murmured in my ear. 'Let me just . . . just let me . . . okay?'

His hands moved purposefully. I will say this for us; we put each other under a spell in bed together. Our troubled pasts and our uncertain future had no place in that bed.

Later, in the darkness, my fingers traced the muscles and skin and bones I knew so well. Jack is strong and scarred, like me, but his is visible all the time, a single thin puckered line running from the hairline by his right eye down to his jaw. Jack used to be a policeman; he used to be married; and he used to smoke and drink too much, too often.

I started to ask him how his case, the one that had taken him to California, was going; I thought of asking him how his friends Roy Costimiglia and Elizabeth Fry (also Little Rock private detectives) were doing. But all that really mattered was that Jack was here now.

I drifted off to sleep, Jack's breathing even and deep by my side. At eight, I woke up to the smell of coffee perking in the kitchen. Across the hall I could see the bathroom door opening, and Jack stepped out in his blue jeans and nothing else. His hair was wet and dragging over his shoulder. He'd just shaved.

I watched him, not thinking of anything, just feeling: glad to see him here in my house, comfortable with the warmth in my heart. His eyes met mine, and he smiled.

'I love you,' I said, without ever meaning to, as if the sound of the words was as natural as breathing. It was something I'd held inside myself like a secret code, refusing to reveal it to anyone, even Jack, who'd devised it.

'We love each other,' he said, not smiling now, but this look was better than a smile. 'We have to be together more.'

This was going to be the kind of conversation we needed to be dressed to have. Jack looked so clean and buff that I felt sleazy and crumpled in contrast.

'Let me get a shower. We'll talk,' I said.

He nodded, and padded down the hall to the kitchen. 'You want some pancakes?' he called, as though the earth had not just shifted to another axis entirely.

'I guess,' I said doubtfully.

'Cut loose,' he advised me as I stepped into the bathroom. 'It's not every day we work up enough guts to talk about how we feel.'

I smiled to myself in the bathroom mirror. It was still cloudy from Jack's shower. In it I saw a softer, gentler version of Lily; and since I'd hung it at just the right height, I couldn't see most of the scars. I avoided noticing them from long habit, avoided looking at them and thinking of what my body would look like without them. I did not remember exactly what my torso had been like with no white ridges, or my breasts without circles incised around them. As I did from time to time, I caught myself regretting I didn't have something more beautiful to offer Jack, and as I did, every time, I reminded myself that he seemed to find me beautiful enough.

We eyed each other cautiously as we sat down to eat. Jack had opened the kitchen window, and the cool morning air came in with a gust of smells that meant spring. I heard a car start up and glanced at the clock. Carlton was going to the Singles Sunday-school class at First Methodist, and he'd be home at twelve-fifteen, right after church. He'd change and then drive over to his mother's house for midday Sunday dinner; it would be pot roast and carrots and mashed potatoes, or baked chicken and dressing and sweet potatoes. I knew all that. I'd spent over four years learning this town and these people, making a place for myself here.

Before Jack and I even began our conversation, I knew I wasn't ready to leave. True, I had no family here in Shakespeare; true, I could clean houses as well in Dubuque (or Little Rock) as I could in Shakespeare. And true, my business had suffered a lot in the past year. But I'd won some kind of battle here in Shakespeare, and I wanted to stay, at least for now. I began to tense in anticipation of a fight.

'I don't have to live in Little Rock,' Jack said. I deflated as though he'd stuck a pin in me.

'I do a lot of my work by computer anyway,' he continued, looking at me intently. 'Of course, I'd still need to be in Little Rock part of the time. I can keep my apartment up there, or find a smaller, cheaper one. That'd be more to the point.'

We were being so careful with each other.

'So you want to live with me here in Shakespeare,' I said, to be absolutely sure I was hearing him right.

'Yes,' he said. 'What do you think?'

I thought of what I'd done yesterday. I closed my eyes and wished a lightning bolt would hit me now, to prevent me from ever telling Jack. But that didn't happen. We'd always been honest with each other.

'I kissed someone else,' I said. 'I won't let you hit me, but if it'll help you feel better, you can break something.'

'You kissed someone,' he said.

I couldn't look at his face. 'It was an after-funeral thing.'

'You didn't go to bed with . . . ?'

'No.' Did I really need to elaborate? Hadn't I been honest enough? Yes, I decided.

I stole a glimpse at Jack. I saw Jack's face tighten. Instead of hitting something, he looked like he himself had been hit. He was gripping the edge of the table.

'Is this someone . . . would this happen again?' he asked finally, his voice very hoarse.

'No,' I told him. 'Never.'

Gradually, his grip on the table relaxed. Gradually, his face looked human.

'How old are you, Lily?' he asked, out of the blue.

'Thirty-one,' I said. 'Thirty-two, soon.'

'I'm thirty-six.' He took a deep breath. 'We've both been through some times.'

I nodded. Our names still cropped up in the news every now and then. ('After a brutal gang rape mirroring that of Memphis resident Lily Bard's, a Pine Bluff woman was admitted to

University Hospital . . .' or 'Today Undercover Officer Lonny Todd was dismissed from the Memphis police force after charges he had an improper relationship with an informant. Todd is the latest in a string of dismissals in the past four years on similar charges, beginning with the firing of Officer Jack Leeds, whose relationship with the wife of a fellow officer led to her murder.')

'This is the best I've ever had it,' Jack said. He was turning white as a sheet, but he went on. 'You had a . . .' and he floundered there, stuck for a word.

'I had a moment of sheer stupidity.'

'Okay.' He smiled, and it wasn't a funny smile. 'You had a moment of stupidity. But it won't ever happen again, because you said it wouldn't and you always keep your word.'

I hadn't ever thought of myself as the epitome of honor, but it was true that I kept my word. I was trying not to be surprised that Jack was being so calm and level about this.

He seemed to be waiting.

'I said it wouldn't,' I repeated. 'And I always keep my word.'

Jack seemed to relax just a little. He gave himself a little shake, picked up his fork and took a bite of his pancake. 'Just don't ever tell me who,' he said, not looking at me.

'You're getting so wise.' Jack had a real problem with impulse control.

'It's taken me long enough.' But his smile this time was a real smile. 'So, you never answered me.'

I took a deep breath. 'Yes. I want you to move in. Do you think we'll have enough room here?'

'Could I put an office in the exercise room?'

A little stunned by how easily it had been settled, I nodded silently. I'd hung a punch-and-kick bag in the middle of the second bedroom. I could live without it. I'd use the kicking pads in the aerobics room at Body Time.

Then I tried to imagine Jack sharing my bathroom full-time. It was very small, and counter space was next to none. I wondered what we would do with his furniture. How would we divide the bills?

We had just complicated our lives enormously, and I was scared of the change. There were so many details to work out.

'You don't look very happy,' Jack said. He was eyeing me from the other side of the table.

'But I am.' I smiled at him, and he got that witless look on his face again. 'I'm scared, too,' I admitted. 'Are you, a little?'

'Yeah,' He confessed. 'It's been a while.'

'At least one of us has had prior experience. I've never done this.'

Jack took a deep breath. 'Would you rather just go on and get married?' he asked, every muscle in his body rigid. 'That might be good, huh?'

I had to take my own deep breath while I groped for the right words to tell him what I felt. I hate explaining myself, and only the fact that I simply couldn't hurt Jack impelled me to go through the discomfort of it.

'If it wasn't for other people, I would marry you today,' I said slowly. 'You know how happy the papers would be if they found out? You know how people would pat us on the backs and con-gratulate us? "Those two poor wounded souls, they've found each other".'

Jack's face was beginning to collapse, so I hurried on with the rest. 'But that's no reason for us to bypass any happiness we can have. You know what I would really like? I'd like to be married to you with not another soul in the world knowing about it, at least until it was old news.'

Jack didn't know if I'd said yes or no. He was struggling to understand. I could tell by the way he learned toward me, his eyes focused on my face.

'It would be just for us,' I said, sure I'd failed in what I was trying to convey. I had always been a private person.

'Married is what you would like?'

'Yes,' I said, surprised at myself. 'That's what I would like.'

'To be kept secret?'

'Just for a while. I'd just like to get used to it before we told anyone.'

'Now?'

'No.' I shrugged. 'Anytime. But they put the names of people who've applied for marriage licenses in the paper. How could we get around that? Providing you . . . ?' I felt very anxious as I waited for him to speak.

'Yes,' he said slowly. 'I'd like that, too.' He looked sort of surprised to discover that he would, though. He put his hand over mine where it was resting on the table. 'Soon,' he finished.

I tried to imagine that Jack did not feel about me the way I felt about him. I tried picturing Jack tiring of me in a month or two, opting for some woman in Little Rock who was more convenient and less prickly. I projected myself into that position of pain and rejection.

But I couldn't imagine it.

I didn't count on much in this life, but I counted on Jack's love. Though he'd just confessed it this morning, I'd known Jack loved me, and I'd known it with certainty.

I wasn't going to jump up and down and scream and run home to tell my mother we needed to pick out china and reserve the church. The time in my life I might have done that had long since passed by. Now that I had Jack, I had everything I needed. I didn't need the congratulations and gifts of other people to confirm that.

'Damn,' Jack said, grinning like a maniac. He jumped up and began swinging his arms as if he didn't quite know what to do. 'Damn!'

I felt as radiant as if I'd been painted with light. Without knowing I was standing or moving I found myself glued to Jack from head to foot, our arms wrapped around each other, the smiles on our faces too silly for words.

We'd always had electricity between us, and the high emotion we felt turned us into dynamos.

We celebrated exceptionally well.

Afterward, the kitchen was in an even worse mess. Since he'd cooked, I cleaned while Jack made the bed. Then, with the unusual prospect of a free day stretching ahead of us, we decided to take a walk together.

It was a perfect morning, both in the perimeters of our life together and in the weather outside. The spring morning was just warm enough, and the sky was bright and clear. I hadn't felt this way in years. I hadn't even come close. I was so happy it almost hurt, and I was scared to death.

After we'd gone a few blocks, I began telling Jack about Deedra. I told him about the new sheriff, and her brother; about Lacey asking me for help, and the embarassing items I'd found in Deedra's apartment; about Becca and Janet and the funeral, and the fire at Joe C's house; about the will Bobo had read when he was prying in the rolltop desk.

'Joe C's not leaving Calla anything?' Jack was incredulous. 'After she's taken care of him for the past fifteen years or however long he's been too frail?'

'At least fifteen,' I said. 'According to what she's told me. He's leaving the more distant kids, the great-niece and great-nephews – Bobo, Amber Jean, and Howell Three, the Winthrop kids – an item of furniture apiece. Of course, that's probably not going to happen now, though there may be something worth saving in the house. I don't know. And the direct descendants are going to split the proceeds from the sale of the house.'

'Who are the direct descendants again?'

'Becca and her brother, Anthony,' I began, trying to remember what Calla had told me weeks before. 'They descended from—'

'Just give me the list, not the begats,' Jack warned me. I remembered Jack had gone to church as a child; I remembered that he'd been brought up Baptist. I wondered if we had some other things to talk about.

'Okay. Also there are Sarah, Hardy, and Christian Prader, who live in North Carolina. I've never seen them. And Deedra, who's out of the picture.'

'And you think the house and lot are worth what?'

'Three hundred and fifty thousand was the figure I heard.'

'Seventy thousand apiece isn't anything to sneer at.'

I thought of what seventy thousand dollars could do for me.

In the newspaper, almost every day, I read about corporations that have millions and billions of dollars. On the television news, I heard about people who are 'worth' that much. But for a person like me, seventy thousand dollars was a very serious amount of money.

Seventy thousand. I could buy a new car, a pressing need of mine. I wouldn't have to scrimp to save enough to pay my property taxes and my gym membership and my insurance payments, both car and health. If I got sick, I could go to the doctor and pay for my medicine all at one time, and I wouldn't have to clean Carrie's office for free for months afterward.

I could buy Jack a nice present.

'What would you like me to get you when I get seventy thousand dollars?' I asked him, an unusual piece of whimsy for me.

Jack leaned close and whispered in my ear.

'You can get that for next to nothing,' I told him, trying not to look embarrassed.

We'd walked to the front of Joe C's house, and I pointed, drawing Jack's attention to the blackened front windows. Without commenting, Jack strode up the driveway and circled the house. Through the high bushes (the ones that hadn't been beaten out of shape by the firefighters) I glimpsed him at different points, looking up, looking at the ground, scoping it out. I watched Jack's face get progressively grimmer.

'You went in there,' Jack commented as he rejoined me. He stood by my side, looking down at me.

I nodded, not quite focusing on him because I was assessing the damage. The upstairs looked all right, at least from the sidewalk. There was debris scattered on the yard, charred bits of this and that. When the breeze shifted direction, I could smell that terrible burned smell.

'You *went in there*,' Jack said.

'Yes,' I said, more doubtfully.

'Were you out of your fucking *mind*?' he said in a low, intense voice that gathered all my attention.

'It was on fire.'

'You don't go *in* buildings on fire,' Jack told me, and all the anger he'd suppressed this morning erupted. 'You walk *away*.'

'I knew Joe C was in the house!' I said, beginning to get angry myself. I don't like explaining the obvious. 'I couldn't let him burn.'

'You listen to me, Lily Bard,' Jack said, starting down the sidewalk almost too swiftly for me to keep up. 'You listen to me.' He stopped dead, turned to face me, began waving a finger in my face. I stared down at my feet, feeling my mouth begin to purse and my eyes narrow.

'When a house is on fire, you don't go in,' he informed me, keeping his voice low with a visible effort. 'No matter who is in that house . . . if your mom is in that house, if your dad is in that house, if your sister is in that house. If I am in that house. You. Don't. Go. In.'

I took a very deep breath, kept focused on my Nikes.

'Yes, my lord,' I said gently.

He threw his hands up in the air. 'That's it!' he told the sky. 'That's it!' Off he strode.'

I wasn't about to pursue him, because I'd have to scramble to keep up, and that just wasn't going to happen. I took off in the opposite direction.

'Lily!' called a woman's voice behind me. 'Lily, wait up!'

Though I was tempted to start running, I stopped and turned.

Becca Whitley was hurrying down the sidewalk after me, her hand wrapped around the bicep of a huge man with pale curly hair. My first thought was that this man should get together with Deputy Emanuel and form a tag-team to go on the wrestling circuit.

Becca was as decorated as ever, with rhinestone earrings and lips outlined with such a dark pencil she looked positively garish. When she was in full war paint, it was always a little jarring to remember she was so graceful and precise in karate class, and managed the apartments quite efficiently. I was pretty sure that meant I was guilty of stereotyping, something I had good reason to hate when people applied it to me.

'This is my brother, Anthony,' Becca said proudly.

I looked up at him. He had small, mild blue eyes. I wondered if Becca's would be that color without her contact lenses. Anthony smiled at me like a benevolent giant. I tried to focus on my manners, but I was still thinking of Jack. I shook hands with Becca's brother and approved of the effort he made to keep his grip gentle.

'Are you visiting Shakespeare long, Anthony?' I asked.

'Just a week or so,' he said. 'Then Becca and I might go on a trip together. We haven't seen some of my dad's relations in years.'

'What kind of work do you do?' I asked, trying to show a polite interest.

'I'm a counselor at a prison in Texas,' he said, his white teeth showing in a big smile. He knew he'd get a reaction from that statement.

'Tough job,' I said.

'Tough guys,' he said, shaking his head. 'But they deserve a second chance after they've served their sentence. I'm hoping I can get them back outside in better shape than when they came in.'

'I don't believe in rehabilitation,' I said bluntly.

'But look at that boy who just got arrested,' he said reasonably. 'The boy who vandalized Miss Dean's car last year. Now he's back in. Don't you think an eighteen-year-old needs all the help he can get?'

I looked to Becca for enlightenment.

'That boy who works over at the building supply,' she explained. 'The sheriff matched his voice to the one who made those phone calls to Deedra, the nasty ones. Deedra had saved the little tapes from her answering machine. They were in her night-table drawer.'

Then Deedra had taken the calls seriously. And their source

was a real nobody of a person, a man everyone seemed to call a boy.

I told Anthony Whitley, 'See how much he learned in jail?'

Anthony Whitley seemed to consider trying to persuade me that saving the boy through counseling was worthwhile, but he abandoned the attempt before he began the task. That was wise.

'I wanted to thank you for rescuing Great-grandfather,' he said a little stiffly, after an uneasy pause. 'Becca and I owe you a lot.'

I flicked my right hand, palm up; it was nothing. I glanced down the block, wondering how far Jack had gotten.

'Oh, Lily, if you could come by the apartment later, I need to talk to you about something,' Becca said, so I guess I looked like I was ready to go. I murmured a goodbye, turned in the other direction – maybe I'd follow Jack after all – rendering the two Whitleys out of sight and out of mind.

Jack was coming back. We met in the middle of the next block. We gave each other a curt nod. We wouldn't repeat the same quarrel. It was a closed subject now.

'Who was that?' he asked, looking past me. I glanced back over my shoulder.

'That's Becca Whitley, you know her,' I said. 'And her brother, Anthony. I just met him. Big guy.'

'Hmm. Brother?'

'Yep. Anthony. Brother.'

Jack put his arm around me and we strolled off as if he'd never been angry.

'They don't look much alike,' he said after a moment.

'Not much, no,' I agreed, wondering if I'd missed something. 'Do you look like your sister?'

'No, not anything,' Jack said. 'She's got lots more pink in her complexion, and she's got lighter hair than I have.'

We didn't talk much on our way back to my place. The fact that we loved each other seemed enough to contemplate for the moment. Jack decided he wanted to go work his abs while Body

Time was open, but I was awfully sore after wrestling Joe C through his bedroom window.

'I'll start your laundry if you want to go on,' I said.

'You don't have to do that,' Jack protested.

'It's no trouble,' I knew Jack hated doing laundry.

'I'll make supper,' he offered.

'Okay, as long as it's not red meat.'

'Chicken fajitas?'

'Okay.'

'Then I'll go by the Superette on my way home.'

As Jack pulled out of my driveway, I reflected on how domestic that little exchange had been. I didn't exactly smile, but it hovered around my heart somewhere as I opened Jack's suitcase, which was really a glorified duffel bag. Jack didn't look as though he'd be neat, but he was. He had several days' worth of clothes compactly folded in the bag, and they all needed washing. In the side pockets Jack kept his time-fillers: a crossword puzzle book, a paperback thriller, and a *TV Guide*.

He always carried his own when he traveled because it saved him some aggravation. This week's was new and smooth; the one for the week just past was crumpled and dog-eared.

I was about to pitch the older one in the garbage until I realized that this was the same edition as the one missing from Deedra's coffee table. I flipped through the pages of Jack's magazine as if it could tell me something. Once more, I almost tossed it into the trash, but I reconsidered and put it on my kitchen table. It would serve as a reminder to tell Jack the odd little story of the only thing missing from Deedra's apartment.

As I sorted Jack's laundry, my thoughts drifted from Deedra's apartment to Becca's. She'd wanted to talk to me. I glanced down at my watch. Jack wouldn't be home for another hour, easy. I started a load of his jeans and shirts and put my keys in my pocket, locking my door behind me as I went to the apartments. It was a cooler evening after a cool day, and I wished I had thrown on a jacket. Taking the driveway to the rear of the apartment building, I strolled through the parking lot with its numbered shed – one stall for every apartment. Because it was a beautiful Sunday afternoon and because two of the apartments in the building were temporarily vacant, there were only two vehicles parked in the shed, Becca's blue Dodge and Claude's new pickup.

Looking at Deedra's empty stall, I was seized by a sudden idea. I don't like loose ends. I went into the open wood structure – really a glorified shed – and began examining the items hanging from nails pounded into the unfinished walls. Some long-ago tenant had hung tools there. Deedra had left an umbrella, and on a shelf there was a container of windshield-wiper fluid, a rag for checking the oil, an ice scraper, and some glass cleaner. I unhooked the umbrella from its nail, upended it, and out fell . . . nothing. Deedra's spare key was no longer in its usual hiding place.

I found that even more peculiar than her purse being missing from the crime scene. Her killer had known even this about Deedra, the small secret of where she kept her extra key. Now the killer could have in his possession *two* keys to Deedra's apartment, the other keys on the big ring in her purse, the other contents of the purse, and Deedra's *TV Guide*.

There didn't seem to be anything to do about this missing key. I'd tell the sheriff when I saw her next. I shrugged, all to myself.

I went to the rear door of the apartment building and stepped in. Becca's was the rear door to my left; Claude Friedrich lived in the front apartment next to it. Claude and Carrie were due to return from their mini-honeymoon this evening, and I assumed they'd go to Carrie's house permanently. Three apartments empty, then; I hoped Becca would be too busy to clean them for the next tenants. I could use some extra money.

I rapped on Becca's door. She answered almost instantly, as if she'd been standing right inside. She looked surprised.

'You said you needed to talk to me,' I prompted her.

'Oh, yes, I did! I just didn't think . . . Never mind. It's good to see you.' Becca stood aside to let me come in.

I tried to remember if I'd ever been in her apartment before. Becca had left it much the same as it had been in her Uncle

Pardon's day. She'd just rearranged the furniture, added a small table or two, and bought a new television (Pardon had had a small, old model).

'Let me get you something to drink?'

'No, thank you.'

Becca urged me to sit down, so I perched on the edge of the couch. I didn't want to stay long.

'Anthony's gone to the car wash,' Becca told me. 'I was sure it was him when you knocked.'

I waited for her to get to the point.

'If Anthony and I do go on this trip he's planning,' she began, 'would you be interested in being responsible for the apartments while I'm gone?'

'Tell me exactly what that means.'

She talked at me for some time, giving me details, showing me the list of workmen who kept a tab for the apartment-building repairs, and explaining how to deposit the rent checks. Becca was a sensible woman under all that makeup, and she explained things well.

The extra money would be welcome, and I needed the job just for the visibility. Used to be, I cleaned maybe four out of the eight apartments in the building, but that was a couple of years ago. And Pardon had hired me to clean the public parts of the building from time to time. I told Becca I'd do it, and she seemed pleased and relieved.

I stood up to go, and in that moment of silence before Becca began the courtesies of saying good-bye, I heard something upstairs.

From Deedra's apartment.

Becca said, 'Well, Lily . . .' and I raised my hand. She stopped speaking immediately, which I liked, and she mouthed, 'What?' I pointed at the ceiling.

We stood looking up as if we had X-ray vision and could see what was going on overhead. Again, I heard movement in the apartment of the dead woman. Just for moment, my skin crawled.

'Is Lacey here?' I breathed, trying to catch any sound I could.

Becca and I stood together like statues, but statues whose heads were rotating slightly to hear as well as possible.

Becca shook her head, and the ribbon she'd tied around the elastic band holding back her long blond hair rustled on her shoulders.

I jerked my head toward Becca's door. I looked questioningly.

She nodded and we went quietly across to her apartment door. 'Police?' I asked in the lowest voice that would carry.

She shook her head. 'Might be family,' she whispered, with a shrug.

Nothing could creep like Becca and I up those stairs. We were familiar enough with the apartment building to know what creaked and what didn't, and we were at Deedra's door before I was ready for it.

We had no gun, no weapon of any kind besides our hands, while the person inside might have an armory. But this was Becca's property, and she seemed determined to confront the intruder here and now. We both became comfortable with our stance, and I rotated my shoulders to loosen them.

Becca knocked on the door.

All movement inside the apartment stopped. There was a frozen silence as we two, hardly breathing, waited to find out what the intruder's next move would be.

That silence went on too long for Becca's taste, and she rapped on the door again, more impatiently.

'We know you're in there, and there's no way out but this door.' That was true, and it made the apartments something of a fire hazard. I remember Pardon handing out rope ladders to the tenants of the second floor for a while, but he got discouraged when they all left taking the rope ladders with them, so the second floor people would just have to fend for themselves if there was a fire. I had time to remember the rope ladders while the silence continued.

More silence.

'We're not going away,' Becca said quite calmly. I had to admire her assurance. 'Okay, Lily,' she said more loudly, 'call the police.'

The door popped open as if it were on springs.

'Don't call my sister,' Marlon Schuster begged.

Becca and I looked at each other simultaneously, and if I looked like she did, we looked pretty silly. Becca's bright blue eyes were about to pop out of her head with astonishment and chagrin. To trap the brother of the sheriff in such a position, in the apartment of a murder victim . . . We'd cut our own throats with our bravado. No one, but no one, would thank us for this.

'Oh, hell,' Becca said, disgust in her voice. 'Come down to my place.'

Like a whipped puppy, Marlon slunk down to the landlady's apartment, looking smaller than ever. His black hair had been cut very short, I was guessing for the funeral, and now that I could watch him for a minute I realized that the young man was fine-boned and spare. I doubted if he could lift seventy-five pounds. I'd hoped we were catching Deedra's murderer, but now I didn't know what to think.

Without being told, Marlon sank onto the single chair that was squeezed in across from the couch. Becca and I faced him, and Becca told him to start talking.

Marlon sat staring at his hands, as if answers would sprout on them. He wasn't too far from crying.

'How'd you get in?' I asked, to get him rolling.

'Deedra gave me a key,' he said, and he had a trace of pride in his voice.

'She didn't give out keys.' I waited to see what he'd say next.

'She gave me one.' The pride was unmistakable now.

Becca shifted beside me. 'So why didn't you turn it in?' she asked. 'I had to give the cops my key, and I own the place.'

'I kept it because she gave it to me,' Marlon said simply. I scanned his face for the truth. I am no human lie detector, but it looked to me like he believed what he said. I'd noticed before that Marlon was more like his father than his mother, at least as far as looks went. But Sheriff Schuster's size had been belied by his ferocious reputation as a lawman who swung his nightstick first and asked questions later. If there was a similar ferocity in his son, it was buried mighty deep.

'So, you went in with a key given you by the tenant,' Becca said thoughtfully, as if she was considering the legality of his entry.

Marlon nodded eagerly.

'Why?' I asked.

Marlon flushed a dark and unbecoming shade of red. 'I just wanted to . . .,' and he trailed off, aware that a sentence that began that way wasn't going to end up sounding convincing.

'You went to get . . . ?' Becca prompted.

Marlon took a deep breath. 'The film.'

'You and Deedra made a video?' I kept my voice as neutral as possible, but the young man flushed even deeper. He nodded, and buried his face in his hands.

'Then you're in luck, because I have all the home videos at my house,' I said. 'I'll go through them, and when I find yours, I'll give it to you.'

I thought he would collapse from relief. Then he appeared to be screwing up his courage again. 'There were other things,' he said hesitantly. 'Mrs Knopp shouldn't see them, you know?'

'It's taken care of,' I told him.

Becca's eyes flicked from me to the boy, absorbing this information.

'You found her, Miz Bard,' Marlon said. He was staring at me longingly, as if he wanted to open my head and see the images there. 'What had happened to her? Marta wouldn't let me go see.'

'Marta was right. If you cared for Deedra, you wouldn't have wanted to see her like that.'

'How was it?' he asked, pleading.

I felt very uneasy. I tried to keep looking the boy steadily in the eyes, so he'd believe me. 'She was naked in the car with no visible wounds,' I said carefully. 'She was sitting up.'

'I don't understand.'

What was to understand? The plainest explanation of the scene was probably the true one, no matter what problems I had accepting it. Deedra had had one man too many. That man had lured her out to the woods, become angry with her or simply decided she was expendable, and killed her.

'Had she been raped?' he asked.

'I don't do autopsies,' I said, and my voice was too hard and angry. Deedra had been so quick to have consensual sex that it would be hard to even theorize she'd been raped unless there was a lot of damage, I was sure. Maybe the insertion of the bottle covered up damage from another source? Maybe it indicated the man couldn't perform normally?

And maybe it was just a gesture of contempt.

Becca told him, not unkindly, 'You know, Marlon, that Deedra had lots of friends.' Her tone made it clear what kind of friends Deedra had had.

'Yes, I know. But that had changed, she told me it had. Because of me. Because she really loved me and I really loved her.'

I believed that like I believed Becca's hair was really blond. But everyone should have some illusions . . . well, maybe other people. I felt about a million years old as I sighed and nodded at Marlon Schuster. 'Sure,' I said.

'You have to believe me,' he said, suddenly on fire. He straightened on Becca's chair, his eyes flashed, and for the first time I could see what Deedra had seen, the passion that made the boy handsome and desirable.

Becca said, 'She told me that.'

We both stared at her. Becca looked quite calm and matter-of-fact as she went on. 'The last time I talked to Deedra, she told me she'd finally met someone she cared about, someone she thought she could love.'

Marlon's face became radiant with relief and pride. Seeing a chance to act, I silently extended my hand and he put the key in it without thinking. I slid it out of sight, and he didn't say a word of protest.

A couple of minutes later, he left the apartment a happier man than he'd entered it. He'd been told not to worry about the video he and Deedra had made, he'd had the key removed so he no longer had that guilt weighing on him, and he'd had the ego-stroking consolation that his latest love had also loved him, enough to change her life for him.

Who wouldn't feel good?

'Did you make all of that up?' I asked Becca when the door had closed behind Marlon.

'Mostly,' she admitted. 'The last time I talked to Deedra, she was still complaining about the rent going up. But when I said something about seeing Marlon real often, she did say that she'd decided to be monogamous for a while.'

'I wouldn't think she'd know that word,' I said absently.

'Well, maybe she didn't use the term "monogamous", but that's what she meant.'

'When was that, Becca?'

'I know exactly when that was, because the police asked me over and over. It was Saturday afternoon. We were both bringing in groceries at the same time.'

'Who was here that weekend?'

'They asked me that, too. Your friend the chief of police spent the weekend over at his fiancée's. The Bickels were out of town, too, at their mother's in Fayetteville.' Daisy and Dawn Bickel were twin sisters who worked at junior management level, Daisy at the local branch of a big chain of clothing stores and Dawn at Goodnight Mattress Manufacturing. 'Terry Plowright was gone Saturday, to a monster truck rally somewhere on the other side of Little Rock. He didn't get in 'til about one in the morning and as far as I could tell he slept most of Sunday. He lives right across from me. That's the first floor.'

I nodded.

'The upstairs front apartment by Deedra's is vacant. The one across the stairwell from her is a woman who works at Wal-Mart, and she was working most of the weekend – at least Sunday, I know, and I think some hours on Saturday. And the other front apartment is Tick Levinson, and you know how he is.'

'How he is' was alcoholic. Tick was still managing to turn up to work at the local paper, where he was a pressman, but if there wasn't a dramatic intervention, Tick wouldn't be doing that in a year.

'So out of those, who do you think had anything to do with Deedra?'

'Well, Terry, for sure. He had a lot to do with her, real often. But I don't think either of them took it to heart,' Becca said slowly. 'Terry just isn't serious about anything besides cars and trucks. He loves being single. I don't think the Bickel twins even speak – even spoke – to Deedra, besides hello. Claude . . . well, you know, actually I think Claude might have visited Deedra once or twice, if you get my drift.'

I could not have been more surprised. I was sure my face showed it.

I was disgusted, too.

'You know how men are,' Becca said dryly.

I did, for sure.

'But from what Deedra said, I think it was a long time ago, maybe after he first moved back to Shakespeare from Little Rock. Before he kind of knew what was what. Right after his divorce.'

Still.

'Anyway, nothing recent. And Tick? I don't think Tick lusts after anything but the next bottle, you know? You ever see him coming down the stairs after the weekend, trying to go to work? It's grim. If he smoked, I'd worry about being burned up in our beds.'

That was only sensible.

'And before you ask me just like the cops did, I didn't see any strangers around that weekend, but that's not to say there weren't any. Everyone's got their own key to the outside doors.' Those doors were locked at ten at night, after which the residents used their own keys.

'Speaking of keys,' Becca said suddenly, and went to the desk by the door. She opened the top drawer, pulled out a key. 'Here's the outside door key for when Anthony and I go on our trip.'

I put it in my pocket and stood to leave as Anthony came in. He'd been to Stage, where one of the Bickel twins worked, I could see from his bag. He'd bought a lot of clothes. Getting excited about his trip, I guess.

'Where are you-all going?' I asked. I was trying to be polite.

'Oh, who can tell!' Becca laughed. 'We might go to Mexico, we might go to the Dominican Republic! If we really like someplace, we might just stay there.'

'You'd sell up here?'

'I think that's a possibility,' Becca said, more soberly. 'You gotta admit, Lily, I'm a fish out of water here.'

That was true enough.

'Becca needs to see the world,' Anthony said proudly.

They sure were excited. The idea of travel wouldn't make me happy at all, but I could tell Becca was ready to leave town. She'd never really been at home in Shakespeare.

I went home to find a baffled Jack squatting by the television, two stacks of tapes to his right. 'Lily, would you like to tell me where you got these tapes?' he growled, staring at the episode of The Bold and the Beautiful unfolding on the screen. 'Some of these are homemade porn, and some of them are *Oprah* or soaps.'

I smiled. I couldn't help it. I explained about Deedra and about my desire to help by getting the tapes out of the apartment.

'I think you better tell me the whole story about Deedra from the beginning, all over again,' he said. 'Wasn't she that girl with no chin who lived across the upstairs hall from me?'

The previous fall, Jack had rented an apartment when he was working in Shakespeare undercover, on a job.

'Yep, that was Deedra,' I told him. I sighed. The girl with no chin. What a way to be remembered. I began telling Jack, all over again, about finding Deedra in her car – the call of the bobwhite, the silence of the forest, the gray dead woman in the front seat of the car.

'So, how long had she been dead?' Jack asked practically.

'In the newspaper article, Marta is quoted as saying she'd been dead for somewhere between eighteen and twenty-four hours.'

'Still got the paper?' Jack asked, and I went to rummage through my recycle bin.

Jack stretched out on the floor, pretty much filling my little living room, to read. I recalled with a sudden start that he was moving in with me, and I could look at him as much as I liked, every day. I didn't have to fill up with looking so I could replay it while he was gone. And he'd be taking up just as much space, much more often. We had a few bumps in the road ahead of us, for sure.

'So, the last one to see her was her mother, when Deedra left church on Sunday to walk home to her apartment.' Jack scanned the article again, his T-shirt stretching over his back, and his muscle pants doing good things for his butt. I felt pretty happy about him being displayed on my floor like that. I felt like taking the paper away from him. Tomorrow morning he had to leave, and I had to work, and we were not making the best use of the time we had.

'I wonder what she was doing,' Jack said. He was thinking things through like the former cop he was. 'Did she make it home to her apartment? How'd she leave?'

I told Jack what I knew about the population of the apartment building that Sunday afternoon. 'Becca was in town but I don't know exactly where she was then,' I concluded. 'Claude was gone, the Bickels were gone, Terry Plowright was gone. Tick, I guess, was drunk. The woman who works at Wal-Mart, Do'mari Clayton, was at the store, according to Becca.'

'Where was Becca?'

'I don't know, she didn't say.' I had no idea what Becca usually did on Sundays. She wasn't a churchgoer, and though she often made an appearance at Body Time, she didn't stay long. Maybe on Sunday she just slopped around in her pajamas and read the papers, or a book.

'Had that brother of hers gotten here yet?'

'No, yesterday was the first time I'd seen him.'

'So he never even knew Deedra.' Jack rested his chin on his hands, staring at the wood of the floor. While he thought, I fetched the old *TV Guide* from my bedroom – our bedroom –

and opened it to Saturday. This would have been the one day pertinent to Deedra, since she'd died on Sunday.

I read all the synopses, checked all the sports listings, pored over the evening shows. When Jack snapped out of his reverie long enough to ask me what I was doing, I tried to explain it to him, but it came out sounding fuzzier than it was.

'Maybe the *TV Guide* had blood on it or something, so the killer took it with him,' he said, uninterested. 'Or maybe Deedra spilled ginger ale on it and pitched it in the garbage. It's the purse that's more interesting. What could have been in her purse? Did she carry those big bags you could put bricks into?'

'No. Hers were big enough for her billfold, a brush, a compact, a roll of mints, and some Kleenex. Not much else.'

'Her apartment hadn't been tossed?'

'Not so I could tell.'

'What's small enough to be carried in a purse?' Jack rolled onto his back, an even more attractive pose. His hazel eyes focused on the ceiling. 'She have jewelry?'

'No expensive jewelry. At least nothing worth staging that elaborate death scene for. If she'd been knocked on the head with a brick while she was at an urban mall, that would be one thing. She had some gold chains, her pearls, they would be worth that. But this, this arrangement in the woods . . . it seemed personal. And her pearls were there, hanging on the tree.'

'Then we're back to her sex life. Who did she actually have sex with, that you know of?' Jack looked a little uncomfortable as he asked. That was sort of strange.

'Anyone she could,' I said absently, beginning to think suspicious thoughts. 'Do you want a list?'

Jack nodded, but kept his eyes fixed on the ceiling.

'Marcus Jefferson, that guy who used to live in the top front – the apartment you had for a while.' I thought a little. 'Brian Gruber's son, Claude, Terry Plowright, Darcy Orchard, Norvel Whitbread, Randy Peevely while he was separated from Heather, plus at least' – I counted on my fingers – 'four others. And those are just the ones I saw there, actually saw in her apartment. But I wasn't about to give Marta Schuster a list.'

'You didn't tell the police?'

'It wasn't their business. One of those men may have killed Deedra, but that's no reason for all of them to go through hell. And I'm not convinced any of them *did* kill her.'

'Based on?'

'Why?' I asked, leaning forward, my hands on my knees. 'Why would they?'

'Fear of exposure,' Jack said, starting out assured but ending up uncertain.

'Who would fear exposure? Everyone in town knew Deedra was . . . really available. No one took her seriously. That was the tragedy of her life.' I surprised myself, with my intensity and my shaking voice. I had cared more than I knew, for reasons I couldn't fathom. 'Jack, were you lonely enough when you came to Shakespeare?'

Jack turned dark red. It was slow and unlovely.

'No,' he said. 'But it was a near thing. It was only because I thought of AIDS that I didn't. She had condoms, and I was horny, but I'd been tested and I was clean and I . . . could tell she was . . .'

'A whore?' I asked, feeling rage building up in me. And I could not understand it.

Jack nodded.

It's amazing how easily a good afternoon can evaporate.

'Can you tell me why you're so mad?' Jack asked my back. I was kneeling in the bathroom, scrubbing the floor by hand.

'I don't think so,' I said curtly. My hands were sweating inside the rubber gloves, and I knew they'd smell like old sweat socks when I peeled the gloves off.

I was trying to figure it out myself. Deedra hadn't valued herself. That was not the fault of the men who screwed her. And she offered herself to them, no doubt about it. She asked nothing in return except maybe a little attention, a little kindness. She never asked for a long-term relationship, she never asked for money or gifts. She had wanted to be the object of desire, however fleeting, because in her eyes that gave her worth.

So could the men be considered at fault for giving her what she wanted? If something was freely offered, could you grudge the takers?

Well, I could. And I did.

And I was just going to have to swallow it. There were too many of them, among them men I liked and a very few I respected. Men just following their natures, as Deedra had been following hers. But I regretted not giving the sheriff their names. Let them sweat a little. It might be uncomfortable for them, but after all, Deedra was the one who'd suffered.

And yet, in the end, Deedra had finally found Marlon Schuster. He seemed to be a weak reed, but he wanted to be her reed. Would she have been strong enough to turn her back on her way of life and stick with Marlon? Did she even care for him? Just because he offered what she'd always been searching for didn't mean she was obliged to take it.

Now we'd never know. Two years down the road from now, Deedra might've been married to Marlon, a whitewashed woman, maybe even pregnant with their child.

But that option had been taken away from Deedra, and from Marlon.

And that made me *angry*.

I felt better when the bathroom shone. I had relaxed by the time we went to bed, and as I listened to Jack's heavy, even breath beside me, I decided that somehow Jack's near-brush with Deedra absolved me of mine with Bobo. Though Jack hadn't known me well at the time, he'd known me, and now I felt as though my sin had been canceled by his.

I tossed and turned a little, unable to get to sleep. I thought of having to go to work in the morning, of Jack leaving to go back to Little Rock. I wondered if Birdie Rossiter would need me to bathe poor Durwood; I wondered if Lacey would need more help in Deedra's apartment.

Finally, it occurred to me that the remedy for my sleeplessness lay right beside me. I snuggled against Jack's back, reached over him, and began a gentle massage that I knew would wake him up in no time.

I was right.

Chapter Eleven

It was warmer the next day, with just a hint of the sweltering heat of summer: a wake-up call to the inhabitants of southern Arkansas.

Jack and I had gotten up early and gone to work out together at Body Time. We'd done triceps; I was sure to be sore after working triceps with Jack, because I tried heavier weights when he was with me, and I pulled harder for that extra set of reps.

Janet was there, and after she greeted Jack and went back to her leg presses, I noticed that Marshall himself came out of his office to spot her. I was pleased. Marshall needed to notice Janet, who had long had a soft spot for him.

Jack, on the other hand, would never be very partial to my *sensei* because he was well aware that Marshall and I once shared some time together. He wasn't ridiculous about it, but I noticed a stiffness in the way he chatted with Marshall.

Marshall seemed to be in a very good mood, laughing and joking with Janet, and generally going around the room in a circuit to meet and greet.

'What's up?' Jack asked when Marshall reached us.

'My ex is getting remarried,' Marshall said, beaming, an expression that sat oddly on his face.

I'd had some dealings with Thea, who was tiny, lovely, and widely respected. So are small poisonous snakes.

'Who's the unlucky man?' I stood up straight after my second set of tricep pushups. Jack and I usually did them against the rack that held the heavier weights. We would put our hands close together on the top rack, and with our feet as far back as our height allowed, we would begin to lean down until our noses touched the weights, and then we'd push back up. I shook my arms to relieve the ache.

'A guy from Montrose,' Marshall said, actually laughing out loud. 'And I stop paying alimony when she remarries.'

'When is the wedding?' Jack asked, planting his hands to do his set.

'Three months.' Marshall beamed at me. 'No more Thea. And he owns the John Deere dealership, so she'll be set. She's not even going to go back to work.' Thea had been a child-care worker, and a very poor one, at the SCC day-care center.

'That sounds good,' I said. 'I hope nothing happens to the man before she marries him.'

'He's in my prayers,' Marshall said, and he wasn't being facetious. He slapped me on the shoulder, nodded at Jack, and strolled back over to Janet, who was patting her face with a towel. She was trying to restrain her pleasure at being singled out by Marshall, but it wasn't working. She was glowing with something besides sweat.

Back home, I showered and put on my makeup for work while Jack repacked and ate some breakfast. Then he took his turn in the bathroom while I ate some toast and made the bed.

We could make cohabiting work, I figured. It might take some adjustments, since both of us were used to living alone, and it might take some time, but we could do it.

Jack and I pulled out of the driveway at the same time, he to head back to Little Rock, and me to work for Birdie Rossiter.

Birdie was in full spate that morning. Unlike most people, who'd leave when they saw me pull up to their house, Birdie looked on me as a companion who was incidentally a house-cleaner. So from the time I entered until the time I left, she provided a constant accompaniment, chattering and questioning, full of gossip and advice.

It wore me out.

I wondered if she talked to Durwood when I wasn't there. I figured Durwood qualified to be some kind of dog saint.

But sometimes, in the middle of all the inconsequential gossip,

Birdie let drop a nugget of something useful or interesting. This morning, Birdie Rossiter told me that Lacey Dean Knopp had made Jerrell Knopp move out.

'I guess she's just got unhinged since poor little Deedra got killed,' Birdie said, her mouth pursed in commiseration tinged with pleasure. 'That Deedra, she was the light of Lacey's life. I know when Jerrell was courting her, he was mighty careful not to say one thing about Deedra. I bet he was after Lacey's money. Chaz Dean, the first husband, he died before you came to Shakespeare . . . Well, Chaz left Lacey one nice pot of money. I knew she'd get remarried. Not just for the money. Lacey is pretty, no doubt about it, and not "for fifty" or whatever age. Lacey is just plain pretty. If you marry somebody good-looking who has money, you just get a bonus, don't you?'

I didn't know which element would be the bonus, the money or the looks. Lacey, who had both, did not seem to me to be a particularly lucky person.

While Birdie went to pour herself another cup of coffee, I thought about Lacey making Jerrell move out, and I thought about the nasty speculation Janet and I had developed. I'd thought no one would worry if Deedra said she was going to make a relationship public, but I'd temporarily forgotten Jerrell. If she'd endangered his relationship with his wife, Deedra would have to be ruthlessly eliminated. Jerrell was crazy about Lacey. I'd never liked the man, and from my point of view it would be a great solution to Deedra's murder if her stepfather could be found guilty.

But I caught myself scowling at the sponge mop while I squeezed it out into the mopping bucket. I couldn't make a convincing case against Jerrell, no matter how much I tried. While I could see Jerrell hitting Deedra with a handy two-by-four, even taking a gun to shoot her, I couldn't see Jerrell planning the elaborately staged scene in the woods. The strewn clothes, the positioning of the body, the bottle . . . no, I didn't think so.

Birdie was back and babbling again now, but I wasn't listening.

I was mentally examining what I'd just said to myself, and I was forming a little plan.

It was a Monday eerily like that other Monday; it was clear and bright, and the air had a little touch of hotness to it, like standing just the right distance away from the burner on a stove.

Instead of parking out on Farm Hill Road, I turned into the graveled trail. I didn't want to risk my worn-out suspension on the ruts, so I parked right inside the edge of the woods. I sat in my car, just listening for a minute or two. No bobwhite today, but I heard a mockingbird and a cardinal. It was a little cooler in the shade.

I sighed and got out of my car, removing the keys and stuffing them in my pocket for safekeeping. It never hurts to be careful.

Then I was moving down the trail again, telling myself that this time there wouldn't be a car sitting in the middle of the woods, knowing there was no way a car would be in the same spot again . . .

But there *was* a car there, parked just where Deedra's had been, and like hers it faced away from me. I stopped dead in my tracks.

It was a dark green Bronco, which explained why I hadn't picked it out before. There was someone sitting in it.

'Oh no,' I whispered. I shook my head from side to side. This was like one of those dreams in which you are compelled to do something you dread doing, something you know will end in horror. When my feet began moving forward, my teeth were clenched to keep them from chattering, and my hand was over my heart, feeling it hammer with fear.

I drew abreast of the driver's window, standing well back so I wouldn't catch the smell again. I didn't think I could stand that without throwing up, and I didn't want to put myself through it. I leaned slightly to look in and then I froze. I was looking into a gun.

Clifton Emanuel's eyes were just as round and black as the barrel of the gun, and almost as frightening.

'Don't move,' he said hoarsely.

I was too shocked to say anything, and I wasn't about to move a muscle. A lot passed through my mind in a second. I saw that if I acted instantly I could disarm him, though he was equally ready to pull the trigger. But he was a law-enforcement officer and my tendency was to obey him, though I knew from experience that some people in law enforcement were just as wrong headed or corrupt as the sociopaths they arrested.

On the whole . . . I remained frozen.

'Step back,' he commanded, in that eerie voice that told me he was wound as tight as a coil could be wound.

If I stepped back I wouldn't be frozen anymore, but I decided it wasn't the time to quibble with him. I stepped back. Marshall had always warned us that no matter how skilled you became in martial arts, in some situations the man with the gun would rule.

I watched, hardly breathing, as Clifton Emanuel opened the car door and emerged from the car. Though he took great care to keep the gun trained on me, there was one point at which I could've begun to move, but my uncertainty held me paralyzed.

Though I just didn't think the deputy was going to shoot, I remained tense and strung up for action. His eyes were showing a little too much white to suit me. But when I figured he'd heard me coming up the trail, drawn his gun, and sat in the car waiting for me to approach, it wasn't surprising he was squirrelly.

'Up against the car,' he ordered. Now that I felt sure he wasn't going to shoot me out of hand, I began to get mad. I put my hands against the car, spread my legs, and let him pat me down, but I could feel my tolerance draining away with my fear.

He frisked me as impersonally as I could want, which was saying a lot.

'Turn around,' he said, and his voice was not so hoarse.

I faced him, having to look up to gauge his emotional state from his expression. His body was relaxing a little, and his eyes looked a trifle less jumpy. I focused on looking nonthreatening, trying to keep my own muscles from tensing, trying to breathe evenly. It took a lot of concentration.

'What are you doing out here?' he asked.

He was in plainclothes, though I noticed that his khaki slacks and brown plaid shirt were not too far from the uniform in spirit.

'I could ask the same,' I said, trying not to sound as confrontational as I felt. I don't like feeling helpless. I don't like that more than I don't like almost anything else.

'Tell me,' he said.

'I wanted to look at the spot again because . . .' I faltered, not happy at explaining what had really been an unformed feeling.

'Why?'

'Because I wanted to think about it,' I finished. 'See, I was thinking . . .' I shook my head, trying to formulate what I wanted to say. 'There was something wrong about this.'

'You mean, besides the murder of a young woman?' he asked dryly.

I nodded, ignoring the sarcasm.

He lowered the gun.

'I think so too,' he said. Now he looked more astonished than anything, as if it amazed him that I would think about what I'd seen that day, think about Deedra's last moments after I'd reported her death. It appeared that in Clifton Emanuel's estimation, I was so tough that the death of a woman I'd known for years wouldn't affect me. It would be wonderful, I thought, to be that tough.

He holstered his gun. He didn't apologize for drawing on me, and I didn't ask it of him. If I'd been in his shoes, I'd have done the same.

'Go on,' he invited me.

'I found myself thinking that . . .' I paused, trying to phrase it so he'd understand me. 'We're *meant* to think that a man came out here in Deedra's car with her.'

'Or maybe arranged to meet her out here,' he interjected, and I nodded, waving a hand to show I conceded that.

'Howsoever. So, she's out here, and so is the murderer, however he got here. And then, we're supposed to think that this killer got Deedra out of the car for a little sex, told her to take off her clothes. She strips for his pleasure, tossing her clothes at random,

panty hose here, blouse there, pearls, skirt . . . and she's out here
in the middle of the woods naked as a jaybird. Then she has sex
with him, and he's using a condom unless he's a complete moron.
Or maybe they don't have sex? I don't know what the autopsy
said. But at that point, something goes wrong.'

Clifton was nodding his big head. 'They argue about something,' he said, taking over the scenario. 'Maybe she threatens to
tell his wife he's screwing her. But that doesn't seem likely, since
everyone agrees married men didn't appeal to her. Maybe she tells
him she thinks she's pregnant, though she wasn't. Or maybe she
tells him he's a lousy lay. Maybe he can't get it up.'

That had crossed my mind briefly before, when I'd considered
Deedra's artificial violation with the bottle. When Clifton Emanuel said it, the idea made even more sense. I looked up at the
deputy in surprise, and he nodded grimly. 'For some people, not
performing would be reason enough to go off the deep end,' he
told me darkly.

I looked off into the shadows of the woods and shivered.

'So he *shows* her potency,' Emanuel continued. 'He strikes her
hard enough in the solar plexus to kill her, and while she's dying
he hauls her into the car and then shoves the bottle up her . . . ah,
up her.' He cleared his throat in a curiously delicate way.

'And then he leaves. How?' I asked. 'If he arrived in her car,
how does he leave?'

'And if he came in his own car, it didn't leave any trace that we
could find. Which is possible, especially if it was a good vehicle
with no leaks. The ground was dry that week, but not dry enough
to be powdery. Not good for tracks. But it just seems more likely
that he was in the car with her, that he wouldn't risk being seen
pulling in here with her. So he must've had his car already parked
somewhere close. Or maybe he had a cell phone, like yours. He
could call someone to come pick him up, spin some story to
explain it. Someone he trusted wouldn't go the police with it.'

I spared a moment to wonder why a law-enforcement officer
was being so forthcoming with speculation.

'She wasn't pregnant,' I muttered.

He shook his heavy head. 'Nope. And she'd had sex with someone wearing a condom. But we don't know if it was necessarily the killer.'

'So you think maybe he couldn't do it, and she enraged him?' But that kind of taunting didn't seem in Deedra's character. Oh, how the hell did I know how she acted with men?

'That's possible. But I did talk with a former bedmate of hers who had the same problem,' Deputy Emanuel said, amazing me yet again, 'He said she was really sweet about it, consoling, telling him next time would be okay, she was sure.'

'That wouldn't stop some men from beating her up,' I said.

He nodded, giving me credit for experience. 'So that's still a possibility, but it seems more unlikely.'

Emanuel paused, giving me plenty of eye contact. He had no interest whatsoever in me as a woman, which pleased me. 'So,' he concluded, 'we're back to the question of why anyone would do in Deedra if it wasn't over some sexual matter? Why make it look like the motive was sex?'

'Because that makes so many more suspects,' I said. Emanuel and I nodded simultaneously as we accepted the truth of that idea. 'Could she have learned something at her job? The county clerk's office is pretty important.'

'The county payroll, property taxes . . . yes, the clerk's office handles a lot of money and responsibility. And we've talked to Choke Anson several times, both about how Deedra was at work and about his relationship to her. He looks clear to me. As far as Deedra knowing something connected to her job, something she shouldn't know, almost everything there is a matter of public record, and all the other clerks have access to the same material. It's not like Deedra exclusively . . .'

He trailed off, but I got his point.

'I'm going to tell you something,' I said.

'Good,' he responded. 'I was hoping you would.'

Feeling like this betrayal was a necessary one, I told him about Marlon Schuster's strange visit to Deedra's apartment.

'He had a key,' I said. 'He says he loved her. But what if he found out she was cheating on him? He says she loved him, too, and that's why she gave him a key. But did you ever find Deedra's own key?'

'No.' Emanuel looked down at his enormous feet. 'No, never did. Or her purse.'

'What about you and Deedra?' I asked abruptly. I was tired of worrying about it.

'I wouldn't have touched her with a ten-foot pole,' he said, distaste making his voice sour. 'That's the only thing I have in common with Choke Anson. I like a woman who's a little more choosy, has some self-respect.'

'Like Marta.'

He shot me an unloving look. 'Everyone else in the department thinks Marlon did it,' Deputy Emanuel said quietly. He leaned back against his car, and it rocked a little. 'Every single man in the department thinks Marta's blind for not bringing her brother in. They're all talking against her. You can't reason with 'em. He was the last to have her, so he was the guilty one, they figure.'

So that was the reason Emanuel was confiding in me. He was isolated from his own clan. 'Marlon was with Deedra Saturday night?' I asked.

The deputy nodded. 'And Sunday morning. But he says he didn't see her after he left to go to church on Sunday. He called her apartment several times, he says. And her phone records bear that out.'

'What calls did she make?'

'She called her mother,' Clifton Emanuel said heavily. 'She called her mother.'

'Do you have any idea why?' I asked, keeping my voice soft, because it seemed to me Clifton was about to pull the lid back on top of his loquacity, and I wanted to get everything I could out of him before the well ran dry.

'According to her mother, it was a family matter.'

That lid was sliding shut.

'About Jerrell fooling around with Deedra before he dated Lacey?'

His lips pursed in a flat line, Clifton gave an ambiguous movement of his head, which could mean anything. The lid was down
now.

'I'm gonna go,' I said.

He was regretting talking to me now, the luxury of speculating
with another skeptical party forgotten, the fact that he was a
lawman now uppermost in his mind. He'd talked out of school
and he didn't like himself for it. If he hadn't been so enamored of
Marta Schuster, if he'd been in good standing with his fellow
deputies, he'd never have said a word. And I saw his struggle as he
tried to piece together what to say to me to ensure my silence.

'For what it's worth,' I said, 'I don't think Marlon killed her.
And rumor has it that yesterday Lacey told Jerrell to move out.'

Deputy Emanuel blinked and considered this information with
narrowed eyes.

'And you know those pearls?'

He nodded absently.

I inclined my head toward the branch where they'd dangled.

'I don't think she would have thrown them around.' The pearls
had been bothering me. Clifton Emanuel made a 'keep going'
gesture to get me to elaborate. I shrugged. 'Her father gave her
that necklace. She valued it.'

Clifton Emanuel looked down at me with those fathomless
black eyes. I thought he was deciding whether or not to trust me.
I may have been wrong; he may have been wondering if he'd
have a hamburger or chicken nuggets when he went through the
drive-through at Burger Tycoon.

After a moment of silence, I turned on my heel and went down
the road, all too aware that he was staring after me. I didn't get
that uneasy feeling with Deputy Emanuel, that prickling-at-the-
back-of-the-neck feeling that some people gave me; the feeling
that warned me that something sick and possibly dangerous
lurked inside that person's psyche. But after our little conversation
I was sure that Marta Schuster was lucky to have the devotion of
this man, and I was glad I was not her enemy.

★

On my way into town, I was thinking hard. Now more than ever, it seemed to me – and I thought that it seemed to Clifton Emanuel, too – there was something phony about the crime scene in the woods. Though Deputy Emanuel had run out of confidence in me before we'd run out of conversation, he too had seemed dubious about the scenario implied by the trappings left at the scene.

At my next job, Camille Emerson's place, I was lucky enough to find the house empty. I was able to keep thinking while I worked.

That implied scenario: though I'd gone over it with Emanuel, I ran it again in my head. Deedra and a flame go out to the woods in Deedra's car. The flame gets Deedra to strip, which she does with abandon, flinging her clothes and jewelry everywhere.

Then a quarrel occurs. Perhaps the man can't perform sexually, and Deedra taunts him (though Emanuel had testimony and I agreed that such taunting was unlike Deedra). Maybe Deedra threatens to tell the flame's wife, mother, or girlfriend that Deedra and the flame are having sex, period. Or possibly the flame is just into rough sex, killing Deedra in a fit of passion. But would that tie in with the catastrophic blow that stopped her heart?

I was so tired of thinking about Deedra by that time that the last explanation tempted me. I didn't want to think Deedra's death was anything more than passion of one kind or another, passion that had gotten fatally out of hand.

But as I finished dusting the 'collectibles' on Camille Emerson's living-room shelves. I caught sight of myself in the mantel mirror. I was shaking my head in a sober way, all to myself.

The only injury Deedra had sustained, according to every source, was the killing blow itself. I knew all too well what rough sex was like. It's not one blow or act or bit of brutality, but a whole series of them. The object of this attention doesn't emerge from the sex act with one injury, but a series of injuries. The bottle insertion had happened after Deedra was dead. Therefore, I realized, as I carried a load of dirty towels to the laundry area, that little nasty, contemptuous act was no more than window dressing. Maybe the equivalent of having the last word in a conversation.

That said something about the person who'd performed the insertion, didn't it? I covered my hand with a paper towel and pulled a wad of bubble gum off the baseboard behind the trash can in the younger Emerson boy's room.

So, we had someone strong, strong enough to kill with one blow. The blow was probably purposeful. Evidently, the person had *meant* to kill Deedra.

We had someone who despised women. Maybe not all women, but women in some way like Deedra. Promiscuous? Attractive? Young? All of the above?

We had someone who had no regard for human life.

And we had someone clever. When I turned it over in my mind yet again, I could see that the staging was successful if you didn't really know Deedra. Deedra wouldn't throw things around like that, even if she were stripping for someone, which I could very well imagine her doing. Even then, she might sling a blouse, but it would land on something that wouldn't tear or dirty it. She wouldn't toss her pearls around. And the woods . . . no, she wouldn't do that in the woods! Where was the lap robe or blanket for the lovers to lie on? Why ask Deedra to strip if the goal was a quick screw in the backseat of the car?

I concluded that whoever'd killed Deedra hadn't thought anything at all about her character, had only known facts: that she was promiscuous and biddable. He hadn't thought of her fastidiousness about her surroundings, hadn't thought about her care for her possessions, the care that had never extended to cover her own body.

As I closed the Emersons' door behind me, I realized that now I knew much more than I had this morning. What to do with it, how to make it work for me, was still mysterious. These pieces of knowledge were not evidence to which anyone else would give credence, but at least Clifton Emanuel had listened. I was relieved to know he had been wondering, as I had been, if the whole scene in the woods was a setup.

A setup to serve what purpose?

Okay, the purpose had to be, as the deputy and I had hinted to each other in our conversation, to misdirect. The scene had been staged to make it appear that Deedra had been killed for a sexual reason; therefore, if the scene was false, Deedra had *not* been killed because she was sexually active.

She had been killed because . . . she worked at the county clerk's office? She was Lacey Dean Knopp's daughter? She was the granddaughter of Joe C Prader? She was easily led and promiscuous, so she was an easy target? I'd hit a mental wall.

It was time to dismiss Deedra from my thoughts for a while. When I was sitting in my kitchen at noon, that was easy.

My house felt empty and bleak without Jack in it. I didn't like that at all. I ate lunch as quickly as I could, imagining him riding back to Little Rock, arriving at his own apartment. He'd return his phone messages, make notes on the case he'd just finished, answer his e-mail.

I missed him. I seemed to need him more than I ought to. Maybe it was because for so long I had done without? Maybe I valued him more deeply because of what I'd gone through all those years ago? I saw Jack's faults; I didn't think he was perfect. And that didn't make a bit of difference. What would I do if something happened to Jack?

This seemed to be a day for questions I couldn't answer.

Chapter Twelve

At karate class that night, I wasn't concentrating, which called down a scolding from Marshall. I was glad we didn't spar, because I would've lost, and I don't like to lose. Janet teased me as I tied my shoes, accusing me of being abstracted because I was pining for Jack. I managed to half-smile at her, though my impulse was to lash out. Allowing thoughts of a man to disrupt something so important to me was . . . I subsided suddenly.

It would be quite natural. It would be normal.

But picturing Jack in the shower wasn't what had distracted me. I'd been thinking of Deedra – her face in death, her positioning at the wheel of her red car. I didn't know what I could do to help her. I had done all I could. I finished tying my shoes and sat up, staring across the empty room at Becca, who was laughingly instructing her brother in the correct position of his hands for the *sanchin dachi* posture. She motioned me to come over and help, but I shook my head and gathered the handles of my gym bag in my fist. I was ready to be by myself.

After I got home I resumed the task of scanning Deedra's tapes, since I had promised Marlon that if I found the one that featured him I would give it to him. I found myself feeling a little sick at the idea of him keeping a video of him having sex with a woman now dead, but it was none of my business what he did with it. I disliked Marlon Schuster, though that was maybe stating my feeling for him too strongly. It was more accurate to say I had no respect for him, which was quite usual for me. I had found nothing in him to like except his tenderness for Deedra. But that was something, and I had made him a promise.

I almost dozed off as I looked at the videos. I found myself looking at things I'd never seen before: talk shows, soap operas, and 'reality' shows about ambulance drivers, policemen, wanted criminals, and missing children. After viewing a few tapes I could predict what was coming next, her pattern. It was like an up-ended time capsule for the past couple of weeks in television land. When I'd transferred the videotapes into a box, the most recent ones had ended up on the bottom.

Most of the videos weren't labeled – the ones she'd already watched, I guessed. The labeled ones had abbreviations on them that only gradually began to make sense to me. I discovered that 'OLTL' meant *One Life to Live* and that 'C' meant *Cops*, while 'AMW' was *America's Most Wanted*, and 'Op' was *Oprah*.

After I'd scanned maybe ten of the tapes, I found the one of Marlon and Deedra. I only watched a second of it, enough to confirm the identity of the couple. (That was all Marlon needed, to get a tape of Deedra with another man.) I put the tape aside with a discreet Post-It.

Since I'd started the job, I kept on with it out of sheer doggedness. I was able to weed out one more home movie – Deedra and our mailman, in partial uniform. Disgusting. All the other videos seemed to contain innocuous television programming. When I got to the bottom, I realized that I could match these shows with the synopses in Jack's old magazine. These were things Deedra had taped during the week before she died. There was even an old movie Deedra had taped on Saturday morning at the end of one tape.

Deedra had had at least two tapes with previous Saturday night shows on them in her film library. She'd taped the same pattern of shows each weekend. So where was the tape from last Saturday night? She hadn't died until Sunday; she'd been alive when Marlon had left her Sunday morning, he'd said. Even if I didn't want to believe Marlon, she'd talked to her mother at church, right? So where was the Saturday night tape?

It was probably an unimportant detail, but unimportant details are what make up housecleaning. Those details add up. A shiny sink, a neatly folded towel, a dustless television screen; this is the visible proof that your house has been labored over.

I was beginning to get a rare headache. None of this made sense. I could only be glad I wasn't on the police force. I'd be obliged to listen to men tell me day after day about their little flings with Deedra, their moments of weakness, their infidelities. Surely watching a few seconds of homemade porn was better than that, if I was still obliged to clean up after Deedra in some moral way.

It was a relief when the phone rang.

'Lily!' Carrie said happily.

'Mrs Dr Friedrich,' I answered.

There was a long pause over the line. 'Wow,' she breathed. 'I just can't get used to it. You think it'll take people a long time to start calling me Dr Friedrich?'

'Maybe a week.'

'Oh boy,' she said happily, sounding all of eighteen. 'Oh, boy. Hey, how are you? Anything big happen while we were gone?'

'Not too much. How was Hot Springs?'

'Oh . . . beautiful,' she said, sighing. 'I can't believe we have to go to work tomorrow.'

I heard a rumble in the background.

'Claude says thanks for standing up for us at the courthouse,' Carrie relayed.

'I was glad to do it. Are you at your house?'

'Yes. We'll have to get Claude's things moved soon. I told my parents about an hour ago! They'd given up hope on me, and they just went nuts.'

'What do you and Claude need for your wedding present?' I asked.

'Lily, we don't need a thing. We're so old, and we've been set up on our own for so long. There's not a thing we need.'

'Okay,' I said. 'I can see that. What about me cleaning Claude's apartment after he gets his stuff out?'

'Oh, Lily, that would be great! One less thing we have to do.'

'Then consider it done.'

Carrie was telling Claude what I proposed, and he was objecting.

'Claude says that's too much on you since you clean for a living,' Carrie reported.

'Tell Claude to put a sock in it. It's a gift,' I said, and Carrie giggled and gave him the message.

'Lily, I'll see you soon,' she said. 'Oh, Lily, I'm so happy!'

'I'm glad for both of you,' I said. Sooner or later, someone would tell Carrie about the fire, and she'd chide me for not telling her myself. But she didn't need to come down from her cloud of happiness and be retroactively worried about me. Tomorrow she'd be back at work and so would Claude. The lives of a doctor and a chief of police are not giddy and irresponsible.

The next morning I found myself wondering why I hadn't heard from Lacey. She'd wanted me to work some more in the apartment. Her marriage crisis must have changed her agenda, and I wasn't surprised. I worked that morning after all. The gap caused by losing Joe C as a client was filled when Mrs Jepperson's sitter called to ask me to come over.

Mrs Jepperson was having a lucid day, Laquanda Titchnor told me all too loudly as she let me in. Laquanda, whom I held in low regard, was the woman Mrs Jepperson's daughter had had to settle for when better aides had all been employed.

Laquanda's greatest virtues were that she showed up on time, stayed as long as she was supposed to, and knew how to dial 911. And she talked to Mrs Jepperson, rather than just staring at the television silently all day, as I'd seen other baby-sitters (of both the young and the elderly) do. Laquanda and Birdie Rossiter were sisters under the skin, at least as far as their need to provide commentary every moment of every day.

Today Laquanda had a problem. Her daughter had called from the high school to tell her mother she was throwing up and running a fever.

'I just need you to watch Mrs Jepperson while I run to get my girl and take her to the doctor,' Laquanda told me. She didn't sound very pleased I was there. It was clear to both of us we weren't exactly a mutual admiration society.

'So go,' I said. Laquanda waited for me to say something else. When I didn't, she pointed out the list of emergency numbers, grabbed her purse, and hightailed it out the kitchen door. The house was still clean from my last visit, I noticed, after I cast a glance in the master bedroom at the sleeping lady. For something to do, I gave a cursory scrub to the bathroom and kitchen surfaces. Laquanda always did the laundry and dishes (what little there was to do) in between monologues, and Mrs Jepperson was bedridden and didn't have much occasion to litter the house. Her family visited every day, either her daughter, her son, their spouses, or any of the eight grandchildren. There were great-grandchildren, too, maybe three or four.

After I'd written a brief list of needed supplies and stuck it to the refrigerator (the granddaughter would pick it up and take it to the store) I perched on the edge of Laquanda's chair set close to the bed. She'd carefully angled it so she could see the front door, the television, and Mrs Jepperson, all in a single sweeping glance.

I'd thought Mrs Jepperson was still asleep, but after a minute she opened her eyes. Narrowed by drooping, wrinkled lids, her eyes were dark brown and cloudy, and since her eyebrows and eyelashes were almost invisible she looked like some old reptile in the sun.

'She's really not so bad,' Mrs Jepperson told me, in a dry, rustling voice that increased her resemblance to a reptile. 'She just talks to keep her spirits up. Her job is so boring.' And the old woman gave a faint smile that had the traces of a formidable charm lingering around the edges.

I couldn't think of any response.

Mrs Jepperson looked at me with greater attention.

'You're the housecleaner,' she said, as if she'd just slapped a label on my forehead.

'Yes.'

'Your name is . . . ?'

'Lily Bard.'

'Are you married, Lily?' Mrs Jepperson seemed to feel obliged to be social.

'No.'

My employer seemed to ponder that. 'I was married for forty-five years,' she said after a pause.

'A long time.'

'Yep. I couldn't stand him for the last thirty-five of them.'

I made a strangled noise that was actually an attempt to stifle a snort of laughter.

'You all right, young woman?'

'Yes ma'am. I'm fine.'

'My children and grandchildren hate me talking like this,' Mrs Jepperson said in her leisurely way. Her narrow brown eyes coasted my way to give me a close examination. 'But that's the luxury of outliving your husband. You get to talk about him all you want.'

'I never thought of that.'

'Here I am, talking,' she said undeniably. 'He had an eye for other women. I'm not saying he ever actually did anything about it, but he looked aplenty. He liked stupid women.'

'Then he made a mistake.'

She laughed herself, after a second of thinking that through. Even her laughter had a dry and rustling sound. 'Yes, he did,' she said, still amused. 'He did right well in the lumber business, left me enough to last out my lifetime without me having to go teach school or do some other fool thing I wasn't meant to do. 'Course, I had to run the business after he died. But I already knew a lot, and I learned more right smart.'

'I guess you know who owns all the land hereabouts, since you were in lumber.' It occurred to me I had a valuable source of information right here in front of me.

She looked at me, a little surprised. 'I did. I used to.'

'You know Birdie Rossiter, widow of M. T. Rossiter?'

'Audie Rossiter's daughter-in-law?'

'Right. Know where she lives?'

'Audie gave them that land. They built right off of Farm Hill Road.'

'That's right.'

'What about it?'

'There's a few acres of woods right outside the city limits sign, just south of the road.'

'Hasn't been built on yet?' Mrs Jepperson said. 'That's a surprise. Less than half a mile past the city limits, yes?'

I nodded. Then, afraid she couldn't make that out, I said, 'Yes.'

'You want to know who that belongs to?'

'Yes, ma'am. If you know.'

'You could go the county clerk's office, look it up.'

'It's easier to ask you.'

'Hmm,' She looked at me, thinking. 'I believe that land belongs to the Prader family,' she said finally. 'Least, it did up until maybe five years ago.'

'You were working up till then?' I figured Mrs Jepperson was in her late eighties.

'Didn't have nothing else to do. I'd make those men I hired ride me around. Let 'em know I was checking on what they were doing. You can believe I kept them on their toes. They need to keep on earning money for those worthless great-grandchildren of mine.' She smiled, and if I needed another clue that she didn't really think her great-grandchildren were worthless, I got it then.

'Joe C Prader owns that land?'

'Sure does, if I remember correctly. He lets his family and friends hunt on it. Joe C's even older'n me, so he may not have any friends left. He didn't have a whole lot to start with.'

Mrs Jepperson fell asleep without any warning. It was so alarming that I checked her breathing, but she was fine as far as I could tell. Laquanda came in soon afterward and checked on the old lady too. She'd dropped her daughter off at home with instructions to take some Emetrol and ginger ale and go to bed.

'She okay while I was gone?' Laquanda asked.

'Fine. We had a conversation,' I reported.

'You? And Miz Jepperson? I wish I coulda heard that,' Laquanda

said skeptically. 'This lady knows everything, and I mean everything, about Shakespeare. At least about the white folks, and a lot
of the blacks, too. But she doesn't share it, no sir. She keeps her
mouth shut.'

I shrugged and gathered my things together. If I'd asked her
about old scandals and personalities, I wouldn't have gotten the
same cooperation I'd gotten in asking about land. Land was
business. People weren't.

When I got back to my house to eat lunch, I had a message on
my answering machine from Becca. She'd thought of a couple of
bills that would come due while she was gone, and wanted to
leave checks with me to cover them. After I'd eaten a tuna sandwich, brushed my teeth, and checked my makeup, I still had thirty
minutes until my next appointment, so I decided to oblige.

There was a pickup truck backed in toward the rear door of the
apartment building. It was half-full of boxes. Separated from Lacey
or not, Jerrell was helping to empty the apartment. He wasn't
anywhere in sight, so I assumed he was up in Deedra's place.

Anthony answered Becca's door. He looked as though he'd just
stepped out of the shower and pulled on his clothes.

'Becca here?' I asked.

'Sure, come on in. Pretty day, isn't it?'

I nodded.

'She'll be right out. She's in the shower. We've been running,'
he explained.

I finally sat down to wait when a moment or two didn't
produce Becca. I thought I heard the bathroom door open at one
point, but if she'd peeked out she'd gone right back in. Becca
was a high-maintenance woman. Her brother kept up his end of
the small-talk convention with considerable determination, but
I was glad when Becca showed and we could both give up.
Anthony didn't seem to want to talk about anything but his
experiences with the prisoners he counseled. He was on the
verge of sounding obsessed, I thought.

Becca emerged from the bathroom wrapped in a robe. Even
fresh from the shower, she was groomed.

'Lily,' she said, surprised to see me. 'When did you get here?'

'About ten minutes ago,' I said.

'You should have called me,' Becca told Anthony, punching him in the shoulder. 'I could have hurried.'

I waited for her to work her way around to the reason she'd wanted me to come over. She had arranged for the bank to send me a check for the building maintenance, and she assured me the checks would keep arriving until she returned to town and rescinded the order. She'd arranged for the utilities to be paid by automatic withdrawal, and she'd included extra in my check to pay for unexpected repairs.

Then I noticed that Anthony Whitley was looking at me a little too long, making more of a response to everything I said than it was worth. Could Becca have asked me to come over because her brother had an attraction to me? Could that have been the reason for her prolonged stay in the bathroom? The idea made me very uneasy. Some women enjoy all the male attention shown them. I am not one of those women.

I gradually worked my way out of the conversation and closer to the door. I had it half-open when Becca asked me if I had the tapes from Deedra's apartment. I nodded, and kept right on inching out of the apartment.

'If you come across a tape I'm in, would you please let me know?' Becca asked.

I stared at her, thinking of the kind of home movies Deedra had made. 'Sure,' I said. 'But I've almost finished looking at them, and you weren't in a one. Remember, I had to go through them for Marlon?'

Becca looked puzzled. 'That's funny. I borrowed Deedra's camera to tape myself doing the first five *katas* so I could see what I was doing wrong. When I returned it, I'm afraid I left the tape in the camera. I wondered if it was up there.'

She looked so sincere. I was perplexed. Was she covering up in front of her brother, not wanting to say that she and Deedra had engaged in some girl-girl activities? Or was she serious about filming her *katas* so she could improve her form?

'The sheriff opened the camera and it was empty. If I come across a tape featuring you, I'll bring it over,' I told her, covering all the bases. That made a good closing line, so I shut the door and turned to leave the building. I glanced down at my watch. I would be late for my next appointment if I didn't hurry.

When I looked up, there was a large, angry man standing in my way.

Jerrell Knopp looked twice as big and three times as mean when he was angry, and he was very, very upset.

'Lily, why you stickin' your nose in somebody's business?' he asked furiously.

I shook my head. This was my day for confusion. What could I have done to Jerrell?

'You gone and told the police about that day I fought with Deedra, that day the boy wrote on her car.'

'I did no such thing,' I said promptly.

Jerrell didn't expect that. He looked at me suspiciously.

'You shittin' me, girl?' He'd certainly taken off the polite face he wore around his wife.

'I would never,' I told him.

'Someone told the police that I fought with Deedra. Would you consider that morning as fighting? I told her a few home truths that she needed to hear from someone, sure enough, but as far as fighting . . . hell, no!'

That was true enough. He'd told his stepdaughter quite bluntly that she needed to keep her pants on, and she especially needed to be discreet if she was sleeping with a man of another color. He'd also, if I was remembering correctly, told her she was nothing but a whore who didn't get paid.

'I didn't tell anyone about that morning,' I repeated.

'Then how come the police know about it? And why the hell did Lacey just pack my bag and tell me to go to a motel?' Jerrell's face, rugged and aging and handsome, crinkled in baffled anger.

The sheriff's department could only have found out from someone else who'd been in the apartment building at the time the quarrel had occurred. My money would be on Becca. Voices had been raised, and she lived right below Deedra. But I had my own idea about why Lacey had told Jerrell to move out. 'Maybe Lacey'd heard that you slept with Deedra before you started dating her,' I suggested. This was strictly a stab in the dark, but it looked like I'd hit an artery. Jerrell went white. I saw him sway as if I'd struck him. If he got any shakier, I'd have to grab hold of him so he wouldn't fall, and I didn't want to do that. I just plain didn't like Jerrell Knopp, any more than he liked me.

'Who's been saying that?' he asked me, in a choked voice that made me more worried about him than I wanted to be.

I shrugged. While he was thinking of more words, I was walking away.

I was sure he wouldn't follow me, and I was right.

There was a message on my answering machine when I returned home about five o'clock. Jump Farraclough, Claude's second-in-command, wanted me to come to the police station to sign my statement about the night I'd pulled Joe C from his house, and he wanted to ask me a few more questions. I'd forgotten all about signing the statement; too much had happened. I replayed the message, trying to read Jump's voice. Did he sound hostile? Did he sound suspicious?

I was reluctant to go to the police station. I wanted to erase the traces of Deedra Dean from my life, I wanted to think about Jack coming to live with me, I wanted to read or work out – anything, rather than answer questions. I performed a series of unnecessary little tasks to postpone answering Jump's summons.

But you don't ignore something you're told to do by the police, at least if you want to keep living and working in a small town.

Shakespeare's police station was housed in a renovated ranch-style house right off Main Street. The old police station, a squat redbrick building right in front of the jail, had been condemned. While Shakespeareans balked over raising the money to build a new station, the town police were stuck in this clumsily converted house about a block from the courthouse. This particular house had formerly been the perquisite of the jailer, since it backed onto the jail.

I came in quietly and peered over the counter to the left. The door to Claude's office was closed and the window in it was dark, so Claude hadn't yet come back to work, or maybe he'd left early. I didn't like that at all.

An officer I didn't know was on desk duty. She was a narrow-faced blonde with crooked teeth and down-slanting, tobacco-colored eyes. After taking my name, she sauntered to the partitioned rear of the big central room. Then she sauntered back, waving a hand to tell me I should come behind the counter.

Jump Farraclough was waiting in his own cubbyhole, marked out with gray carpeted panels, and the fire chief was with him. Frank Parrish looked better than he had the last time I'd seen him in his working clothes, sweating in their heat and streaked with smoke from Joe C's fire, but he didn't seem any happier. In fact, he looked downright uncomfortable.

I reminded myself there were other people in the building, while at the same time I made fun of myself for the sense of relief that gave me. Did I seriously fear harm from the assistant police chief and the fire chief? I told myself that was ridiculous.

And it might be. But I'd never feel comfortable in any kind of isolated situation with men. A glance out the window told me the sun was setting.

Jump indicated an uncomfortable straight-back chair opposite his desk. Frank Parrish was sitting to Jump's left.

'Here's your statement,' Jump said brusquely. He handed me a sheet of paper. It seemed like years since the fire; I barely remembered giving this statement. There hadn't been much to include. I'd been walking, I'd seen the person in the yard, I'd checked it out, I'd found the fire going, I'd extricated Joe C.

I read the statement carefully. You don't want to just scan something like that. You don't want to trust that it's really what you said. But this did seem to be in my words. I thought hard, trying to figure if I'd left anything out, trying to remember any other detail that might be important to the investigators.

No. This was an accurate account. I took a pen from the cup on the desk and signed it. I returned the pen and stood to leave.

'Miss Bard.'

I sighed. Somehow I'd had a feeling this wasn't going to be that easy.

'Yes.'

'Please sit down. We want to ask you a few more questions.'

'This is everything.' I pointed at the sheet of paper on the lieutenant's desk.

'Just humor us, okay? We just want to go over the same thing again, see if you remember anything new.'

I felt wary all of a sudden. I felt my hair stand up on my neck. This wasn't just routine suspicion. They should have asked me this before I signed my statement.

'Any special reason?' I asked.

'Just . . . let's us go over this thing again.'

I sat down slowly, wondering if I should be calling a lawyer.

'Now,' Jump began, stretching out his legs under the small desk, 'you say that when you went to the back door at the Prader house, you used your key to get in.'

'No. The door was unlocked.'

'Did you ever know Joe C to leave the door unlocked at night?'

'I'd never been there at night before.'

For some reason, Jump flushed, as if I'd been making fun of him.

'Right,' he said sarcastically. 'So, since the back door was unlocked, you didn't need to use your key. Did you have it with you?'

'I've never had a key to the Prader house.' I blessed all the times Joe C had so slowly come to let me in. I blessed him for his suspicion, his crotchety nature.

Jump permitted himself to look skeptical. Frank Parrish looked off into the distance as if he were willing himself to be elsewhere.

'Your employer didn't give you a key to the property? Isn't that unusual?'

'Yes.'

'But you're still sure that's what happened?'

'Ask Calla.'

'Miss Prader would know?'

'She would.'

For the first time, Jump looked uncertain. I pressed my advantage. 'You can ask any member of his family. He always makes me wait while he comes to the door as slowly as he can manage. He really enjoys that.'

Parrish turned his head to look at Jump with surprise. I began to worry even more.

'Are you planning to charge me with anything?' I asked abruptly.

'Why, no, Miss Bard.'

The fire chief hadn't said anything since I'd come in. Parrish still looked uncomfortable, still sat with arms crossed over his chest. But he didn't look as though he was going to gainsay Jump Farraclough, either.

'Just tell us everything from the beginning . . . if you don't mind.' The last phrase was obviously thrown in for padding, as Southern and soft as cotton.

'It's all in my statement.' I was getting a feeling I couldn't ignore. 'I have nothing new to add.'

'Just in case you missed something.'

'I didn't.'

'So if someone says they saw you elsewhere, doing something else, they're mistaken?'

'Yes.'

'If someone says they saw you behind the house with a gas can in your hand, instead of in front of it seeing this mysterious vanishing figure, that someone would be wrong?'

'Yes.'

'Didn't you dislike Joe C?'

'Doesn't everyone?'

'Answer the question.'

'No. I don't think I have to. I've made my statement. I'm leaving.'

And while they were still thinking about it, I did.

I would call Carlton's cousin Tabitha if they followed me and arrested me, I decided, keeping my pace steady as I headed toward the door in the police station. Tabitha, whom I'd met once or twice when she was visiting Carlton, was an attorney based in Montrose.

Gardner McClanahan, one of the night patrol officers, was fixing a cup of coffee at the big pot next to the dispatcher's desk. He nodded to me as I went by, and I nodded back. I'd seen Gardner the night I'd been walking, the night of the fire. I was sure that Farraclough knew that. Gardner's seeing me didn't prove anything either way except that I hadn't been trying to hide myself, but knowing he'd seen me and could vouch for at least that little fact made me feel better.

I crossed the floor, keeping my eyes ahead. Now I was almost at the front door. I tried to recall if Tabitha Cockroft's Montrose phone number was in my address book. I wondered with every step if a voice would come from behind, a voice telling me to stop, ordering Gardner to arrest me.

I pushed the door open, and no one grabbed me, and no one called after me. I was free. I hadn't realized how tense I'd been until I relaxed. I stood by my car fumbling with my keys, taking big gulps of air. If they'd put handcuffs on me . . . I shuddered when I thought of it.

Logically, there was no reason for the assistant police chief, or the sheriff, to suspect me of anything. I'd reported Deedra's death, and I'd saved Joe C's life. I'd called 911, twice, as a good citizen. But something in me persisted in being frightened, no matter how firmly my good sense told me Jump Farraclough had just been on a fishing expedition.

'Hey, Lily.'

My head snapped up, and my fingers clenched into fists.

'Did you hear the news?'

Gardner was standing on the front porch, blowing on his hot coffee.

'What?'

'Old Joe C Prader died.'

'He . . . died?' So that had been the reason for the

requestioning. Now that the arson was murder – despite Joe C's age, surely the fire had caused his death – the investigation would have to intensify.

'Yep, he just passed away between one breath and the next while he was in the hospital.'

As I'd anticipated, I'd lost another client. Shit.

I shook my head regretfully, and Gardner shook his right along with me. He thought we were both deprecating these terrible times we lived in, when an old man could have his house burned around him. Actually, I thought, if Joe C had lived in any other age, someone would have done him to death long before this.

Gardner strolled down the steps and stood beside me, looking around at the silent street, the night sky, anything but me.

'You know, they ain't got nothing on you,' he said, so quietly someone a foot away from me would not have heard. 'Jump just took against you, I don't know why. No one said they saw you in any backyard with any gas can. You saved that old man's life, and it ain't your fault he died of the fire. Nothing wrong with you, Lily Bard.'

I took an uneven breath. 'Thank you, Gardner,' I said. I didn't look into his face, but out into the night, as he was doing. If we looked at each other, this would be too personal. 'Thank you,' I said again, and got into my car.

On my way home, I debated over calling Claude. I hated to intrude on his time with Carrie. On the other hand, they'd be married for years, and a few minutes' conversation now might save me some unpleasant encounters with Jump Farraclough. He wouldn't have tried to scare me into saying something foolish if Claude had been aware of his purpose.

Now that Joe C was dead, his estate would be divided up. I found myself speculating that the half-burned house would just be bulldozed. It was the lot that was worth so much, not the house. The arsonist had just taken a shortcut to eliminating the factor of the house and its stubborn inhabitant. Possibly he hadn't intended Joe C to die? No, leaving a very elderly man in a burning house certainly argued that the fire-starter was absolutely indifferent to Joe C's fate.

Once home, I hovered around the telephone. Finally, I decided not to call Claude. It seemed too much like tattling on the kids to Dad, somehow; a whiney appeal.

Just as I withdrew my fingers from the receiver, the phone. rang.

Calla Prader said, 'Well, he's dead.' She sounded oddly surprised.

'I heard.'

'You're not going to believe this, but I'll miss him.'

Joe C would've cackled with delight to hear that. 'When is the funeral?' I asked after a short pause.

'He's already in Little Rock having his autopsy done,' Calla said chattily, as if Joe C had, been clever to get there that fast. 'Somehow things are slow up there, so they'll get him back tomorrow, they say. The autopsy has to be done to determine exact cause of death in case we catch whoever set the fire. They could be charged with murder if Joe C died as a result of the fire.'

'That might be hard to determine.'

'All I know is what I read in Patricia Cornwell's books,' Calla said. 'I bet she could figure it out.'

'Is there anything I can do for you?' I asked, to get Calla to come to the point.

'Oh, yes, forgot why I called you.'

For the first time, I realized that Calla had had a few drinks.

'Listen, Lily, we're planning on having the funeral Thursday at eleven.'

I wasn't going. I knew that.

'We wondered if you could help us out afterward. We're expecting the great-grandchildren from out of town, and lots of other family members, so we're having a light luncheon at the Winthrops' house after the service. They've got the biggest place of us all.'

Little touch of bitterness, there. 'What would you like me to do?'

'We're having Mrs Bladen make the food, and she'll get her nephew to deliver it to the house on Thursday morning. We'll need you to arrange the food on Beanie's silver trays, keep replenishing them, wash the dishes as they come into the kitchen, things like that.'

'I'd have to rearrange my Thursday appointments.' The Drink-waters came first on Thursday; Helen Drinkwater was not flex-ible. She'd be the only problem, I figured as I quickly ran down my Thursday list in my head. 'What kind of pay are we talking about?' Before I put myself out, it was best to know.

Calla was ready for the question. The figure was enough to compensate me for the amount of trouble I'd have to go to. And I needed the money. But I had one last question.

'The Winthrops are okay with this?' I asked, my voice carefully neutral. I hadn't set foot in the Winthrop house for five months, maybe longer.

'You working there? Honey, it was Beanie who suggested it.'

I'd been the means of sending Beanie's father-in-law to jail, and she'd taken it harder than her husband, Howell Winthrop's only son. Now, it seemed, Beanie was going to sweep the whole incident under her mental rug.

For a dazzling moment, I visualized Beanie hiring me again, her friends picking me back up, the much easier financial state I'd enjoyed when she'd been my best client.

I hated needing anything that much, anything I had to depend on another person to supply.

Ruthlessly, I clamped the cord of that happiness off and told Calla that I'd call her back when I'd seen if I could arrange my Thursday schedule.

I'd be needed from around eight o'clock (receive the food, arrange the trays, wash the breakfast dishes, maybe set up the table in the Winthrop dining room) to at least three in the after-noon, I estimated. Service at eleven, out to the cemetery, back to town . . . the mourners should arrive at the Winthrop house around twelve-fifteen. They'd finish eating about – oh, one-thirty. Then I'd have dishes to do, sweeping and vacuuming . . .

When Helen Drinkwater found that by releasing me from Thursday morning, she'd be obliging the Winthrops, she agreed to my doing her house on Wednesday morning instead of Thursday. 'Just this once,' she reminded me sharply. The travel agent I usually got to late on Thursday I should be able to do with no change, and the widower for whom I did the deep work – kitchen and bathroom, dusting and vacuuming – said Wednesday would be fine with him, maybe even better than Thursday.

I called Calla back and told her I accepted.

The prospect of money coming in made me feel so much more optimistic that I didn't think again about my problem with Jump Farraclough. When Jack called, just as I was getting ready for bed, I was able to sound positive, and he picked up some of that glow from me. He told me he was looking into getting a smaller apartment, maybe just a room in someone's house, in Little Rock, giving up his two-bedroom apartment. 'If you're still sure,' he said carefully.

'Yes.' I thought that might not be enough, so I tried again. 'It's what I really want,' I told him.

As I was falling asleep that night I had the odd thought that Joe C had already given me more happy moments in his death than he had ever given me in his life.

As if in punishment for that pleasure, that night I dreamed.

I didn't have my usual bad dreams, which are about the knife drawing designs in my flesh, about the sound of men grunting like pigs.

I dreamed about Deedra Dean.

In my dream, I was next door, in the apartment building. It was dark. I was standing in the hall downstairs, looking up. There was a glow on the landing, and I knew somehow that it came from the open door of Deedra's apartment.

I didn't want to go up those stairs, but I knew I must. In my dream, I was light on my feet, moving soundlessly and without effort. I was up those stairs almost before I knew I was moving. There was no one in the building except whatever lay before me.

I was standing in the doorway of Deedra's apartment, looking in. She was sitting on the couch, and she was lit up with blue light from the flickering television screen. She was dressed, she was intact, she could move and talk. But she was not alive.

She made sure I was meeting her eyes. Then she held out the remote control, the one I'd seen her hold many, many times, a big one that operated both television and VCR. While I looked at her fingers on the remote control, she pressed the PLAY button. I turned my head to the screen, but from where I stood I could only see an indistinct moving radiance. I looked back to Deedra. She patted the couch beside her with her free hand.

As I moved toward her, I knew that Deedra was dead and I should not get any closer to her. I knew that looking at the screen would cause something horrible to happen to me. Only dead people could watch this movie, in my dream. Live people would not be able to stand the viewing. And yet, such is the way of the subconscious; I had to walk around the coffee table and sit by Deedra. When I was close to her, I was not aware of any smell; but her skin was colorless and her eyes had no irises. She pointed again at the screen of the television. Knowing I couldn't, and yet having to, I looked at the screen.

It was so awful I woke up.

Gasping and straining for breath, I knew what I'd seen in a deathly X-ray vision. I'd seen Deedra's view. I'd seen the lid of a coffin, from the inside, and above that, the dirt of my grave.

Chapter Thirteen

I felt sullen and angry the next morning. I tried to trace the source of these unjustifiable feelings and discovered I was angry with Deedra. I didn't want to dream about her, didn't want to see her body again in any manifestation, dead visionary or live victim. Why was she bothering me so much?

Instead of going in to Body Time, I kicked and punched my own bag, hanging from its sturdy chain in the small room that was meant to be a second bedroom. The chain creaked and groaned as I worked out my own fears.

There'd been no semen in Deedra's body, no contusions or bruises in the genital area, only indications that she had sex at some time before she died. But in a way she'd been raped. I took a deep breath and pummeled the bag. Right, left, right, left. Then I kicked: one to the crotch, one to the head, with my right leg. One to the crotch, one to the head, with my left leg.

Okay. That was the reason, the source, of the burrowing misery that spread through me when I thought of Deedra. Whoever had jammed that bottle into her had treated her like a piece of offal, like flesh in a particular conformation with no personality attached, no soul involved.

'She wasn't much,' I said to the empty room. 'She wasn't much.' I back-fisted the bag. I was getting tired. It hardly moved.

An empty-headed girlish woman whose sole talents had been an encyclopedic knowledge of makeup and an ability to deal efficiently with a video camera and related items, that was the sum of Deedra Dean.

I marched back to my tiny washing area and stuffed clothes in my washer. I felt something hard through the pocket of a pair of blue jeans. Still in a rotten mood, I thrust my hand into the pocket and pulled out two objects. I unfolded my fingers and stared. Keys. I labeled all keys, instantly; where'd this come from?

I shut my eyes and thought back through the week. I opened them and peered at the keys a little more. Well, one was to the apartment building doors; Becca had given it to me yesterday. The other? Then I saw another hand dropping the key into my palm, my own hand closing around it and sliding it into my pocket. Of course! This was the key to Deedra's apartment, the one she'd given to Marlon Schuster. Becca and I had made him give it up. Becca hadn't asked for it; that was unlike her. She was so careful about details. I would take it over to her.

Then I remembered I was supposed to go to the Drinkwaters' this morning instead of the next day, and I glanced at the clock. No time to stop by Becca's now. I thrust the key into the pocket of my clean blue jeans, the ones I'd pulled on for today, and I started the washer. I had to get moving if I was going to clear all my hurdles this morning.

As if to punish me for asking for a different day, Helen had left the house a particular mess. Normally, the Drinkwaters were clean and neat. The only disorder was caused by their grandchildren, who lived a few doors down and visited two or three times a week. But today, Helen hadn't had a chance (she explained in a note) to clean up the debris from the potted plant she'd dropped. And she'd left clean sheets on the bed so I'd change them, a job she usually performed since she was very particular about how her sheets were tucked. I gritted my teeth and dug into the job, reminding myself several times how important the Drinkwaters were to my financial existence.

I gave them extra time, since I didn't want Helen to be able to say I'd skimped in any way. I drove from the Drinkwaters' home directly to Albert Tanner's smaller house in a humbler part of Shakespeare.

Albert Tanner had retired on the day he turned sixty-five, and one month later his wife had dropped dead in Wal-Mart as the Tanners stood in the checkout line. He'd hired me within three weeks, and I'd watched him mourn deeply for perhaps five months. After that, his naturally sunny nature had struggled to rise to the surface of his life. Gradually, the wastebaskets had been less full of Kleenex, and he'd commented on how his phone bills had dropped when he called his out-of-town children once a week, rather than once a day. In time, the church women had stopped crowding his refrigerator with casseroles and Albert's freezer filled up with Healthy Choice microwave dinners and fish and deer he'd killed himself. Albert's laundry basket had gotten fuller as he showered and changed more often in response to his crowded social calendar. And I'd noticed that his bed didn't always need making.

As I let myself in that morning, Albert was getting ready to take his wife's best friend to an AARP luncheon.

'How does this look, Lily?' he asked me. He held out his arms and unselfconsciously offered himself up for inspection. Albert was very shaky on color coordination, a sartorial problem he'd left to his late wife, so I was often asked to give advice.

Today he'd worn a dark green golf shirt tucked into pleated khakis and dark green socks with cordovan loafers, so it was easy to nod approval. He needed a haircut, but I figured he knew that. I was only willing to give him so much monitoring. Carry it too far, it amounted to mothering. Or wifing.

In a few minutes he was gone, and I was going about my business in my usual way. I knew Albert was actually pleased I would be here when he had a solid reason to go out; he didn't like to see me work, felt uncomfortable with me moving about his house. It made him feel like a poor host.

As I was dusting the family room, where Albert spent most of his time when he was at home, I automatically began the familiar task of boxing his videos. Albert Tanner was a polite and pleasant man, and seldom made truly big messes, but he had never put a video back in its box in the months I'd worked for him. Like Deedra, he taped a lot of daytime television to watch at night. He rented movies, and he bought movies. It wasn't too hard to figure that if Albert was home, he was in front of the television.

When I finished, I had a leftover video box. A quick scan of the entertainment center came up empty; no extra tape. I turned on the VCR, and the little symbol that lit up informed me that Albert had left the tape in the machine, something he did quite often. I pushed the EJECT button, and out it slid to be popped into its container after I checked that it had been rewound. If it hadn't been, I would have left it in the machine on the off chance Albert hadn't finished watching it.

As I opened the cabinet door in the entertainment center to shelve the movies, I had a thought so interesting that I put the movies away with no conscious effort. Maybe that was where the missing tape was – the tape of Becca that she'd left in Deedra's apartment. Maybe it was in Deedra's VCR. As far as I knew, no one had turned the machine on since Deedra had been found dead.

That would be the last tape Deedra had watched. I am not superstitious, especially not about modern machinery, but something about that thought – maybe the mere fact that I'd had it – gave me the creeps. I remembered my dream all too vividly.

What it probably was, I figured as I folded Albert Tanner's laundry with precision, was the tape of Deedra's regular Saturday-night shows. She'd had company (Marlon) for Saturday night and Sunday morning, and after she'd come home from church Sunday and after she'd talked to her mother on the phone, she'd be anxious to catch up on her television viewing. She'd play her tape. Or maybe she'd had time to watch all she'd recorded and put in the tape of Becca for some reason.

I wondered if Lacey would want me back anytime soon to finish packing Deedra's things. I could check then.

The key was in my pocket.

I could check now. I'd been so virtuous and self-protective in turning in my copy of Deedra's key to the police, but here was another key that had almost literally dropped into my hands.

Would it be wrong to use it? Lacey had given me the videos, so there should be no problem with me taking one out of the machine, presumably. The problem lay in using this set of keys to enter.

It would be better to have a witness.

I went home to eat a late-ish lunch and observed through my kitchen window that Claude was stopping in at his apartment. I watched his car turn in to the back of the building. That solved my problem, I figured; what more respectable witness could there be than the chief of police?

Claude was opening his door as I raised my hand to knock fifteen minutes later.

He jumped a little, startled, and I apologized.

'How was the trip?' I asked.

Claude smiled. 'It was great to get away for a few days, and we tried a different restaurant every meal. Unfortunately, my stomach's been upset ever since.' He grimaced as he spoke.

After we'd talked about Hot Springs and the hotel where he and Carrie had stayed, and about how much of his stuff he had left to pack up to move into her house, I explained my errand while Claude absently rubbed his stomach. He listened with half his usual attention.

'So,' Claude rumbled in his slow, deep voice, 'you think this tape is the one Becca is missing?'

'Might be. And she and her brother are leaving on vacation tomorrow, I guess after the funeral. Would you mind just going in the apartment with me to see?'

Claude pondered that, then shrugged. 'I guess that'd be okay. All you're doing is getting the one tape. If there isn't anything in the machine?'

'Then I'll shut the door behind me and take these keys to the sheriff.'

Claude glanced at his watch. 'I told Jump I'd be in sometime this afternoon, but I wasn't real specific. Let's go.'

As we went to the stairs, through the narrow glass panes on either side of the back door, I saw the Whitleys getting out of Becca's car. They'd been to the gym, I figured from their clothes. Becca's hair was braided. The brother and sister were talking earnestly.

By the time I heard them coming in the back door, we had unlocked Deedra's apartment and stepped in.

Half-dismantled, dusty and disordered, the apartment was silent and dim.

While Claude fidgeted behind me, I turned on the television and the VCR. The voice of the man on the Weather Channel sounded obscenely normal in the dreary living room, where a few boxes remained stacked against the wall and every piece of furniture subtly askew.

The tiny icon lit up. There was a tape in the machine. I pressed the REWIND button. Within a second or two, the reverse arrow went dark, and I pushed PLAY.

John Walsh, host of *America's Most Wanted*, filled the screen. I nodded to myself. This was one of the shows Deedra always taped. In his painfully earnest way, Walsh was talking about the evening's roundup of criminals wanted and criminals caught, of the things he would show us that would make us mad.

Well. I was already mad. I started to pop the cassette out and give up on my search for Becca's tape, but instead I thought I'd fast-forward through the commercials and see if there was something else on the recording.

Ads went by at top speed. Then we were back into *America's Most Wanted*, and John Walsh was standing in front of mug shots of a man and a woman. Walsh shook his head darkly and jerkily, and the film of a crime reenactment began to play. I hit another button to watch this segment.

'. . . arson,' Walsh said with finality. In the reenactment clip, an attractive brunette woman with hawklike features, who somewhat resembled one of the mug shots, rang a doorbell. An elderly man answered, and the young reenactment actress said, 'I'm from TexasTech Car Insurance. Your car was named by one of our insurers as being involved in an accident that dented his car. Could you tell me about that?'

The elderly man, looking confused, gestured the young woman into his living room. He had a nice home, big and formal.

The actor playing the older man began to protest that his car hadn't been involved in any accident, and when the young woman asked him if she could have an associate examine the car, he readily handed over his keys.

He was a fool, I thought.

So was I.

On the screen, the young woman tossed the keys out to her 'associate', a large, blond young man with impressive shoulders. He strode off, presumably in the direction of the homeowner's garage, but the camera stayed inside the house while the owner continued expostulating with the woman. To show us how shifty this woman was, the camera dwelled on her eyes flicking around the attractive room while the homeowner rattled on. She drifted closer and closer, and when the man announced his intention of calling his own insurance agent, the young brunette dropped into a classic fighting stance, drew back her left fist into the chamber position, and struck the man in the spot where the bottom ribs come together. He stared at her, stunned, for a second or two before collapsing to the floor.

I was barely conscious of a shuffling of feet behind me.

'Excuse me, Lily,' Claude said abruptly. 'I'll be in the bathroom.'

I didn't respond. I was too shocked.

Now the camera showed the man lying limp. He was probably meant to be dead.

'While their victim lay on his own living-room floor, breathing his last, Sherry Crumpler and David Messinger systematically looted his house. They didn't leave until they had it all: money, jewelry, and car. They even took Harvey Jenkins's rare-coin collection.'

Show the mug shots again.

As John Walsh went on to detail the couple's string of similar crimes, and urged viewers to bring these two murderers to justice, their heads filled the screen once more.

I peered at the face of the woman. I paused the picture. I put my hands on either side of her face. In my imagination I painted all the colors in brightly.

'I thought I heard someone up here,' Becca Whitley said from the doorway.

I hit the OFF button immediately. 'Yeah, Lacey asked me to work up here some more. I shouldn't have been watching television,' I said, trying to smile.

'Watching television? You? On the job? I don't believe it for a second,' Becca said blithely. 'I'll bet you found another tape.'

She turned and spoke into the hall behind her. 'Honey, she knows.'

Her brother came in. He was the other mug shot. He was much more recognizable.

'Where is the real Becca Whitley?' I asked, glad they couldn't hear how loudly my heart was pounding. My knees bent slightly, and I shifted my feet for better balance. 'And the real Anthony Whitley?'

'Anthony got into a little trouble in Mexico,' David Messinger said. 'Becca is a pile of bones in some gulch in Texas hill country.'

'Why did you do this?' I asked. I waved my hand to indicate the apartment building. 'This isn't riches.'

'It just dropped from heaven,' the woman I still thought of as Becca said. 'David had been romancing Becca for months when he had to leave the country for a month or two. Things were getting too hot for us to stay together. David talked Anthony into going with him. Becca was a real straight arrow, but Anthony was a bad boy. You ever wonder why the apartment building was left to just Becca? Because Anthony was in jail. In fact, that's where Dave and Anthony met. While they were down in Me-hee-co, the guys went boating together, and when the boat came back in, why, there was only one man on it. And that man had all Anthony's papers.' Becca smiled at me, her hard, bright smile that I'd grown nearly fond of. 'I'd remade myself, as you can see. The best wig I could buy, and a lot of makeup. While I was hanging around with Becca in Dallas, being her best friend since I was gonna be her sister-in-law, she thought, her uncle died here in Shakespeare. She'd told me about him, about his apartment building and his little pile of cash. And she told me about the great-grandfather,

too. I needed a place to be, a quiet place where no one would
bother me. So after she'd quit her job and given up her apartment
to move here, Becca and I took a little drive together.'

Her smile was genuine and bright.

Sherry Crumpler and David Messinger were between me and
the only door, and as I watched, David shut the door behind him.
He was really big. She was really good at combat.

They were wary.

'What about the keys, did you take the keys?' How long would
Claude's stomach be upset?

'I knew I'd have to give mine up to the sheriff, at least temporarily, and I couldn't be sure Deedra hadn't left some kind of
message. So I stole the whole purse, and I took her extra key
from the umbrella in the car stall. I came up here right when I got
back from the woods, and took the *TV Guide*, because it was
marked. But people started coming back from the weekend then,
and I had to stay in my apartment. After that, I had a chance to
come up here twice trying to find any trace she'd left about us,
but I decided she hadn't left anything. Until I saw you carry out
all the tapes. Then I realized she'd probably taped the show. I was
watching AMW that night. You can imagine how I felt. But I
was sure no one would recognize me. Then I saw Deedra on the
stairs the next morning when she left for church. I was shocked
when I could tell she knew who I was.'

'It's incredible how much difference the makeup makes,' I said,
as they split up and began to approach me from both sides.

'You know, I hate the stuff,' Sherry said frankly. 'And I hate this
damn wig. At least I could take it off to sleep, but during the day I
have to wear it every minute. That time you dropped in and I was
in the shower – if I hadn't trained myself to put it on perfectly the
second I could, I would've strolled out of the bathroom in my
bare head. But I've got discipline, and I had my hair on and my
makeup in place.'

She'd gradually been easing into, a fighting position, her side
turned toward me, her knees bent, her fists held ready. Now she
struck.

But I wasn't there.

I'd stepped to the side and kicked her right knee.

She made a gagging noise, but she recovered and regained her stance. David decided to slip up behind me and circle me with his arms from behind, and I threw my head back and caught him on the nose. He staggered back and Sherry attacked again. This time her strike hit me in the ribs, and through the pain I grabbed her fist and twisted.

I was just prolonging the inevitable, but I had my pride.

I lost it when David clouted me upside my head.

'Claude!' I yelled through the ringing in my ears. 'Claude!'

Becca – Sherry – was in the act of starting her kick when Claude came out of the hall bathroom with his gun drawn. She had her back to him, but David saw him, and I was at least vaguely aware Claude was there as I shook my head to clear it. Claude managed to knock Sherry off target by shoving her shoulder, and she sprawled onto Deedra's couch while Claude kept the gun steady on David. I scrambled, minus any dignity, from between Claude and the man and woman, taking care to keep low so Claude could shoot them if he wanted to.

He spoke into his shoulder radio, got back a lot of surprise, and repeated his orders in the calm, steady, *Claude* way that kept him in office.

'I can't even leave the room, much less the town, you get in trouble,' he said to me when he figured I'd gotten my breath back. 'You want to tell me what this is all about?'

'She killed Deedra,' I said. I opened the door David Messinger had closed, so the cops could come in. I could hear sirens coming nearer.

'Becca killed Deedra? Why?'

'She's not Becca. Deedra found that out.'

The woman didn't say anything. She just glared and clutched her knee. I hoped I'd put it out on her. I hoped she was in tremendous pain. David had blood streaming from his nose, but Claude wouldn't let him reach for a handkerchief. David wasn't talking, either. Far too experienced a criminal for that.

'Well, while we chat with them about Deedra, we can book them for assault on you,' Claude said thoughtfully.

'You need to watch this video.' I gestured toward the VCR. 'After your backup arrives,' I added hastily, because I wanted Claude to stay focused on the moment.

He smiled in a grim, unamused kind of way. 'Ain't a nasty video, is it?' he asked, his gaze never leaving David.

And Becca, Sherry, whatever-her-name-was launched herself from the couch. She would've flown right over the spot close to the door where I crouched if I hadn't caught desperate hold of her calf. My hands weren't large enough to get a good grip, but I slowed her down and managed to get a better one on her left ankle, the ankle of her uninjured leg. She went down half on top of me and I gathered myself and rolled. I put my forearm across her throat and she began gagging, her hands clawing at my shoulders and head. I kept my eyes shut and my head tucked, as much as was possible, and I pinned her legs with my own. I knew I had to do this myself; Claude couldn't take the gun off the bigger man.

'I'll kill you!' she said weakly.

I didn't believe she would. I believed she wanted to.

But she had tricks left. She concentrated her strength: Instead of fighting like a windmill, she fought like a trained fighter. She gripped my ears and twisted, trying to force me to roll over. I was wearing out, and wasn't as desperate as this woman, and I was going to go over any second. But I summoned the last bit of resolve I had and fisted my left hand, struggling to draw it back as far as possible. She was so intent on getting on top that she never saw what I meant to do.

I hit her in the head as hard as I could.

She made a funny noise, her grip relaxed, and her eyes went blank.

Then two men lifted me off.

It took a minute or two for things to straighten out about who the bad woman was and who the good woman was. Once Jump Farraclough and Tiny Dalton realized I was on the side of law and order (though it took some telling to convince them) they abandoned their intention of handcuffing me and instead cuffed the groggy Becca. Sherry. Whoever, Her wig had gone askew in the struggle, even as securely pinned as she'd had it. Underneath, her hair (dyed the same blond in case it happened to show, I assumed) was about an inch long. I wondered if her outstanding chest was her own, and what she would look like when the makeup was cleaned from her face; all the outlining, highlights, shadowing, and bright colors had recontoured her features until only an expert in makeup could tell what she really looked like. An expert like Deedra Dean. Deedra had seen beyond the blue contacts, the push-up bra, the paint, the wig.

'Why didn't Deedra tell someone?' Claude asked me later that day. We were sitting in his office at the police department.

'Maybe she just couldn't believe the evidence of her own eyes. She must have been still unsure about what she'd seen; maybe she wanted to look at Sherry Crumpler again, real carefully, to make absolutely sure that what she suspected was true.'

'Sherry is real clever, and she doesn't seem to have any problem with killing people if half of what she told you pans out,' Claude said. 'I guess she figured she better kill Deedra before her partner came into town, because David is much more like he looked on TV than Sherry is. Seeing David would have clinched all Deedra's suspicions.'

'Maybe they'll tell on each other,' I said, my voice as tired as the rest of me was.

'Oh, they already are. They each got a lawyer from the phone book, both of whom want to make a name for themselves so they can be in the update on television. I expect to hear from *America's Most Wanted* tomorrow at the latest.'

'Can you tell me what they're saying?' I wanted to be as far away from the jail and the police station and Claude as it was possible to get when the media showed up.

'David's saying they would've been out of here a week ago if Joe C had died when he was supposed to. She set the fire, of course – Sherry did. She wanted to get that $70,000 inheritance. Then she figured if David showed up claiming to be her brother, instead of her boyfriend, he'd get another share of the money. Once she'd killed Deedra, she knew she better accelerate their plan to get the money and then she better get out of town. She'd planned, he says, to sell the apartment building once they were safely away, hire someone to handle the legal work. Just send her the paper for her signature. Then she could vanish. No one would think much of it.'

I examined this idea for holes, finding only a few. 'She could forge the real Becca's signature?'

'Just beautiful, apparently.'

'And since no one from here, including family, had seen Becca or Anthony since they were little, no one ever imagined that she wasn't Becca? It never crossed anyone's mind to question her?'

'Seems to me,' Claude rumbled, 'that the real Becca must have been a lonely sort of girl. I guess Sherry, in disguise, matched a superficial description of the real Becca; blond, athletic, blue-eyed. But David says the original Becca had some emotional problems, had real trouble making friends. I guess she thought David was a godsend, and when his "sister" was willing to pal around with her, and David was already buddies with Becca's bad-ass brother, she thought her lonely days were over.'

'Why did David pick a fictional job as a prison counselor?'

'Well, he'd know all about it, wouldn't he? If you'd been able to concentrate on the AMW story, you would've heard that David's been in and out of prison all his life. For that matter, Sherry too.'

'She sure had a lot of nerve, living here as Becca for so long.'

'It took nerve, but it was great cover. And if she could wait it out until David felt it was safe to join her, they stood to make a bunch of money – a combined $140,000 from the sale of Joe C's lot, plus what they got eventually from the sale of the apartment building. Until the story on television, which broke only days before David was due to arrive. He says she should've gotten in touch with him and made him stay away; she says she tried but he wasn't at the prearranged phone spot. So he came. On the whole,

I think they felt pretty safe, pretty anonymous. Sherry's attempt to burn Joe C's house was only partly successful, but he ended up dying, and they thought it'd look funny if they left town before the funeral. But then you interfered.'

'I just wanted to know what had happened to Deedra.'

'According to David . . . do you really want to hear this, Lily? It's strictly what David says Sherry told him.'

I nodded. I looked down at my hands so I wouldn't have to watch his face.

'Sherry drew a gun on Deedra that Sunday afternoon, a couple of hours after Deedra came home from church and encountered her on the stairs. Sherry'd done a lot of planning in those two hours, when she saw Deedra wasn't going to call the police right away. The apartment building was empty, and though she couldn't be sure someone wouldn't show up any moment, it was a risk she had to take. She had to get Deedra away from the building; if Deedra died in her apartment, the investigation might focus more on the only person, around that afternoon – the landlady. Sherry got Deedra to drive out to the trail off Farm Hill Road, which Sherry knew would put them right out of the city limits, so Marta Schuster would be heading the investigation. That would complicate things real nice, since Marlon had been hanging around Deedra so much lately. Once down the track in the woods, Sherry made her stop the car and get out and strip.'

I could feel my face twisting. 'Made her throw her clothes.'

'Yep.' Claude was silent for a long time. I knew Claude was trying, and failing, as I was, to imagine how Deedra must have felt. 'Then, Sherry had made Deedra strip, she backed her up against the car, and when Deedra was in place, she struck her. One blow to the solar plexus. With all she had.'

I drew in a long, slow breath. I let it out.

'While Deedra was dying, Sherry forced in the bottle and positioned her in the car. It took a lot of doing, but Sherry's a martial-arts expert and a right strong woman. As you know.'

I breathed in. I breathed out. 'Then what?'

'Then . . . she walked home.'

After all the talk about switching cars or having an accomplice, it was that simple. She walked home. If she'd stuck to the edge of the woods, she would've been all the way in town before she had to show herself. In fact . . . I tried to look at Shakespeare in my head, from an aerial view. By some careful planning, she could've come out in the fields beyond Winthrop Sporting Goods, and then it would be a stroll back to the apartments.

'Thanks to you,' Claude continued after a long pause, 'my wife is sitting in the house by herself, wondering when her brand-new husband is going to make it home.'

I managed a smile. 'Thanks to me, you're going to have your fifteen minutes of fame,' I reminded him. 'You caught two of "America's Most Wanted".'

'Because I had the trots,' he said, shaking his head ruefully.

'Maybe you could leave that part out.'

'I'd like to figure out a way.'

'Let's say you were suspicious when we heard footsteps coming up the stairs and you concealed yourself in the bathroom so you could take them by surprise.'

'That sounds better than telling them I ate some bad fish.'

'True.'

'Think that's the line to take.'

'You got it.'

'Now what, for you, Lily?'

'I have to work tomorrow.' I sighed heavily, and heaved myself out of the extra chair in Claude's office. 'I have to receive food and serve at Joe C's funeral.'

'No, I mean . . . longer-term.'

I was surprised. Claude had never asked me a question about my life.

'You know Jack is the one.' I said it plainly and quietly.

'I know. He's a lucky guy.'

'Well, I just see that going on.'

'Think you two'll get married?'

'Maybe.'

Claude brightened. 'I never would have thought it. I'm glad for you, Lily.'

I wondered briefly why that idea cheered Claude. Well, they say newlyweds want everyone else to get married.

' 'Cause my wife' – and he said that phrase so proudly – 'called him when she found out you were involved in this showdown, and he's sitting outside in the waiting room.'

'Carrie . . . called Jack?'

'She sure did. Just when you think she's a shy woman, she pulls something like that on you.'

'He's here,' I said, relieved beyond measure, and happier than I'd been in days.

'If you just open the door,' Claude said astringently, 'I wouldn't have to be telling you, you could see for yourself.'

And I did.

Later that night, when the only light in my house was moonlight, I sat up in bed. Next to me, Jack lay only on his side, his hair tangling around him and his chest moving silently with his breath. His face, asleep, was peaceful and relaxed, but remote. Unknowable. I could only know the man he tried to be when he was awake. Who knew where his dreams took him, how far into his mind and heart? Farther than I could ever penetrate.

I stood, parted my curtains, and looked out the window. The lights in the upstairs apartment that had been Deedra's were still on; I guess the police had left them that way. It was a strange feeling, seeing those lights on again. On occasions I'd noticed them before, I'd always had a contemptuous reaction; *she's entertaining again*, I'd thought, and reviewed once again the host of risks she'd run in her promiscuity.

But it was not her weakness that had caused her death; it was one of her strengths that had killed her.

I wondered what that meant, what lesson could be drawn from Deedra's death. I considered for a moment, but it was either meaningless, or its moral beyond me. I remembered Deedra as she'd appeared in my dream, the remote control in her hand. Looking at a film of the inside of her coffin.

I let the curtains fall together and turned back to the bed.

Shakespeare's Counselor

This book is dedicated to the memory of
Elizabeth Daniels Squire,
who was many things – all of them good.

Chapter One

I connected with a hard blow to the nose, rolled on top of him, gripped his neck, and started to squeeze. After the pain, the unfathomable humiliation, this rage was completely pure and good. His hands gripped my wrists, struggled to pull my fingers away. He was making noises, hoarse and pleading, and I gradually realized he was saying my name.

That wasn't part of the memory.

And I wasn't back in that shack in the cotton fields. I was on a firm wide bed, not a sagging cot.

'Lily! Stop!' The grip on my wrists increased.

I wasn't in the right place – or rather, the wrong place.

'Lily!'

This wasn't the right man . . . the wrong man.

I released my grip and scrambled off the bed, backing into a corner of the bedroom. My breath was coming in ragged pants, and my heart thudded way too close to my ears.

A light came on, blinding me for the moment. When I got used to the radiance, I realized with agonizing slowness that I was looking at Jack. Jack Leeds. Jack had blood streaming from his nose and red marks on his neck.

I'd done that to him.

I'd done my best to kill the man I loved.

'I know you don't want to do this, but maybe it'll help,' Jack was telling me, his voice altered by the swelling of his nose and throat.

I tried very hard not to look sullen. I didn't want to go to any damn therapy group. I didn't like to talk about myself, and wasn't that what therapy was for? On the other hand, and this was the decisive hand, I didn't want to hit Jack again, either.

For one thing, hitting was a terrible insult to the one you loved.

For another thing, eventually Jack would hit me back. Considering how strong he was, that was not an unimportant factor.

So, later that morning, after Jack left to drive to Little Rock to talk to a client, I called the number on the flyer we'd seen at the grocery store. Printed on bright green paper, it had caught Jack's eye while I was buying stamps at the office booth at the front of the store.

It read:

HAVE YOU BEEN SEXUALLY ASSAULTED?

ARE YOU FEELING ALONE?

CALL TODAY 237-7777

ATTEND OUR THERAPY GROUP

ALONE NO MORE!

'Hartsfield County Health Center,' said a woman's voice.

I cleared my throat. 'I'd like to find out about the therapy group for rape survivors,' I said, in as level a voice as I could manage.

'Of course,' said the woman, her voice scrupulously neutral and so consciously nonjudgmental it made my teeth hurt. 'The group meets Tuesday nights at eight, here at the center. You don't have to give me your name at this time. Just come in the end door, you know, the door that opens on the staff parking lot? You can park there, too.'

'All right,' I said. I hesitated, then asked a crucial question. 'How much is it?'

'We got a grant to do this,' she said. 'It's free.'

My tax dollars at work. Somehow that made me feel better.

'Can I tell Tamsin you'll be coming?' the woman asked. Definitely a local; I could tell by the number of syllables in 'tell.'

'Let me think about it,' I told her, suddenly frightened of taking a step that would undoubtedly add to my pain.

*

Carol Althaus lived in the middle of chaos. I had dropped all but three of my customers, and I wished Carol had been one of them, but I'd had one of my rare moments of pity and kept her on. I was only cleaning Carol, the Winthrops, and the Drinkwaters, and Monday was the day I did all three. I went back to the Winthrops on Thursday, and I remained open for the odd errand or special cleaning job other days, but I was also working for Jack, so my schedule was complicated.

Carol's chaos was of her own making, the way I saw it, but it was still chaos, and I like order.

Carol's life had gone out of control when she'd married Jay Althaus, a divorced salesman with two sons. To Jay's credit, he had custody of his sons. To Jay's debit, he was on the road all the time, and though he may have loved Carol, who was anemically attractive, religious, and stupid, he also needed a live-in baby-sitter. So he married Carol, and despite all their previous experiences with the two boys, they had their own babies, two girls. I'd begun working for Carol when she was pregnant with the second girl, throwing up intermittently every day and sitting limply in a recliner the rest of the time. I'd kept all of the children for a day and a half, only once, when Jay had had a car wreck out of town.

Probably these children were not demonic. Possibly, they were quite typical. But collectively, they were hell.

And hard on a house, too.

Carol needed me to come at least twice a week, for maybe six hours at a stretch. She could afford four hours a week, just barely. I gave Carol Althaus the best value for her money she would find anywhere.

During the school year, it was nearly possible for Carol to cope. Heather and Dawn were still at home, only five and three years old, but the boys (Cody and Tyler) were in school. Summers were another kettle of fish.

It was late June, so the kids had all been home for about three weeks. Carol had enrolled them in four Bible schools. The First Baptists and the Central Methodists had already completed their summer programs, and the house was even more littered with paper fish and bread glued to paper plates, sheep made from cotton balls and Popsicle sticks, and lopsided drawings of fishermen pulling in nets filled with people. Shakespeare Combined Church (a fundamentalist coalition) and the joint Episcopalian/ Catholic Bible schools were yet to come.

I entered with my own key to find Carol standing in the middle of the kitchen, trying to get the snarls out of Dawn's long curls. The little girl was wailing. She had on a nightgown with Winnie the Pooh on the front. She was wearing toy plastic high heels and she'd gotten into her mother's makeup.

I surveyed the kitchen and began to gather dishes. When I reentered the kitchen a minute later, laden with dirty glasses and two plates that had been on the floor in the den, Carol was still standing in the middle of the floor, a quizzical expression on her face.

'Good morning, Lily,' she said, in a pointed way.

'Hello, Carol.'

'Is something wrong?'

'No.' Why tell Carol? Would she be reassured about my well-being if I told her I'd tried to kill Jack the night before?

'You could say hello when you come in,' Carol said, that little smile still playing across her face. Dawn looked up at me with as much fascination as if I'd been a cobra. Her hair was still a mess. I could solve that with a pair of scissors and a brush in about five minutes, and I found the idea very tempting.

'I'm sorry, I was thinking of other things,' I told Carol politely. 'Was there anything special you needed done today?'

Carol shook her head, that faint smile still on her face. 'Just the usual magic,' she said wryly, and bent to Dawn's head again. As she worked the brush through the little girl's thick hair, the oldest boy dashed into the kitchen in his swimming trunks.

'Mom, can I go swimming?' Carol's fair complexion and brown hair had been passed on to both the girls, but the boys favored, I supposed, their own mother: they were both freckle-faced and redheaded.

'Where?' Carol asked, using a yellow elastic band to pull Dawn's hair up into a ponytail.

'Tommy Sutton's. I was invited,' Cody assured her. 'I can walk there by myself, remember?' Cody was ten and Carol had given him a range of streets he could take by himself.

'Okay. Be back in two hours.'

Tyler erupted into the kitchen roaring with rage. 'That's not fair! I want to go swimming!'

'Weren't invited,' Cody sneered. 'I was.'

'I know Tommy's brother! I could go!'

As Carol laid down the law I loaded the dishwasher and cleaned the kitchen counters. Tyler retreated to his room with a lot of door slamming and fuming. Dawn trotted off to play with her Duplos, and Carol left the room in such a hurry I wondered if she was ill. Heather appeared at my elbow to watch my every move.

I am not much of a kid person. I don't like, or dislike, all children. I take it on an individual basis, as I do with adults. I very nearly liked Heather Althaus. She would be old enough for kindergarten in the fall, she had short, easy-to-deal-with hair since a drastic self-barbering job that had driven Carol to tears, and she tried to take care of herself. Heather eyed me solemnly, said 'Hey, Miss Lily,' and extricated a frozen waffle from the side-by-side. After popping it in the toaster, Heather got her own plate, fork, and knife and set them on the counter. Heather had on lime green shorts and a kingfisher blue shirt, not a happy combination, but she'd gotten dressed herself and I could respect that. In acknowledgment, I poured a glass of orange juice for her and set it on the table. Tyler and Dawn trotted through on their way out to the fenced-in backyard.

For a comfortable time, Heather and I shared the kitchen silently. As she ate her waffle, Heather raised her feet one at a time when I swept, and moved her own chair when I mopped.

When there was only a puddle of syrup on the plate, Heather said, 'My mama's gonna have a baby. She says God will give us a little brother or a sister. She says we don't get to pick.'

I leaned on my mop for a moment and considered this news. It

explained the unpleasant noises coming from the bathroom. I
could not think of one single thing to say, so I nodded. Heather
wriggled off the chair and ran to the switch to turn on the
overhead fan to dry the floor quickly, as I always did.

'It's true the baby won't come for a long time?' the little girl
asked me.

'That's true,' I said.

'Tyler says Mama's tummy will get real big like a watermelon.'

'That's true, too.'

'Will they have to cut her open with a knife, like Daddy does
the watermelon?'

'No.' I hoped I wasn't lying. 'She won't pop, either,' I added,
just to cover another anxiety.

'How will the baby get out?'

'Moms like to explain that in their own way,' I said, after I'd
thought a little. I would rather have answered her matter-of-factly,
but I didn't want to usurp Carol's role.

Through the sliding glass doors to the backyard (doors that
were perpetually decorated with handprints) I could see that
Dawn had carried her Duplos into the sandbox. They'd have to
be washed off. Tyler was firing the soft projectiles of some Nerf
weapon in the general direction of a discarded plastic soda bottle
he'd filled with water. The two seemed to be fine, and I couldn't
see any danger actually lurking. I reminded myself to check again
in five minutes, since Carol was definitely indisposed.

With Heather at my heels, I went to the room she shared with
her sister and began to change the sheets. I figured that any
second, Heather would exhaust her attention span and go find
something else to do. But instead, Heather sat on a child-sized
Fisher Price chair and observed me with close attention.

'You don't *look* crazy,' she told me.

I stopped pulling the flat sheet straight and glanced over my
shoulder at the little girl.

'I'm not,' I said, my voice flat and final.

It would be hard to pin down exactly why this hurt me, but it did. What a senseless thing to waste emotion on, the repetition by a child of something she'd apparently heard adults say.

'So why do you walk by yourself at night? Isn't that a scary thing to do? Only ghosts and monsters are out at night.'

My first response was that I myself was scarier than any ghost or monster. But that would hardly be reassuring to a little girl, and already other ideas were flickering through my head.

'I'm not afraid at night,' I said, which was close to the truth. I was not any more afraid at night than I was in the daytime, for sure.

'So you do it to show them you're not afraid?' Heather asked.

The same wrenching pain filled me that I'd felt when I saw Jack's bloody nose. I straightened, dirty sheets in a bundle in my arms, and looked down at the little girl for a long moment.

'Yes,' I said. 'That's exactly why I do it.'

I knew then and there that I would be at the therapy session the next night. It was time.

For now, I taught Heather how to make hospital folds.

Chapter Two

I slid through the designated door the next night as though I'd come to steal some help, not to get it for free.

There were four cars in the parking lot, which was only partially visible from the street. I recognized two of them.

The side door we were to use was a heavy metal door. It slid shut behind me with a heavy thud, and I walked toward the only two rooms that were well lit. All the other doors up and down the corridor were shut, and I was willing to bet they were probably locked as well.

A woman appeared in the first open doorway and called, 'Come on in! We're ready to get started!' As I got closer I could see she was as dark as I was blond, she was as soft as I am hard, and I was to find she talked twice as much as I'd ever thought about doing. 'I'm Tamsin Lynd,' she said, extending her hand.

'Lily Bard,' I said, taking the hand and giving it a good shake.

She winced. 'Lily? . . .'

'Bard,' I supplied, resigned to what was to come.

Her eyes got round behind their glasses, which were wire framed and small. Tamsin Lynd clearly recognized my name, which was a famous one if you read a lot of true crime.

'Before you go in the therapy room, Lily, let me tell you the rules.' She stepped back and gestured, and I went into what was clearly her office. The desk and its chair were arranged facing the door, and there were books and papers everywhere. The room was pretty small, and there wasn't space for much after the desk and chair and two bookcases and a filing cabinet. The wall behind the desk was covered with what looked like carpeting, dark gray with pink flecks to match the carpet on the floor. I decided it had been designed for use as a bulletin board of sorts. Tamsin Lynd had fixed newspaper and magazine clippings to it with pushpins, and the effect was at least a little cheerful. The therapist didn't invite me to sit, but stood right in front of me examining me closely. I wondered if she imagined herself a mind reader.

I waited. When she saw I wasn't going to speak, Tamsin began, 'Every woman in this group has been through a lot, and this therapy group is designed to help each and every one get used to being in social situations and work situations and alone situations, without being overwhelmed with fear. So what we say here is confidential, and we have to have your word that the stories you hear in this room stop in your head. That's the most important rule. Do you agree to this?'

I nodded. I sometimes felt the whole world had heard my story. But if I'd had a chance to prevent it, not a soul would've known.

'I've never had a group like this here in Shakespeare, but I've run them before. Women start coming to this group when they can stand talking about what happened to them – or when they can't stand their lives as they are. Women leave the group when they feel better about themselves. You can come as long as I run it, if you need to. Now, let's go to the therapy room and you can meet the others.'

But before we could move, the phone rang.

Tamsin Lynd's reaction was extraordinary. She jerked and turned to face her desk. Her hand shot out and rested on top of the receiver. When it rang again, her fingers tightened around the phone, but she still didn't lift it. I decided it would be tactful to step around the desk and look at the clippings on the wall. Predictably, most were about rape, stalking, and the workings of the court system. Some were about brave women. The counselor's graduate and postgraduate degrees were framed and displayed, and I was duly impressed.

The manifestly intelligent Tamsin had picked up the phone and said, 'Hello?' as though she was scared to death.

The next thing I knew, she'd gasped and sunk down into the client chair in front of the desk. I abandoned my attempt to look like I wasn't there.

'Stop this,' the therapist hissed into the phone. 'You have to stop this! No, I won't listen!' And she smashed the receiver into its cradle as though she was bashing in someone's head. Tamsin took several deep breaths, almost sobbing. Then she was enough under control to speak to me.

'If you'll go on next door,' she said, in a voice creditably even, 'I'll be there in a minute. I just need to collect a few things.'

Like her wits and her composure. I hesitated, about to offer help, then realizing that was ludicrous under the circumstances. I eased out from behind Tamsin's desk and out the door, took two steps to the left, and went into another.

The room next door was probably a lot of things besides the therapy room. There was a large institutional table, surrounded by the usual butt-numbing institutional chairs. The room was windowless and had a couple of insipid landscapes on the walls as a gesture toward decoration. There were women already waiting, some with canned drinks and notepads in front of them.

My almost-friend Janet Shook was there, and a woman whose face was familiar in an unpleasant way. For a moment, I had to think of her name, and then I realized the formally dressed, fortyish big-haired woman was Sandy McCorkindale, wife of the minister of Shakespeare Combined Church, known locally as SCC. Sandy and I had clashed a couple of times when I'd been hired by the church to serve refreshments at board meetings of the SCC preschool, and we'd had a difference of opinion at the Ladies' Luncheon, an annual church wingding.

Sandy was about as pleased to see me as I was to see her. On the other hand, Janet smiled broadly. Janet, in her midtwenties, was as fit as I was, which is pretty damn muscular. She has dark brown hair that swings forward to touch her cheeks, and bangs that have a tendency to get in her eyes. Janet and I sometimes exercise together, and we are members of the same karate class. I sat down by her and we said hello to each other, and then Tamsin bustled into the room, a clipboard and a bunch of papers clutched to her big bouncy chest. She had recovered quite well, to my eyes.

'Ladies, have you all met each other?'

'All but the latest entry,' drawled one of the women across the table.

She was one of three women I didn't recall having met before. Tamsin performed the honors.

'This is Carla, and this is Melanie.' Tamsin indicated the woman who'd spoken up, a short, thin incredibly wrinkled woman with a smoker's cough. The younger woman beside her, Melanie, was a plump blonde with sharp eyes and an angry cast to her features. The other woman, introduced to me as Firella, was the only African American in the group. She had a haircut that made the top of her head look like the top of a battery, and she wore very serious glasses. She was wearing an African-print sleeveless dress, which looked loose and comfortable.

'Ladies, this is Lily,' Tamsin said with a flourish, completing the introductions.

I got as comfortable as the chair would permit, and crossed my arms over my chest, waiting to see what would happen. Tamsin seemed to be counting us. She looked out the door and down the hall as if she expected someone else to come, frowned, and said, 'All right, let's get started. Everyone got coffee, or whatever you wanted to drink? Okay, good job!' Tamsin Lynd took a deep breath. 'Some of you just got raped. Some of you got raped years ago. Sometimes, people just need to know others have been through the same thing. So would each one of you tell us a little about what has happened to you?'

I cringed inside, wishing very strongly that I could evaporate and wake up at my little house, not much over a mile from here.

Somehow I knew Sandy McCorkindale would be the first to speak, and I was right.

'Ladies,' she began, her voice almost as professionally warm and welcoming as her husband's was from the pulpit, 'I'm Sandy McCorkindale, and my husband is the pastor of Shakespeare Combined Church.'

We all nodded. Everyone knew that church.

'Well, I was hurt a long, long time ago,' Sandy said with a social smile. In a galaxy far, far, away? 'When I had just started college.'

We waited, but Sandy didn't say anything else. She kept up the smile. Tamsin didn't act as though she was going to demand Sandy be any more forthcoming. Instead, she turned to Janet, who was sitting next to her.

'Lily and I are workout buddies,' Janet told Tamsin.

'Oh, really? That's great!' Tamsin beamed.

'She knows I got raped, but not anything else,' Janet said slowly. She looked at me out of the corner of her eye. She appeared to be concerned about the effect her story would have on me. Ridiculous. 'I was attacked about three years ago, while I was on a date with a guy I'd known my whole life. We went out parking in the fields, you know how kids do. All of a sudden, he just wouldn't stop. He just . . . I never told the police. He said he'd tell them I was willing, and I didn't have a mark on me. So I never prosecuted.'

'Next, ah, Carla?'

'I was shooting pool at Velvet Tables,' she said hoarsely. I estimated she was approaching fifty, and the years had been hard. 'I was winning some money, too. I guess one of them good ole boys didn't like me beating the pants off of 'em, put something in my drink. Next thing I know, I'm in my car buck naked without a dime, my keys stuck up my privates. They'd had sex with me while I was out. I know all of 'em.'

'Did you report?' Tamsin asked.

'Nope, I know where they live,' Carla said.

There was a long silence while we chewed that over. 'That feeling, the need for vengeance, is something we'll talk about later,' Tamsin said finally. 'Melanie, would you tell us what happened to you?'

I decided that Tamsin didn't know Melanie that well, just from the timbre of her voice.

'I'm new to anything like this, so please just bear with me.' Melanie gave a nervous and inappropriate giggle that may have agreed with the plump cheeks and pink coloring, but clashed with the anger in her dark eyes. Melanie was even younger than Janet, I figured.

'Why are you here, Melanie?' Tamsin was in full therapist mode now, sitting with her clothes arranged over her round form in the most advantageous way. She crossed her ankles, covered with thick beige stockings, and tried not to fiddle with the pencil in her clipboard.

'You mean, what incident?' Melanie asked.

'Yes,' Tamsin said patiently.

'Well, my brother-in-law done raped me, that's why! He come to my trailer all liquored up, and he busted in my door, and then he was on me. I didn't have time to get my .357 Magnum, I didn't have time to call the cops. It was so fast you wouldn't believe it.'

'Did the police arrest him?'

'Sure they did. I wouldn't leave the police station until he was in it, behind bars. The police tried to talk me out of it, said it was a family feud gone wrong, but I knew what I was doing and I know what he was doing, which was nothing I wanted him to do. His wife had told me he made her do it, too, when she was sick and didn't want to. They was married, so I guess she didn't feel like she could complain, but I sure could.'

'Good for you, Melanie,' Tamsin said, and I mentally echoed that. 'It can be hard to stand up for what you know is right. Firella?'

'Oh. Well . . . I moved here from New Orleans about a year ago,' Firella said. 'I'm an assistant principal at the junior high school here in Shakespeare, and I had a similar job in Louisiana.' I revised my estimate of her age upward. Firella was probably closer to fifty than to the thirty-five I'd originally assumed. 'When I lived in New Orleans, I got raped at the school, by a student.' Then Firella's lips clamped shut on the rest of her story, as if she'd given me enough to think about, and she was right. I remembered the smell of school, chalk and lockers and dirty industrial carpeting, and the silence of the building after the children had gone home. I thought of someone, some predator, moving silently through that building . . .

'He broke my arm, too,' Firella said. She moved her left arm a little as if testing its usability. 'He knocked out some of my teeth. He gave me herpes.'

She said all this quite matter-of-factly.

She shrugged, and was silent.

'And they caught him?'

'Yeah,' the woman said wearily. 'They caught him. He told them I'd been having sex with him for months, that it was consensual. It got really ugly. It was in all the papers. But the broken arm and the missing teeth were powerful testimony, yes indeed.'

Tamsin cut a glance toward me to make sure I was absorbing the fact that I wasn't the only victim in the world who'd gone through an extraordinary ordeal. I've never been that egotistical.

'Lily, do you feel able to tell us your story tonight?' the therapist asked.

Fighting a nearly overwhelming impulse to get up and walk out, I forced myself to sit and consider. I thought about Jack's nose, and I thought about the trust the other women had extended to me. If I had to do this, it might as well be now as any other time.

I focused on the doorknob a few feet past Tamsin's ear. I wished that some time in the past, I'd made a tape recording of this. 'Some years ago, I lived in Memphis,' I said flatly. 'On my way home from work one day, my car broke down. I was walking to a gas station when I was abducted at gunpoint by a man. He rented me to a small group of bikers for the weekend. That was what he did for a living. They took me to a – well, it was an old shack out in the fields, somewhere in rural Tennessee.' The fine trembling began, the nearly imperceptible shivering that I could feel all the way to the soles of my feet. 'There were about five of them, five men, and one or two women. I was blindfolded, so I never saw them. They chained me to a bed. They raped me, and they cut patterns on my chest and stomach with knives. When they were leaving, one of them gave me a gun. He was mad at the guy who'd rented me to them, I can't remember why.' That wasn't true, but I didn't want to explain further. 'So the gun had one bullet. I could have killed myself. I was a real mess by then. It was real hot out there.' My fists were clenched, and I was struggling to keep my breathing even. 'But when the man who'd kidnapped me came back – I shot him. And he died.'

It was so quiet in the room that I could hear my own breathing.

I waited for Tamsin to say something. But they were waiting on me. Janet said, 'Tell us how it ended.'

'Ah, well, a farmer, it was his land, he came by and found me. So, he called the police, and they took me to the hospital.' The condensed version.

'How long?' Tamsin asked.

'How long did they keep me? Well, let's see.' The shivering increased in intensity. I knew it must be visible by now. 'Friday afternoon and Friday night, and all day Saturday, and part of Sunday? I think.'

'How long before the farmer got there?'

'Oh! Oh, sorry. That was the rest of Sunday, and Monday, and most of Tuesday. Quite a while,' I said. I sat up straighter, made my fists unclench. Tried to force myself to be still.

'I remember that,' Melanie said. 'I was just a kid, then. But I remember when it was in all the papers. I remember wishing you had had a chance to shoot them all.'

I flicked a glance at her, surprised.

'I remember thinking that you were asking for it, walking after your car had broken down,' Firella said. We all looked at her. 'That was before I found out that women had a right to walk anywhere they wanted, with no one bothering 'em.'

'That's right, Firella,' Tamsin said firmly. 'What's the rule, people?'

We all waited.

'Don't blame the victim for the crime,' she said, almost chanting.

'Don't blame the victim for the crime,' we chorused raggedly. I thought some of us got the idea better than others, judging by their expressions.

'Baby-sitter accepts a ride home with the father of the kids, he rapes her. Is she at fault?' Tamsin asked us fiercely.

'Don't blame the victim for the crime!' we said. I have to admit this was an effort for me. I was about to decide Jack owed me big time when I remembered the blood running out of his nose.

'A woman's walking on a street alone at night, she gets grabbed and raped,' Tamsin said. 'Is it her fault?'

'Don't blame the victim for the crime!' we said firmly.

'A woman's wearing a tight skirt and no bra, goes to a bar in a bad part of town, gets drunk, takes a ride with a stranger, gets raped. Is it her fault?'

The chorus died out. This required more thought.

'What do you think, Lily?' Tamsin asked me directly.

'I think wanting to look attractive, even provocative, doesn't mean you deserve to get raped. I think even the stupidity of getting drunk with people you don't know doesn't merit the punishment of being raped. At the same time, women should be responsible for their own safety . . .' I trailed off.

'And what does being responsible for your own safety mean?'

That was something I could answer. 'It means learning to fight,' I said with certainty. 'It means being cautious. It means taking care of your car so it won't break down, making sure your doors are locked, and evaluating the scene around you for danger.'

Some of the women looked dubious when I mentioned fighting, but the rest of my measures met with approval.

'How responsible for your own safety were you before you got raped?' the therapist asked. Her dark eyes were fixed on me intently. She leaned forward, and the blouse gaped slightly because she filled it up too much.

I tried to remember. 'Not very. I made sure I always had enough money to make a phone call. When I was going on a first date with someone I didn't know, I made sure a friend or two knew where I was going and who I was with.'

'So wouldn't you say that most of this wisdom is hindsight?'

'Yes.'

'Can you blame other women for not having the same sense?'

'No.'

The talk went on, and I confined myself to listening for the rest of the hour. The problem of responsibility was a knotty one. Women dress provocatively to attract sexual attention and admiration, because that's gratifying. I believed that very few women would wear a push-up bra, a low-cut blouse, high heels, tight skirts, if they were going to stay home working on the computer, for example. But sexual attention does not equate with rape. I knew of no woman who would walk out the door for an evening of barhopping with the idea that maybe she would enjoy being forced at knifepoint to give a blow job to a stranger. And very few women walked alone at night hoping a man would offer them a choice between sex and strangulation.

The fact remained that stupidity and/or poor judgment are not punishable by rape. And that was the bottom line, as far as I was concerned, and as far as Tamsin was, I thought, by the way she seemed to be steering the group.

What about the great-grandmothers and children who got raped? They were only sex objects to the eyes of the hopelessly warped. They could hardly be accused of 'asking for it'.

This pattern of thought was familiar to me, an old treadmill. Once I'd reconfirmed where we were going, I thought about the therapist herself. By her bearing and presence, Tamsin Lynd was forcing us to think about events and issues we found it hard to face. What a job – having to listen to all this! I wondered if she'd ever been raped herself, decided it was none of my business to ask since she was the natural – and neutral – leader of the group, at least ostensibly. Whether or not Tamsin had survived a rape, she definitely had problems to face now. That phone call had not been from a friend.

When the session was over, Tamsin ushered us out, remaining behind in the empty building to 'clear some things up,' she said. Once we were outside in the parking lot, the cocoon of mutual pain dissolved, and Melanie and Sandy scooted off immediately. Carla got in an old boat of a car and lit a cigarette before she turned the key in the ignition. Firella said, to no one in particular,

'I live right down the street.' She arranged her keys between her fingers in the approved face-ripping position and strode off into the dark.

Janet gave me a hug. This was not typical of our relationship and almost made me flinch. I held rigidly stiff and pressed my hands against her back in an attempt at reciprocation.

She took a step away and laughed. 'There, that better?'

I was embarrassed and showed it.

'You don't need to pretend with me,' she said.

'What's the story on Tamsin?' I asked, to get off the subject.

'She's had this job about a year,' Janet said, willing to go along with my drift. 'She and her husband have a little house over on Compton. They're both Yankees. He has a different last name.' Janet clearly saw that as evidence that the couple had a very un-traditional marriage.

'Does that bother you?'

Janet shook her head. 'She can screw alligators, for all I care. Coming to this group is the most positive step I've taken since I got raped.'

'It doesn't seem like you, not reporting,' I said carefully.

'It's not like me now. It was like me then.'

'Do you ever think of reporting it, even now?'

'He's dead,' Janet said simply. 'It was in the paper last year. You may remember. Mart Weekins? He was trying to pass on a yellow line on that big curve outside of town on Route Six. Semi was coming the other way.'

'So,' I said. 'He wasn't taking responsibility for himself, I guess. Would you say his being there was – unwise?'

'I wonder if he was dressed provocatively,' Janet said, and we both laughed like maniacs.

As it happens so many times, once I'd met Tamsin Lynd, I saw and heard of her everywhere. I saw her at the post office, the grocery store, the gas station. Sometimes she was with a burly man with dark hair and a beard and mustache carefully shaved into a pattern. Each time, she gave me a friendly but impersonal nod, so I could acknowledge or ignore her as I chose.

As Jack and I drove to Little Rock the next week, after my second therapy session, I tried to describe her character and found I had no handle on it at all. Usually, I know right away if I like someone or not, but with Tamsin I just couldn't tell. Maybe it didn't make any difference, if the person was supposed to be helping you get your head straight. Maybe I had no business liking her or hating her.

'She's smart,' I said. 'She always gets us to talking about different sides to our experience.'

'Is she likable?' Jack smoothed his hair back with one hand while gripping the steering wheel with the other. His wiry black hair was escaping from its band this morning, a sure sign he'd been thinking of something else while he got dressed. I wondered if my job performance was the issue on his mind.

'Not really,' I said. 'She's got a strong character. I just don't know what it's made up of.'

'You usually make up your mind about someone faster than that.'

'She puzzles me. Maybe it's a part of being a counselor, but she doesn't seem to want to focus right now on how we feel about the attacker, just about the problems we have adjusting to being attacked.'

'Maybe she's assuming you all hate men?'

'Could be. Or maybe she's just waiting for us to say it. I guess none of us are in the "Men Are Wonderful" club, and I think one or two in the group really hate all men, to some extent.'

Jack looked uncomfortable. I wasn't sure how much he wanted to hear about this new experience of mine, and I wasn't sure how much I was willing to share.

'You sure you're okay at this new job?' he asked, for maybe the hundredth time.

'Jack,' I said warningly.

'I know, I know, I just . . . feel responsible.'

'You *are* responsible. But I'm fine, and I'm even enjoying myself some.' Jack had this idea that I should be a private detective, like him. To achieve this, I had to work with an experienced investigator for two years. This job was my first step, and the experienced investigator was Jack.

We pulled up in the parking lot of a strip mall in the western part of Little Rock. This was the second Marvel Gym to open in the city, and it had taken over about three store widths in the strip mall. Mel Brentwood was risking a chunk of investment money in opening a second gym, especially since Marvel was no back-to-basics weightlifting place. Marvel was a deluxe gym, with different classes all day, a special room for aerobic equipment (treadmills and stair climbers), a sauna and tanning beds, a whirlpool, and lots of free weights for people who actually came to the gym to pump some iron.

I went in the women's changing room, which also contained the women's bathroom, and peeled off my shirt and shorts, folding them to stack in my tiny locker. Underneath, I wore what I considered a costume, since I wouldn't ever wear it otherwise: a Spandex unitard patterned in a leopard print. It came to mid-thigh and was sleeveless. Across the chest, MARVEL was printed in puffy letters, with the word 'gym' centered underneath in smaller type. Though this so-called garment was brief and showed every ounce I had on me, it covered the scars left from the knifing I'd taken. I wore heavy black socks and black Nikes to look a little more utilitarian. After a moment's thought, I left my purse out when I pushed my locker shut, then went out to the main floor to punch in my time clock. My job, the lowest paid as the newest employee, was to check 'guests' in, that being the gym's euphemism for people who'd paid for a year's membership. The rest of my job consisted of showing new guests how to use the equipment, spotting for someone who'd come without a buddy, pushing the drinks and clothes the gym sold, and answering the phone. There were always two people on duty, always a man and a woman. If the man who shared my shift wanted to go work out, I was supposed to watch the desk. He was supposed to do the same for me.

I had never shown quite so much of myself to so many strangers, on a day-to-day basis. Even before what I labeled my 'bad time', I'd been modest. But I had to blend in with the other employees, most of whom were younger. If any of them had had a body like mine they would have flaunted it much more than I was doing, Jack had assured me.

To minimize my self-consciousness about appearing in this getup, I kept my makeup to a minimum, avoided direct eye contact with the men, and tried to squelch any interest manifested by any of the guests.

Since the front door had been opened already, I knew the manager was there. Sure enough, the light in her office was on. Linda Doan didn't like me and was determined to get rid of me the first chance she got. But Linda couldn't fire me, though she didn't know that yet. She didn't know why I was really at Marvel.

I was *undercover*. The very term had a tendency to make me snicker, but it was true. Since its opening seven months before, the gym had been plagued by a thief. Someone was sneaking into the changing rooms and stealing items – cash, jewelry, cell phones – from the guests. It wasn't impossible that the thief was a guest, but Jack thought the culprit was one of the staff, given the territory the thief had covered.

'The men's changing room, the ladies' changing room, the storage cubes outside the sauna,' Mel Brentwood had moaned. 'Drinks, watches, chains, cash. Never a lot, never anything awfully expensive, but it's just a matter of time. And the guests will hear about it and they won't come. If we don't find out who's responsible, I'll fire everyone working there and replace all of them, I swear I will.'

I was pretty sure such drastic action was illegal, but it wasn't my business to say so, and I noticed Jack glanced out the window and kept his face blank. Mel couldn't be the idiot he projected himself to be. He had started this string of gyms with money he'd begged and borrowed from skeptical friends of his parents, and he'd made the gyms prosper by thinking of ever-new ways to get them in the news without actually burning them down.

'Can we install a camera in the changing room?' Jack asked.

'Hell, no! How do you think these people, most of 'em trying to take off weight, would react to discovering they'd been on camera? There's no way to put one in there that no one would notice.' But I could tell the idea had caught Mel's interest. 'If I didn't want to take the thief to court . . . ,' he said slowly. 'If I just wanted to catch the bastard and fire him . . .'

'The camera would never come up,' Jack said. 'We could take it out, destroy the tape, no one the wiser. I can run by Sneaky Pete's. I'm not crazy about the idea of filming people who don't know about it, but it would work.'

'So, do I need Lily?' Mel Brentwood eyed me like I was a gunslinger who might draw on him.

'Sure. There are things cameras won't catch,' Jack said. 'And we have yet to figure out a way to disguise them.'

'Okay, girl,' Mel said, whacking me on the shoulder to get me fired up for the big game. 'You start work as soon as you can get your tights on.'

I eyed him balefully. I wasn't happy about working for Mel, but I'd worked for plenty of people I hadn't liked. I told myself to ease up. Politically correct he wasn't, but Mel would pay Jack to do this, Jack would have another client who would call him when he got in a jam, and Jack's business would prosper.

So there I was, in Marvel Gym, in glorious leopard print Spandex, making sure guests swiped their green plastic cards as they came in so their presence would be recorded on the computer. I handed out small towels to the guests who'd forgotten theirs, I checked the supply of bath-sized towels in the locker rooms, and I sold the expensive 'health' drinks displayed in the cooler behind the counter. Those tasks were constants, but every day there was some specific problem to solve. In the first hour I worked today, I unstuck the weight-setting peg on a leg-extension device. Then I discreetly sprayed cleaner on a weightlifting bench after a particularly sweaty guest had used it, and got the vacuum out to suck up clods of dirt tracked in by a guest who'd been running in the mud yesterday.

Mostly, I grew angrier by the second at Byron, the twenty-four-year-old man who shared my shift. I watched Byron loaf his way through his workout, making himself friendly with every female in the place except me. Me, he tried to dodge.

Byron was sculpted. You could tell he thought of himself that way; sculpted as a Greek statue, sensuous, masculine. That is, if Byron knew any of those words. Byron was a waste of space, in my opinion. In my two weeks at Marvel, I couldn't count the times I had hoped he was the thief. Unless people would pay the high membership fee just to gaze upon Byron, he was a poor employee: pleasant to those people he liked, people he felt could help him, and rude to the guests who couldn't do anything for him, guests who expected him to actually work. And he'd fondle anything that stood still. Why Linda Doan had hired Byron was a mystery to me.

'I need to go put some more towels in the women's locker room,' I told him. 'Then I'm going to start my own workout.'

'Cool,' said Byron. Mr Articulate. He began doing another set of ab crunches.

I took the pile of towels into the tiled locker room. Someone was taking a shower when I walked in, which was surprising because it was a little early for the rush we got about ten, ten-thirty. The water cut off as I reached the shelves where I stacked the towels. I was walking lightly because I always do.

I caught a guest red-handed. She was going through my purse, which I'd left temptingly propped against an extra pair of shoes by my locker. It took me a minute to mentally leaf through the pictures I'd tried to commit to memory, and finally I came up with her name: Mandy Easley.

Mandy became aware of me after I'd watched her get a twenty out of my wallet and flip open the credit card compartment. Mandy was only in her twenties, but she looked like a hag when her eyes met mine. Her dark brown hair was still wet from the shower, her narrow face was bare of makeup, and her towel was wound around her modestly, but she still didn't look innocent. She looked guilty as hell.

'Oh! Ah, Lily, right? I was just getting some change for the Tampax machine,' she said, in a jittery voice. 'I hope you don't mind. I didn't have the right change, and your purse was just sitting here.'

'Machine takes twenties now?'

'Ah, I . . .' The twenty fluttered from her fingers as she stared down at the purse, exactly as if it had just materialized in her hands. 'Oh, that fell out! I'm sorry, let me just put it back in . . .' and she fumbled for the bill. She was one big twitch.

'Ms Easley,' I said, and by my voice she knew I wasn't going to smooth it over.

'Oh, shit,' she said, and covered her face with her hands as if she was overwhelmed with shame. 'Lily, honestly, I never did anything like this before.' She tried to squeeze out some tears, but couldn't quite manage. 'I just have such bad money problems, please don't call the cops! My mom would die if I had a record!'

'You already have a record,' I observed.

Her face flashed up from her hands and she glared at me. 'What?'

'You have a record. For shoplifting and passing bad checks.' The computer had told us what employees and guests had been present at Marvel during the time the various thefts had occurred, and twenty-three-year-old divorcee Mandy Easley's name had recurred. Jack had run a check on her.

'We'll be glad to refund your membership money by mail after you hand us your card,' I said, as I'd been instructed to do. 'When I have your card in my hand, you can go.'

'You're not going to call the police?' she asked, unable to believe her good luck. I felt exactly the same way.

'If you return your card, then you can go.'

'All right, Robocop,' she said furiously, relief shoving her over the edge of caution. 'Take the damn card!' She turned to yank it out of the pocket on her shorts, which were draped over the bench behind her. She extricated the plastic card and threw it at me. Mandy didn't look like a well-groomed young matron any more as she yanked my twenty out of my purse and thrust it into the same pocket. She was sneering in my face.

I had seldom seen anyone look quite so ugly, male or female. I thought Mandy Easley was just as much a waste of space as Byron, and I wished her out the door. I was sick to death of her.

She read something in my face that stopped her manic rant. Yanking off the towel, she let it drop to the floor while she pulled on her shorts and a T-shirt and thrust her feet into sandals. She gathered up her purse, spitefully knocked over the stack of towels as her parting shot, and headed out the door to the hall leading to the main room. She spun on her heel to fire some comment my way, something that could be heard by everyone in the weights room, but I began moving toward her with all my disgust in my face. She hurried out of the gym for the last time.

I had to straighten up the locker room, of course, and though it made me sick to do so, I had to pick up the card Mandy had thrown at me. While I was refolding the towels and placing them in the resurrected rack, I pictured many gratifying ways to make Mandy pick up her own card. By the time I had to take my place beside Byron again, I was in at least an equitable mood.

'What happened to Mandy?' he asked casually, taking a moment away from his absorbed fascination with his own face reflected in the gleaming counter. 'She took outta here like a scalded cat.'

I couldn't tell him she'd been stealing. That would jettison the whole idea. But I could tell him something else. 'I had to take her membership card,' I said, even more seriously and quietly than normal.

He goggled with curiosity. 'What? Why?'

I was drawing a blank.

'Did she . . . make a pass at you?' Byron supplied his own scenario. I could practically see the steam coming out of his ears. 'Did she actually . . . was she actually *doing* something? In the shower?'

I wasn't supposed to disclose Jack's business arrangement with Mel Brentwood. I looked away, hoping to indicate embarrassment. 'I don't want to talk about it,' I said truthfully. 'It was really ugly.'

'Poor Lily,' Byron said, laying his hand on my shoulder and giving it a squeeze. 'You poor girl.'

Was he *blind?*

Biting the inside of my lips to keep from snarling, I managed to indicate to Byron that I wanted to go work out, and he let his hand trail off my shoulder while I went to the leg press. After I'd warmed up and put the first set of forty-fives on, I dropped down into the sleigh-type seat and placed my feet against the large metal plate. Pushing up a little to relieve the pressure, I flipped the prop bars outward, and let the plate push my knees to my chest. I pushed, and felt everything tighten in a surprisingly relaxing way as I exhaled. Legs to chest, inhale. Legs out straight, exhale. Over and over, until the set was done and I could add another pair of forty-fives.

Toward the end of my workout, I realized I should be feeling proud that I had successfully completed my first assignment as a private investigator. Somehow, television and the film industry had not prepared me for the mundane satisfaction of detecting a thief. I hadn't gotten to run after anyone waving a gun; the police hadn't threatened me; Mel Brinkman hadn't tried to sleep with me. Could it be I had been misled by the media?

As I pondered this, I noticed that Byron had been so anxious to start spreading the 'news' about Mandy that he'd actually gotten the glass spray out and begun cleaning some of the mirrors that lined the gym walls. This brought him into murmuring distance of some of his cronies and the many sideways glances at me were a clear indication that my brush with Mandy was being mythologized.

At least I'd gotten some good workouts, being on this job. I wondered how long Mel would want me to work after this; this might be the last time I'd have to come to Marvel Gym.

Jack picked me up at the end of my shift. I was so glad to see him it made me feel almost silly. Jack is about five foot ten, his hair is still all black, and his eyes are hazel. He has a scar, a very thin one – a razor scar – running from the hairline close to his right eye down to his jawline. It puckers a very little. He has a narrow, strong nose and straight eyebrows. He's been a private detective since he got urged to resign from the Memphis Police Department about five years ago.

'I like the outfit,' he said, as we walked to his car.

'In this heat, I feel like one big smell,' I said. 'I want to shower and put on something cotton and loose.'

'Yes, ma'am. You just happy to see me, or did something interesting happen at the gym?'

'A little bit of both.'

When we were in the car and on our way back to Shakespeare, the town where I've lived for five years, I began to tell Jack about my day. 'So it was Mandy Easley all along,' I concluded. 'I guess I found myself a little disappointed.'

'You just want to catch Byron doing something,' Jack said. I turned, huffing in exasperation, in time to catch the amused curl of his lips flatten out into a serious expression.

'Being a stupid jerk isn't a jailable offense,' I admitted.

'Jails wouldn't be big enough,' Jack agreed.

'What will happen now?'

'I'll call Mel when we get home.'

While Jack was on the phone, I peeled off the nasty unitard and dropped it in the hamper. The shower, in the privacy of my own bathroom, cramped as it was, was just as wonderful as I had anticipated. Drying off was sheer bliss. I fluffed up the wet blond curls that clung to my head, I checked to make sure I'd gotten my legs very smooth, and I put on a lot of deodorant and skin cream before I came out to join Jack. He was putting steaks in a marinade. We didn't eat much beef.

'Special occasion?'

'You caught your first thief.'

'And you're going to congratulate me with dead cow?'

He put down the pan and eyed me with some indignation. 'Can you think of a better way?'

'Ah . . . yes.'

'And that would be?'

'You're slow on the uptake today,' I said critically, and took off my robe.

He caught on right away.

*

We'd returned to Shakespeare too late to attend karate class, so later that night we took a walk. Jack had spent most of the day sitting down, and he wanted to stretch before bed.

'Mel says thanks,' Jack told me, after we'd been clipping along for maybe twenty minutes. 'I think he'll call us again if he has any problems. You did a good job.' He sounded proud, and that lit an unexpected glow somewhere in my chest.

'So, what next?' I asked.

'We've got a Workman's Comp. job I'm sure you can handle,' Jack said. 'I get a lot of that kind of case.'

'The person is claiming he can't work any more?'

'Yeah. In this case, it's a woman. She fell on a slippery floor at work, now she says she can't bend her back or lift anything. She lives in a small house in Conway. It can be hard watching a house in some neighborhoods, so you may have to be creative.'

That was not the adjective that sprang to my mind when I thought of my abilities, so I felt a little anxious.

'I'll need a camera, I'm assuming.'

'Yes, and lots of time fillers. A book or two, newspapers, snacks.'

'Okay.'

We paced along for a few more minutes. A familiar car went by, and I said, 'Jack, there's my counselor. And her husband, I think.'

We watched the beige sedan turn the corner onto Compton. That was the way we'd planned to go, too, and when we rounded the same corner, we saw the car had stopped in front of an older home. It was built in a style popular in the thirties and forties, boxy and low with a broad roofed porch supported by squat pillars. Tamsin and the man with her had already left their car, and he was at the front door. She was standing slightly behind him. Under the glare of the porch light, I could see he was partially bald, and big. The clink of keys carried across the small yard.

Tamsin screamed.

Jack was there before I was. He moved to one side as I caught up, and I saw that there was a puddle of blood on the gray-painted concrete of the porch. I cast my gaze from side to side, saw nothing that could have produced it.

'There,' Jack said, still one step ahead of me.

Following his pointing finger, I saw there was a squirrel hanging from a branch of the mimosa tree planted by the porch. The heavy scent of the mimosa twined with the hot-penny smell of blood.

Since I didn't have a bird feeder or fruit bushes, I happened to like squirrels. When I realized the squirrel's throat had been cut and the little animal had been hung on the tree like an out-of-season Christmas ornament, I began a slow burn.

I could hear Tamsin sobbing in the background and her husband saying, 'Oh, not here, too. Honey, maybe it was just some kids, or someone playing a sick joke . . .'

'You *know* it was him. You *know* that,' Tamsin said, choking and gasping. 'I told you about the phone calls. It's him, again. He followed me.'

Jack said, 'Excuse me, I'm Jack Leeds. This is Lily. We were just out walking. Sorry to intrude, but can we help?'

The man with his arm around Tamsin said, 'I'm sorry, too. We can't believe . . . excuse me, I'm Cliff Eggers, and this is my wife, Tamsin Lynd.'

'Tamsin and I know each other,' I murmured politely, trying not to look at Tamsin's face while she was in such distress.

'Oh, Lily!' Tamsin took a long, shuddering breath, and she appeared to be trying to pull herself together in the presence of a client. 'I'm sorry,' she said, though damned if I could think for what. 'This is just very upsetting.'

'Sure it is,' Jack agreed. 'Don't you think we ought to call the police, Ms Lynd?'

'Oh, we'll call them. We always do. But they can't do anything,' her husband said, with sudden violence. He ran a big hand across his face. He had one of those neatly trimmed beards that frames the mouth. 'They couldn't do anything before. They won't do anything now.' Cliff Eggers's voice was choked and unsteady.

He was fumbling with the keys to the door and he managed to open it.

They stepped in their hall, and Tamsin beckoned me in behind them. I caught a glimpse of a large, friendly room. There were pictures hung over an antique chest to the right of the door. In the framed grouping I saw a wedding picture with Tamsin in full white regalia, and her husband's business college diploma. There was a big brass bowl of potpourri on the chest, and my nose began to stop up almost instantly.

Tamsin said, 'We'll call them tomorrow morning.' Her husband nodded. Then he turned back to us. 'We appreciate your coming to help us. I'm sorry to involve you in something so unpleasant.'

'Excuse us, please,' Tamsin said. She was obviously just barely containing her anguish. I felt she knew she'd made a mistake asking us in, that she was just waiting for us to leave so she could drop that facade, crumble completely.

'Of course,' Jack said instantly. He looked at Cliff. 'Would you like us to . . .' and he nodded toward the squirrel.

'Yes,' Cliff said with great relief. 'That would be very kind. The garbage can is at the rear of the backyard, by the hedge.'

We stepped back out on the porch, and Cliff and Tamsin had closed the door before Jack and I chanced looking at each other.

'Huh?' I said, finally.

'Double huh,' Jack said. He fished a pocketknife out of his jeans and leaned over the waist-high railing to cut the string. Holding the little corpse at arm's length, he went down the steps and around the house to the garbage can. Cliff's telling Jack that the garbage can was 'by the hedge' was unnecessary, since everything in the Eggers-Lynd yard was 'by the hedge'. It was an older home, and the original owners had believed in planting. The front yard was open to the street, but the clipped thick growth followed the property line down both sides and across the back of the yard. The surrounding greenery gave the yard a feeling of enclosure. While I waited, I thought I heard voices, so I went around the house to look into the backyard. In the darkness by the hedge at the rear of the property, I saw two figures.

Jack came back after a few more seconds. 'Their neighbor was outside, wanted to know what had happened,' he explained. 'He's a town cop, so at least law enforcement will know something about this.' I could tell Jack had suspected Cliff Eggers wouldn't call about the incident.

I wondered belatedly if I should have tried to deduce something from the state of the squirrel's body. But I was clueless about squirrel metabolism, especially in this heat, and it would be way beyond me to try to estimate how long the poor critter had been dead. After a last glance at the blood, and a pang of regret that I had nothing with which to swab it up, I joined Jack on the driveway and we resumed our walk.

We didn't say anything else until we were a block away from the house, and then it wasn't much. Someone was stalking Tamsin Lynd, and from all the cues in the conversation we'd had with the couple, this persecution had been going on for some time. If Tamsin and her husband were unwilling to ask for help, what could be done?

'Nothing,' I concluded, straightening up after washing my face in the bathroom sink.

Jack picked up on that directly. 'I guess not,' he agreed. 'And you watch your step around her. I think this therapy group is good for you, but I don't want you catching some kind of collateral fallout when her situation implodes.'

As I composed myself for sleep thirty minutes later, I found myself thinking that it hardly seemed fair that Tamsin had to listen to the group's problems, while her own were kept swept under the rug of her marriage. I reminded myself that, after all, Tamsin was getting paid to do her job, and she had been trained to cope with the inevitable depression that must follow hearing so many tales of misery and evil.

Jack wasn't yet asleep, so I told him what I'd been thinking.

'She listens to a lot of bad stuff, yeah,' he said, his voice quiet, coming out of the darkness. 'But look at the courage, look at the toughness. The determination. She hears that, too. Look how brave you all are.'

I couldn't say anything at all. My throat clogged. I was glad it was dark. At last, I was able to pat Jack's shoulder; and a minute later, I heard by his breathing that he was asleep. Before it could overcome me, too, I thought, *This is why Jack is here beside me. Because he can think of saying something like he just said.*

That was a fine reason.

Chapter Three

By my third therapy session, Tuesday night was no longer a time I dreaded.

I'd had hours sitting in a car, standing in a convenience store, and drifting around a mall – all in pursuit of the Worker's Comp. claimant – to analyze our counseling sessions. I had to admit I couldn't tell if Tamsin Lynd was following some kind of master plan in directing us along the path to recovery. It seemed to me that often we just talked at random; though from time to time I could discern Tamsin's fine hand directing us.

Not one of the women in the group was someone I would've picked for a friend, with the exception of Janet Shook. Sandy McCorkindale made me particularly edgy. She tried very hard to be the unflawed preacher's wife, and she very nearly succeeded. Her veneer of good modest clothes and good modest makeup, backed by an almost frenzied determination to keep the smooth surface intact, was maintained at a tremendous, secret cost. I had lived too close to the edge of despair and mental illness not to recognize it in others, and Sandy McCorkindale was a walking volcano. I was willing to bet her family was used to living on tiptoe, perhaps even quite unaware they were doing so.

The other women were OK. I'd gradually learned their personal histories. In a town the size of Shakespeare, keeping identities a secret was impossible. For example, not only did I know that Carla (of the croaking voice) was Carla Preston, I knew that her dad had retired from Shakespeare Drilling and Exploration, and her mom took the lunch money at the elementary school cafeteria. I knew Carla smoked like a chimney when she went out the back door of the Health Center, she'd been married three times, and she said everything she thought. She'd become a grandmother when she was thirty-five.

Melanie Kleinhoff no longer looked quite as sullen, and despite her youth and pale doughy looks, she set herself goals and met them (no matter how difficult) to the point of idiocy. She had never graduated from high school and she was still married to the man whose brother had raped her. Firella Bale, probably the most educated of all of us – with the exception of our counselor – seemed baffled sometimes by how to fit in; she was black, she was smart and deliberate, she had taught others, and she worked in a position of authority. She was a single mother and her son was in the army.

Sandy, Janet, and I had never doubted that we could share our problems with a woman of another race. Tamsin seemed a little more careful of Carla and Melanie. We would all have known right away if Carla was uncomfortable with Firella, since Carla had few thoughts she didn't set right out in front of us. Luckily, she seemed to have passed that particular rock in the road. Melanie hadn't, and we could watch her prejudice struggle with her good sense and her own kindness. Our common fate transcended our color or economic status or education, but that was easier for some of us to acknowledge than others.

I had neither witnessed any more incidents nor heard any rumors about Tamsin and her husband. I had not spoken a word about what Jack and I had seen that evening while we were out walking. As far as I could tell, no one in Shakespeare knew that someone was stalking our counselor.

Sandy McCorkindale was waiting outside when I arrived for our third evening together. While I knew more about Sandy's life than I knew about almost any of the others – I'd met her husband, seen her sons, worked in her church, walked by her home – I realized I understood her less than any member of our little group. Waiting in the heat with her was not a happy prospect.

In the two weeks since our first meeting, the season had ripened to full-blown summer. It was hotter than the six shades of hell standing on the asphalt, maybe the temperature was down to ninety-four from the hundred and four it had been that afternoon. At eight o'clock, the parking lot wasn't dark; there was still a glow from the nearly vanished sun. The bugs had started their intense nightly serenade. If I drove out of town right now and parked by the road in an isolated place and tried to talk to a companion, the volume of bug and frog noise would put a serious crimp in the conversation. Anyone expecting nature to be silent – especially in the South – was plain old nuts.

I got out of my car reluctantly. It had been a fruitless day on stakeout in Little Rock, and Jack was out of town on a missing-persons job, so I wasn't having the mild glow of accomplishment I usually enjoyed after a long day. When I went home after the therapy hour, I promised myself, I would take a cool shower and I would read. After a day spent dealing with others, television was just one more batch of voices to listen to; I'd rather have a book in my hands than the remote control.

'Evening, Sandy,' I called. At that moment, the pole-mounted security lights came on. With the residual daylight creating long shadows from behind the trees, I was walking across a visual chessboard to reach the woman standing by the side door we always used. As I drew closer, I could see the preacher's wife had sweat beaded on her forehead. She was wearing the current young matron uniform, a white T-shirt under a long sleeveless, shapeless khaki dress. Sandy's streaked hair was still in its slightly teased-with-bangs Junior League coiffure, and her makeup was all in place, but there was definitely something happening in her head. Her brown eyes, dark and discreetly made up, darted from my face to the cars to the bushes and back.

'Tamsin didn't leave the door open,' Sandy said furiously. She was carrying her straw shoulder bag in the usual way, but with an abrupt gesture she let the strap slide down her arm and she swung the bag, hard, against the side of her car. That made me jump, and I had to repress a snarl.

I wondered, for maybe the fifth or sixth time, why Sandy kept coming. She'd never talked in any more detail, or with any more feeling, about what had happened to her, but she kept showing up. She was making a real effort to keep herself separated from the common emotional ground. But every Tuesday night, there she was in her chair, listening.

I leaned against the wall to wait for Tamsin to unlock the door. I didn't feel up to any more emotional outbursts from Sandy McCorkindale.

Melahie and Carla arrived together. I had decided they'd known each other before coming to the therapy group. In conversation, I'd heard them refer to common acquaintances.

'Good! I got time for a cigarette,' Carla said in her harsh voice. She had one lit and puffing in a flash. 'My car done broke down today in front of Piggly Wiggly, and I had to call Melanie here to give me a ride.'

Normally I would have expected Sandy to pick up the conversational ball, but not tonight.

'What's wrong with the car?' I asked, after a beat.

'My boyfriend says it might be the alternator,' Carla said. 'I sure hope it's something cheaper. Tamsin not here yet?'

'Her car is over there,' Sandy said resentfully, pointing to Tamsin's modest Honda Civic. 'But she won't open the door!'

Melanie and Carla gave Sandy the same kind of careful sideways look I'd found myself delivering.

Firella came walking from the darkness at the other end of the small parking lot, pepper spray in one hand and keys in the other.

'Hey, y'all!' she called. 'We meeting out here in the parking lot tonight?' Carla laughed, and Melanie smiled. As Firella drew closer, she counted us and observed, 'One of us hasn't made it here yet.'

'Oh, Janet's car's here, too,' Sandy snapped. 'See?'

We all looked over to note that Janet's dark Camaro was half concealed by Tamsin's Honda.

'So where's Janet, and why won't the back door open? You think Tamsin and Janet are in there doin' it?' asked Carla. She didn't sound angry about the possibility – only ready for them to finish and unlock the back door, so she could get in the air conditioning.

Sandy was almost shocked out of her odd mood. 'Oh, my gosh,' she said, rattled to the core. 'I just never believed I could know anyone that . . . oh, my Lord.'

Though I was pretty sure Carla had just been blabbing – for the pleasure of hearing her own voice, and to shock Sandy – I didn't comment. I got a phone book from the front seat of my car, pulled my cell phone from the pocket of the drawstring sheeting pants I was wearing because they were cool, and dialed the health center number.

Inside the building, we could hear the phone ring, very faintly. That would be the one at the main reception desk, inside the front door.

A voice came on the line. 'You have reached the Hartsfield County Health Unit. Our office hours are nine to five, Monday through Friday. If you know the extension of the person you're calling, please press it now.' I did.

From inside the building, we heard another phone begin to ring, this time closer. We counted the rings. After four, the female voice came back on the line, to tell me that the party I wanted to contact was away from her desk and to ask me to call back during office hours. She also told me what to do in case of emergency.

'This seem like an emergency?' I asked, not sure I'd said it out loud until Firella said, 'It's getting to be.'

I stood back and looked at the door. Made of a heavy metal and painted brown, it was intended for staff use, so therapists wouldn't have to enter and exit through the reception area. It was kept locked every evening but Tuesday, as far as I knew, though there might be other kinds of therapy groups that met using the same arrangement. Tamsin always locked the door when the six of us were assembled inside, and something she'd said once had made me think she only unlocked it about ten minutes before group time.

The light wasn't crystal clear in the area around the door, but I could tell when I aimed my tiny key-ring flashlight at the crack that the deadbolt was not actually engaged.

So the door wasn't locked, after all. I tugged on it again, baffled. It didn't budge.

While the other women watched, I again punched the 'on' button of my tiny flashlight. My insurance agent would be glad to hear I'd found his giveaway so useful. This time, I shone the light all the way around the edges of the door, trying to spy something that would give me a clue as to why the door was being so stubborn. I was rewarded maybe the second or third time around, when I realized a chip of wood was protruding from the bottom.

'There,' I said, and squatted. I heard Melanie explaining to the others and many exclamations, but I ignored them. I tried to grip the sliver of wood in a pincer formed by my thumb and middle finger, but I didn't have much success. Tonight was the first time I'd ever wished I had long fingernails. I checked out the hands around me. 'Firella,' I said, 'your nails are the longest. See if you can grip this little piece of wood, here. That's what's got the door wedged shut.'

Sandy was suggesting in an increasingly nervous voice that we call the police right now, or at least her husband, but Carla put a hand on Sandy's arm and said, 'Hush, woman.' I noticed, while Firella crouched and tried to wriggle the strip of wood from its lodging, that Carla had put out her cigarette before it was smoked down to the filter. She was worried, too.

After a lot of shaking of her head and several little whispers of 'No, not quite . . . almost . . . damn thing!' Firella said, 'Got it!' and held up the thin strip of wood. About four inches long and two wide, it could have been no more than two millimeters thick, if that. It was just the right size to slip in the crack in the door, just thick enough to get wedged there when the first person tried to open the door to go to Tamsin's office.

I reached out to turn the knob, hesitated.

'What you waiting for?' Carla asked, her voice raspier than ever. 'Now we're late.'

I was waiting because I'd thought of fingerprints, but then I shrugged. By her own account, Sandy had already touched the door. 'Remember, she didn't answer the phone,' I said, my voice as quiet and calm as I could make it. I opened the door. The other women clustered around me.

The hall light was on, and Tamsin's office door was open, but not the door to the therapy room.

'Tamsin!' called Carla. 'You and Janet in there? You two stop messing around, you hear! The rest of us'll get jealous!'

Carla was trying to sound jaunty, but the atmosphere in the hall was too thick with anxiety for that.

Melanie said, 'I'm scared.' It was an admission, but it didn't signal that she was going to run away. She'd planted her feet and had that bulldog look on her face that meant she wouldn't back down.

'We're all scared,' Sandy said. Oddly, she'd gotten calmer. 'Do you think we had better just stay out here in the parking lot and call the police?'

'No,' I said.

They all turned to look at me.

'You can all stay outside,' I said, amending my words. In fact, I would've preferred they all stay out. 'But I have to see if they're . . . okay.'

Even slow Melanie read between the lines on that one. To my surprise she said, 'No. You go, we all go.'

'We all go,' Firella said, in a voice even more certain. Sandy didn't say anything, but she didn't walk away, either.

Oh, wonderful, I thought. The five musketeerettes.

We shuffled down the hall in a clump. I couldn't control my anxiety any longer and stepped out ahead of them, pivoted on my left foot and faced into Tamsin's office, my hands already floating up into the striking position. I was ready for something, but not for what I saw.

Behind Tamsin's desk, on the fuzzy wall where all the clippings had been stuck up with pins . . .

'Oh, dear God,' said Sandy, miserably.

'Shit, shit, shit!' Carla's blackbird voice, hushed with shock.

. . . was a body, and the whiteness of it was the first thing I noticed, the whiteness of the chest and arms and face. Then the blackness of her hair.

'Holy Mary, Mother of God,' Firella said, her voice more steady than I would have believed. 'Pray for us now, and at the hour of our death.'

But then there was the redness of it; that was startling, and considerable. The glistening redness mostly issued from the – stake? Was that really a metal stake? Yes, driven through the heart of . . .

'Who *is* that woman?' Carla said, more struck by this shock than by any of the others, apparently.

That naked woman, I amplified her statement.

'The naked and the dead,' I said, drawing from somewhere in the attic of my mind.

'So,' Firella said. Her voice was unsteady, and I heard her gulp back nausea. 'She's actually pinned to the wall?'

There was a groan practically under my feet, and I was shocked enough to lurch back, knocking everyone else into confusion.

Janet was lying on the floor in front of the desk. We'd been so transfixed by the dead woman that we hadn't even seen her. Janet rolled, with great effort, from her back to her front, and I saw a darkening bruise on her forehead. But her hand went to the back of her head, moving slowly and painfully.

In a moment, Firella was on her other side, and we tried to raise her. Though we believed we were the only ones in the building (at least I did) I wanted to get Janet out of there as fast as possible, as if the woman's deadness was contagious.

Janet began mumbling something, but I couldn't make it out. She moaned, though, as we tried to pull her to her feet. Without discussion, we lowered her back to the carpet.

'We gotta get out of here,' Carla said urgently, and I agreed. But we couldn't all go. I handed my cell phone to Melanie, who was silent and shocked.

'Go outside and call the police,' I said.

'Can't we just leave and call it in later?' Carla asked.

We all stared at her. She shrugged.

'I mean, take Janet to the hospital ourselves. Just so we won't be connected to the police side of this. I mean, someone offed this gal, someone really, really seriously sick. Right?'

Sandy said, 'That's true.'

'Look,' I said, and they did all look at me. I was feeling Janet's pulse, trying to decide if her pupils were even. I stopped and collected myself. 'We're listed on some schedule as coming here tonight, you know. All of us. Our names are written down somewhere, no matter how confidential Tamsin promised us this would be. I don't think we can opt out of this.'

'Do you think whoever killed this woman put her there for us to see?' Sandy asked in a quavering voice. 'Or for Tamsin?'

It was a funny question if you weren't there. If you were there, you could see the intention of display that had gone into arranging the body. To see the poor woman pinned up there, among the articles about rape and the empowerment of women, the accuracy of DNA testing and the heavier sentences being handed down to men who raped . . . we were meant to know we were powerless, after all.

We tried to look anywhere but at the body. 'White as a sheet' was a phrase that came to mind when I looked at my therapy group . . . except Firella, and she had turned an ashen color.

'So we can't dodge this,' Carla admitted. 'But . . . no, I guess, we just have to face the music.'

'After all, we didn't kill her,' Sandy said briskly – as if that cleared up the whole thing, and assured smooth sailing ahead.

When there was a long, thick pause, she said, 'Well, *I* didn't.'

'Enough of this, we have to get help for Janet.' I looked at Melanie. 'You and Carla and Sandy go out the door we came in,' I said. 'Call nine one one. Firella and I will stay here with Janet. Be sure to tell them we need an ambulance.'

'We haven't found Tamsin,' Sandy said.

The rest of us had forgotten all about Tamsin in the turmoil of finding the naked impaled woman and the unconscious Janet.

'She might be in here somewhere,' Sandy whispered. 'She

might be the one who did this.' We stared at Sandy as though she'd sprouted another head.

'Or she might have been killed, too,' Carla reminded her.

'I don't think we better wander around here looking for her,' Firella said sensibly. 'I think we better call the cops, like Lily said. Janet needs an ambulance bad.'

Carla, Melanie, and Sandy turned to go, when Firella said, 'Just for the hell of it, any of you know this woman?'

'I do,' Melanie said. She started out, not looking back. 'That's my sister-in-law, who was married to the man who raped me.'

After a moment of stunned silence, Carla and Sandy hurried after her, down the hall and out into the parking lot. They stood holding open the door so we wouldn't be shut off from them, a piece of thoughtfulness I appreciated. I could hear Carla placing the phone call, having to repeat herself a few times. Firella and I stared at each other, side-swiped by the identification of the dead woman and uncertain how to react to it.

I turned my attention from what I couldn't understand to what I could, the fact that my friend had been attacked. But there didn't seem to be much I could do for her. Janet made little movements from time to time, but she didn't appear to be exactly conscious.

'She's not really stuck up there, is she? Like the newspaper clippings?' Firella said after a moment. Of course, the white-and-red display on the wall was what we were really thinking about.

'I don't see how the wall could be soft enough to drive the stake in far enough to actually hold her up.' Janet's color was awful, a sort of muddy green.

'I see what you're saying. I'm looking behind the desk.' Firella, proving she was tougher than I – I guess years of the school system will do it – stood and peered over the top of the desk.

She abruptly sat down on the floor again.

'I think she's kind of propped up,' she reported, 'with string around her arms in loops, attached to nails that have been driven into the wall. Her bottom half's kind of sitting on the back of Tamsin's rolling chair. There's a wadded-up doctor coat stuck under the wheels to keep the chair from moving.'

I couldn't think of anything to say to that.

'I wonder if one person could fix her that way. Seems like it would take two,' Firella said thoughtfully.

'I guess if one person had enough time it could be done,' I said, so she wouldn't think I was shucking her off. 'That's a lot of preparation. The wedge to keep us out until the scene was set, and the coat to keep the chair from moving.'

'I'm worried about Tamsin,' Firella said next.

'Me, too.' That was easy to agree with. I was wondering if Tamsin was in the therapy room. I was wondering if she was alive.

'Janet, help is coming,' I told her, not at all sure she could hear me or understand. 'You hang on one minute more.' It was true that I could hear sirens. I didn't think I'd ever been happier to know they were coming.

I hadn't talked to my friend Claude Friedrich in a while, and I'd just as soon not have talked to him that night. But since he's the chief of police, and since it was a murder scene in the city limits, there wasn't any way around it.

'Lily,' he greeted me. He was using his police voice; heavy, grim, a little threatening.

'Claude.' I probably sounded the same way.

'What's happened here tonight?' he rumbled.

'You'll have to tell us,' I said. 'We got here for our therapy group—'

'You're in therapy?' Claude's eyebrows almost met his graying hair.

'Yes,' I said shortly.

'Accepting help,' he said, amazement written all over him. 'This must be some doing of Jack's.'

'Yes.'

'And where is he, tonight?'

'On the road.'

'Ah. Okay, so you were here for your therapy group. You and these women?'

'Yes.'

'A group for . . . ?'

A very tall African American woman appeared at Claude's shoulder. Her hair was cut close to her scalp. She was truly almost black, and she was wearing a practical khaki pantsuit with a badge pinned to the lapel. A pale yellow tank top under the jacket shone radiantly against her skin. She had broad features and wore huge blue-framed glasses.

'Alicia, listen to the account of this witness. I know her, she's observant,' Claude said.

'Yes, sir.' The magnified eyes focused on me.

'Lily, this is Detective Stokes. She's just come to us from the Cleveland force.'

'Cleveland, *Ohio*?' Cleveland, Mississippi wouldn't have been surprising.

'Yep.'

Alicia Stokes would have to be classified as a mystery.

Focusing on the more pertinent problem, I explained to Claude and Detective Stokes that we were a group composed of rape survivors, that we met every Tuesday night at the health center, that we were led by a woman who was missing and might be somewhere in the building.

'Tamsin Lynd,' said Stokes unexpectedly.

I stared at her. 'Yes,' I said slowly. 'Tamsin Lynd.'

'I knew it,' the detective said to herself, so swiftly and in such a low voice that I wasn't sure I'd understood her correctly.

Stokes turned to a man in uniform and gave him some quick orders. He stared back at her, resentment all over his face and in his posture, but then he turned to obey. I shook my head. Stokes had her work cut out for her.

She caught the headshake and glared at me. I don't know how she interpreted my reaction, but she definitely didn't want sympathy.

Claude made a 'go-on' gesture, so I went on to explain how we hadn't been able to get in, had finally managed to do so, what we had found. I was glad to see the ambulance team taking Janet out, before I'd finished my account.

Stokes, who was at least four inches taller than my five foot six, said, 'Do you know the victim?'

'No.'

'Did any of you know her?'

'Ask them.'

Stokes clearly was about to come down on me like a ton of bricks when I caught sight of something that made me weak-kneed with relief. The officer Stokes had sent into the building was leading Tamsin Lynd out, his arm around her, and Tamsin appeared to be in good physical shape. She was walking on her own. She was crying and shaking, but she seemed to be unhurt. Not a drop of blood on her.

Following my gaze, Stokes and Claude saw her, too.

'She's your missing counselor?' Claude asked.

'Yes,' I said, relief making me almost giddy. I strode over to her and didn't even think about the other two, right on my heels.

'Lily, are all of you okay?' Tamsin called, pulling away from the officer to grip my arms.

'Except Janet,' I said. I told her Janet had gone in the ambulance.

'What on earth happened here?'

I became aware that the audience had grown quite large around us, listening to this exchange. One glare from Stokes sent them scattering, but she and Claude flanked me.

And at that moment, looking into Tamsin Lynd's eyes, I remembered the phone calls and the slit throat of the squirrel, and the fear she lived with. I had been very upset, deeply upset, but in that second I drew myself under control. 'There was a dead woman in your office,' I said, after a little pause to let the two cops stop me, if they would. 'Where were you?'

Only someone who'd witnessed at least part of Tamsin's problem would have understood her reaction.

'Oh, my God,' she moaned. 'Not again!'

'Again?' I repeated, because that hadn't been quite what I

expected. Then, I said more harshly, '*Again?* You've found women killed in your office more than once?'

'No, no. I just mean . . . the whole cycle. You know, I called you about the squirrel being left hanging on my front porch,' she said tremulously, her shaking hand pointing to Claude.

'I know about your past problems,' Detective Stokes said curtly. Claude rumbled, 'I'd gotten a sort of outline picture.' Tamsin nodded. She made an effort to control her ragged breathing and tears.

After a moment, she went on. 'I was hiding in the therapy room,' she confessed. She looked at my face as if it were up to me to absolve her of this piece of self-preservation.

'Saralynn got there early so I could give her my little orientation speech. I said hi to her and then I remembered I'd left some papers in the therapy room, so I went in there to fetch them, and while I was in there, I heard . . . I heard . . .'

'You heard the woman being killed?'

Tamsin nodded. 'And I shut the door,' she said, and shuddered and gasped. 'As quiet as I could, I shut the door and then I locked it.'

That was hard to swallow. We had ventured into a building we thought contained danger, to help Tamsin. But from her own account, Tamsin wouldn't open the door to try to save a woman's life. I made myself choke this knowledge down, shove it aside. Fear could make you do almost anything: I had known fear before, and I was willing to bet this wasn't Tamsin's first experience of it. 'Didn't you hear Janet come in?' My voice was as even as I could make it.

'That room's pretty soundproof,' she said, pushing her dark hair out of her eyes. 'I thought I heard someone calling down the hall, but for all I knew it was the same person who'd killed poor Saralynn, so I was too scared to answer. That was Janet, I guess. Then, later, I heard other sounds, other people.'

I'd have said we'd made enough noise to establish our identities, but it wasn't my business. Now that I knew the situation was more or less under control, I would be glad to leave, if Claude would give me a green light. I was finding that the idea of Tamsin cowering in a safe, locked room – while one woman was killed and another popped over the head – was not agreeing with me.

I had opened my mouth to ask Claude if I could go when another car pulled into the parking lot, toward the back where the police cars weren't as thick. Cliff Eggers sprang out as though he'd been ejected. He hurried to his wife.

'Tamsin!' he cried. 'Are you all right?'

'Cliff!' Our therapist hurled herself into the big man's arms and sobbed against his chest. 'I can't stand this again, Cliff!'

'What's happened?' he said gently, while Stokes, Claude, and I stood and listened.

'Somebody killed a woman and left her in my office!'

Cliff's dark eyes bored into Claude, another large white male.

'Is this true?' he asked, as though Tamsin often made up fantasies of this nature. Or as though he wished she had.

'I'm afraid so. I'm the police chief, Claude Friedrich. I don't believe I've had the pleasure?' Claude extended his hand, and Cliff disengaged from Tamsin to shake it.

'Cliff Eggers,' he responded. 'I'm Tamsin's husband.'

'What do you do, Mr Eggers?' Claude asked in a social way, though I could practically see Detective Stokes twitch.

'I'm a medical transcriptionist,' he said, making an obvious effort to relax. 'I believe your wife is one of my clients. Mostly I work out of our home, my wife's and mine.'

We must all have looked blank.

'Doctors record what they find when they examine a patient, and what they're going to do about it. I take the recordings and enter the information into a computerized record. That's paring my job down to the bare bones.'

I had no idea Carrie employed a medical whatever, and from his face Claude had either been ignorant of it, too, or had forgotten; he wasn't happy with himself. I was probably the only one present who knew him well enough to tell, though.

'You live here in Shakespeare?' Claude said.

'Right over on Compton.' Cliff Eggers's big hand smoothed Tamsin's hair in a cherishing gesture.

I was about to ask Tamsin if she'd heard anyone leave the building before our group had broken in, when I heard a voice calling, 'Lily! Lily!'

I peered around the parking lot, trying to find its source. Full dark had fallen now, and the lights of the parking lot were busy with insects. The people buzzed around below them, looking as patternless as the bugs. I was hoping all the police were more purposeful than they appeared. Claude was no fool, and he'd sent everyone in his department through as much training as he could afford. No wonder he was so quick to snap up a detective from a big force, one who was sure to have more experience than anyone he could hire locally. And though he'd never spoken to me of it, I was aware that Claude had quotas he had to meet, and his force was probably always trying to catch up on the minority percentage, especially since Shakespeare had had some racial troubles about eighteen months ago.

'Lily!'

And there he was; the most handsome young man in Shakespeare, prom king, and thorn in my side, Bobo Winthrop. My heart sank, while another part of me reacted in a far different way.

I turned a hose on myself mentally.

'Bobo,' I said formally.

He disregarded my tone and put his arm around me. Out of the corner of my eye I could see Claude's bushy eyebrows escalate toward his hairline.

'You okay?' Bobo asked tenderly.

'Yes, thank you,' I said, my voice as stiff as I could make it.

'Is this your friend, Lily?' Tamsin asked. She'd recovered enough to try to slip back into her therapist role, and the neutral word *friend* suddenly seemed to have many implications.

'This is Bobo Winthrop,' I told her. 'Bobo: Tamsin Lynd, Cliff Eggers.' I had done my duty.

'What happened here?' Bobo asked, giving Tamsin and Cliff a

distracted nod. I was glad to see that Detective Stokes had drawn Claude away to huddle with him on real police business.

I wanted to be somewhere else. I started walking to my car, wondering if anyone would stop me. No one did. Bobo trailed after me, if a six-foot-tall blond can be said to trail.

'A woman got killed in there tonight,' I said to my large shadow when we reached my car. 'She was stabbed, or stuck through somehow.'

'Who was she?' Bobo loomed over me while I pulled my keys out of my pocket. I wondered where the rest of my therapy group had gone. The police station? Home? If Melanie didn't tell the police the identity of the corpse herself, they'd find it out pretty quick. She'd look bad.

'I didn't know her,' I said accurately, if not exactly honestly. Bobo touched my face, a stroke of his palm against my cheek.

'I'm going home,' I said.

'Jack there tonight?'

'No, he's on the road.'

'You need me to be there? I'll be glad—'

'No.' Clipped and final, it was as definite as it was possible to be. Dammit, when would Bobo find a girlfriend or stop coming home during the summer and the holidays? There must be a special word for someone you were fond of, someone who aroused a deep-rooted lust, someone you would never love. There was nothing as idiotic, as inexplicable, as the chemistry between two people who had almost nothing in common and had no business even being in the same room together. I loved Jack, loved him more than anything, and reacting to Bobo this way was a constant irritant.

'I'll see you around,' he said, abandoning his hope that I would prolong our encounter. He took a step back, watched me get into my car and turn the key. When I looked out my window again, he was gone.

Chapter Four

When Jack called that night, he sounded weary to the bone. He was following the trail of a sixteen-year-old runaway from Maumelle, a boy from the proverbial good home who'd become caught up in the subculture of drugs and then prostitution. His family hadn't seen him in a year, Jack told me, yet they kept getting hang-up phone calls from different cities and towns around the South. Convinced their son was on the other end of the phone, sure the boy wanted to come home but was ashamed to ask, this family was getting into seriously shaky financial shape in their search for him.

'How can you keep it up?' I asked Jack, as gently as I could.

'If I don't look, they'll hire someone else,' he said. Jack sounded older than thirty-five. 'People this driven always do. At least I'll really try my best to find the boy. Ever since we found Summer Dawn Macklesby, I'm the guy to see for missing kids.'

'Have you even had a glimpse of this kid?'

'Yes.' Jack didn't sound happy about it. 'I saw him last night, in the Mount Vernon area, on Read Street.' Jack was in Baltimore. 'He looks awful. Sick.'

'You didn't get to talk to him?'

'He went off with a man and didn't come back. I'll be out there again tonight. I might have to pay him for his time, but I'll have that talk.'

There was nothing to say.

'How is the surveillance going?' he asked, ready for some good news.

'She won't bend over. She's wearing a neck brace and walking with a cane, and any bending she does, she must be doing it where I can't see her. Maybe Bonnie Crider's really hurt. It would be nice to find an honest woman.'

'Not a chance. All the warning signs are there. She's a fraud. We gotta think of a way to catch this woman. Put your mind to it.'

'Okay,' I said. I said it very neutrally, because I am used to taking orders, but I am not used to taking them from Jack. However, I reminded myself in a flattening way, he was my boss now.

'Please,' Jack said suddenly.

'Okay,' I repeated, in a more agreeable tone. 'Now I have a thing or two to tell you.'

'Oh?' Jack sounded apprehensive.

'Therapy group was unexpectedly exciting tonight,' I told him.

'Oh, new woman?'

'Yes, in a way.'

'She'd gotten raped in some new way?'

'I don't know about the rape. She never got a chance to tell us. Someone killed her dead and left her in Tamsin's office.'

After Jack exclaimed for a minute or two, and made sure I hadn't been in personal danger, he became practical. 'That's all your group needed, right – a dead woman, on top of dealing with a pack of traumas. Who was she, did anyone know?' Jack was interested in my story, even more so when I told him about the dead woman, Tamsin's actions, and the new detective, Alicia Stokes.

'I can see why Claude would snap up a woman that qualified, but why in hell would a woman that qualified want to come to Shakespeare?'

'Exactly.'

'I don't know anyone on the Cleveland force, but maybe I know someone who does. I might make a few phone calls when I get back.' Jack's curiosity, which made him such a good detective, could also make him a little uncomfortable to be with from time to time. But in this case, I was just as curious about Stokes as he was.

I tossed and turned that night, seeing the wound in the woman's chest, the pale body and the red blood. I kept wondering why the body had been arranged in Tamsin's office. That was sending a message, all right: a woman murdered and displayed in the middle of all those articles about how women could overcome violence and keep themselves safe.

I thought time was overdue for Tamsin to give us a rundown on the stalker that was going to such lengths to terrorize her. After all, now the whole group was involved in Tamsin's problem, though we had come to her to get rid of our own.

Finally, I got out of bed and pulled on shorts and a T-shirt, socks and walking shoes. Jack wasn't home, and I couldn't sleep, so it was back to the old pattern. I slipped my cell phone and my keys into my pocket and left my house, making a beeline across the street to the arboretum that filled the whole block opposite mine. Estes Arboretum is one of the town's less popular bequests, since the land will only belong to Shakespeare as long as it remains in its leafy state. If the trees are cut down for another use, the city loses the land to the nearest living descendant of Harry Estes. Every now and then there's a flurry of resentment in the local paper about Estes. A group will protest that the city should either sell it or let it revert to the family because the trails through it are not being maintained and the trees are not properly labeled. Then there'll be a storm of cleaning up across the street, and dead branches and leaves will be carted off and new plaques affixed to the trees. The trails will be edged and new trashcans will be positioned discreetly. An elementary school class or two will visit the arboretum and collect leaves in the fall, and a few women from one of the garden clubs will come to plant some perennials in the spring. Then lovers and druggies will start visiting the park at night, trashcans will be vandalized, signs will disappear, and the whole cycle will begin again.

Right now the arboretum was in the upswing, and the petunias were being pinched back by the women of the Shakespeare Combined Church every week, Sandy McCorkindale among them, I was sure. The paths were free of downed branches and debris, and there weren't any used condoms decorating the bushes. I went over all the trails quickly and silently.

Suddenly and without warning, my right leg cramped. I hit the cement of the path a lot faster than I wanted to, and I made an awful noise doing it. The pain was intense. I knew if I could get up and stretch the leg I could recover. It was easier to imagine than to do, but I finally managed to push myself to a kneeling position, and from there I lurched to my feet. I almost screamed when I put my right foot to the ground, but within seconds the cramp had lost its hold on me.

I staggered home, my leg weak and aching. My face was covered with sweat and my hands were shaking. When I got into the house, I went to the kitchen and took an Advil. I didn't know if it would help, but a pain like that would surely leave soreness in its wake. Limping a little, I made my way into the bathroom and washed my face, patting a wet hand along the back of my neck as well.

I was grateful to be back in bed, and stretching the leg out felt so good that I was asleep within minutes of crawling between the sheets.

By the next morning I had almost forgotten about the incident. When I got out of bed to get ready to drive to my surveillance job, the muscle that had cramped was only a faint shadow of discomfort. I wondered if the cramp had anything to do with the approaching onset of my period, which was due any day, judging by my symptoms. I slipped a couple of plastic pouches in my purse to be on the safe side.

Bonnie Crider, the Worker's Comp. claimant, lived on a busy suburban street in Conway. The ranch-style homes, the small lots, the one-car garages all said 'lower middle class'. Crider had been the supervisor of a crew of men whose job consisted of shifting large boxes around a warehouse, more or less. The boxes left, the boxes arrived, but all the boxes were moved to correct areas on forklifts. Crider told the operators what to do, filled out paper-work on each and every transfer, and generally ran the place, except for the hierarchy she answered to. She'd been turned down for a promotion, and her raise hadn't amounted to what she felt she was due, according to her personnel file. So it had aroused her superior's suspicions when she'd had an 'accident' in the warehouse that had led to unverifiable back and neck injuries. A forklift driver had taken a turn too sharply and bumped Crider with the box he was shifting. She'd been knocked to the hard floor of the warehouse, and the frightened driver had called the ambulance when Crider didn't scramble right to her feet.

Crider now said she was too hurt to ever work again. She had a sore back, a stiff neck, and severe pain in one shoulder. All these conditions, she said, were chronic.

It would have been pleasant to believe her, but I didn't.

Even if I hadn't gotten the job trying to prove that very thing, I still wouldn't believe her. I had enough time, sitting there in my car, to reflect that this probably said something about me that most people might find unpleasant. So be it.

I'd alternated my car with Jack's, and now was back to mine. I'd pretended to visit the house for sale, which was on the opposite side of the street; I'd canvassed door-to-door for a nonexistent political candidate; and, I'm sorry to say, no one who was at home called me on that. They were all sufficiently uninformed to accept my assertion that there was a candidate they'd never heard of running for Congress in the district. I'd visited the convenience store, and I'd gotten gas. Bonnie Crider didn't go out much, and when she did, she stuck doggedly to the collar and cane. She didn't even go for walks. Hadn't the woman ever heard of exercise?

Of course, for all I knew, she had a home gym and was in her house now, minus all aids, bench-pressing up a storm.

I hated that idea, but when I thought of snooping closer, I was sure that any pictures I took through her window would not be admissible as court evidence. I would have to ask Jack about that.

After a couple of hours watching, I had expected to be antsy with pent-up energy. Instead, I found myself draggy and melancholy, inclined to think fruitless thoughts about situations beyond my control or affect. I wondered if the woman killed the night before had a big family. I wondered if Janet was all right, and if Tamsin could explain her behavior a little better than she had. I felt like I could take a nap.

Now, where the hell had that come from? Since when did I take a nap, or even think of doing so? I shook my head. I must be getting older. Well, of course I was. But lately I'd been thinking and feeling unlike myself. Was the difference my new living arrangement with Jack, or my new work, or the therapy?

I was doing a lot of new stuff at one time; that was for sure. Maybe all these new patterns and activities were having some kind of cumulative effect. Maybe I was being squeezed through a tube and would come out someone different.

The idea was deeply unsettling. I had perfected living the life I'd framed before I met Jack. Maybe that life had started to alter, to become more involved with the lives around it, even before he'd first come to Shakespeare on a job. But ever since I'd known him, change had become the norm.

I sat and brooded over this low-grade anxiety of mine, rousing myself every now and then to change the position of the car. I was beginning to worry about my mental state when I had a mild revelation. Of course, this was just a variation on PMS! Instead of my ordinary pattern of diminished patience, tender breasts, and backache, I was having all those plus cramps and mood swings.

But this deviation from my own body's norm was proof that my body was changing, that time was passing.

I finally convinced myself that the sanest response was, 'So what?'

Letting myself into my silent house in Shakespeare, I peeled off my sweaty clothes and headed for the shower. Fifteen minutes later, fluffing up my curls with my fingers, I checked my answering machine. My friend Carrie Thrush's voice said, 'When you come in today, give me a call, please. I know you're in the middle of learning a new job, but I have a cleaning crisis. Plus, I just want to talk to you.' I wrote her name on the notepad by the phone. The second message was from Melanie. 'Hey, I guess I got the right number, that sounded like your voice on the message. Listen, we all need to talk. Give me a call.' She read off her number, hesitated as if she was going to add something, then hung up.

For the first time, I looked at the message counter. Eight. I'd never had so many before.

A smoky voice began, 'Ms Bard, I hope you're over your shock today. This is Detective Stokes. I need you to come in to make a statement about last night.' Alicia Stokes bit out each word as though it would dissolve her mouth if it weren't perfectly enunciated.

The next call was from Tamsin, who wanted to reschedule our interrupted therapy session. I had to laugh out loud at that.

Firella had called. And Janet, sounding weak. And Carla. Everyone but Sandy. Her husband had called.

'Lily, this is Joel McCorkindale.' He had a rich, sincere voice that I would have recognized anywhere. 'I would like to speak with you about this therapy group you've been attending with my wife. I hope you don't think she broke whatever confidentiality you have to keep with the group; I just recognized you walking in last week when I dropped Sandy off. Please call me back at the church at your earliest convenience.'

I glanced at my watch. It was five-thirty. I looked up the church number and dialed.

He picked up the phone himself. His secretary must have gone home. This must be an important conversation to the Reverend Mr McCorkindale.

'Lily' he said with elaborate pleasure, when I identified myself. 'I was hoping you could come down here and we could have a talk?'

I thought about it. I'd had my shower, and felt better, though still very tired.

'I guess,' I said reluctantly. 'I can be down there in a couple of minutes.'

I put on a little makeup to obscure the dark circles under my eyes, brushed my hair, and set out. Locking my front door behind me, I plodded down the front steps and over to the sidewalk, turning right. Watching my feet carefully because the sidewalk was cracked in many places, I went past the Shakespeare Garden Apartments and then around the corner (the big squared U that went around the arboretum road bearing three names was actually a cul-de-sac) to the parking lot and redbrick buildings of Shakespeare Combined Church. Joel McCorkindale's office was upstairs over the expanded Sunday school wing, and the daycare program it housed was closed for the day. The gym was busy, judging by the cars parked outside, but it was a separate facility on the other side of the church proper. So the big building was silent when I opened the glass door at the bottom of the stairs.

I plodded up, gripping the handrail, feeling more and more exhausted as I mounted. I didn't think I'd ever felt as washed-out in my life. I managed to get to the reverend's office and knock on the door without stopping to rest, but I had to push myself. And it was karate night, too, I groaned to myself. I'd just have to miss.

Joel came to the door to open it and usher me in. It was one of those little courtesies that endeared him to so many of his congregation, especially women.

I sat down in the comfortable chair he indicated, and I was happy to do it. Joel sat in a matching chair a careful distance away – no desk between us for this conversation, another signal – and steepled his hands in front of him, his elbows resting on the arms of the chair.

'Lily, I don't know if you feel you're getting anything out of this therapy group, but I'm concerned about Sandy.'

'You should probably talk to the counselor about this.'

'I don't think she would be objective. She'll maintain Sandy needs her services, no matter what.'

'Now you've lost me,' I said, after a pause during which I tried to make sense of his words. I wondered if my mind were going through some sort of trough the way my body seemed to be.

'I have heard, not through idle gossip but through the concerns of members of my flock, that Tamsin Lynd has strong views about the relationships between men, women, and the church.

Views that don't coincide with our interpretation of the Scriptures.'

I would have left then if I hadn't been too tired to get up.

'And this is my problem . . . how?'

'I come to you for your . . . advice.'

'I'm just not understanding you.'

'I understand that y'all know each other.'

I stared at Joel's smoothly shaved face, his carefully trimmed mustache, and his razor-cut hair. He wore a very good suit, not so expensive that the people of the church would whisper, but nice enough for sure.

'Joel.' He didn't like me using his first name. I'd always found him distasteful, but fair, and I didn't want to be as ugly as my first inclination led me to be.

'Joel,' I said again, trying to pick my words carefully. 'I don't think I've ever heard Tamsin say one word about any religion in our therapy group.' I took a deep breath. 'It seems to me you should be more concerned about your wife's mental health than about the possible theological opinions of her counselor.'

'Of course, Sandy's well-being is my primary concern,' Joel said. 'I'm just – why does she feel the need to go to this group at all?' he burst out, seeming genuinely puzzled. Suddenly, Joel looked like a real man, not like a little impervious god. 'We've prayed about it and asked for her healing and her forgiveness of the one who did such a terrible thing to her. Why does she need to talk about it?'

'Because your wife was raped,' I said, as if I was telling him this for the first time. 'She needs to talk to other women who've lived through the experience. She needs to be able to express her own true feelings about what happened to her, away from people who expect so many different things from her.'

He tilted back in his chair for a moment. At that second, he looked more vulnerable than I'd ever seen him. I didn't doubt that Joel McCorkindale loved his wife. I did doubt that he knew what a burden his public persona was on his wife's shoulders and what a struggle it was for her to preserve the image of the kind of wife she thought he deserved.

'My wife was accosted in college, over twenty years ago, from what little she's told me,' he said. 'Why would she need help now?'

Accosted? He made it sound as unthreatening as a panhandler asking you for spare change – though under some circumstances, that could be pretty damn scary. And I noticed that even Joel didn't seem to know exactly what had happened to his wife. 'Don't you ever counsel members of your congregation who've been raped?' I asked.

He shook his head. 'I'd be glad to help if someone came to me with that problem, but it hasn't happened.'

'Then you're not doing your job,' I said, 'in some sense. Because believe me, Reverend, your congregation contains rape victims.'

Joel looked unhappy at the idea, though what caused that unhappiness I couldn't guess. 'How many women are in your group?' he asked, staring at his fingers so evenly matched together in front of him.

'More than me and your wife, I can tell you that,' I said sadly. 'And we're just a fraction. How many women in yours?'

He blinked. Considered. 'Two hundred fifty, more or less.'

'Then you have about twenty-five victims,' I told him. 'Depending on whose estimates you use.'

He was shocked, no question.

'Now, Joel, I have to leave. I don't think I was any help to you. But I hope you can be to Sandy, because she definitely has some heavy problems.' I pushed myself to my feet, thinking this had been a waste of time and energy, and I left.

He was still sitting in the chair when I shut the door behind me, and unless I was completely wrong, Joel McCorkindale was deep in thought. Maybe he was praying.

I had more phone calls to return, so I ate a salad and some crackers to get supper out of the way. I was hungrier than I thought I'd be, and it was a little later than I'd planned by the time I called Carrie.

Claude answered the phone and bellowed Carrie's name. I could hear her telling him she'd be there in a minute, then the sound of water being shut off.

'It's my night to do the dishes,' she explained. 'Listen, the reason I called you, the woman who's been coming in to clean every day – Kate Henderson – has taken a little sabbatical because her daughter had a baby. So I was wondering . . . I hate to mix friendship and business, but is there any way you can come in for a few minutes a day until Kate gets back from Ashdown?'

I'd cleaned Carrie's office until about eighteen months ago, when she'd found her increased patient load called for a daily cleaning, an obligation I couldn't schedule in at the time. 'I'm working in Little Rock this week,' I told her. 'But I can come Thursday and Saturday for sure. The other days, I'll have to see. I may finish up my job in Little Rock pretty soon.' That was probably optimistic thinking, but it was possible.

'I appreciate any time you can give me,' Carrie said. 'So, I'll see you tomorrow?'

'Sure. I'll get there first thing tomorrow morning before you start seeing patients, then I have to go to the Winthrops. But I can come back after you close.'

'So it'll be clean for Thursday morning and Friday morning, and you'll come in on Saturday so it'll be looking good on Monday. Great.' Relief was running high in Carrie's voice. I heard a rumbling in the background at her house.

'Claude wants to know if Alicia Stokes called you,' Carrie relayed.

'Tell him yes, and I'm just about to call her back.'

'She did,' Carrie called to Claude. 'Lily's returning her call after we hang up.'

'He says good.' Carrie listened to some more rumbling. 'He says to tell you Alicia Stokes might be almost as tough as you.'

I could hear from her voice she was smiling. 'Tell him, from me, that in that case I'll be extra careful,' I said.

Chapter Five

Alicia Stokes had her own little cubicle at the Shakespeare Police Department, which for the past three years had been 'temporarily' housed in an older home after the jail and the police station had been declared substandard and put on notice to meet the state requirements. The city had responded sluggishly, as Shakespeare always did when money was involved. After a couple of years, the new jail was completed. Prisoners could march extra yards and be incarcerated in a decent facility. To no one's surprise, the police station in front of it had run into work delays.

It was sort of nice to walk up onto a front porch to go in to see the police, but the old house really wasn't suited to the purpose, and it would be abandoned within the next two months. Alicia's cubicle was at the back of the former living room, and she'd already hung pictures of some of her heroes there. All her heroes were black and female. Alicia Stokes, obviously, had the courage to be different. And she was dedicated. She'd told me to come on in when I'd called, even though it was getting dark.

She stood to shake my hand, which I liked, and she gestured me into a chair that wasn't too uncomfortable. Unlike Joel McCorkindale, Stokes seated herself firmly on the power side of the desk. Then we both had to pretend that no one else could hear us, which wasn't easy, since the partitions were about as high as the detective's head.

'I'd like to review what happened last night,' the detective said to open the interview. 'And then, we'll get a statement typed up for you to sign before you leave.'

So I'd be here a while. I nodded, resigned.

Detective Stokes had a legal pad in front of her. She opened it to a fresh page, wrote my name at the top of it, and asked, 'How long have you been attending this survivors' therapy group?'

'This would have been my third session. My third week.'

'And all the members of the group have been raped and are in the process of recovery?'

'That's the idea.' The air conditioning, probably as old as the house, could barely keep up with the heat.

'How were you contacted to join this group? Were you already a patient at the center?'

'No.' I told her about the flyer at the grocery store and described coming to the first meeting.

'Who was there?'

'The same people that were there last night.' I went through the list.

'Did Ms Lynd say anything about others who were supposed to come?'

'No, but that wouldn't be surprising.' I remembered my own reluctance. 'I'd expect someone to have second thoughts, or back out entirely.' I remembered Tamsin looking out into the hall that first night, as though she were waiting to hear someone knocking on the door at the end of the hall.

'I guess whoever killed that woman wore a lab coat,' I said. I hadn't been able to stop speculating about that lab coat, the one used to prop the rolling chair in place. 'Was it the nurse's?' There was a staff nurse who did drug testing.

She appeared not to hear me. 'Did you pass around any kind of sign-up sheet?' Her glasses magnified her dark eyes, which were large and almond shaped. Right now, they were fixed on me in a take-no-prisoners stare.

'No, we were supposed to have the illusion of confidentiality.'

'Illusion?'

'How could we remain secret from each other in this town?'

'True enough. Has Ms Lynd ever said anything to you about her own history?'

I shook my head. 'Well, not directly.' My inner thermostat

seemed to have gone haywire. I took a tissue from the box on the desk and patted my face with it.

'What do you mean?'

'We saw the squirrel that was killed at her place. And I was there in the office when she got a phone call that seemed to upset her pretty badly.'

Of course I had to go over both incidents with the detective, but I'd expected that.

'So you had already formed the idea that Ms Lynd was being stalked?'

'Yes.'

'Did you report that to the police?'

'No.'

Detective Stokes looked at me almost archly, which was an unnerving sight. 'Why not? Wouldn't that have been the logical thing to do?'

'No.'

'Why not? You don't trust the police to help citizens?'

I was baffled by her manner. 'It would have been *logical* for Tamsin or her husband to call the police themselves. It was their business.' I shifted around in the chair, trying to get comfortable.

'Did you ever think that if you had called us, that woman might not be dead?'

I was in imminent danger of losing my temper. That would be very, very bad in this situation. 'If I had called here yesterday, and said that someone had killed a squirrel and hung it in a tree, what would you have done? Realistically?'

'I would have checked it out,' Alicia Stokes said, leaning forward to make sure I got her point. 'I would have warned Ms Lynd not to go anywhere by herself. I would have begun asking questions.'

I was figuring out things myself. 'You already knew, too,' I said, thinking it through as I went. 'You knew someone was stalking Tamsin Lynd. What did *you* do about it?'

For a long moment, I thought Stokes was going to lean across the desk and whop me. Then she collected herself and lied. 'How could we possibly know anything like that?' she asked.

'Huh,' I said, putting a lot of disgust into it. If Alicia Stokes was playing some kind of hide-and-seek, she could do it on her own damn time.

'She did look like Tamsin, didn't she?'

Detective Stokes laid her pen down on top of her yellow tablet. 'Just what do you mean, Miss Bard?'

'You know what I mean. The dead woman. She looked like Tamsin.'

'Who mentioned that to you?' Her interest was keen now.

'No one. I'm not blind. She was pale, she was plump, she was brunette. She looked like Tamsin.'

I had no idea what the detective was thinking as she regarded me.

'But as you know, I was told by . . . ,' she checked a note on the tablet, 'Melanie Kleinhoff that the dead woman was her sister-in-law, that is, the wife of her husband's brother.'

'Melanie did say that,' I admitted. 'Saralynn, wasn't that her name?'

'And yet you told me last night you didn't know the name of the dead woman.'

'No, I told you I hadn't known her. You asked me if the others had recognized her, and I told you to ask them.' Splitting hairs, but I had technically told her the truth. 'I don't like repeating what other people tell me, when I don't know it for myself.'

Detective Stokes's face told me what she thought of that, and for once I wondered if I wasn't just being balky, like a stubborn mule.

'So where is Saralynn's husband, the one who raped Melanie?' I asked. 'I guess he raped Saralynn, too, since she was going to join our group?'

'Tom Kleinhoff's in jail,' Detective Stokes said, not confirming and not denying my assumption. 'He didn't make bail on the rape charge, because he already had other charges pending.'

It would have been good if he had been the guilty one. That would have been simple, direct, and over.

'Too bad it wasn't him, isn't it?' said Stokes, echoing my thoughts. I guess that wasn't too great a leap to take.

I nodded.

'So let me just ask you, Miss Bard. Since your boyfriend, I understand, is a private eye.' The distaste in her voice told me she knew all about the circumstances of Jack's becoming a private eye; he'd left the police force in Memphis under a black cloud. 'If you think the dead woman was killed in mistake for Tamsin Lynd . . . why? Was that supposed to send a message to Tamsin Lynd herself, that a woman resembling her was killed in her office? Was it a genuine mistake – the killer finds a dark-haired fat woman in the right place so he's sure he has the right victim? Or was the message for your group?'

I hadn't speculated that far, wasn't sure if that was a conclusion I'd have reached.

'Hadn't thought about that? Well, maybe you'd better.' Alicia Stokes's expression was definitely on the cold and hard side. 'Someone thinks they've killed the woman supposed to be helping five rape victims, you've got to ask yourself why.'

She was so far ahead of me all I could do was gape at her.

'How does your boyfriend feel about you being in this group?' she asked, pounding on down the track.

'He was the one who wanted me to go to it.'

'You sure he doesn't resent you giving such a big part of your time to a group of women? Maybe he doesn't like some of the advice Tamsin gave you? Maybe Tamsin told you to stand up to him? How long has he lived here?'

Scrabbling for the most recent question, I said, 'He's lived here in Shakespeare for only a few weeks. He lived in Little Rock for a few years.'

Angry with myself for babbling, I realized just how battered I felt.

Then I began feeling angry.

Even as I tried to remember all the other questions she'd asked so I could begin to respond, I thought, Why bother? I got up.

'You sit your butt back down in that chair,' Alicia Stokes told me.

I fixed my eyes on her face.

'Before I make you,' she added.

Rage hit me like fireball. 'You can't make me do shit,' I said, slow and low. 'I came in to give a statement. I gave it. Unless you arrest me, I don't have to sit here and answer any questions.'

Stokes loomed over me, leaning across her desk, her knuckles resting on its surface. A patrolman I'd never met, a wiry freckled man, peered in the entrance to the cubicle, went wide-eyed, and backed away.

'This looks like the gunfight at the O.K. Corral,' Claude's voice said behind me.

I let out my breath in a long gust. I speculated on what could've happened if the new patrolman hadn't fetched him – would Stokes have launched herself across her desk at me? Would I have hit a police officer?

'I was just leaving,' I told Claude. I edged past him and strode out the front door, picking my way through the desks and chairs and a few assorted people with my eyes fixed on the floor. The freckled patrolman held open the front door for me. His name-tag read 'G. McClanahan'. I made a mental note that I owed G. McClanahan a free house cleaning. Right now, getting in the car and driving away appeared to be my best move.

I wondered if Claude would have a talk with Stokes now, and what that talk would be like. I knew she would have no cause to like me any better afterward, that was for sure, and I didn't know if I'd care or not. What was more certain was the fact that as fast as I could think, the detective could think faster, and I added that to the list of her sins, as I was sure her fellow officers would. Stokes was northern, black, a woman, aggressive, very tall (and I'd bet strong), and smart as hell. She would have to perform like a one-woman band to be popular, or even tolerated.

How would she live in Shakespeare? Why had she taken the job?

To my mind, that was as much a puzzle as the woman pinned to the wall in the health center. Maybe the city paid better than I'd assumed, or maybe Stokes had a master plan that included some time in a small force – a very small force. Maybe Stokes had family in the area.

But it hadn't escaped my attention that a puzzling and bizarre murder had occurred in Shakespeare (where the norm was a Saturday night knifing) just when a puzzling and mysterious detective had turned up to solve it.

Some might think that suspicious, too.

I felt groggy when I woke up. I had to force myself to obey the clock. This was one of my days in Shakespeare, and I had to clean Carrie's office in addition to putting in a stint at the Winthrops' house. Forcing myself every step of the way, I got dressed and ate; though my head was aching and the rest of me felt exhausted already, as if I'd already put in a hard day. I wondered if I had dreamed a lot – dreams that were best forgotten – and had therefore slept restlessly. I caught no echoes of it as I cleaned my teeth and fluffed my hair. I expected my new sneakers to make me perk up; I don't often get new things, and these black high-tops had been on extreme sale.

But after they were laced and tied I stared down at them as if I'd never seen them before; or my feet, either, for that matter.

I saw a car already parked in the lot to the rear of Carrie's office, and I had a feeling I'd seen it before. I just couldn't place where and when. It was an hour earlier than any of the staff should appear. When I tried the back door, it was already unlocked.

'Hello?' I said cautiously, not wanting to scare anyone.

'Good morning!' called a horribly happy voice. Cliff Eggers stuck his head out of one of the doors on the left. 'Carrie left a message you'd be coming in.'

I brought in my cleaning caddy and a few other things. I didn't know what Carrie's new cleaner kept here, so I'd piled my car with stuff. I had to do a great job for Carrie.

'And you're here so early to do medical transcriptions?' I said in a voice that would carry down the hall as I deposited my burdens.

'That's right.' Cliff appeared in the doorway again, beaming at me as though I'd said something very clever. 'It works out better for me this way. I can do the rest of my doctors at home.'

'And you like your job,' I prodded.

'It's fascinating. I learn something every day. Well, I'd better get back to it.' Cliff retreated to his desk, and I started with the waiting room. Dust, straighten, polish, vacuum, mop. In short order, the magazines were lined up on the square table in the middle of the room; the chairs were sitting in neat rows against the wall. The large mat in front of the door where most of the dirt from patients' shoes was supposed to fall had been shaken out the front door and replaced, exactly square with the door.

Cliff squeaked down the hall in rubber shoes, and I cleaned the glass barrier between the patient sitting room and the clerks' office. I saw with disapproval that Carrie's new maid had been slacking off there. And the counter in the reception clerk's area was just nasty.

'Want a cup of coffee?' he called to me after a few minutes had passed.

'No, thank you,' I said politely.

I was able to get on with the other rooms and the hall, and cleaned as fast as a dervish whirls until I reached the room in which Cliff was working.

The burly man was sitting at a desk, a headset on, and his fingers flying across the keys of a computer. His leg was moving slightly, and as I mopped behind him, I saw that he was operating a pedal. He wasn't listening to music on a CD player, as I'd at first believed. He was listening to Carrie's voice. I could barely hear it while I dusted. Carrie was saying, 'temperature of one hundred and one. Mr Danby said he'd had episodes of fever for the past two days, and his stomach had become very sore and tender to the touch. Upon examination, when the lower left quadrant of his abdomen was palpated . . .'

'You know anything about medicine?' Cliff said out loud, as I wiped the picture frames.

'No, not much,' I confessed.

'It's like listening to a soap opera every day,' he said, as if I'd asked.

'Ummm,' I said, lifting an open magazine to wipe underneath, ready to set it down exactly the same way.

'How's Tamsin doing?' I asked, just to stop him from asking me any more questions. I had seen his lips begin to form a phrase.

'She's doing well, considering what a shock she got,' Cliff said, his heavy face grim. He hesitated for a second, then said, 'And considering this has ruined our new life here.'

That seemed a strange way to put it. Here I was thinking it was Saralynn's life that had been ruined.

'It's awful about the woman who was killed,' Cliff went on, echoing my thoughts. 'But I'm Tamsin's husband, so I can't help worrying about her more than anyone. For someone whose joy is to help others, her life has been full of trouble this past couple of years.'

From what I'd seen, that was certainly true.

'You moved here from the Midwest?' I asked, trying to confirm the accent. I realigned a stack of insurance forms and put a stapler in the drawer below.

'I'm originally from northern Kentucky,' he said. 'But we've moved a lot these past few years since we both got out of school. It's been hard to find a place where we both can have the jobs we like and a good lifestyle.'

Jack and I were facing the same sort of problem right now. 'So you've been here in Shakespeare for how long?'

'A little over a year, I guess. We really like it here, and Tamsin's finally making friends.'

I wondered how long Detective Stokes had lived here. Quite a Yankee invasion we were having, here in little Shakespeare. And there was the new freckled officer G. McClanahan at the police department. I had no idea where he'd come from.

As I cleaned around Cliff Eggers's bulk, as I bundled all my things back into the car, I deliberated over asking Tamsin about her allusions to problems in the past. Cliff seemed more than willing to talk, but I knew I'd feel uncomfortable discussing Tamsin's secrets without her permission or presence.

The silent Winthrop house was just what I needed after the unexpected and aggravating presence of Cliff Eggers at Carrie's office. Since school was out, I was a little surprised to find no one at home, and quite pleased. I was able to do things exactly in the order I wanted, up to the point when Amber Jean came in the back door escorted by about six of her friends.

Amber Jean was a whole different shooting match from her oldest brother, Bobo. She cast me a casual hello, as did two of her buddies, while the rest of them behaved as though I were invisible. Actually, I didn't mind that so much. I'd rather be ignored than the center of attention.

The three boys in the group were around fifteen or sixteen, and they were going through the goofy, pimply awkward phase where they could be adults one moment and silly children the next. I'd met Bobo when he'd been around that age.

The girls were more mysterious to me. Since I'd been one, and I had a sister, I should have understood these teenagers better. But with these particular girls, maybe it was the money their parents gave them, maybe it was the 'freedom' they had (which was really lack of supervision), maybe it was their mobility . . . they all had their own cars . . . Any or all of these factors made their lives different from any experience of mine.

I was relieved when the whole group trooped out to the pool. The boys pulled off their shirts and sandals and the girls took off various things. I supposed the shorts the boys were wearing could double as swimsuits, and the girls were already suited up under their clothing. They had small swimsuits on. Really, really small.

Amber Jean's two-piece was screaming pink with a pattern of green leaves. She looked very attractive in it. She stuck her head in the sliding glass door and called, 'Lily, could you bring us some lemonade and some snacks out to the pool?'

'No.'

She gaped at me. 'No?' she repeated, and the closest of the boys began sniggering.

'No. I clean. I don't serve.' I finished mopping the floor and squeezed out the mop.

Amber scrambled to catch hold of some superiority. 'Okay, no problem,' she said in a clipped, cold voice. 'Come on, guys!' she called over her shoulder. 'We got to get the food ourselves!'

I invented something for myself to do in the master bedroom to get out of their way, and when I heard the sliding glass door shut again, I ventured out. The floor had still been damp, and they'd tracked all over it. I'd have to mop again. Well, that was my payoff for not serving. Taking a deep breath, I took care of the floor for the second time. I thought it possible Amber Jean would invent a second reason to come in, and I waited for a few minutes just in case. When she and her friends stayed out, I scrubbed the sink and polished it in uninterrupted industry.

Just as I'd cleaned the counters, Howell Three came in. This second son was Howell Winthrop the Third, but he'd been called Howell Three since birth thanks to his mother, who thought the nickname was cute. Reedy, slender, plain, and an honor-roll student, Howell was the bridge between Bobo (beautiful and moderately book smart) to Amber Jean (fairly pretty and book dumb).

'Hi, Lily,' Howell Three said. 'Oops, sorry, the floor.' He took huge steps to get across the linoleum as quickly as possible.

'Quite all right,' I said. 'It's almost dry.' Now that he was on the carpet in the living room area, Howell Three heard the noise from the pool and looked out. A look of disgust crossed his face. 'Amber Jean,' he said angrily, as though she was right by him. 'She's sunning with her top off,' Howell Three told me, sounding about ten years younger than his age, which I realized with some surprise was seventeen. 'Lily, she shouldn't do that.'

'Will she listen to you?' I asked, after some hesitation. I felt a little responsible in a roundabout way. If I had brought her drinks and chips, Amber Jean would not be exposing her breasts now. That made no sense, but it was a fact.

'No. I'm gonna call Mom,' he said, reaching a resolution. 'I hate to rat on her, but this is embarrassing. She thinks she's being cool, that they won't talk about her, but that's not true. Those girls and those guys, they'll tell everyone.' He looked at me with some appeal in his face, but I had no authority to assume the role of Amber Jean's mother. I doubted if Amber Jean would listen to me, even if I did speak; she'd probably just strip off her bikini bottom, too, to spite me.

So while Howell Three called his mother (she was at one of the family businesses meeting with an accountant) and got her promise that she was on her way home instantly, I gathered up my stuff and got out of there. The last thing I wanted was to witness a Winthrop family blowup.

And to think, I'd been so happy a month or two before when Beanie had called me to come back to work for the family. I'd missed the income the Winthrops had given me, and in a weird way, I'd missed them. What had I been thinking? Was I falling victim to the Mammy syndrome?

Shaking my head at myself, I went home for lunch.

The afternoon was supposed to be free, but I had messages on my answering machine.

'Lily, hey, we're going to try to have our meeting tonight, since Tuesday didn't work out. I hate to lose our momentum,' Tamsin said. 'Oh, this is Tamsin Lynd calling. I hope I see you tonight, same time as usual.'

Tuesday didn't work out? That was one way to put it.

I trudged unwillingly into the building that night. It was still light, of course, but the day was lying on my shoulders like a heavy coat. I craved sleep, and the aching of my back and breasts reminded me that my cycle was coming full circle.

I saw Janet getting out of her car when I entered the parking lot.

'How are you?' I called.

'Lots better,' she said, trying to smile normally and failing. 'I still have a headache, but there wasn't any fracture and everything looks normal in the X rays.'

'What does the doctor think happened to you?' I fell into step beside her and tried to slow my steps to match hers.

Janet heaved a deep sigh. 'He thinks that someone hit me with something hard on the back of the head, that my head bounced forward and hit another hard surface, and that was all she wrote. I was completely out for maybe five minutes, total. I could kind of hear you and Firella when you were waiting with me. So I wasn't really out of it that long.'

'It felt like a long time to us,' I told her. 'We were pretty worried about you.'

'I'm glad you all came in. The detective told me what happened. I don't remember seeing the dead woman, so I guess I should thank the person who bopped me. That's not a memory I want.'

'So you don't remember seeing anyone in the building?'

'Nope. I just barely remember getting here Tuesday evening. It seems to me I sort of recall walking down the hall, but even that's not exactly clear.'

The rest of the group trickled into the therapy room in near silence. Janet and I were sitting on the left side of the table, Melanie and Carla on the other. Firella came in and pulled out a chair on my other side, and Sandy scooted in the room with her gaze cast on the floor. She worked her way down to the end of the table without meeting anyone's gaze. Tamsin came in last and sat at the end closest to the door.

'We needed to meet tonight to find out how everyone's handling what happened. As you all know by now, the woman you found dead was Melanie's sister-in-law, Saralynn. She used to be married to the man who raped Melanie. They'd just gotten divorced.'

Firella shook her head. 'Sunday dinners must be hell in that family.'

Melanie nodded. Her plump, doughy face looked pinched and her eyes were definitely red. Her hair was frizzy as though she'd tried a home permanent that didn't work. But the same determination that had led her to prosecute her attacker when no one else in the world wanted to seemed to be getting her through this latest crisis.

'How are you getting along with your husband after all this?'

'We're fine,' Melanie said. 'He loves me and I love him, more than anything in the world, and he's not going to let me down. His brother is a no good piece of trash and Deke's always known it. Ain't Deke's fault his mom and dad turned out a bad 'un.'

'That's wonderful, Melanie,' Tamsin said. She didn't sound convinced, though. I leaned forward a little to get a good look at our counselor. 'Do you think your brother-in-law could be responsible for the death of his wife?'

'No, seeing as how he's in jail,' Melanie responded tartly.

I noticed that the ones who hadn't known this looked disappointed. Everyone, it seemed, would have been glad to have Tom Kleinhoff to blame for this murder.

'Why aren't you telling us how you feel about this?' Firella asked. She leaned forward so she could look right into Tamsin's face. 'Why aren't you telling us what happened in here Tuesday night?' This sudden aggression surprised almost everyone except me.

Tamsin flushed a deep plum color. 'I've admitted I was hiding in the therapy room when Saralynn Kleinhoff was killed,' she said in a low voice. I saw Sandy lean across the table to hear. 'I've admitted to being scared when I knew there was a killer in the building. I don't think that's too surprising.'

'But . . .' I began before I thought. I had leaned forward to focus on her myself. I stopped before I voiced my doubts.

'What, Lily?' Tamsin asked. But only because she had to; you could tell she was scared about what I was going to say. We were supposed to bare all to Tamsin; what about her being honest with us?

'Tell us exactly what happened,' I said, with careful emphasis.

'As far as we can tell, it could have been any one of us pinned to that wall in your office. How come Melanie's sister-in-law and Janet got attacked, and you didn't?'

'Are you blaming Tamsin for not getting hurt, Lily?' Firella asked. 'Are you blaming the victim for the crime, so to speak?'

'Yeah, where are you going with this, Lily?' Carla croaked.

Good question.

'I just want to know exactly what happened. We come here every week.' I simmered for a minute. 'We're supposed to feel safe here. How did this person who killed Saralynn get in? How'd he get out without us seeing him?'

Everyone around the table looked thoughtful after hearing my questions. I wasn't sure why I was maneuvering our therapist into telling us something that would surely upset her, but I was determined to do just that.

'As I told you the night of the incident, Lily,' Tamsin said with reluctance, 'Saralynn was supposed to come early so I could give her the little talk I give everyone before she joins the group. I'd asked her to come in at seven fifteen, a little earlier than I'd asked you to come. You were the last one to get the lecture the first night you all came, and I remembered I'd had to rush through.

'I was a little worried about Saralynn having such a close relationship with Melanie, how that would impact the group, and we talked about that a little bit.'

'You didn't hear anyone else in the building?' Firella asked.

'I may have. Now, I think I did. But it could have been someone staying late, or coming back in after something he'd left . . . anything.'

'The end door was locked?' Sandy wanted to be sure.

'No, the end door wasn't locked,' Tamsin flushed red. 'I knew you guys would be coming in. So I didn't lock it behind her.'

'Did you hear the door while you talked?'

'No. I don't think so.'

When I looked skeptical, she said, 'That's the most normal noise in the world, to me. I'm not sure I would have noticed!' She was getting angry.

'So there was a reason you had to leave Saralynn in your office?' Melanie said, to get Tamsin back on the track.

'Yes, I'd left the group list on the table in here, and I had to get it to enter Saralynn's name – just her first name – and phone number. You remember, I took that information from all of you in case we had to cancel sometime.'

'So while you were in the therapy room . . . ?' Melanie prompted.

'Okay, while I was in there I dropped everything. I spilled all my papers from my notebook and knocked my pop over.'

After a brief vision of Tamsin pushing down an old man with white hair, I realized she meant she'd spilled a soft drink. Maybe it was a northern or midwestern thing? We all waited, watching her. Janet's mouth was pulled tight against her teeth. Anger? Skepticism?

'I started picking everything up, and while I was doing that I heard someone going into my office.'

'Did you hear this person pass the door of the therapy room, or come from the direction of the end door?'

'I don't remember either way,' she admitted. 'I've tried and tried, but I don't remember.'

Sandy interrupted. 'What difference would that make, Lily?'

I shrugged. 'The difference between someone hiding in this building until he was able to catch a woman alone, and someone coming in from the parking lot – maybe after Saralynn – on purpose.'

An interesting difference, their faces said, and they turned to Tamsin again. She shook her head. 'No use, I just can't recall it. After I heard someone go into my office, I heard Saralynn say something, but I couldn't make it out. She sounded surprised but not scared. But after that, she said, 'What?' and she made an awful sound. Then there was a lot of scuffling and grunting, and I knew what was happening. I was so scared. I know I should have gone to help her, but I was so scared. I crawled over to the door to the therapy room. It was shut, you know how it falls shut? So as quietly as I could, I locked it.'

She got a chorus of sympathy from everyone in the room except me. Her eyes traveled around the group of women, coming to stop at my face.

'Lily, I think we have to get this out in the open. Are you blaming me for not going to Saralynn's aid?'

'No,' I said. 'I think that was good sense.'

'Then are you angry I let Janet come in without warning her?'

'No. If you don't go help one, why go help another?' She winced, and I knew that had sounded as if I thought her callous. 'I mean, if you expected to be killed when he killed Saralynn, you would still have been killed if you'd tried to help Janet, I guess.'

'Then what issue do you have with me?'

I thought for a minute. 'You seem . . . already scared,' I said, picking my way slowly. 'Don't you think you should tell us the rest?' I could see the fear in her face, read it in the tightly drawn line of her mouth and the way her shoulders were set. I know a lot about fear.

'That don't make a lick of sense, Lily,' Carla said.

'Well, yeah, it does,' Janet said in her unnaturally husky voice. 'Like Tamsin's already been a victim and she's anticipating being a victim again.'

'The therapist isn't supposed to talk about her own problems,' Tamsin reminded us. 'I couldn't, even if I wanted to.'

'And why wouldn't you want to? We share our big problems with you,' Carla said illogically.

'This is where you come to get help,' Tamsin began.

'Oh, yeah, like the help we got Tuesday night?' Sandy's voice was bitter and shrill. The rest of us tried to look at her without actually turning our heads to stare, because Sandy was the least forthcoming of the group by far. We didn't want to startle her, or she'd run; it was like having a wounded deer in your backyard, a deer you felt obliged to examine. 'Seeing that dead woman in your office was the scariest thing that's happened to me in a long time, and if you know anything about it or if it happened because of you, I think we have a right to know that. Because what if it's connected to one of us?' I exchanged glances with Janet, not quite following Sandy.

'Sure,' said Carla, who evidently hadn't had the same problem. 'Think about it!' I was hopelessly confused.

'You're saying,' Firella clarified, 'that maybe if Saralynn's murder ties up with something in Tamsin's past, it hasn't got anything to do with us. Maybe we'd all been scared it did? Like maybe one of the bikers who raped Lily following Lily here and killing Saralynn as a lesson to Lily?'

'Right. Like that.' Carla sounded relieved that someone understood her.

'Or like whoever raped Sandy, not that Sandy has chosen to reveal that to the rest of her sisters in the group, which every one of the rest of us has,' said Melanie, and I thought through that sentence for a moment.

Sandy flushed a deep red. 'Well, then, missy, I'll just tell you that it couldn't be connected to me because the man who raped me was my grandfather, and I'll tell you what I did about it. I put rat poison in his coffee and that son of a bitch died.'

We all gazed at her with our mouths hanging open. In a million years, not one of us could have predicted what had come out of Sandy's mouth.

Firella said, 'Way to *go*, Sandy.'

So I had a sister under the skin. Another killer. I felt myself smile, and I was sure it was a very unpleasant smile to see. 'Good for you,' I told her.

Tamsin's face was a sight. A professional excitement that Sandy had spoken up was mingled with subdued dismay at Sandy's revelation, and concern over Tamsin's own situation.

'Didn't expect that, did you?' Carla jeered.

'No,' Tamsin admitted readily, 'I never suspected Sandy would share with us, especially to this extent. Sandy, do you feel good now that you've told us what happened to you?'

I observed that attention had turned away from Tamsin, which was undoubtedly what Tamsin had wanted.

Sandy looked as though she was rummaging around inside

herself to discover what was there. Her gaze was inward, intensely blue, blind to all around her.

'Yes, I feel pretty good,' she said. Surprise was evident in her voice. 'I feel pretty *damn* good.' She looked happily shocked at herself. 'I hated that old man. I hated him. I was eighteen when it happened. You'd think an eighteen year old could fight off a grandfather, wouldn't you? But he was only fifty-eight himself, and he'd been doing manual labor all his life. He was strong and he was mean and he had a knife.'

'What happened afterward?' Tamsin asked. She kept her voice very even and low, so Sandy's flow would continue.

'I told my mother. She didn't believe me until she saw the blood on the bed and helped me clean up. He'd been living with us since my grandmother died. After my mom and dad talked, they took Grandpa to a hospital. They told him he had to stay in the mental hospital till he died, or else they'd tell what he'd done to me and he'd have to go to regular jail.'

'Did he believe them?'

'He must have, because he agreed. Oh, he tried to say no one would believe me. That was what I was afraid of, but then I turned up pregnant and of course,' and Sandy's face was too awful to look at, 'I would have had the baby to prove the paternity with.'

I felt nauseated. 'What happened with the baby?' I asked.

'I lost the baby, but only after Granddaddy was committed. And I thank God for that every day. Two days after I lost the baby, I visited Granddaddy in the hospital and I took him some coffee. It was spiked, so to speak. I was scared he'd talk his way out if he knew I wasn't pregnant anymore.'

Telling the bare and horrible truth takes its toll, and I could read that in the woman's face.

'You weren't prosecuted?' Firella, too, was keeping her voice very even and low.

'It's funny,' Sandy said, in an almost detached way. 'But though I wasn't trying to sneak in, no one saw me. Like I was invisible. If I'd sat and planned it a week, it couldn't've gone like that. No one at the front desk.' She shook her head, seeing the past more clearly than she could see the present. 'No one at the wing he was in. I pushed the button that opened the door myself. I went in. He was in his room alone. I handed him the cup. I had a plain one. We drank coffee. I told him I'd forgiven him.' She shook her head again. 'He believed that. And when the coffee was all gone – the tranquilizers had pretty much destroyed his sense of taste – I got up and left. I took the cups with me. And no one saw me, except one nurse. She never said a word. I just didn't register.' Sandy was lost in a dreamlike memory, a memory both horrible and gratifying.

'Have you ever told your husband?' Tamsin asked, and her more recent world came crashing back to Sandy McCorkindale.

'No,' she said. 'No, I have not.'

'I think it's time, don't you?' Tamsin's voice was gentle and insinuating.

'Maybe,' Sandy admitted. 'Maybe it is. But he may not want someone who's been through something so . . . sordid . . . my sons . . . the church . . .' And Sandy began crying, her back arching with huge, heaving sobs.

'He really loves you,' I said.

Her head snapped up and she gave me an angry look. 'How would you know about that, Lily Bard?'

'Because he called me into his office yesterday to ask me if I could tell him what was wrong with you. He doesn't know why you're in therapy, and he doesn't have the slightest idea how to help you.'

She stared at me, stunned. 'My husband is worried about how to help me? My husband wonders why I need therapy?'

I nodded.

Sandy looked intensely thoughtful.

Tamsin glanced down at her watch and said, 'This has already been a big night. And our time is up. Why don't we save the rest of this discussion until next Tuesday night?' She'd escaped from any further questioning, and her whole body relaxed as I watched.

With some grumbling, the rest of the group agreed. Sandy

hardly seemed to be in the same room with us any more, her thoughts were so distant. As we left the building, I saw Sandy go to the end of the parking lot and slide into the car, where Joel sat in the front seat, waiting for her. I saw him lean over to give her a kiss on the cheek, and when he did, she gripped his arm and started talking.

Chapter Six

Some days everything just works out wonderfully. I didn't have many of those, and I enjoyed one when I got it.

I got two phone calls the next morning before I started for Little Rock and the stakeout. One was from Mel Brentwood, the owner of Marvel, who asked if I would work that day. I tried explaining to Mel that since the thief had been captured I had moved on to another job. Mel replied that he hadn't been able to find anyone to fill my position and if it was at all possible, he really wanted me to come in for my former shift. It would be worth the extra pay to not have to worry for one day.

'It might be a little awkward, Mr Brentwood, having me back now.'

'Oh, they don't know you were there as a private eye,' Mel reassured me. 'As far as they're concerned, you're a regular employee who had another job offer. I told Linda to put you on the substitute list.'

I wished Jack were there to advise me. I didn't want to alienate an important client of Jack's, but I didn't want to miss a day watching Beth Crider, either. Perhaps it might be good to lull her into security for a day? Maybe she'd been feeling watched; a day free from observation might make her careless. 'Okay, Mr Brentwood, I'll be there,' I said. I laid down the phone and it rang immediately.

'Yes?' I asked, a little apprehensive.

'Babe, it's me,' Jack said.

'How are you? Where are you?'

'Still at the hotel, but we're about to leave for the airport.'

'We?'

'He's agreed to come with me,' Jack said in a low voice. 'He's in the bathroom right now, so I can talk for a minute.'

'He just caved?' I asked, incredulous.

'He's sick and scared,' Jack said. 'And a trick beat the shit out of him two nights ago.'

If the boy had been fated to be beaten, this was the right time for it to happen, I thought, but I kept it to myself. I wasn't always sure if I believed in fate or not, but sometimes it was comforting to believe in something.

Jack went on to tell me he planned to drive the boy home after they landed. Then he'd come to Shakespeare. 'No matter how late it is,' he said.

So I was already feeling unusually chipper when I parked my car at Marvel, even though I was back to wearing the loathsome leopard-print unitard. As I slung my purse and lunch bag into my locker, Linda Doan, wearing a zebra-striped workout bra and puffy black shorts, asked me if I'd had a boob implant. Since she was pinning on her 'Manager' label at the time, I was tempted to ask her what she'd leak if she stuck her breast, but I abstained, which made me proud of myself.

'No, just me in here,' I said so cheerfully that I checked the mirror again to make sure I was myself.

Even Linda looked surprised.

'You musta gotten some last night,' she observed. 'You're mighty perky today.'

I sure was. Perky. Lily Bard, perky?

As long as I was being such a cheerful team member, I asked, 'Did you get any feedback from the calisthenics class?' That had been my idea. I got tired of the cute little classes taught in the aerobics room; they all pivoted around some gimmick. The set of calisthenics we did before karate class had seemed exotic to this bunch. And extremely painful.

Linda's face took on a reserved expression. Linda was brown from the tanning bed, streaked from the hairdresser, and hard bodied from exercise. She was a little cautious, too, when she perceived that her interest was at stake. 'A couple of the women said it was the hardest workout they'd ever had,' Linda said. 'And at least one of them wanted to try it again.'

'Great.'

'Byron was telling me you know Mel?' Linda was striving to keep her voice casual, but I could tell we'd come to the crux of the conversation.

I nodded.

'Did he send you here to keep an eye on me?' she asked, abandoning all pretense of having a normal conversation.

'No,' I said. My shoelace was loose, so I squatted down to retie it.

'You stop trying to dodge me,' Linda said in a furious whisper.

'I'm not. I'm just tying my shoe.'

'Well, I don't believe that you're just here to work this job.'

'Believe what you want,' I said. I picked up the bottle of spray cleaner and the paper towels and went over to the nearest mirror to begin my cleaning round. I glanced at Linda's reflection while I worked, and when I saw her expression I knew that she really hated me. I didn't particularly care, but it would have cleared the air if I'd been able to tell her why I'd really been hired. Mel Brentwood had been clear about that point, though. He wanted me to remain just an occasional employee to the staff at Body Time.

One of the regular clients, Jay Scarlatti, a tall, lean, bony man, had taken a shine to me. He came in every morning after his run to lift some weights; afterward, he'd shower and go to work in a suit his wife had brought in the afternoon before.

Jay was interested in me physically. He had no idea what my character was like. Today, as always, he saw the body in the unitard and not the person who was wearing it.

'Hello, you beautiful thing,' he said this morning, coming up behind me while I was spraying the upholstery of one of the weight benches. 'How are you today?'

I wasn't supposed to beat on the customers, so I replied mildly that I was fine, and I hoped he was well.

'And Mrs Scarlatti?' I asked.

'Katy's fine,' he said stiffly.

'That's good. She seems like such a nice lady, when she brings in your clothes in the afternoon. It's really too bad you never have time to do that yourself.'

Jay Scarlatti was scowling.

'Being a little emphatic, aren't you?' he asked, biting the words out.

'Seems like I need to. Are you going to try calisthenics today?'

He looked startled. 'Sure, I guess so.'

'Then let's get into line.'

I stowed away my cleaning things, blew my whistle, and collected a small crowd right away. Linda and Byron got in line, too, since I'd told Byron he might have to lead this exercise when I was off.

'You'll see,' said a young muscle-builder to his pal. 'This is gonna make you sore in places you didn't even know you had muscles.' He looked excited at the prospect.

So we began, and the first time I asked them to touch the floor right in front of their toes, I heard a chorus of groans and cracking joints. But gradually they improved, and since I'd insisted on discipline from the beginning, I heard no complaints. Linda and Byron were red and panting, but they made it through the rest of the class.

Now that I wasn't watching for a thief, I actually enjoyed being in the gym all day. And I was so thankful not to be loitering in Beth Crider's neighborhood that I was extra-friendly all day.

Jack had thought he'd get home about ten, so I left some food out on a microwavable plate for him. I got ready for bed and read for a while, then heard the familiar snick of the key in the lock of the front door.

While Jack ate and brushed his teeth, I kept him company. He talked a little about the boy he'd found, about how halfway home the boy had decided he felt a little better and wanted to go back to the streets. He and Jack had had some conversation, and the boy had decided to stick to his original plan.

'What did you say to him to persuade him?' I asked.

'I just told him I'd carry him home, kicking and screaming if necessary. When he told me I wasn't capable of that, I pinched a nerve in his neck for a minute.'

'I bet that shut him up.'

'That, and me telling him I'd found and shipped plenty of runaways – just like him – home in coffins. And they never came back from *that*.'

'You've seen a lot of runaways.'

'Yeah. Starting back when I was a cop, I've seen way too many. The ones like him, the ones that started selling their butts, didn't last three years. Sickness, or a client, or self-disgust, or drugs . . . mostly drugs.'

Every time Jack tracked a runaway, he went through a spell of depression; because the fact was, the kid often ran off again. Whatever grievance had led a child to leave home was seldom erased by life on the streets. Sometimes the grievance was legitimate; abuse, mental or physical. Sometimes it was based on teen angst; parents who 'just didn't understand'.

Catching a runaway often led to repeat business, but it wasn't business Jack relished. He'd rather detect a thieving employee or catch someone cheating on a disability claim any day.

'Did you get a chance to call anyone about the new detective here?' I asked, as Jack slid into bed.

'Not yet. Tomorrow,' he said, half asleep already. His lips moved against my cheek in a sketchy kiss. 'Everything tomorrow,' he promised, and before I switched off the lamp by the bed, he was out.

The next morning when I returned from cleaning Carrie's office, Jack was in the shower. He'd already worked out, I saw from the pile of clothes on the floor. Jack didn't believe in picking up as he went, a tenet that my mother had instilled in me when I was knee-high. I took a deep breath and left his clothes where he'd dropped them.

When he came out of the steamy little bathroom fifteen

minutes later, vigorously toweling his hair, I was working on a grocery list at the kitchen table. He was well worth the wait. I sighed when Jack pulled on a pair of shorts and a T-shirt and began to brush through his long hair.

'When I got up, I called this woman I know on the force in Memphis, and she knew someone on the job in Cleveland,' Jack said.

'And?' I said impatiently, as he paused to work through a tangle.

'According to this detective in Ohio, Alicia Stokes was a rising star in the office. Her clearance rate was spectacular, she handled community appearances well, and she was on the fast track for promotion. Then she got involved in a case she couldn't solve and it all kind of fell apart.' Jack frowned at the amount of hair that came off in his brush.

'What was the case?'

'One she wasn't even the primary on,' Jack muttered, still preoccupied by his hair loss. 'That is, she wasn't the detective in charge. She did some of the related interviews, that's all. No one knows what set her off the deep end about this case. Which,' he added, seeing the exasperation on my face, 'involved a woman who was being stalked.'

I felt a deep twinge of apprehension. 'Okay. What exactly happened?'

'I heard this secondhand, remember, and I don't know how well my friend's source actually knew Detective Stokes.'

I nodded, so he'd know I'd registered the disclaimer.

'In Cleveland, this woman was getting threatening letters. Stuff was being nailed to her door, her house got broken into, she got phone calls, her purse got stolen three times, her car was vandalized . . . everything happened to this poor gal. Some of it was just annoying, but some of it was more serious, and all of it was scary when you added it up.'

'What about the police?'

'They were onto it right away. But they couldn't catch anyone. This guy, who was like Stokes's mentor, was the primary, and he pulled her in to do some of the questioning of neighbors – had they seen someone they didn't know hanging around the neighborhood? Which of the neighbors had been home when the incidents happened? You know the kind of thing.'

'So she got wrapped up in it, I gather?'

'More so than was healthy. She began to spend her off time watching the house, trying like hell to catch the guy. She was so furious about what was happening to this woman . . .'

'I can understand why.' How would it feel to think that some-one was watching your every move? Someone was waiting for you to be alone, your fear his only goal.

And that someone was able to get away with it. The police couldn't stop him; the officers who had sworn to protect you couldn't do their job. Despite everything, he would get you eventually.

Shaking my head, I leaned forward to rub my aching back. 'So she got as obsessed about finding the stalker as the stalker was about his victim?'

'Yes, that's about the size of it.'

'So, what happened?'

'She was warned off three times. The department gave her a lot of slack, because she was a good detective, she was a woman, and she was a minority. They didn't want to have to fire her. After a while, when she seemed to be watching the victim as much as the stalker was, they gave her a long leave of absence so she could get her head on straight.' Jack looked disapproving; no one had suggested he be extended the chance of a leave of absence when he'd misbehaved. They'd wanted him gone. If he hadn't resigned, he would've been fired.

'So, no matter what Alicia Stokes told Claude, she's really still an employee of the Cleveland Police Department.'

'Yes,' said Jack, looking surprised. 'I guess she is. Surely Claude called up there when she applied for a job here; that's one of the first steps, checking references. You call and get the official story. Then you use the network of cops you know to get the real story, like I did this morning. So Claude must know about her problems.'

But I wondered if Claude, chronically understaffed, had taken the extra time.

I shook my head free of problems that really didn't concern me and returned to work on my grocery list. It was taking me an awfully long time to finish my task. I couldn't seem to concentrate. Truthfully, I was feeling less than wonderful. When Jack showed signs of wanting to make up for his inattention the night before, I had to wave him off. It was the first time for that, and when he looked surprised I felt obliged to tell him I was about to have my monthly time, and that somehow it felt worse than usual. Jack was quite willing to leave our discussion at that; I think he feels it's unmanly to ask questions about my femaleness.

After thirty more minutes, my list was complete and I'd figured out the weekly menu. Also, I was in pain. Jack agreed to go to the store for us, and when I saw the worry on his face, I was embarrassed. I was seldom ill, and I hated it; hated going to the doctor, spending the money on prescriptions, not being my usual self.

After Jack left – after many admonitions and a lot of scolding – I thought I might lie down, as he'd suggested. I couldn't remember the last time I'd lain down during the day, but I was feeling very strange. I went back to our room and sat down very carefully on the edge of the bed. I swung my legs up and lay on my side. I couldn't get comfortable. I had a terrible backache. The weird thing was, it was rhythmical, I would feel a terrible tense clenching feeling, then it would back off. I'd have a few minutes of feeling better, then it would start again.

By the time I heard Jack unloading groceries in the kitchen, I was sweating and scared. I was lying with my back to the bedroom door, and I thought of turning over to face him, but it seemed like a lot of trouble to move. His footsteps stopped in the door.

'Lily, you're bleeding,' he said. 'Did you know?' There was lot of panic behind the calm words.

'No,' I said, in the grip of one of those pulses of pain. 'Gosh, and I put a pad on, just in case. I've never had this much trouble.' I was feeling too miserable to be embarrassed.

'Surely this isn't just your period?' he asked. He went around to the side of the bed I was facing and crouched down to look at me.

'I don't think so,' I said, bewildered. 'I'm so sorry. I'm just never sick.'

He glared at me. 'Don't apologize,' he said. 'You're white as a sheet. Listen, Lily, I know you're the woman and I'm the guy, but are these pains you're having . . . have you by any chance been timing them?'

'Why would I do that?' I asked, irritated.

'Your back hurts?' he asked, as though he were scared of the answer.

I nodded.

'Low down?'

I nodded again.

'Are you late?'

'I'm never very regular. Hand me the calendar.' Jack got my bank giveaway calendar from the nail in the kitchen and I flipped back to the months before. I counted. 'Well, this one is late. I don't know why it's so painful, my last one was just nothing. A couple of spots.'

If I was as white as a sheet, we were a matching set. Jack lost all his color.

'What did you say?' he asked.

I repeated myself.

'Lily,' he said, as if he was bracing himself. 'Honey, I think you . . . I think we need to get you to the hospital.'

'You know I don't have insurance,' I said. 'I can't afford a hospital bill.'

'I can,' Jack said grimly. 'And you're going.'

I was as astonished as I could be. Jack had never spoken to me that way. He said, 'I'm going to call an ambulance.'

But I balked at that. It would take us only four minutes to get to the hospital in Shakespeare, and that's even if we caught the red light.

'Just put the bath mat down over your car seat,' I suggested, 'in case I leak any more.' Jack could see I wouldn't go unless he did as I'd said, so he grabbed the bath mat and took it out to his car.

Then he returned to help me up, and we went out to the car during a moment when I wasn't actively in pain. I got in and buckled up, and Jack hurried around to his side of the car and jammed the key into the ignition. We went backward at a tremendous rate, and Jack got out into the street as though there were never any traffic.

After a minute, I didn't care. I was really hurting.

Suddenly, deep inside me, I felt a kind of terrible wrench. 'Oh,' I said sharply, bending forward. I took a deep breath, let it out . . . and the pain stopped.

'Lily?' Jack asked, his voice frantic. 'Lily? What's happening?'

'It's over,' I said in relief. I looked sideways at Jack, but he didn't seem to think that was good news. Just when I was about to ask him if he'd heard me, I felt a gush of wet warmth, and I looked down to see blood. A lot of blood.

I felt very tired. I thought I would lean my head against the car window. It felt cool against my cheek. Jack glanced over and nearly hit the car ahead of us.

'What's happened to me?' I asked Jack from a far distance, as we pulled into the emergency room carport and he pushed open his door.

'Stay right there!' he yelled, and disappeared inside the building. The bath mat underneath me turned red. I congratulated myself on my foresight, trying not to admit to myself that I was terrified. In seconds, a nurse came out with a wheelchair. Jack helped me out of the car, and the minute I stood up my legs were drenched in a gush of fluid. I stared down at myself, embarrassed and frightened.

'What's happened to me?' I asked again.

'Hon, you're miscarrying,' the nurse said briskly, as if any fool should have known that.

And I guess she was right.

Chapter Seven

Carrie was there in five minutes, and she confirmed what the nurse had said. I was so shocked I didn't know which piece of knowledge was more stunning; the fact that I'd gotten pregnant without knowing it, or the fact that I'd lost a baby.

'Our baby,' I said to Jack, trying to absorb the loss, the impact of the facts. Tears rolled down my cheeks and I was too tired to blot them. I didn't know if I was exactly sad or just profoundly astonished.

He was just as amazed as I was at the whole incident. He left the cubicle in the emergency room abruptly, and I was left staring after him from the gurney.

Carrie re-entered. 'He's crying,' she whispered to me, and I could not imagine that. Then I remembered that when Jack's previous lover, Karen Kingsland, had been murdered, she had been pregnant. Carrie said, 'Did you really not know?'

'I never even thought of it,' I admitted. 'I never put everything together. I guess I'm just dumb.'

'Lily, I am so sorry. I don't know what to say.'

I shook my head. I didn't know what she could say, either.

'I thought I had too much scar tissue,' I told Carrie. 'I thought between the indications that I wouldn't be very fertile, and the fact that we used birth control every single time, I was safe as I could be.'

'Only abstinence is a hundred percent safe,' Carrie said automatically. Her round brown eyes fixed on me from behind her big glasses. 'Lily, I have to do a D and C.'

That meant operating room fees and an anesthesiologist and an overnight stay in the hospital. I began to protest.

'You don't have an option,' she told me firmly.

Jack said, 'You do what you have to do, Carrie. We're good for it.' He'd come back through the curtains behind her. His eyes were red. He took my hand.

'You know,' Carrie said very slowly, propping her bottom against the wall and hugging a clipboard to her chest, 'If this has happened once, this could happen again.' She rested her chin on the clipboard, and I could tell she was thinking of saying something she knew she ought not to say.

I looked over at Jack. His hair was hanging in tangles around his shoulders, and his scar almost gleamed in the harsh overhead light. He didn't seem to know what to think, and I couldn't even figure out how I felt about what had just happened to me, or at least how I fully felt. But the truth was, it was like being at the bottom of a deep pit of sorrow.

'A baby,' Jack said tentatively. 'A baby.'

'Lots of work,' I said, thinking of the Althaus home.

Carrie braced herself. 'Of course,' she interjected in a very low voice, looking anywhere but at us, 'I think it's always nice if a baby's parents are married.'

'Oh, no problem,' Jack said absently. Then he snapped to, and his eyes met mine. I shrugged.

Carrie perked up. Her glasses glistened as she raised her head. 'So, you guys are going to get married?'

'No,' I said. 'We already are.'

After all that 'parents should be married' preaching, Carrie gave us hell because we were married. I'd been her only bridesmaid, and I should've returned the compliment; Claude would've liked to have been at the ceremony; they would've welcomed the chance to give us a wedding present; etc.; etc. Blah, blah, blah.

'Listen, Carrie,' I told her. 'I am going to say this once because I am your friend. We don't want to talk about being married, we don't want to change the way we are, we don't want to put it in the papers. I haven't even told my parents, though Jack did tell his sister, since he can't seem to stop hinting.' I cast a look at Jack, who had the grace to look abashed. 'This isn't a good day for us anyway, right? Wait and hop on us when I feel better.'

'I'm sorry.' Carrie apologized thoroughly. 'Listen, Lily, I'm going to do your D and C in . . . ,' she looked at her watch. 'About an hour. The operating room'll be free then, Dr Howard's in there now.'

'What can I expect afterward?'

We went over that for a while, and I began to feel better. Carrie was sure I'd be feeling physically well very soon.

When she ducked out from the curtain, Jack took my hand. He hooked a chair with his foot, drew it closer, and settled in by the bed, resting his head against it. We were still and quiet together for a while, and it was wonderful after the hubbub of arriving at the hospital, the struggle to remove my jeans, the shock of the miscarriage. I felt drained, mentally and physically. I'd lost a lot of blood. After a while, I think I dozed a little, and Jack may have, too.

As I drifted in and out of uneasy napping, I was thinking that this was the first time I'd felt really married. It felt like a cord ran between Jack and me, an umbilical cord, pulsing with life and nutrients. Then I thought of the baby, the baby who'd been attached to me with a real umbilical cord, and I thought of Jack leaving this brilliant white cubicle to cry for our lost child. I stared at the wall, at the incomprehensible medical things attached to it, and I considered that if I had not allowed Jack into my life, none of this pain would have been mine or his. Dry eyed, I stared at the wall, from time to time stroking his dark hair, and I did not know if I was glad or miserable that I'd ever seen him.

That evening Tamsin and Cliff came to my room. It was a double, but there wasn't another patient in there, which was a relief I was sure I owed to Carrie. Jack had left to spend a little time at the house cleaning up the disorder we'd left behind us that morning and to shower and change. I'd been dozing again, this time from the anesthesia, and I was startled to open my eyes and see the couple standing in the doorway.

'Tamsin,' I said. 'Cliff.'

'I was visiting a client on my lunch hour and I saw your name on the admissions list,' Tamsin explained. She had a little arrangement of daisies and baby's breath in her hand. 'Are you feeling all right, Lily?'

'Yes, much better,' I said, being careful not to move. 'Thanks for coming by.'

Tamsin placed the flowers on the broad windowsill, and Cliff came to the side of the bed and peered down at me. 'We've had a miscarriage, too,' he said. 'Tamsin lost our baby about three years ago.'

Tamsin looked away, as if the mention of the loss was a reproach.

'How are you doing?' I asked her.

'You mean, about the death of Saralynn?'

I nodded.

'I'm adjusting,' she said. 'Her mother came to see me. That was bad.'

'I can well imagine,' I lied.

'I brought you some magazines.' Tamsin fumbled with a bag. 'Here, maybe one of them will distract you for a while.' She arranged a stack on my rolling table. She'd been smart enough to avoid *House Beautiful* and *Vogue*.

'Thank you,' I said.

'Then, I guess, we'll see you later. I hope you feel better.'

'Thank you.'

After they'd left the room, I was ashamed of my eagerness to have them gone. I didn't want to see anyone, not a soul, but normally I would have expended some effort to be more polite.

Between the slit left between the curtains, I could see the late summer sun setting on one of the longest days of my life. I was seeing only a slice of the brilliant ball of glory, the briefest flare of red and orange. I looked for a long time. Then I pressed my call button.

The nurse eventually arrived to help me to the bathroom. She was a burly middle-aged woman who had no sympathy for me at all . . . kind of a relief after the emotional fire-walking I'd had that day.

As I shuffled back to my bed across the bright linoleum, I realized that Tamsin herself must be going through much the same difficulty. Her life was churned and risky, and she and Cliff most probably could not see any end to that risk.

In my self-protective way, I wanted to hold my counselor at arm's length because I had too much trouble of my own to help her out of hers.

Whatever Tamsin was doing, or whatever was being done to her, I wanted no part of it. I had worked myself into a state of revulsion for my increasing entanglement in the lives of others, even Jack. This was where it led, to this hard white bed in this hard white place, where pieces of me bled out of my body.

I caught my breath, revolted by my own self-involvement.

When Jack returned, he tried to hold my hand, but I pulled my fingers away and turned my eyes to the wall.

'I'll feel better before long,' I promised the wall. I forced myself to go on. If there was anything I hated, it was explaining myself. 'I'll just brood for a while and get it over with.'

I just couldn't, shouldn't, treat Jack this way. I was ashamed. I did my second least favorite thing, and began crying. My tears felt hot against my face. I bit my lips to keep from making a sound, but it didn't work.

'I'm sorry,' I said, 'I'm sorry I couldn't hold on to our baby.'

'Move over.'

I scooted as much as I could in the narrow bed. I heard Jack's shoes hit the floor and then the mattress took the weight of his body. He wrapped himself around me. There was not anything to say, but at least we were together.

Chapter Eight

The next morning, right after Carrie checked me over, I went home. Jack was silent for the short drive, and so was I. When we got to the house, he came around the car and opened my door. Slowly, I swung my legs out and got up, glad he'd brought me clothes to replace my ruined jeans. Trying to be modest in a hospital gown would've been just too much. I was a little shaky, but he let me make my own way into the house.

When I looked around the living room, I was stunned.

'Who?' I asked. Jack was focused on my face, his own dark and serious. 'What . . . ?'

A vase of pink carnations was on the table by the double recliner. Three white roses graced the top of the television. A small dried bouquet was arranged in a country basket on my small bookshelf.

'Go lie down, Lily,' he said.

I shuffled into our bedroom, saw two more little flower arrangements and two cards. I sat gingerly on the edge of the bed and eased back. I swung my legs up.

'Where'd these come from?' I was realizing that my initial idea, that Jack had gotten them all, was just plain crazy.

'Carrie and Claude. Janet, the dried arrangement, and she brought some chicken. Helen Drinkwater left a card in the door. Marshall brought you a movie to watch; a Jackie Chan. Birdie Rossiter sent flowers and included a card from her dog Durwood.' Jack's voice was very dry. 'The Winthrops sent flowers, Carlton from next door dropped by and left a card, the McCorkindales brought flowers.' Jack picked up a notepad he'd dropped on the night table. 'Let's see. Someone named Carla brought you a sweet-potato pie. Someone else named Firella called, said to tell you she'd be bringing by a ham tonight.'

People here in Shakespeare had been kind to me before, helped me out when I needed it, but this was a little overwhelming. The Drinkwaters, for example. Since when had they cared about my well-being? The McCorkindales? I'd been beaten black and blue before and they hadn't noticed. Something about my losing a baby had struck a chord.

'How did they find out so fast?'

'You were brought up in a small town and you haven't figured that out?' Jack tried to sound teasing, but couldn't quite manage it.

I shook my head, not feeling smart enough to figure out how to untie my shoes.

'McCorkindale, the minister, visits at the hospital every evening. Beanie Winthrop is a volunteer Pink Lady. Raphael Roundtree's oldest daughter is an admissions clerk, so Raphael carried the news to Marvel. I had to call your clients and tell them you couldn't come in this week, so they knew. I arranged with the sister of the woman who does Carrie's office for the Winthrops and the Althauses to be covered this week, and she's best friends with Carla's little sister.'

'You did?' I was so startled by all this that I was caught off balance. 'I won't go to work this week? But Carrie said I would be okay tomorrow,' I said. I could feel the blood rush into my face. 'I could—'

'No,' Jack said flatly.

There was a long silence.

'What?' My fingers began to roll into fists.

'No.' Jack's face was quite expressionless. 'You are not. And before you get that look on your face, listen to me. What Carrie actually said was, you would be feeling fine tomorrow if you took it easy. That means no work. That means you really do stay home and take it easy. Now,' and he held up a warning hand, 'I know you're going to get into the "I have to earn my living" speech, and I know you're going to get mad.'

He was quite right about that.

'But, I am telling you, you are finally going to take the time you need to recover from something, and I am going to make sure you do it.'

'Who are you to tell me anything?' I was starting off low, but I could feel the pressure building.

'Lily, I am . . . your . . . husband.' With the emphatic spacing of someone who wants to be clearly understood.

And all at once, like the tidal wave that precedes a hurricane, understanding washed over me. As though it would hold me in the room, my fingers clenched the bedspread as I stared without focus, the stunning facts washed off my anger. I had lost *our baby*. This man was *my husband*. I gasped air in desperately, fearing I would choke.

Jack stepped closer to the bed, obviously worried.

I felt tears run down my cheeks. I couldn't seem to let go of the bedspread to get a Kleenex.

'Lily?'

Wave after wave of complete comprehension swept over me, and it felt as though no sooner did I rise to my feet in the surf than another surge swamped me. I was weeping for the second time in two days. I hated it. Jack handed me tissue after tissue, and when the worst had passed, he stayed there, not moving, clasping me against his warmth.

'I'm sorry,' I said, trying hard not to care that I sounded quavery and weak. 'Jack, I'm sorry.' I felt guilty that I hadn't been able to carry his child, guilty I hadn't managed better than Karen Kingsland, though there was no comparison between us. 'This is so stupid,' I managed to say, and was grateful when he didn't agree.

I didn't know I'd gone to sleep until I woke up. Jack had had a bad night, too, and I could tell from his breathing that he was dozing behind me. I thought over what he'd said to me. I made myself admit that he'd made sense. I made myself admit that before, when I'd gone back to work early after an injury, I'd done myself harm.

Even though I'd known I loved Jack for months, I was shocked by the power he had in my life. I hadn't thought this through; I guess you can't, you love someone without counting the change. I began to wonder what influence I exerted over Jack. He didn't smoke or drink; though he'd formerly done both to great excess. He'd hardly had time to think about another woman, and I knew ahead of time how I would handle that: it would be very bad.

I couldn't think of anything that I wanted Jack to do, or not do, differently. So . . . Jack was perfect? No, that wasn't really how I felt. I knew Jack was imperfect. He was impatient, which meant he didn't always take time to plan things out. He relied too much on intuition. He had a hard time handling his pride.

I rolled over to face him. I looked at his eyelids, at the relaxed face with its thin nose and slightly puckered scar. Jack had been divorced twice, and he'd had the disastrous affair with Karen Kingsland, a cop's wife. Karen had been in her grave for five years now. For the first time, I wondered what the other wives had looked like, where they were now. For the first time, I was admitting to myself that I was one of those wives. One result of keeping our marriage secret was that I hadn't had to consider myself really Jack's wife, hadn't had to acknowledge the whole load of baggage and implication that was carried in the word *wife*.

Well, we could make of it what we would.

Sooner or later, I had to tell my parents.

I could picture them doing cartwheels in the streets, but I could also imagine them sobering up when they thought of the fact that Jack had been married twice before. And they'd have to consider Jack's notorious affair with Karen, whose husband had ended up shooting Karen dead in front of half the Memphis Police Department – and on television.

Well, all those women – including Karen, who'd been using Jack to make her husband pay attention – were idiots. Anyone who let Jack go was, by definition, a fool.

I didn't often think of cosmic systems, but in this instance I had to conclude that these other women had only parted with Jack so I could have him.

The doorbell rang, and when Jack didn't twitch, I eased off the bed and padded barefoot down the hall through the little living room, to answer the front door.

Carol and Heather Althaus were wearing matching short sets, pink-and-purple plaid cotton camp shirts tucked into pink shorts. Carol was holding Heather's hand, and in her other hand she had a Hallmark gift bag. Carol looked far uneasier than her daughter.

'Oh, I'm afraid we woke you up!' she said, eyeing my rumpled hair.

'I was awake. Come in.' I stood to one side, and Heather was across the threshold in a flash, tugging at Carol to follow. Once the two were seated, Heather said socially, 'This is such a nice little house, Miss Lily.'

'Thank you.' I wasn't often called upon to show company manners. 'Can I get either of you a glass of ice water or some cranberry juice?'

'Thanks, no, we can only stay a minute. We don't want to wear you out.'

'Are you feeling better?' I asked Carol.

'Oh, yes! You know how it is. Once the morning is past, I'm fine.' Then she realized I certainly did not know how it was, and she closed her eyes in mortification. She made a little waving motion with her hand, as if she were erasing what she'd said. Heather was looking at her mother like she'd grown horns.

'If I'm not up to par by next Monday, I believe Jack called you to say he'd arranged for someone else to help you out?' Social talk was definitely uphill work for me.

'You're gonna come back, though, aren't you, Miss Lily?' Heather's narrow face was tense as she leaned toward me.

'I plan on it.'

Her shoulders collapsed with the weight of her relief. 'We brought you a present,' she said, and slid off the loveseat to carry the bag over to me. She gave it to me ceremoniously, her face serious.

Jack came from the hall to sit on the arm of my chair. He introduced himself while Carol eyed him much as she would have a pet tiger. Heather seemed less anxious and more interested.

There was a card in the bag, one with a teddy bear on the front. The bear's arms were spread wide and the legend inside read, 'Big Hug'. Okay.

The gift had been picked out by Heather, I knew as soon as I extricated it form the nest of yellow tissue. It was a figurine of a harassed-looking blonde with a dustcloth in one hand and a broom in the other.

'That's you,' Heather explained. 'Do you like it?' She edged very close while she waited for me to speak.

'That's just the way you stand at the end of the day,' Jack said, over my shoulder. I could tell he was smiling from the sound of his voice. I re-examined the slumped posture of the figurine and suppressed a snort. 'I like it very much,' I told Heather. I glanced at Carol to include her in my thanks. 'I'm going to put it on these shelves over here, so my company can see it.'

Jack was off the chair arm and carrying the figurine very carefully over to my small bookcase. He positioned it dead center on top, looked to me for my approval.

'Thanks,' I said. 'Heather, does that look okay?'

'I want a hug,' Heather said.

I tried to shove my surprise aside quickly. I scooted forward in the chair and opened my arms. It was like holding a bird. A sharp grief lanced through me, and I had to restrain myself from holding the child tightly to me. I sighed as silently as I could, patted Heather on the shoulder, and gently let her go.

Jack drove in to Little Rock on Monday morning, leaving me with a long list of restrictions: only a light amount of exercise, only a little driving, no cleaning.

After I ate a slow breakfast, I realized I felt much better – physically, anyway. It was still only seven fifteen, and I was already at loose ends. So I went to Body Time and got on the treadmill for a while, and did a little upper body work. Marshall Sedaka, the owner of the gym, came out of his office to talk to me, looking more muscled up than ever. I thanked him for giving me the Jackie Chan movie. After he'd commiserated with me awkwardly over the miscarriage, he told me about the woman he was dating now. I nodded and said, 'Oh, really?' at the right intervals, wondering if he'd ever look at Janet Shook, who'd been doing her best to attract him for years.

Tamsin and Cliff were being shown the ropes by one of the young men who seemed to stream through Body Time on a regular basis. They liked working out, Marshall had told me one day when he was feeling discouraged, so they thought they'd like working at Body Time. The fact was, as I'd found myself from my recent experience at the gym in Little Rock, that working for low pay in a gym is just the same as working for low pay at any other job. This particular young man was one I vaguely recognized as being a friend of Amber Jean Winthrop. In fact, I was almost certain he was one of the crowd by the Winthrops' pool, the day Howell Three had gotten so upset.

Tamsin was looking lumpy and lost in her Wal-Mart workout ensemble of cotton shorts and black sports bra, topped with a huge T-shirt that must have been borrowed from her husband. Cliff was not faring any better, projecting discomfort and uncertainty though he was wearing an old pair of sweatpants that he must have saved from college and an equally ancient T that was full of holes.

'What a role reversal,' Tamsin said, with a wan smile. 'Here we are in your place of power, instead of mine.'

She hadn't taken the words right out of my mouth, since I never would have said that out loud, but she'd taken the thoughts right out of my head. And it was interesting that she thought of the health center as her 'place of power'. The assault that had taken place in her own office must have shaken her to her mental and emotional foundations. Considering that, she'd made a great recovery.

'You're gonna start coming in every morning?'

'Well, we're going to try. Cliff and I both have been eating too much; we've just been so nervous. That's what I do when I'm nervous, I head for the doughnuts. Jeez, do you have any body fat at all?'

'Sure,' I said, feeling awkward.

'I'm glad you feel well enough to come in this morning,' Tamsin said, her dark eyes uncomfortably sympathetic.

'Thanks for your visit while I was in the hospital,' I said dutifully. 'I enjoyed the flowers.'

'When I lost my baby . . . ,' she began, to my discomfort. But just at that moment, Cliff gestured to her to rejoin him, since the young man was explaining yet another piece of equipment.

I left before Tamsin could speak to me again, on purpose. At the moment, I didn't want to assume anyone else's problems, since my own were bearing down on me.

But later that day, I would've been glad to have listened to Tamsin talk her heart out. Correction. Maybe not glad, but I would have tolerated it with a much better grace. Hanging around doing nothing was not a state of affairs I was used to. I cleaned my kitchen cabinets, slowly and carefully, only slightly violating Jack's dictum. I was in a silent house, since Jack had assumed my stakeout on Beth Crider. He called home once on his cell phone to find out how I was feeling and to tell me he was having no more luck catching her out than I'd had.

That night, when he was drying the dishes while I washed, Jack expressed disgust that we hadn't closed the books on Beth Crider.

'Maybe she's really hurt,' I said, without conviction.

'Huh.' Jack didn't seem troubled by doubt about that. 'In the years I've been a private detective, I've investigated one case where the guy was really hurt as badly as he claimed. One. And every now and then, I still drive by his house to check, because I can't quite believe it.'

'The level of cynicism here is pretty deep.'

'Absolutely. Did you have any time to check Beth's credit rating today?'

'Sure did,' I said. Jack had a computer program that seemed able to call up anything about an individual's financial history. To me, it seemed frightening that he didn't have to produce any kind of ID, or explain his purpose, in buying this program. Joe Doe could buy one as easily as law enforcement personnel. 'If I did everything right, nothing seems to have changed on her credit history.'

'Then she's smarter than most of them, but we'll nail her,' he said, confidence running strong in his voice. 'Next week, you can take over surveillance, if you feel well enough. I should spend some time in the office, returning phone calls.'

I managed to keep my face still, but I had to acknowledge to myself that I was feeling gloomy. Jack would be spending some nights in Little Rock next week. He had rented a room in his friend Roy Costimiglia's house, the room vacated by Roy's son when he'd gotten married the year before. Jack could come and go as he pleased and not bother with renting an apartment, so the arrangement suited him perfectly. I'd known when Jack moved in with me that he would have to stay in Little Rock some of the time. I just hadn't counted on missing him.

'Sure,' I said. 'Listen, did you find out anything else about Saralynn's murder?' Jack and Claude had shared a beer the night before while Carrie and I talked. Claude had kind of taken to Jack, since there were few people in town he could talk to freely. Jack, an outsider experienced in law enforcement and married to a woman who didn't gossip, was heaven-sent to Claude.

'I don't think they're making any progress on the case,' Jack said, 'though maybe I'm reading in between the lines. And the new detective – well, everyone except the new guy, McClanahan, has come to Claude to complain about her. Too Yankee, too black, too tough.'

'You'd think they'd want a fellow officer to be tough.'

'Not if she's a woman, apparently. She ought to be able to back them up on the street, but then she ought to let them take the lead in everything else. And she ought not to want to be promoted as much as they do, because they deserve it more, having a wife and children to support.'

'Oh,' I said, enlightened.

'Right.'

'You think she's crippled as a police officer, down here?'

Jack mulled this over, as he brushed back his hair and secured it at the nape of his neck.

'No, but she'll have to try like seven times as hard as a guy, and probably twice as hard as a Southern white woman,' Jack said. 'I'm glad I'm not in her shoes.'

That very day, who should drop by to see me but Detective Alicia Stokes. I opened the door, hoping I didn't look as surprised as I felt. Instead of her career clothes, Stokes was looking good in walking shorts and a sleeveless T-shirt, serious walking shoes instead of sandals at the end of her long legs.

'You feeling better?' Stokes asked, but not as if she actually cared.

'I'm fine,' I said with equal enthusiasm.

'I need to talk to you.'

'Okay.' I stood back and let her into the (by now) spotless little house. 'Would you like a Coke?' Letting Jack do the grocery buying had had its consequences. He had gotten a bag of Cheetos, too.

'Sure.'

'What kind?'

She stared at me.

'You said Coke. That's what I want.'

I didn't bother explaining that I called all soft drinks 'Coke', like most Southerners. I just got her some. I didn't often drink carbonated drinks, but I joined her in a glass. Once I'd gotten her settled in a chair, and had satisfied the dictates of hospitality, I asked Alicia Stokes what I could do for her.

'You can tell me what you think about Tamsin Lynd.'

'Why do you care what I think?'

'Because everyone in the damn town says you are the one to ask.'

I found that inexplicable. But it seemed to me that it would look like I was being falsely modest if I asked for her to tell me more about that, so I shrugged and told her I hardly knew Tamsin well.

'And she's your counselor?'

'Yep.'

'Because you were raped.'

'Yes.'

'All right. What kind of job do you think she's doing?'

'A pretty good one.'

'How do you figure that?'

I said carefully, 'Those of us who weren't talking at the beginning are talking now. I don't know how she did it, and maybe she didn't have a lot to do with it at all, but it's a fact that we're all dealing with what happened to us, in some way or another.' There, hadn't I put that well?

'You think I'd fit in the group?'

'No.'

'Why not? Cause I'm Yankee? Cause I'm black?'

'Tamsin's a Yankee. Firella is black.'

'Then why?'

'Because you haven't been raped.'

'How do you know that?'

I shook my head. 'You wouldn't have to worry about fitting in with the counseling group if you had been raped.' And that mark just wasn't on her, though I wasn't about to say that. She'd ask me how I knew, and I just couldn't tell her. The mark was not on her.

'So, in your opinion, how can I get close to this woman?'

'Why do you want to?'

'I need to watch her.'

I was getting a growing feeling of doom.

'It's her,' I said.

'What?'

'It's her. You took a leave of absence from the Cleveland force to watch her.'

'How did you know that?'

I shrugged.

'You better tell me now.'

'Jack made a few phone calls.' I didn't want her to think I'd had a look at her personnel records or learned something out of school from Claude.

She sat back in her chair, tall and black and tense and angry.

'I know about you, too.'

'Most people do.'

She didn't like that. I didn't like her. I felt a certain grudging admiration for someone who would pursue a case with such relentless determination. At the same time, it seemed kind of nuts. Like the man who'd pursued Jean Valjean . . . what was his name? Inspector . . . Javert, that was it.

'What about this has you so hooked?' I asked, in honest puzzlement.

'I think she's doing it herself,' Alicia Stokes said. She sat forward, her long hands capping her knees, her Coke forgotten on the table beside her. 'I think she's fooling everyone, and I can't let her get away with it. The man hours we wasted in Cleveland . . . enough to work four extra cases, cases where people really needed us. As opposed to trying to protect one neurotic woman who's actually persecuting herself. She had everyone else fooled. Everyone.'

I gave Stokes a long hard look. 'You're wrong,' I said.

'On what basis?'

'She's done good. She can't be that crazy. We would know.'

'Oh yeah? You a licensed shrink? You know there have been cases like this before. They're almost all women. All the men, they feel sorry for the poor persecuted woman. They feel frustrated because they can't protect her from the evil demon who's doing this to her. Then it turns out she's doing it all herself!'

Alicia Stokes certainly believed what she was saying. I looked down at my hands, considering. I was trying to reconfigure my world, trying to see Tamsin as Stokes saw her. Tamsin, with her medical transcriptionist husband and her little old house. Tamsin, with her nice conservative clothes and her plump belly, her good mind, her compassionate nature. Nothing I got from Tamsin added up to the kind of emotional horror that could plan and execute such clever schemes against herself.

But I could be wrong. As the detective had pointed out, I was no therapist.

What if Stokes was right? The consequences – to me, to the whole group – would be devastating. We had all placed our trust in each other and begun to build on that; but the basis of this trust was the foundation laid by Tamsin Lynd.

I looked up to find the detective leaning forward, waiting patiently for me to finish my thoughts.

'Could be, couldn't it?'

'I guess,' I said, my voice reluctant and unhappy. 'I guess you realize that your own behavior is pretty damn fishy.'

Stokes was startled, and almost lost her temper. For a long, tense moment, I could see the war in her face. Then she pinched her lips together, breathed in and out, and collected herself. 'I know that,' she said.

'It's not my business,' I said slowly, surprising myself by telling her what I was thinking, 'but what are you going to do when this is over? Sooner or later we will know the truth. The Cleveland Police Department may not take you back. Claude will be very angry when he finds he hired you under false pretenses. How did you get past his checking your references?'

'My superior owed me the biggest favor in the world,' Alicia Stokes said. She put the palms of her big hands together, bumped her chin with the tips of her fingers. I'd seen her make the gesture before, and it seemed to indicate that she was feeling expansive. 'So I knew when Claude called him, he'd get a good recommendation from Terry. I passed the physical and psychological tests, no problem.' She smirked. 'The others were glad I was going. They wouldn't say anything – or I might stay.'

I tried not to let my surprise show on my face. Quite a change of heart, here: Stokes was sharing more than I wanted her to. But then I thought, Whom else could she talk to? And she must want to talk, want it desperately.

Detective Stokes needed a good therapy group.

Something twittered in the room. I looked around, startled.

'It's my phone,' Stokes said. She pulled it from a small pouch clipped to her belt. 'Yes?' she said into the unfolded phone, which looked very small in her hand.

Her face became hard as she listened, and the fire burned hotter in her eyes. 'I'll be there,' she said abruptly. The phone went back into the depths of her purse. 'Take me to Tamsin Lynd's house,' she said.

So she'd walked to my place. As I grabbed my keys, I looked back at the detective. Oddly, Stokes looked almost happy – or at least, less angry.

'Is Tamsin all right?' I asked, venturing onto shaky ground.

'Oh, yes, little Miss Counselor is just fine. It's her husband, Cliff, who's hurting.' Stokes was positively grinning.

I could find out what had happened without leaving my car, as it turned out. Cliff was on the lawn bleeding, and the ambulance attendants were bent over him, when we arrived within three minutes of the call.

'Stay here,' Alicia ordered, so I sat in the car and watched. I think her goal had been to keep me out of the crime scene, or the situation, whatever it was. If she'd been thinking straight, instead of being so intent on the scene, she would've sent me home. What did she need me for, now that I'd provided transportation?

It wasn't too hard to read the evidence. Cliff's leg was gashed and bleeding, as they say, profusely. In fact, the medics had cut away his pants leg. I could see that one of the steps going up to the side door of the house, the door nearest the garage, was missing its top. Splintered wood painted the same color as the other step was lying on the ground.

Well, this could have been an accident. Hefty man meets weak board. Cliff's leg could have gone through the step, scraping his shin in the process. However, that wouldn't really fit the facts. The leg was gashed, not scraped; I could see that much, more clearly than I really wanted to. And surely, for that kind of ordinary accident, one wouldn't call an ambulance.

Someone tapped on my window, making me almost jump out of my skin. It was the new policeman, Officer . . . there was his nametag, McClanahan. I lowered the window and waited.

'Ma'am? You need to move on,' he said apologetically. He laid his hand on the door. He was wearing a heavy gold ring, and he tapped it against the car door as he stared off at the paramedics' activities.

I looked at him, really looked at him, for the first time. He wasn't tall, or fat, or pumped, or handsome. In fact, he was a plain pale man with freckles and red hair, a narrow mouth, and light green eyes that were much the color of a Coke bottle. But there was intelligence there, and assurance, too, and then there was the odd coincidence of his always being at hand whenever I was with Detective Stokes.

'Then you will have to tell Detective Stokes that you told me to go home, since she told me to stay right here,' I said.

We took each other's measure.

'Oh, really,' he said.

'Really.'

'Lily Bard, isn't it?'

'You know who I am?' People never looked at me in the same way once they knew. There was always some added element there: pity, or horror, or a kind of prurient wonder – sometimes even disgust. Curiosity, too. McClanahan was one of the curious ones.

'Yes. Why did the detective ask you to wait here?'

'I have no idea.' I suspected she'd just plain forgotten she didn't need me any more, but I held the knowledge to myself.

He turned away.

'Where are you from?'

It was his turn to jump. 'I haven't lived here long,' he said noncommittally. His bottle green eyes were steady and calm.

'You're not . . .' But I had to stop. To say, 'You're not an ordinary cop,' would be unbearably patronizing, but it was true that Officer McClanahan was out of the general run of small town cop. He wasn't from around here; he wasn't from below the Mason-Dixon Line at all, or I'd lost my ear completely. Granted, the accents I heard every day were far more watered down than the ones I'd heard in my youth; a mobile population and television were taking care of that.

'Yes, ma'am?' He waited, looking faintly amused.

'I'll leave,' I said, and started the car, I had lost my taste for sparring with this man. 'If Detective Stokes needs me to come back, I'll be at home.'

'Not working today?'

'No.'

'No cleaning jobs?'

'No.'

'Been ill?' He seemed curious, mildly amused.

'I lost a baby,' I said. I knew I was trying to erase 'Lily Bard, the victim' from his mental pigeonhole, but replacing that version of me with 'Lily Bard, grieving Madonna' was not much better. If I'd been fully back to myself, I would've kept my mouth shut.

'I'm very sorry,' he said. His words were stiff, but his tone was sincere enough to appease me.

'Good-bye,' I said, and I pulled away. I went to Shakespeare's Cinema Video Rental Palace, picked out three old movies, and drove home to watch them all.

Maybe I would take up crocheting.

Chapter Nine

Bobo Winthrop stopped by that night. He knew the whole story about Cliff Eggers.

'There was a stake hidden under the steps,' he told me, the relish of the young in his voice. We were sitting on my front steps, which are small and very public. I wanted the public part. There were good reasons I should not be alone in a private place with Bobo. I had my arms around my knees, trying to ignore the ache in the pit of my stomach and the unpredictable flares of misery.

'Stake a-k-e, not steak e-a-k?'

He laughed. 'A-k-e. Sharpened and planted in the dirt under the steps, so when the step gave way, his leg would go down into the area and be stuck by the stake.' He pushed his blond hair out of his face. He'd come from karate class, and he was now in his *gi* pants and a white tank top.

'I guess that would've happened to anyone's leg,' I suggested.

'Oh. Well, yeah, I guess so. If his wife had come home before he did, she would've gotten hurt instead of him.'

I hadn't thought of that, and I winced as I pictured Tamsin going through the step and being impaled on the stake. 'Did he have to stay at the hospital?' I figured if Bobo knew all this, maybe he knew even more.

'Nope, they sent him home. It was really an ugly wound, Mary Frances's aunt told me – she's an emergency room nurse, Mrs Powell is – and she said it looked worse than it really was. But it's going to be really sore.' Mary Frances was one of Bobo's former girlfriends. He had a talent for remaining on their good side.

Janet Shook came jogging down the street then, her small

square face set in its determined mode, and her swinging brown hair darkened with sweat around her ears and temples.

'Stop and visit for a minute,' I called, and she glanced at a watch on her left wrist and then cast herself down on the grass. 'Want a lawn chair?'

'No, no,' she panted. 'The grass feels good. I needed to stop anyway. I'm still not a hundred percent after that knock on the head. And I had karate class, tonight. You should have been there, Lily. Bobo and I got to teach two ladies in their sixties how to stand in *shiko dachi*. But I missed running. I've signed up for a ten K race in Springdale next month.'

Janet and Bobo began a conversation about running – wearing the right shoes, mapping your route, maximizing your running time.

I laid my cheek on my knee and closed my eyes, letting the two familiar voices wash over me. At the end of a day in which I'd done mighty little, I managed to feel quite tired. I was considering Cliff's leg going through the step – what a shock that must have been! – and the hostile visit of Detective Stokes. I mulled over green-eyed Officer McClanahan. I wondered if he'd seen the body of poor Saralynn Kleinhoff, if he'd looked at her with the same cool curiosity with which he'd eyed me.

Surely his face was familiar to me, too? Surely I had seen him before? I had, I was sure, after a moment's further thought. I began to rummage around in my memory. He hadn't been in a police uniform. Something about a dog, surely? A dog, a small dog . . .

'Lily?' Janet was saying.

'What?'

'You were really daydreaming,' she said, sounding more than a little worried. 'You feeling okay?'

'Oh, yes, fine. I was just trying to remember something, one of those little things that nags at the edges of your mind.'

'What Marshall doesn't realize,' Bobo said to Janet, evidently resuming a conversation that my abstraction had interrupted, 'is that Shakespeare needs a different kind of sporting goods store.'

I could feel my eyebrows crawl up my forehead. This, from a young man whose father owned a sporting goods store so large there was a plan to start producing a catalog.

'Oh, I agree!' Janet's hands flew up in the air to measure her agreement. 'Why should I have to drive over to Montrose to get my workout pants? Why shouldn't the kids taking jazz at Syndi Swayze's be able to get their kneepads here? I mean, there are some things *you just can't get* at WalMart!'

I'd never seen Janet so animated. And she sounded younger. How old could she be? With some astonishment, I realized Janet was at least seven years younger than I was.

'So, are you totally satisfied with your job?' Bobo asked, out of the blue.

'Well.' Janet scrunched up her face. 'You know how it is. I've run Safe After School for four years now, and I feel like I've got it down. I'm restless. But I don't want to teach school, which is the only thing I'm trained for.'

'My family, we're all merchants,' Bobo said.

It was true, I realized, though I'd never have thought to put it that way. Bobo's family had made their money selling things; the sporting goods store that leaned heavily toward hunting and fishing equipment, the lumber and home supplies store, and the oil company that had supplied the money to build the Winthrop empire.

'So,' he resumed, 'I guess it's in my blood. See, what I've been thinking lately – now you tell me if you think this is a good idea, Janet, and of course you, too, Lily – I think that the sporting goods store isn't really the kind of place most women and kids want to come into. What they want, I think, is a smaller store where they can come in without going through a lot of crossbows and fishing rods and rifles, a smaller store where they can find their running shorts and athletic bras and those kneepads you mentioned – the ones you need to wear when you take jazz dancing.'

'Tap shoes,' said Janet, longing in her voice. 'Ballet slippers.'

'I think we really have an idea here.'

'It would be great,' she said, philosophically. 'But ideas aren't money to underwrite a store start-up.'

'Funny you should mention that,' Bobo said. He was grinning. He looked about eighteen, but I knew he was at least twenty-one now. 'Because my grandfather's will just got probated, and I happen to have a substantial amount of money.'

Janet gaped at him. 'We're talking serious? You weren't just dreaming? You really think there's a possibility of doing this?'

'We need to do a lot of figuring.'

'We?' Janet asked, her voice weak.

'Yeah. You're the one who knows what we need. You're the idea woman.'

'Well.' Janet sounded out of breath. 'You actually mean it?'

'Sure I do. Hey Lily, would you mind if we finished Janet's run and went over to her place to talk? What do you think about this idea?'

I felt rueful and old. 'I think it's a great idea for both of you.'

Janet's face lit up like a torch. Bobo's was hardly less excited. In a second, they were stretching before they began running. I noticed Bobo's eyes running over Janet's ass when she bent over. He gave a little nod, all to himself. Yep, it was a nice ass.

As they set off down the street, I had to smile to myself. All those hours I'd worried about Bobo's inappropriate affection for me, all the times I'd tried to repulse him, hate him, fight my own shameful physical attraction to him . . . and all it took was Janet Shook's brain, ass, and a dash of mercantile blood.

I went inside, and when I'd locked the door behind me, I laughed out loud.

The next morning – the next boring, boring, morning – I went to the library. I needed to swap my books, and I thought I might do some research on runaways. Jack had discussed printing a small pamphlet on the search for runaways, since so much of his business came from such searches. It would be good to feel I'd accomplished something.

The modest Shakespeare library was in the oldest county

building, which was about the rank at which most Shakespeareans placed reading. In the summer, it was hot, and in the winter, the pipes clanked and moaned and the air was warm and close. The ceilings were very high. In fact, I believed the building had been a bank at one point in time. There was a lot of marble.

To humanize the building, the librarians had added curtains and area rugs and posters, and on pretty days the attempt worked. But today was not such a day; it was going to rain, and the uniform sullen gray of the sky was echoed in the marble. I stepped from the damp heat of the morning into the chilly marble interior and shivered. Through the high windows, with the happy yellow curtains pulled back to show the sky, I could see a silver maple tossing in a strong wind. The rain would come soon.

I consulted one of the computers, and began scribbling down a list of books and magazine articles. One article was very recent. In fact, it should still be in the current magazine area, a sort of nook made comfortable by deep chairs and an area rug.

After I'd read the article and made some notes, I picked up a copy of *People* and flipped through it, amazed all over again that the reading public would be interested in the outsider's view of the life of someone they would never know. Why would a hairdresser in Shakespeare care that Julia Roberts had worn that designer's slacks to the premier of a new movie? Would a bartender in Little Rock ever be the richer by the knowledge that Russell Crowe had turned down a part in that film?

Of course, here I was, reading the same article I was deriding. I held the magazine a little closer to peer at a ring some singer had paid a third-world budget to purchase. A ring . . . a celebrity magazine. Suddenly, some synapsis fired in my head.

The picture I remembered wasn't in this magazine in particular, but I associated the picture with a magazine very like it.

How had I happened to see the picture? These things weren't on my normal reading agenda. I pulled and prodded at my faint memory until I'd teased a thread loose. I'd seen the picture when I'd been at Carrie's office, when I'd been dusting. The magazine had been left open in one of the rooms – which one? I could almost see the cover after I'd automatically flipped the magazine shut and returned it to a pile. The cover had been primarily ivory, with the picture of an actress – maybe Julia Roberts again – dressed in jeans and boots and a handkerchief, looking brilliant against the neutral color. Carrie's office!

Trying to keep hold of the image in my memory, I drove to Carrie's. Of course, her office was open and full of patients, and I explained to the receptionist that I wasn't there to see the doctor, that I was trying to find something I'd lost the last time I'd cleaned. Gennette Jenks, the nurse, gave me a suspicious look, but then Gennette was always suspicious of me. A hard-faced woman in her fifties, Gennette was chemically brunette and naturally efficient, which was the only reason Carrie kept her on. I looked around the small front office, which was crammed with a fax machine, a copier, a huge bank of files, and mounds of paper everywhere. No magazines.

And no magazines in Carrie's office besides a tattered old *Reader's Digest* left there on the little table by the chair in front of the desk. That was the bad-news chair; because most often when Carrie invited patients into her office and sat behind her desk, that meant she was about to deliver bad news. I twitched the chair to a more hospitable angle.

The magazine I'd been seeking was in the big pile on the table by the waiting area, a few chairs at the end of the hall where caregivers could wait while their charges were being examined. I shuffled through the stack and extracted the cover I'd been searching for. I stepped sideways into the little room where the part-time clerk, a milkmaidish blonde with a lust for Twinkies, worked on insurance claims. This was the same room where Cliff Eggers had been working the morning I'd cleaned, and this was where I'd picked up the magazine and returned it to the pile. That explained why I'd remembered the magazine. I'd stood in there for such a long time while he talked to me, I'd had time to memorize the cover.

After nodding to the clerk, who gave me an uncertain smile in return, I began paging through the magazine. Once, twice . . . I was beginning to doubt myself when I noticed the jagged edge. Someone had removed a page from the magazine. Maybe it had had a great recipe for chicken salad on the other side – but on the whole, I doubted that. Someone besides me had found the picture interesting.

Now that I knew what issue of what magazine I needed, I returned to the library, dashing through the first blast of rain to push through the heavy glass doors. Lightning was making patterns in the sky and the wind had increased in pace, so the view through the high windows was ominous. Mary Lou Pettit, the librarian working the circulation desk, was clearly unhappy about the violence of the weather. As I crossed the large open area in front of the desk to reach the periodicals area, she caught my eye and gave an exaggerated wince, inviting me to share her anxiety. I raised my hand to acknowledge her, and shrugged,

To tell you the truth, I've always liked a good storm.

I'd checked the date on the magazine at Carrie's office. Now I found that the one I wanted had been put away. I filled out a slip, handed it in, and waited ten long minutes while an aide looked in the periodicals storage room. I passed the time by watching the rain lash the windows in irregular gusts.

Refusing to peek until I was by myself, I sought out a half-concealed table in a corner behind the stacks. I turned to the page that had been clipped from the copy I'd checked. 'Author protects privacy' was the uninspired headline, and I checked the other side to see if there was anything more interesting there. But it turned out to be an ad for a diet supplement, one I'd seen in many, many other periodicals, so I flipped back.

The author in question was a man of medium height and build, swathed in a track suit and baseball cap, further shielded with sunglasses. He was holding leashes with two little dachshunds trotting at the ends.

Okay. So this wouldn't be an instant answer. I scooted my chair closer to the table and began to read. There was only one other person in sight, a bony and lashless young man who worked as a bagger at one of the grocery stores. He was reading a computer magazine. He seemed completely engrossed.

So I began scanning. Author of true-crime bestsellers *Baby Doll Dead* and *Mother and Child*, reclusive Gibson Banks . . . blah, blah, blah . . . real name kept completely secret by his publisher . . . only picture his publisher is allowed to release . . . 'He probably rented the dogs for the picture,' said Gary Kinneally, the photographer. 'He didn't seem to care for them at all.'

I examined the picture again. I whipped out the little magnifying glass that attached to my key chain, a stocking stuffer last Christmas from my sister. I'd never had occasion to use it before, but now I was glad I had it. It took a moment's practice to learn how to use it effectively, but finally I had it on the man's face. I looked at his skin very carefully. The picture was not in color, but I could tell the hair was not dark. No mustache. I analyzed his body.

He was probably five foot ten, maybe one fifty-five or one sixty. I moved the magnifying glass over his hand, the one extended holding the leashes.

I looked at his hand real close. And then I looked again.

And then I got mad.

He wasn't at the police station. It was his day off, the dispatcher told me. I was lucky not to encounter Claude on my way out.

How'd I know where his house was? I'd seen him coming out of it as I took one of my night walks. At the time, I hadn't realized who he was, or at least what his cover identity was. At the right modest house on Mimosa Street, I pulled up in front, not caring that I was halfway onto his lawn. I was across the sodden grass and onto his front porch before you could say, 'Traitor.' I was too angry to raise my hand to knock. I turned sideways, raised my leg, and kicked.

Officer McClanahan looked up from his computer in understandable surprise.

Chapter Ten

'Miss Bard,' he said, getting up very, very slowly. 'Are you all right?'

'I think not,' I said, softly. The rainwater was trickling down my face. I shivered in the air conditioning because my clothes were soaking wet.

'I have no intention of attacking you,' he pointed out, and I realized I had dropped into fighting stance, my body aligned sideways to him, my knees bent, my hands fisted; the left one in chamber, the right one poised in front of me.

'I might attack you, though,' I said. I circled to the right a little. He was stuck behind his computer desk, and it was hard to see what he could do about it. I was interested to find out. 'I know who you are,' I told him.

'Damn. I ripped the picture out of the magazine at the doctor's office when I was there for my allergy shot. I knew there were lots more copies around town, but so many people could see that one.'

I sensed movement and glanced toward the door that led into the back of the house. Two little dogs stood there, the dachshunds from the picture. They didn't bark, but stared at me with round brown eyes and wagged their tails in a slow and tentative way.

I looked back quickly to 'Officer McClanahan'. He hadn't budged.

'Was it them that gave me away?' he asked. His voice was calm, or he was working mighty hard to make it seem so.

'The ring.'

He looked down at his finger. 'I never even thought of it,' he said, his voice heavy with chagrin. 'The dogs, yes. But I never thought of the damn ring.' It was heavy and gold, with a crest of some kind with one dark blue part and one white, as background; I hadn't been able to tell the colors from the picture, of course, but I could tell dark and light. 'My college ring,' he told me.

'The dogs weren't just props,' I said.

'No, and I laughed like hell when I read that story,' Gibson Banks said. He pointed at the dogs. 'This is Sadie, and this is Sam.' His face relaxed into a smile, but mine didn't. If he thought cute names for his dogs would charm me, he had the wrong woman. 'I can tell you're very angry with me,' he continued, the smile fading.

'No shit,' I said. I moved a little closer and the dogs came in to sniff me. I didn't react to their cold noses pressing my ankles, and I didn't take my eyes off him.

'Well, what are you going to do? Are you going to hit me, or what?'

'I haven't made up my mind,' I said. I was at ease with standing and thinking about what to do, but he was getting jumpy. My breathing was even and good, the discomfort in my pelvis now only a slight ache, and I was fine with kicking him. I wondered if Jack would come back to Shakespeare to bail me out of jail, and I wondered if the trial would take very long.

'You betrayed me, and my friend Claude,' I said.

'I misled you.'

'You came to write about my life, without telling me.'

'No, not your life.' He actually looked indignant.

I found myself feeling strangely embarrassed, guilty of some form of hubris. 'Jack's?'

'Not even Jack's, as fascinating as it is to any aficionado of true crime that you two are a couple.'

'Who, then?'

'Tamsin Lynd,' Gibson Banks said.

'Does Claude know who you are?' All the fire left me, abruptly and without warning. I eased into a chair close to the desk.

'He knows I'm Gerry McClanahan, a police officer who wanted to live in a small town.'

'That's who you really are? Your real name?'

'Yes. I spent fifteen years on the St. Louis force before I found out I liked writing just as much as I liked being a cop. Since then, I've lived all over America, moving from case to case. Europe, too.'

I held up my hand to stop his digression. 'But Claude doesn't know you're also Gibson Banks.'

Gerry glanced down, and I hoped he really was feeling a little ashamed. 'No. I've never taken a real job to be closer to a story before. I figured it was the only way to stay hidden in a town this small.'

I ran a hand over my face. Claude had one cop who was a writer in disguise, another who was obsessed with proving her own version of a current case. 'I'm going to tell him,' I said.

'I wish I could persuade you not to, but I hear Chief Friedrich and his wife are your friends.'

'Yes.' Gerry McClanahan, aka Gibson Banks, didn't sound upset enough to suit me.

'What about Tamsin Lynd?'

'She's my counselor.'

'What do you think about what's happening to her?'

'I'm not giving you a quote. If you think you're going to put me in your book, you deserve anything you get.' I felt like someone was boring through me with a giant awl. My poor life, so painfully reconstructed, and it was all about to be destroyed. 'Don't write about me,' I said, trying not to sound as though I were begging. 'Don't write about Jack. Don't do it.' If he could not hear the despair, he was a stupid man.

If he had smiled I might have killed him.

But – almost as bad – he looked cool and detached. 'I'm just here in Shakespeare following the Tamsin Lynd story,' he said after a long pause, during which the sound of the rain dripping from the roof became preternaturally loud. 'A middle-class woman of her level of education, in her line of work, being stalked by a madman as she moves around America? That's a great story. You know Tamsin and Cliff have moved twice to escape this guy? But somehow he always finds out where she is and begins leaving her tokens of his – what? His hatred of her? His love of her? And she's this perfectly ordinary woman. Bad haircut, needs to loose some pounds. It's amazing. It could happen to anyone.' Gerry McClanahan was speaking with such gusto that I could tell he was delighted to have someone to talk to.

'But it's happening to her. She's living this. You're not watching a movie,' I said, slowly and emphatically. Talking to this man was like talking to glass. Everything I said bounced off without penetrating.

'This case has even more twists than even you can imagine. Look at finding you, such a name in true crime books already, and Jack Leeds, whose television clip is a true piece of Americana.'

He was referring to that awful footage of Karen's brains flying all over Jack's chest when her husband shot her. I had a moment of dizziness. But McClanahan hadn't finished yet.

'And you're just sidebars! I mean, think. One of the counselees getting killed in the counselor's office? That's amazing. This case has turned upside down. When it's over, and I wrap up my book, think of how much women in America will know about being stalked! Think of all the resources they'll have, if it ever happens to them.'

'You don't give a tinker's damn about the resources available to the women of America,' I said. 'You care about making money off of someone else's misery.'

'No,' he said, and for the first time I could tell he was getting angry. 'That's not it. This is a great story. Tamsin is an ordinary woman in an extraordinary situation. The truth about this needs to be told.'

'You don't know the truth. You don't know what is really happening.'

He put his hands on the yellow legal pad on his desk and leaned on it as if he were guarding its contents. He focused on me. 'But I'm very close. I'm right here; working on the investigation into the murder that took place in Tamsin's office! The death of a woman who was killed just to make some weird point to Tamsin!

How much closer can you get?' He was flushed with excitement, the bottle-green eyes alight with elation.

I thought of many things to say, but not one of them, or even all of them, would have made any impression on this man. He was going to ruin my life. I once again thought of killing him.

'I'll bet that's how you looked before you pulled the trigger,' he said, his eyes eating me up. For an interminable moment I felt exposed before this man.

'Listen,' he said. 'Keep quiet, let me see this through, and I'll leave you out.'

I stared at him. Bargaining?

'I'm doing as good a job as any other policeman on this force. I'm really working, not just playing at it. If you let me follow this story to the end . . . you're home free.'

'And since you're so honest, I should believe you?'

He pretended to wince. 'Ouch. The truth is, I've done more watching out for Tamsin than any cop could ever do. In case you hadn't realized it, I bought this house because it backs catty-cornered to Tamsin and Cliff's. I watch. Every moment she's home and I'm not at work, I watch.'

'Let me get this straight,' I said slowly. 'You're stalking her, too?'

His face flushed deeply. He'd never put it that way to himself, I was willing to bet. 'I'm observing her,' he said.

'No, you're waiting for someone to get her.'

I got up and left his house.

'Remember!' he called after me. 'If I get to keep my job, you get to keep out of the book!'

I went right to Claude. I was in that period of grace, the time between the moment the bullet hits and the moment you begin to feel the pain; in that period of grace, you actually felt numb, but you knew something dreadful was coming. (At least, that was what some gunshot victims had told me.) If I waited, I would consider Gerry McClanahan's offer. I couldn't let myself hesitate.

The old house, temporary home of the chief of police's office, looked especially forlorn in the renewed rain. I was so wet that getting out again hadn't posed a hardship, and I walked into the station with my hair dripping in streams to the floor, much to the amusement of the desk clerk. She went into Claude's office after I asked for him and ushered me in after a brief consultation. She also handed me a towel.

It was hard to know what to dry first, but after I rubbed my face and hair, I began to work my way down. Then I folded the towel, put it in the uncomfortable chair that faced Claude's desk, and sat on it.

Claude was wearing his work face, serious and hard, and I was wearing mine, blank and equally hard. We were just two tough people, there in that little office, and I was about to tell my friend Claude some tough things. Before I opened my mouth to speak, I found myself wishing I were rich enough to hire someone else to come in here and tell Claude all this unpleasant news. And I was still undecided about whether or not to talk about Alicia Stokes.

In the end, I only broke the news about Gerry McClanahan. If Claude had researched a little more he would've found out about Stokes's obsession. Or maybe he did know. Maybe he needed her more than he cared about her quirks.

At least I told myself that was my reasoning; but actually, I suspect I just didn't want to give Claude so much bad news at one time.

'So,' Claude rumbled, when I'd finished, 'My newest officer is a famous writer?'

I nodded.

'He's a qualified police officer, right? I mean, his references checked out.' These words were mild, giving no hint that Claude was truly and massively angry.

'Yes, he is a qualified police officer.'

'He told me he had taken a few years off to travel on some money he'd inherited.' Claude swiveled his chair to look out at a dripping world. 'He didn't have a record.' Claude kept staring out the damn window for a good while. 'And he intends to write about the murder of Saralynn Kleinhoff?'

'He's writing a book about the stalking of Tamsin Lynd.'

Another shock for Claude, who ran a hand over his seamed face. 'So, though she never told us squat and I wouldn't know about it to this day if Detective Stokes hadn't remembered it from her former job, Tamsin Lynd has been stalked for a while. Persistently enough to make it a notable case.'

'According to McClanahan, yes. He says she's moved twice.'

'And whoever this is, just keeps following her.'

'Alicia Stokes has a theory about that.'

'Yeah, Alicia said she thinks Lynd is doing all these things herself. She played me a tape about a similar case that occurred a few years ago, the woman was doing it all herself. Smearing manure on her own door, setting off smoke bombs on her porch, sending herself threatening hate mail.'

I couldn't help but realize that Tamsin's stay in the conference room while Saralynn was killed and Janet attacked was much more explainable if it had been Tamsin doing the attacking. I tried to imagine Tamsin pinning the body of Saralynn up on the bulletin board, and I just couldn't. But I knew better than anyone did what could be inside someone, unsuspected. However . . . I shook my head. I just couldn't see it. I didn't want to see it.

'Lily, what did he threaten you with?'

'What?'

'You told McClanahan you were coming over here?'

'Yes.'

'He didn't try to stop you?'

I didn't answer.

'I know he did, Lily. Don't you lie to me. There's been enough of that.'

The numbness had worn off by then, and Claude's question drew my attention to the wound. The pain hit me broadside. I realized, fully, that my new life was gone. Possibly Jack's, as well. We would go through the whole thing again, both of us, and I didn't know if we were strong enough to withstand it.

'Lily?'

Looking down at my hands folded in my lap, I told him.

After a moment of silence, Claude said, 'Damn him to hell.'

'Amen to that,' I said.

We sat in silence for a moment.

'What about telling Tamsin?' I asked.

Claude rubbed a finger over the surface of his badge. 'Lily, you go home and rest up,' he said finally. 'That isn't your responsibility. I'm sorry it's mine, but I guess it is. It's someone I employed who's watching her.'

'But not illegally,' I said, having thought it over. 'He stays on his property. He doesn't trespass. He's just . . . observing Tamsin's life. From a safe distance.'

'He doesn't communicate with her or try to scare her?' Claude asked, thinking it through.

'No. He just watches and waits for something else to happen to her.' I couldn't help it; I shuddered.

'Maybe I should just tell her husband, that Cliff.'

'Cliff Eggers, martial medical transcriptionist? I don't think that'd do a lot of good.'

'Me, either.' Claude reflected for a moment. 'Well, Lily, I'm sure Jack will track me down and beat me up if you don't go home to rest.'

For whatever reasons, he wanted me to go. There was nothing else I could say or do. I just had to wait, and watch the consequences coming at me. Nothing I could do would stop what was going to happen. I had sworn to myself that I would never again feel helpless in this life; to that end, I had trained myself and remained vigilant. But now, all over again, I was a victim.

I felt very tired. I returned the towel to the receptionist on my way out, and when I got home I was happy to get in a shower, get even wetter, and then put on some dry clothes. I sat in my reclining love seat, began rescreening one of the movies I'd rented, and without a premonitory blink I fell asleep.

Someone had hold of me, and I wrenched my arm away.

'What? Stop!' I mumbled, heavy with sleep.

'Lily! Lily! Wake up!'

'Jack? What are you doing here?' I focused on him with a little difficulty. I wasn't used to napping, and I found it disagreed with me.

'I got a phone call,' he said, his voice clipped and hard. 'Telling me I better get back fast, that you were in trouble.'

'Who would have said that?'

'Someone who didn't want to leave a name.'

'I'm okay,' I said, a little muddled about all this, but still pretty sure I was basically all right. 'I just fell asleep when I left Claude's office. You won't . . . you're going to be really mad when I tell you what's happened.'

'It must have been something, to make you sleep through karate class,' Jack said. I peered past him at the clock. It was seven thirty. I'd been asleep about two hours, I realized with a great deal of astonishment. I could count the naps I'd taken as an adult on the fingers of one hand. 'How are you feeling?'

'Pretty good,' I said. 'Let me go clean up a little. My mouth is gummy. I can't believe I fell asleep.'

When I came back from the bathroom I was sure I was awake, and I knew I felt much better. I'd washed my face, brushed my teeth, and combed my hair. Jack looked calmer, but he was angry now, the false phone call having upset him badly.

'Did you try calling me before you rushed back from Little Rock?' That would have left the puzzle of who had called him, but relieved his anxiety.

Jack looked guilty, 'Once.'

'No answer.'

'No.'

'Did you try my cell phone?'

'Yes.'

I took it from the table and looked at it. I'd never turned it on that day. 'Okay, let me tell you where I was.' I could hardly upbraid Jack because he had rushed back to Shakespeare under the impression I was in deep trouble, either physically or emotionally. 'I was at the police station.'

Jack's dark brows arched up. 'Really?' He was determined not to overreact, now.

'Yes. I was there because of the new patrolman.'

'The red-haired guy?' There wasn't much Jack didn't notice.

'The very one. It turns out he's Gerry McClanahan, all right, but he's also the true-crime writer Gibson Banks.'

'Oh, no.' Jack had been standing by the window looking out at the darkness of the cloudy night. Now he came and sat beside me on the love seat. He closed his eyes for a second as he assessed the damage this would do us. When he opened them, he looked like he was facing a firing squad. 'God, Lily. This is going to be so bad. All over again.'

'He's not after us. We're only an interesting sidelight to him, something he just happened on. Serendipity.' I could not stop my voice from being bitter or my face from being grim.

Jack looked at me as though I better not draw this out. So I told him quickly and succinctly what Gerry McClanahan, aka Gibson Banks, had proposed to me. And what I had done.

'I could kill him,' Jack said. I looked at Jack's face, and believed him. 'I can't believe the son-of-a-bitch made you that offer.' When Jack got mad, he got mad all over; there was no mistaking it. He was furious. 'I'm going to go over and talk to him right now.'

'No, please, Jack.' I took his hands. 'You can't go over there mad. Besides, he might be on patrol.' I had a flash of an idea, something about Jack and his temper and impulsive nature, but in the urgency of the moment it went by me too fast for me to register it.

'Then I'll find him in his car.' Jack shook my hands off. I could see that something about my becoming pregnant had smothered Jack's sure knowledge that I was a woman who could definitely take care of herself. Or maybe it was because our brief life together was being threatened; that was what had shaken me so badly.

'You can come with me if you're afraid I'll kill the bastard,' Jack said, reading me correctly. 'But I'm going to talk to him tonight.' Again, I felt as if I ought to be drawing a conclusion, as if somewhere in my brain a chime was ringing, but I couldn't make the necessary connections.

I didn't feel as though I had enough energy left to walk to the car, much less trail after Jack over to the writer's house. But I had to. 'Okay. Let's go,' I said, getting to my feet. I pulled my cheap rain slicker from the little closet in the living room, and Jack got his. I grabbed my cell phone. 'We need to take the car,' I said, trying not to sound as shaky as I felt. 'I don't want to walk in the dark.'

That didn't fool Jack. I could see he knew I was weak. He shot me a sharp look as he fished his car keys from his pocket, and I saw that even concern for my well-being was not about to divert him from his goal of confronting the writer. Jack waited, barely holding his impatience in check, until I climbed in the passenger's seat, and then we were off. Jack even *drove* mad.

There were lights on in the small house. Oh, hell, McClanahan was home. No matter how he'd upset me that day, I'd found myself wishing he'd be at the police station, or out on patrol, anything but home alone. I got out of the passenger seat to follow Jack up the sidewalk to the front door. He banged on it like the cop he'd formerly been.

No answer.

The author could have looked out to see who was visiting, and decided to remain silent. But Gerry had struck me as a man who would relish such a confrontation, just so he could write about it afterward.

Jack knocked again.

'Help!' shouted a man's voice, from behind the house. 'Help me!'

I vaulted over the railing around the porch and landed with both feet on the ground, giving my innards a jolt that sent them reeling. Oh, God, it hurt. I doubled over gasping while Jack passed me by. He paused for a second, and I waved my hand onward, urging him to go to the help of whoever was yelling.

I was sure I needed to go home to wash myself and change my pad. I felt I was leaking blood at the seams. But the pain abated, and I walked to the voices I was hearing at the back of the house.

I could barely make out Jack and – was that Cliff Eggers? – bent over something huddled in the darkness by the corner of the hedge that separated the rear of this house from the house behind it. I could see the back of Tamsin's house to my right, and its rear light was shining benignly over the back door. There was a bag of garbage abandoned on the ground beside Cliff, who was covered with dark splotches. I'd only seen him dressed for work, but I could make out that Cliff was wearing only a formerly white T-shirt and ancient cutoff shorts.

'Don't come closer, Lily,' Jack called. 'This is a crime scene.'

So I squatted in the high grass next to the house, while I eased the cell phone out of my pocket. I tossed it to Jack, who punched in the numbers.

'This is Jack Leeds. I'm at 1404 Mimosa,' he said. 'The man living here, Gerry McClanahan, a police officer, has been killed.'

I could hear the squawk of the dispatcher over the phone. I pushed myself up and leaned over the steps at the back porch, which was covered by a roof. There was a light switch. I flipped it up, and the backyard was flooded with a generous amount of light.

Gerry was on his stomach, and underneath his head was a thick pool of blood.

'Yes, I'm sure he's dead,' Jack said, circling his thumb and forefinger to thank me for turning on the light. 'No, I won't move him.'

Jack pressed 'end' on the phone and tossed it back to me. Cliff, big burly Cliff, was crying. He rubbed his eyes with the back of his hand, staring down at the body on the ground beside him, his face contorted with strong emotions. I couldn't figure out which feeling would get the prize for dominant, but I figured shock was right up there. There was a hole in the hedge to allow passage between the yards, and in that hole lay another white garbage bag cinched at the top.

'I came out to put the garbage in the can,' he said, his voice thick with tears. 'I heard a sound back here and I came to look.'

'What's happened to him?' I felt I should know.

'There's a knife in him,' Jack answered.

'Oh my God,' Cliff said, his voice no more than a whisper, and the night around us, the pool of light at the back of Cliff's house, became alien in the blink of an eye, as we all thought about a knife and the person who'd wielded it. I have a particular fear of knives. I found myself crossing my arms across my breasts, huddling to protect my abdomen. I was feeling more vulnerable, more frightened, than I had in years. I thought it was because my hormones were bouncing up and down, perhaps, unbalanced by my lost *pregnancy*, a word that still gave me a jolt when I thought of it.

I made myself straighten up and walk into the dark front yard. Looking up into the sky, where there was a hole in the clouds through which I could see an array of stars, I realized that I wanted to go home, lock the door, and never come out again. It was a feeling I'd had before. At least now, I wanted Jack locked in with me. That was, I guess, progress. I could hear the sirens growing closer. I slipped back to my previous post.

'Where's Tamsin?' I heard Jack ask Cliff.

'She's inside taking a shower,' Cliff said. 'Oh God. This is just going to kill her.'

I was horribly tempted to laugh. Tamsin wasn't the one who was dead, her biographer had died in her place. Instead of writing the last chapter in Tamsin's story, Gerry McClanahan had become a few paragraphs in it himself! Was that poetic justice? Was that irony? Was that the cosmic balance of the universe or the terrible punishment of a god?

I had no idea.

But I did know taking a shower would be a good idea if, say, you had bloodstains on your hands.

I was glad that I hadn't exposed Alicia Stokes to Claude, because he certainly needed her that night. One of his other detectives was on vacation and the third was in the hospital with a broken leg, suffered that very afternoon at the home of a man arrested for having a meth lab on his farm. The lab had been set up in an old barn, one with rotten places in the floorboards, as it turned out.

Alicia's dark face was even harder to read in the dramatic light provided by the dead man's back porch fixture. I wondered if she would automatically assign guilt to Tamsin Lynd. Her suspicions had well and truly infected me.

When Jack and Cliff had been ordered away from the heap on the ground, I had seen more than I wanted to see of what was left of Gerry McClanahan. Dressed in shorts and a T-shirt, he lay in a heap, a terrible wound in his throat. From it protruded the wooden handle of a knife. He had no wounds on his out-flung hands, or at least none that I could see. There were no weapons in his grip. As we stood there in the tiny backyard, the rain blew in again. The sky was a solid dark mass of clouds. They let go their burden, and soon our hair was again wet and plastered down. So was the red hair of the corpse. It was too bad about the crime scene; though plastic tents were put up as quickly as possible, I was sure if there were any small clues in the hedge and the yard, they were lost. A portable generator powered lights that exposed every blade of grass to a brilliant glare, and people up and down the street began coming out of their back doors to watch, despite the rain.

It was very lucky I'd told Jack I'd come with him, since Jack would have made a dandy murder suspect, given the mood he'd been in after he'd learned Gerry McClanahan's other identity. Claude had thought of that, too. I could tell from the way his eyes kept returning to Jack. The two men liked each other, and they were well on their way to being as good friends as Carrie and I were – but I'd always known Claude recognized the wild streak that more than once had led to Jack's downfall.

I said, 'I was with Jack every second until we heard Cliff yelling.'

'I believe you, Lily,' Claude said, his voice deceptively mild. 'But I know why you were coming over here in the first place. This man could've caused you no end of trouble.'

'That's why Jack got the call,' I said, feeling as if I'd just seen a piece of machinery crank up smoothly.

'What?'

I told Claude – and Alicia Stokes, too, since she drifted up at that moment – about the anonymous call Jack had gotten at his office in Little Rock. It was hard to tell if Detective Stokes believed me or not, but I made myself assume that Claude did. It was a pretty stupid story to tell if it wasn't true, since Jack's phone records could be checked.

Stokes seemed more interested in questioning Cliff Eggers. Someone who was spying on Tamsin would naturally be in Cliff's bad graces, but Cliff gave no sign of realizing that the policeman had been leading a double life. It was a piece of information Claude seemed to be keeping under his hat, at least for the moment. It would have to come out soon. Most often, writers aren't celebrities the way movie stars are, but Gibson Banks had very nearly attained that status.

Cliff was telling Alicia (for the third time) he'd just come out to put two bags of garbage in the can when he'd heard a moan, or anyway some kind of sound, in the backyard catty-cornered to his. That noise, of course, had prompted him to investigate. If I had been the object of as many vicious attacks as Cliff and Tamsin had, I am not sure I would have been so quick to find out what was making the noise.

Just as Cliff wound up his explanation, Tamsin emerged from the house wrapped in a bathrobe with wet hair. The bathrobe and hair made her look faintly absurd when she crossed the backyard under an umbrella. Predictably, she crumbled when she learned why we were all out in the rain. Stokes showed her the knife, encased in a plastic bag. 'I never saw it before,' she said.

'Did you know Officer McClanahan?' Stokes asked, her voice cold and hard. Did Stokes know, yet, about Officer McClanahan's secret identity? I thought not.

'Yes, we'd talked over the hedge. It made me feel so much safer to have a policeman living so close!' Tamsin said, which struck me as the height of irony. I could feel my lips twitch, and I had to turn my back to the group clustered in the yard, a group at that moment consisting of Alicia, Claude, Cliff, Tamsin, and a deputy I didn't know.

Stokes sent Tamsin over to stand by me to clear the way for

the hearse. Tamsin was shivering. 'This is so close to home, Lily. First Saralynn gets killed at my office, and now this Officer McClanahan gets killed right behind my house. I have got to start carrying something to protect myself. But I can't carry a gun. I hate them.'

'You can get some pepper spray at Sneaky Pete's up by Little Rock,' I said. 'It's on Fontella Road.' I told her how to get there.

After all the recent rain, the heat of the night made the atmosphere almost intolerable. The longer we stood in the steamy night, the less inclined we were to talk. I could feel the sweat pouring down my face, trickling down the channel between my hips. I longed for air conditioning, for a shower. These small concerns began to outweigh the far more important fact that a man had died a few feet away, a man I'd known. I closed my eyes and leaned against the house, but the aluminum siding still felt hot from the day and I straightened back up. Tamsin seemed to have control of herself and she pulled a comb out of her pocket and began trying to work it through her hair.

She spoke once again before Jack and I were allowed to leave. She said, 'I don't know how much longer I can live like this. This . . . terrorism . . . has got to end.'

I nodded, since I could see the strain would be intolerable, but I had no idea what to reply. You couldn't stop it if you didn't know the source.

Jack came over to me and held out his hand. Though it was almost too hot for even that contact, I took it, and with a nod to Tamsin, went back to his car with him. We were glad to get home, take a blissful shower, put on clean things, and stretch out in the cool bed, to lie there close to each other with sufficient air conditioning to make that pleasant. I don't know what Jack was thinking about, but I was acknowledging to myself how glad I was that Gerry McClanahan wouldn't be writing his book now. Jack and I could lead our lives again, and we would not be exposed. Tamsin, at least for a while, would be spared some scrutiny, though if it were ever discovered who was stalking her, there was sure to be some newspaper articles about her persecution. As of now, she and Cliff had come out of it well, too. Only Gibson Banks and his publisher were permanently inconvenienced.

I could live with that.

Chapter Eleven

I went to Little Rock with Jack the next morning. I couldn't stand another day in the small house doing nothing.

I had to promise Jack I wouldn't do anything too vigorous. I was absolutely all right, and I was chafing a little more each day under the weight of his protectiveness. Since I was just going back to surveillance on Beth Crider, it was easy to swear I'd limit my exertions.

I was beginning to hate Beth Crider.

Jack dug in at his office to begin clearing up backlogged paperwork and returning calls. I organized my campaign and drove to Crider's neighborhood yet again. Maybe we should just buy a house close to her. Maybe when Jack was pushing my wheelchair down the street she might slip up and discard her walker.

Today I'd come prepared. I'd brought a hand vacuum, a load of cleaning materials, and a bucket, plus some Sneaky Pete paraphernalia. I parked in front of a house with a For Sale sign in the yard, about three doors west of Beth Crider's, and I got out.

After I got everything set up, I began to work. In no time at all, sweat was trickling down my face and I was fighting an urge to pull off my socks and shoes. Jack's car had never been cleaned more slowly and thoroughly. When I needed water, I got it at the outside faucet. I was lucky they hadn't had the water turned off, since I had to go back and forth several times refilling the bucket.

I received my reward when Crider came out of her front door, with envelopes in her hand. It didn't take a genius to figure out she was going to put some outgoing letters in her mailbox. In this neighborhood, they were on posts by the ends of the driveways. With my back to her, I watched her progress in the passenger-side rearview mirror, while I polished it with a rag and glass cleaner. I

880 — The Lily Bard Mysteries Omnibus

reached inside the car to turn on the movie camera I had set up, loaded and ready. It came inside a stuffed panda. I had the panda propped and positioned to cover just that area, since Beth normally mailed her letters at about this time.

She slid her letters into the box, shut it, and raised her red flag. Then she hesitated, and I could see she was looking at the ground.

'Come on, bitch,' I whispered, polishing the rearview mirror yet again. 'Fall for it.'

She looked back and forth, up and down the street. I was the only person out, and I had my back to her.

Down she squatted, supple as you please, to pick up the ten-dollar bill I'd torn and stuck to a tattered Arkla bill next to the curb. I'd tossed this out the window on my way down the street. I'd hoped it would seem as though the stiff morning breeze had picked up some of the trash from the car, and lodged it in front of her home on the ground.

Beth Crider straightened and walked back to her house, only remembering to resume her halting gait when she was about five feet from the steps. I knew the camera would catch the transition from robust to rehabilitative. Inside, I laughed my ass off.

And Jack's car was clean, too.

He looked up when I came in the office, having his own little transition from businessman and detective to my lover. I had the panda tucked under my arm.

'I did it,' I said, knowing I sounded proud but unable to keep it out of my voice.

'Yes!' He was up like a shot and hugged me. 'Let's see!'

Together we watched the film of the temptation of Beth Crider.

'So what will happen now?' I asked.

'Now, United Warehouse will approach Beth and ask her to drop her suit. She'll probably accept. United will give her some cash, she'll sign some papers, and that'll be it.'

'She won't be prosecuted?'

'Staying out of court saves money and time and publicity.'

'But she cheated.'

'Saving time and money is more important than vindication, in business. Except in very special circumstances, when public punishment will ward off more troublemakers.'

I wasn't as happy any more. 'That's not right,' I said, not caring if I sounded sullen.

'Don't pout, Lily. You did a good job.'

'Pout?'

'Your bottom lip is stuck out and your eyes are squinted. Your hands are in fists and you're swinging your legs. You look like I'd just told you about Santa Claus. That's what I call pouting.'

'So, United Warehouse will pay you lots of money?' I said, reforming my mouth and unclenching my fists. I opened my eyes wide.

'They'll pay. You'll get a percentage, like any trainee.'

I felt deep relief. Now, I could feel better about having quit my cleaning jobs.

'Let's go eat lunch,' Jack said. He turned off his computer after saving what he'd been working on. 'We're meeting Roy and Aunt Betty.'

I tried to be pleased about having lunch with Jack's friends, but I just didn't know the two older detectives well enough to take a personal pleasure in their company. I'd met them both before, and talked to them on the telephone several times.

As we were led to their table in the Cracker Barrel (a favorite of Roy's) I spied Aunt Betty first. With her fading brown hair, nice business suit, and sensible shoes, Elizabeth Fry certainly did look like everyone's favorite aunt. She had the kind of slightly wrinkled, well-bred, kindly face that inspires universal trust. Betty was one of the best private detectives in the Southeast, Jack had told me.

At the moment, Betty was telling Roy some story that had him smiling. Roy doesn't smile a lot, especially since his heart attack. Though he has a sense of humor, it leans toward the macabre.

When I sat across from him, I could look Roy right in the eyes. He's not tall.

'Hey,' I said.

Betty leaned over to pat my hand, and Roy looked stricken.

'Hey, baby, you feelin' okay?' He reached over with one of his stubby hands and patted the same place Betty had. 'Thelma and me, we're sorry.' Thelma was Roy's wife, to whom he was devoted.

Of course, Jack had told them about the miscarriage. I should have expected that.

'I'm feeling much better,' I said, trying very hard not to sound cold and stiff. I failed, I could see, by the glances Roy and Aunt Betty exchanged. Personal exchanges with near strangers in public places are just not my thing, even though I knew I was being a pill. I made a tremendous effort. 'I'm sorry, it's hard to talk about.' That was truer than I'd realized, because I could feel tears welling up in my eyes. I grabbed up a menu and began trying to focus on it. It persisted in being blurry.

'Lily caught Beth Crider this morning,' Jack said. I knew he was diverting them, and from their hasty exclamations I could tell they were glad to be diverted. I recovered, after a minute or two, and was able to look pleasant, if nothing else.

I had my back to the entry, so I couldn't see what made Roy stiffen and look angry a moment or two after we'd ordered. 'Crap,' he said under his breath, and his eyes flicked to my face, then back over to Jack. 'Trouble coming,' he said, a little more audibly.

'Who is it?' Jack asked, sounding as though he were afraid he already knew the answer.

'Her,' Aunt Betty said, her voice loaded down with significance.

'Why, it's the private detective table, isn't it?' said a voice behind me, a youngish woman's voice with a Southern accent so heavy you could have used it to butter rolls. 'My goodness me, and I wasn't invited along. But who have we here, in my old place?' A navy-and-beige pantsuit, well packed, twitched by me, and I looked up to see a pretty woman, maybe a couple of years my senior, standing by the table. She was looking down at me with false delight. The perfect makeup and honey-colored shoulder-length tousled hair were designed to distract attention from a nose that was a little too long and a mouth that was a little too small.

'You are just too precious,' said this sleek newcomer. I don't believe anyone had called me 'precious' in my life, even my parents. 'Let me introduce myself, since Jack seems to have lost his tongue. His *wonderful* tongue.' She gave me a roguish wink.

Well, well, well. I didn't dare to look at Jack. I wavered between amusement and anger.

Roy said, 'Lindsey, this is Lily. Lily, Lindsey Wilkerson.'

I nodded, not extending my hand. If I shook with her, some of my fingers might come up missing. You don't often meet people who will lay an unattractive emotion out on the table like that. Showing your hand so clearly is a big mistake.

'Dear old Betty, how you been doing?' Lindsey asked.

'Fine, thank you,' said "dear old Betty", her voice as weathered as old paint. 'And I hear you're flourishing on your own.'

'I'm paying the rent,' Lindsey said casually. She was carrying a leather handbag that had cost more than two of my outfits, which mostly come from Wal-Mart. Her beautiful shoes had two-inch heels, and I wondered how she walked in them. 'Lily, how do you like working under Jack?'

I shrugged. She was about as subtle as a rattlesnake.

'You watch out, Lily, Jack's got himself a reputation for fooling around with his co-workers,' Lindsey warned me with mock concern. 'Then he just leaves 'em high and dry.'

'Thanks for the advice,' I said, my voice mild. I could feel Jack relax prematurely.

'Where'd he find you?' she said. Her southern Arkansas accent was beginning to grate on my nerves. 'You' comes out 'yew', and 'where'd' was awful close to 'whar'd'.

Not under the same rock he found you, was my first, discarded answer. I exercised my option of not speaking at all. I looked into her eyes, instead. She began to shift from pump to pump, and her nasty smile faded.

But she rallied, as I'd been willing to bet she would.

'Jack,' she said, leaning over the table right in front of me, 'I need to come by your place and pick up some clothes I left there.'

Her throat was exposed, right in front of me. I felt my fingers stiffen into Knife Hand. At the same time, the part of my brain that hadn't lost its temper was telling me that it's not right to hurt someone just because she's a bitch.

'I don't believe I have anything of yours,' Jack said. From the corner of my eyes I could see his hands clenching the edge of the table. 'And I don't live in that apartment any more.'

She hadn't known that. 'Where'd you move to?'

'Are you a detective, too?' I asked.

'Why, yes, honey, I sure am.' She straightened up, now that she knew I'd had a good time to look at her impressive cup size.

'Then you can find out.' She would also find out we were married.

'Listen, bitch . . .,' she leaned back down toward me, extending a pointing finger. People around us were beginning to stop eating in order to listen.

My hand darted up, quick as an arrow, and I seized her hand and dug my thumb into the pit between her thumb and first finger. She gasped in pain. 'Let go of me!' she hissed. After a second's more pressure, I did. Tears had come into her eyes and she stood there nursing her hand until she understood that she had become ridiculous, and then she did what she had to do – she walked away.

Aunt Betty and Roy began talking about something else right away, and the other diners went back to their own concerns, leaving Jack and me in a sort of cocoon. I picked up a long-handled spoon and stirred my iced tea. It was too weak. I like tea that's something more than colored water.

'Uh, Lily,' Jack began, 'listen, I . . .'

I made a chopping motion with my hand. 'Over and done.'

'But she never meant—'

'*Over and done.*'

Later, when Aunt Betty and I were discussing a recent court

verdict, I heard Roy ask Jack if I'd really meant it when I'd said we'd never talk about Lindsey again.

'Absolutely,' Jack's voice somewhere between amused and grim.

'That's a woman in a million,' Roy said, 'not wanting to hash over every little thing.'

'You said it.' Jack didn't sound totally delighted.

Later, when we'd eaten, paid, and gone back to Jack's car, we found a long scratch down the paint. I looked at Jack and raised my eyebrows.

'Yeah, I figure it was her,' he said. 'Vindictive is her middle name. Lindsey Vindictive Wilkerson.'

'Will this be the end of it?'

'No.' He finally looked me in the eyes. 'If Betty and Roy hadn't been there, maybe. But she got beat, and in front of witnesses she cares about.'

'If she keeps this up,' I told him, 'she'll be sorry.'

Jack gave me a look. But at length, his troubled face gave way to a smile. 'I have no doubt of that,' he said, and we went back to the office for the afternoon. He filed, and I cleaned. He gave me another lesson on the computer, and a lecture on billing procedures. As a kind of treat for Jack, on our way back to Shakespeare we stopped at Sneaky Pete's, one of Jack's favorite businesses. Jack wanted to report to Pete on the success of the panda-bear camera.

As was often the case, Pete's was empty of customers but crammed with goods. Most of the store's income came from a stock of high-end cameras and home security systems, but Pete Blanchard had founded the shop with the idea that you could buy any sort of expensive electronic surveillance device there.

Pete Blanchard hadn't made up his mind about me yet, and I wasn't sure what to think of him, so our conversations tended to be tentative and oblique. Mostly, I was content to watch Jack prowl around and have fun, but Pete seemed to feel it was his duty to entertain me while Jack shopped. The fact that Jack seldom bought anything didn't seem to bother Pete. He'd known Jack for several years, and he liked him.

Every time I'd seen him, Pete had been wearing the same sort of clothing. He wore a golf shirt and khakis and Adidas. He seemed to have several versions of this outfit, but he liked it and that was what he wore. I could respect that. A former cop, Pete had probably had trouble fitting into a patrol car; he had to be six foot four or five. His mustache and hair were graying, but his toffee-colored skin had few wrinkles, and I couldn't begin to guess his age.

This particular afternoon, Pete's son was working in the store. A college student who picked up some money wherever he could, Washington Blanchard considered himself much smarter than his father and vastly more sophisticated. Jack had told me he just hoped Wash, as the young man was called, would learn better before too long. Otherwise, in Jack's opinion, someone was likely to sock Wash in the mouth. Jack had had a gleam in his eye that had said the sight wouldn't be unwelcome.

Though I hadn't noted it on my calendar that morning, today had apparently been designated as Pick a Fight with Lily Day. Most men are put off by me. I just don't seem, I don't know, womanly or something. Especially if they know what happened to me. A small sampling of men, the ones that are sick, are turned on by that very same thing. Wash Blanchard was a member of that small group.

While Pete showed Jack a pair of glasses that took pictures, Wash asked me questions about the woman who'd been murdered in Tamsin Lynd's office. That death had made the Little Rock paper mostly due to its bizarre circumstances. Little Rock as a whole seems to try to forget there's anything south of it in the state.

I hadn't checked this morning to see if Gerry McClanahan's death had made the paper, but I figured it hadn't, since it had occurred so late. At any rate, Wash didn't bring it up, so neither did I.

Wash wanted to know if I'd known the health center murder victim.

'No.'

'There can't be that many women in Shakespeare, Lily.'

'I didn't know her.'

'What was she doing in that building, I wonder. The paper didn't make that clear.'

'She was coming to attend an evening self-help group.'

Wash was astonished. He said, 'How do you know that?'

I shrugged, sorry I'd said anything at all.

'Did you see her?' he said. Wash had the usual prurient desire to hear secondhand about blood and death. If he'd ever happen to see it close up, he'd lose that in a jiffy.

'Yes.'

'What did she look like? Was she really impaled?'

I looked longingly at the door.

'Don't talk to me any more,' I said. I began to look at a rack of cameras, the kind that did everything but snap their own buttons. That was my kind of camera. I liked photographs, as aids to memory and as art, but I was not interested in taking them myself.

'Because I'm black? Huh?' And there he was, right in front of me again, determined to bother me. It's like people don't understand English, sometimes.

'It doesn't have a thing to do with your skin. It has to do with your obnoxious character,' I said, my voice still under control but inevitably rising.

Big Pete interposed. I felt the presence of Jack behind me.

'Something wrong, here?' Pete was trying to sound calm.

'She's treating me like trash, ignoring me and calling me names,' Wash said, though his voice was not as full of righteous wrath as it might have been.

'I can't imagine Lily doing that,' Pete said.

Explaining. People always want you to explain. I yearned to walk out speechlessly, but this was one of Jack's favorite places.

'I don't care to discuss crime scenes and how this woman died. The woman who was killed in Shakespeare.'

Pete stared at his son. 'Wash, you want to talk about dead

bodies, remind me to show you some pictures of things I saw in Viet Nam.'

'You got pictures, Dad?' Wash sounded stunned and happy.

' 'Scuse us, Jack, Lily. Wash and I got some talking to do.'

Jack and I left in a hurry.

I tried to figure out if I needed to apologize to Jack, but no matter how I looked at it, this little run-in was not my fault. However, Jack wasn't talking, and I wondered if he was angry.

'It's really weird, isn't it,' he said suddenly. 'You'd think nice people like Pete and Marietta, his wife, would have such great genes their kids couldn't turn out bad. And then, look at Wash. He has to learn every lesson over and over, lessons he shouldn't even have to be taught. Things he should know by . . . instinct.'

Where had that come from? I followed the trail of that thought for a moment. Genetics. Kids turning out differently from their parents. Okay.

'Do you want a baby, Jack?' We'd been dodging this conversation ever since I'd lost the baby.

'For the life of me, Lily, I don't know.' It was clear he'd only been waiting for me to open the subject. 'If you had kept the baby, if everything had gone okay, I would have been proud to have a baby with you. When the baby . . .' He hesitated.

'Miscarried,' I supplied.

'When the baby miscarried, I guess you could tell how sad I was. But the next day, I maybe felt a little relief, too. What changes that would have made in our lives, huh?'

I nodded when he glanced over to check my reaction.

'Can you tell me how you feel?' he said.

'Like you.'

'No elaboration on that?'

'It surprised me when you cried. It made me love you more.' If we were going to say things, we might as well say everything.

'I hated to see you bleeding and weak. It scared me to death. And I would have loved to have been the father of our baby.'

'Didn't ever want to be the dad of Lindsey Wilkerson's baby?' I asked, keeping my face poker-straight. I was able to dodge Jack's hand when it slapped in my direction, because I was waiting for it.

'The world's best argument for birth control,' he said.

I didn't laugh out loud, but I smiled. His sideways glance caught it, and he grinned at me, that wicked look I loved.

Tamsin and Cliff came over that night. They called first, and I said it was all right, but I shouldn't have. I really didn't want to see them, didn't want to hear about Tamsin's multiple problems. But she had helped me, so I was obliged to her, a yoke I found nearly intolerable. I reminded myself not to ask for help again.

I should have been ashamed of my grudging attitude. And maybe I was, a little. But being close to Tamsin now seemed a risky thing.

'How are you feeling?' Tamsin's question seemed on the perfunctory side, especially since she didn't meet my eyes to hear my answer.

'I'm all right. You and Cliff?' I motioned them to chairs and offered them drinks, as I was obligated to do. Jack got Cliff a Coke, but Tamsin waved the query off.

'You can imagine how strange it is to find out that this policeman was really a famous writer,' Tamsin told me.

I nodded. I could imagine that.

'And then I finally recognized that woman last night. Detective Stokes.'

Jack reached over my shoulder to hand Cliff his drink.

'And, Lily, what I want to know is, why me?'

I couldn't believe I'd heard her correctly. Tamsin Lynd, of all people, was asking the unanswerable. Was this something some victims were just bound to go through, no matter how smart or clearly victimized they were?

That couldn't be true. And why had she decided to talk to me about it? Because I was Supervictim?

I thought for a minute, but I decided there was no way to get around this but to talk to Tamsin about it.

'Why are you different?' I asked her.

'What do you mean?'

'Would you let us ask that question in counseling group?'

She flushed red. 'I see what you mean.'

'Do you think you're better than us, because you're being stalked instead of being raped?'

Cliff looked horrified and upset, and his hand moved as if he were going to get my attention to signal to me, but I gave him a quelling look. Tamsin had dragged him along, and Jack was in the room, but this conversation was between me and her.

'Oh, Lily, I hate to see that in myself!' Tamsin was really upset, now. But upset in a more intelligent way.

'Why not you, Tamsin? What makes you superior or invulnerable?'

'I've got it, now,' she breathed. 'I see that. But I guess what I was thinking, was not that I should be spared because I was superior, but because I'm not. I'm an overweight, nearly middle-aged woman in a crowded and poorly paid profession. There's nothing remarkable about me. How did I attract the attention of someone so determined?'

'There is plenty special about you, honey,' Cliff said, his voice desperately earnest. 'You are the most sweetnatured, kindest—'

'Oh, Cliff.' Tamsin's face was radiant with pleasure, but deprecating. 'You're the only one who believes that,' she added with a little laugh.

I wasn't going to sit here and bathe Tamsin in compliments. She was quite right. I liked her – a little – and I appreciated her, but there was nothing exceptional about Tamsin Lynd in my eyes . . . except her victimization.

'You just got picked by the Claw.' That was as good an explanation as I could come up with.

'The Claw?'

'You know that game they have out in the Wal-Mart entryway? The one where you put in some quarters and the metal claw swings down over a bin of stuffed animals and swoops down at random, and maybe picks one up, maybe not? That's the Claw.'

'Lily!' Tamsin looked at me with the oddest quizzical, expression. 'That's the most depressing philosophy I've ever heard.'

I shrugged. I wasn't in the Pollyanna business. 'The Claw picked you up, Tamsin. So you have a stalker, and Janet doesn't. I got raped, you didn't. Saralynn was murdered, Carla wasn't. The claw passed her over.'

'So you don't believe a divine plan runs the universe?'

I just laughed. Some plan.

'Don't you believe that most people are innately good?'

'No.' In fact, I found the fact that some people did believe that to be absolutely incomprehensible.

Tamsin looked really horrified. 'You don't believe that we're only given the burdens we can handle?'

'Obviously not.'

She tried again. 'Do you believe in the eventual punishment of evildoers?'

I shrugged.

'Then how do you go on living?' Tamsin was tearful, but not as personally tearful, as she had been before.

'How do I go on living? A day at a time, like everyone else. A few years ago, it was an hour at a time. For a while, it was minute by minute.'

'What for?'

Cliff looked like he wished he was anywhere but here. But Jack, I saw, was leaning forward to hear what I was saying.

'At first, I just wanted to beat the . . . ones that attacked me.' I picked my words carefully. I was being as honest as I knew how. 'Then, I couldn't add to my parents' miseries any more by dying. Though I did think about suicide, often. No more fear, no more scars, no more remembering.

'But after a while, I began to get more involved in trying to make living work. Trying to find a way to make my days, if not my nights, productive and make a pattern to stick to.' I took a drink from my glass of water.

'Is that what you think I should do?'

'I don't know what you should do,' I said, amazed anyone would ask advice of me. 'That's for you to figure out. You're a professional at helping people figure out what they should do. I guess that doesn't really help you right now.'

'No,' she said, her voice soft and weary. 'It's not helping, right now.'

I gave her the only piece of advice, the only philosophy, that I cherished. 'You have to live well to defeat whoever's doing this to you,' I said. 'You can't let them win.'

'Is that the point of living, to not let him win? What about me? When I do I get to live for myself?'

'That is entirely up to you,' I told her. I stood up, so she'd go.

'I thought you, of all people, would have the answers, would have more sympathy.'

'The point is, that doesn't make any difference.' I looked Tamsin straight in the eyes. 'No matter how much sympathy I have for you, it won't heal you faster or slower. You're not a victim of cosmic proportions. There are millions of us. That doesn't make your personal struggle less. That just increases your knowledge of pain in this world.'

'I think,' said Tamsin, as she and Cliff went through the door, 'that I should have stayed at home.'

'That depends on what you wanted.' I shut the door behind them. I could see Jack's face. 'What?' I asked, sharp and quick.

'Lily, don't you think you could have been a little more . . .'

'Touchy-feely? Warm?'

'Well, yeah.'

'I told her exactly how it is, Jack. I've had years to think about this. I don't know why everyone feels like they're supposed to be safe all the time.'

Jack raised an eyebrow in a questioning way.

'Think about it,' I said. 'No one expected to be safe until this century, if you read a little history. Think of the thousands of years before – years with no law, when the sword ruled. No widespread system of justice; no immunizations against disease. The local lord free to kill the husbands, husbands free to rape and kill their wives. Childbirth often fatal. No antibiotics. It's only here and now that women are raised believing they'll be safe. And it serves us false. It's not true. It dulls our sense of fear, which is what saves our lives.'

Jack looked stunned. 'Why have you never told me you feel this way?'

'We've just never gotten around to talking about it.'

'How can you even share a bed with me, if you hate men that much?'

'I don't hate men, Jack.' *Just some of them. I despise the rest.* 'I just don't believe – no, let me turn that around. I do believe that women should be more self-sufficient and cautious.' That was probably the mildest way I could put it.

Jack opened his mouth to say something else, and I held up my hand. 'I know this isn't fair, but I've talked as much as I can for one evening. I feel like I pulled my guts out for inspection. Can we be quiet from now on? We can talk more tomorrow if you want to.'

'Yes, that would be okay,' Jack said. He looked a little dazed. 'You sure you want me sharing the bed tonight?'

'I want you in the bed every night,' I said, forcing myself to reveal one more bit of truth.

And for the first time since the miscarriage, that night I gave him proof of that truth. After a long, sweet time, we slept that night back to back, me feeling the comfort of his warm skin through the thin material of my nightgown. I never felt he was turning away from me when our backs touched; we were just attached in a different way.

I lay awake, thinking, longer than I liked. Since I was on a roll with the truth, I had to think of what I hadn't told Tamsin, what I couldn't tell anyone else in the world. My healing had accelerated when I began to love Jack. Love weakens, too, makes you vulnerable; but the strength, the power of it . . . it still amazed me when I considered it. I would die for him, be hurt for him, give anything I owned for his happiness; but there were parts of me that could not change for him. There were traits and attitudes I required for my hard-won survival. Knowing this left me with an uneasy feeling that some day I would have to face this fully and in more detail, an idea that I detested.

Jack gave a little gasp in his sleep, much like the one he often gave when I surprised him in lovemaking. It was a sound I found infinitely comforting, and hearing it, I fell asleep.

Chapter Twelve

I woke the next morning feeling very clearheaded and relaxed. After Jack had left for a meeting with a client in Benton, I decided stretching and mild calisthenics would do me a world of good. When that was done, and I felt much better overall, I changed the sheets, taking pleasure in the order of clean smooth percale.

The phone rang just when I was wondering what to do next.

'This is Dani Weingarten,' announced the caller. There was a silence.

'Yes?' I said finally.

'Dani Weingarten, the mystery writer,' said the voice, less firmly.

'Yes?' I read very little fiction, so her identity was not an exciting fact, which the caller soon seemed to realize.

'I'm the fiancée of Gerry McClanahan,' she said, by way of redefinition.

'Okay.' Sooner or later, she'd get to the point.

'I'm flying in from Florida tomorrow to take charge of the arrangements for having Gerry's body flown back to Corinth, Ohio . . . his hometown.' So far, Dani Weingarten had not given me one bit of information that interested me. There was a long pause. 'Did you hear me?' she asked, in a testy way.

'I didn't realize that required a response.'

Another long pause. 'Okay,' she said, 'Let's try this. I have talked to the police department there in Shakespeare, and the chief of police there recommended you as the best housecleaner in town. Whatever that means. So, if you have time, I'd like you go to over to Gerry's little rental house and start packing up his things. I'll ship them to my house to go through them.'

I almost turned her down. I'd spent enough time sorting

through the detritus of the dead. But I thought of the hospital bills coming soon, and of my improved health, and I said I would do it. 'Key?' I asked.

'You can pick one up at the police station,' Dani Weingarten told me. Her voice sounded softer now, as if she'd used up all her forcefulness. 'I told them it was okay. Did you know Gerry?'

'Yes,' I said. 'I knew him a little.'

'He told me Shakespeare was a fascinating little town.' She sounded on the verge of tears.

'He talk about his work much?' I asked cautiously.

'Never,' Dani Weingarten told me. 'He only discussed it when his first draft was ready.'

So she didn't know I was one of the fascinating things in Shakespeare. Good. 'Will you be staying at the house?' I couldn't pack up all the bed linens, if so.

'No, I couldn't stand it.' Her voice was getting heavier and heavier with unshed tears. 'I'll check into a motel. If you have motels in Shakespeare.'

'We have one. It's a Best Western. Do you want me to make a reservation for you?'

'That would be great.' She sounded surprised, and I didn't blame her. 'I'm going to rent a car at the airport. I should get there about three thirty.'

'I'll tell them.'

'You know,' she said suddenly, 'I don't believe any of this.' And she thunked the receiver down.

She would believe it by tomorrow. I called the motel, and went over to the police department yet again. Claude had left the key with the dispatcher, along with a verbal message that the police department would finish its search of the house by eleven. I could have the house to myself once they were out.

I felt energized at the idea of money coming in, and I had time to kill, so I drove to the Winthrops' house. Bobo's car was there, but no one else's. I let myself in, calling for him, but got no answer. The pool was empty. Maybe he'd gone somewhere with a friend.

After glancing around at the mess in sheer disbelief, I got to work. There was so much to do I hardly knew where to start. Just in case Bobo was asleep upstairs, I decided to concentrate on the ground level.

Living room, kitchen, game room, wash room, pantry. Master bedroom and master closets, master bath, smaller hall bath. In due time, they were gleaming and dustless. A couple of times, I thought I heard a voice; maybe Beanie had left the radio on? But I checked, and found nothing.

As I closed Beanie's walk-in closet door (with its newly polished mirror) I was beginning to feel a little tired. Well, pretty tired. But it went against my grain to stop without finishing. I wondered if I could just do a little straightening upstairs? Just as I started up, I heard a sound above me, and I looked up to see a very startled Janet, followed by an equally surprised Bobo, coming down the carpeted steps.

Since Janet was buttoning her blouse, it was impossible for her to pretend they'd been up there planning their sporting goods store. They had certainly been engaged in another joint venture.

I raised my eyebrows.

'Hey, Lily,' Janet said, squeezing the words out as though they were toothpaste. She looked anywhere but my face, which I was struggling to keep neutral.

'Lily,' Bobo said. 'Ah, we didn't hear you come in.' His face was scarlet from the awkwardness of it; if he'd been observed by anyone in the world but me, this would be easier for him. Janet, not knowing that Bobo had harbored feelings for me once, was free of worry. She was suppressing laughter; her eyes swung over to mine and she made a little face.

'No, I guess you didn't.' I was really glad I hadn't decided to do the upstairs first. I nodded gently, trying very hard not to smile, and began to make my way up the stairs. Bobo seemed to wake up from his shock, then followed Janet across the living room. They made it to the kitchen in silence, then I heard Janet begin to giggle, and Bobo join in.

I laughed myself, once I was safely up the stairs. It would be tacky of me, I decided, to go in Bobo's room and make the bed or change the sheets. So I cleaned the upstairs bathroom, leaving all three bedrooms as they were. Beanie would be glad I'd come at all. I didn't think she'd be overly upset about the kids' bedrooms. A little order is better than none at all.

A little later, after lunch and some rest, I let myself into Gerry McClanahan's house on Mimosa. It is never a pleasure to deal with the belongings of the dead. But the dealing would be nominal in this case: as I'd noticed on my previous visit, the furniture was very sparse. I wondered if it was rented like the house. The dispatcher at the police department had told me the dachshunds had gone home with Officer Stuckey, who had two small boys, so I knew they were okay; but somehow their abandoned toys seemed more desolate than Gerry McClanahan's abandoned computer.

I walked through the quiet house. All the rooms were empty except for the front room, with its big desk and couch and television, and the larger bedroom, which had the usual furnishings. In a kitchen drawer was the rental agreement for the furniture, so I left that out for Dani Weingarten to see. A quick examination told me there'd be precious little to pack. I called the older couple who'd rented the house to Gerry McClanahan. They hadn't turned on their radio that morning, so they hadn't heard the news. I had to hear lots of exclamations and lamentations before I was able to ask the pertinent questions about to whom the linens and pots and pans belonged. Those items, I found, were Gerry's. I wondered a little about the cage I found just inside the back door; it didn't seem large enough for one of the dogs, though it had definitely been used. I might ask Dani Weingarten if she recognized it. Now that I had an idea about the scope of the job, I went to the garage that was the local outlet for a big moving company and bought some boxes, keeping the receipt so Ms Weingarten could reimburse me.

I turned on a radio at the rental house, just so I could have some company while I packed up the dead man's clothes. Normally, I don't like distractions. But this house was sad. Though it had been years since I had a pet, I almost wished the little dogs were there.

Folding McClanahan's clothes didn't take long. I packed his uniform carefully, wondering if he'd be buried in it. What had this man been, in his core: a policeman or a writer? He had certainly been a researcher. There were at least three shelves of nonfiction books, like Gavin de Becker's *Gift of Fear*, and David Simon's *Homicide: A Year on the Killing Streets*. I looked at de Becker's book, repressing a snort. McClanahan hadn't read that carefully enough: he hadn't known to be scared, when he should've been. The only thing I was sure of about his death was that he had seen it coming and not recognized it.

A trio of books actually piled on the desk were more disquieting. They were thinner and had a scholarly look, like books you wouldn't get in a regular store unless you ordered them. The one on top was titled, *The Psychology of Two; the Selection of a Mate* by Lauren Munger, and the thinner black and blue one underneath it was by Steve Coben and called *Pathological Pairs: Duos with Bad History*.

I felt a flash of rage so intense I had to sit down. Despite everything he'd said, it was evident that Gerry McClanahan had planned to write about Jack and me. He had been studying us. Maybe his interest had begun as a sidelight to the stalking drama of Tamsin Lynd, but that interest had evolved. I took some deep breaths, told myself over and over that nothing could be done about it now, and packed those books along with the rest.

I found a biography sheet, I guess one that his publicist was preparing; Gerry had made little corrections here and there. He'd won prizes and awards, and his books had been translated into twenty different languages. I'd had other things on my mind when I'd scanned the *People* story. Reading the biography sheet, I understood for the first time what a furor there would be when it was discovered that Patrolman Gerry McClanahan was also Gibson Banks. I wondered how much time we had before that connection was made; not much, I was sure. There was an accordion file, full of notes for other projects. Gerry was tentatively planning a book on a serial killer in Minnesota. That would have been a change of climate, for sure.

The house had been gone over by the police, and I knew I wouldn't find anything remarkable they hadn't already seen. Plus, they would've taken anything interesting with them. But as I picked up a pen that had rolled onto the floor, I saw the edge of a sheet of yellow paper torn from a legal pad, protruding very slightly from under the desk. I remembered that Gerry had had a legal pad in front of him while we talked. A legal pad and a computer; that had seemed like overkill to me at the time. Why both?

Now, I pinned the paper to the floor with the point of the pen, and raked it out. It was a sheet covered with tiny black handwriting.

I peered at it and switched on the desk lamp to see it better. It was a log of the comings and goings at Tamsin's house. Nothing much, it seemed, had happened at Tamsin's that particular day. The Lynd-Egger couple had gone to work, come back home. Various lights had gone off and on. Tamsin had swept the back porch, and Cliff had spent five minutes in the little tool closet by the back porch some time after that. The date was the night before Jack and I had heard Tamsin yell on her front porch.

I was sure the rest of this log, which was a terrible document in and of itself, had been taken by the police. Perhaps Gerry had ripped this day's observations out to discard because nothing much had happened, and I hoped that the other notes he'd made proved of more value. The person stalking the counselor – it was hard not to think of this person as some kind of evil entity, since he was so invisible – hadn't liked anyone else stalking them, I was willing to bet. Gerry's obsession with the stalker's obsession had led to his own death.

As I locked the door behind me, my job completed, I suddenly realized that Gerry must have found out, there at the end, who the stalker was. I hoped, after all he'd sacrificed for the knowledge, he'd had a moment's satisfaction. Had he been dreadfully surprised . . . or had the killer's face been well known to him?

I was glad to lie down when I got home, but it was a good, tired feeling; not exhaustion. I watched a few shows on television: a biography of an actor I'd only heard of in passing, a documentary on the CIA. It was embarrassing to realize that the phone ringing actually woke me up.

'Yes?'

'Lily.' Jack.

'Hi.'

'I won't be home tonight. I'm going to start this job right away. If the CEO likes the job I do, there'll be more business from this firm.'

'What does he want you to do?'

'She.' I felt embarrassed. 'She wants me to do very thorough background checks on the applicants for this very sensitive job.' He was telling me the essence without the particulars, but that was all right with me. 'Have you been taking it easy?' Jack asked, suspicion evident in his voice.

'Well, I did do a little work today.'

'You know what Carrie said, Lily!'

'I just couldn't stand it any more. I had to do something or die of boredom.'

'Lily, you have to mind the doctor.'

'Yes,' I said, keeping my voice gentle.

'I love you.'

'I know. I love you, too. I got to go, Jack. Someone's at the door.'

'Answer it while I'm on the phone.'

I went to the door and looked through the peephole Jack had installed for me. 'It's Bobo, looks like.'

'Oh, okay,' Jack said, relieved. I cocked my head as I opened the door. Jack, who was sometimes jealous, had never gotten the fact that there was actually something to be jealous of with Bobo. I was grateful for his lack of acuity where this particular Winthrop was concerned. I sometimes felt very guilty when I caught an unexpected glimpse of Bobo and experienced a definite physical reaction to the sight of him.

'Bye, Jack,' I said, and he told me he would see me the next day.

I waved Bobo inside, feeling unusually curious about what he would have to say. This time, sure I was safe from – well, safe – I let him in and shut the door behind him.

'Are you okay with . . . ?' he tried just waving his hands a little, not wanting to come right out and say it.

'With you having sex with a friend of mine?'

'Yeah, that.'

'Of course, Bobo. You're over eighteen and so is Janet.' Not for anything in the world would I have explained my more complicated feelings. I would hardly admit them to myself.

But, as he often did, Bobo surprised me. And this was why I never quite lost a link to this unusual golden boy, this was why despite the difference in our ages and our lives there was a relationship between us. 'It's not just that, and you know it,' he said, his anger evident in the way he was standing, the tension in his arms.

I held up my hands in front of me, palms outward. I meant him to stop; we were not going to get serious, here. I'd had enough of that the night before. My long talk with Tamsin Lynd still griped me.

'You have to tell me if it's true.'

Suddenly, everything grew clear. 'You heard I was married.'

'Yes. Is it true?'

'Tell me you didn't take Janet to bed out of spite.'

'Is it true?'

'Yes, it's true.'

'How long?'

'A month.'

'Why were you keeping it a secret?'

'It isn't anyone's business,' I said, not caring if I sounded harsh.

'But it is,' he said. 'It is. You should have told me.'

I lost my temper. 'Why? Were you going to marry me?'

'No! But a married woman, you shouldn't even think about her!'

'So, if I'm married, I'm sacred to you, you can't lust after me.'

'That's right! That's exactly right!'

'Then end this, right here and now. I am married.'

'Can you give up thinking of me? Has being married made any difference to you? Because I know you. I know you think of me.'

'Bobo, this is too weird. Neither of us has any business thinking of the other. This is all wrong.'

'And now you're married.'

'Yes.'

'You love him?'

'Of course. More than anything.'

'But—'

'But nothing. This – we have to seal this off. This is over.'

'We've said this before. Or you have.'

'Are you saying I'm encouraging you in this idea you have, that we should go to bed together?'

'No, I'm not saying that. What I'm saying is, I can tell in your eyes that you know that if we did it would be great, that you want to fuck me as much as I want to fuck you.'

'But we can't do that, because there are trails leading up to and away from any act of sex.'

He took a deep breath. 'That's right.'

'So we won't talk about this again.'

'No,' he agreed, more slowly, with less conviction.

'I don't want to answer this door when my hair has gone gray, to find you still talking about it.'

He laughed a little. 'No,' he said. 'I have to get on with my life.'

'And Jack and I have to get on with ours.'

'Lily,' he said. He reached out and brushed his knuckle down my cheek. 'Do you love me just a little?'

'Yes,' I said. I owed him that. 'Just a little.'

I closed the door.

My unremembered dreams must have caused me to toss and turn in the night, because I woke up tired the next day. I took a cup of coffee out onto the tiny back porch and sat listening to the birds. My rosebush, growing up a cheap plastic trellis to one side of the porch, was in bloom. The rose had been chosen for smell, not appearance, and I closed my eyes to enjoy it to the fullest. My neighbor, Carlton Cockroft, waved at me from his back porch, and I raised my hand. We knew it was too early to talk to each other. The slope up to the railroad tracks was covered with flowering weeds that were full of bugs of all sizes and dispositions. I didn't know much about bugs, but I could appreciate their industry and appearance when they weren't in the house. I watched a butterfly, and a small bee, as each made the rounds of the flowers. When I'd had enough of that, I unrolled the small local paper that I'd gotten from the end of the sidewalk.

Man Stabbed by Stranger read the lead headline. I began to read what I assumed was going to be an account of Gerry McClanahan's murder, which had occurred too late to be featured in yesterday's paper. Stabbing is rare in Shakespeare, and stabbing by a stranger almost unheard of. Most killings in Shakespeare are male-on-male violence, of the Saturday-night-drinking-binge variety. I was actually shaking my head, anticipating the national news stories about Gerry's double life, when my eyes caught the name in the story.

CLIFF EGGERS of 1410 Compton was taken to the hospital late yesterday evening after he said he was stabbed by a stranger, local police stated. Eggers, who has been a resident of Shakespeare for about a year, said he was walking out to his car after dark when an assailant rushed from the hedge to the side of his property. The assailant struck Eggers in the back and ran away. Hampered by a bandaged leg, Eggers did not pursue. At first, Eggers said, he didn't realize he'd been stabbed.

'It just felt like he hit me,' Eggers said. 'I called my wife, and she called the police.'

A city policeman, Gerry B. McClanahan, was stabbed to death almost to the rear of Eggers's house two nights before. (See related article, page 2)

'We may have a deranged person in the neighborhood, or we may have someone who's targeted the Eggers household,' said Claude Friedrich, chief of police. 'We have every available officer assigned to the case.'

Asked if he had any leads in the case, Friedrich responded, 'New information is coming in constantly.'

Eggers was treated and discharged from Shakespeare Regional Hospital.

I assumed Claude's comment meant that he didn't have a clue. Carrie had called me the night before to thank me for cleaning her office. 'I knew it was you,' she'd said, 'because you always make the magazine stacks so neat.' She'd confessed her regular cleaner had gotten held up, and she was up a creek. But she hadn't said anything about Cliff Eggers.

Of course, she couldn't. I could see that now. She couldn't blab any more about her husband's business than I could about Jack's. I was glad, just the same, to see Carrie's old car parked behind her office. She often came in on Saturday mornings to catch up on paperwork.

'No one in the hospital?' I called as I went in the back door.

'Not a soul, can you believe it?' She came out of her office with a mug in her hand. She was wearing her weekend outfit of cutoffs and T-shirt.

'Not even Cliff Eggers,' I said.

'No, he bled like a stuck pig, but it wasn't that deep.'

'Where was he cut?' I asked, since Carrie seemed to be in a chatty mood.

'In the back, oddly enough,' Carrie said. 'It was a funny kind of wound. Started here,' and she touched a point just above my waist slightly left of my spine, 'and ended here,' which turned out to be a spot about midway down my right hip. 'It was deeper toward the end.'

'Kind of low for a blow from another man,' I said, after I'd considered it.

'Yes, isn't it. I don't think I've ever seen a knife wound quite like that.'

'Maybe . . .' I thought for a minute. 'Okay, what if Cliff was walking away, and the knifer was swooshing down.' I raised my arm with an imaginary knife in it, and brought the arm down in an arc. 'So if Cliff stepped away just then, the end of the knife would slice through the hip, rather than penetrating him higher up by the spine, as it was intended to.'

'Could be. Could be,' Carrie said, looking at my back doubtfully. 'Of course, Cliff's at least six inches taller than you. But still, I would say his assailant had to be shorter than Cliff. Or kneeling, but I can't quite visualize that.'

I couldn't either, but it was an interesting idea. 'What was Tamsin doing while all this was going on?' I asked, trying to sound casual. I assumed that since Tamsin and Carrie were both in some sense medical professionals, they would know each other, and I was right.

'In the kitchen cooking, she told me,' Carrie said, still staring at my back as if it would tell her the answer.

'I guess she came to the hospital with Cliff.'

'Oh, yeah, as upset as she could possibly be. I don't know how much longer she's going to be able to do her job, if things like this keep happening around her. She said something about moving again.'

I looked at Carrie. 'What was she wearing?'

'Oh, I don't know. Ah, a pair of old jeans and an Arkansas Razorbacks T-shirt, seems like.'

'No apron?'

'No. Either she's one of these women who cooks without, or she pulled it off before she came. Why?' Carrie seemed to realize that this was an odd question.

'Just wondered.' I was relieved when the phone rang, because Carrie once more immersed herself in work. I didn't want to have to explain to Carrie what I didn't even want to admit to myself, that I'd been infected with Alicia Stokes's suspicions. I was wondering if it was my mental health counselor who had stabbed her husband in the back.

As I polished the sink in the women's bathroom, I longed for Jack. It was always easy to talk things over with him. He seemed to enjoy the process, too. Jack understood people a little better than I did. I was repulsed by people who were messy with their emotions; just look at the tangled mess of Bobo and me. It felt good to have encapsulated and pushed away our mutual attraction.

I had a sudden and unprecedented flight of fantasy. I pictured myself telling Beanie Winthrop that Bobo and I were going to be married, and the expression I could just imagine on her face tickled me all morning. Though Beanie had some admirable characteristics, we had never liked each other. It almost seemed worth telling her the lie just to see her face. I wondered if her only daughter, Amber Jean, would turn out to be a good woman. Her teen years were obviously shaky ground. Amber Jean had her picture in the paper this morning, helping with the canned goods drive for the soup kitchen maintained by Shakespeare Combined Church, Calvary Baptist, and First Presbyterian. She'd looked glossy and preppy in the picture; not the kind of girl who would take off her shirt in front of a group of boys, not the kind of girl who would try to subordinate a woman older than herself. 'A picture is worth a thousand words' did not apply in Amber Jean's case.

What about my mental picture of Tamsin? Tamsin looked like the average young professional, the kind who didn't care terribly about money, the kind who really, really wanted to help. But she'd been stalked, or so it seemed, through three jobs and two states. Small animals around her died, unpleasant things happened to her everywhere, and people around her were beginning to drop like flies. She was in the center of a circle of destruction; she was the eye of a storm.

I drove to the gym thinking hard about Tamsin and her situation. She was the first person I saw when I stepped into Body Time. She was talking to Marshall, and she was looking haggard and unkempt. Her sweats looked dirty, and her hair was disheveled. Marshall gave her a dismissive pat on the back and glided over to me. Marshall is so fit that you could bounce a dime off his abs, so dangerous as a martial artist that he's made me cry from pain. I was glad to have him for a friend.

I could tell he wanted to ask me if it was true that Jack and I were married, but he couldn't quite bring himself to do it. He knew I hated personal questions, so he was determined to avoid that most personal one.

'Since Jack's not here, why don't we work out together?' he suggested. I agreed, since it's always nice to have a spotter, and the workout always goes better with a partner to challenge you. It was triceps day for me, though I was so far behind my normal schedule I could start just about anywhere. Triceps were fine with Marshall, so we went over to the heavy weights rack to begin. Assuming the pushup position, my hands on the pair of seventies on the top rack, I began my first set, concentrating on my breathing. Marshall was propped on the hundreds farther down the rack, and his body moved as though he had springs embedded in his arms.

'Tamsin was telling me about Cliff,' Marshall said, as we rested between sets. 'She came in this morning because he finally fell asleep and she didn't know what to do with herself.'

I nodded.

'Yeah.' Marshall did some stretches, and then we did our second set of pushups. 'I guess you knew she has been followed by this crazy person,' he said, when we were through.

'Yeah, I heard about that,' I said carefully. 'Hard to believe in a town this size, we wouldn't notice someone new.'

Marshall turned an inquiring face to me as we assumed the pushup position for the third and last time. 'That's true,' he said, 'but what other explanation is there? I guess you've thought of something.'

'What if it's her?' I asked.

Marshall gave a derisive snort. 'Yeah, right. She's a nice enough woman but she doesn't have enough grit in her to say boo to a goose. You think she's doing this to herself so she can get a lot of sympathy as Velma Victim? That seems a little far-fetched.'

I shrugged as I stood up and shook my arms out to relieve the ache. 'Who else could it be?' I really wanted to know what Marshall was thinking.

'I hadn't given it a thought,' he said. 'Ah . . . , Cliff, but he'd hardly want to stab himself in the back, and he's nuts about Tamsin. Okay, not him . . . well, what about the new police detective? The tall black woman?'

'She worked on Tamsin's case when Tamsin lived in Ohio,' I said. 'If Stokes stabbed Cliff, believe me, he'd be dead.'

I was serious, but Marshall laughed as though I were joking.

'There was the other new cop, the patrolman, but he's dead now, too,' Marshall said, thinking out loud. 'Oh, there's Jack! He's new in town.'

'Ha-ha-ha,' I said, my voice showing clearly how unfunny I found this.

'And there's the guy that's started dating my ex.'

'I thought Thea was getting married.'

'Me, too. But he got to know her a little too well.'

'And now she's dating someone else?'

'Sure. You know Thea. She's nothing if not flexible, when it comes to men.'

I disliked Thea intensely. She gave women a bad name.

'Who's the guy?'

'The new mortician at the funeral home.'

'Oh, that's right up Thea's alley,' I said. 'I bet she loves that.'

Marshall laughed again, but less happily. This time he knew I was serious, and he agreed with me. Thea had a cruel and macabre streak, and making love in a funeral home would suit her sexual playbook, if all I'd heard were true. 'But he and Thea were in Branson when Saralynn Kleinhoff was killed,' Marshall said.

So I'd developed and eliminated a suspect in the space of five minutes. I was sure all these crimes had been committed by one person. Anything else would have been too much of a. coincidence.

Not that I didn't believe in coincidence. I did. But I thought it

would be stretching, in this case, to even entertain it as a
possibility.

Jack's car was in the driveway when I got home. I was very glad to
see it there.

He was cooking something when I went into the kitchen,
something that smelled good.

'Bacon sandwiches for lunch. I have tomatoes picked right off
the vine,' he told me, his voice unmistakably smug.

I don't eat much bacon, since it's not good for you, but a bacon
and fresh tomato sandwich was just too good to pass up.

'Where'd you get 'em?' There were at least six tomatoes on the
kitchen counter. Two were green.

'From Aunt Betty,' he said. 'Can we have fried green tomatoes
tonight?'

Two fried things in one day was really a lot, but I nodded. I
stood behind him, watching him cook.

'Hold still,' I said.

'What are you going to do?'

'Pretend to stab you.'

'I guess that wasn't the answer I was wanting to hear.' But Jack
obligingly stood still.

I raised my hand above my head as though it held a knife
pointing downward. My hand whizzed through the air, and I
mentally marked the point at which the blade would have grazed
Jack's back.

'Hmmm.'

'Can I help?' Jack asked. He picked some of the bacon out of the
skillet with some small tongs, and put the bacon to drain on a pad
of paper towels. I got out the small cutting board and a knife, and
began to slice a tomato.

'Let me stab you again,' I said, and this time, with the knife in
hand, I held it straight out in front of me. The wound Carrie had
described simply couldn't be made, if the knife was held like this.

While Jack put ice in two glasses, I explained what I was doing.

'Okay, let me try.' He turned me around, and taking the

precaution of using a dull table knife, he began to experiment. 'A graze at the top, a true stab at the bottom, going from the left side of the back to the right.' he said. 'So I think you're right, it would have to be an overhand blow.'

'An overhand blow from someone much shorter, right?' I put our plates on the table and folded a paper napkin beside each plate. Jack got out the bread and mayonnaise, my mother's home-made. 'Cliff's a little taller than you, huh?' Jack nodded, as he used a fork to put tomato slices on his bread. 'Maybe six feet?'

Jack said, 'Just barely.'

I could think of no one involved in the episodes who was short, besides a couple of the women in the group, and Tamsin herself. 'Maybe Tamsin did it by accident? And they were too embarrassed to say it?'

Jack even looked good to me when he chewed, which is one of the more unattractive activities for a human being. He swallowed. 'She could have mistaken Cliff for someone else, I guess, but there's a streetlight practically in front of their house. He was attacked in the driveway, right? So how, in good light and in a place where she would expect him to be, could she knife him by accident?'

'There's only one other new person in town,' I said, not able to think of any rebuttal. I told Jack about my conversation with Marshall, about Thea's new lover. Jack said, 'I've met him. He runs in the evening.'

'Joel McCorkindale does, too.' I tried to make something of that. Joel ran, Talbot ran, Joel's wife was in the support group, and she was short. That didn't add up to anything. This made as little sense as one of those logic problems the first time you read it through. 'If Mary has a poodle, and Mary is taller than Sarah and Brenda, and Brenda's dog is brown, read the following state-ments to figure out who has the dachshund.' Besides, Sandy McCorkindale might be half nuts, but I simply could not picture her catching a squirrel and hanging it in a tree. It was actually easier to imagine Sandy stabbing someone.

We ate in silence, enjoying our first summer BLT. While we washed the dishes, I asked Jack what would happen next.

'I don't know. Stalking's just not that common a crime, and I have no big backlog of experience with it. When I first started my apprenticeship, Roy was handling a case a little like this. The woman couldn't get the police to take her seriously, because the intruder wasn't doing anything to her.'

'Intruder?'

'Yeah, he was actually coming into her apartment while she was gone, sifting through her stuff. Leaving her presents.'

I made a face. Disgusting and scary.

'I agree.' Jack looked grim as he scrubbed the skillet. 'Finally, she scratched up enough money to pay for around-the-clock surveillance. The spot-checking we were doing just wasn't effective. But it didn't take long after that. We caught him jacking off on her underwear the second day. It was her apartment manager. It was a tough case to take to court, because he had a legal key.'

'Did you win?'

'Yes. But of course she had to move, and she found she couldn't stay in the city even after she'd moved. So he got a slap on the wrist, and her life was changed dramatically.'

Gee, that sounded familiar. I had only heard stories like that about a million times. I sighed, and asked Jack what he planned for that afternoon.

'First, I'm hitting the computer to see what background Alicia Stokes has. Then, we're going over to Tamsin's house and look at their driveway. Then, at some point, I plan on us having a serious session in the bedroom, there.'

I got caught between a smile and a frown. 'Why are you looking into this?' I asked.

'Because it's got you going crazy, and I can't have that. I like you happy. We started this whole thing so you wouldn't have nightmares any more, and I hate it that this has turned into something that makes you feel even more angry.'

It surprised me that Jack saw me as perpetually angry.

It was true, but I hadn't wanted him to know that.

So I was being a deceiver, something I despised.

'It's not you,' I said.

'I know that.'

'I love you.'

'I know that.'

'Does it really bother you?'

'It worries me, sometimes. If it keeps on eating at you, some day it might include me.'

'I can't see that happening.'

'I wish I couldn't.'

I looked down, unable to meet his eyes. Maybe he was right. He'd taken a big chance. 'Thanks for helping, Jack.'

'We'll get this solved,' he said.

'Do we have to do those things in the order listed?'

'Why, no, I guess not.'

'Could we reverse the order?'

'I bet we could.' He grinned. The scar crinkled, and his hazel eyes narrowed, the crow's feet at their corners spreading until the smile affected his whole face.

I took a deep breath. 'I'll beat you to the bed,' I said, and got a head start.

It ended up being a tie.

Later that afternoon, Jack had to confess he was coming up empty. Alicia had no previous record. She had good credit and paid her taxes on time. Her income was not great, but adequate for the time and place. She had once been married, was now divorced. She had never been named as the mother of a child. She had never served in the armed forces.

I decided to mow the lawn that afternoon, while Jack was busy on the computer. It was easy to think while I was mowing, and I liked the look of the small yard when it was even and trim. I even used the weedeater and then swept away the clipped grass from my sidewalk. During all this work, I thought and thought, and I could not come up with any clearer understanding of the vicious cycle surrounding Tamsin Lynd. I must have been looking at it wrong, but I couldn't seem to find a new perspective.

Jack came outside when the sun was making deep shadows. I lay on the newly cut grass, disregarding the likelihood of fire ant bites and the certainty of grass stains, and stared up into the vast blueness. My backyard is very small and runs into the slope up to the railroad tracks, and it's overlooked by the second-floor windows of the apartment building next door and by Carlton's rear window, but it does give the illusion of privacy. Carlton was gone, anyway, because I'd seen him pull out in his car, and the apartment on the end closest to me was vacant at the moment. So maybe we really were unobserved.

Jack stretched in the grass beside me. His hair was loose, had been since our session in the bedroom, and I knew we'd have to pick the grass bits out of it before we went to bed. But there was nothing I would rather do.

It was hot, and quiet, and the smell of the grass was sharp in our noses.

'Let's review,' Jack said, his voice slow and sleepy.

'Okay.' I sounded just about as peppy as he did.

'Tamsin moves to Shakespeare because she's been stalked at her previous home in Cleveland.'

'Right.'

'A detective on that case, not the primary, but one assigned to do some of the legwork, is a young detective named Alicia Stokes.'

'Check.' I closed my eyes against the relentless blue.

'Alicia Stokes becomes so fascinated by the case, so obsessed, that when Tamsin Lynd and her husband, Cliff Eggers, move to Shakespeare, eventually Alicia finds herself compelled to follow.'

'"Compelled to follow". I like that.' I turned on my side and raised myself up on my right elbow. 'Also, within a matter of months, a true crime writer whose real name is Gerry McClanahan signs on with the city police in Shakespeare. He's a real policeman, so this doesn't seem fraudulent to him. His secret life as a writer isn't known to anyone . . . anyone we're aware of.'

'Gerry, aka Gibson Banks, knows not only about Tamsin and Cliff, but also about the obsessed policewoman. He's come to watch the showdown.'

I nodded.

'And, once again, things start happening to Tamsin Lynd . . . and tangentially, to Cliff.'

'Tangentially. I love it when you use big words.' I bent over to kiss Jack's forehead. He wiggled closer to me.

'Expeditious. Arraignment. Consequence. Territorial . . .' Jack smiled, his eyes closed against the glow of the sky, and I leaned over to kiss him again, this time not on the forehead.

'So, she gets phone calls,' he resumed. 'We happen by when they find the dead squirrel.'

'Then Saralynn Kleinhoff is killed – and put on display – and put in Tamsin's office. While Tamsin is still in the building. But Janet, who interrupts the killer, is not murdered, but rendered unconscious.'

'Then, the writer who is planning to do a book on both the stalking and the detective who can't stop stalking the stalker, so to speak, is murdered while he watches the stalkee.'

'That's one way to put it.'

'Then Tamsin's husband, her last stronghold, falls into a booby-trap. Shortly thereafter, he's attacked in their own driveway.'

'And that's where we are now.' I lay down with my head on Jack's chest, my arm thrown over him. I closed my eyes, too, and felt the sun kiss my cheek. I knew in a minute I'd be uncomfortable and itchy, but this moment was idyllic.

'And though we figure the stalker also has to be someone who's new in town, the only other new person is a strange, possibly perverted, but apparently guiltless mortician.'

'That's it in a nutshell.'

'And we're nowhere.'

'Well, it's not you and it's not me.'

'Oh, good, just about ten thousand more people to go.' Sure enough, I was beginning to get itchy. I sat up and started to brush off the cut grass. I thought about packing up Gerry McClanahan's house, the life he'd left behind him. His awards and accomplishments, his ties with people in small worlds and big worlds, his notes of projects yet to come, projects that now would never be completed unless his estate hired someone to finish the work he'd started.

The notes. All those notes. I wished now I'd had a chance to read them before the police gathered them up. Gerry McClanahan, after all, had been a trained detective with lots of experience. What had he concluded about the stalking of Tamsin Lynd? All I could remember was that he'd called it a fascinating case. That wasn't a help.

'What are you thinking so hard about?' Jack asked. He was propped up on his elbows.

I explained my line of thought to him.

'Fascinating,' he said, 'he called it fascinating?'

'Yeah. And he said, "This is a case turned upside down. No one will forget this one." '

'Turned upside down.'

I nodded. 'So let's see,' I said, mostly to myself. 'If a case is upside down . . . the victim is the perpetrator? That would mean Tamsin has been responsible for the whole thing.'

'Or it could mean that whoever is guilty looks innocent.'

'Whoever loves Tamsin actually hates her.'

That gave us both a jolt. We looked at each other. 'Who loves Tamsin?' Jack asked, almost in a whisper.

'Cliff loves Tamsin.'

After a wide-eyed moment, we both shook our heads in disbelief.

'Nah,' I said. 'Did you see how he cried when he picked her up in the parking lot after Saralynn was murdered? And the gash on his leg after he fell through the step?'

'Let's go look at their driveway,' Jack said.

We walked, because it was beautiful, and because it might make the visit look less rehearsed. But we need not have been concerned about that; no one was home at the house on Compton Street.

Up the driveway we went, as though we'd been invited. We gave a perfunctory knock to the front door, and then turned away to enact the attack of the night before.

'You be Cliff,' I told Jack. 'Remember, your leg is still sore from going through the steps.' Jack pretended to emerge from the house. He limped down the front steps, and walked slowly over to where the couple parked their cars. Jack got his keys out, as someone naturally would if they expected to drive off. Then he stopped. I came up behind him as quietly as possible, but the driveway was loose gravel. Even the grass strip running between the driveway and the hedge was full of the stuff.

'I can hear you coming a mile away,' he said over his shoulder. 'No way anyone snuck up on Cliff.'

Of course, if you heard someone coming up behind you when you were outside, you'd turn around to look. Anyone would. You wouldn't just keep on with what you were doing.

But I raised my hand, again pantomiming the knifing. This time, I crouched a little until I approximated Tamsin's height. I made an awkward swing, and was very close to the wound area as Carrie had described it to me. But the angle was all wrong, straight down instead of left-to-right. 'That didn't work,' I told Jack, almost cheerfully.

'You know, and I know, that when someone's coming up behind you, you're going to turn around to see what they want.' Jack's face was getting grimmer and grimmer as he spoke. 'And if the stabber was really determined he'd stick around and try again.'

Jack turned his back to me again. He bent his hand up behind his back as far as he could bend it. He had a pocketknife clenched in his right fist, with the end pointing down. Jack made a chopping, downward motion. The point of the knife grazed his rump in an arc from left to right. If he hadn't been careful, it would've gouged the flesh of his right hip.

It was exactly as Carrie had described the wound.

'Oh, no, Jack.' I felt almost as though I was going to cry, and I couldn't say why.

'It might not be that way,' Jack said. 'But it looks like it to me.'

'So what'd he do with it?' I asked. 'Put it in his pocket?'

'They'd find it at the hospital,' Jack said. He pantomimed the self-mutilation again, he put out a hand to rest on an imaginary car, and with the other he pitched his pocketknife into the depths of the hedge. Then we both got down on our hands and knees and searched, very carefully.

Jack found a splotch of dried blood in the bed of old leaves below the hedge, right after I'd retrieved his knife.

'Of course, his attacker could've thrown it in here and retrieved it later. It didn't have to be Cliff that did the tossing and retrieving,' Jack said.

I nodded. I felt about twenty years older, all in a flash. This was betrayal on a grand scale. And on an incredibly mean scale, too.

'Do you think Claude has figured this out?' Jack and I strode down the sidewalk. Jack had thrust his hands in his pockets and he was scowling. 'Or do you think he's been too distracted by the upheaval in his department?'

We stopped at the next corner. Tamsin was at the stop sign facing us, and through the windshield of her car I could tell she was looking haggard. The plump and assured woman I'd met a few weeks earlier had simply vanished.

We'd finished our little experiment just in time. She waved us through the intersection, and tried to summon up a smile for us, but it failed. We nodded and kept on walking. I felt like a traitor to her. First I thought she'd been persecuting herself, and now I suspected her husband was her tormentor.

'We have to go talk to Claude,' I said.

Jack nodded unenthusiastically. Neither of us is happy in a police station. Since my ordeal, I'd become shy of the police, who were first to initiate me into the range of human reactions to my victimization that I now knew so well. And Jack is still ostracized by some cops for his involvement in the scandal that led to his leaving the force in Memphis.

Claude was in and willing to see us. I had half hoped he'd be outfighting crime or swamped in paperwork.

We went into his office. Claude looked puzzled, but glad to see us, a reaction so far off base that I came pretty close to turning around and leaving. But conscience demanded that we take the wooden chairs in front of Claude's old desk and state our business.

I glanced at Jack, took a deep breath, and launched in to our theory.

Claude said, when he was sure I'd finished, 'That's pretty interesting stuff, there. What do you have to prove it?'

My heart sank. 'You haven't found any evidence to point to Cliff, or Tamsin . . . or anyone else?'

'You mean, in general? Or in the death of Saralynn Kleinhoff? In the murder of my police officer? Let's just take Saralynn's murder. Let's see,' Claude rumbled, scooting lower in his chair and crossing his ankles. 'Got to be someone that had a key to the health center. That's forty present and past employees, plus their families.'

I hadn't even thought of that.

'Got to be someone who doesn't mind getting their hands messy. Well, who knows? My grandmother, the most finicky woman on God's green earth, could butcher a chicken as fast as you can say Jack Robinson,' Claude continued. 'Got to be someone with a personal dislike of Tamsin Lynd. Mental health workers get all kinds of enemies, right? And as for thinking it has to be the same person here as was stalking her in Illinois – well, why? Could be a copycat. Doesn't have to be someone who followed her down here. As far as hanging the squirrel, anyone could've done that at any time. You could tie up the squirrel ahead of time and take it over there, get it strung on the branch in a minute or less.'

This wasn't going the way I'd hoped. Jack was looking pretty bleak, too.

'Then, Gerry. Now that I know about Gerry, I can understand a lot of things about him better. But that doesn't stop me from being mad at him for deceiving me, and I'll bet a lot of other people were mad at him, too. Just because he told you that he was watching Tamsin's house doesn't mean that was why he was killed. And Cliff is the only one giving Tamsin an alibi for that one; he says she was in the shower. Well, maybe she was and maybe she wasn't.'

I closed my eyes and wished I were somewhere else.

'About this scenario you two have worked out – you may be right. May be. But if Cliff did stab himself, that doesn't necessarily mean he killed Saralynn and Gerry. That doesn't mean he's been terrorizing his own wife. We have no proof either way.'

'No forensic evidence?' Jack was leaning forward in his chair.

'There were fibers on Saralynn that came from a pair of slacks a lot like the ones Cliff was wearing that day. Khaki Dockers. Everyone's got a pair of those. And Cliff readily told us that he'd been in there earlier in the day, when he'd brought Tamsin her lunch. Fibers could've been left there then.'

'Say we're right,' Jack said. 'Say that the one behind everything is Cliff. What do you think he'll do next?'

My eyes flicked to Claude, who was thinking the matter over.

'If he follows his pattern, he'll quit. They'll move. It'll start all over again.'

Jack nodded.

Claude continued, his face looking as seamed and careworn as that of a man ten years older. 'But he's escalated and escalated. From nasty pranks, to small deaths like the squirrel, to human deaths like Saralynn's and Gerry's. What could be left? Next time, I reckon he'll try to kill her.'

With regret, I agreed.

Chapter Thirteen

'We might as well not have gone to Claude,' I said to Jack.

We were on our way home from Body Time the next morning when I reopened the subject.

'Yeah.' He stared straight ahead, his face like a thundercloud and his posture just as aggressive as mine. 'We can't just wait for her to be killed.'

'What else can we do? We can't stay outside her house for days or weeks. We can't follow her everywhere she goes, or kill Cliff before he kills her.'

Jack looked at me sidelong, and I could see the idea of taking Cliff out appealed to him. 'We can't,' I said, in the voice my fifth grade teacher had used when she recited the Golden Rule to us every morning. 'We are not going to get in trouble with the law again.'

When we got home, at least part of our problem was solved. There was a message on the answering machine from Tamsin. Even her voice sounded quavery. 'Lily, this is Tamsin. I just can't get up the energy to do any housework, and the place is a wreck. If you're feeling better – only if you're well enough – I would really appreciate hearing from you.'

I called her back right away. 'This is Lily,' I said.

'Oh. Oh, Lily! Can you come to help me clean house today? I don't know if I can go in to work this week . . . and I'm definitely staying home today. I'm so shaken up.'

'I think I can come over,' I told her. After all, it was Sunday morning, when I never scheduled anything so I could have a break from work. But I'd definitely had enough down time this week.

'Oh, thank God!'

We talked a little more – well, she did – and I hung up. Jack, standing beside me for the whole conversation, was sunk in thought. We looked at each other for a second or two.

'Do you have to go over there?' He ran a hand through his hair to push it over his shoulders.

'Yes. I owe her.'

'Do you think Cliff's there?'

'She didn't say.'

'I don't know about this, Lily. I hate for you to be anywhere close to the woman. I feel sorry for her, but she's a human lightning rod.'

I wasn't too enthusiastic about Tamsin's request myself. 'Maybe she really wants me over there to clean. But I'm thinking maybe she needs company, and doesn't know anyone well enough to just ask for it.'

'So, you're going to go?' Jack was still reluctant.

'Yes, but I'll call you when I get there. If you don't hear from me, come over to see how everything's going. I don't know if I could take a lot of weeping.' At odd moments, the loss of the baby still struck me with a peculiar pain.

'You won't forget to call?' Jack touched my hair.

'No, I won't forget.'

I showered and changed, so it was about ten when I left my house, ten o'clock on a hot and peaceful Sunday morning. Shakespeare was at its best. The church parking lots were full. A little towheaded boy was in his driveway operating a remote-control car. Everything looked absolutely normal on Tamsin's street. Both the cars were parked in the drive, and I wedged in behind them.

I wasn't too pleased that Cliff was home, but I had only suspicion, after all. Lugging my cleaning-material caddy, I went up the front steps and knocked. With professional eyes I examined the porch; it needed to be swept, if not hosed down.

Tamsin came to the door immediately. She looked as awful as she had the day before. Her hair was straggly and dirty, her cutoff jeans and truncated sweatshirt were anything but pristine, and she was free of makeup and jewelry.

'Thank you for coming,' she said, in a limp voice. 'I just can't stand for everything to be so dirty, with people dropping by all the time. I can't ever tell who'll be seeing my house, with the police coming in all the time.'

'Cliff home?' The litter of the big edition of the paper and a couple of stained coffee mugs in the living room were like a tableau called 'Sunday morning'.

'Yes, he's in the small den back there where we keep the TV.' This living room, decorated in inexpensive American comfortable, did not contain a television or music system. Shelves hung on the wall held little china statues of wide-eyed children.

'Aren't they darling? I love those things,' Tamsin said, following my gaze. 'My folks started giving me one a year when I was little. Then, Cliff took over.'

Despite her dishevelment, Tamsin seemed calm and in control. I felt encouraged. Maybe this wouldn't be too bad. As soon as she explained the program, I'd call Jack. 'Where do you want me to start?' I stood before her with raised eyebrows, just waiting for her word.

'How about in there?' Tamsin pointed to the hall leading to the back of the house, and I preceded her down the dark corridor.

'In here?' I asked, and turned the knob of the door at the end.

'Yep,' she said, and I just had time to turn the knob and push the door open, all the while thinking she was sounding so cheerful. I was met with a burst of sunlight, and the sight of Cliff Eggers bound and gagged with duct tape and lying on the floor.

Then she did something horrible to me, something that made every atom in my body surge, and I fell down beside him.

I had some seconds of complete disorientation. Or maybe I lost minutes. My legs had no bones in them. Talking was simply impossible, even if I'd been able to formulate a sentence. My mouth was open and I was drooling. I felt wet at my crotch; I had wet my pants. When I became aware that I was still thinking, that my thoughts could form patterns and make sense, my first clear concept was that I should avoid having that – whatever it was – done to me again, no matter what the cost. My wandering gaze happened to meet Cliff's desperate brown eyes, and I slowly became anchored in the here and now, as unpleasant as that was.

I was still alive. That was the important thing. And I hadn't called Jack, so I figured he'd be coming sooner or later – unless Tamsin had done something while I was mentally out of the room, something to fool Jack, too.

Of course, I felt like the biggest idiot.

Cliff's eyes stared into mine. He was scared shitless. I didn't blame him. But I was just as glad the duct tape across his mouth made talking impossible. I didn't need anyone else's fear. I had plenty of my own.

'What you gonna do?' I asked Tamsin, after tremendous effort. It was the first sentence that managed to make it out of my lips. She was holding something in her right hand, a black narrow shape, and I finally recognized it as a stun gun. I took a deep breath of sheer bitterness. Oh, gosh, who had told her where to buy one? Could it have been me? It would have been hard for me to be more angry with myself than I was at this moment, or more sickened by the human race.

'If you're not outraged by what he's done to me, I'm going to have to do it myself,' Tamsin said. 'Then, I don't know what I'll do about you.'

'Why?' Though that was probably a pointless question.

Oddly, she looked like she was thinking of answering me.

'I just realized the past few days. At first, it just didn't seem possible. That someone living with me, someone sleeping with me, someone who took my dresses to the cleaners, was trying to drive me crazy. The first stuff, the stuff in Cleveland, even that was Cliff.' Instead of looking at me, she was staring off into space, and I swear she had the most disillusioned, heartbroken expression. I would have felt sorry for her, if she hadn't just disabled and humiliated me. 'I figured out just this week that after I lost our baby, Cliff was out to kill me. He thought I did things to kill the baby. And he knew I had a lot of insurance – one big policy through work and another on my own. He thought, in my profession, getting killed wouldn't be so strange. He was doing my transcripts for me, then. In fact, that's where we met, at that clinic.' The narrow black device swung in her hand like a television remote control. 'So Cliff transcribed my sessions with a patient who had potential for great violence, one who actually might think of killing me. I think Cliff planned to beat me to death.' She got right in my face to confide this. If I'd had the energy, the hair would have been lifting on my neck. 'He could count on the investigators going through my patients, finding – this man – and arresting him.'

'And?' If I didn't try to say too much, it came out okay. My legs were slowly feeling a little more functional. Cliff was moving a little more. She'd bound his hands in front, which wasn't too competent. He was picking at the duct tape across his mouth.

'We moved once, in the Cleveland area, after I found a snake nailed to the door. Moving didn't help. Then, as I've come to realize these past few days, Cliff stretched his fun out a little too long. Charles, my patient, died in a bar fight. Cliff had to stop. Of course, I didn't put two and two together then.' Her face became blank, her eyes opaque. 'I really thought Cliff suggested this move to Shakespeare because he was concerned about me. He gave up his business and everything to move south with me, and I believed we would be happy here. I didn't put Charles's death together with the end of the persecution, the end of the horrible messages on the answering machine. But Cliff told me just a few minutes ago that the police up there did make the connection, did mention – to *Cliff* – the possibility of my stalker being Charles. They would've wondered if the calls had kept coming. So here we are, and we get settled, and I think everything is going so good, and I start getting the calls again. The house is entered. There's . . . poop . . . smeared on the door.'

Cliff had succeeded in ungagging himself. 'Lily,' he said in a weak voice 'don't let her kill me.'

I didn't even glance at him. 'Yeah?' I said to Tamsin, to encourage her to talk. The longer she talked, the more time I had to recover.

'So we decided the police had been wrong. That someone else

had followed me down here. It still didn't occur to me to suspect the most obvious person.' She shook her head at her own naïveté. 'We figured – that is, I figured, and Cliff pretended to – that since the calls only came when Cliff was gone, that meant the guy was watching me, knew when I was alone. That made it more scary. Notes slid under the door, notes in my clothes – oh, God!' She shuddered and wept.

My sympathy would have been deeper if I hadn't been sitting there in wet pants.

'Lily,' Cliff said, 'I didn't do those things. I love my wife . . . even though she planted the stake in the step for me to get hurt on. If you'll just let me go, we can work this out.' He was plucking awkwardly at the duct tape around his wrists, but that was going to be much harder.

I said, 'Tamsin, why'd you call me here?'

'Because you can kill him.'

I shook my head.

'You can kill him,' she repeated persuasively. 'You killed a man before. This one deserves it, too. Think of what he's done to me. He shouldn't live!' Her face grew crafty. 'What if he gets off and does this to someone else? I know from our therapy group that you have a sense of justice.'

Unhampered by the rules of law, she meant.

'You could kill him for me. We'd all be safer.'

She had condensed Cliff into every man who'd hurt a woman.

'Please do this for me! My mind is too fragile, too delicate, to sustain killing him.' She made it sound like her mind was made out of old lace. 'I just don't have the guts, the determination. I need you to do this favor for another woman.' The empty hand touched her chest. 'Help your sister out.'

'You – stunned me.'

'I was afraid you'd run away before I could talk to you if I didn't do something,' she told me, and her voice was so reasonable that I winced. 'I know you, from the group. You wouldn't sit and listen to me unless I made you. Would you? Just think about it, Lily. You have to understand this. I loved him more than anyone else in the world. He took everything away from me. I think he did something to make me lose the baby. I don't believe in anything any more.'

And she should have made him unconscious, because he was eyeing me frantically, shaking his head to deny what she was telling me. 'Lily, Tamsin has just lost her mind. Don't cater to her when she's clearly off her rocker. I love my wife, and I've done everything I can to help her through this. Please don't let her do something worse than this.' I noticed he was making progress on loosening the duct tape binding his wrists. It was difficult, but he was managing. The next time I wanted to secure someone, I wouldn't call Tamsin to do the securing.

Tamsin went on enumerating her wrongs. Since I was still too weak to move, I had plenty of time to think. I thought it was pretty lucky their baby hadn't been born, whatever had caused the miscarriage. What if what Tamsin was telling me wasn't true? She was deeply disturbed. She might be mistaken, and she might just be a liar. What if she just wanted an excuse to kill Cliff, with a reasonable chance of an acquittal, or at the most a light sentence? Pretending he'd confessed his long persecution of her, pretending he'd told her he'd killed Saralynn and Gerry McClanahan, would provide an excellent story to tell a jury.

Especially with a witness like me.

She could have no serious hope that I would take the bait and do Cliff in, but she could provide a good case for herself if I was there to witness her frenzy and her anguish, even if she had to immobilize me to make me watch it. I was pretty sure Tamsin was not quite as crazy as she was making out; I was pretty sure she was making a case for temporary insanity.

But I wasn't *completely* sure.

The only certainty I had was that I hated Tamsin, my counselor, who was twisting what she'd extracted from our therapy sessions to serve her own ends: my disregard for the letter of the law, my strong sense of justice. She'd ignored other things about me that were just as important, like my absolute and total hatred of people who made me feel helpless, my loathing of being physically unclean, and my dislike of being bested.

'What happened in your office when Saralynn was killed?' I asked. My speech was better, too.

'I swear to God, exactly what I told the police,' Tamsin said.

'You knew I was there,' Cliff said, his voice ragged. 'You knew someone was killing Saralynn. And you hid. I wondered the whole time, does she even care enough to come out? If she'll come out, if she'll be brave, I won't finish . . . and she yelled for you, Tamsin. You heard her. And you stayed shut in that conference room, doing nothing.'

'Lily, he's trying to take you in just like he took me!' She was all but wailing, rocking back and forth, the stun gun still in her hand.

'You knew she was being killed,' Cliff repeated, 'and you knew it was me.'

Tamsin was breathing like she'd been running, and she was pale and sweating.

'I hear what you're saying,' I said, unable to stop myself from registering that Tamsin wasn't the only one who had had a sad disillusionment here.

I was feeling stronger by the minute. I was going to take that stun gun away from her if I had to beat her senseless to do it. In fact, that was starting to sound very appealing.

'I'll help you out, Tamsin,' I said, staring into Cliff's eyes. I noticed, as I pulled myself up to my knees, that Cliff had made great progress unwrapping his wrists. In a minute, he would be much more of a factor than he was right now. I gripped the arm of a couch, and pushed myself up. I thought my muscles would all work. Upright had never felt so good.

Cliff began rolling around on the open floor like a giant bowling pin. He had given up plucking subtly at his wrist bindings. His fingers were tearing at the last wraparound of the silver tape, yanking so hard they sometimes broke his skin.

Tamsin, standing in the open doorway, looked absolutely crazed. 'Kill him, Lily!' she shrieked. 'Kill him kill him kill him!'

They were both using up valuable oxygen, as far as I was

concerned. While Tamsin had been enumerating her woes earlier, I'd been learning the room. A sofa and an armchair divided by a small table, a television on an oak stand, and my cleaning caddy; and in it, my cell phone. It was awfully close to Tamsin, too close, I'd decided. I wouldn't willingly get within range of that stun gun again. Somewhat closer, there was a telephone on the table between the couch and the chair.

I snatched up the phone and hit nine one one before Cliff crashed into me from behind. I went sprawling on the couch, rapping my nose sharply on the edge of the wooden arm. Suddenly there was blood everywhere, and a blinding pain.

I scrambled up as quickly as the pain permitted. Tamsin was shrieking and darting at Cliff with the stun gun, only to dodge away when he got near enough to kick at her. Seeing Cliff still rolling on the floor, his hands still bound, I realized that he was looking for something to roll up against, to provide stability so he might be able to struggle upright. I brought back my foot and kicked him as hard as I could, just as he ripped his bonds apart. I didn't have time to choose, but my foot connected with his lower back. The jolt ran all the way up to my face and made my nose hurt even more. He bellowed in pain, and I very nearly joined him.

'That's it, Lily! Kick the son of a bitch!' yelled Tamsin, delighted. She actually had her arms up in the air in a cheerleader gesture. No way she could get the stun gun down in time. I hoped fervently that I'd recovered enough strength to finish this. I took two strides, drew back my fist and hit her in the pit of her stomach as hard as I've ever hit anyone in my life. To my intense pleasure, Tamsin finally shut up. I stood swaying on my feet, watching her gag.

The moment of silence was as refreshing as a cool shower, but it ended when Jack dashed in. He stood in the doorway panting, his face dripping with sweat. 'You didn't call. How are you? Your nose is broken.' I nodded. He surveyed the floor, and looked at me. 'Well, which one of them did it?'

'Hell if I know,' I said, and called the police.

*

Because he is a good and merciful man, Claude let Alicia Stokes interview Tamsin. 'If you're smart,' he told Alicia in his deep, rumbly voice, 'you'll learn more about being a cop in the next two hours than you have in the last year.' Jack and I were sitting in the designated waiting chairs as they came through on their way to the interview rooms. Alicia gave me a long, thoughtful look as she went into one interview room.

Claude was in charge of Cliff, whom the hospital had treated and released.

The only part I had left to play was that of incidental victim. My misery and my trembling muscles were the byproduct of the secret war between Tamsin and Cliff. They were victims of each other; at least, that's how I figured it. How a man and a woman who both set out to do good, at least by their choices of professions, could have gone so far into the red zone of human torment is not something I care to understand.

I had gone to the hospital to have a nose X ray, and then home to shower, before I was due at the police station. I was still shaky and felt very much like some other person who bore only a distant relationship to Lily Bard. Jack made it clear I wasn't going anywhere without him. I gave him no argument when he said he was going to drive me to the police station.

I was feeling much more like myself by the time Alicia and Claude sat down with me to go over what Tamsin had said before Jack came in like the cavalry. From the direction their questions took, I pieced together the public line they would take in their prosecution.

Claude believed that most of what Tamsin had said was true. But he thought that Tamsin must have realized Cliff's intentions earlier than she alleged. In fact, he thought the move to Shakespeare had been conceived by Tamsin, who believed a small town's less experienced and sophisticated police department would not be able to solve any crimes committed on its turf, provided the criminal was clever. Well, as Claude put it, the hell with her.

On one level, their marriage had proceeded at a predictable pace. They made love, worked, fought sometimes, and each made their own plans. On another level, they were engaged in a life-and-death struggle.

'I don't know what happened in their early marriage, but Cliff's deep problems with his wife seem to have started because of the miscarriage. Tamsin seemed to enjoy the sympathy it earned her, to a real suspicious extent,' Claude said, recrossing his ankles. His feet were propped up on the edge of his desk in his favorite pose.

'Tamsin said she thought he wanted to collect on her insurance money, too,' I said.

Claude shook his head. 'I just don't see money as an important part of this, and I guess it's the first time I ever said that.'

I shrugged.

'But somehow, at some point, he decided to make a game out of retaliation. Tamsin was fun to scare. She had more education than Cliff, more pretensions; he enjoyed getting the edge back.'

'Cliff upped the ante when he killed Saralynn,' Alicia Stokes said. She'd been sweating. Her skin gleamed like highly polished mahogany. 'Tamsin admitted to herself, then, that she suspected her husband. Maybe his footsteps in the hall were too familiar for her to block the knowledge from herself.'

'She told you that?' I asked.

Stokes nodded, slowly and deliberately. 'Yes, she figured Cliff had access to her keys to the building, knew its layout and her routine, and also knew she was meeting a new group member early.'

'Janet's appearance was a real shock.' The chief of police resumed his part of the narrative. After all these months of silent struggle, talking must have been a relief to both Tamsin and Cliff. I would have called a lawyer, myself, and clammed up, but that was not as much a stretch for me as for most people. 'And the fact that Tamsin stayed in the conference room. I think he'd looked forward to her reaction to finding the body; he'd planned on at least listening to the sound effects from out in the lobby. But she stayed low, and he had to leave. He knew the members of the group would be arriving soon. He went out the front door and to his car, which he'd parked at Shakespeare Pharmacy about half a block away. He didn't think anyone would particularly remember his car at the pharmacy, and he was right. Then he showed up at the health center. He expected his wife to completely collapse. But she bore up under it pretty well. Cliff's reaction, in the parking lot, you remember how upset he seemed? He really was.'

'What about Gerry McClanahan?' Jack took another drink from his plastic foam cup of station-house coffee. He'd be up all night. I would be too, unless the pills Carrie had given me packed a true wallop. I had had many painful things happen to me, but the broken nose ranked right up there in the top three. I had tomorrow to look forward to, when Jack said my face would be even more arresting. But at least I was clean and dry, and the soiled clothes were in the washer back at the house.

I was putting my money on Gerry having pegged Cliff as the stalker, but as it turned out I was half wrong.

Claude had just finished reading Gerry McClanahan's notes about the odd behavior of his neighbors. In fact, when Jack's call had come into the station, Claude and Alicia had been discussing what they could prove, and who would be charged with what. Tamsin's mental collapse had settled some of their questions.

As the surveillance log showed, Gerry had noticed Cliff going to the toolshed at what Gerry considered odd times. The writer had thought it was strange that Cliff always emerged empty-handed. Gerry had sneaked over to check out the shed once or twice when Cliff and Tamsin were both gone. He'd seen an animal cage, but didn't question its presence until the dead squirrel was found hanging from the tree. After reading the police report on the incident, Gerry had retrieved the squirrel corpse from the garbage where Jack had put it. Then he'd stolen the cage (I'd later seen it in Gerry's house after his death), which contained plenty of squirrel hairs. Gerry planned to get a lab to test the creature's DNA.

Claude didn't know if such a test was possible, or if it was, if the results would be admissible in court. But from Claude's voice I could tell he admired Gerry's tenacity and his willingness to put his money where his mouth was.

The page of Gerry's log I'd found had noted that Cliff went to the toolshed the night before we'd found the poor squirrel murdered.

Gerry had planned to return the cage so Cliff wouldn't get suspicious. But before he could act, he witnessed something even stranger. He'd seen Tamsin sabotaging her own back steps. The worm had turned.

Gerry had been completely gripped in the drama he saw unfolding before him. He'd acted like a writer instead of a cop, and when Cliff had noticed the missing cage and followed the faint traces of footsteps in the damp yard, he'd come across Gerry. Maybe Gerry had already been out in his backyard, filling out his log; maybe Cliff had knocked on Gerry's back door and demanded an explanation or created some excuse to get Gerry outside. And he'd killed him. Later, reasoning that two stabbings would throw the police off even more than one, he'd staged the clumsy attempt on himself. A hastily arranged mistake, that self-stabbing; Tamsin could not have had any doubt after that, no matter how much she had blinded herself to the truth.

'But she backed Cliff up,' Jack said incredulously. 'When he said he'd never seen the knife before, the one in Gerry's throat. Surely she recognized it? And Cliff had called me, to have me back in Shakespeare so maybe I'd get blamed for Gerry's death.'

'The world would've been a better place if those two had never met,' Claude said.

'Uh-huh, you got that right,' Alicia said, trying to cover her yawn with her hand.

'As for you, Detective Stokes, we need to have a private conference. Cliff Eggers has told me he recognized you from Cleveland. I have reason to believe you've been far more aware and involved in this case than you saw fit to tell me. According to you, Tamsin's case was one you'd heard about while you were on the Cleveland force, not one you'd worked on.'

Alicia suddenly looked wide awake.

'Well, Lily and I will be going home now,' Jack said. He held out his hand, and I took it gratefully. He gave me a gentle pull to help me up. Having help was such a luxury. I hoped I never would grow to take it for granted. At least I could be sure that Jack and I would never become like Cliff and Tamsin. Our hard times and aggressive impulses had been flashed to the world. Everyone knew what we were capable of. We didn't have to prove ourselves in any secret way.

Claude clapped Jack on the shoulder, just when Jack was almost out of the room. Claude said, 'By the way, a little bird told me you married this woman.' He was not smiling and he did not look happy. Something pretty old-fashioned and definitely paternalistic had surfaced in Claude. 'You better treat her right.'

'I'll do my best,' Jack said.

'He hasn't done too bad the first three months,' I said.

Claude began smiling at us. Behind him, I saw Stokes was sitting in the old office chair with her mouth hanging open. 'When are you planning on letting the rest of the world in on this?' Claude asked.

'It's seeping out gradually,' I said. 'We just wanted to get used to the fact ourselves, first.'

'Was my wife the first to know?' Claude still sounded proud saying 'my wife'.

'Yes, my wife told your wife,' Jack said, grinning like an idiot.

As the door began to close behind us, we heard Claude open a conversation with his detective. 'You want to tell me who you're really working for, Stokes?' he began, and then the door thudded into place.

Though the next day was Monday, Jack and I lay in bed late. My face was swollen and bruised and I looked like hell. I still felt a bit weak from the stun gun, which the police had regarded with great respect. They'd charged Tamsin with use of a prohibited weapon, in addition to all the other charges. I wondered if Sneaky Pete would get into trouble, but I couldn't summon up enough energy to get really worked up about it.

'How could two people who are supposed to love each other get so crossed up?' Jack asked. 'They could have just gotten a divorce, like other couples.'

'They must have enjoyed their little war, somehow. Perfectly matching pathologies.' I'd been thinking of getting up and changing our sheets, but it was so nice to have a reason to lie in bed, so pleasant to have Jack beside me. I was sure I would get used to that pleasure, in time; waking up beside Jack would become routine. I'd begin to notice the little things that irritate any spouse. But because of the tenor of my life, I appreciated the simple fact of love. So did Jack.

I couldn't help but feel convinced that if Tamsin and Cliff had deserved each other, so did Jack and I. Gazing up at my white ceiling in my clean bedroom, I pictured a panorama of centuries of mating: of men and women looking for the perfect match, and finding pairings that were at best convenient – at worst, the product of one twisted psyche calling to another equally perverse.

I had been a child of love. My parents were lucky in their marriage, and I had been the beneficiary of that luck. After I'd been forced into a different kind of mating, I'd changed irrevocably into someone my former self would hardly have recognized. It seemed to me that now I had a chance to change back. I wondered if that was really possible.

But I am not a woman who can sit and think theoretically for long stretches of time, and I am not a woman who can change philosophy easily. In fact, I floated away from that vista of pairings and sank back into myself on the bed with a distinct feeling of relief.

'Today,' I said, 'we're going to clean the gutters.'

Acknowledgments

Shakespeare's Champion

My thanks to Larry Price and Pat Downs, who described being blown up; and to members of my karate class, who kindly enacted fight sequences and offered various lethal suggestions. Dr John Alexander has also been polite about answering some very peculiar questions.

Shakespeare's Christmas

My thanks to all who gave me information and advice while I was writing this book: retired police chief Phil Gates, go between Ann Hilgeman, private detective Norma Rowell, and fingerprint expert M. Nolte.

Shakespeare's Trollop

My thanks to the usual suspects: Drs Aung and Tammy Than and former police chief Phil Gates. My further thanks to an American icon, John Walsh.

Shakespeare's Counselor

My thanks to Laura Lippman, Phil Gates, Susan McBride, and Officer Kelly Blair, who all were kind enough to answer more or less peculiar questions.